RAVEN SON: BOOKS 1-3

NICHOLAS KOTAR

THE SONG OF THE SIRIN

Raven Son: Book One

THE SONG OF THE SIRIN

(Raven Son: Book One)

Copyright © Nicholas Kotar 2017

All rights reserved. No part of this book may be reproduced, stored in a retrieval system, or transmitted in any form, or by any means, digital, electronic, mechanical, photocopying, or otherwise, without prior permission of the publisher.

This is a work of fiction. All the characters and events portrayed in this book are either fictitious or are used fictitiously.

Cover Design by Books Covered Ltd.

Published by Waystone Press, 2017

ISBN: 9780998847917

LCCN: 2017908889

❦ Created with Vellum

To my princess

The song of the Sirin can overthrow kingdoms. I know. I have seen it. I have seen the song make gods of men. The song carved the eternal city of Vasyllia out of the mountains. The song transformed queens into healers, so that thousands were made well with a single word. But ever it comes as a harbinger of affliction. Only in the fire of adversity does the pure water of healing flow.

-from "The Journals of Cassían, Dar of Vasyllia"
(The Sayings, Book II, 3:35-43)

CHAPTER 1
THE SONG

The song teased Voran at the first hint of sunrise. His sister Lebía still slept, and he rose quietly, trying not to wake her. Outside his window, the trees were encased in overnight ice. Branches, like freshly-minted blades, clanged against each other in an almost military salute. As Voran leaned against the sill, the sun breached the summit-lines, and the ice-encased branches glowed from within. The song rose in a vast crescendo, then faded again. It stopped his breath short like a punch to the chest.

"Ammil," said Lebía from across the room, her hair rumpled from sleep.

"Ammil, little bird?" he whispered, hoping she would turn over and fall asleep again. It cut him deeply that she still could not sleep on her own, despite her sixteen years.

"The sun's morning sparkle through hoarfrost," she said, laboring through a yawn. One of her eyes remained stubbornly closed. "That's how the Old Tales call it. Ammil. The blessing of Adonais, you know."

Voran smiled, though there was little to smile about in the purple shadows under her eyes. She needed to sleep if she were ever to find her joy again.

"What is that?" She indicated the parchment lying on the sill, garish in its profusion of purple and red.

"One of the Dar's huntsmen claims to have seen the white stag." Personally, Voran doubted it.

Her second eye opened. "The white stag? Dar Antomír wishes to hunt the deer of legend?"

"He's anxious to begin as soon as possible," said Voran. Too anxious, he thought, but kept it to himself. "His advisers are less sure. The Dar's called together a small council this morning."

Privately, Voran wondered at the Dar's eagerness. Yes, catching the white stag was supposed to bring prosperity to the hunter's city for seven generations. But although legends grew in Vasyllia with the same profusion as lilac trees, they mostly stayed bound to the page.

"Why does he want the approval of his advisors? Couldn't he just announce the hunt, and be done with it?" she asked, rubbing her right eye with the heel of her palm.

"It's complicated..." Only last week, the Dar's head drooped in sleep during a small council. "Dar Antomír is of a different time. Most of his advisers are young, and they would prefer to leave old tales and superstitions behind. In fact, I think there are some who wouldn't mind so much if Dar Antomír retired from public life and allowed Mirnían to take a more active role in Vasyllia."

"I see. Meddling nags."

Voran laughed. "I agree with that sentiment wholeheartedly." He would much rather wander the wilds than sit in council with the representatives of the three reaches of Vasyllia.

"Do you have to be there? Why not stay at home for once?"

She looked away as soon as she said it. His conscience pricked him. Lebía was practically begging him, and he knew how much she hated to beg. It had been far too long since he stayed with Lebía at home, helped in the kitchens, took a long walk through the family vineyards, or actually read something with her. But Dar Antomír depended on him. Even more than he depended on his son, Mirnían.

"I wish I could..."

"Oh well." She put on a feeble smile like a mask. "Never mind. Only please don't stay at court the whole day. You can't imagine how oppressive this house can be."

Yes, I can, he thought. Why do you think I avoid it so much? Nothing like an empty house to remind you of your parents' absence.

"I expect I'll be back before evening," he said, and his conscience pricked him again. He doubted he'd return before night. "Sleep now, my swanling. You need to rest."

She looked at him without blinking for what seemed an inhumanly long time.

"Voran, do you think...maybe if I had done something differently—"

"Lebía, don't." He hurried to her and sat by her on the bed. "You were the least problematic child in Vasyllia. Mama's disappearance wasn't your fault."

"I remember there were times when Papa looked at me with those heavy eyes, you know? Like he was trying to remember what it was like to love me. To love Mama. Could he have really—?"

"Lebía, don't believe the gossip. The bruises on Mama's arms were part of the disease."

She nodded, thoughtfully.

"I don't know why she left when she did, swanling. But the fact that he went to find her proves that he loved her, don't you think?"

Her look only mirrored his own thoughts. *He didn't love us enough to stay.*

"Please, Lebía, you need your sleep."

She hugged him and turned over. Within a minute, her breathing had deepened into sleep.

May all the Powers damn him for leaving you, Lebía.

The curse did not give him the pleasure he hoped. It gave him no sudden illumination about the nature of Aglaia's disease. It suggested nothing new about Otchigen's madness and subsequent disappearance after implication in the mass murder of other Vasylli. Nothing but questions, as always.

At this early hour, he went out the back door of the wine cellar, chary of waking the servants. He managed to close the door with no noise, but the gate at the end of the overgrown back garden moaned like a thing diseased. It always did, but Voran always forgot. Cursing inwardly, Voran looked back at the house. No one seemed to stir within.

The house's two stories lurched over him, the shadows thrown back by the morning sun, threatening him. As though the house itself were angry that Voran was master instead of his lost father Otchigen. As though it were Voran's fault that his mother had fallen prey to a strange illness, then disappeared inexplicably.

The song appeared again, hardly more substantial than the red alpenglow on the underside of the clouds. Voran's heart swelled as he turned away.

Otchigen's house was nestled among the other estates of the third reach of Vasyllia. Voran loved to walk the flagstoned road through the reach as it crisscrossed the cherry groves of the noble families. Amid the trees, the mansions—each a fancy in carved gables, lintels, and columns—stared at each other as though they, like their masters, were jealous of each other's status. Some of the most extravagant even sported gilded cockerels on the roof. Voran was grateful that it was generally considered in bad taste.

Every house was built on a small mound, to better overlook the other two reaches that extended downward and outward along the slope of the mountain, like the skirts of a great dress. Voran knew that, if looked at from below, the houses sparkled like jewels every morning: a reminder to the lower reaches that such opulence was as far out of their reach as the Heights themselves.

Voran stopped at a crossroads where stairs carved into the mountain led down to the second reach. Just to his left was the Dar's palace, its seven onion-domed towers carved out of marble blocks, each larger than a single man. He hesitated, unwilling to brave the nagging of the small council yet. The second reach spread out beneath him in clean lines of austere homes set apart by stone hedges, staircases, and canals, all in keeping with the military calling of most of the inhabitants.

"Make way," said a voice behind him. Before Voran could turn around, a mail-shod shoulder pushed him off the path. Voran landed knee-first in mud.

"Well, well, it's the son of Otchigen," sniggered Rogdai, the chief warden of the gates of Vasyllia. "You seem to have lost your warriors' edge. No graduate of the seminary should ever allow himself to be surprised by an enemy in the open. I'll have to speak to the elders about it. Maybe they can find you a post in the Dar's library."

The two sub-wardens flanking him laughed, but their knuckles were white on their pommels.

"Ever the paragon of civility, Vohin Rogdai," said Voran, forcing his tone to remain calm. He would have preferred to knock the idiot's teeth into the back of his head. "Thank you for pointing out the weakness in my defense. I will gladly accept your further instruction in the sword-ring." *Where I'll poke more holes into you than a sieve.*

"A pleasure. It's been years since my sword has tasted traitor's blood. Shall we say... this evening? I've always thought swordfights are best done in torchlight."

Where fewer people can see how bad you are, Voran thought, *or how you cheat.*

"I'm afraid today I'll be too busy hunting and catching the white stag."

"You?" Rogdai spit. "You'll catch that beast as soon as the sun sets in the middle of the day."

"I smell a wager," said Voran. "My father's entire wine collection if I don't bring it back by midnight."

Rogdai's face twisted in indecision. The superstitious idiot was afraid of drinking the wine of a suspected traitor. On the other hand, it was the best wine in Vasyllia...

"Done," growled Rogdai. "I wager a public feast hosted in the central square by my family in your honor."

"No, in my father's honor." Voran smiled at the way Rogdai twitched. Voran was sure he would just walk away. The coward.

"Done." Rogdai's teeth sounded ready to break from the strain of his jaw. "Not one minute past midnight, mind."

Voran inclined his head.

Rogdai and his flunkeys walked by, their shoulders not quite as straight as before.

The wind picked up and whipped Voran's hair into his face. Annoyed, he pulled it back. As he did, the song rose as though it were carried by the wind. He gasped for a moment, it was so intense. And it seemed to whisper a thought to him.

Go now. Forget the small council. Go find the stag now. Leave the blind to lead the blind.

Voran was running even before he realized it, but not toward the palace. He angled away away from it, toward the headwall of Vasyllia Mountain.

Voran avoided the streets, sprinting along dirt paths behind the gardens of the third reach. Here, the trees were wilder—native fir and spruce for the most part. Sometimes avoiding the paths outright, Voran veered toward the largest of many canals that watered the three reaches, all of them fed by Vasyllia's twin waterfalls. As he reached the canal, all signs of domestication faded, replaced by mossy rocks and tree roots. Even the air smelled differently here. The spicy smells of the nobles' kitchens gave way to the cool scent of pine. Though he knew the way well enough, it took him a moment to find the ivy-encrusted archway that led to a staircase going up, away from the city.

Dar Antomír would forgive him, Voran was sure. Especially if he found the stag. An honor for his family, a boon to his disgraced name. Seven generations of prosperity to his city. If the legends were to be believed, of course. Did he believe them? Voran wasn't sure any more.

The wind gusted, dousing him with the spume of Vasyllia's twin waterfalls, thundering on either side of the ancient stairway. With it came the music, louder than ever. He closed his eyes, savoring. Only when he clung to the face of the mountain was the melody this vivid. It sounded as if the mountain, the trees, the clouds all sang. And only for him.

He reached a ledge and pulled himself up. He was soaked from the exertion and the mist. Falling on one knee, he raised both arms toward the rising sun.

"Adonais, accept the prayer of this scion of the dishonored house of Voyevoda Otchigen. May my hunt not prove futile."

The song hung on the air like a memory, then faded. He leaned back against one of the stone chalices that collected the water from the falls, each taller than Vasyllia's famed birches. The chalice hummed with the steady rhythm of the waterfall pounding it. At Voran's feet, a stone mouth faintly reminiscent of a dragon's head spit the gathered water toward the city's canals.

How mad and beautiful, he thought, considering the dragon. In the old times things were made with beauty in mind, not merely usefulness. How unlike these times. With the passing of the song, Voran felt emptied, hungry for a recurrence of the song. It did not return.

Voran stretched his shoulders, relief flooding into the popping joints. He sat at the ledge's lip, resting his feet on the dragon's ears. Miles upon miles of the woods beyond the city lay carpeted at his feet. It was the perfect vantage point.

As he stared into the spaces between the trees, Lebía's shadowed eyes kept intruding on his thoughts. He really should spend more time with her, not conjure up excuses to remain at the warrior seminary after hours, training the boys. Her plea pained him. He had not realized that she was so lonely at home. But of course she was. She had few friends, tainted as she was with their father's assumed guilt, their mother's inexplicable disappearance. He promised himself he would take her to the forests more often. Maybe even let her spend the night under the stars with him, as he so loved to do.

He was so wrapped up with the image of her smiling at the innumerable falling stars on a late summer night that he nearly missed it. Something gold flashed in the woods far beneath him. Voran's heart stopped, then raced forward. A white streak passed through the trees. Fearful of moving even a muscle lest the vision fade, Voran continued to stare. It moved again, now clearly visible. A white stag.

It took Voran a maddening hour to get through the city's reaches and out the gates. Another half hour away from the paths as he tried to get his bearings in the forests beyond the city. He was intent on his path like a pointer on the scent. But when the howling started, his blood turned to ice in his veins.

He had heard wolves before. This was no mere wolf. The sound was deeper and darker, like the buzz of a hornet compared to a fly. He tried to recall the details of the many stories of the white stag. Was there a legendary predator to accompany the legendary quarry? Not that he could remember.

A blur of white raced before his eyes, so close he could spit at it. In an instant, it was gone.

The sun showered the foliage with dappled light. Something that was not the sun—a strange golden mist-light—flickered through the trunks, as though the stag had left a trail of light behind it. The mist beckoned him deeper into the forest.

Voran plunged headlong into the deepwood. The strange light continued before him for a mile or so, then blinked out. Voran looked around and realized he had never been in this place before. He stood on the edge of a clearing awash in morning sun, so bright compared to the gloom of the woods that he could see nothing in it but white light. He stepped forward.

The light overwhelmed him, forcing him to crouch over and shield his eyes. Fuzzy at first, then resolving as Voran's eyes grew accustomed to the light, the white stag towered in the middle of the clearing, almost man-high at the shoulder. Its antlers gleamed gold, so bright that they competed with the sun.

Voran froze in place and adopted the deep, silent breathing pattern that an old woodsman taught him in childhood. Inch by inch, he reached for his bow. His quiver hung at his side in the Karilan manner, so taking the arrow would be the work of half a second, but extricating the bow strapped to his back was another matter. A single bead of sweat dropped from his forehead and slid down the side of his nose, tickling him.

The deer turned its head to Voran, showing no inclination to flee. As though Voran were nothing more than a fly, it flicked both ears and continued to graze.

The howl repeated, just to Voran's right. Out of the trees crept a black wolf the size of a bear, its fur glistening in the light of the antlers. It paid no heed to Voran, leading with bristling head toward the grazing deer. It lunged, blurring in Voran's vision like a war-spear, but the stag leaped over it and merely moved farther off to continue grazing. The wolf howled again and lunged again. Back and forth they danced, but the stag knew the steps of this death-dance better than the wolf. His nonchalance seemed to infuriate the hunter.

The wolf charged so fast that Voran missed its attack. The deer flew higher than Voran thought possible, and its golden antlers slammed the wolf's flank like a barbed mace. The wolf screamed. The sound ripped through Voran, an almost physical pain.

The stag trotted to the other end of the clearing. Looking back once more, it waited. Gooseflesh tickled Voran's neck. The stag called to him, teasing him to continue the hunt. Voran ran, and the deer launched off its back legs and flew into the waiting embrace of the trees.

Voran stopped. His body strained forward, intent on the hunt, but his heart pulled back. The wolf. He could not leave a suffering creature to die, even if it was the size of a bear, even if it would probably try to kill him if he approached. With a groan for his lost quarry, Voran turned back.

The wolf dragged itself forward with its forepaws. Each black claw was the size of a dagger. As Voran approached, its ears went flat against its head, and it growled deep in its throat. Voran's hands shook. Gritting his teeth, he balled his hands into fists and willed himself to look the wolf in the eye. Its ears went up like an inquisitive dog's. It whined.

In the eyes of the wolf, Voran saw recognition. This was a reasoning creature, not a wild animal.

"I can help you," he found himself saying to the wolf as to a human being. "If you let me."

The wolf stared at him, then nodded twice.

Voran pulled a homemade salve—one of Lebía's own making—from a pouch on his quiver. Tearing a strip from his linen shirt, he soaked it with the oils and cleaned the wound of tiny fragments of bone. The wolf tensed in pain, then exhaled and relaxed. Its eyes drooped as the pungent odor suffused the air, mingling with pine-scent. Soon the wolf was snoring.

As Voran watched the sleeping wolf, something stirred in his chest—a sense of familiarity and comfort he had only felt on rainy evenings by the hearth. For a brief moment, the wolf was a brother, closer even than any human. Perhaps it was better that he had given up the chance to hunt the stag. This stillness was enough.

A rustle of leaves distracted Voran. He turned around to see the white stag returning into the clearing with head bowed. Voran could not believe his good fortune. He *would* be the successful hunter. His family's dishonored name would be raised up again on Vasyllia's lips. Trembling, he reached for his bow.

The stag stopped for a moment, as if considering. More boldly, he walked to Voran. Voran's heart raced at how easy this kill would be, but the excitement died when the stag didn't stop. He stared right at Voran as he strode. Voran pulled out an arrow and nocked it. The stag walked closer.

No. He couldn't do it. This beast was too noble, his eyes too knowing. Killing him would be like killing a man in cold blood.

The stag stopped close enough that Voran could touch him. To Voran's shock, he bowed his two forelegs and dipped his antlered crown to the earth, a king of beasts making obeisance to a youth of a mere twenty-four summers. Gathering courage, Voran approached the stag. His hands shook as he reached out to touch the antlers.

Something shook the branches in the trees ahead. Voran looked up, shoulders tensed. Something, some sort of huge bird, much bigger than a mountain eagle, perched in the crown of an orange-leaved aspen. No, not a bird, something else. Then Voran understood, and terror and excitement fought inside him, leaving him open-mouthed and rooted to the ground. The creature had a woman's face and torso, seamlessly blending with the wings and eagle body. Her head was adorned in golden-brown curls, and each feather shone like a living gem. A Sirin.

She opened her mouth and sang. It was *his* song, but he had never heard it like this.

Voran no longer felt his body. It soared above the clouds; it plumbed the depths of the sea; it hovered on the wings of a kestrel. The song pinioned him like a spear to the earth, but raised him on a spring breeze above the world's confusion. He was once again in the arms of his mother as she nursed him, her breath a soft tickle. He was inside the sun, and its music weaved him into existence. The earth shuddered, and he knew that he could turn it inside out.

The song of the Sirin stopped, and life lost all meaning. It was all grey, ugly, useless without her song.

When he came back to himself, the stag, the wolf, the Sirin were all gone, though her song lingered on the air. It seemed he would never rest, never sleep until he found her again.

The prince, beguiled by the aspen grove, sat down to sleep. A sleep that lasted three hundred twenty-seven years...

From "The Sleeping-Wood"
(Old Tales: Book I)

CHAPTER 2
THE PILGRIM

It was a few hours after midday on the same day, as far as Voran could tell in the enormous dark of leaves. He walked in a direction he hoped would lead him back to known paths, but he still recognized few of the trees or hills. The undergrowth was so thick that Voran suspected he had stumbled on a true wildwood. He didn't know there were any left in Vasyllia, for though there were few outlying villages outside the city proper, many Vasylli had been woodsmen in their time, and hardly an inch of copse, plain, or grove was undiscovered.

One thought niggled the back of his mind, where he tried in vain to keep it contained. It whispered that he was no longer in Vasyllia at all, that he had entered a different realm from the human. Though he had just encountered not one, but *three* legendary creatures, Voran was not yet ready to believe all the Old Tales to be true.

He stumbled out of the murk of oaks into the breathing space of an alder-grove. He was exhausted. Laying down his bow, quiver, and sword, he sat at the base of a young tree and leaned back.

He should be more worried about losing his way. His provisions were few, he had drunk all his water before midday, and poor Lebía would be frantic with worry. But he found he cared little for any of that. He was not even anxious to find Vasyllia. Nothing mattered so much as finding the Sirin, as hearing her song again.

A kind of echo of the music thrummed through him stronger than his own heartbeat. Whenever he stopped moving, everything around him moved with the rhythm of the Sirin's song. The wind tossed the branches in her cadence; the birds chirped in unison. His own heart and breath began to move with it, until he thought he would go mad with its insistence.

It was not the music itself, he realized. It was the incompleteness of it. The Sirin had sung, but not to him. To the trees and the beasts, perhaps, to the summits and rivers, but not to his heart. The thought held a creeping dread. If her incomplete song had caused him to go half-mad, what would happen if she directed her song at him? Nevertheless, to contemplate the possibility of not hearing the song again terrified him, like a childhood dream of a parent's death.

As for finding her, none of the Old Tales were particularly helpful. The Sirin were capricious, appearing in their own good time, in their own chosen place. You did not seek out the Sirin, they sought you out. But he had no intention of waiting patiently for the song to return. He needed to do something.

The stag. Somehow, the white stag and the Sirin were connected. He couldn't exactly understand how, but it made sense on a level of intuition. The stag was of a different world, the world of the tales, the world that never encroached on everyday life. At least until today. If he found the stag again, perhaps it would lead him to the Sirin.

His heart accelerated. Why had he not considered it before? The Dar would have already gathered the hunting party to search for the stag. All of Vasyllia—rich third-reacher and poor first-reacher alike—would be lounging in pavilions and on wool blankets before the city, feasting and awaiting the return of the hunters. Perhaps they had caught the trail already? He must stop them at all costs.

He tried to jump up, but found that his limbs were not responding to the commands of his mind. His eyelids were heavy, his head drooped, hungry for sleep. What had come over him? He had hardly been out for half a day!

Then the realization speared him. He was stuck in a sleeping-wood. By the Heights, surely *that* old story wasn't true as well?

Out of the corner of his vision, a hairy creature waddled toward him. He couldn't move his head to see it clearly. He heard a porcine snuffle, though it was far too large to be a tree-pig. It stood up on two hind legs, growing in the process, all matted hair and dirt and encrusted leaves. It growled.

Something changed in the music of the grove. At first, Voran couldn't place it, then he realized it was the birds. They no longer sang in rhythm to the Sirin's song, but to another music, more somber and ancient. Every branch in his vision hopped with purple, red, golden, brown songbirds.

There was even a firebird trilling on one of the larger branches. The hairy creature snuffled back into the oaks.

"You shouldn't amble through these woods, young man. The Lows of Aer are not to be lightly entered. All manner of strange things are possible here."

Voran strained to move his jaw, and realized that nothing held him in place any more. He jumped up so suddenly that the speaker took two alarmed steps back and raised a walking stick in warning.

"I'm sorry, master," said Voran, eager to make amends. "I didn't mean to startle you."

"No harm done, young man." The voice was as harsh as rock grating on rock, though it had an uncanny melody. It oddly harmonized with the birdsong. "Tell me, what brings you to the Lows?"

The man's face was wrapped in some coarse grey fabric, though a beard poked out of it here and there. He was a huge man, out-gaining Voran by at least a head, and Voran was of the warrior caste. Something about him suggested incredible age, but he moved confidently, like a young man. Voran urgently wanted to make friends with this strange man.

"I am lost. My name is Voran, son of Otchigen of Vasyllia."

The man's grey eyes flashed like the sun reflecting off new snow. "The son of Otchigen? You are far from home, young man. How long have you traveled, then?"

Something in the pit of Voran's stomach twisted. "Only this day. I hunted the white stag."

Voran expected the man to laugh, but instead he unwrapped his face, revealing a smile of recognition. Like the beard, the man's entire face resembled carved stone.

"Ah, a fellow seeker. What good fortune. I am a Pilgrim, young Voran."

Voran could not believe his luck. Pilgrims were unnamed wanderers who traveled all lands searching for the beautiful and the terrible. They were whispered to have a special grace of Adonais. Meeting a Pilgrim in the wild was more valued than catching a questing beast; hosting a pilgrim brought one's family years of prosperity. Many a well-bred housewife would brave open war with her neighbors for the sake of a Pilgrim's visit.

"Good fortune indeed, master! Where do your feet take you this day?" Voran hoped he remembered the correct traditional address to a Pilgrim from his seminary days.

"My feet go where they will, young Voran." The Pilgrim bowed his head, acknowledging the formality gratefully. Voran's shoulders relaxed. "But meeting you perhaps has indicated a surer path. You wish to return to Vasyllia? It will take a week, at least, if you take the usual paths."

Voran's mouth must have dropped open in shock, because the Pilgrim laughed—if harsh rock can be imagined to laugh—and tapped his chin with his stick.

"You meddled with the Powers, young man. No telling what sort of trouble you've gotten yourself into."

"Pilgrim, what do you know of the Sirin?"

The Pilgrim stiffened in suspicion. "Why do you ask? Have you not been chastened enough for your curiosity?"

"Forgive me. It is just…I have seen a Sirin. I have heard her song."

The Pilgrim's eyebrows rose a fraction and his eyes widened a jot, but his body remained still. Voran imagined it took great effort to appear so little moved.

"White stag," the Pilgrim murmured, more to himself than to Voran, "Sirin-song…Is it that time already?" He seemed to make up his mind about something, and now his gaze was firm. "Come, Voran, I will take you to Vasyllia a different way."

Everywhere the Pilgrim went, holloways seemed to carve themselves through the trees. Where Voran saw nothing but trees, the Pilgrim picked out alleys between birches, passages through beeches, and doors through sage-brush. It was like the land belonged to him. As though seeing with new eyes, Voran was inundated with details of the forest he had never before bothered to notice, and he wanted to stop to breathe in the warm birch-smell, to pick out the male sparrow's call from the female's, to run his fingers through rain-soaked juniper for the joy of the sticky drops. But he had to run to keep up with the long strides of the Pilgrim.

"Pilgrim, what was that thing in the sleeping-wood? How did you scare it off?"

The Pilgrim stopped walking, turning to Voran. "That? Oh, nothing but a harbinger." He smiled at something. "Things stir in the deepwoods. Things you Vasylli have not seen, or even heard of, for a very long time."

He continued forward with even more determined tread.

"Voran, tell me something. While traveling, I have heard tales about your father. Are any of them true?"

The anger rose in Voran with the suddenness of nausea.

"Which tales, Pilgrim?" he asked, unable to hide the quiver of anger in his voice. "That he massacred innocent people? Or that he beat my mother, forcing her to run away from Vasyllia in a half-mad state?"

The Pilgrim stopped, abashed.

"Surely *that* is not what is said of Aglaia?"

Voran stopped in mid-stride. The Pilgrim had knowledge of his mother. The possibility made his heart run circles in his chest.

"Pilgrim, do you know what happened to my mother?"

The Pilgrim smiled, but did not answer the question.

"Voran, am I wrong to believe that you have never spoken of these things to anyone? Will you consider it brazen of a Pilgrim to ask your confidence?"

Voran's mouth began speaking even before he gave it permission.

"There is no one I can confess to, Pilgrim. Lebía—my little sister—is still haunted by nightmares. She was only eight years old when we lost both our parents. The Dar is eternally sympathetic, but I don't feel comfortable burdening him with personal worries. His daughter Sabíana, my...intended..." The heat rose in Voran's cheeks. "Well, she is very protective of Lebía, and has a flinty nature. I find it better not to speak of it in her presence."

The Pilgrim smiled knowingly. He pointed forward with his staff, offering Voran to continue speaking while they walked. Voran nodded, and they both walked forward as the carpet of fallen leaves rustled comfortably underfoot.

"Pilgrim, have you heard of the Time of Ordeal?"

"Who has not? Vasyllia's warrior seminary is famed for it. Though I believe my knowledge of it to be several hundred years out of date." He laughed, with a faraway look, as if remembering. Surely he was not *that* old. "Tell me, how many houses are still extant of the original seven?"

"Three remain. All three are segregated, as you know, coming together only for the training and vigils of the Ordeals. The gates of the seminary close, and no one is allowed in or out, not even with messages from family members. The Dar himself has no right to open the gates, except in times of war. The vigils, physical training, and period of intense contemplation are every bit as grueling as the tales have it.

"Eight years ago, I volunteered for the Ordeal of Silence four years before my allotted time. It's a vow that few take, and hardly ever in their sixteenth year, but I sought out the opportunity with pleasure."

"Voran, did you know that some of the oldest legends claim that the successful Ordeal of Silence fulfilled before its time is rewarded with a Sirin's song?"

It explained a great deal. "No, Pilgrim. I did not."

The Pilgrim's smile was knowing. Chills ran down his spine. It was strangely pleasant.

"A week into the ordeal, my mother fell ill. None of the physicians understood it. There were lesions and bruises, and she just withered away. Then she disappeared. No note, no sign of departure, nothing. She just vanished. When I successfully finished the ordeal, the Otchigen I found was half the man he used to be. He had recently returned from a week of searching the wilds, but had found no sign of her. His state grew steadily worse, until I was forced to beg release from my studies, something I hated to do.

"Soon after, Father volunteered for a commission to Karila. There were unfounded rumors of nomad uprisings in far Karila, and it had led to a worsening of tensions between Vasyllia and Karila. He joined the garrison guarding a group of ambassadors who hoped to strengthen Karila's ties to the throne of Vasyllia. I was against Father's going from the start, but the Dar insisted. Said it would do him good."

Through the haze of memory, Voran saw that he and the Pilgrim walked along a more recognizable path than before, and the aspens interspersed with pines hinted that they were coming nearer home.

"You never saw him again," said the Pilgrim.

Voran nodded. He didn't have the heart to speak of the murder of the ambassadors to Karila, or of his father's assumed guilt in their murders.

"Voran, I thank you for your confidence. You may not understand yet why a Pilgrim would be so interested in your family history. I hope, when the trials begin, that you will find some solace in our shared confidence."

Before Voran could answer, he was distracted by a white streak to his left. The stag.

The path turned sharply and led them to a bald patch in the wooded hills, where they entered open sunlight for the first time since leaving the sleeping-wood. The white stag walked toward them in a straight line. He stopped a foot in front of them, and Voran saw that there was a shimmer in the air between them. Voran touched it, and his hand could not pass through. A transparent wall.

"Never mind, old friend," the Pilgrim said to the stag. "We have need of you after all."

The deer raised his head and shook it. Snorting, he pawed the ground with a foreleg. The Pilgrim smiled at Voran.

"He's annoyed with you. He would much rather remain in Vasyllia. Good country, he says, even if a bit on the forgetful side."

Voran was dumbfounded. "Vasyllia is on the other side of that...transparent wall?"

The stag bowed as he had in the clearing, and the gold light from his antlers burst out. Voran raised an arm to his face, but the stag was already gone.

The mustiness of Vasyllia's birches inundated Voran's senses. He and the Pilgrim stood next to a saddle-shaped branch that Voran often slept on during the hot afternoons.

"The white stag is a bearer," the Pilgrim explained, "a sort of...doorway. Between the worlds, you know. But to bear us to Vasyllia, he had to return to the Lows of Aer."

Voran felt no more enlightened than before, but the Pilgrim only rumbled hearty laughter and strode uphill toward Vasyllia.

All of Vasyllia feasted before the gates. Close to the walls, rows of wedge-pavilions marked the families closest to the Dar's regard, all from the third reach. Farther downslope, canvas tents flapped on sturdy frames. First and second-reacher families gathered around makeshift hearths. Heavy pots boiled over with stew. Carts pushed by pantalooned merchants wended their way among the feasters, regardless of social standing. In the midst of it all, a smaller replica of the market day stage had been built, and a storyteller had all the children in stitches, while their parents feigned seriousness, though most couldn't hide their abashed smiles at the ribaldry their children didn't catch.

On any other day, the spectacle would have cheered Voran. He loved a good pageant, as did any Vasylli. To see the entire city together like this, the reaches mingling, was a rare thing. And yet, something was lacking. Somehow, everything about Vasyllia now seemed half-empty, devoid of meaning.

The master bell roared in the palace belfry, announcing the return of the unsuccessful hunting party. Copper bells followed in syncopated chorus, beating in rhythm to the bay of the hunting dogs. Silver bells clamored in the rhythm of a thousand blackbirds.

"Pilgrim," he said, straining to hear himself over the din of the bells, "Will you do my house the honor of staying with us while you visit Vasyllia?"

"Of course, Voran. I thank you for the offer." His voice was more resonant than the bells. For a quick moment, Voran thought that the grey cloak and the stony visage were a kind of mask that the Pilgrim chose to assume for his own purposes, and that his real face was different. But the moment of intuition faded. Voran shook his head, befuddled.

The mountain city loomed before them, many-tiered and many-terraced. Its houses and streets hugged a sloping peak that curved upward like a saber to a pinnacle high above the mists. Amid the pines and spruces, the city of Vasyllia seemed to have grown from the mountains' bones many ages ago. Towers were extensions of crags. Alleys, bridges, and archways were natural hollows and caves, gently bent to human will.

Something deep within the city compelled Voran. Not the Vasyllia built of wood, cobbled with stone, and planted in earth. No, that was little more than a mask, like the mask of the Pilgrim. The real city lay beneath it. For the first time in his life, Voran sensed there was something living, something vital in the heart of Vasyllia, something no one knew about or even suspected. The hidden Vasyllia whispered to him, though he could not parse out the words.

"You surprise me, young Voran," said the Pilgrim. "How quickly you pierce to the heart of things. Whatever happens, my falcon, do not forget this. Vasyllia is everything. You must never let Vasyllia fall. She is *everything*."

Vasyllia is the Mother of Cities. Nebesta, our first daughter, will forever be jealous of her second place. Karila, the runt of the three city-states, will seek every opportunity to thrust thorns into the side of her mother. But I charge you, my sons, remember this. A true mother always slaves for her children...

From "The Testament of Cassían, Dar of Vasyllia"
(The Sayings: Book II, 15:3-5)

CHAPTER 3
THE MARKET

To Voran's annoyance, the Pilgrim plunged into the middle of the assembled throng of Vasylli. Voran had hoped that he could have the Pilgrim to himself for a time, before the tide of adoration inevitably took him. But Voran's worries were unfounded.

The Pilgrim walked among the people of all reaches, speaking to none and being addressed by none. It was almost as if the people could not quite see him. And yet, everywhere he went, faces brightened and conversations turned boisterous. Even the colors of fabrics seemed brighter after he had passed.

Walking unnoticed among the people, Voran and the Pilgrim reached the gates of Vasyllia. As they did, Voran's heart skipped a beat. He had forgotten that they would have to pass through the first reach.

"Pilgrim, shall we go up another way?" He pointed at one of the smaller gates at a higher elevation. It avoided the first reach entirely.

The Pilgrim looked at Voran, and it seemed that he looked through him.

Voran was ashamed of himself and of Vasyllia, ashamed that this splendorous city still hid the poor of the first reach in dim alleyways where dogs and children lay side by side in filth.

"Lead as you will, Voran," said the Pilgrim. His eyes seemed to chide Voran, and he felt his face burning. Voran's heart gently inclined away from his desire. To his own surprise, he found himself leading the Pilgrim *into* the first reach, not away from it.

The gates of Vasyllia yawned to accept them. They passed under the arch—two massive beech-trees carved out of marble, leaning toward each other, locked in an embrace of branches and leaves. The refined perfection of the carvings seemed worse than a mockery compared to the squalor of the first reach.

Voran's senses were overcome, as though he were experiencing the first reach truly anew. Smells of horse-dung and freshly baked bread mixed together. The chatter of playing children and the barking of old mongrels joined in a strange cacophony. Most of the houses were hardly more than sticks leaning against each other, with a board for a door. They were not built along any ordered streets like the second reach. Instead, they seemed to be thrown about randomly. Foul-smelling dirt roads meandered between the houses and towering dung heaps, some of which smoldered with fire that never went out.

And yet, behind all that Voran sensed something he never felt in the third reach. Some native vitality belied the filth and poverty. Yes, the suffering around him was obvious. Every street corner was littered with beggars. Some of them fought for territory out in the open, pummeling each other with no care for the glances of others. A few children had a glint in their eyes as they assessed the contents of his pocket. But most of the people here seemed more *real* than in the other reaches. There was something natural and unconstrained in their interactions with each other. It contrasted sharply to the careful conventionality of the merchants, the sour disdain of the nobles, and the constipated piety of some of the priests.

Voran approached the opulence of the third reach with conflicted emotions. From his newfound perspective, he saw his father's house as a sprawling monstrosity, inundated by peach and cherry trees like weeds.

Among them, Lebía danced, arms outspread. The setting sun lit up three singing firebirds on her shoulder and arms.

"Lebía?"

She turned, startled, and the birds flew up at once, giving her a red-gold halo. She smiled, and her smile's warmth was even more astonishing than the firebirds.

Lebía ran up to him and embraced him, her golden curls pouring all over his shoulders.

He picked her up and twirled her as she loved. She laughed, as though she had not a care in the world. Years of tension sloughed off his shoulders like old skin.

"I'm sorry I took so long, swanling."

"Oh, Voran," she said, ignoring his words completely. "I've been trying for *months* to get the firebirds to come down to me. And today, they all came at once, singing. Can you imagine?"

Voran was astounded. What had happened to his sad Lebía?

"Lebía, dear, run and tell cook to prepare something to eat, quickly. We are honored with a Pilgrim's stay tonight."

Lebía was suitably impressed as she assessed the Pilgrim towering behind them in the shadows of the cherries.

"You grace our house, Pilgrim," she said formally, with a touch of uncertainty.

"The honor is mine, little swan," he said with disarming tenderness. "May the blessing of the Heights be forever yours."

Lebía smiled a little, stealing a quick glance at Voran that said, "I am not quite sure what to make of him." Voran inclined his head toward the house. She bowed to the Pilgrim in the formal Vasyllian manner before running into the house, hair streaming behind her like a banner catching the wind.

Voran sat the Pilgrim at the place of honor, in Otchigen's own high-backed oak chair, then bowed to one knee before him, a supplicant in the traditional ceremony of welcome.

"Pilgrim, I greet you for Vasyllia. I greet you in the name of my father Otchigen (may his honor be restored). I greet you on behalf of my sister and myself, the Dar and his family. I beg you to bestow upon us Adonais's grace, given to all who choose to wander the wilds in search of the beautiful and the terrible."

The Pilgrim looked briefly uncomfortable at the mention of Adonais, but he laid two hands on Voran's head and said, "Sometimes the Heights are moved by our fervent supplication, sometimes they are silent for our hidden good. I wish that Voran will find the strength to choose the right way among all ways, though it be the most painful."

A wave of heaviness lifted from Voran's shoulders. He felt younger than he had in years, worn down as he had been by his family's situation. His head was clear and bright as after a full night's sleep. Still, a shadow lurked behind the final words of the Pilgrim's blessing.

Voran and Lebía served the Pilgrim with their own hands while the servant girls stood in the doorway, gawking at the sight. The Pilgrim hardly ate anything, though he constantly thanked them for the morsels he did eat. He enjoyed the drink in greater quantities. Only after he put his horn down for the final time did Voran and Lebía sit down on either side to begin their own meal.

As they ate, the Pilgrim grew more and more somber. By the time Voran and Lebía had finished, he stared at Voran intently with a pained expression. It unnerved Voran, making the space between his shoulder blades itch wildly. He wanted to pelt the Pilgrim with his questions as soon as possible, but convention would not allow it. At table, a Pilgrim spoke first.

"Voran, tell me about Vasyllia's Great Tree."

Voran's ears pricked up at his tone. There was no doubt—the Pilgrim was testing him. Something told him that much would depend on his answer. He tried to feign calmness.

"Well, it's a bit of a misnomer, isn't it? It's hardly even a tree. It's an aspen sapling. But...well, it's on fire. Every year, the priests officiate a ceremony that summons fire from the Heights. It keeps the tree's fire fresh, and the sapling eternally young."

The Pilgrim looked annoyed.

"No, tell me what it *is*."

Something stirred in Voran's memory, an old story his nanny used to tell him.

"It used to be called the Covenant Tree." The details escaped him, no matter how hard he tried. "A seal of Adonais's promise to Vasyllia."

"What promise?" whispered the Pilgrim, his tone urgent.

"A promise of...protection. Yes, a girdle of protection against...oh, Heights, I don't remember."

The Pilgrim sagged into his chair, a look of open despair in his face.

"The stag was right. How forgetful Vasyllia is. I had not realized how forgetful."

Voran slept badly and lay awake before the sun rose. The morning fog promised to dissipate, though the clouds in his mind threatened to remain the whole day. Something must be done about it.

Not bothering to dress, Voran slipped on his boots and wrapped his bare chest with his old travel cloak. Lebía didn't stir, even when he climbed out the window and slid down the carved lintel to the gardens below, to the brook that Otchigen, with the Dar's blessing, had redirected from one of the city's canals. Their own private river.

At least I can thank you for this one good thing, Father, Voran thought.

Throwing off his boots and cloak, he flung himself into the water, bracing for the icy shock. It was immediate and glorious, the sun inside his head bursting apart his huddled thoughts. As he rose again into the cold, he laughed with pure exhilaration.

Afterward, he sat by the river, wrapped in his cloak, which did little to stave off the late autumn chill. The momentary euphoria of the swim had faded, leaving behind nagging unease. The song of the Sirin, which would often tease him after his morning wash, had stopped entirely since his encounter with the stag.

"Early riser, Voran?" The Pilgrim materialized out of nowhere, making Voran's heart attempt a desperate leap out of his chest. Voran laughed, shaking with more than the cold.

"Good morning, Pilgrim." He gestured for the Pilgrim to sit. "I could not sleep. Too many questions."

"Have you considered that you may not understand the answers yet, even if I told you everything? In any case, I am eager this morning to take part in the feasting before the walls. Will you come with me?"

Inwardly, Voran groaned, but he nodded. "It would be my honor."

Though it was early, already many people were huddled around their makeshift hearths in the fields, busy with breakfast. There was a joyful tenseness in the air; Vasyllia had not yet tired of waiting for the success of the hunt. Already a bustling marketplace stood ramshackle around the storytelling stage.

The married women in headscarves with temple rings, the young women with their hair unbound or in the tell-tale single braid—they all regarded Voran and the Pilgrim with smiles that rarely lit their eyes. The men, in tall beaver hats and wide, sweeping coat-sleeves, barely looked at them before passing on to the more important business of the day.

Pipers and fiddlers danced and spun about among the people, sometimes narrowly missing colliding with them, to general comic effect.

Again, that nagging sense that something was missing bothered Voran. It was as though Vasyllia were a woman far past her prime, who still painted her face in the fashion of newly-married youth.

The Pilgrim showed little interest in the usual wares—ceramics, fabrics, trinkets fashioned from wood, some of which sang on their own, some of which moved about in choreographed figures. The chalices of gold did not hold his attention; the woven tapestries may as well have been rags. He walked past the most ornate stalls with hardly a glance, though many of the merchants' wives, impressed with his mien, tried their loudest to attract his attention.

Like hens flapping their wings to attract a cockerel, Voran thought.

The only stall that seemed to interest the Pilgrim was that of an old potter. It was hardly a stall at all, rather a tattered canvas hung over a frame of grey wood. It stood at the farthest edge of the market, surrounded by refuse. The potter, who smelled as bad as his teeth looked, could not even speak from surprise when the Pilgrim approached him.

All of his wares were plain, unglazed, though Voran sensed that they were made with great skill. The Pilgrim seemed to think so as well. He pointed at an urn of perfect proportion, smooth and undecorated. A handwritten rag sported the price: two copper bits. Voran winced at the price. This potter must have no business at all, if he was willing to sell his handiwork for so little.

"May I buy this?"

The potter stuttered something unrecognizable.

"I'm sorry, my brother," said the Pilgrim. "I did not hear you."

The potter's eyes changed. Their dull yellow cleared to white, and something in them sparked. To Voran's surprise, the potter seemed to shed his years before their eyes. He wasn't old at all. He was hardly more than forty.

"From a traveler, I ask nothing but blessing," he said. "Take it with my thanks."

Voran was taken aback. The man spoke in a beautiful accent, similar to how the old priests spoke. It was a pleasure merely to listen.

"May you be blessed, my brother," said the Pilgrim.

The potter continued to watch after them as they walked back to the center of the market. Shame nagged at Voran, though he couldn't exactly explain why.

The Pilgrim returned to the center of the marketplace, where the tallest hats and the shiniest temple-rings congregated. Approaching a ceramics merchant, he pointed to an urn twice the size of the potter's, glazed and hand-painted with fanciful images of animals and plants interweaving so tightly it made the head spin.

"Ah, you have quite the eye, good sir," simpered the merchant, his five jowls quivering with subservience. "Best Nebesti make, that is."

The Pilgrim raised the decorated urn in his right hand, the potter's simple clay in his left. The crowd stilled. Just before it happened, Voran saw it in his mind's eye, and he had to stop himself from laughing.

"Sudar," said the merchant, using the honorific of respect for a person of indeterminate social class, "may I ask what you intend…"

All the ladies gasped in unison as the Pilgrim dropped both urns to the ground. The Nebesti urn shattered with a beautiful noise. Next to it, the potter's vessel lay as though no one had even touched it.

"And so falls Nebesta," whispered the Pilgrim. His eyes bored into Voran. "But will Vasyllia prove to be as strong as the potter's urn before the coming darkness?"

Voran's stomach churned at the Pilgrim's words, but the Pilgrim merely turned and walked out of the market, accompanied by shocked silence. Voran picked up the potter's urn and turned to pay the merchant.

"Will a silver suffice for your trouble?" Voran asked, abashed.

The merchant glared at him. "Five silver ovals. Not a lead jot less."

Voran chuckled at the merchant's willingness to take advantage of the situation. But he still pulled out only two silvers. He handled them for a moment, looking over their rough edges. These coins were little more than slivers cut from a long bar of grey metal. How strange that they were more cherished in Vasyllia than the life-earned work of an artisan like the poor potter. Shaking his head at his own muddled thoughts, Voran dropped the silvers down in the bulbous palm of the merchant. He rewarded Voran with cursing eyes.

The Pilgrim was already halfway back to the city, his shoulders bent and his step labored. Voran had no trouble gaining on him this time.

"Sudar!" called a voice behind them. It was the potter. "Please," he said, running up to them, "I know you must be a Pilgrim. Forgive me, but...would you honor my house..." He seemed to run out of words, though his hands continued to gesture expressively until he noticed and laughed at himself. Voran had never seen such unguarded simplicity in any man. Everyone he knew seemed to plan every gesture, every word spoken in public. This spontaneity was strangely refreshing.

"Yes, we will come with pleasure," said the Pilgrim.

In the beginning was the Darkness. The Darkness covered the earth. Yet an ember of light there was in the high places. In Vasyllia, upon the mountain, the Harbinger found a people worthy of the Light. He blessed their leader, a man named Lassar, and he made a Covenant with them. As a sign of their calling, he summoned fire from the Heights upon an aspen sapling. As long as the fire burns, as long as the Covenant Tree remains young, Vasyllia remains blessed by the Heights, and the Darkness shall not touch it.

- From "Lassar the Blessed and the Harbinger"
(Old Tales: Book I)

CHAPTER 4
AT THE POTTER'S

The potter's house stood wedged between two taller buildings—a common mead-house and a smithy. It seemed built of shadows more than wood. But the open door revealed a different picture. A bright hearth illumined a much longer interior than Voran expected. At the far end, the house grew into a two-story loft swarming with small children. Their clamor was far more pleasantly inviting than the sour smell of the mead-house next door. The potter's wife, dressed in simple but clean grey homespun, laughed with her eldest daughter as they cooked something tinged with thyme and mint in the cauldron over the hearth. The potter's many wares adorned every nook and cranny in the long house. Some pots clearly contained stores, but many more overflowed with flowers. Colors in mad profusion burst from unexpected corners—fabrics, blossoms, the bright eyes of a ruddy child. Voran was breathless with unexpected pleasure at the harmonious madness of it all.

The Pilgrim seemed to grow taller and wider as he entered, and his eyes lit up with more than the light of the hearth. He sighed in relief.

"Come, come, my dears," called the potter, clapping his hands as though herding a flock of turkeys. "It is as we hoped. A Pilgrim comes to our home! You will take part in the day's celebration, yes, Pilgrim?"

The Pilgrim laughed—a full-throated guffaw that encircled everyone with affection. Even the hearth seemed to leap.

"What an unexpected joy!" he said. "And I thought no one in Vasyllia remembered this day." Voran wondered what he meant.

The simmering household boiled over, and all the children exploded into movement that looked perfectly rehearsed. Two girls, their braids pinned to the top of their heads, carried an embroidered hand towel to the Pilgrim. A boy of about ten years floated over with a silver basin of water—where did a potter manage to find himself a *silver* basin? —and spilled only a few drops on his way to the Pilgrim. The Pilgrim washed his hands, then lowered his head. The boy's eyes sparkled with delight. He had obviously been hoping for this moment. He threw the remainder of the basin over the Pilgrim's head. The Pilgrim exploded into laughter, and the two girls with the hand towel could hardly keep their hands steady for their own giggling.

The eldest daughter brought a loaf the size of her head, still warm by the smell of it. The eldest son carried a frothing tankard of mead carved in the shape of a mallard. It was exquisite workmanship. The smallest boy—no more than two or three—stood by them with a ceramic cup full of salt. The Pilgrim tore off a piece, dipped it in the ale, then in the salt. He smelled it with his eyes closed, savoring. Then he threw it over everyone's head directly into the hearth. Everyone cheered. Then he downed the tankard, leaving a sip for the boy who brought it. The boy looked like he had been given gold coins for his birthday.

Pleasant gooseflesh tingled Voran's back and neck. He had never seen anything like these rituals. They were rustic, but clearly ancient. How pitiful his own words must have sounded to the Pilgrim when he welcomed him into Otchigen's cold, empty feasting hall.

The potter walked around his children, tucking in a shirt-tail here, fixing a stray hair there. His wife gestured with eloquent hands to two more girls coming down from the loft so insistently that one of them fell before reaching the final rung. The entire family presented itself to the Pilgrim. But instead of bowing before him as Voran had expected, they exploded into a complicated line dance that weaved in and out of a circle of which the Pilgrim was the center. It felt spontaneous, and yet no one stepped on each other's feet. Not even the smallest children. Above the noise of stomping feet, a song rose as if from the depths of the earth. Everyone sang it, even the Pilgrim.

"*We greet you, distant traveler!*
Rejoice, beloved brother!
You've come from behind the mountain,
You've risen to the high places.
Now bless our grass, our flowers blue,
Our bluebells with your words, your eyes.
Warm our hearts with gentle words,

Look into the heart of these brave children,
Take out the evil spirits from their souls,
Pour into them your living water,
Whose source is locked, and the key is in Evening's hands.
Evening the bright took a walk and lost the keys.
And you have walked the road and found it.
May you bless us, if you will,
for many years, for the long harvests,
for the endless ages of ages!"

Voran found himself inching away from the song and the dance, since he was not party to its mysteries. But the eldest girl took him by the hand and led him into the pattern. To his own surprise, he melded into it without a thought. Something about the steps, the shape of the dance seemed natural, intrinsic, as though his feet already knew what to do. He even found himself singing the song, which they repeated three times.

Finally, they all ended up in a rough circle around the hearth, seated.

"Will you say the incantation, Pilgrim?" asked the potter.

The Pilgrim stood up and raised his hands and began to chant:

"The Evening of the year has come,
And the joys of sun will fade to naught.
Now sleep in earth, our fathers dear,
Kept warm by our remembrance, tears.
We'll give you joy again anon,
When the rising sun sees snow no more."

The potter handed him a bowl filled with oil. The Pilgrim poured it over the fire. It was scented with lavender. Voran breathed in as long as he could, savoring the symphony of herb, cooked fowl, and sour mead.

Now, platters of food passed from one to the next around the circle, and everyone ate with their hands. A large horn full of mead was also shared by all. Voran's head spun from all the constant movement, but his heart was warm and content.

Was he even still in Vasyllia? Nothing in the third reach compared to this simple joy in life. He had thought that the scholars and warriors of the seminary had preserved the mores and traditions of old Vasyllia. But there, everything was formalistic, strict, conventional to a fault. Repeated movements without inner content. Everything in the potter's world was replete with significance.

"Thank you, my friends," said the Pilgrim from his seat, "for celebrating the departed with me. It is fitting. I had thought no one kept the Evening anymore."

He looked at Voran, his eyes probing. Voran felt the flush creep up his cheek.

"Tell me," Voran whispered.

"The Evening, my falcon. It is the old festival of the dead. The remembrance of our departed parents. The send-off of the world into the sleep of winter."

Two of the younger girls giggled at Voran's stupidity. He was surprised to find himself smiling.

"I have never heard of this festival. How many others have I not heard of?"

"There's the Day of Joy," said a boy with a shock of white hair, probably no more than three or four. "Then the Presentation of the Bride, the Awakening of the Ground, the Cleansing of the Harvest, the Summoning of Fire..."

"*That* one I know," said Voran, abashed at the child's precocity.

"There is much that you third-reachers don't notice, I'm afraid, Vohin Voran," said the potter, laughing. "And even more that you've forgotten."

Voran was mortified. The potter had named him, and he had no idea what the potter's name was.

"Sudar, forgive my rudeness. What is your name?"

"I am called Siloán, Vohin Voran. You are welcome at my hearth."

Again, Voran wondered at the purity of the potter's accent. Priest-like, it was. As though speaking the language of Vasyllia had sacred meaning in and of itself.

The conversation weaved in and out of Voran's hearing as he descended into brooding. Shame uncoiled itself inside him. There was so much he didn't know about his own city. So much beauty wasted in the putrid alleyways of the crumbling first reach.

Siloán put a rough hand on Voran's shoulder and looked him in the eye. It lifted the fog from Voran's heart. They conversed. Easily, without constraint. Siloán spoke about things Voran never expected a potter to know—about ancient songs, about the ways of craft that Voran thought long lost, handiwork that required creativity of mind as well as skill of hand.

"You see, Voran...I am sorry, may I call you by your godsname?"

Voran hadn't heard the term "godsname" since he was in school. It was an archaism, a term found more often in the Sayings than in daily conversation.

"Yes, of course, Siloán. It would be my honor."

"I thank you. As I was saying, your bewilderment at the richness of our life here in the first reach is understandable. It is all connected with our general sickness as Vasylli. You must have noticed how the people of our great city prefer cheap, gaudy wares to the beauty of a craft well done."

"Yes," said Voran, thinking of the shattered Nebesti urn. "Things are not made with beauty in mind anymore."

"Have you considered why this is?" The potter seemed eager to share his own theories, so Voran extended an open palm to him, encouraging him to speak on. "Creating something truly beautiful requires labor pains. Vivid as childbearing. Not many willingly choose such a path, especially if every craftsman is encouraged to churn out cheap trinkets by the dozen."

"Yes, I see," said Voran, warming to the topic. "Without the time of labor, there will be no pleasure from the fulfillment."

"You both reason well," said the Pilgrim. "But I want you to think it through to its end. Imagine if every person in the entire city-state avoided these labor pains, as you've called them. Not just craftsmen, but fathers and mothers, priests and elders, Dars and representatives."

"It is like a disease," said Voran, feeling the gaze of the Pilgrim like fire on his cheek. "A disease that would weaken Vasyllia. Not only as a nation. All would become weak in spirit. If not already dead."

"And consider this," said the Pilgrim, his every word carefully enunciated. "What if Vasyllia were faced with an enemy. Not any enemy, but one that lived for an ideal. That was ready to die for it. What if this enemy were a follower of a dark power, servants of another god?"

"We would not stand against them," whispered Voran, his voice heavy. "Not for long."

"Voran, that is what I fear as well," said Siloán. "We are a trivial people if we only come to Temple services because Dar's law closes trade on holy days. A people with dead hearts."

"And so we must do everything we can to reawaken that flame in the heart," said a new voice from the doorway.

The potter beamed at the newcomer. "Otar Gleb! We only needed you to make this evening perfect. Come, come!"

The newcomer was a young priest whom Voran didn't know. He was dressed in a linen cassock with no adornment other than a red embroidered belt. Blond ringlets and short beard with a few white streaks framed a sharp face with exaggerated features. At first glance, he seemed fantastically ugly, especially with a broken nose that covered half his face. But his smile came easily and illumined his pale-blue eyes. When he smiled, he was beautiful.

"Vohin Voran," he said, approaching Voran and taking his forearm in the traditional warrior greeting. "We have not met, but I have long wished to know you. How fitting that it should be this day, and in such illustrious company."

When he saw the Pilgrim, he went a little pale, as though he saw something in him that Voran did not. The Pilgrim smiled in acknowledgement and nodded once.

"By the..." Otar Gleb cleared his throat and chuckled. "What an honor to meet a Pilgrim. Truly you bless this day, when we bring joy to all our dead."

"Vasyllia is blessed while its clerics still zealously labor for the flame in the heart," said the Pilgrim enigmatically.

The conversation around the hearth grew even more boisterous, if that was possible. Voran watched the young priest intently. He was different from most priests he knew. Less concerned with outward appearances. When he spoke to someone, even the smallest child, he looked them in the eye and didn't flinch or allow his eyes to flick away. His smile was always ready, always present in the corner of his eyes, but he only let it blossom fully when he felt joy in himself. Everyone seemed physically drawn to him, despite his ugliness.

"Otar Gleb," said Voran in a rare lull in the conversation, "please forgive my rudeness, but are you a first-reacher?"

"No, Voran. I am a second-reacher. Merchant stock, as it happens. But with no interest or ability in the fine art of trading. And in any case, you know, I'm sure, that one of our priestly vows is the rejection of reacher status."

Siloán chuckled. It seemed that he and Gleb shared a private jest.

"But now that you mention it," said Gleb, "I find the division into reaches to be a crippling reality for the city, don't you think, Siloán?"

"No, not in the least," said the potter. "Only in our segregation can we hold to the traditions that are so fast disappearing, even in your second reach."

"But the separation limits the reach of your wares, does it not?" said Voran. "Not many third-reachers will buy first-reacher work these days."

In answer, the potter reached behind himself and pulled out an urn, very similar to the one he sold to the Pilgrim. Except it was more beautiful. At first glance, it seemed no more than a simple clay urn. But the longer Voran looked at it, the more perfect it seemed. Its proportions were flawless. Its form and color were unique. The gradations of the natural clay had been manipulated with purpose, but to look as though it were the work of nature. There were even words and figures in between the swirls of clay, invisible to the careless eye.

"Yes, I see you understand," said the potter. "If this urn were to appear in a third-reacher stall at the market, it still would only sell to the discerning eye. And those are rare in any age. Especially our decadent one."

"You do realize that by limiting yourself thus you are depriving your family of comfort and riches?"

"Oh, you third-reachers!" laughed Siloán. "You have so much that your hearts have become small. You can live very well with very little. Sometimes, it is better this way."

Voran wondered if that were really true.

They spent most of the day at Siloán's. Afterward, Voran was morose and unwilling to talk. He meandered through the first reach's dingy streets, wondering at how few trees remained in these levels. The only greenery he saw was the occasional kitchen garden. The Pilgrim took his arm and led him up a staircase leading into the second reach. Just before entering the archway to the clean and orderly streets of the military sector, they stopped at a naked outcrop with a perfect view of the crowd in the plain still feasting in front of the city. From this vantage point, the embroidered designs of the pavilions of the rich took on a life of their own. Here was an embroidered dragon, there a longboat with sail unfurled, even owl eyes staring from butterfly wings. Everywhere the colors danced as the mist from the waterfalls showered the feasters with drops of gold and opal.

"Beautiful, is it not?" The voice behind them was low and musical.

"Good eve, Mirnían," said Voran, feeling oddly abashed. "I had hoped you would be about. I wanted you to meet the Pilgrim in person."

"A Pilgrim in Vasyllia," said Mirnían, his right eyebrow barely rising.

Voran felt like a hump-backed invalid next to Mirnían, though the prince was not much taller than he. Curling gold hair resting on his shoulders, eyes grey as a storm, perfectly straight teeth—Mirnían had everything that Voran did not have, but desired greatly.

"My father the Dar will be pleased to see you, though he is much engaged with matters of state at the moment. I can walk you through the market in the meantime."

"We spent most of the morning there, Mirnían," said Voran.

"Well," said Mirnían as though brushing off a mosquito, "I hardly have time today, in any case. Pilgrim, surely you have tales to tell of the other lands. Yesterday's storyteller was a disaster. Would you honor us on the stage? Tomorrow will be the last triumphal day before the Dar calls off the hunt for the white stag. Your story may help alleviate the disappointment the city will feel at our famed hunters not finding any trace of it." Mirnían stared at Voran significantly.

"I would like nothing more, Prince Mirnían," said the Pilgrim.

"Excellent. I will send for you at the proper time. You must forgive me, but matters of state, you know."

Voran breathed a sigh of relief at Mirnían's departure.

"Why do you dislike Mirnían?" asked the Pilgrim.

Voran was annoyed at the Pilgrim's astuteness.

"We were very close as children, and soon I am to be his brother. And yet...I don't dislike him, it's only..."

"Tell me, did he take the Ordeal of Silence with you that year, Voran?"

Voran's heart sank. He nodded.

"He did not last, did he?"

"No, he broke after two weeks. But there is no shame in that. It is a very difficult ordeal."

The Pilgrim stared without expression at Voran, until Voran looked down in shame.

"Voran, do you know why the Nebesti urn cracked so spectacularly, while the potter's vessel did not?"

Voran shook his head, not daring to raise it yet.

"It was baked in too hot a fire."

Voran looked up.

"I thought the heat strengthened the clay, Pilgrim."

"The right amount of heat does, just as the right amount of adversity strengthens any relationship between two people. But there is one fire that is always too hot. Do you know what that is?"

Voran did not answer.

"Envy."

They joined the main road of the second reach that led through the open marketplace—now empty of stalls—toward the center of Vasyllia. Ahead of them stood the large central square, at the heart of which stood the Covenant Tree. Pale flames danced over the translucent leaves of the aspen sapling, which stood barely taller than a man. For a moment, Voran thought the fire was low. But that was unlikely. It was months still until the day of the summoning of the fire.

"Pilgrim. Do you think the potter is right? Can we restore the ideal of Vasyllia? Or are we just idealistic dreamers?"

The Pilgrim exhaled a long, wheezy breath, all the while staring at the sapling. Finally, he looked at Voran with heavy eyes.

"Come, I will show you."

The Pilgrim took Voran's arm, his grip like an eagle's talon. A white light enclosed them, rising out of nowhere, and for a moment Voran saw nothing but the light. Then it dimmed, and the aspen burst into wild color. The aspen was surrounded by red and silver fire—firebirds and moonbirds frolicked and sang with the kind of joy one sees in a one-year-old child just awoken from a full night's sleep. Surging waves of purple, red, orange, blue, brown pulsated around the tree—songbirds unable to contain themselves enough to sit on a branch. All their music interweaved as though imagined by a single mind, harmonized from a single melody.

The single melody came from far above the aspen sapling. Three Sirin reigned over their kingdom of lesser birds, flying a distant circuit around Vasyllia. One wept, one laughed, one remained stern and impassive. All three sang, each her own variation of a single melody, each weaving in and out of the other, first a motif of joy, then a shadow of grief, replaced by a long moment of introspection. Then all three sang in unison, and Voran fell on his knees, unable to bear the weight of the music pressing down on him.

All around, Vasylli walked with heads high, backs straight, quiet joy and hidden song evident in each face. Strange flowing robes adorned both men and women. It was as though one of the old Temple frescoes had come to life.

"This is Vasyllia as it used to be, yes?" Voran asked the Pilgrim, his voice hardly above a whisper. The Pilgrim inclined his head, looking around with an expression Voran couldn't quite define.

As he looked at them, Voran was amazed at the faces of these past Vasylli. Nearly everyone in his own Vasyllia walked with bent shoulders, eyes turned inward, faces full of cares. In *this* Vasyllia, joy burst forth from the eyes of every person. But there was something more. Voran tried to focus above the music of the Sirin, and suddenly he saw.

"Pilgrim! I can see every one of their talents. That man. With his own hands, he will carve the great stone chalices catching the falls, working days and nights without end. When I look at that girl with the long hair, I see an embroidered banner that will be carried in battle, sparking inspiration in the hearts of many warriors. That woman will raise a Dar long to be remembered. That man will raise a temple in a land far away, a land of endless fields of undulating grass. And their hearts! Every person has a flame in their hearts, burning steadily. What is that flame?"

"It is the soul-bond with the Sirin. This is the Vasyllia of the days of the Covenant. Over one thousand years ago. Lassar of Blessed Memory is Dar."

Voran gasped in pleasure. No time was more decorated with legends. No time gave more of the Old Tales and Sayings than the reign of Lassar. But the pleasure was short-lived, as his own Vasyllia returned to his thoughts, so grey and drab compared to this place.

"How much beauty has been lost, Pilgrim. Every person here is a maker, a creator of vast potential. I can see every man, woman, and child shine with beauty, beauty made and beauty lived. Now all we care about is the latest trinket from Karila sold at market."

Voran sat down on the bare earth, hugging his knees. He felt exhausted, emptied, confused. Why did the Pilgrim show him so much? Was something expected of him in return?

"Why did we lose it all, Pilgrim?"

The Pilgrim's half-smile faded as he looked down at Voran. "Many reasons, my falcon. Chief among them, you forgot your part of the Covenant."

"We have always been taught that the Covenant between Vasyllia and Adonais was merely an instructive tale. A reminder of Vasyllia's greatness, surely, but not literally true. What have we forgotten?"

The light faded as though the sun were obscured by a cloud. Voran looked up at the sky, but there were no clouds in the sky. Yet the darkness deepened. A chill crept up his arms and down his back. He shivered.

"You forgot the Darkness, Voran. It has been so subtle, these centuries. So wise. And now, no one even remembers it. But it lives. Look up, Voran."

He pointed at the sun, looking at it directly, to Voran's amazement. Squinting in expectation, Voran turned to the sun.

It was almost completely gone, a creeping darkness devouring it. The darkness ate and ate, until nothing was left. Voran began to shake with fear.

"It comes, Voran. The Darkness comes."

All around Voran, men and women were running about, hands shielding their faces in fear. Mothers clasped their children, husbands encircled the waists of their wives. They were no longer in the flowing robes of Lassar's time. Voran's heart plunged.

"Yes, Voran," said the Pilgrim. "This omen is not of the vision. It is happening now."

Vasyllia roiled around them. A river of people rushed through the gates back into the city. Guards in the Dar's black livery ran past Voran, trying to restore order.

"Come, Pilgrim, we must go." He took the Pilgrim by the arm, but the big man did not budge. Voran turned back at him, questioning.

"Voran, it begins. So soon, and so much yet unsaid. They move so quickly against us. If you remember anything, remember this. Find the Living Water. They must not find it first."

The prince lay dead, his heart pierced by his own brother's arrow. The wolf and the falcon watched over him.

"Fetch the Living Water," said the wolf.

The falcon flew beyond the thrice-nine lands, into the thrice-tenth kingdom. He found the Living Water under the shade of a young apple tree in the first garden of the world. He poured it over the prince's wounds, and they faded away as though they never were. The prince came to life again...

From "The Tale of the Deathless and the Living Water"
(Old Tales: Book II)

CHAPTER 5
THE STORY

Though the darkness that swallowed the sun soon dissipated, it took the greater part of the day to calm Vasyllia. After ensuring Lebía was well, Voran put on full armor and joined the ranks of his brother-warriors as they attempted to calm the people and prevent any outbursts of public violence. Only a few young men, their blood up, tried to take advantage of the mêlée to settles scores, but they were easily contained.

Voran returned late to find the house asleep. Not bothering to take off his mail, he crumpled in exhaustion at Lebía's side and feel into a deep sleep.

He dreamt that he walked back to the center of Vasyllia, toward the Great Tree. The path widened into the square, paved in large flagstones, all four sides lined with the gabled inns and taverns of the second reach of Vasyllia. The burning aspen seemed small, its flames sputtering.

Walking around the sapling, the Pilgrim caressed its leaves as one caresses a lover before a long separation. His singsong rumble was nearly in unison with the hum of the twin waterfalls, which from this vantage point appeared to plunge directly on either side of the aspen, framing it. His words were inaudible, but chant-like. His joy-pierced tones were tinged with grief.

The flames of the tree flared for a moment, then died.

The song of the Sirin flooded the air. Voran's Sirin flew once around the sapling, chanting with the Pilgrim. Voran's chest ached as though his heart were torn out. He was desperate to run to her, to beg her to sing to him, but as is the way with dreams, he was immobile as stone.

Voran awoke to clanging pots and shattering crockery. The house was in an uproar, servants rushing about and whispering nervously to each other.

"Cook, what is all this racket?" Voran asked as he entered the kitchens, still in yesterday's mail.

The cook, thin as a reed—everyone jokingly called her "your lardship" behind her back—did not even stop to look at him.

"Prince Mirnían sits in the high hall with the Pilgrim, breaking his fast. There is to be a city-wide storytelling today. The Dar hopes it will calm the people after yesterday's omen."

"And you did not think to wake me?" Voran growled.

She flashed him a knowing smile and turned the piglets spinning over the hearth. "Lady Lebía said you've not snored so loudly in weeks. It would've been a crime to wake you."

By the time Voran dressed and made his way down to the hall, Mirnían and the Pilgrim were already mounting horses in the courtyard.

"Voran," said Mirnían with a sardonic smile, "so good of you to see us off. I had quite an appetite today. Her lardship tells me there are no more partridges in your cellars, I'm afraid. Do tell her how much I enjoyed them."

Voran cursed inwardly. Partridge was his favorite.

"I will see you at the storytelling, I hope. Don't forget that it's in the main square today. All festivities outside the city walls have been canceled after the omen." Mirnían turned his horse around and rode off. The Pilgrim followed, surrounded by an honor guard of twelve black-cloaked spear-bearers in helms.

As he joined the crowd of all reaches walking to the storytelling, Voran was pleased that he had an opportunity to walk alone. In his worn travel cloak, he easily blended in with the crowd, affording a rare pleasure of hearing the latest rumors.

Most of what he heard was nervous tattle, the people still nagged by yesterday's fear. Voran let those conversations wash over him, seeking a word or phrase that would force his attention. There! The words were innocuous enough on their own, but there was something unnerving about them.

"You don't believe me?" She was a matronly sort, fat from much childbearing. "He *saw* it, I tell you. That's why I'm braving this morning, what after the omen, you know. I want to see it for myself."

"Your husband is always seeing things." The second speaker was an older woman, probably unmarried, at least judging by a bitterness that sounded long-established. "He's as reliable an observer as he is a teller of tall tales. Every time he tells that story about hunting the boar, he adds to the number of his wounds."

"You *never* give him the credit he deserves. You will see. He said it quite clearly. The fire on the aspen is nearly out. And we're nowhere near the day of summoning."

Voran's skin crawled. Perhaps what he had seen was not a dream, but a vision? Had the Pilgrim sung a funeral dirge for the tree?

Straining for the sight of the tree through the houses, Voran pushed forward through the crowd. As he entered the square, he stopped, hardly noticing the grumbling of the people who jostled past him. There was no mistaking it. The fire on the tree was simmering, no more. It looked as though a gust of wind would put it out.

Voran found himself stranded, the square too full for him to push his way closer to the stage at the foot of the tree. The tension stretched around him like a viol string at its snapping point.

"Friends!" Mirnían spoke from the stage, and the crowd's noise lessened. "Some of you have already heard of our unexpected honor. Vasyllia is visited by a Pilgrim."

All around Voran a murmur of appreciation rose. The tension eased palpably, and Voran breathed out with it.

"He has traveled alone for many days, and all for the pleasure of seeing our land. Let us welcome him."

More tension released in the music of their clapping hands. Even Voran, who liked to think himself impervious to mob mentality, felt his heart swelling.

"Yesterday was a dire day, my friends, there can be no doubting it. Though I am loath to say it, the hunt for the white stag has been canceled, and the omen of the darkened sun is enough to chill the heart of the bravest. But lest we think our own misfortunes too great, let us hear of the horrors and wonders of the other lands. I put it to you, dear friends. Shall we let the Pilgrim take the mantle of the storyteller for the day?"

Once again, universal cheers.

The Pilgrim walked forward and assessed the crowd. All cheering stopped as the people shriveled under his gaze. Some even began to mutter in discomfort. An awkward chuckle broke out somewhere, but was cut off immediately. The Pilgrim seemed to be searching for someone or something. His eyes caught Voran's, and Voran heard the Pilgrim's voice clearly in his mind: *I am sorry, my falcon. I am sorry for everything.*

Voran's breath grew labored. A sense of inescapable calamity seized him. He tried to still his breathing, but the more he tried, the tighter his chest constricted. It was painful just to stand there. He needed to escape, to be anywhere but here. But he was hemmed in on all sides.

"I once knew a man who owned a great wealth of cherry trees," the Pilgrim began in a storyteller's sing-song. "His cherries were legendary—they were just sour enough, just sweet enough, just red enough. But one year the cherry orchard produced no fruit at all. Some gardeners blamed the warm weather; others blamed the soil. The rich man was greatly saddened by this.

"He walked through his favorite cherry orchard, amazed at the beauty of the trees. The leaves were the same transparent green they were in early spring; a faint fragrance rose with every breath of wind. They were a sight to behold, but they had no cherries, and it was nearing the end of the picking season.

"And the rich man grew more and more sad at the failure of the orchard. But there was nothing to be done. The ground was expensive; he could afford no fruitless trees. And so, with tears in his eyes, he took an axe and chopped down every tree himself."

The Pilgrim stopped. Slowly at first, then rising like the wind before a thunderstorm, the crowd gave rein to its disappointment. The Vasylli never liked parables, thought Voran. The sense of impending calamity lessened, but it took a great force of will to unclench his fists. There were white marks on his palms where the nails bit.

Mirnían approached the Pilgrim, apparently encouraging him. The Pilgrim's shoulders sagged an inch further with each of Mirnían's words. He seemed a man broken by grief. It was strangely incongruous—the scene was one of festival, with banners fluttering on every windowsill and the people dressed in their finest. And yet, the fire on the tree sputtered.

Mirnían seemed to have won the argument, because the Pilgrim faced the people again with a story on his lips.

The Tale of the Prince and the Raven

Beyond the thrice-nine lands, in the thrice-tenth kingdom, there lived a restless prince. He had everything he could ever want—riches, health, a beautiful princess as his intended bride. But despite all this, wanderlust ate at him constantly.

So he left behind his love to climb the mountains, to explore the forests, to swim the rivers, seeking to slake the thirst of his restlessness. But nowhere did he find the peace he sought.

One day he stopped to drink from a pure mountain spring. It was a taste of paradise.

"Do you like the water?" croaked a voice behind his back.

It was a withered old man, all tawny beard and hair, twisted and resembling a tree stump more than a person.

"Yes, I do," said the prince. "I do not think I have ever tasted such water."

The creature leered with a leathery, lipless mouth. "Hah! That is nothing. I have water that will make this water taste like sand. Not only will you never thirst again, but your greatest desire will be fulfilled instantly. What do you desire most, young man?"

The prince could not believe his ears. Could this be the end of his quest?

Just then he looked up and saw a great eagle lounging on a spruce branch like a monarch on a throne. What exhilaration there must be in soaring through the infinite sky!

"I wish to fly as the eagle," said the prince.

"A very worthy desire. The Raven can provide that."

The prince had heard of the Raven, a mysterious spirit of the forest, though he supposed it nothing more than a story in the shriveled imagination of a village hag. He remembered the tales he heard in childhood—stories tainted with blood and loss. A creeping fear wrapped itself around his heart, but he laughed it to scorn.

"What do you require in return?" the prince asked.

"Oh, I require nothing. The virtue of my enchantment is such that I will partake, in small measure, of your pleasure."

"Is there nothing else?"

The Raven shook his head, and the trees began to quiver, and the wind moaned like a crying woman.

"So be it," said the prince.

The Raven pulled a carved wooden flask from his dirty robes, and the prince drank. Fear suddenly flashed in dreadful clarity as he saw the face of his beloved in his mind, pale as death. He gasped as his breathing grew more painful. Terror gripped him. He could not breathe. A light stabbed his eyes, and he fell.

It took him a blank eternity to realize he was flying. His feathered arms caressed the waves of wind as they hugged his eagle body. His eyes met the sun's rays, and he did not need to look away. Through his eagle eyes, the sun was a spinning furnace of purple, orange, even green tongues of flame.

A dark streak dimmed the sun for a moment. A swan, feathers black as a mountain's peak at midnight, flapped toward the mountain stream. Her beauty enraged him, impelling him to destroy this usurper of his glory. He screamed and plunged on the unsuspecting swan.

An alien emotion disturbed him. Pity, a frantic desire for mercy. The eagle recognized the prince still inside him, and he unleashed his anger to drown out the vestiges of man. A warm stream of blood poured over his talons. He could smell the swan's life oozing out. Dropping her corpse with disgust, he turned once again to the dancing wheel of fire.

An intense pain clutched his chest. The colors of the sun turned grey and the whirling dance froze; the air cut his lungs like daggers. His arms lost their feathers; pudgy nobs replaced them.

He came to himself near the stream, a man again. He crawled to its edge. There, propped against a boulder, lay his beloved princess. Her face was white with death. He touched her cheek and took her hand. It was slippery; blood streamed down her arm. Her shoulder had the unmistakable imprints of an eagle's talons.

A noxious croak jolted him. On a swinging branch above him, a raven was laughing, its black head nodding insanely. The prince lunged at it, but it flew without effort up to the sun, laughing still. Near the roots of a nearby tree lay the wooden flask, taunting him.

Silence. Then whispers bubbling up like a pot of stew reaching a boil.

"What a horrible story."

"Is that a Karila story? Never heard anything so absurd."

"What a disappointment. They don't make Pilgrims like they used to, it would seem. What tripe."

The whispers rose into a dull groan, the mass of people rocking back and forth like a river in the wake of a longship. Then they parted in the middle. Voran was confused at first, not being able to see, but as the parting reached him, he saw Rogdai and a few other wardens leading a young man, dressed in brown and green woodsman's garb. Voran had a vague memory of the boy—he was a few years his junior in the warrior seminary. A dreamy, odd sort of boy. Not good for battle. What was his name? Tolnían, he remembered. A scout.

He felt cold as he realized what that meant. The chief door warden was leading a simple scout directly to Mirnían in the middle of a storytelling. Voran pushed some very annoyed old people aside and joined the small party approaching the stage. Rogdai saw him and looked as though he wanted to say something cutting, but he nodded curtly and looked forward.

"Rogdai," said Mirnían, simmering with rage. "I hope you have sufficient reason to disrupt the storytelling."

Rogdai bowed silently and moved aside, prompting Tolnían to walk forward.

"My prince," said the young scout in a soft voice barely heard over the crowd's commotion. "Living Water has been found in Vasyllia. They say a blind man has already been healed."

"Rogdai," said Mirnían, no longer trying to keep his anger contained, "you are a fool if you think this sort of rumor was worth stopping the storytelling."

"But, Highness..."

"Don't interrupt me. You know the proper protocol. It should be the elders in private counsel that gave us this information."

"Mirnían," said Voran, his heart dropping to his heels. "Rogdai is right. The Living Water is never spoken of in the Old Tales without mention of the Raven and his eternal quest to seek out the Living Water. To become the Deathless One."

Just two days ago all that would have seemed little more than childhood silliness to Voran. But no longer.

"The Raven?" Mirnían looked like he couldn't decide whether to laugh or fume in anger. "Deathless ones? Voran, have you gone mad?"

"Whether or not those old stories are historically accurate, they all contain deep truths that we should never ignore. Living Water never appears without—"

"Enough!" cried Mirnían, now red in the face. "Rogdai, you and the scout are to report immediately to the Dar. Voran, go home before you embarrass yourself any further. Is this the sort of behavior befitting the future consort of the Darina Sabíana?"

The words echoed in the square and in the eyes of the crowd

surrounding them. Voran was struck dumb. Mirnían had never yet chosen such a public stage to humiliate him. He turned to seek out the Pilgrim on the stage. Maybe the Pilgrim could speak some sense to Mirnían. But there was no one there. The Pilgrim was gone.

Lassar's days are long gone. Four hundred ninety-six years to the day of his death. And again, the darkness preceding his Covenant gathers. It reveals itself in the plague that already rages in the outer reaches of the Three Lands. The Raven escaped Vasyllia. For all I know, he is at the brink of finding Living Water. But no Harbinger has come to give light to my reign. Am I wrong, then, to seek a renewal of covenant with Adonais for my people, though it cost me my very soul?

From "The Apocryphal Diary of Dar Cassían"
(The Sayings, Appendix D:6e)

CHAPTER 6
THE DAR'S DAUGHTER

Sabíana despised high day afternoons. Once a week, it behooved Adonais—or at least the clerics who spoke in his name—to confine all members of the Dar's household to the palace. All anyone wanted was to be outside for as long as possible before the winter, especially since today was a day of story. Instead, they were ordered to dedicate the half-day to the restoration of the Temple holies. Today—a day of deep winter-blue sky, crisp air, and birdsong—Sabíana's sacred work was the restoration of an ancient banner. She tried to remember how many weeks in a row she had slaved over this half-tattered rag. She lost count at seven.

It was a large square banner depicting a Sirin in flight. The style was archaic: the Sirin was flattened, her face oddly twisted toward the viewer. Her woman's head was badly fitted to her eagle body by an almost nonexistent neck; the wings were far too widely outstretched, the talons looked too long with respect to the rest of the body. The face was long gone, and even in the weeks of her work, Sabíana had managed only to finish the eyes.

To her dismay, she saw that one of the eyes was bigger than the other. How had she not noticed it before? She silently groaned.

Two other girls joined her soon after she began, sitting opposite her at the long table brought into her chamber once a week. They sat demurely, not daring to speak, though the stifled smiles warned that soon decorum would fail, and the gossip would begin. Sabíana wondered if she would even have five minutes of silence with her thoughts.

"What a fine figure that Yadovír made at Temple today, did he not?" attempted one of them, a pale girl of thirteen.

"Yado—who? Do you mean that *first-reacher?*" hissed the other, appalled.

Sabíana groaned, audibly this time. The girls' heads snapped back to their work, and she won another few minutes of blessed silence.

Now that her fingers overcame their initial clumsiness to act of their own accord, Sabíana could finally give a little rein to her thoughts. She told herself she would not think of Voran. Immediately his green eyes invaded her mind. They were striking in his pale face, framed by dark, shoulder-length hair. Sabíana ground her teeth in frustration.

He had changed. For days, he had not so much as sent her a note, much less seen her. Not for the first time, the dark thought nibbled at her mind. If she had not pursued him, would Voran have found the courage to seek her out himself? Immediately, she felt guilty and tried to push the thought away. A sickly sweet after-pain remained in her stomach.

"My father told me that the traitor's son got what his father deserved!" The younger girl's face was red with annoyance. Sabíana realized that she had stumbled into the middle of a heated argument.

"Your father is an upstart second-reacher who speaks far more than he should," said the other girl, smirking.

"Silence, both of you," Sabíana said, smacking her palms on the table. Both girls jumped, and the younger immediately melted into tears.

"Enough of that, Malita." Sabíana tried to make her voice soothing, but it came out raspy. She patted the younger girl's hand. The girl jerked it away. "Tell me, what traitor's son are you talking of?"

Malita flushed and shook her head, continuing to sob.

"Go on, I won't bite you, I promise." *But I may bark some more, if you don't speak quickly.* "Surely you don't mean Vohin Voran, son of Otchigen?"

It was as if the girl's face were brushed over by white paint, then quickly repainted again in dark red.

"Malita, I am ashamed of you, to be spreading rumors. Do you not realize how much Vohin Voran has lost in his life?"

Malita looked up, lips pursed in exasperation. "I am only repeating what everybody knows. Mirnían himself..."

"Do not presume to name the prince without his honorific."

Malita stamped her foot, and the tears flowed anew. The other girl, embarrassed to be the cause of her friend's fit, interjected, though not looking up from her embroidery.

"What Malita was trying to say, Lady Sabíana, is that *Prince* Mirnían was absolutely justified in his public rebuff of Vohin Voran this morning..." The girl's voice tapered off. She gathered the courage to look at Sabíana, but immediately faded back into dumbfounded fear. Sabíana realized her fury must be visible in her face. She would have to work on her composure. Later.

"Public rebuff? What in the Heights do you mean, girl?"

Malita sensed she had a chance to gain ground. "After the storytelling today, my lady. Vohin Voran and Prince Mirnían had a very public confrontation. The prince threatened him."

Sabíana rose abruptly, pushing back the wooden bench so fiercely that it flipped over. Both girls, shoulders tensed and hunched over, looked very attentively at the embroidered clouds above the Sirin's head. Without giving them another thought, Sabíana pulled the door open as hard as she could. It crashed, and the young sentry at the door, a boy of no more than fifteen, jumped half a foot into the air.

"That will teach you to sleep at your post, soldier," she said as she passed him. "Let that be the last time, or your elders will hear of it."

The boy straightened and saluted, fist to chest. Two beads of sweat streaked down his cheek.

Sabíana hid a smile as she hurried down the tapestried hallway. She really should not enjoy rattling the boys so much, but the pleasure never lessened for its frequent repetition.

Her mirth quickly subsided. Mirnían. Arrogant, pathetic weakling! She knew how deeply he still felt his failure at the Ordeal of Silence, and how greatly he resented Voran's success. Was this how low he would stoop to get his revenge?

Past a rounded archway, a wall of icy wind slapped her face before she could descend the stairs hugging the sides of her turret. Perhaps it would be best to avoid the outdoors. Reaching the new rushes strewn on the bare ground below, she turned left through a heavy oak door that creaked with disuse. A curving staircase stood beyond the door, rising to a latticed hallway lined with white stone pillars in the form of trees, with nothing but the clouded sky as a roof. At the end of the open passage stood another wooden door with a carved Sirin in a tree. Her father's private room.

She raised her fist to knock, but stopped. Voices, raised. She put her ear to the door and closed her eyes. Mirnían, his tone plaintive, petulant in his most childish way. Father's answer. Angry. Gooseflesh prickled her neck. Father had not been this angry in a long time. She closed her eyes and held her breath, trying to make out the words. Her father spoke.

"You dare to excuse..." Something muffled, maybe *reason*? "Can't understand. How..." again incomprehensible... "without my knowing?"

Sabíana pushed gently, and the door opened a crack.

"It is not for you to determine, Mirnían!"

"Father, these rumors come from the wilds every five minutes. Do you remember when all of Vasyllia was in a flurry over a rumor about nomadic armies massing in the Steppelands? When was there ever a nomadic army that threatened anything?"

"Oh, Mirnían. You will not stand there and tell me you see no difference with this situation."

Silence, tense as the lull before a storm.

"Father, I really don't see how I should be held responsible for..."

"A Dar is always responsible, you fool!" Father sighed audibly. Sabíana heard more in that sigh than exhaustion. It was old age. "If you will not take responsibility for your lapse in judgment, perhaps you will be kind enough to explain how it is that a future Dar allows himself to publicly berate a future member of his own family?"

"Pah! You don't actually think Sabíana will go through with it."

Sabíana pushed the door and advanced on Mirnían. Seeing her, Mirnían's eyebrows shot up, and he blanched. He retreated three steps and raised his hands in self-defense.

"You idiot, Mirnían! Why is it that I, a *woman*, can see the ramifications of your actions better than you can yourself? Have you stopped to think for even half a second? You know what sort of element likes to feed the rumors about Voran's family. You have publicly allied yourself with the babblers. You appear weaker than my future husband. Is that a good vantage point for a Dar-to-be?"

Mirnían stiffened. Sabíana had a sharp desire to strike him across the face.

"Enough, Sabíana," said Dar Antomír, but his voice was gentle. "He has enough to think about without you berating him." He pulled her toward him, then leaned on her, grimacing with pain. She helped him sit back down.

"Tell her, Mirnían," he said, wheezing. "That will be punishment enough. And it is time you learned to respect her counsel more. You will have no better counsellor when I am gone."

Mirnían looked at her as he did so often in childhood. It was a silent cry for help. How often she had seen that face, whenever he was at his wits' end, whenever he knew he couldn't do without her. Poor Mirnían. So talented with people, so generous of heart, so beloved for his beauty and his charm. But just enough wit to know that he lacked the wisdom needed to be Dar. He was once again a little boy in her eyes, face unwashed and eyes wide. She smiled at him, the pity nearly overwhelming her.

"About a month ago," began Mirnían, "I was finishing an inspection of the door wardens. It was late evening. The doors were already shut when a merchant caravan came into sight at the far end of the plateau. It was one of our second-reachers, one of the more prosperous ones, I believe. I ordered the doors open, though it was after the closing horn-call.

"Everything seemed in order. The Karilan wares—the silks in particular—were exquisite, and the merchant reported nothing amiss with the journey. Just when I was about to send them home, the merchant's daughter, a little sprightly thing, probably five or six, took a liking to me. She ran up to me. Told me she had a big secret. She said she saw a hawthorn tree weeping tears of water."

Sabíana failed to understand the significance of the story. Dar Antomír smiled mischievously. "So, you do not know everything, do you, my swan?"

She felt a flush creep up her cheek. "I'm missing the key to the cipher, Father. What does this story have to do with what happened today in the square?"

"Then today," said Mirnían, more boldly, "Tolnían, a young scout, reports that Living Water has been seen in the form of a weeping tree. At least one healing has been recorded."

"Oh, by all the Heights," she whispered in shock. "This is not your fault, Mirnían, but how terrible that you said nothing."

"I don't understand why everyone is so disturbed by this news," complained Mirnían.

"Do you not?" said Sabíana. She shook her head. "Mirnían, what happened after the last appearance of the Living Water?"

Mirnían's whole body sagged and he raised both hands to his face. They were shaking. "Internecine war between the city-states," he said. "But how was I to know? It was just a little girl's story."

"Enough of that," said Dar Antomír, more firmly. "No time for it. Now, lest someone in Nebesta or Karila decides to start another internecine war, we must act. Mirnían, stay with me and help me see through this mess. Sabíana, I want you to find Voran. Bring him here."

She was grateful. Father always knows what I need, she thought. She walked out without another word.

Sabíana found Voran wandering the streets aimlessly, seeing nothing and no one. He looked thinner than he had in weeks, with dark shadows under his eyes that made their green color shine with an eldritch light. Where were his thoughts? Would he be upset to see her after Mirnían publicly insulted him?

He caught her eye standing across a cobbled street in the second reach amidst the merchant homes and public houses. People walked between them, only pretending not to see the daughter of the Dar and her future intended. It was not normal for them to appear in public together, certainly not like this. Luckily, he hurried across the cobbles to her.

"My love, I'm sorry, I didn't see you there," he said, breathless, though he had not been walking fast. His face was grey and sickly. He took her hand in both of his. They were hot to the touch.

"Voran, what has happened to you? You don't look well."

"Don't mother me yet, dear," he whispered, flashing his usual smile. It was brief, but enough to warm some of her doubts away. "There will be plenty of time for that later."

"Voran, I came from the Dar. He needs to see you now. Will you come?"

A storm cloud passed over his face for a moment, but he nodded. His eyes glazed over again, and she felt no responding warmth from him when she took his arm.

Sabíana led Voran toward the waterfalls, up a narrow path hugging the headwall of the mountain, overlooking the empty marketplace of the second reach. The path rose gradually until it entered the mountain's wall through a thick curtain of ivy, near the canals flowing from the twin chalices. It was her private way back home, a secret path in a city full of them. She vaguely remembered that her nanny never liked her taking this way. Apparently, there was an old tale about the Raven escaping Vasylli prisons through this passage.

"Sabíana," Voran whispered as they walked through the torch-lit passage within the mountain. "What do you make of all this?"

"I don't know, Voran, I haven't had time to think."

"Did you know the Pilgrim has been staying with us these past nights?"

It explained much of Voran's absence. "No. No one bothered to tell me."

He was silent, though she was sure she could smell his embarrassment in the dim light. Good. It was high time he apologized for neglecting her.

"Do you remember what your nanny used to say about this passage? About the Raven's escape?"

She stifled her annoyance. She would make sure he would apologize later.

"Yes. She would still tell me the tale now, given half a chance."

"You were not at the storytelling, were you?"

She had been expecting something about Mirnían's outburst. She braced herself. "No. I'm sorry, Voran. Mirnían has so little self-control, sometimes."

Voran looked at her with a confused expression. "Oh, that? I had forgotten about it already. No, I mention it because the story the Pilgrim told was about the Raven. One I have never heard before. It's certainly not in the Old Tales."

As if on purpose, a chill wind howled through the passage, dimming the torches. Sabíana's blood chilled.

"Pilgrims don't say anything without good reason," she said.

"Yes, exactly. Just after the story, Tolnían came with news of Living Water. It made me think."

"About the traditional link between the appearance of Living Water and the Raven's eternal quest for immortality?"

"Yes. What if it's true?"

Sabíana guffawed, but stifled her laugh. He actually looked upset.

"Voran, you don't believe those stories are actually true?"

He looked about to continue, but a thought occurred to him and he stopped, dropping Sabíana's arm. He assessed her with cold eyes, the eyes of a stranger. She felt frigid and half-naked before his gaze.

He turned away without saying another word.

"I don't think there is any way of preventing mass pilgrimage to the weeping tree," Mirnían said as Sabíana and Voran entered.

"There's nothing wrong with pilgrimage, my son," said Dar Antomír, faintly disapproving. "I would go myself, had not Wicked Woman Age grabbed me by the left ankle."

The room was tense with expectation. Dar Antomír, never more bent and careworn, insisted that Voran and Mirnían exchange the brotherly kiss. He beamed at them with sanguine eyes, though Sabíana could not help noticing how thin was his white beard—once an avalanche on his chest. They grudgingly embraced, and only the pleasant babble of the Dar's speech managed to ease their tension as they stood around a small table, staring down at a map of Vasyllia.

"There must be military presence, of course," said Mirnían, though he offered his counsel carefully now, as if expecting Sabíana to contradict him immediately. She kept her peace.

"Yes, and more than a few warriors," said the Dar. "Do you see the opportunity, my children? I've long wanted to gauge the response to a strong military show on the outliers, especially those with Nebesti blood ties."

"Have there been any rumors of discontent from that quarter, Father?" asked Sabíana.

He smiled ruefully. "Only Vasylli are simple enough to think that all lands relish to be under the lordship of Vasyllia. The purported place of the weeping tree is very near the Nebesti border. I know Lord Farlaav of Nebesta well, and I do not think he is the opportunistic kind. But the same cannot be said of others in his court. Do not forget Nebesta is traditionally governed by a kind of mass fist-war they call a representative assembly. Nothing like our Dumar. Voran, what do you think?"

Voran seemed mesmerized by something on the map, his concentration so great Sabíana expected the map to go up in flames. He seemed not to have heard the Dar.

"Voran?" she asked, touching his shoulder. He recoiled from her as though her touch were hot iron.

"I'm sorry, my love," he whispered, shocked at himself and probably also at the livid flush she could not hide. "I am not myself."

He looked away from Sabíana, shimmering with barely-repressed energy.

"Highness, I beg you to allow me to lead the pilgrims."

He trembled feverishly, his face white except for a crimson smear on either cheek. A thin sheen of sweat gathered on his hairline.

"I don't think so, Voran," said the Dar, assessing Voran through half-closed lids. "I would be much comforted by your presence at my side, especially now that the Pilgrim has disappeared. Too many dark omens."

Voran did not seem to have heard a single word.

"Highness, my family is indebted to you for everything, I know that. You have given far more generously than I or Lebía have ever deserved. You know I have never asked anything for myself." He paused, seemingly out of breath.

"No, Voran, you have not," said the Dar, his frown deepening.

"I ask it now. I must seek the Living Water. It is not merely for myself. The Pilgrim told me to. For Vasyllia."

Mirnían snickered and rolled his eyes. To her surprise, Sabíana found herself agreeing with her brother's reaction.

"Voran, you are not well," said Mirnían, his voice lathered in sarcasm. Voran did not even acknowledge him. It was not that he ignored him; he seemed not to have heard him at all.

"Highness, I beg you." Voran's voice was no more than a whisper, but it seemed to echo.

Dar Antomír's eyes began to fill with tears. Sabíana knew why. This whole situation was a repetition of Otchigen's ill-fated command of the embassy to Karila. It filled her with dread.

"I sense this is something I cannot prevent. May Adonais bless it."

Voran fell on one knee and bowed his head. Dar Antomír placed his right hand on his head and kept it there for a moment. When he lowered it, Voran couldn't help notice how covered it was with brown spots, how gnarled beyond recognition.

"Go, my child. Choose what warriors you wish. The pilgrimage will set out one week from tomorrow."

Voran stood, bowed, and kissed Sabíana's hand. He looked at her with a fleeting glance that refused to engage her eyes. She had the disconcerting sense that she had slipped into a dream. Everything moved slowly, and the loudest sound in the room was her own heart beating. Voran walked out without waiting for her.

"Father, am I the only one who sees?" Her throat had gone completely dry. "Or have I gone mad? Does no one else see the parallel?"

Dar Antomír would not look at her. "Voran sees a chance to redeem his family's name, Sabíana. Would you deny him that?"

"Father," said Mirnían. "You once assigned a half-mad Otchigen to the Karila embassy. Now you assign a half-mad Voran to take charge of tens, if not hundreds, of city-folk, right after an omen of the skies. You expect a different result?"

"I hope for one, yes," said the Dar. He sat down again, exhausted. "My children, I fear that dark times are coming. After the omen of the skies, the Pilgrim came to me. Pilgrims are not as other men. They are closer to the Heights, and some barriers of the natural world are but trifles to them. Some of them live for three hundred years or more. So when he came, I listened.

"We spoke of many things, most of which you will know soon enough. He told me a darkness is coming the likes of which Vasyllia has not seen in hundreds of years. He spoke of a plague that would afflict man, beast, tree, blade of grass. He spoke of a fountainhead of healing flowing from a heart of stone."

Sabíana gasped. "A heart of stone. Voran means stone in Old Vasylli."

Dar Antomír smiled and closed his eyes, leaning back into his chair. "You understand, Sabíana. That is why I have hope for Voran."

And yet, the dread in her chest tied itself into knots over and over again, until she feared she would never be able to untie it.

The soul-bond between man and Sirin is unlike any other bond of love. It defies clear explanation, but it is known by its fruits. The soul-bonded man can withstand inordinate pain, can carry burdens which no man can lift, can survive in battles, though he be the lone warrior in the field. But the true nature of the bond is that it removes a man from earthly wants, calling him to desires of eternity. No man, once bonded, will find rest until he has undergone the seven baptisms of fire and climbed to the very Heights of Aer.

From "On the Nature of the Soul-Bond"
(The Sayings, Book XI, 4:1-5)

CHAPTER 7
SISTER OF THE PARIAH

On the third morning of the pilgrimage, the fog glimmered, pregnant with the coming sun. The birth of the sun brought spring warmth in the midst of early winter. A steaming tarn in winter usually meant one thing—dreadful cold—but the children knew before anyone else that this steam was different. It meant warmth. By the time Lebía had made breakfast for Voran, three boys already blattered in the water with their dogs, while the girls, skirts hiked up, stood at the edge, toes longingly nibbling the water. Lebía had a giggling desire to push the girls in, then to jump in herself. Instead, she sat by the porridge to wait for Voran. She would not be welcome among the laughing children, not the daughter of Otchigen, not the sister of Voran. *We are pariahs.*

She began to plait a new set of bark shoes, humming to herself. Already some of the younger children's shoes were wearing down on the hard roads. It was pleasant to do something for them, even if they might not want to accept a gift from her hands because of her association with Otchigen. She would have to think of a way of gifting them without being noticed.

The music she hummed was a new song, she realized. That often happened to her. She would hear snatches of music already formed in her heart. It never seemed strange to her; how could it? She had been hearing music since she was a small child. Only later did she realize its source.

She had seen her first Sirin when she was ten, on a day when her heart-pain at her mother's loss was like a wedge splitting apart an ash log. It was only a glimpse, but she knew it was no accident, because the shards of her heart grafted together and blossomed. After that, whenever the pain threatened to break her, the memory was enough to bring her back to herself.

The Sirin had continued to visit her, though always at a distance. Lebía sensed that the distance was more for her benefit. She had no illusions about the Sirin's love. It was not gentle; it was fierce as fire. More often the Sirin sent her gifts of music.

The tent shivered behind her. Voran pushed through the flap, sodden with sleep. How strange that their roles should be reversed now. He was always the early riser in Vasyllia, but since they had begun the journey, he seemed incapable of getting up with the sun.

"Porridge again, swanling?" He complained, but with enough of a smile to make rejoinder unnecessary.

It was the first time since they left that he called her by his "little name," and it warmed her more than the unseasonable sun. He had been categorically against her going on the pilgrimage. Only the most convincing stubbornness she could muster—never easy for her, especially toward Voran, who was almost a father to her—managed to sway him. He punished her with dour silence for the first day, and only spoke to her in clipped phrases the second.

"I've added dried apples this morning, Voran."

He ate with the relish of a famished wolf. Poor Voran. He had changed so much since the coming of the Pilgrim. He was restless by nature, but this unquiet bordered on manic.

"Voran, what happened with Sabíana?"

Lebía couldn't help noticing that Sabíana had left their house that morning weeping. She was not even there to see them out of the city with Dar Antomír.

"Lebía, why do you ask me such things?" His face was beet-red. "You are too young to understand."

"Am I? Too young to see that you deliberately wounded the woman you claim to love?"

"It was not..." He stopped, breathed, and sagged a bit in the shoulders. "You are right. It was deliberate. I have not been able to put her face out of my mind since then. I do not know why I spoke to her like that."

"Voran, I am not accusing you. I just want to understand. You know I love you."

The creases in his forehead smoothed into his quick, winning smile. "Oh, swanling. Sometimes I forget about the weight of pain on your sixteen years. You want to know the truth?"

Lebía nodded, purposely not looking at him, intent on her fingers plaiting the rough bark. There were a few cuts on them, but only in the uncallused places.

"When I asked Sabíana to marry me, I did it like a madman jumping off a cliff. I never thought she would consider me, not after..."

He closed his eyes and sighed. His usually thick, curly black hair was mangy, hanging in strands around his shoulders. He had not shaved in weeks, but he looked the better for it, his angular features set off pleasantly by the messy chin-beard.

"Swanling, it's a terrible thing, our human nature. We spend all our energies on getting things we never expect to receive, but if by some miracle we receive them, they start to lose their luster very quickly."

"You didn't expect her to say yes?"

"Well, I hoped she would. But then the Dar had to agree as well. I was sure she was being kept for some Lord something-or-other in Nebesta. When he agreed, and blessed our union wholeheartedly, I thought my joy complete. I saw my life then as it would be. Lord Protector to Darina Sabíana, a life of luxury in the palace, the love of a passionate woman whose beauty has no compare in Vasyllia, children on the bear rug before the hearth."

"Sounds like our father's life when we were children."

"Exactly. That was the first thought to give me pause. Then the small, still voice deep inside me. *Not enough*, it said. I still longed for something with no name, or someone whose name I had not yet found. That was the first time I heard the song of the Sirin."

Lebía's heart raced. She thought she was the only one who knew the longing that sometimes comforted, but sometimes emptied.

"Everything changed after that?"

"Not immediately. I was always with Sabíana in the palace, walking the secret cloisters and the summit cherry groves. Those were moments of happiness I had never known. Poor Sabíana. She doesn't know what longing is. She is all fire, all desire, all forward movement."

"Voran, do you love her?"

He stared at his porridge, his eyes never more green. He plucked at his chin-beard.

"I do, Lebía. I always have. I just didn't know there could be a feeling more powerful than the love of a man for a woman."

It took the better part of an hour for the mothers to convince the boys to come out of the tarn to begin the morning leg of their journey. As it was, the crowd of pilgrims usually left far later than was probably necessary, but there were nearly a hundred people on the pilgrimage of all ages, and it seemed some had come more for the change of scenery and the joy of good company than for a religious experience.

Lebía loved watching Voran race back and forth on his black charger every morning, tightening up discipline among the warriors. She was proud of him, even if she laughed at him silently for being a touch pompous in his manner. He had no idea how ridiculous he looked.

That entire day, Lebía walked alone. By the evening, she had grown lonely again, and almost regretted coming. Finally, Voran rode to her and dismounted, handing his reins over to one of the younger warriors. Voran looked eager to speak, his mood lightened by the warmth of the day.

"How much longer, do you think, until we reach it?" Lebía asked.

"Well, the weeping tree is supposed to be not far from the Nebesti border on the side of Vasyllia's lands. Roughly one hundred miles through mostly mountainous terrain. At the rate we're going? Two weeks, maybe more."

"Will we come near Nebesta, the city?"

"No. The Dar's road splits in two at the Nebesti border. We go straight, the road to Nebesta goes left, hugging the border along a narrow valley until you hit the city at the end of the valley. It's beautiful, you know. All wood where Vasyllia is stone. A confluence of two rivers and some of the most gorgeous forests you've ever seen."

"I wish I could see it."

"You can see the border range over there." Voran pointed at a series of jagged peaks that started at their left and reached all the way to a point directly ahead of them. They looked like the rotting teeth of an old man. Fog encircled the tips of the left-most peaks, and something darker than fog swirled there as well.

"Strange," said Voran. "That looks like smoke."

He stared at the column of cloud reaching toward Vasyllia from the Nebesti side. It was pinkish in the late morning sun. Then he shook his head, thoughtful, before turning back to Lebía with a smile.

"Lebía, here I am blabbing away. And you have not yet told me why you so wanted to see the weeping tree."

Their road led straight ahead to a dip between two drum-hills, the left crowned with aspens, the right with birches.

"It's easier for you, Voran. You are an intimate of the Dar. I sit at home.

Sometimes the pain of our parents' absence is like a physical illness. There are mornings when I can't rise from bed."

"You hope the Living Water will heal that wound?"

"To be honest, I don't think it will. But yes, I hope."

"There is something else, then?"

She found a barrier between her thoughts and her words. To speak was as hard as to move a boulder covered with moss from a riverbed.

"Voran, there is something very wrong in Vasyllia. The omen merely confirmed it for me."

"Yes, I have begun to feel it as well, swanling."

"It sounds terrible, what I am about to say. It has hurt so much, seeing how everyone was willing to attack our father in his absence, when he couldn't defend his name. With such obvious enjoyment, too. People who allow that cannot be good. Now, I don't even care much for Vasyllia anymore. I'm going on this pilgrimage because I can no longer stay in the city."

Voran looked thoughtful.

"Lebía, I agree with you. But do you know what the Pilgrim told me? He told me Vasyllia was *everything*. He told me I must never let it fall. As if *I* could do anything about it."

The last sentence was said more for himself than for her, she thought.

"Is that why you seek the Living Water?" she asked

"Well, the Pilgrim told me to find it. But there's also something else. In the Dar's chambers, when I saw that the weeping tree is at the top of a tor called Sirin's Peak, I felt a summons as strong as the music ever was."

"You hope to find the Sirin?"

He nodded.

The first of the pilgrims had reached the narrowing pass between the drums, being forced to walk only three or four abreast. Voran and Lebía were still on the downslope of the road, and for a moment the sun hid behind the right drum, only visible in the golden leaves of the birches crowning it. When the sun came up over the trees, it was fire-white, brighter than Lebía had ever seen. It rose with a faint music, as though singing. Then it hit her. The light was not the sun. A Sirin perched on the top of the central birch, bathed in her own light.

Yearning pierced Lebía's heart with a keen, pleasant pain. She knew, in that knowledge that surpasses a movement of thought, being something already formed in the heart, that the Sirin on the mount offered Lebía a choice to meet face to face. No more distant visits, no more hints of music.

She could have the soul-bond only read about in tales. She could be consumed in the fire of the Sirin.

She desired it as much as she had desired anything in life. It all welled up inside her—all the injustice, all the pain, all the promises never kept. Had she ever asked for anything for herself? Did she not deserve this consolation more than anyone? No one else even believed in the Sirin.

But then, she looked at Voran, and something inside her balked. He was so unhappy. And he was so incapable of being unhappy. She was used to it. He needed this more than she did.

"Voran, do you see the birches on the top of the hill there?" she said, her voice heavy. "It's a good vantage point, is it not? Would you do me a favor? Go up there and see what waits for us on the other side."

Immediately, the light faded, the music faded, the world faded. Voran's eyes widened and he gasped in pleasure. She knew that now the Sirin sang for him alone. She had made her choice, and the Sirin had accepted it. Voran rode off without looking back. Lebía wept.

If man is to brave the Heights of Aer, to face the Throne of the Most High, he must endure the seven baptisms of fire. The soul-bond is the first baptism of fire. The second is the passage from Earth to the Lows of Aer. The third is the shedding of the skin of the old man. The fourth is the first death. The fifth is the great sacrifice. The sixth is the second death. The seventh...is a mystery.

From "On the Emulation of the Powers"
(The Sayings, Book VII, 7:1-7)

CHAPTER 8

THE SIRIN

The song of the Sirin rang out, drowning out the noise of the pilgrims. Everything else faded from Voran's mind. It was even more intense than in the forest the first time. He left his horse in the hands of one of the warriors. He felt it would be somehow blasphemous to encounter a Sirin on horseback.

"Lead them on," he said, not even realizing who it was he was talking to. "I'm going to take a look from the top of that hill."

Voran climbed, slogging through cold mud to a stand of birches leaning upward along the incline of the hill toward the sun. Their exposed roots held the earth like grubby hands. Voran slipped over them, finding the way harder than it looked. As he reached the head of the drum-hill, he cleared the line of trees and entered a small clearing, in the middle of which stood three white birches, taller than the rest, still clad in autumn gold. His Sirin perched on top of the middle tree and sang. Voran found that his cheeks were wet with tears, and his heart sang in unison with the Sirin. Approaching her was nearly impossible, as though ten strong men were pushing back against him with all their force.

He could go no further and went down on his knees, the linen shirt under his mail sweat-soaked and sticking to his skin. The Sirin no longer chanted, but Voran feared to look at her. She flew down, alighting in front of him, so that her face was directly in line with his. Mastering himself, he forced his eyes to lock with hers. Something inside him shifted. He heard a soft, regular thumping, as of another heart, and a small flame came to life in the center of his chest, radiating warmth to the rest of his body. He heard many musics—joyful, haunting, terrifying—all at the same time, but with no disharmony. He was covered in golden flame, warm and dew-like, and he did not burn. His mind lurched with terror; his heart raced with joy.

"Voran." Even when she spoke, she sang. "I am named Lyna."

Voran could find no words for a long time, content only to look into the abyss of her eyes. It was never easy for him to look into another person's eyes. It was dangerously intimate, and he was squeamish about that kind of intimacy. Looking into her eyes was like staring from a peak at a river at the bottom of a valley, jumping down without closing his eyes, and then plunging into the river, only to find it had no bottom. There was no single word for it.

After a long time, he retreated from her eyes and saw that she had an oval face framed with auburn curls, a mouth that seemed incapable of laughter, an expression of austere sorrow, like a living statue. Under her collarbone, undulating blue-green feathers shimmered down to her golden feet and talons and ended at the black tips of her outstretched wings.

"What a blessed and cursed day this is, Voran." Her wings moved with her speech like human hands. "Sirin and man are joined once more, though it comes at the time of testing."

"Why have you waited so long to greet me, Lyna?" His voice sounded crude compared to the music of her voice, like two rocks tapping each other.

"My falcon, the love of the Sirin is a blazing fire. We cannot force it on anyone. For generations, none have been ready for the soul-bond. It is a glorious thing, but it is heavy, as any true love must be."

Never had confession of love sounded so simply, and yet if the earth gaped and volcanoes erupted around him, he would not have been surprised. After the soul-bond, he felt nothing could ever surprise him again.

"Lyna, can I stay here with you? Must I continue my journey to the Living Water?"

"You do not know what you are saying, my falcon. No love can exist where there is no forward movement. If you stayed here too long with me, you would be consumed. You are not ready for the full bond."

"There is so much I do not understand, Lyna. So many questions. What is happening to Vasyllia? With the Covenant Tree?"

"The tree's fire is fading, Voran."

"Is it the Covenant, Lyna? All we Vasylli remember is hints of old stories."

"They contain much truth, those old stories. The Covenant was a simple thing. Vasyllia was to protect the Outer Lands against all darkness, caring for and nurturing all peoples. In return, Adonais girded them with power. Nothing could touch Vasyllia. The Harbinger summoned the fire that confirmed the Covenant. While the aspen is on fire, the Covenant stood. When he returned, he witnessed the covenant broken. The fire will fade until it is no more."

Voran's heart chilled. The Harbinger. The greatest of Adonais's allies; a name never spoken above a whisper, so great was the reverence attached to it. Did she mean that the Pilgrim was the Harbinger? It would explain his strange powers.

"No one in Vasyllia believes in the Covenant, Lyna. Even I find it hard to fathom with my mind alone."

"Do you wonder, then, that no Vasylli is bound to a Sirin anymore? In the time of Lassar, nearly every Vasylli was bound to a Sirin. Five hundred years later, in the reign of Cassían, less than half were. Now, four hundred years after the death of Cassían, no one seeks the old beauty."

"How could something this important be forgotten, Lyna?"

She was silent for an age. She seemed to be searching for the right words.

"When love grows cold, my falcon, eternal truths darken."

"You are saying that we have not done our part to care for the Outer Lands? But we have enough troubles in our Vasyllia. The separation of the reaches—it is a terrible thing. How can we be held responsible for the welfare of outsiders, if we cannot keep our own house in order?"

Lyna sighed heavily and shook her head. Her curls danced in the wind.

"Your own heart can answer that question, Voran. But there is so much noise there, so much confusion."

"Lyna, you must speak to me as though I were a child. Please, I want to understand. Be patient with me."

"Yes, my falcon, I will try. Recall the image of Lassar's Vasyllia that the Pilgrim showed you. Was there anything unusual about the people you saw?"

"They were more joyful than any people I have ever seen."

"Do you imagine that their Vasyllia had fewer problems than your Vasyllia? You would be a fool if you did. You know your histories. Lassar was a man of war; only after many trials, much blood, did the Harbinger come to him with an offer of Covenant. And yet, the joy in their faces. You saw it. Joy like that comes from only one source. Pain."

Voran nodded, remembering his talks with the potter.

"Yes, pain. Did you not suffer pain during the Ordeal of Silence? Were you not rewarded for that pain a hundred-fold? Does not the artist suffer his creation? Do you not think all those people you saw suffered pain in the making of those works of beauty whose loss you so lamented?"

Voran was surprised that he did not wonder at Lyna's deep knowledge of his thoughts and emotions. Truly the bond they shared was soul-deep.

"Tell me, Voran. What is the most beautiful thing a man can mold and form, though it is not of his own creation?"

How many times had he pondered the same question while sitting half-frozen on the banks of their river of a morning?

"His own life," he said.

"To make his own life beautiful, what must he do?"

It came to him like floodwaters, overwhelming.

"A human being can only become truly human if he lives for others. That way, the way of love, is by necessity the way of pain. Shared pain. Co-suffering."

He felt the dew-flames flare up around him again. A darkness of which he had never been aware lifted from his heart, and he was calm. He could not remember the last time he felt so calm.

"Where do you think Vasyllia received its name?" she asked. "The Vasylli is the one who gives his life for another. You all know it; you all repeat it endlessly. But meaning is lost in endless repetition."

"Vasyllia was named *after* the Covenant," Voran whispered to himself.

"Yes. There are few true Vasylli left, Voran."

"Lyna, what can I do?" He felt small, like a child called to account for his older siblings' misdeeds.

"Seek the weeping tree, my falcon, before it is found by one who has sought it for ages." She shimmered and began to fade. "We must part now, but know that I am always with you, even if you cannot see me. You are unformed yet, Voran, only crude clay in the hands of the potter. There is risk and loss in every meeting, so choose carefully when you seek to see me again. I leave you with hope. The Harbinger walks the earth once more. If he finds true Vasylli, as he did in the time of Lassar, he may reforge the forgotten Covenant. But I fear much pain and loss must transpire before then."

He heard the sound of wind whistling through reeds as Lyna flew up to the sun. She was gone, but her song remained in the flickering flame warming his heart.

When Voran came to himself, it was already late evening. Nowhere did he see any sign of the pilgrims; even their racket, which he thought could be heard for miles, was absent. How long had he been with Lyna? He shivered with cold and rising dread.

Then he remembered how his encounter with the white stag seemed to move him to a different place entirely. The Lows of Aer. Only entered in certain places and times, and always perilous. He looked around in consternation. Truly, this was not a place he recognized. There was no road, only an overgrown path such as a woodsman might use. The peaks of Vasyllia's main range were much closer than they should have been and in *front* of him. In the dim light, it was difficult to make out much.

He must have entered into the Lows of Aer during his encounter with Lyna. Coming out of them, he must have been displaced again. He would have to be more careful about crossing that threshold in the future.

He heard something behind him. A cry or a moan. Could be an animal, but it sounded human. He ran toward it, along a path cresting to a grassy knoll. When he looked over its edge, he gasped.

As far he could see, a beech wood extended to the horizon, rising and falling gently. A mass of people labored through the trees, their number greater than he could count. Some were already rising up the hill to meet him. They were bloody and hobbled. Then he understood the sound. The wailing of grieving women.

Leading them was a tall middle-aged woman leaning on a branch. She saw him about a stone's throw away, stopped, her expression confused, but not frightened. Next to her walked a skeletal girl no more than six years old.

"Matron," Voran called to her. "What is all this? Who are you and what has happened?"

"Are you but the skin of another changer, come to devour what is left?" She threatened with the branch. Her voice was like dried peas rattling in a box. She had a strange accent. Nebesti, probably.

"I do not understand you. I am Vohin Voran, the son of Otchigen of Vasyllia. I bear you no ill will, Matron."

Her eyes seemed to shift somehow, as though she had not fully seen him until now. He felt the flame in his heart surge toward her, and she gasped in surprise. When she could speak again, her voice had more power to it.

"They are all dead and burning, dead and burning. Blood, fire everywhere. Like...living torches..." She shuddered. "Son of Otchigen, we are all that remains of the ancient and glorious city of Nebesta. The Second City is destroyed."

The world is not as it seems. You think there is only the visible world for the living, and the invisible for the dead and the immortal? You are wrong. There are many realms interweaving with each other like the threads in a tapestry. Most are invisible most of the time. But sometimes, some people fall into other realms or encounter the denizens of those places. Some of these Powers are good. Many are not...

From "A Primer on Nebesti Cosmology"
(The Lore of Nebesta, Book I, 3:6-8)

CHAPTER 9
THE FALL

Among the ubiquitous women and children—some walking but most hanging on their mothers—Voran found no men at all. The implication was chilling—whoever did this had killed or captured the men and sent the women forward to spread tales of terror in their wake. Whoever this enemy was, they were cunning beyond Voran's experience.

The woman who spoke to him called herself Adayna, daughter of Farlaav. Once she seemed satisfied Voran was not a "changer"—Voran had no idea what that was—she took him into the mass of refugees, eager to share something, a secret of some kind.

"I managed to save the Voyevoda, my father. But he will not last long."

He was an old man, though his beard was still black with two streaks of white, like a badger-pelt. He lay on a makeshift litter pulled by a horse half as dead as he was. Only his face was visible in the mountain of furs keeping him warm.

"Lord Farlaav," said Voran. "I am Voran, son of Otchigen."

"Voran? I knew your father." He looked suddenly lost, gazing about wildly, hoping to find something to orient him. "Are we near Vasyllia?"

"No, I suspect we are a week or so away. But you need not worry, Vasyllia will care for your people. You have my word. Please, what happened to Nebesta?"

"I do not quite know what to tell you first, Voran. There was no warning. In the weeks leading to this attack, some of our rangers disappeared in the wild. It should have alerted us to our danger.

"It happened in the dead of night, and suddenly most of the city was burning. How they breached the walls I will never know. An army of mounted men, screaming in a foreign tongue I've never heard. Their skill with the arrow is not human. They are like men possessed, with supernatural strength and cruelty. They call themselves Gumiren."

Voran had never heard of them. In the back of his mind he remembered an old rumor, from about ten years ago, that nomad armies were assembling in the far Steppelands. Could this be the result of that muster?

"But even they are not the worst danger," said Lord Farlaav. "In every shadow of the fallen city, unspeakable things lurked—monsters the like I've only read about in stories. I would not have believed it without the witness of my two eyes. Huge wolf-men and bird-creatures and many-headed snakes with wings."

"Lord Farlaav, are you sure? Perhaps in the heat of the—"

Lord Farlaav lifted himself up from the litter with a groan and grabbed Voran's arm, gasping with the effort.

"Listen to me! I saw what I saw. If you do not believe me, there will be nothing to stop him."

"Him? Who?"

"This is not a human enemy we strive against, Voran. The Raven is coming."

The effort was too much, and he collapsed in a dead faint. A pool of red seeped into the furs at his back. Adayna pushed Voran aside and called for help.

Voran's mind reeled, but his instincts took over. He seemed to hover over himself, watching as he ran back and forth, cajoling here, ordering there, pushing, pulling, jostling, and helping along. Within an hour, he and Adayna—she had a new stick and had tied a wolf-fir around her chest with a leather thong, giving her the appearance of a nomadic priestess—led the mass of wounded Nebesti toward Vasyllia. He carried the skeletal girl on his shoulders. She was Farlaav's great-granddaughter. Both of her parents, Adayna's daughter and her husband, had been killed.

For the first day, Adayna spoke little, leaving Voran to his thoughts. He was almost unnaturally calm after his encounter with Lyna, but his mind told him that he was courting disaster for seeming to abandon the pilgrims, even for the sake of these thousands of refugees. Anyone else would be lauded by Vasyllia for saving the remnant of Nebesta. But it was more likely that the son of Otchigen would be imprisoned for abandoning his charge and leaving the pilgrims to an untamed wilderness crawling with creatures from nightmares and an enemy that slaughtered people just to make an impression. The Dar would be right to imprison him.

Worse still, he had lost Lebía. Agonized worry for her gnawed at him—he was sure he would have a red gaping hole in his chest by the time he reached Vasyllia. The desire to turn back and find her was so strong that a few times his feet seemed to turn aside of their own accord. Every time he moved back to the path, he imaged Lebía's corpse riddled with arrows.

Another fear was the realization that the only way he could justify himself before the Dar and Dumar would be to tell them of the Sirin. But that was impossible. No one believed in the Sirin anymore. Actually claiming soul-bond with a legend? Impossible.

Yet he saw no other possible solution. He could not abandon the refugees. Neither could he fathom abandoning the pilgrims. But he had no idea where they were. To make matters worse, the farther he traveled from his encounter with Lyna, the more his sense of loss and yearning deepened. The flame in his heart remained alight, but it did not fill him, only leaving him warm enough to live.

On the second day, Adayna was more inclined to speak. He was glad of the change. Speaking to himself was becoming tiresome.

"Adayna, does your father still live?"

"He fades, Voran. I hope he will survive to Vasyllia. To see Dar Antomír would ease his passing, I think."

"Tell me, what did you mean when you thought I was a changer?"

She looked at him with the gaze of those who have seen too much to care about social niceties. Voran felt a flush creep up his cheek.

"Did you believe my father's account of the Raven's army of horrors? I saw it myself, Voran, too clearly to doubt. A warrior, seemingly human, who changed shape before my eyes. Where a nomad archer stood one moment, the next lurched a creature with a human body and a lion's head."

Voran said nothing, though the dread inside him deepened.

"Nebesti lore tells of changers, spirits of the abysses who wield the power of transformation. Vasyllia has no such legends?"

"I have never heard of such a thing."

"Nevertheless, it is spoken of. The Raven is the first of these."

"The Raven I know, though many think him merely a cautionary tale." But if the Sirin were real, could not other legends walk the earth as well? Find the Living Water, said Lyna. If the Raven walked the earth, it was clear that he came to Vasyllia to find the Living Water. How would Voran ever convince the Dar of the need to protect the weeping tree from a monster out of stories?

"That carn ahead of us," said Adayna, "the one red with sun-blood. Is that not Vasyllia Mountain?"

"Yes, it is." Voran smiled at her use of the word "carn"—an archaism in the Vasylli language. "A few more days, and your people will find refuge."

"But for how long? Surely you cannot doubt that the Gumiren come for the jewel of the Three Cities?"

There was faint irony in her voice, and Voran recognized Nebesta's old jealousy at being the Second City. He could not blame her. If what Lyna said about Vasyllia's responsibility to care for all Outer Lands was true, then the Vasylli had much work before them to restore goodwill with Nebesta, Karila, and the lesser cities. Too many years of bad blood. Housing the refugees of fallen Nebesta would be a good start.

Vasyllia Mountain grew by the day, and on the seventh morning they were within sight of the city. Here, the dirt paths they had taken finally merged with the Dar's road. As soon as Voran and Adayna, walking a bowshot ahead of the others, had stepped on the road, something slipped in and out of view at a point where the road dipped down and out of view.

"What was that?" said Adayna, tense with fear.

"Vasylli scouts. Don't be afraid. They are only performing their duties. Now the city will be informed, and we will be met at the gates." Voran's even tone belied his perturbation. Why had the Vasylli scouts allowed themselves to be seen so easily? Were things truly falling apart so badly in Vasyllia that even the scouts couldn't stay off the Dar's road?

By mid-day, they approached Vasyllia, wading through the stubs of reaped wheat, still poking through the half-frozen soil in the fields of harvest that lay before the city. The gates stood open, and three companies of warriors in black were arrayed before them, banners—gold sun on black field—unfurled, spears glistening in the late autumn sun.

"You said we would be met," said Adayna, "but I did not think you meant armed warriors."

Voran walked ahead with Adayna, his hand tight on his pommel. Two mounted guards cantered toward them, both swordsmen. To Voran's disgust, one of them was Rogdai.

They had not spoken since their wager. Rogdai had seemed eager to avoid Voran, and Voran had been happy to oblige.

Rogdai took off his helm.

"Vohin Voran, I charge you in the name of Dumar with abandoning your charge of protecting the pilgrims. You must come with me immediately."

Voran was struck speechless. He had expected at least some banter about his father's wine, at least, before things got unpleasant.

But to be charged by the name of the Dumar, the assembly of the people? That was interesting. The Dar was still on his side, it would seem. That gave Voran a measure of courage.

"Vohin Rogdai, I will come with you as soon as you can give assurances to the daughter of Lord Farlaav, Adayna, that the remnant of Nebesta will be given refuge in Vasyllia."

Rogdai hesitated, then dismounted. He fell on one knee awkwardly before Adayna.

"Forgive me, lady," he said. "Remnant? Is what Vohin Voran says true?"

Adayna stood tall and straight, through Voran sensed her exhaustion.

"It is. We are all that remains of Nebesta, Vohin Rogdai. I cannot speak for our outlying villages, though I fear the worst. I hope Vasyllia will remember her hospitality in this time of need."

Rogdai looked down at the ground, unable to hold her gaze. He seemed embarrassed to continue speaking.

"I am… sorry, my lady. The Dumar has made it clear that all refugees must remain outside the city until further notice."

"Apparently, the Dumar did not inform the first reach, Rogdai," said Voran, pointing to the city.

A mass of first-reachers poured through the gates, bearing tents, blankets, pots, and sundry other daily necessities. They were led by the potter from the marketplace, the one who made the perfect clay urn. Voran was pleased to see Rogdai seething with impotent anger.

"Lady Adayna," said Voran, "the poor of Vasyllia offer you hospitality, even though her leaders have forgotten what the word means. When you have settled your people, I invite you to lodge at my own home. I will speak to the Dar on your behalf, have no worry. Rogdai, the Lord Farlaav of Nebesta is lying wounded among the refugees. Lady Adayna will show you where he lies. Of course, you will want to accompany him to the Dar's palace yourself."

Rogdai looked like he wanted to bind Voran with chains on the spot, but he merely turned to Adayna and bowed his head in agreement.

"Oh," said Voran, as though it were an afterthought, "and please arrange for my father's wine to be served to the Nebesti. They have need of refreshment."

Voran turned away, not waiting for a reply. He felt Rogdai's hatred like a hot poker in his back. As he walked through the ranks of warriors, he expected to be stopped by one of them at any moment. But they let him pass.

As he approached the gates, tents were already springing up like mushrooms after an autumn thunderstorm. Voran saw not a single second or third-reacher among them. Only the poor of Vasyllia had come outside the city to help the Nebesti in their hour of need.

Voran spent most of the day arranging for food and more tents to be sent out to the Nebesti outside the city walls. As he feared, none of the rich wanted anything to do with the refugees. Even in the second reach—many second-reachers themselves had known poverty at some point in their lives—only a few families, most of them from the warrior caste, opened their doors to him.

※

That evening, he sat in his own kitchens enjoying the last of his father's wine. He had only drunk half the chalice when the pounding on the doors threatened to splinter them.

Her lardship came into the kitchen, her face red with annoyance.

"Voran, it's the palace guard."

Voran smiled and nodded.

Four black-liveried warriors in full armor, led by Rogdai, stood outside the door.

"You will leave your sword here, Vohin Voran," said Rogdai. "Accused traitors are not allowed arms in the palace."

The Monarchia of Vasyllia is first concerned with the care and welfare of its citizens. Therefore, we have found it necessary to form a representative body, the Dumar.

I. Dumar representation will be based upon population density.

II. Twenty will come from the first reach, fifteen from the second, five from the third.

III. Let the reaches choose their own.

IV. The Dumar will assist the Monarchia in an advisory capacity.

V. According to the discretion of the Dar, the Dumar may also legislate certain internal matters.

VI. The Dumar may, in extreme cases of dynastic turmoil, call for a Council of the Reaches to choose a new Dar.

Official edict of Dar Aldermían II, year 734 of the Covenant

CHAPTER 10
THE DUMAR

The heavy double doors of the Chamber of Counsel opened inward to reveal a fresco of the Covenant Tree adorning the entire far wall. Just as the doors opened, sunlight pierced through the colored glass in the windows, and the flames danced on the painted tree. Gooseflesh prickled Voran's arms at the sight. On either side of the rectangular room stood tiered wooden galleries filled to the brim. Every one of the forty representatives of the three reaches of Vasyllia, the full Dumar, looked at him with undisguised hatred. Of course, Voran thought, he had chosen to aid Nebesti over Vasylli. He understood their hatred, but he deplored it. It shocked him how deeply entrenched Vasyllia had become in its insularity.

In each of the four corners of the room stood a great stone likeness of a tree—a birch, an oak, a beech, and an aspen. For a moment, he thought he saw a Sirin in the branches of the birch, but he was mistaken. Even so, the flame in his heart surged, and he felt new strength blooming from his chest.

Dar Antomír sat in a simple throne of white marble under the fresco of the aspen sapling. Mirnían—his face an inscrutable mask—stood before a throne of malachite a step lower than the Dar. Sabíana sat on the Dar's left on a throne of pink granite. She seemed to look at Voran, but as he approached, he realized her eyes were directed at a point beyond his left shoulder. He had hoped she had forgiven him; it appeared he was wrong.

"The Dumar may be seated," said Mirnían. "Chosen speakers of the Dumar, step forward for counsel."

These were two military men, the willowy chief cleric Otar Kalún, and a young courtier Voran did not know. He could smell lavender on him, even from this distance, and his silver cloak shimmered as he moved. Voran disliked him immediately. He knew the type—a social climber who would not hesitate to sell his own grandmother for advancement in the Dumar.

The chosen speakers stood on a step lower than Mirnían and Sabíana and faced Voran. At that moment, when even Sabíana looked at him with the eyes of a statue, Voran finally realized the full seriousness of his situation.

"Vohin Voran," said Mirnían, "son of Otchigen, the former Voyevoda of Vasyllia, you are charged with dereliction of duty. Before you speak in your defense, know that it was the Dumar's wish that you be clapped in irons upon your return to Vasyllia. Only the Dar's clemency grants you the freedom you now enjoy."

"Something you hardly deserve," hissed Otar Kalún. His pupils were abysses in eyes of pale grey.

Dar Antomír tensed, as if he were about to rebuke the chief cleric. But he did not. Sabíana looked down at her hands, cupped on her knees. The tips of her mouth curled down, either in anger or in sorrow. Voran couldn't decide which. He wanted her to look at him again. He was sure it would give him strength. But she did not.

"Highness and Dumar assembled," Voran said, his voice shaking in spite of himself. "Nebesta is fallen. Your scouts doubtless spotted the refugees days ago. What they did not tell you is that the Second City is no more. Every male Nebesti has been slaughtered or captured." He felt anger rising, his voice hardening. "The invader has sent their women and children ahead, doubtless to spread fear and to *burden* Vasyllia with their care." This last phrase he spat out with contempt. Every face but the Dar's twisted. In an upsurge of emotion, Voran went on the offensive.

"But that is nothing!" Voran's voice echoed. "Nebesta was invaded not merely by an army of men, but by something the Nebesti call changers. Dark creatures, half-man, half-beast, capable of changing physical form to suit their needs. They are led by the Raven."

The hall erupted in noise—laughter, shuffling cambric, frantic whispers, hands wringing sword-hilts. Voran kept his gaze firmly on the Dar's. He saw understanding there and the beginning of fear.

The older military man boomed over the noise. "Highness, must we listen to stories? This man is charged with treason."

"Perhaps Vohin Voran would care to elucidate?" It was the courtier. He did not even try to hide his derision. Voran's gut twisted. This man was wrong, somehow. Voran had a compulsion to run him through with a sword. It was so strong that he had to physically restrain himself.

"Fools," Voran said more quietly, but his voice echoed still. "Are you blind to the dying of the tree? The fire on the aspen sapling is dying, far earlier than its allotted time. Does this bother no one?"

Voran turned slowly to look at the rest of the Dumar. Some faces were paler than when he entered. A few did not return his gaze.

"*We* have caused Nebesta's fall. *We* have broken Covenant with Adonais, and now the fire on the tree will fade, and we will not be able to bring it back. The ancient protection girding Vasyllia will fade, and our city will fall."

"Father, will you do nothing?" Mirnían shook with anger. "This man is charged with abandoning innocent pilgrims in the wild, and he is raving about covenants."

Dar Antomír continued to stare at Voran. Voran returned his gaze, willing himself to be still. He focused on the flame in his heart. It burned strongly. Dar Antomír nodded slightly and seemed to come back to life.

"Peace, my children." He raised his hands and the clamor died. "These are serious things Vohin Voran speaks of. Otar Kalún. Is what Voran says possible? This covenant between Adonais and Vasyllia. Is it anything other than an old story? And if it is, under what circumstances can it be broken?"

"Well," said the cleric, feeble voice dripping with disdain, "in the more recent redactions of the Old Tales there are several obscure references to the Vasylli being a 'High People, chosen by Adonais,' but it would be very difficult to extrapolate any covenant from those few passages. I cannot account for the older collections of tales; they have serious textual inconsistencies. As for the Sayings, there are a few references to a covenant, yes, but the writers of the Sayings seem to assume the reader knows of such a covenant as established fact. They never describe it explicitly."

"Then there is reason to believe that the Covenant exists?" asked Mirnían, his face once more an impassive mask.

"Highness, if I may speak?" said the courtier. He reminded Voran of a snake with his insinuating and effeminate gestures.

"Speak, Sudar Yadovír," said the Dar.

"I have studied the Sayings," said Yadovír. "If one reads them literally, then yes, the Covenant is an established fact. But if so, then we must take every verse in the Sayings as literally true, must we not? In that case, animals can speak with human tongues and Sirin are still flying around in the deepwoods." He laughed, and his neck muscles stuck out obscenely.

Voran had a nagging sense that Yadovír knew more than he should, that he was challenging Voran to make a compromising admission. He had a sensation of panic, like a drowning man with legs cramping in pain. Yadovír continued.

"It makes a great deal more sense to read the sections concerning the Covenant as a metaphor for the mutual love between Adonais and Vasyllia."

"I agree with Yadovír," said Kalún.

"Do you really, Otar Kalún?" Rumbled the younger military man, huge and red-faced and red-bearded. Until that moment, Voran hardly noticed him, he was so silent. "I am not a learned man, but I know that if you start subjecting all the old truths to the test of your own fallen mind, everything collapses."

He looked at Voran and nodded, though his expression was still guarded.

"Dumar," said Voran, heartened by the big warrior's support. "Tell me, did our scouts give us any indication of this enemy that razed great Nebesta in a single night?"

No one answered.

"This is not a normal enemy we face. Surely there have been enough omens, even for your doubts! I have spoken to Lord Farlaav. He is a man known to many of you. He himself told me of the monsters in Nebesta…"

"You do seem to know a great deal, Vohin Voran," said Yadovír. "But why must we submit to your superior knowledge in this? You abandoned your own people in the wild. And you say nothing of that."

Voran felt backed into a corner. He was still sure, somewhere deep within, that Yadovír wanted him to admit to seeing the Sirin, though why, he could not say. As Voran spoke, his own body tried to stop him from speaking. But it was too late to turn back.

"Highness, Dumar assembled, I did not abandon them. On the third day after we left, I encountered a Sirin by the road. She sang to me, and our souls are now bound. But it is a perilous thing—to encounter the Higher Beings. I passed into another place. Another time. When I came to myself, I found myself in a completely different part of Vasyllia, more than twenty miles away from the Dar's road. It was there that I found the refugees. Ask the scouts. They know how far the refugees traveled, and by what woodsmen's roads. I lost the pilgrims, yes. But not through my own volition."

They didn't believe him, Voran saw it immediately. All he heard was silence, intense as the hum that follows the ring of blade against blade. Mirnían's expression shifted subtly, and Voran thought there was a glimmer of something behind it, maybe yearning. Sabíana now looked straight at Voran's eyes, her cheeks barely touched with pink. When he met her gaze, she did not look away. He found he could not hold her gaze for long.

"Chosen speakers of the Dumar," said Dar Antomír, his voice touched with finality, as though he were condemning a man to death. "Have you anything further to say before I speak in judgment?"

No one answered, and the silence echoed.

"Very well. Vohin Voran, we hereby find you guilty of dereliction of duty. You are exiled from Vasyllia, you and any children you may come to have, until your death, under the pain of public execution."

Voran remained in his own home, a prisoner, for three days. Outside, Vasyllia mustered. The great marketplace of the second reach—clearly visible from the high room in Otchigen's house—was cleared of its ornate booths, and long planks were set on trestles. Women and girls sewed, gathered, and packed provisions on the tables. Men and boys sharpened swords and spears, polished mail, brushed the horsehair tails of the peaked Vasylli helmets. Merchants gathered food in barrels and granaries that were built overnight. Voran sat at the window, his body itching for action.

On the evening of the third day, they came. A swarm of guards, spearpoints catching the half-moon's light. Three waiting-women in furs surrounded Sabíana, who stood a head taller than all of them. Ahead of all walked the Dar, erect and proud, giving no sign of his many years. Voran's heart warmed with love at the sight, then frosted over with regret. Would the Dar ever embrace him as a father again?

Voran put on his finest kaftan—sleeveless, the collar and shoulders tipped with rabbit fir—and tried to brush the dirt off his boots. He left his head uncovered, quickly tied his now shoulder-length hair back into a tail, and rushed to the hearth-hall. The Dar entered alone, his face drawn in anger. He stood in the doorway for a long moment, looking at Voran, waiting for something. Voran bowed his head and dropped to his knees, then fell on his face in a full penitential bow. He remained there.

Nothing happened. The Dar spoke no word, but Voran did not dare move until the Dar released him.

Something metal clanged on the floor. Voran looked up in alarm, thinking the Dar had fallen. The first thing his eye glanced on was the ancient crown wrought by the smiths of Dar Cassían's rein almost five hundred years ago—cloudy silver with white-gold flowers blooming. It was on the ground. The Dar had thrown it down. His eyes were brimming with tears.

"Highness," whispered Voran in shock.

"My son," the Dar said, voice broken by a sob. "How you remind me of your father. He was so sure of himself, so brazen. Until the time for penitence. Then he was a lamb. How I miss him."

Voran stood up and ran forward. He grasped the Dar's outstretched forearms as he began to go down on his own two knees before Voran.

"No, Highness, not before me." Voran's tears rose at the sight of the bent, careworn Dar.

"Voran, you break my heart. If the Pilgrim had not so much as commanded me to send you after the Living Water, I would never have allowed it. Do you not see? If even one of the pilgrims is found dead, you will be cursed with your father's guilt for all time."

Voran mused on his first memory of Antomír. Voran was eight years old at the time and had been sick for weeks. Breathing through his nose had been impossible, and so he had not really slept for days. He was blowing his nose with all the vigor of his warrior blood when Otchigen and the Dar walked into the house after a week's hunt. The Dar, his laughing, dark eyes a better cure than all the horrid-smelling mustard wraps that Mother tried on him, turned to Otchigen.

"He has a nose like a horn," Antomír had said. "Next time, bring him to the hunt. He could prove useful with such a horn." At which point they both laughed until the tears flowed. Voran had loved him intensely from that moment.

"Highness, you must think me touched by madness," Voran whispered. He led the Dar to the high place and returned to pick up the fallen crown. He placed it on the Dar's head—it was colder than ice—and stood to his right on both knees. "You must believe me. I have seen the Sirin. I have spoken to her. I have soul-bonded with her."

A knot of muscle stood out on Dar Antomír's jaw. "Tell me everything, Voran."

And Voran did, beginning with the echoes of the song. He spoke of the white stag, at which the Dar tutted, smiling. He tried to describe the Lows of Aer, which left the Dar pensive. He spoke of the Pilgrim, the Covenant Tree, the Living Water, and the soul-bond with Lyna.

"Lyna?" asked the Dar, his eyes wide with surprise. "She is of the eldest Sirin. Older far than the Covenant, older far than the Three Cities."

Voran's heart leaped in his chest. "You do believe me, Highness."

Dar Antomír sighed with a rueful smile. "Yes, my son. I have seen the Sirin myself, in the deepwoods, many years ago. Sometimes I think I still hear a song, but I can no longer catch the melody." He seemed a hundred years older at that moment. "Nonetheless, no one else will understand. I can grant you no more clemency, Voran. The Dumar is on edge as it is. They want you imprisoned. Some want you publicly flogged. It must be exile for you."

Voran's heart plunged to his ankles.

"Voran, tomorrow Vasyllia's armies go to seek out the enemy in the open field. You cannot go with them; indeed, I think you might find a knife in your back if you did. But I will give you a chance at restitution. You will follow the trail of the pilgrims you lost. If Adonais wills it, you will find them before any enemy—human or not. Mirnían insists on going with you, though I threatened to have *him* imprisoned for self-will. I will also give you the young warrior who spoke at the council. The red-bearded one, Dubían. He has uncommon strength, though he is gentle as a maiden in peacetime."

"Highness, I do not deserve your..."

"That is right, you do not," said the Dar, with a flash of youthful anger. Then he smiled again. "I do not do this for you. For whatever reason, both the Pilgrim and the Sirin have indicated that *you* must find the Living Water. If you do, and if you see the pilgrims safe to one of the outlying strongholds, I will recall you to Vasyllia. If we live that long.

"Now," he said, standing up and wincing in pain. "You have a much less pleasant task before you. Sabíana has the strength of a she-wolf, but you wounded her deeply, Voran. Put it right."

Sabíana's eyes were a rare dark brown that warned of deep unhappiness. Voran steeled himself against a conversation he would have given years of his life to avoid. She refused to speak first or even to look at him for longer than a second.

"Sabíana, I—"

"Voran, what has possessed you? You have become strange to me. Half-mad with phantasms and omens."

Her every word was a hot knife-thrust.

"This Covenant you seem so intent on," she continued, now jeering. "How do you imagine it happened? Adonais's hand descended from the clouds and signed a parchment with letters of fire?"

"Sabíana, a broken Covenant explains the death of the tree, the omen of the skies, the burning of Nebesta, the invasion..."

"Voran, these are but the aberrations of history. They *happen*. It's our misfortune that they all conspire to happen now, but there's no need to seek for mystical causes. It is unbecoming of you."

"You saw how the Dumar welcomed the refugees, Sabíana. The Covenant commands us to care for the Outer Lands' people as we would for our own. A camp of refugees denied entry into the richest city in the world? What more confirmation do you need?"

"The Covenant is a fairy tale! Yes, in the stories it makes sense, but you cannot apply it literally. Even if we have failed in some sacred duty, what sort of a god punishes his own people only for forgetfulness? Is that our gentle, loving Adonais?"

On some level, Voran agreed with her. But he had already considered the implications of that line of reasoning. If faith in a gentle god had led the Vasylli to neglect the good of others, then perhaps they imagined Adonais to be different than he really was. Perhaps Adonais was a jealous god.

"Has your father told you?"

"Of his plan for you? Yes." She turned away from him and folded herself into her black shawl.

"I suppose you wish me to release you from our promise?"

She turned back to him, her eyes blazing. "I would sooner run you through with your own sword!" She seemed shocked at her own vehemence, but only for a moment. "Why can you not give me your heart, my bright Voran? I have tried so hard to dispel the restlessness that keeps driving you away from me, but you have built a wall around your heart. I can comfort you; I can be your joy. But you must let me."

"Sabíana, you're upset, I understand."

"You understand very little, for all your new-found importance. Why do you keep shutting yourself from me?"

Voran found no words. She was right. He felt deflated, more tired than he had in years.

"What would you have me do?" He asked.

She slowly released the muscles tensing her body like a bowstring. The beauty seemed to seep back into her relaxing curves, the warrior princess transforming into a sinuous black swan. She took his hand and kissed it, caressing it gently.

"It is not for me to tell you what to do," she said.

His stomach lurched, and warm desire groped him. His head began to swim. His heart raced like a deer through the trees. He enfolded her into his embrace—how small and brittle she seemed! For a moment, everything was foolishness—the Raven, the Living Water, the coming war. It was all even mildly amusing. What else mattered except her embrace?

A kind of madness was on him, a savage excitement. The brittle thing in his arms was now not Sabíana, but a thing. He could do anything he wished with her. He kissed her violently. She shuddered for a moment, then melted into it. His hands itched to caress her.

Cutting through the noise of blood rushing in his ears, Voran heard the song of the Sirin, faint, plaintive. In his mind, he saw Lyna as she had met him, wings outstretched in the birches. She shone in a delicate light that sharply framed her feathered outline, but now she wept. The desire faded, and Voran felt a rush of tenderness for Sabíana. He pulled away from her, laughing gently. Sabíana's face was flushed, rosy. She smelled faintly of tuberose. She rested her head on his chest.

"I adore you, my Voran. I've never had so little control over my own heart. Even in your absence, you fill me. I see you even with my eyes shut. All the memories, brilliant as the sun shining through the rain."

For the first time in his life, he felt calm in her presence.

"I thank Adonais for every moment I've shared with you," she said. "You've been carved into my heart, every moment of you. How your eyes soften when you laugh, rare as that is. How your voice sparks when you become inspired with an unexpected idea. How your head droops when you wander in thought. Most of all, I love seeing you forget yourself when faced with a thing of beauty—a wildcat leaping from a boulder or an eagle soaring above the summits. How did I come to be tied to you, Voran?"

"Sabíana, what do you desire most?"

The final traces of her pain were expunged, and she shone from within. It only made the reality of their parting twist deeper into him.

"We are living in such an uncertain time. I hope for safety, permanence, not only for Vasyllia. I feel a need to find a place and root into it. Our future is dark, I know, but I have strength. I can use it if I know your heart is mine, though you are far away from me."

"I am with you always," he said, and thought of Lyna. "When this is all done, I will come back for you, my love."

They remained still for a long time, entwined in each other, content.

A pounding on the door jolted them both.

"Could they not have allowed us at least this evening?" Voran ground his teeth so hard his jaw flared in pain. "I'll teach them…"

Before he reached the door, it flew open. The hallway on the other side bristled with spears. Mirnían stood at the head.

"Sabíana! You and Voran must come now. The flames on the aspen sapling are going out. Otar Kalún has called for the Summoning of Fire to be performed today."

Usually, the many-hued dusk was the most beautiful part of the day. But now the silence of the evening fog oppressed Voran. The orchards were black and white parodies of trees, looking more like sinister old men reaching up with knobby fingers, as though enraged at the gathering gloom. They seemed unnaturally still, almost bewitched into nightmarish sleep. The sight clashed with Sabíana's gentle warmth next to him.

Down the road from the central square in the second reach, their company entered through a rounded archway into the oblong Temple Plain —a clearing in a grove of ancient red-bark pines that ended in a sheer drop thousands of feet deep. At the far end of the Temple, a small circle of aspens, glowing in orange-yellow vesture, stood guard over the altar stone.

A sense of presence inundated Voran, a barely-evident energy, something between sound and light. It was stronger than usual, fed by the tense expectation of the crowd, many of whom were openly weeping. This is like a funeral, he thought, not a supplication.

Voran and Sabíana took their place at the front, near the quivering aspens. Voran turned back to see two files of longhaired youths robed in black, carrying square banners with embroidered images of Dars, Sirin, and High Beings whose names had long ago faded into legend. Passing through the Temple, they cleared a path to the grove of aspens, then stood in two lines with their backs to the crowd on either side. The clerics followed, robed in deep burgundy, the color of recent sorrow. They chanted an ancient lament.

The melody haunted Voran; for a moment, it seemed that the mountain itself sang. The voices weaved into the melody and out of it in an increasingly complex pattern. One moment the rich tenors predominated, then the dark-toned basses, and finally the middle voices rang out, lush as stringed instruments. The voices united in harmony, then fought each other in unexpected dissonance, only to resolve in chords that echoed over the tops of the red-barks. Images flashed through Voran's mind—falling water, shaking branch, and whispering fields of wheat.

Torchlight flickered beyond the stone archway. Ten warriors in mail and crimson robes preceded Dar Antomír. They approached the altar table, solemnly bowed before it, and stood on their knees encircling the aspens, swords drawn and placed into the ground point-down. Dar Antomír met Otar Kalún inside the circle and kissed him three times on the cheeks. Both then bowed to the altar.

The tenors wailed over a drone in the basses, massive as a full spring torrent. The words of the ancient hymn echoed crisply in the cold air.

"O, gentle light of Adonais and his numberless hosts, radiant and glorious. From

the rising to the setting of the sun, you illumine the mountains and valleys. Shine out for us wandering in darkness, show us the merciful gaze of morning. O Lord Adonais, we praise and glorify you until the Endless Age."

The crowd joined in with a rumbling noise at once dissonant and moving. Voran felt no longer merely himself, as though the minuscule creature he called "himself" was nothing but a stone in a much larger edifice, a tower reaching with song and flesh and bone to the Heights. He felt small, but also part of something majestic and glorious, a note in a complex harmony that rose to the ears of Adonais himself.

The hymn was twice repeated, ending in a long, groaning note of lamentation. Silence prevailed as Kalún chanted alone in his watery voice. The words were completely unintelligible. Voran's ecstasy crashed to earth. Why must the chief cleric of Vasyllia always be such a terrible celebrant of the mysteries?

When Kalún's mumbling ceased, he turned around to face the people.

"People of Vasyllia," he said. "It is not the day for the Summoning. But our beloved sapling is already fading. Let us all come together in prayer so that we, your priests, may find the inner strength to call down fire from the Heights, as our forefathers did in the days of Lassar the Blessed."

Voran's stomach soured. That wasn't right. It wasn't the priests who had summoned the first fire. Not according to the Old Tales. It was the Harbinger. What was Otar Kalún up to?

The priest led the procession back through the middle of the Temple and out into the main square. In the evening darkness, the mansions of Vasyllia's third reach—all lit with lanterns—were like jewels lit on fire. Above them, the twin waterfalls fell in perfect lines framing the palace, which from this vantage point looked like it floated in the air directly above the sapling. The sapling! Its upper leaves were no longer aflame. The flames that remained in the lower part of the tree were bluish, barely moving.

One gust of winter wind, and the whole tree would go out. Voran was sure of it.

The procession arrived at the tree, and everyone fell silently to their knees. Only Otar Kalún stood, visible to all in the center of the square.

"As you visited our fathers in their darkest time," he intoned, "so heed our request on this day, Adonais, though it is not the day allotted for your grace. Send down fire. Let it illumine our hearts and give life to the eternal tree of Covenant."

The chanting rose again, bleak and stark in the night. Kalún circled the tree, mumbling to himself with arms raised.

A huge gust of wind lashed the Temple from the summit, as if Vasyllia

Mountain had opened its maw and begun to blow with all its might. The remaining fire on the tree sputtered and died, as did most of the lanterns in the city. Darkness seemed to pour over the assembled crowd.

Another omen, thought Voran, his hands shaking with more than mere cold.

"People of Vasyllia!" roared a voice in the half-darkness. "Your hearts are nothing but stone. Do you think you can buy the Heights' favor by forcing the hand of the Most High?"

The Pilgrim stood to the right of the aspen, impossibly tall, arms held high. He glowed with a golden light.

"It is not too late, Vasyllia. You can win back the regard of the Heights. Behold! All Nebesta sprawls at your feet, but you do not give her entry. Take her children's care into your hands."

Many moaned with fear, and many more cried out in agreement. But an angry throng surged at the Pilgrim—mostly young men. They dragged him, screaming, stomping, spitting on him as they dragged him back into the Temple, to try to throw him off the edge of the Temple Plain. Voran rushed forward, but there were too many of them. The mass surged, pushing down whatever was in its way, closer and closer to the far end of the Temple.

Two ranks of warriors appeared and rammed the crowd from either side of the Temple, coming into the open space from the darkness of the redbarks, where they had been silently standing guard. Swords drawn, they beat down the mob. They surrounded the bloody Pilgrim and carried him back toward the square. A wall of people surged to block their way, and only when the priests with their oak staffs joined the warriors did the wave crest and fall back toward the archway. The warriors rushed to the third reach, leaving trampled humanity in their wake.

Vasyllia is fallen, thought Voran. It is too late.

Know this, my dears. Our realm is full of doorways. Doorways into other realms. You may have seen them sometimes. A curtain of water falling where there is no waterfall. A metal gate standing in the middle of a field. A pool of water in the middle of a desert. Do not enter them. If you do, you will be taken to a perilous place, the Lows of Aer. If you ever come out again, it will be to a different place entirely! Many are the children who have entered the Lows. Few have come back...

From "A Child's Retelling of the Sirin's Tale"
(Old Tales, Book VI)

CHAPTER 11

THE CHANGER

The day that Voran and his companions left Vasyllia, it began to rain—a steady, insistent kind of rain that chilled deeper than snow. It never stopped long enough for the three travelers to dry their clothes, and soon they gave up altogether. Saddle sores became an ever-present reality, despite the cold. Voran forgot to take the necessary precautions, for which he silently cursed himself in language he never used in public. Judging by Mirnían's stiffness, Voran was not the only one. Dubían merely sulked. In their mutual discomfort, all remained silent.

Mirnían's guard of ten warriors traveled with them for the entire first day. But they were not trained woodsmen. They were slowing Voran down, and their racket could be heard for miles. After conferring with Dubían and Voran, Mirnían ordered them to return to Vasyllia. Voran knew what Dar Antomír would think about Mirnían's decision. He also knew how little Mirnían cared about that.

It took them three days to reach the place where Voran bonded with Lyna. Voran hoped that he would see her again, though his rational mind told him that was unlikely. There was no change in his inner flame, no surge in his yearning as they approached. If anything, the closer they came, the less he felt anything, as though something were dulling his emotions from without.

"Why can't it make up its mind?" roared Dubían, face red as his beard. "I can understand rain; I can understand fog. I hate both of them, but at least

I can understand them. This...this is like sweat. It's not raining, it's sweating!"

Voran pushed his exhausted charger up through a cleft between two tree-crowned hills. When he came to the other side, he hoped to see clear indications of the pilgrims' passage through that region.

"Voran, what is it?" asked Mirnían.

Voran could not understand. There was no sign of the pilgrims. Nothing. Until that moment, their trail—old food-scraps, strips of torn fabric hanging on black hawthorn, trampled earth—was unmistakable. But here, in the place where he last saw them, their trail veered off the road toward a wood, where it vanished.

Mirnían laughed. Dubían looked near to tears. Voran wanted to vent his frustration by hacking down the nearest tree with his sword.

"Well, now what?" said Mirnían pointedly, as though this was all Voran's fault.

"I don't know," Voran said. "It's too late to go on in any case, especially if we're going into those woods. The morning is wiser than the evening." *Or at least I hope so.*

"I knew you would have some sort of inspirational nonsense from the Tales, you fool," burbled Mirnían. He walked off, head down and shoulders slumped. His words stung Voran like the slap of a birch-switch.

As their mounts munched on the last few greens remaining among the ascendant browns, Voran gathered wood for the fire. Like the insistent buzzing of a fly, he felt Mirnían's anger, though the prince pointedly refused to look at him.

In the failing light, swarms of swallows kept him company. They wheeled low, almost at ground level. It's going to rain, thought Voran. But the sky was already planted with stars, and no cloud obscured their glint. Neither was there any heaviness in the air. And yet, the birds seemed weighed down. There was something chaotic about their flight, nothing elegant about their circles. A few almost flew into each other, and there was none of the usual playfulness in it. Voran shivered with unease.

All three of them took turns trying to light the fire. All three failed. It seemed to break something in Mirnían's resolve. Voran felt a wave of anger slap him a split second before Mirnían spoke.

"Voran, I have long wanted to ask you. You must have thought of this much over the years. Why do *you* think Otchigen murdered all those innocent people in Karila?"

Voran's nails bit into his palm as he balled his fists. What a coward, he thought. Mirnían could find nothing to attack Voran with directly, so he struck in his soft place, in the place that he could not defend.

"You as well, Mirnían?" asked Voran, pushing the nails deeper into his palm, hoping the pain would keep the anger at bay.

Dubían tried to play conciliator. "Never mind what other people think." He glared at Mirnían. "I've always been sure Otchigen was also killed in the wild, only his body was never found."

"I don't know," said Voran. "Somehow, if he were dead, I think I would be more sure of it. No, he's alive, but something prevented him from saving those people. It's not an easy choice to willingly return home only to face judgment."

Mirnían chuckled, clearly understanding Voran's implication, but he said nothing.

"Voran, tell me. What sort of a man was Otchigen?" asked Dubían. "I would be honored to hear it from you. All the seminary rumors smacked of jealousy. He was a great man, and great men are not often liked."

The unexpected kindness of the big man touched Voran.

"Everyone seems to think that my father was the Dar's enforcer, a man who thought better with his axe than with his head. But they never saw him tell stories. Every evening he would gather us around the hearth. Some evenings it was something from the old tales, sometimes he told us of his youth. I loved it when he spoke of his first meeting with my mother. He had a particular way of speaking. It was almost in song."

Like the Sirin. The thought struck him with unexpected revelation. He had always known it, but in some deep recess of the mind. Truly, there was something otherworldly about Otchigen when he told stories, leaning on one of the carved columns in their hearth-hall, always the same column. He would shed his years as he spoke, and every time he recalled his early days courting Aglaia, she would sit on her bench, rocking herself gently as she sewed something, pretending not to look at him. Her eyes looked different in those moments: they shone with intense color, revealing a wealth of shared remembrance, pride, and something deep, strong, poignant. The memory made Voran think of Sabíana.

Dubían put a hand as big as a cauldron on Voran's shoulder in what he intended as a gentle caress. It nearly bowled Voran over.

"You must miss them very much," whispered Dubían. There were tears in the big man's eyes.

"Yes." The tightness in his chest lessened for a moment, but as it did, the old yearning for Lyna flared up. He missed Lyna even more than he missed his parents, even more than he missed Sabíana. *I'm so confused,* he thought. Bonding with her was supposed to make the wistful itch disappear. She was supposed to order my inner world. Instead, I'm more lost than I ever was.

The morning was no wiser than the evening. At first light, Voran followed the trail of the pilgrims into the woods. As soon as he stepped into the trees, the trail vanished. But there was something else. Something crackling behind his ears, like a lightning bolt beyond his peripheral vision. Something wrong with the wood. It was not quite *there*.

Mirnían noticed it as soon as he joined Voran, a few minutes later.

"Did you feel that?" he asked. "What is wrong here?"

Dubían was more enlightening in his reaction. "There was a doorway here," he said, with quiet certainty, "into the Lows of Aer."

Voran nodded, while Mirnían shook his head and rolled his eyes.

"What do you mean *was*?" asked Mirnían. "Can these doorways move?"

Dubían smiled, clearly pleased at knowing something Mirnían did not.

"I thought everyone knew. Once entered, a doorway into the Lows shuts forever. Then you are forced to wander in that perilous realm, filled with all manner of strange beasts and people, until either you find another doorway, or you are forcibly taken out of it."

"Do you not hear how ridiculous you sound?" Mirnían turned back to the camp.

"Wait," said Voran. Something stirred inside him. They needed to go forward.

The wood rose ahead of them for a short stretch up a hilltop. At the top of it, the trees ended like a bald patch. The downslope on the other side was a sheer wall of ragged slate. Voran climbed down, finding plenty of footholds to bear him. A few feet away from the ground, he jumped onto ground covered in dead leaves, but his foot slipped, and he realized that what he thought was flat ground was another slope, though not as steep. He fell in a cloud of brown and landed hard, his breath knocked out of him. When the stars stopped dancing in pairs with the dead leaves, he realized that he lay in front of a large cave. Something beckoned to him from inside.

"I've found something," he called to his companions, who were still standing on the hill above him.

It was a natural cavern in the rocky hill, probably a shelter for wolves. Shards of yellow and brown bones seemed to confirm this. To Dubían's great delight, there was dry wood strewn about aplenty. He set about to build a fire, and soon a weak flame sputtered to life.

For the first time in what seemed ages, their stiff hands prickled with warmth.

"Well, this is much better," said Mirnían, flexing his finger over the flames. "The stories have got it all wrong. There is nothing glorious about questing. The only glory I want is a bath-house, a roaring hearth, and a piglet dripping on a spit."

"You're right," said Voran, warming on the inside. "What would our exploits be called? The aimless wandering of three soaked froglings?"

Dubían threw his head back, opened his cavernous mouth—several teeth were broken or missing—and exploded in a torrent of laughter. It was so unexpected, and yet so natural, that both Voran and Mirnían laughed together with him until the tears flowed.

But they were far away from home in a distant part of Vasyllia, and they were at an impasse. It quickly sapped their mirth. Soon they were silent and tense again. Voran felt the inner stirring again, more intently this time, as if someone were looking at him. He turned around, but there was nothing there. Something was different, though. Was that rock on that ledge before? Voran couldn't remember.

"I wonder how the Pilgrim is doing," said Voran. "He was a big man, but that was quite a mob that attacked him."

"Well, serves him right. What sort of a fool lectures a mob after a failed summoning? What was he thinking?" Mirnían chuckled.

"How can you be so callous? He is a Pilgrim. And he was our guest. Nothing can excuse that kind of violence. And in the Temple!"

"Oh, Voran. Always such a purist."

"And what about you, *prince*? Always so presentable in public, so careful about your people's needs. But as soon as anyone turns around, you laugh and scoff and throw them all to the ravens. Should you not actually care for your people if you are to make an even passable Dar?"

"How dare you!" Mirnían's face contorted with rage. "You, a traitor's son, a spineless leech who depends on my father for everything. You have the gall to pass judgment on me? I should slit your throat right here."

"Careful, Prince Mirnían," growled Dubían, his hands hovering over his knife-hilt. "You go too far."

"And you!" An angry vein throbbed in Mirnían's temple. "Are you so blind that you take Voran's side in everything? You think Voran saw the Sirin? You actually believe in some forgotten Covenant? Voran made all of it up himself. Apparently, the attention of the Dar's own daughter is not enough."

Voran's hands trembled. He grabbed his knees until his knuckles turned white.

"Men like you pollute the earth, Voran. You sit on rocks and ponder questions with no answers, while Vasyllia crumbles around you. What have you ever accomplished? Everything you touch is blighted, and now even Sabíana withers under your caresses."

Voran struck Mirnían with the back of his hand, then pounced on him and pinned him to the ground. He felt the point of Mirnían's dagger tickling the skin under his right ear. Mirnían's smile was feral. The feel of the metal thrilled and enraged Voran, and he reached for his sword.

Something rustled behind them. A shrieking, frenzied fear crushed Voran to the mud next to Mirnían, face-first. Every muscle froze, but tore at itself in a wild desire to flee. His heart pulsed hysteria with the blood through his body. His mind demanded that he fly from the unknown horror behind them, but his body was locked in place. He could not even speak. Damp with sweat, Voran willed with all the strength he could muster to turn his head out of the muck.

The rock he had noticed before moved of its own accord off its ledge. It fell, struck the ground, bounced, and *changed*...

...into a monstrous creature, over seven feet in height, standing on two rippling, hairy legs. Its arms and chest had the shape of a man's, but larger and covered in a thick tangle of grey fur. Instead of a face, it had the slavering maw of a wolf. Its eyes were the source of the screaming fear. They were the eyes of a demon with pits of emptiness instead of pupils, black like a bottomless abyss. Brown saliva dripped from its fangs. It growled, but it also laughed. Voran's blood felt like ice in his veins.

"I come as bidden, prince," the creature spoke with a guttural bass. "What would you have me do?"

"I... did not..." Mirnían sounded like he had pebbles in his mouth. "What are you?"

"The sound of strife calls to me like fresh blood. Malice sings to my ears like a lamb in death-throes. I am hungry, fair prince. Will you kill the offending wretch, or will you let me?" He pointed at Voran with a twisted black claw.

Mirnían did not answer.

Hissing with excitement, the changer approached Voran. Its eyes, dull yellow with black absence in the center, darted up and down. Its jaws panted with expectation. Black claws twitched as they reached for Voran's eyes. The wolf ears lay flat against its monstrous head.

"Such young blood I have not tasted in centuries," it whispered, then grimaced. "Is that the stink of Sirin on you? Never mind. I am *very* hungry. Your eyes first, my beautiful boy."

It reached for Voran's face. He lay without power, fear choking him. His breath gasped frantically, but his body was in a vise, helpless, as though laid out in a blasphemous sacrifice to this demon.

Something growled behind the beast, and Voran heard a nauseating crunch. The changer howled. It snapped Voran awake, like falling out of a nightmare. The changer was on the floor, scrabbling at something colossal and black. A wolf the size of a bear. Voran felt the flame surge inside him. He drew his sword. Tense and ready, he waited for an opening.

The changer managed to throw off the black wolf and faced Voran. It screamed and it screamed.

"I do not fear you, creature of the Darkness," whispered Voran. He feinted, waited for the changer to defend himself, then plunged the sword into the creature's chest, underneath its arm. The beast *dissolved*. Voran's sword clattered on the rocks. A stench of rotting flesh filled the cave, and a column of black smoke oozed out into the forest, puss-like.

The black wolf shook its head, as if disgusted. It stood up and padded toward the three travelers.

Voran laughed and extended his arms to the huge wolf. It cuddled against him with its huge head like a house cat.

"I was hoping I would see you again," said Voran, smiling. "It seems you have paid off your debt to me handsomely."

The wolf harrumphed. "You have a high opinion of yourself, cub. Your debt to me is now lifelong. Do you even realize what that thing was?" She spoke with a woman's voice. When Voran got over the initial shock of hearing the wolf actually talk, he realized there was something vaguely familiar about the wolf's voice.

"A changer, is it not?" Voran said.

"You say that as though you know what that is. You have no idea."

Voran turned to the others. Their eyes were bigger than their faces, especially Mirnían's, who was clearly having a hard time convincing himself that the talking wolf was a figment of his imagination.

"Cub," said the wolf. "That creature is the least of your problems. The army of the Vasylli has been routed."

"What?" Mirnían snapped out of his stupor. "What do you mean, routed? Impossible!"

"As impossible as wolf-men prowling the woods, my prince?" She turned on Mirnían, snarling. "As impossible as a prince of Vasyllia calling on a creature of the Raven in the anger of his heart?"

Mirnían flushed.

"I don't understand," said Voran. "Mirnían *called* that thing? How? Why?"

Mirnían moaned, answering as if against his will. "I wished your death, Voran. You drove me to such a passion that I lost all self-control. I wanted to kill you with my own hands."

"Why, Mirnían?"

"You really are that thick-headed, aren't you?"

The wolf growled. "Envy, Voran. That creature smelled his envy like a wolf smells blood."

"Wolf!" Dubían visibly trembled. "How do you know that the Vasylli were defeated?"

"Do you doubt the word of Leshaya?" She bared bloody fangs at Dubían.

"No, Leshaya," said Voran, placating. "But tell us nonetheless."

"Come, I will show you. I watched the battle."

"You did nothing to intervene?" asked Mirnían.

"I have little love for Vasyllia," she said and loped out of the cave.

She took them deeper into the woods, to a craggy hill overlooking the tree line. Voran climbed it before the rest. All around he saw nothing but forest, except in one direction. To the west stood a high plateau, a mile away at most. Even from this vantage point, he saw a horrific mound of piled bodies, their mail glinting in the morning sun. The ravens looked like flies swarming a dung-heap. Voran felt sick.

"What happened?" Mirnían stood next to Voran. His face was chalk-white.

"They never had a chance," said Leshaya. "This is a new kind of enemy, like nothing ever seen in these woods. They have no fear. They sidle up to death as if it were a life-long companion. Pain affects them little. But the Vasylli destroyed themselves. They were too arrogant. It was almost laughable. The initial skirmish was bloody, and the invaders took to their heels and ran away. Thinking this was a rout, the Vasylli ran after them with no semblance of order, giving up the high ground. As soon as they entered the deepwood, the marauders turned around and counterattacked. Reinforcements were waiting in the trees. In seconds, they surrounded the Vasylli. It was a calculated move. A trap. They left none alive."

The reality seeped into Voran slowly, like waking to realize a nightmare was real. That was at least three, four thousand lives snuffed out. How many of them were his friends, his cohort elders? He stood staring at the mound of death, trying to make sense of the disaster. If the pilgrims were also dead, the three of them could be the last Vasylli in the forest.

Voran felt a song rise up from the depths of the earth through him and up to the Heights, a dirge from the time of Lassar of Blessed Memory. He sang.

Peace eternal to your servants,
in your bosom, Adonais,
grant this.

Sobs spluttered through the song. When Voran could sing no longer, Mirnían repeated the dirge with his resonant baritone. Dubían wept aloud, his tears streaming down his beard and hissing as they fell on the cold earth. The wind picked up as they sang, harmonizing. Rain dropped on them, slowly and heavily, then clumped into feathery bunches of snow. The trees swayed back and forth, in time with the flow of the dirge. Then all fell silent.

Voran fell on his knees and bowed his head as his tears continued for his fallen brothers, for all the orphaned children, for Vasyllia's dark time.

Do not joke with giants. Their humor can get you killed.

Old Karila proverb

CHAPTER 12
THE WAYSTONE

They followed Leshaya for a week, heading east. The distant shimmer of the last Vasyllian ridge remained on their right for the first few days, then they turned away, and the mountains faded into mist. By the end of the week, the peaks were no longer in sight. This was completely unfamiliar territory for Voran.

They no longer pitched tents, sleeping instead under the stars, wrapped in wools that kept every part of their bodies warm, except their faces. At least once a night, Voran woke from the numb burning of his frozen nose.

Dubían had insisted that he return to warn Vasyllia. Voran could not stop the big man, but he thought him foolish. Mirnían agreed.

"No, there is no wisdom in returning now," Mirnían had said. "There is as much likelihood of you being captured as arriving in Vasyllia in time. And the scouts will have seen the enemy already."

But Dubían would not be deterred. Seeing the back of him brought Voran more grief than he expected. He feared he would never see him again.

On the eighth day after encountering the changer, the mountains lessened into rolling hills. Voran's ears began to pop as they descended. That day, they stopped early, before the sunset. They laid out their food and furs at the shores of a glass-clear lake.

"You might think that the lake is shallow," said Leshaya, "but it is not. Do not be fooled. That is one of the deepest lakes in this part of the world."

"That should be the slogan of our journey," grumbled Mirnían. "*Nothing is as it seems.* Never in my life did I think I would follow a speaking wolf on a journey to a doorway that exists, but only sometimes."

"What choice do we have?" asked Voran. "It seems obvious that the pilgrims entered the Lows of Aer. We have no other trail to follow." And perhaps he would find Lyna. The need to see her pierced even the veil of sleep. He only dreamed of her now.

"You would be wise to practice a little humility, prince of Vasyllia," said Leshaya. "You Vasylli are not equipped to battle the enemy now approaching your city. Try to learn something. It might prove useful."

Mirnían ignored her.

In the morning, the lake was frosted over with thin tendrils of mist.

"There lies our way," Leshaya said, pointing with her muzzle at the mist.

"What, over the lake?" Mirnían said. "It is not frozen yet."

"Not over the lake. Over the mist."

Voran smiled. He felt unusually eager this morning.

Leshaya led the way, and Voran followed. Mirnían, shaking his head and muttering under his breath, came last. As Voran stepped on the mist, it seemed to be hard ground. He waded knee-deep in what looked like milk. No ice, no water. When they all reached the center of the lake, a wind raised the mist around them until they were bathed in it. Something seemed to shift in the shapes just beyond the white. As the mist lifted, a high plain revealed itself ahead of them. Not a stone's throw away lay the strangest thing Voran had ever seen—a slumbering giant's head, the size of a three-story house, bearded, wearing an ancient helmet made of a curious silver-copper metal. It snored. Every time it snored, a cloud of starlings flew up, only to alight back on the helmet as soon as it stopped.

"Everyone is usually so taken with the head, they never notice the waystone," said Leshaya.

She was right. Voran had missed the ragged plinth. It had carved scratches on its face, too dim to be made out from this distance.

"This cannot be real. I am dreaming." Mirnían stood a few steps behind them, his face pale.

Upon closer inspection, the scratches on the waystone were legible, though barely, after what seemed many centuries of erosion.

If left you go, there love awaits
    If right you go, there gold awaits
    If straight you go, there death awaits

. . .

"What wonderful choices!" Mirnían spat on the ground.

"Maybe the head will be more enlightening," said Voran. He picked up a rock the size of his head.

"Voran, what are you...No, stop!" said Leshaya.

Voran hurled the stone at the giant, just as it was breathing in to snore. The stone flew up the giant's nose, and the head jolted awake, then sneezed like a gale. When Voran picked himself up, the head was awake. It looked very annoyed, but there was also something else in its eyes. The kind of amusement a bear might feel when faced with a charging ant.

"Voran, you idiot," whispered Leshaya. Her tail was stuck out straight behind her and her ears were at full alert.

"Well," the head bellowed. "You have my attention, tiny creatures. What do you want with me?"

A sense of the scene's absurdity struck Voran, and he spoke without even thinking.

"Giant, what happened to you? Why does your head continue to live without...well, the rest of you?"

Mirnían looked at Voran as though Voran had mushrooms growing up his nose.

"UGGH!" The giant's groan was like an earthquake. "Always the same stupid question. It's not fair. It's not as though I can, you know, *walk* away from stupid conversations. No. I'm stuck here, forever subject to witticisms and imbecilities."

"Buyan, ignore him. He's but a cub." Leshaya's eyes flashed at Voran.

"Oh, Leshaya, I didn't see you there. You're so small, you know. Can you remove these pimples from my presence, please? I am sleepy."

"Buyan, have you seen or heard anything of Vasylli pilgrims seeking the Living Water?"

One huge eyebrow shot upward.

"Ah! Always seeking information, aren't you, Leshaya? What makes you think that a big oaf like me knows anything in the wide world?"

"You're right," said Voran, turning away. "This is a waste of time. He's obviously half-man...I mean, mad."

"Oh, thank you for that, annoying little person. I may know something of these pilgrims, or I may not. You'll have to take that chance."

"Oh, by all the..." Mirnían looked ready to burst with frustration. "This is too much like a story. I hate it. Listen, whoever you are. What do we have to do to earn the chance at your knowledge?"

"Finally," the giant head sighed with pleased relief. "A little person with a brain slightly larger than a pea. I will tell you whatever you want to hear if you can guess a riddle." It smiled thoughtfully. "I haven't played at riddles in ages. Oooh, this will be fun. Here's the first one:

Above mighty water most often I mount,
Trying the hearts of heroic men.
I peer over cliffs and perilous jaunts,
Sounding the sum of all of my strength.
Don't think I'm a dragon, though indeed I breathe fire,
A thousand sparks, like scales, rise up from my soul.
I weep among welkin, though always keep watch
To help, never hinder, the poor helpless man."

Voran couldn't believe how easy this one was. "Beacon. The answer's *beacon.*"

The eyebrows came down like a drawbridge, and huge rotten teeth tried to chew the lower lip. In its disembodied state, the head found this difficult, which only made it angrier.

"How did you?...Well, never mind. Something harder, then."

"We guessed correctly," said Mirnían. "Now tell us!"

"There are three of you. Three riddles. Each of you answers one. Here's the next:

My place is high perched apart from all favor
To watch all the workings of this worrisome world.
Well covered and cloaked in midnight's dark color,
I sing all the songs my bright cousins dread."

Voran's skin prickled. That was not an accidental riddle.

Mirnían scoffed. "It's *raven,* you overgrown cabbage."

The giant head opened its mouth wide and tried to bite Mirnían.

"The third!" commanded Leshaya. The head smiled daggers at the wolf.

"I'm hopefully well held, lest I harass all my neighbors,
For fierce am I found, oft forcing my way blindly.
I borrow much beauty of all that's about me,
A shimmer and shine amidst the world's show,
Yet I terrify the toughest amidst my great temper.
Having beheld the beginning of all this world's bounty,
I sing its great song on all sides of the world,
Yet sit happily in stillness, in silence of mind."

Voran was stumped. Mirnían's face fell. Leshaya remained tense.

"That's not funny, Buyan." She growled, deep in her throat. The giant head laughed. There was no mistaking the malice in that laugh. Voran's skin crawled all over his body.

"He will not help us," said Leshaya. "We must choose a path on our own."

"Why do I have the nagging sense that you are going to suggest we go straight?" asked Mirnían.

"Because it's the only possible way," said Voran. "Unless you have something else to say, Leshaya?"

"Why can we not turn back?" asked Mirnían.

"There is no way back," said Voran. He did not look back, but he knew that he would find no trace of the mist-covered lake they had just crossed.

"And we can afford the risk of the path leading to our death?" Mirnían nearly shrieked.

The head snored.

"Do you fear death, Mirnían?" asked Voran.

Mirnían screwed up his eyes and pursed his lips. "Voran, you will rue this day." He shouldered his pack with a grunt and walked past the head to the silvery path leading to the horizon. The head snored on. Voran followed.

That entire day, and the next, Mirnían refused to speak to Voran. Leshaya was not much for conversation, either. She spent most of every day hunting. Sometimes she would be gone for hours. Voran's loneliness ate at him.

Soon the trees became smaller and rarer, until they gave way to shrubs and carpets of grass. Everything was bright green from constant moisture, even this late in the year. Their road led into a narrow dale, both walls of which sloped sharply upward and ended with three jagged peaks directly ahead. A narrow pass was barely visible between two of the teeth. The ascent did not look strenuous, but it was late evening by the time they reached the foot of the slope, so they stopped for the night. The rain picked up again by midnight, and with no shelter of trees anywhere for miles, the night was miserable.

In such weather, even Leshaya seemed uncomfortable. Halfway through the night, she crawled toward Voran and lay at his side. He fit himself against her belly. Her warmth suffused his aching joints, banishing much of the cold to the edges of his hands and feet and nose.

"Leshaya," Voran whispered, unable to sleep. "There is something I don't understand about the Lows. When I first hunted the stag, I had no trouble entering through the invisible doorway. I did not even realize I was in the Lows until it was too late. But in order to leave the Lows, the Pilgrim and I had to cross paths with the white stag. The Pilgrim called the stag a "bearer". Why did we not just find another doorway out of the Lows?"

Her words slurred in the haze of the state preceding sleep.

"There are doorways, and there are bearers. Doorways work only in one direction. If you enter, you cannot leave the same way. If you leave, you cannot enter the same way. Bearers, like the white stag, are two-sided doorways, so to speak. They can bear anyone in or out, but only if they are on opposite sides."

"Seems strange, does it not? Why are there such restrictions placed on the Lows?"

Leshaya panted. It took Voran a moment to realize she was laughing at him. "If you do not yet realize the peril of entering the Lows of Aer, I am sure there will be ample opportunity to find out. Silly cub."

In the morning, Voran and Mirnían started the climb. Leshaya was not with them, and Voran assumed she was out hunting again. As they rose, they waded through small waterfalls, not a dry stone to be seen. They snaked the tortuous way up the hill, which became more and more shrouded in rain and mist. By midday, Voran thought they had entered another doorway into a different level of the world, until they stumbled onto two cairns lining the road. The summit-marks.

At that moment, the clouds parted, and the sun warmed their wet backs. Voran turned to look back. The dale stretching behind them was a pure emerald green, sparkling everywhere as the rivulets and waterfalls seemed to be showing off to the sun. It was a stark, gorgeous landscape. For a moment, it seemed that he and Mirnían were the only beings in existence on the earth. Had Adonais himself descended on a horse of fire from the Heights at that moment, Voran would not have been surprised. In such a place, Vasyllia and her trials were somehow absent. Or rather, Vasyllia did not belong in this world at all; this was a different place, a different time.

"Why do so few of the priests ever talk about Adonais in the right way, Mirnían?"

Mirnían seemed to forget his days-long silence. "What do you mean?"

"Do you not see? The curve of that mountain. The thunder of that waterfall."

"Yes, I do." Mirnían smiled for the first time in weeks. "It's almost as if Adonais is here, present in these natural beauties."

"If the chief priest knew him as he claimed to," said Voran, thinking of Kalún's mumbling of the prayers, "he would spend his days singing the wonders of his craft with the best poetry. Not try to call down fire from heaven by his will alone. You know, it's all written down in the Old Tales.

The priests in those stories were poets who sang from the tops of hills as the snow pelted their faces."

The fire burned brightly in Voran's chest. He felt Lyna's nearness, but he had no idea how to call her to himself. It was maddening.

Then the sun swaddled itself in fog, and the cold and wet became all too real again.

"Look at this," said Leshaya, barely visible in the fog down the road.

As they approached, a wrought iron gate seemed to form itself out of the tendrils of mist. It was decorated in shapes of strange animals and plants, none of whom Voran had ever seen or even read about in the stories.

"Is this the doorway out of the Lows?" asked Voran.

"Let's find out," said Mirnían and pushed it open. It opened with little resistance. Nothing changed. The downslope remained ahead of them, leading to another valley where trees of changing colors surrounded a village of thatch houses settled along a snaking river, brown with the recent rains. The village looked empty.

They walked through the entire village without meeting another creature, except for the wild rabbits that fled from them in panic.

"Is that...music?" said Mirnían.

Voran heard the unmistakable strumming of a hand-held harp. Then the smells struck him like a fist across the nose—pork, cherries, apple, bacon. Had he gone mad?

Whether real or not, the source of the sound and the smell seemed to be a wooden hut, crookedly constructed, as though it were stuck in an eternal shrug. From this vantage point, the two dark windows only intensified the house's puzzled look.

The front door was open. The music stopped, but the smells were even more intense. A head popped out of the doorway, belonging to a young girl, buxom, red curls messy on her shoulders. Voran felt an uncomfortable lurch in his stomach. She was very beautiful.

"Come in, my lords! Oh, what joy! I hoped to have company this day. Dinner is almost ready."

It was a meal fit for a king. There was soup of a soft, red fish, unexpectedly tangy and salty from an excess of chopped pickled cucumbers. The first course was a white river-fish garnished with mushrooms that burst with juice at every bite. Lightly steamed vegetables— salty with a smoky aftertaste—followed. Finally, the boar—succulent, tender at the first bite. With it came a purple hash of some semi-sweet root, dripping with juice dark as blood. The ale was sweet, tinged with cinnamon and nuts.

Voran ate with relish. Mirnían waited before eating, staring at Voran as though he expected him to transform into yet another legendary creature. When nothing happened, he ate—tentatively at first, then as ravenously as Leshaya, whose slurping could be heard outside the hut, though she sat some ways off, feasting on the boar's entrails.

They remained silent through the entire meal.

Afterward, Voran and Mirnían walked to the brook to wash their hands and faces. The water had a faint smell of old cheese. Leshaya lay asleep near the door, snoring.

"Voran, I can't rest easy," said Mirnían, unexpectedly friendly. "There's something happening here that I do not understand. Something is very wrong."

Voran said nothing, but plunged his entire head into the brown water. It was unpleasantly warm.

"Is it not all a bit convenient?" continued Mirnían. "An entire village abandoned except for one hut with a girl making dinner especially for us? How does she live in this village? How does she support herself?"

Voran laughed. Such mundane details seemed irrelevant in the Lows of Aer.

"And I can see how you stare at her, Voran." There was a hint of a growl in Mirnían's voice. "Do not forget you are promised to another."

"I don't know what you mean," said Voran, lying through his teeth. The girl was beautiful, *too* beautiful in a way, as though some poet had imagined her into existence. Yet he desired her; lust for her pulsed through his body. He was again on the cusp of that madness when nothing matters, when reason falters. He had to have her.

"You are tired, Mirnían. Sleep with your sword by your side. I will take the first watch. If there is even a hint of something untoward, I will call for you."

Voran stood by the river, deep in thought. Heavy clouds roiled in the sky, churned by warm gusts, pregnant with rain. The river gurgled like an overfull stomach. The trees twitched with each gust as though awakened into a bewitched half-life, only to fall back to uneasy sleep. As each gust heaved and died, the air seemed to bloat, giving off the same acrid odor as spoiled milk. Voran sweated under his cloak, but neither the river nor the wind relieved him.

"It's quite full with storm tonight," said the redhead, somehow appearing next to him. She wrapped herself in a thin shawl, her arms crossed over her belly. Her linen shift was unbuttoned at her throat, just enough to reveal the swell of the breast underneath. Voran looked away quickly.

"Strange for this time of year," he said, lamely. His teeth chattered, but not with cold.

"It is that." She sighed and closed her eyes in contentment. Her lips were unnaturally red. Her hand barely grazed his. It was the touch of white-hot iron.

"You are not lonely here, all by yourself?" he asked.

She lowered her eyes. Even in the dark, he could see a flush creep up her cheek. Her lower lip trembled ever so slightly.

"Oh, I am, my lord." She turned away, the picture of demure modesty.

"I hope we have leavened your solitude a little," said Voran, awkwardly fumbling over the words.

She did not answer, instead walking away to an old willow weeping over the river. She sat down on a bed of moss between two outspread roots. She looked up at Voran and smiled, then leaned back against the trunk of the tree and beckoned to him.

He could never afterward recall exactly how it happened. Rather, the memories remained very clear, but as if belonging to someone else. Before he knew what he was doing, he had lain with the girl. After it was done, as the slow realization slithered into him, he lay between the outspread roots embracing her, caressing her. A drowsy slumber enticed him, and he fell asleep.

He dreamed that he saw the girl standing before him, but her face was unrecognizable through a mask of savage hatred. At her feet lay the carcass of some dead animal; a dagger was clenched in her fist. Blood dripped from its tip with insistent regularity. The animal was majestic, its fur spotted with bloody dirt. Its head, twisted grotesquely to the side, sported a pair of antlers still half-luminescent with gold. The white stag.

A wave of nausea throttled him awake. It was still early morning, and his mind felt muddled as if with wine, his limbs like cold fish. A scream of anguish. Mirnían.

Voran sprang to life and reached for his sword. It wasn't there. He ran.

In front of the crooked hut, Mirnían stood on his knees, his face in his hands. He wailed in pain. His arms, hands, neck, everything was flaky-white, gouged with deep sores. Another wave of nausea checked Voran's run. He knew the signs. Leprosy.

Standing over Mirnían, facing Voran, was something that had once been the beautiful red-head, now twisted and gnarled and wrapped in a hairy black cloak. Her curls were gone, replaced with rare wisps of grey. Her eyes were sunken and red, and a toothless leer replaced the former beauty. She leaned on a stone club that bore a sickening resemblance to a pestle, and she cackled, unable to restrain herself, hopping in place.

Voran tried to approach Mirnían, but found he was rooted to the ground. To his left, Leshaya— hackles raised and teeth bared—seemed also unable to move. The hag leered at Voran, as though challenging him to defy her, though he felt no more than a thing in her misshapen hands, to be thrown around and played with before being devoured.

"Oh, how delicious," she cackled. "The sons of Vasyllia are no more than worms writhing in the mud." She twitched her head side-to-side like a deranged crow.

"Voran," Mirnían sounded like an old man. "Whatever you do, do not tell her anything. She tried to seduce me last night, thinking I would be amenable to talk. Keeps asking about our quest. I spurned her. Disgusting hag!" He spit on her. She danced around him, then struck him with the pestle across his face. He fell on the ground, his legs twisted underneath him, but did not cry out.

"Le-per! Le-per! So much for words, princeling."

"You have no power over me, hag," said Mirnían, blood flowing from his mouth as he tried to roll over. "Though you curse me with this leprosy, you will not stop us from completing our journey."

"Well, well. There you are very wrong, princeling. My darling Voran is staying with me, probably for a long time. You see, Voran gave me the power over you all. Gave it willingly, too, the great-hearted warrior. *He* did not spurn me."

Voran vomited. The hag turned to him, crouching, her head cocked sideways.

"You thought you could take your pleasure from my body," she said, "and it would cost you nothing? You do have a high opinion of yourself, Voran, son of Otchigen."

Mirnían's face creased into disgust and fear.

"Voran? Is this true?"

Voran could not meet his eyes, but nodded once, curtly. Sabíana filled his mind, and the regret was like ten swords plunged one after another into his chest.

"What has Sabíana ever done to deserve you as her champion?" Mirnían scraped himself off the ground and crawled to Leshaya. She crouched to the ground and helped him up to her back with her jaws, as though he were no more than a cub. She trembled in fury. Voran could no longer contain himself.

"Yes, I am guilty!" he screamed. "I despise myself for it. Yet I am friend to the Sirin. Lyna loves me, and will intercede for me. She will not forsake you, Mirnían. Do not give up now!"

"What can I do?" Mirnían sounded as old as Dar Antomír. "I don't believe your tales about the Sirin. I don't claim to have heard their song, you madman. Now, I am a leper. The quest lies with you. I have no more strength. Leshaya, take me home to die in peace."

"Yes, yes!" the hag squawked. "Go and die, pointless princeling."

Leshaya looked at Voran, her eyes red and almost human. She looked like she was about to say something, but she only shook her head. In a moment, she and Mirnían were a blur racing back up the mountain.

"As for you, my delicious Voran, I won't kill you yet. You'll do slave duty for a while. And then I'll eat you."

The hag resumed her frenetic dance around Voran, punctuated with several blows from her pestle on his back and legs, just enough to hurt without breaking anything.

"Now, tell me. What were you looking for in the Lows of Aer?"

My beloved is like a cherry tree in the midst of the desert. I delight to sit in his shade. His fruit is a sweet taste on my lips. Take me away with you; let us hurry from this place. The bridal chamber awaits...

From "The Song of the Dar's Beloved" (*The Sayings, Book III, 2:7-9*)

My beloved is like a cherry tree in the midst of the desert. I delight to sit in his shade. His fruit is a sweet taste on my lips. Take me away with you; let us hurry from this place. The bridal chamber awaits...

From "The Song of the Dar's Beloved"
(The Sayings, Book III, 2:7-9)

CHAPTER 13
THE ISLAND

The sweat, mingled with the sting of sea-wind, burned Lebía's eyes. Her fingernails were threatening to pop off with every thrust of her hand into the black soil. The hand-harrow was slowly transforming into lead. Her back reminded her, periodically, that if she did not straighten out soon, she would remain hunched over the ground forever.

It was exhilarating.

She had never felt this alive, this useful. All her life she was served, waited upon, coddled, and worried over. All her life she ached to help others, but her father's assumed guilt branded her, and all Vasyllia shrank from her touch. Here in Ghavan, everyone needed to work, or everyone would starve. She never imagined something as innocent-sounding as preparing the soil for winter would be the hardest work of her life.

"Take a break, dear girl," the voice was firm, despite the age of the speaker. Lebía secretly envied Otar Svetlomír his vigor. Though his nose looked like an old potato, though his eyes had more red in them than white, he labored over the soil longer than anyone else.

"I will not stop while you still work, Otar."

"Oh, I stopped an hour ago, swanling." His smile smoothed out the furrows in his forehead, making him look twenty years younger.

His young smile had been the first thing Lebía saw when the pilgrims arrived on Ghavan Isle. Even now, the events of their coming to this place were as fresh as if they happened yesterday. The disappearance of Voran, the coming of the white stag, the passage into the Lows of Aer, the waiting longboats on the shores of the Great Sea...

"So pensive for a little one," he interrupted her thoughts. "I know the island encourages it, but you must not grow up too fast, Lebía."

"It is not merely the island, Otar," she said.

A howl shattered the air, as though it were made of glass. There was something human in the howl.

"That is no wolf," said Svetlomír, gathering the long hem of robe in his right hand and running off like a ten-year-old boy. Lebía sprinted after him. The entire village already crowded the beach, keeping a healthy distance from an enormous black wolf with nearly human eyes. At its feet lay an emaciated body, milk-white, but spotted with livid red. Lebía gasped and ran to him. It was Mirnían.

"You've grown so much, swanling," said the wolf.

Before Lebía could fully register the fact that a wolf had *spoken* to her, the creature had turned and leaped into the water. Mirnían groaned in pain, and Lebía's attention was snapped away from the she-wolf. Svetlomír picked up Mirnían with no effort at all, he was so wasted away.

"Svetlomír, you are not afraid of the leprosy?" Lebía asked.

"No, little bird." He smiled. "Are you?"

"No," she said, surprised at herself. "Otar, will you do something for me? Let me take care of him. Put him in my home."

Svetlomír's eyebrows momentarily met in the middle, but his expression softened as he looked at her.

"Yes, swanling. That would be a good thing."

Lebía dedicated herself entirely to Mirnían's care. Her presence seemed to ease his pain, her touch to stop the progress of the disease. After only a few days, his emaciated body filled out. Through the petulant lips and the pain etched into the lines around his eyes, Lebía glimpsed something she had never seen in Mirnían—a man of courage and gentleness.

Two weeks later, he awoke for the first time. When he saw her face, he shook his head as though trying to dispel the lingering tendrils of a dream.

"It cannot be," he whispered.

She caressed his head, and he leaned toward her as if she were a hearth-fire. After that moment, he recovered not in days, but in hours. With every one of those hours, to her surprise, Lebía lost another piece of her heart to him. Even when he slept, she sat by him, content merely to stare at him. She pitied him, but it was more complicated than that—something thrilling and joyful, a stirring attraction that went far deeper than physical allure. She sensed his emotions and his pain as though they were her own.

"How did you come here?" asked Mirnían one morning, when he was strong enough to sit up in bed and hold a bowl of soup with his own hands. "You must know that we have been combing the wilds to find you. We thought you were lost, or worse. You've heard about the invasion?"

"Yes, there is talk of little else among the pilgrims."

"What happened to you?"

"When Voran disappeared, chaos erupted among the pilgrims, and none of the warriors—most of whom were barely out of the seminary—wanted to take command. Half of the families clamored to return to Vasyllia, and they would have, if not for the white stag.

"I saw it before the rest, standing still on a hill-top, its antlers sparkling in the sun. It came to me, no one else, and as the people saw it, the noise stopped. Everyone stopped. Everyone stared. It came right up to me and kissed me—that's the only way I can describe it—then moved away into the woods. I felt like it was calling me, so I followed.

"I didn't speak to anyone—who would listen to me, anyway? —I just followed. Soon everyone was following me, even the warriors. We seemed to have passed into another place, because when we walked out of the woods, we were on the shores of a sea. I couldn't see the other end of it.

"Five longboats waited on the shore, and a small group of Vasylli—or so they seemed by their dress, even if it was a little outmoded—greeted us. Otar Svetlomír was at their head, carrying a loaf of bread in an embroidered white towel, with a wooden cup of salt in the middle.

"They welcomed us like family, and before we knew it we were all on the boats. We sailed to a dim dot on the horizon. Ghavan Isle, they call it."

"Are they Vasylli?" asked Mirnían.

"Yes, for the most part. Many came here because they wanted to leave the bustle of Vasyllia for a quiet life. Many of them seemed also to have premonitions of Vasyllia's impending doom, and so left before it was too late."

"But how did they all find it? Were all of them led here like you and the pilgrims?"

"Yes. The call came in different ways for different people. Sometimes they found it as though by accident. Other times creatures—the white stag, a particularly large firebird, or strange chimaeras—appeared to lead them to awaiting boats. The first settlers, it is said, were led here by the Sirin directly."

"Are you not lonely, Lebía?"

"It is a quiet life here, but busy. We live off the land. It is different from what I am accustomed to, but I like it. Though I confess I am lonely in the evenings. I miss Voran a great deal."

Mirnían's face darkened visibly.

"What happened to you two in the wild, Mirnían?" She asked, barely hearing her voice above the thump of her heart.

He looked at the floor for a long time as the last colors of day faded to twilight. She waited.

"We were separated when we entered the Lows of Aer," he said. He looked at her directly with a gaze that puzzled her, even as it stopped her breath with its coldness. "I do not know where he is."

Two more weeks passed. Lebía rejoiced to see Mirnían turn away from his dour thoughts and look outward. She often sat with him in front of the house overlooking the valley, already dusted with snow. Occasionally, she even noticed a tear on his cheek, but he always tried to cover it with a forced laugh. They spoke about small, trivial things, but their intimacy grew. Still, Lebía doubted he would ever see her as anyone other than the little girl he had played with as a child.

No matter what she did, the leprosy still remained on his body. She prayed constantly to Adonais—"Tell me what I must do to heal him!"—but no illumination was forthcoming. While Mirnían improved, even allowing himself the rare pleasure of walking through the woods, he was not well, and soon it weighed him down again. His leprosy precluded any possibility of mingling with the villagers, which did not in the least help his tendency to brood.

One quiet afternoon about three weeks after Mirnían's arrival, Lebía walked home after a long day of preparing vegetables for the winter. As usual, she walked alone, content to be with her thoughts, allowing the twittering girls that walked out with her to take the paths before her. The smell of fresh snow was a welcome relief after hours of sweat and dirt, though even the sea-air could not completely dissipate the ever-present tang of manure. She hugged her fur as she turned toward the setting sun and home. It shone steadily between the trees, but for a moment Lebía thought it moved sideways. She stopped, curious. The light flashed again, but now it was a second sun. Her heart tripped and ran forward as she realized what that light was. The stag had returned.

She ran into the woods. The trees spoke to her in hushed voices, their language caressing and mellifluous, pointing her toward the stag. The golden light of the antlers faded in and out of view, but she followed it easily. Soon she was deep in a part of the island she had not yet explored, where the spruces and pines grew taller and more sparse, allowing much of the sun to filter through columns of bark. On the sun-side, the trees blazed orange, but their shadow-sides were purple, giving her the strange sensation of being in two places at once. The gold antlers stopped. Their light brightened as she approached. The stag turned to face her. Its eyes were full of opal tears.

Lebía saw the sun and the moon facing each other in a darkling sky, but they were Voran and Mirnían also. She saw Sabíana, but with a different face, one she did not recognize for its sternness and warlike aspect. Now the sun was Sabíana, and it was shrouded in black, yet a fiery ring shone around the blackness. She saw smoke and fog and ruins of stone. She saw pearly bones overgrown with rich flora that pulsed with life. Where did she see all this? Was it in the opal tears of the stag?

She snapped back, as if awakening from a dream. The stag stood bowed on two forelegs before her. She felt a summons from it: mount, it said. At first, she was afraid, but the stag's eyes were reassuring. She mounted.

They soared deep into groves that danced in twilight. Music surrounded them like a subtle fragrance, and now the light from the antlers was blinding white. As they entered a small clearing blanketed with snow, the stag slowed to a trot, then stopped at the banks of a stream that still gurgled, despite the winter. Steam rose from it, deepening the sense of mystery humming around her like a song. A curving wall of spruces leaned over the opposite bank of the stream. The air palpitated with a muted presence. Lebía was reminded of the high days in the Temple. In this stillness, she hardly breathed as the stag crossed the stream.

Lebía dismounted between two spruces and continued into the grove alone, through interlacing needles, up a rough footpath crisscrossed by roots. The path sloped upward, and the roots of the trees formed a natural stairway. At the top of the incline, where the path ended in a slight semicircle, stood three of the largest spruces she had ever seen.

"Welcome, Lebía," sang a voice in the trees. A Sirin with golden hair and wings of different shades of green—all the colors of the forest—smiled at her, then sang.

All the spruces seemed to grow upward a hundred feet, covering the sky and the sun. The branches widened into an embrace that smelled of pine and fresh rain and overturned earth. Lebía collapsed into it, closed her eyes, and felt—for the first time in her life—complete and utter stillness.

"You and I are one now, swanling," whispered the Sirin, though that whisper echoed over the trees and into the waters of the Great Sea. "I am called Aína."

"I have waited for you all my life," whispered Lebía. "I lost you once. You still came."

"Dear girl," Aína laughed like spring rain falling on icicles. "When you sacrificed your own need for Voran's, you became the beloved of the Sirin for all time."

"My new family," said Lebía as the tears brimmed over onto her cheeks. She had never known joy to be so pierced through with longing. And yet, her joy was not complete.

"I know," said Aína, answering her thought. "I can give you this grace, for this day only. If it is your desire, you may heal Mirnían of his leprosy."

Lebía searched her thoughts, and realized she knew exactly what needed to be done. She ran off that very second, her excitement was so sharp.

"But Lebía, take care," said Aína in her wake. "Mirnían has a secret wound that he will seek to hide from you. If he does not reveal it, you will not be able to heal him fully. And if he remains unhealed...Well, suffice it to say that the choices of men can sometimes topple mountains."

Mirnían slept when she returned. She let him rest, barely able to contain her excitement. She boiled water and prepared a poultice whose recipe had suddenly appeared in her mind. When it was ready, she sat outside, wrapped in furs, watching the flakes gather on her feet. She tried—but did not succeed—to not think of the following day. All that she lacked now for her complete happiness was Voran. Surely their paths would cross again soon, she hoped.

For a moment, she remembered Mirnían's strange expression when he spoke of Voran last. Did he know more than he was willing to admit?

The Dar of Vasyllia had three sons, none of whom could find suitable brides. So, he ordered them to shoot arrows into the wind. Wherever their arrows landed, there they would find a wife. The eldest son's arrow landed in the courtyard of the richest merchant's house. His daughter was famed for her beauty. The second son's arrow landed in the garden of the high priest's house. His daughter was famed for her virtue. The third son's arrow landed in a swamp. An old hag lived there, famed for her ugliness. The third son complained, but his father ordered him wed. On the wedding night, disgusted with his bride, he threw her into the hearth-fire to die. But she came out of it with only her hag's skin burned off. Underneath was a beauty that no story can relate, no pen can describe. "You could have had me, fair prince," she said. "If only you had borne my ugliness one night. Now you must seek me beyond the thrice-nine lands, in the thrice-tenth kingdom." And she turned into a swan and flew out the window.

From "The Apples of Youth"
(*Old Tales, Book IV*)

CHAPTER 14
HEALING

Mirnían awoke. The stink of his own sweat flushed his nostrils, and his gorge rose. He was just about to curse aloud when a cool touch grazed his hand. Sparks ran up his arm, and he gasped in unexpected pleasure. Lebía stood on her knees, her arms on the edge of his bed. She had a small, mischievous smile. That smile. It made him want to laugh like he had not laughed in years. Warmth spread through his chest, and he couldn't stop an idiotic grin from stretching his face from ear to ear.

Was he falling in love with little Lebía?

Lebía was simply dressed in cream and white, her only ornament a golden headband with two filigreed temple rings. Her unruly curls were forced into a braid that ended at the small of her back. Compared to the third-reacher daughters with their damask and stifling embroidery, Lebía's simple adornment enhanced her natural beauty. But there was something else, a self-confidence absent in her usual manner. She was up to something.

"What a pitiful mess I am, Lebía," he whispered.

"Shall I heal you, Mirnían?" Her eyes positively twinkled.

"Yes, please," he said, taking up her teasing manner.

Lebía rose, opened the curtains, and pushed out the groaning storm-shutters. Powdery snow wafted into the room, sparked into gold by the winter sun. For a moment Mirnían thought he was still dreaming, but the blast of icy air soon convinced him otherwise.

Lebía crossed her arms over her chest and looked at him with an expression he had never seen on her face.

"I will heal you, dear one," she said. Chills ran up and down his back. Yes, she was his dear one as well. He just hadn't realized it until that moment. "But you may not like my methods. I've been a kind nurse, but now you need more serious treatment. Do you give your word that you will do all I say, no matter how absurd it may seem to you?"

"Whatever you do or say, my Lebía, I will follow faithfully." If she wanted to continue to play this part, he would happily oblige.

She raised her right eyebrow the tiniest fraction. "We shall see," one eyebrow seemed to whisper to the other. Was this the same Lebía that sat with downcast eyes on a bench with him only yesterday, never speaking until spoken to?

She glided out to the steam room behind the house. Within half an hour, resin-scented steam, tinged with the headiness of oak, filled the room, making him want to breathe in and never stop. When she returned, her cheeks were ruddy with cold, her eyes shone with the pleasure of physical labor, and the sleeves of her linen shift—rolled up to the elbows—revealed skin glistening like a fresh apple.

"You must wash, my dear," she said. "I've prepared the bunches and the bucket. There should be enough steam even for your pampered tastes."

"Lebía," Mirnían said, tilting his head to one side, "you are not serious, are you? I am covered with sores. As much as I would love a steam, I can't."

"You promised," she said, in a way that clearly settled the matter.

Mirnían pushed down his irritation and hauled himself out of bed. It was excruciating, but he managed to keep from swearing. His feet felt like bloated sausages. He took one step and tripped on something, falling onto sore-gouged knees. He restrained a cry, but only barely. Lebía crouched down to him, his pain reflected in her face, her mask of playfulness dropped. He forced a smile, and she once again put on the chiding, motherly role. Helping him up to his feet, she continued to lecture him.

"I found an old recipe for a poultice that heals leprosy," she said. "Of course, its preparation is a great secret handed down from woman to woman for generations, so you must not ask how it's made. I will treat you with it, but I put a heavy price on it."

"I have already said I will do whatever you ask. Ask it."

"You must promise to marry me."

She looked serious. The game was growing a bit confusing, and a new headache was making him doubt his ability to play along. Still, he would play his part to the last.

"I do hereby pledge to marry you, Lebía, as soon as you heal me."

"We shall see," she said and winked. That wink was the strangest part of the whole charade, and almost convinced Mirnían that he was dreaming everything.

As soon as he entered the steam room, he wanted to jump out. His sores screamed with the heat.

And she wants me to thrash myself with oak? She's crazy.

But he did it. He almost fainted from the pain. The poultice's effect was immediate, however. It cooled his sores at a touch. He even laughed a little.

What other improbable feats could this new Lebía accomplish?

"Lebía," he said, mocking. "You've grown so talented overnight. Are there perhaps some other talents you have found?"

No answer.

"I need a new shirt, Lebía. This one is seeped with disease and sweat. I noticed you put some fresh rushes on the floor. Can you sew me a new shirt from them before I finish here, so I can put on fresh garments, woven by your love?"

The door to the steam room opened, and a scrap of old wood dropped to the floor. A whittling knife followed it.

"What is this?" he asked.

"I will sew you an entire set of new clothes out of the rushes," she said from outside the door, "but only after you carve me a spinning wheel from this scrap of wood."

Mirnían laughed.

He sat in the steam, melting into nothingness, for as long as he could bear it. Then he ran outside, completely naked, and fell into the nearest snowdrift. After his mind reminded him to breathe, he got up and ran back into the house. A linen shirt lay there. As he put it on, he thought he smelled lavender.

Lebía waited for him by the window, absently humming and twirling the end of her braid on her finger. As he came in, she turned and gasped.

"Look," she said, pointing at his arms.

His sores had healed completely. He felt stronger than he had in months.

"Thank you, my love," he said.

Her face blanched at his words. His heart dropped in his chest. *What did I just say?*

He took her shoulders and pulled her into an embrace.

Lebía did not push back.

"I love you too, Mirnían."

She was crying. Mirnían stroked her hair and put his chin on her head, enfolding her completely in himself.

"I feel so safe," she whispered in between the sobs.

"I hope you always will, my love," he said. "So. When shall we marry?"

Beware the man who thinks himself righteous, for he is a liar or a madman.

Seek out the man who knows himself sinful, for in him the light resides.

From "The Wisdom of Lassar the Blessed"
(The Sayings, Book I, 4:20-21)

CHAPTER 15
THE CONSPIRACY

Vasyllia had been shrouded in fog for weeks. It almost seemed alive, a kind of enormous grey snake squeezing the city in its coils until even the air felt unbreathable. Though the air of the Temple was not as restricted, in Otar Kalún's mind it was forever defiled by the violence done to the Pilgrim. Even now, as he tried to bring his unruly heart back to its usual, pleasant, barely noticeable beat, he could not stop the images of blood and mayhem from huddling in on his enforced silence. For the hundredth time this day, he tensed his bone-thin body and breathed out slowly, willing himself into submission to the purity of thought that he had nurtured in himself for many years. Only then did he allow his thoughts to proceed unchecked.

"How could we have allowed this to happen?"

He often spoke aloud in the Temple, though he had never heard an answer. He continued to hope. Surely the day would come that Adonais himself would speak to him?

"Adonais, your house has never been so polluted. How am I to put this to rights? What must I do to make it fitting for your presence again? It is no wonder that we are hemmed in from all sides by the dirty refugees, by disease, by rumors of war. There must be purification. Even if it be by fire."

The words consoled him. How fitting if he, the chief priest of the great, awe-inspiring Adonais, would be the one to purge the filth that had come over his beloved Vasyllia! Who better, after all? He had dedicated his life to the discipline of the purity of the flesh. He had never taken a wife, though

THE SONG OF THE SIRIN

the desires for a woman and a family of his own ran hot in him from his youth. It had taken many years of physical effort, even pain, to extirpate those desires. He had even learned to abstain from excessive food and drink.

Nothing could compare with the inner freedom that was the reward of such willful abstinence. Nothing could replace that lightness, that joy he sometimes felt when he realized the dizzying spiritual heights he had scaled. And yet how far he still had to climb.

A muffled roar intruded on the stillness of his heart. It jarred him. Of course. The execution.

"What a disgusting display the Dar has prepared," he said aloud. "And he expects me to attend. No, I will not befoul the person of your holy one, Adonais. Better for me to be here, to contemplate the Heights of Aer and the depths of human depravity."

Better to prepare for the purification.

Yadovír stood in the palace turret only a few paces behind the Dar himself. He could hardly contain his excitement at being selected from among the commoners. Finally, his hard work was paying off. Finally, all the unbearable flattery, all the sneers, all the demeaning service he had to endure in his rise through the Dumar was bearing fruit. The Dar trusted him. By the Heights, he did not know why, but he did not complain.

Unfortunately, such a place of honor meant a very limited view of the execution itself. Princess Sabíana further complicated matters by wearing a gown with such an absurdly high collar that his view was blocked completely. Oh, how he wanted to grab that collar and yank it backward! But no. Civility. Decorum. No doubt he would see plenty more blades cutting through exposed necks in the near future. The thought warmed Yadovír.

His thoughts were interrupted by a harsh, nasal ox-horn. To Yadovír's relief, Sabíana, face pale with contained emotion, turned aside just enough for him to move forward a step. There they were: ten young third-reachers who dared profane the Temple by doing violence to the Pilgrim. Still dressed in all their gold-fringed finery, those noble born sons of sows! The bright future of Vasyllia. A future soon to be decapitated.

Kalún left the Temple, inspired by an unexpected idea. He would ask

Yadovír to dine with him tonight. Yes, the man was very common, no doubt, but his determination to gain power bordered on manic. That could be useful. And they had forged a kind of unspoken accord at the trial of Voran, being the only rational voices in a sea of believers in myths and fairy tales.

As he passed the Temple arch, he was accosted by some of the Nebesti refugees. He hated their tap-tapping manner of speech, so lacking in the proper aesthetic. They touched his robes as they passed. As though his clothes had healing powers! Stupid folk superstitions. Kalún would never understand why the Dumar had not insisted on keeping the refugees in camps outside the city.

Their hands, most of them brown with dirt, reached for him. He tried to smile and walk through them as quickly as possible. Every touch caused a rush of cold sweat from the small of his back to his neck, and he began to feel nauseous. There had been several cases of a fatal disease in the city recently. What if these were the carriers?

The ox-horn stopped, its retort lingering in diminishing waves. Ten swords flashed up, then down in a blur. The crowd roared, some with outrage, most with approbation. Yadovír watched Sabíana with rapt fascination. She closed her eyes in horror, but then forced herself to turn around at the last minute. He was close enough now to see her expression. There was no feminine softness there. Her pursed mouth was no more than a thin red line and there were unhealthy spots on her cheeks, but the fear was gone from her eyes. They were fierce, eagle-like. Yadovír was mesmerized.

She turned and caught his eye, and her left eyebrow rose up ever so slightly. Then she smiled, trying to cover her disgust with him, but it was too late. He saw it and was devastated. At that moment, Sabíana became the face of all that was rotten in Vasyllia.

Yadovír walked home alone, heavy with regret, not even bothering to push through the crowd still seething after the execution. His only comfort was imagining all sorts of fantastic ways in which he would someday be able to torment Sabíana.

"Sudar Yadovír!"

He looked up absently, not recognizing the voice. When he saw Kalún, he hurried to the priest, then bowed before him and kissed his hand in the customary greeting.

"You look as if *you* were the one condemned today, Yadovír." The priest chuckled. "Come and dine with me. I think a hearty meal will lift your spirits."

Inwardly, Yadovír groaned at the thought of a meal with a man who chronically starved himself.

"Oh, Otar Kalún, I am honored, honored!" he said, assuming his habitual subservience. He was surprised to see the priest's face frost over with scorn.

"Don't pander to me. It is beneath you. I invite you as an equal. Act as one."

Yadovír's heart skipped a beat, as much from exhilaration as from embarrassment. He had never before been acknowledged as an equal by a third-reacher.

Yadovír was amazed at the interior of Kalún's spacious third-reach house. It was bare. Stone walls, a few wooden tables, some benches, and nothing else, even in the expansive hearth-hall.

"Otar Kalún, you live so simply. I admire that."

Kalún smiled. "My family is among the oldest in Vasyllia. It does not follow, however, that I should live extravagantly. I have always prized abstemiousness over excess. I do not believe in even moderate enjoyment of physical pleasures. I seek something else. Dare I say, something higher?"

Yadovír felt a sharp thrill at the words. There was an intangible quality to the priest's tone that Yadovír knew well. This man was a fanatic. Yadovír had uses for such a man.

"How sad that more do not follow such a path," said Yadovír. "Certainly, the refugees do not."

"How true. Until I saw these Nebesti, I did not know human beings were capable of swallowing so much food at once."

"You will be happy to know that the Dumar is considering keeping the refugees restricted to the first reach. What with the pestilence rearing its head."

"Yes, I am glad to hear it. What is perhaps less encouraging, however, is the Dumar's continued inability to stop the spread of rumor. Have you heard the latest stories about our mysterious invaders?"

"How they flay their victims alive and brutalize their women? Yes, yes, I have heard. Nothing particularly interesting in that, is there? It is a tactic as old as time itself to intimidate an enemy with propaganda. It would not surprise me if a few of the refugees are in the pay of the invader."

"Now *that* is interesting. I had not considered it."

Kalún's formality had begun to soften. Yadovír wanted to rush forward with his characteristic enthusiasm, but this fish needed to be boiled slowly, or it would jump out of the pot.

Kalún served Yadovír with his own hands—there was not a servant to be seen anywhere—from a heavy iron pot. The red lentil stew proved to be surprisingly filling and very well-seasoned, even to Yadovír's pampered tastes. Heartened by the food and the conversation, Yadovír decided on a tentative attack.

"I was pleased, Otar Kalún, that we agreed on so many points during the trial of Voran. How shocking to find so little intelligence among any of the other counselors."

"Indeed. Now that you mention it, I had intended to speak to you on this matter."

It took all of Yadovír's honed self-possession not to jump in excitement.

"I hope that we understand each other," said Kalún, lowering his voice, though they were the only people in the entire house. "What I say to you must never leave this room. I do not play court games with you. I know that what you are about to hear will be worth a great deal of money if you decide to betray me. I trust you will not do that."

Kalún's eyes bored into him, assessing, then the priest visibly relaxed. Yadovír assumed he passed the test.

"You were present at the execution, yes? What would you say if I suggested that such punishment is not sufficient?"

"What do you mean, Otar?"

"I believe that we are all at fault for the profanation of the Temple. I believe we must all pay the price. In fact, I welcome the invasion of Vasyllia."

Something twisted uncomfortably in Yadovír's gut. This was not how the conversation was supposed to go.

"You cannot mean that."

"I do, Sudar Yadovír, I assure you. There is more. Vasyllia must be purified by fire. I believe Adonais has provided a refining fire in these invaders."

"Otar Kalún, we do not yet know how the Dar's troops fared against them in the open field. Is it not perhaps a bit early to speak of Vasyllia's fall?"

Kalun smiled knowingly. "I have no doubt the Dar's armies will be routed by the invader. It would not surprise me if Vasyllia itself would be under siege in a matter of days. And I intend to be the hand that wields the invaders as a tool for the purification of our great city."

Yadovír's blood froze. He had been mistaken. Kalún was no mere fanatic; he was a madman.

"Otar, what you suggest is brave, bold. But surely all other measures must be considered before such drastic action?"

Kalún's manner snapped back to formal. The conversation was at an end.

※

Yadovír hardly remembered how he managed to walk back to his house in the second reach. He stood before his door with its gilded hinges and couldn't bring himself to raise a hand to push it open. He shouldn't be this disappointed. This was just one minor setback amid hundreds in his life. But he couldn't help himself. He was devastated.

The door opened before him, as though of its own volition. Immediately, the scarlet hangings and golden braziers seemed to leap out of the house at his eyes, laughing at him. You can pretend all you like, they mocked, but you'll never be a real noble. You can wear silver in your ears, drip lavender oil into your hair, collect painted chests from Negoda and ceramic tiled stoves from beyond the mountains to your heart's content. Go ahead, hang that ancient Vasylli suit of armor in your bedchamber. Hang ten of them! What does it matter? You'll always remain just outside the reach of real power.

"Yadovír? Are you ill?"

Yadovír was so lost in self-pity, he had actually thought that the doors opened themselves. He didn't even see Otar Gleb there.

"What are you doing in my house? I've had enough of priests for today."

"Ah," whispered Otar Gleb with that crook in his smile that endeared so many. "You need to sit by the hearth with me, my friend. I've brought mead."

"I don't drink that first-reacher stuff, you know that."

"Today, you do," said Gleb, and dragged Yadovír into the house and slammed the door behind him. Gleb led him through the hallways like an invalid, with a hand as strong as a cohort elder's. He passed all the smaller rooms, making his way to the end of the corridor, into the noble-sized hearth-hall, Yadovír's pride and joy. It had more wall-sized Nebesti embroideries of High Beings than Otchigen's famed collection. It had higher-backed oak chairs than the Dar himself. It even had a chimney, possibly the only one in Vasyllia. But today, it all had a sheen of falsity. Like a doll's house magicked into abnormally large proportions.

But the two cushions on the stone floor, a hearth crackling and sparking, and a low table laden with a tankard of mead? That was perfection.

"How do you always know?" asked Yadovír.

Otar Gleb guffawed into his eagle-beak nose and said nothing, only pushed Yadovír by the shoulders down on the larger of the two velvet-lined cushions. Yadovír wanted to melt into it, to dissolve into nothingness. But there was mead to be had. Gleb knew how much Yadovír missed it. You could only bear so much of the wine of the rich.

"Gleb, what is wrong with your chief priest? Why does he have such a hard time being human?"

"Ahhhh," Gleb shook his head as he exhaled a long, tired breath. "Poor Otar Kalún. Do you know what's wrong with him? He never, not once, allowed himself to sit by the hearth on a cushion to sip the best mead in Vasyllia."

Yadovír laughed, the first unforced laugh of the last month. It was like poison seeping out of a wound. "Is that it? Excessive strictness?"

"No, I'm afraid it's more than that," said Otar Gleb. "Our dear chief priest is a very righteous man. Very correct. Perhaps even holy, if we were to judge by externals alone. But he forgot a subtle truth long ago."

"What's that?"

Gleb half-closed his eyes at Yadovír, assessing. Yadovír's mouth tasted bitter.

"The heart is what matters. That's what Adonais wants. Your heart. If you spend your entire life cleansing yourself of impurity, and yet your heart does not expand in love for those around you... It's like scouring all the rust off a pot. If you don't stop, you'll rub a hole in the iron."

He shook his head again and clicked his tongue. He always did that when pensive. It was one of the things Yadovír loved most about him.

"But I didn't come here to gossip about my betters," said Gleb, smiling again.

"Why did you come?"

Again the slitted eyelids, the fire in the eyes probing behind pale-blond eyelashes.

"Stop it!" The bitterness in Yadovír's mouth turned sour. "You won't convert me. You've tried for as long as I've known you. It hasn't worked yet."

"Fifteen years. But it's never too late, I say." Gleb smiled again, but without his eyes. "I'm not here to convert you. I only want you to know that there are those who love you. Those who wish you would use your gifts... well, for a better purpose."

Yadovír groaned aloud.

"You have an incredible talent, my friend. Can you imagine if you redirected your endless energy to the refugee problem? You could stop this plague that's beginning to ravage the first reach. Not shut them up like rats in a cellar! You could find places for all the Nebesti. Build makeshift homes in the marketplace, for Sirin's sake! Instead you waste yourself, trying to assimilate power that doesn't belong to you. Why? Haven't you forgotten that you're dying?"

"Dying?" Yadovír almost jumped out of his cushion. "What are you talking about? I'm as healthy as a horse!"

"And yet, you're going to die. We all are. Have you forgotten?"

"You priests are so morbid."

"Yadovír, I have a premonition about you."

"Oh dear, not one of your—"

"I'm not joking with you. I don't know how or why. But I sense that you are on a cliff, and there are abysses to either side of you. There may even be another abyss ahead of you. Some difficult choice that you have to make, or not make."

Gleb leaned toward Yadovír and grabbed him by the shoulders.

"Do not doubt, Yadovír, that evil is more than a state of mind. There are dark powers out there willing to use people against their will. Sometimes, all it takes is one compromise."

"Well, then it's too late for me," said Yadovír, brushing it off with a laugh. But the heaviness in his heart was back.

Gleb said nothing, but his eyes filled with tears. "Here," he said, pouring the last of the mead. "May the morning be wiser than the evening, eh?"

The next morning, the entire city was abuzz with news. The rising sun revealed a fresh onrush of refugees, but these were not Other Landers. These were Vasylli, from outlying villages. Every one of them told the same tale—the invaders had destroyed the Dar's army to the last man.

Yadovír did not consider himself a superstitious man, but the timing of this news rattled him. It was too neat that he should refuse the priest's offer on the eve of such a disaster. In any case, this changed everything. If the army was routed, that meant siege. He doubted he would survive such hardships, and he doubted anyone else in Vasyllia would either. They had all grown too fat and content with their lot. Eventually, someone would betray the city to the invaders rather than be reduced to eating horses and rats. Better for everyone if *he* did it than some half-wit second-reacher. Or an insane high priest.

At that thought, he remembered the cozy pleasure of the evening with Otar Gleb. Maybe the fool was right. What was the point of all this rushing about after power, anyway?

Down the street from his house stood the large courtyard of Sudar Kupian, one of the richest merchants in Vasyllia. It could hold at least a hundred people, and often the old man set up trestles full of food for passers-by, just to show off how little it meant to him. Yadovír envied him. Today, a royal crier stood in the middle of the courtyard. Yadovír hurried to hear what the man had to say. He missed the beginning, but came just in time to hear:

"Effective immediately, the Dar has declared martial law. The Dumar's powers are revoked until further notice."

How dare he? He has no right to deprive the people of their voice!

No. Gleb was wrong. If Yadovír did not take control of things, there would be no more Vasyllia soon.

Yadovír ran up the nearest staircase to the third reach. Absently, he noticed that some of the asters were still hanging on the brown ivy. It made him sad, somehow, but he pushed that thought aside.

The many-gabled house of the high priest glared at Yadovír, and the leafless cherry trees seemed to be reaching out toward him in threat. He banged on the doors of Kalun's house until his hands were red and painful. Only then did he hear the squeak of bolts being pulled back. The door opened a fraction, and was about to close again, but Yadovír pushed it open.

"Otar Kalún. You were right. I want to help you. I want to be the instrument of Vasyllia's purging." Otar Gleb's smile faded in his mind's eye. Yadovír felt himself getting sick at his own words.

The door opened. Kalún beamed. Yadovír's hands trembled at that smile: it was soft and childish, with no trace of guile. This was the face of madness. Yadovír had not seen it before, and for a moment his body clamored at him to flee. Instead, he walked into the tomb-like house, and the door shut behind him.

The lands under the protection of Vasyllia are called "The Three Lands" or "The Three Cities," meaning, of course, Vasyllia, Nebesta, and Karila, with the lands appertaining to them. There are also other smaller principalities that officially owe allegiance to one of the Three Cities, but in fact are largely independent. There is Negoda, an offshoot of Nebesta, which shares the Southern Downs with its Mother City. Tiverna, Bskova, and Charnigal pay tribute to Karila. They make a kind of three-pointed gate to the hilly country that sits at the foot of the Vasylli-Nebesti Mountains. Another five or so cities do not even merit a name, for they stand at the edge of the Steppelands. Only nomads live beyond...

From "A Child's Lesson in Vasylli Geography,"
(Old Tales, Appendix 3c)

CHAPTER 16

THE GUMIREN

The kestrel keened, hung on the air, trembling with ecstasy, then plunged down into the shadows. Sabíana, standing on a palace turret, thought of Voran. Whenever they had walked in the forests or simply sat in silence together, the kestrel had always commanded his attention. He had called it a "windhover." She never really understood why he was so entranced by the small sparrow-hawks. But now, its appearance was enough to make her cry. Again.

For the first three weeks after Voran's exile, Sabíana had rushed about like a madwoman, busying herself in important and unimportant work. She even finished the embroidered Sirin banner. One morning, when the fog seemed ready to smother Vasyllia, she woke up with the realization that she had never been so tired and lonely. She returned to her bed, hoping no one would hear her sobs. She slept the entire day.

That evening, when she woke up, she was refreshed and able to think about Voran without the memory gouging out the remnants of her heart. Until the kestrel.

Once again, the kestrel soared to the clouds, fell backward and caught himself right in front of Sabíana's face. Its mouse-like squeak was almost comical, but she couldn't laugh. Truly, its sleek, mottled shape was beautiful.

It hovered before her, staring at her.

"Go to him, little sparrow-hawk. Tell him to hurry back for me."

The kestrel flew away, and Sabíana saw it ride a wind-gust out over the Covenant Tree—now no more than a normal aspen sapling, naked in the winter cold—into the forests beyond Vasyllia. Perhaps it had understood her. She stared after it as far as she could, until it melted into a dark band of cloud.

Except it was not cloud. It moved toward Vasyllia with supernal speed, and it twitched. She heard them before she realized what they were. The skies crawled—ravens by the thousand circled over Vasyllia, croaking discordantly, calling for the coming of the war to fill their bellies with the flesh of the dead. They remained high above the city, out of bowshot. Sabíana's uneasy apprehension turned into dread.

Then she saw them: shimmering, dancing abysses at the very edge of the plateau. They resolved into a mass of men carrying torches. There were so many of them! Ten thousand strong or more. The enemy was here.

"Come, Sabíana," said the Dar. "I need you at the wall with me."

The Dar, standing outside her chamber door, shimmered in a halo of torchlight. He was surrounded by black-clad warriors in full armor.

"Parley?" she asked.

He nodded once.

She rose and wrapped herself in a wolf-fur before joining her father in the ring of light. It was already dark in the city, and only smoking torches provided illumination—an angry, red glare that bloodied everyone's faces. It all seemed somehow too vivid to be real, the way Sabíana sometimes felt in a dream the moment before awakening.

As they walked—Dar Antomír a few steps ahead of Sabíana—she felt an itch near her left ear. Someone was staring at her. She turned and caught the open glance of the warrior to her immediate left. He blanched and turned away. She recognized him.

"You are Tolnían, yes? The scout who brought us the report about the weeping tree?"

"Yes, Highness," he mumbled in confusion. "Kind of you to remember me."

"How could I forget you? Your tidings were the beginning of all this, were they not?"

The warrior—if he could be called that, for he was no more than a boy—blushed a little.

"Speak your mind, Tolnían. It would give me relief."

"Highness, forgive me. I was only wondering if there is anything I can do to relieve the Dar. I can almost feel the weight of ruling pushing him down."

Sabíana looked ahead at her father, who walked briskly with the head of the company. He betrayed no outward signs of stress.

"You are a bit young to be able to read people so well, Tolnían," she said.

"I never had a childhood, my lady. My mother and father died when I was little. They were ambassadors to Karila."

"Do you mean—"

"Yes, they were among those massacred."

Sabíana was surprised by the calm tone. It was full of warm remembrance, but resigned in a way typical with older men, not youths.

They had reached the turret built into one of the carved trees framing Vasyllia's doors. They climbed onto the platform, and Sabíana's heart grew cold, her limbs heavy, at the sight of the enemy. There was no end to them—torches as far and deep as the eye could see—endless lines across the high plain, into the groves on either side, and all the way down the slopes until they were shrouded in fog. Sabíana nearly despaired. She and the Dar approached the wall, and a banner-bearer raised a large, black banner with the figure of a High Being. Sabíana couldn't remember what sort of being it was. Perhaps someone invoked during wartime.

In the torchlight, details were difficult to distinguish. The invaders were all dressed similarly in loose kaftans cinched at the waist, worn over tight-fitting pants—good riding clothes, Sabíana realized—and no external markings seemed to distinguish the common soldier from the officer. All of them were brown-skinned, squat, well-built, with silky black hair and faces like round bowls. There was some similarity in feature to the Karila, but these had a much more pronounced angle to their eyes. *It looks like they're always laughing,* thought Sabíana with an unpleasant lurch in her stomach.

One of the largest came forward, surrounded by a guard of archers with bows impossibly long, almost the height of two men standing on each other's shoulders. Surely, they were no more than ceremonial, she thought. But the grim set of the archers' jaws changed her mind. This leader had a silk scarf tied to his fur-lined conical hat, probably to designate importance. He looked up at them and bowed to the waist. He then snapped his fingers, and a large band of shirtless, muscular brutes armed with spears pushed a prisoner forward. He looked familiar. Then she recognized him, and she reeled at the edge of abysmal despair, barely holding on. It was Dubían.

"Father, what does this mean? What about..."

"Hush, my dear," he whispered, his eyes set and firm. "We know nothing. Not yet."

Dubían was bloodied and his face was swollen, his eyes barely visible. The brutes pushed him down to his knees with spear-points. The silk-scarfed leader said something in an undertone to Dubían, and to Sabíana's surprise it sounded like the Vasyllian tongue. How could these mysterious enemies from beyond the Steppelands speak Vasyllia's language? Dubían shook his head, stubbornly looking down. The leader took up a heavy horsewhip and beat him twice. Dubían tilted his head up, though Sabíana still doubted he could actually see much, so battered was his face. She pitied him, but the face she saw in her mind—battered and bruised—was Voran's. Her hands trembled.

"Highness," rasped Dubían. "Forgive me. I have failed in my charge before you. I did not come in time to warn you.

The whip cracked again. The leader angrily muttered something at Dubían.

"Dubían, my son," said Dar Antomír with unexpected vigor, though Sabíana couldn't mistake the slight tremor, "do not fear to speak. Whatever they force you to say, say it. You are not accountable. Adonais forgives, and so do I. Speak."

The leader guffawed and slapped the back of Dubían's head, almost as a friendly encouragement. Sabíana's stomach lurched again dangerously.

"I thank you, Highness." Dubían crouched over in pain, then forced himself to straighten. His eyes were now completely shut. "The Gumiren have one condition. They will allow Vasyllia its peace and continued existence. In return, the Dar must recognize the lordship of the Ghan of Gumir, though as a courtesy he will retain the title of Dar. Every ten years, three of Vasyllia's best young men and three of Vasyllia's best young women will be sent to the capital city of Gumir-atlan, to be given in marriage to the clan-lords and ladies of the Gumiren. An additional tribute of timber, furs, gold, and wine will be levied every few months. Furthermore, a representative of the Ghan will preside at all ruling sessions of the Dar. He will have power to supersede the Dar's command, should the Ghan's wishes contradict those of the Dar."

Dar Antomír suddenly took a spear from one of his retainers and hurled it over the wall. It landed point-first at the feet of the leader. Sabíana gritted her teeth, expecting an immediate reprisal. The leader smiled derisively and spit on the spear.

"Vasyllia rejects your offer, Gumir!" cried the Dar. "We know who you are. Tell your Ghan's masters that we will never treat with them. Our blood and our lives first, you filth!"

The leader smiled no more. The Dar turned away from him and spoke to the wall-guard.

"This is the time of testing, my children. Stand fast, and fear no darkness!"

Sabíana sensed the rising of an invisible cloud of anger from the direction of the Gumiren. The air itself seemed poisoned. The leader rattled off a curt command in a guttural language that sounded like spoons beating each other. He pointed at Dubían. The entire army of Gumiren shrieked—a high-pitched, blood-curdling whooping that sounded more beastly than human. Dubían's guards hurled their spears at their prisoner. His face twitched, but not a sound of pain escaped his lips. He half-fell to the earth, the spear-shafts twisting his body awkwardly.

A shout rose among the Vasylli.

"Rogdai," cried the Dar, "now!"

Sabíana felt the shadows widening around her into dancing spots, and everything started to go dark. The shrieks pursued her into the darkness.

"Princess dear! Little one? Wake UP!"

Sabíana woke, finding it difficult to remember where she was, why she was wherever she was, and even for a brief moment *who* she was. A round, wrinkled face with two apple-red spots on her cheeks was not a foot away from hers. There was something familiar about it.

"Well, my chick. Took you long enough."

"Nanny? What are you doing here? I haven't seen you in ages."

"You were not doing so well. They needed my *special* knowledge."

The old face, wrapped and tied elaborately in the manner of widows, had hardly a tooth left in it, but still she smiled in that way only the old have, so full of memory. Sabíana imagined how the old woman must be seeing all her selves—the precocious child, the headstrong girl, the Dar's solemn daughter—in a single moment. It unnerved Sabíana, though the sensation was not unpleasant.

"How long have I been sleeping?"

"Sleep? That wasn't sleep, my little one. Three days. They thought you had caught the pestilence."

Everything came flooding back, especially Dubían's broken body lying askew on the muddy ground. Again spots danced before her eyes, and the world swam around her. Enough of this weakness, she said to herself. I am of Cassían's proud line. We have iron in our hearts, and if all others fall to the madness out there beyond the wall, I will not.

The world righted itself, though Nanny still looked worried.

"Poor Dubían," Sabíana whispered. "How terrible to die within sight of home, but never to enter it a last time."

The corners of Nanny's mouth trembled.

"Adonais is good, my little one. You should have seen them! Our Vasylli went war-mad. They stormed those… whatever-they-call-themselves. Those pigs never expected the mad charge. A hundred of our best men. They fell on the enemy's thousands like bees. Dubían they brought back. Yes, it was at great cost. We lost many, but the enemy lost more."

Sabíana swelled with pride, and the tears gathered. She held them back. "How brave Dubían was. He never cried out. Not once! Though the pain must have been terrible. His wounds…"

"Mmmm. Yes. I washed him, you know, ducky. His face. You should have seen his face. Well, I'm sure you will. You were never one to shrink from death."

"How could I? Mother died so young…" Her poor father. How he must be suffering Dubían's loss. "Nanny, how is the Dar?"

The old woman's breathing became erratic, and a sob escaped.

"Oioioi," she keened, "my Dar, my wonderful Dar. He would not be so badly off if Dubían wasn't killed. He can't ask him—"

"About Voran and Mirnían," Sabíana finished for her. "I must see him, Nanny. Get me my housedress. The green one." She swooped into action, every movement of her body pushing the dangerous thoughts about Voran further away from her mind. The old woman, well-versed in the behavior of the Dar's family, stopped chattering and hurried to be useful. She dressed Sabíana calmly, with firm, quick hands. Sabíana was grateful for it.

"No. First show me the fallen warrior," said Sabíana as they left her bedroom. She would not use his name. To name him would be to personalize him. No more. She must become stone.

He lay in a vaulted room with high ceilings. As in the Dumar's council room, decorating each corner of the room was a tree carved of stone. The air shimmered gold from the many candles surrounding his bier, which stood like an altar in the center of the room. Dubían was arrayed in ancient robes over golden scale-mail. The candlelight ricocheted off his helmet and greaves. His red beard looked almost bloody next to his white face, yet he smiled slightly. He looked so young. The few lines that etched his forehead in life were smoothed away by the hand of death.

Sabíana dismissed Nanny. She had a sudden urge to pull aside Dubían's armor, to see the wounds for herself, to understand the nature of their enemy, but his face stopped her. He was so peaceful. Where was Dubían now? Was his spirit still living? Had it flown away somewhere? Why did his body appear still so vigorous, even in death? It looked like he would open his eyes at any moment and sit up to speak to her.

The candles flared, becoming impossibly bright. Their light rose like a wave, no longer gold, but pure, blinding white. Voices, faint and ethereal. The sound of wind whistling through reeds. The voices arranged into harmony, at first simple, then growing in complexity until it was like a river bearing down on her, like the rush of wind through heath, like the pounding of the sea on stones. Sabíana fell to her knees.

Three Sirin sat over the dead warrior's body and sang. The first—her wings green as the forest—cried tears of fiery joy. The second—her wings like living sapphire and amethyst—cried tears of inconsolable pain. The third—her wings dark indigo like twilight—did not cry, her face grave and reverent. They took Dubían's body with their talons and unfurled their wings, raising him gently, rocking him like a mother would a child. The colors of the gem-feathers burned from within, until they were flames engulfing his body. Sabíana's eyes watered with the pain of looking at this light—so much brighter than the sun—and she was forced to turn away. From the corner of her vision, it seemed to her that Dubían opened his eyes and gasped for breath, but when she turned back to look, they were all gone. The world seemed grey and faded in their absence.

Hag: a shape-shifter of dubious loyalties. She may or may not be immortal.
Leshy: a spirit of the forest, Alkonist. Sometimes goes by the name "Lesnik."
Rusalka: the unquiet soul of a drowned girl. Likes to tickle young men to death.
Bukavach: a six-legged amphibious monster with a taste for human flesh.
Vila: also known as "rain maidens." They feed off the powers of others.
The Storyteller: a large cat with an inordinate love for fairy tales. Alkonist.
Alkonist: a general label indicating any creature of authority in the Lows of Aer

From "A Bestiary of Vasyllia"
(Old Tales, Book II)

CHAPTER 17
AN ORDEAL OF STORIES

"Breakfast time, my darling Voran."

It was the girl's voice, not the hag's. He dusted the night's snow off his filthy rag-blanket. When will she tire of this game?

As usual, he was surprised he slept at all. Every night, as he lay down on the brown straw near the outhouse, he hoped he would simply freeze to death. Every morning he woke up, aching and miserable, but very much alive.

This morning, like all mornings, the smells coming from the lopsided hut were obscenely delicious. His eyes confirmed the promise of his nose—the table was littered with thick, buttery pancakes, stuffed chicken and pike, pickled tomatoes and cucumbers. He groaned slightly. The girl—her red hair a gorgeous mess framing her pale beauty—laughed a little as she blushed. He almost laughed himself. She was so obvious in her attempts to force the information out of him.

"All this I prepared for you," she whispered. "You do not know how hurt I am that you never eat. Please, I beg you, join me today. You must be very hungry."

He sat down next to her, compelled by that invisible string binding him to her will. She took a pancake, doused it in butter, slathered it with red caviar fit to burst, adorned it with dill and parsley. Then she lifted it to his nose. The smell was overwhelming.

Voran turned his face away, though it took a great deal of effort to do so.

"Why do you do this to yourself, Voran? All you have to do is tell me.

Simple. A few words. What do you seek in the Lows of Aer? Then all this food is yours. And so much more." She leered at him, and he nearly vomited again.

It took all his remaining strength—little as there was— to croak out his daily answer to her pleas: "I would sooner gnaw on that table than eat what food is on it."

"Get out, pig!" The hag had returned, brandishing a clawed fist. Voran scurried out of the hut—his stomach reluctantly groaning—the hag after him, now wielding the pestle-club. She contented herself to a mere three blows this morning. *Must be tiring of me*, he thought, and did not know whether to be relieved or afraid.

This was their monotonous routine, their eternal courtship. After withstanding the temptation of food, he experienced a certain reawakening of his heart. He tried to inflame his hatred, hoping it would give him enough resistance to break the hag's power. But the moment he began to gather strength from such thoughts, as if by enchantment his fall with the maiden-hag flashed on his memory, and he stewed in his guilt, trying not to think of Sabíana.

This morning, he was so overwhelmed by despair that he searched for large stones to dash his head against. But the moment that he bent over to pick a particularly jagged rock, total apathy was thrust on him, leaving him powerless. Again, he fumed in impotent anger, and the cycle repeated itself endlessly, until he merely fell over from exhaustion.

That internal war was far worse that the degrading tasks she forced on him—cleaning after her, washing her, dressing her, mending her clothes. Soon, time blurred into a single unending day of drudgery.

"The outhouse needs scrubbing," she growled at him, her hands twitching on the handle of the pestle.

His legs felt more like lumpy rocks than usual, and he rose—too slowly for her tastes, as the pestle-club reminded him—to do her bidding.

To his surprise, Voran heard the unmistakable, and very unexpected, sound of a human voice. A man's voice, apparently speaking nonsense over and over again. Soon some semblance of words reached Voran's ears.

"Broken windows, broken heart
All beyond your feeble art.
Strong you are, but wise are not
If you think to hide your thought
To force that Raven Son to speak
Better drown him in a creek!
Too late! The Lows are here to call

Your naughty actions to account.
If you lose, the cursed goes free,
And his care will come to me."

The speaker was an old man with a curly, matted black beard unevenly streaked with grey. His head was a shock of tangled white bursting from under a woven black cap. His face was remarkably free of wrinkles, his eyes innocent and childlike. He wore a nondescript grey robe, and rough shoes woven from tree bark peeked out from the tattered hem. He held a dark wooden staff with a crooked crossbar on top. As he approached the hag, he placed his hands on the crossbar. A kestrel appeared out of nowhere and sat on his head.

"Oh, there you are, you silly thing," he said, smiling like a child, eyes nearly rolling back into his head in his attempt to look at the kestrel perching on his skullcap.

His behavior was as strange as his appearance. He leaned down and kissed the roots of every tree in the vicinity, as if they were objects of sacred worth, wiping his forehead on the bark of the trunk and jumping up with all his might to reach the leaves, until he ran out of breath. The kestrel held on to his cap the whole time, nonplussed. All the man's movements were punctuated by a clicking of the tongue and an awed murmur, with the occasional hop in place.

The hag stood with her hands on her hips, an expression of half-disgusted indulgence on her face.

"Have you missed me, hag?" he said, as though remembering the reason for his visit.

"Humph," she said.

He walked up to Voran and smelled him, making an exaggerated grimace. He faced the hag and smiled lopsidedly.

"Why are you bothering me again, Tarin?" growled the hag. "I don't want to hear any stories today, especially after the horrific one you sprung on me, for which I paid you a king's ransom."

"Don't lie," he chuckled, "you *loved* that story. But I'm not here to entertain you. I'm afraid you're in a bit of a pickle. You've got the attention of the Authorities. And not for the right reasons. Seems you've annoyed the Alkonist with your mistreatment of this poor specimen."

Voran's heart hammered. He did not quite understand what was happening, but he had heard of the Alkonist. They were Creatures of Aer, High Beings. It seemed they were the ruling authority of the Lows of Aer. Would they take his side over one of their own?

"You have no authority to speak for the Alkonist, Tarin. You're only a man." Voran thought he detected a sliver of fear in the increased shrillness of her voice. "Let them come themselves and speak to me. I dare them."

"Baaaaaah! Do you really?" said one of the trees near the watermill. Except it wasn't a tree at all. It was a giant, covered with matted hair and green moss, with acorns and pinecones sticking out of his long beard. He sniffled like a porcupine. Voran had heard that sniffle before, in the sleeping-wood, what seemed like such an age ago.

"What are *you* doing here?" complained the hag. "Don't you have some travelers to scare with your clapping?"

The giant took an angry step away from the trees and shrank in a second to the size of the grass blades surrounding the hut. "I hate it when that happens," he muttered in a mouse-squeak.

Something laughed in the trees. It was a girlish laugh, uninhibited and slightly insane. She had thick, waving blond hair reaching to her heels. It dripped wet, but still covered her body. Voran was grateful for that, because she was completely naked. She rocked back and forth on an oak-limb, tears of laughter streaming down her face.

"What do you have to laugh about?" complained the former giant, who by now had grown to the height of a tree-stump.

She gasped and fell silent, hands raised to her mouth in mock alarm. It was such an exaggerated gesture, that Voran felt he was watching a very badly-done stage play. The girl broke into laughter again.

"What do you expect, Lesnik?" drawled a bored voice from the roof of the hut. "She is drowned, after all. Can't help herself."

The girl stopped laughing and began to moan, tears of sorrow seamlessly replacing the tears of laughter. The bored voice came from a huge tawny cat with the most cunning eyes Voran had ever seen.

The stump-sized former giant named Lesnik snuffled into his overgrown, mossy beard.

"Hag," said the cat, yawning so hugely that Voran was surprised its jaw remain hinged, "we of the Alkonist have been keeping an eye on you. It seems you're breaking the rules again."

"I haven't done anything illegal," she grumbled.

"Do you know? I never liked liars," said the cat. "I knew you were the worst when we let you into the Lows, but I didn't expect you to be so blatant about it. Yes, we can all appreciate occasionally harassing a human. We all do it! But what you've done with that poor creature is unforgivable. You should know better."

The hag bristled at the cat's manner. "Don't insult me, cat-thing. I demand a trial by ordeal."

Lesnik laughed. It sounded like a pig eating swill. "We thought you would. So we brought the storyteller. It will be an ordeal of story."

"Couldn't I just tickle the human and be done with it?" said the naked girl. To Voran's horror, she had the same expression a wolf might have after being starved for weeks. To his even greater horror, he found himself strangely attracted by that expression. He tried to shake it out of his head.

"Only if the hag wins the ordeal," said Lesnik. "You know the rules."

"An ordeal of story?" The hag groaned. "That's the most idiotic—"

"The ordeal of story is the most ancient ordeal in the world, hag," said Tarin, clicking his tongue. "And who better to judge than the original storyteller?" He bowed to the cat, who graciously acknowledged the compliment. It purred, conceit evident in the fluffing of its tail.

"Perhaps I can tell a story while you decide, hag?" said the cat, its eyes wide and excited. "In a certain kingdom, in a certain land..."

"No!" The hag stomped in frustration. "Your stories are the worst. If I win the ordeal, what do I get in return?"

"You?" said Lesnik, one eyebrow—which was actually a chestnut—raised derisively. "You get nothing. Continued permission to reside here, that is all."

"And if I lose?"

"Tarin takes your slave for himself."

Voran's heart leaped. Tarin was strange, it was true, but anything would be better than bondage to the hag.

"For the benefit of all concerned," the cat drawled, extremely upset at being interrupted, "I will review the ancient rules of the ordeal. Its premise is simple. Two tellers will weave a story of their choosing, and we three Alkonist will decide the winner. We will consider the following criteria: originality, beauty of language, musicality of expression, and truthfulness."

"Truthfulness?" The hag made a sour face. "That's very vague. Very subjective."

No one paid any attention to her.

"Now for the traditional incantation," said the cat.

"Oh, this is too much," said the hag. "I will not say it. It's silly and outdated."

"It will be done in the proper way, or not at all," said Lesnik. He was nearly man-sized again, his voice deepening with the growth.

"Maybe I should just tickle him?" ventured the drowned girl. Everyone ignored her, as though they only tolerated her presence out of necessity. Voran tried not to look at her as her hair waved lazily in the wind.

Tarin drew himself up to his full height, and the kestrel flew up and re-alighted on his shoulder. It looked intently at Voran, as though trying to think something at him. Tarin intoned.

"The art of story is sacred and old,
So, teller, beware, lest your heart be revealed,
For the power of words can turn iron to gold
Or bind fetters as fast as the roots of the elm."

The hag repeated the incantation through gritted teeth. Tarin raised his staff and began to tell his story.

The Tale of the Sirin and the Child

In ages when the earth was untamed and curious as an infant, men were yet a thought in the mind of the Heights. Strange and magnificent creatures inhabited the earth. Wardens of this wild earth were the Sirin, highest of the natural creation, fiercely beautiful and glorious. The Sirin reveled in the delights of mountain and steppe, lake and river, basking in the simple company of the beasts who adored them.

In those days, mankind was created and began to sing their quiet songs. The beasts listened in awe, and man tamed Nature to his gentler hand. But man had yet to meet the Sirin.

A morning bright and fine it was when one of the Sirin beheld a marvelous sight. A giant warrior, mounted on a giant horse, towered over the forest. His mount's shoulder reached the crowns of the trees; its mane flashed like lightning with each shake of its head; the earth trembled with each step. The warrior scowled through a mountainous beard as he spoke aloud to himself, dispersing the hordes of ravens perching on his shoulders.

"Oh, my strength, my curse! Why do I have such power if I find none to test it, none to challenge me? Oh, if only the earth would grow a great ring from its bones, that I might grasp it and turn the earth inside out."

He stopped. In his path lay a rough purse. Hardly giving it a thought, the giant nudged it with his spear, but it would not move. He tried to lift it, yet it was as though rooted to the ground. Intrigued, the giant dismounted, but even his tree-trunk arms could not budge the purse. Pleased by the challenge, he pulled with all his might, and buried himself to the ankles. He pulled again, and buried himself to the knees. He pulled again, and buried himself to his neck.

The Sirin, watching silently, saw a new wonder. A small creature, all softness and grace, approached the trammeled giant. It was a young man, leaning on a stick. He limped as he walked. His beauty pierced the Sirin's heart. The youth reached the purse and lifted it off the ground, as though it weighed no more than a goose feather.

"How is it that you," said the giant, amazed, "a crippled human, can lift what I—mighty as I am—cannot?"

The youth opened the purse and poured its contents to the ground. They were nothing but kernels of wheat.

"The wheat has a great secret, giant. The secret of all power. In order to flower, it must die. True strength is found in that most humble of acts—the death of one's self for the sake of another."

Years passed. The Sirin often returned to look upon the youth, but never revealed herself to him. Over the years, his crippling illness worsened. His grieving mother would carry his emaciated body to a seat near the window, where he would sit and stare with unnaturally round eyes at the world moving past him, paying him no heed. Every day, when his mother left to work in the fields, he repeated the same prayer.

"I give my legs, my life, to all those who sicken and die on this earth. May my sacrifice prove useful to them."

And his prayer was answered. Every day sick children jumped with renewed vigor, every day the dying found life again. And every day the young man faded a little more.

One morning, the youth heard a loud voice outside his small hut.

"Rise up and greet your guest, young man!"

The young man obeyed, and his limbs knit together, and life flowed through them once again. He came outside to greet a bearded ancient in long robes. He held a bowl carved in the likeness of a mallard. The old man presented it to the youth.

"Drink this," he said. "The bees labored over it in their clover-fields, their strawberry-meadows."

The youth sipped thrice.

"How do you feel, young man?"

"I feel life in me again, as I have not these many years."

"Now dip the bowl in the running waters of the river and drink."

The youth did so.

"How do you feel now?"

"I feel the strength of ten men within me."

Suddenly the old man was there no more. A glorious creature—half-woman, half-eagle— stood before him and sang to him. Thus were the Sirin bound forever to their beloved, and while the bond lasted, the earth gave fruit, the mountains gave pure springs, and the Heights reached down to earth in a harmony of endless song.

"I don't think I've ever heard such utter nonsense," muttered the hag. "You expect to win with *that* story? It's a mishmash of several battered horses. But you knew that already. And who ever heard of a Sirin who could transfigure?"

Tarin winked at her and smiled. "Poetic license."

With a loud harrumph, the hag sat on a tree stump and began her story.

The Curious Princess

You have probably heard the horrible story of the prince and the raven. I hate that story. It ignores all the important details and never considers the Raven's point of view. Well, I'll tell you the true end of that story. As you probably already know, after the Raven had his fun with the prince, the Sirin caught the Raven and imprisoned him in Vasyllia.

The prince came home and—somehow getting over the grief of killing his own beloved—married and had a daughter. She must have inherited some of his restlessness, because she could not be prevailed upon to stay in any one place for more than a few minutes. There was too much to be seen! She would disappear from the palace to wander around the city, the fields, the wild forests. The prince finally had enough of his little girl's wanderlust, and he ordered that she be confined to the palace.

Unfortunately for him, the palace itself was an endless labyrinth of discoveries, especially in the dungeons. There, the mountain itself bled into the palace, and some of the rooms were hardly distinguishable from caves. Most were empty, but some had fascinating treasures—ancient tapestries, old rotted chests with moldy drapery and robes woven with dulling gold, drafty armories with rusted swords and mail from the forgotten days of Lassar. The princess was nearly in constant ecstasies.

But her curiosity was insatiable. Naturally, there was a single door that would not open, no matter how hard she pushed. She could not simply ask someone to open it for her. Soon all other rooms lost their charm. She would come to this old wooden door and sit in front of it, staring.

One evening, she was caught prowling the dungeons and brought to her father. He looked grave, but not angry. He didn't even scold her. Instead, he put her on his lap and petted her hair and spoke softly to her.

"You must not seek beyond that door, my dear. There is great evil there. It must never be let out, or many will die."

Well, so much for the prince's wisdom. Anyone knows that for a child as inquisitive as that, a prohibition is little more than an invitation. But the problem was still all too real: how to open the door? She decided to wait. Despite her impatient curiosity, she knew very well that if she really wanted something, there would always be a way to get it. She was a prince's daughter, after all.

So she waited. Every day she would spend at least an hour in front of the locked door, but no idea presented itself on how to open it. Finally, her patience was rewarded. One late evening, a hunchbacked and very deaf servant carried a bucket of water right up to the forbidden door. She managed to hide before he saw her. To her delight, he pulled out a set of keys bigger than his head and opened the door. To her even greater delight, he walked in and left the door open. She sneaked in behind him.

They entered a long passage that ended in another shut door of heavy black iron, bolted in ten places with locks and mechanisms that made her head spin as the servant deftly worked them open. Another passage followed, faintly illuminated by torches, smelling unpleasantly of pitch and tar. This passage ended in a huge stone. Pushing with all his might, the servant managed to budge it enough to open a small enough chink to walk through. She followed.

The room was so dark, she had no trouble hiding. Barely illumined by the torches in the hallway, the old man poured the contents of his bucket into a well in the center of the room, then wiped his forehead with his arm. To her chagrin, he immediately walked out and pushed the stone back into the doorway. Blackness fell. She was shut in.

Eventually, she noticed that there was a thin slit in the wall high above her. As her eyes adjusted to the faint light, she began to look around. It was obviously a dungeon. Old chains lay on the ground and hung from rusty rings on the wall. Then she saw *him* and nearly jumped out of her skin. He was a wretched old man, nary a hair on his head, a wispy white beard barely hanging from a receding chin. There was nothing but skin on his bones. She had never seen such a pathetic creature.

"Water..." he gasped. "Please, give me some of that water."

There was a large bucket next to the well, too far for him to reach. How terrible, she thought. That horrid servant brought in the water just to torture the old man.

"You poor thing," she said. She was, for all her curiosity, rather a soft-hearted girl. "Of course I'll give you some water."

And so she did. At first she was a little put off at how greedily he drank it, bucketful after bucketful. She was a little more unnerved by how his eyes kept getting redder and redder. It's only torchlight, she said to herself. By the fifth bucketful, she was afraid. The bony old man was now a huge, beastly creature with burning eyes. He looked at her with his head cocked to one side. He's going to eat me, she thought, unable to move for sheer terror.

Instead, he hurled himself at the stone door and pounded it to dust. He tore off the second door of iron in one blow. He shattered the third door of wood to splinters.

The Raven turned back once more and looked at the princess. He smiled. It was not a pleasant smile at all. She screamed.

Thus, the Raven escaped his unjust imprisonment and fled Vasyllia to hide and gather his strength for a final, devastating retribution.

"Well, Tarin? Didn't expect me to have a story *that* good in my skirts, did you?"

"Tut, tut." He winked at her. "Our judges have yet to make their choice."

The Alkonist were already conferring under the drowned girl's tree, since it seemed she refused—or was unable— to come down. Voran could not hear what they were saying, or if they were speaking in a human language at all. There were far too many squeaks, burbles, clicks, and whoops for normal speech. Finally, they seemed to agree, though the drowned girl looked morose again. Voran hoped that meant she would *not* be allowed to tickle him to death.

"We judge in favor of Tarin," said the cat. "Hag, you must leave the Lows immediately. Since you seem to like the Raven so much, we suggest you join him. He's in Vasyllia."

Voran froze in place. The Raven was already in Vasyllia? Could that be possible?

The spark in the hag's eyes spewed into angry flames. Starting with a low rumble, she shrieked, louder and louder until Voran thought his ears would burst. Her hair stood on end like a writhing mass of snakes. She pulled a jagged knife out of nowhere and lunged at Voran, arm upraised. She was a mere breath from plunging the knife into his heart, when she jerked backward as though someone threw a rope around her neck and pulled it hard. Voran looked at Tarin, thinking he had done it, but the old man stood a little way off, holding his knit cap to his head, staring up at a lamentation of migrating swans. Lesnik was once more the size of a tree, and one hand was outstretched toward the hag.

"Let me go!" she screamed and thrashed wildly as she began to float above the ground.

"The power of words can turn iron to gold, or bind fetters as fast as the roots of the elm," said the giant Lesnik. "You know the power of incantation, and yet you still defy it. Your kind was always too smart for your own good. Now pay the price."

She began to hiss. Wider and wider grew her eyes, louder and more insistent grew the hissing. A snake's forked tongue darted out of her still human mouth. Voran turned away to find Tarin next to him, looking at him intently.

"What's happening to her?" asked Voran.

"Focus," commanded Tarin. He pulled out an old sword from his robe-skirts. It was only then that Voran noticed the ropy muscle of the man's arm. Tarin was an old warrior; the signs were all there. "Stay alert," he said and gave him the sword.

Voran felt a gust of wind from the direction of the hag. He turned to face her and nearly fell over from the shock. Instead of a hag, he saw two dancing reptilian heads attached to a serpent body as big as a longboat. She flapped two bat-like arms and flew up. One of the heads lunged at him and hot fangs slashed at his neck as he rolled away. Fear paralyzed him. He shook from exhaustion and lack of food. His mind screamed at him—Run! Run! Every joint of the serpent's wings was edged with a claw as long as a dagger. Even her tail was razor-sharp.

She swooped over him, nicking his arm with her tail. The wound bubbled and burned. Tarin grabbed him and pushed him forward with a cry. Voran grasped the old sword and ran at the diving serpent. She evaded his slash and battered him with iron-clawed wings. Again and again he faced her. Again and again she eluded him, punishing him for every miss with another slash of her tail. Soon the ground was black with his blood.

But with every new wound, his old strength, his old freedom clawed its way back, even as his vision began to swim and his arms sagged with fatigue.

The serpent landed as Voran tottered. She slithered toward him, one of her heads reaching forward ahead of the other, eager to deliver the death-stroke. But the other head would not be outdone. It opened its jaw and buried its fangs in the other head, just as it was about to lunge at Voran. The bitten head jerked and thrashed, beating the ground spasmodically. The other head then lunged at Voran, but now he was prepared. With a quick feint, he lured the head forward, leaning back at the last moment. He hacked once, and the head lolled, still half-attached. He kicked the neck aside and hacked again. The head fell away, spraying turbid blood. The bitten head writhed, then stopped.

Tarin laughed until tears poured down his cheeks. He embraced Voran—heedless of all the blood—and danced around him, holding Voran all the while. He kissed his cheeks three times. The Alkonist were nowhere to be seen.

"Well, the first step is taken, Raven Son. How many more until your chains come clanging off? We shall see, we shall see. Come along now."

"Tarin, how long have I been here?"

"Over a month, my Voran. It's deep winter in Vasyllia. Spring is not far coming."

Voran collapsed into Tarin's arms, his legs giving way under him. His hands trembled, and he could not control them. Tarin held him fast as he carried him to the bank of the river. He washed his wounds tenderly. Barely conscious, Voran felt relief as pleasant as a day-long thirst quenched. His eyelids drooped. As they closed, he saw the kestrel on Tarin's shoulder chattering insistently. Tarin smiled.

"Silly bird. He wants you to know that Sabíana misses you. She told you to hurry back."

The story begins from the grey, from the brown, from the chestnut-colored horse. On the sea, on the ocean, on the island of Varian—a baked bull stands with a pounded onion. In the side of the bull, there's a sharpened knife. Now, pull out the knife. It's time to eat! This is still not the story, but only the pre-story. If anyone listens to my story, he will receive a sable and a marten coat, a beautiful wife, one hundred gold coins for his wedding, and fifty silvers more for the party!

From the traditional pre-story of all tales
(Old Tales, Book I)

CHAPTER 18
THE SORE

Mirnían took his place among the villagers for the first time on the day after his healing, standing among them as their equal in the central square. Otar Svetlomír was the first to embrace him with tears in his eyes, then every other member of the village followed suit. Soft snowflakes fell throughout this almost ritual greeting, steaming on his new skin.

"With the blessing of Otar Svetlomír," said Mirnían, raising his voice for all to hear. "I hereby announce my intention to marry the Lady Lebía, daughter of Otchigen of Vasyllia."

All the old women raised their hands to their mouths and laughed, shedding their years in their joy. The children danced around the couple, chanting their names to the rhythm of their feet.

"Ladies!" cried Otar Svetlomír. "Are you waiting for my invitation? Get on with it!"

Mirnían felt his eyes grow wider as every single woman in the crowd surrounded him and pushed him away from Lebía. The younger ones did it while laughing hysterically. The old women—some without a single tooth in their head—sang:

"Away, away! Avert your eyes,
The sacred distance don't despise
For now's the time the bride must die
To all her past. Cry, nightingale, cry!"

They turned him until his head spun and he fell. At that, they chittered like birds and gave him his space. Then they descended on Lebía like a swarm of bees.

"Cry, nightingale, cry!" They sang. "Cry, nightingale, cry!"

Lebía tossed off her heavy fur. Underneath, she wore a white dress. In the light of the winter sun, she was blinding.

Mirnían had to turn away.

"Oh, my single braid, my single braid!" someone sang with a voice like the last songbird in winter. Mirnían sighed involuntarily. It was Lebía. Where did she learn to sing like *that*?

"Is it time for my braid to be split?" Lebía keened, almost wailing. "Is it time to part from my father's house?"

At that, she tottered and stopped. She looked ready to fall over. Mirnían's heart plunged. Of course. Lebía had not had a father in years.

All the young ladies encircled her, their arms entwined. They picked up her song, and Lebía came back to life.

"It is not time yet, nightingale.

Your braid is single still..."

Two young men picked Mirnían up and hoisted him on their shoulders.

At that, the children cheered.

"Wash, wash!" they called. "Wash away the old life, bring to life the new!"

Two more men picked up Lebía and brought her near to Mirnían.

"Now is the time for the last word," said Otar Svetlomir, chanting. "You will no longer speak until the fateful day. Choose wisely."

"The lady first," said Mirnían, remembering the words of the rite.

Lebía looked at him for a long time. She did not even blink. Her presence grew inside him until it was too large to fit in his heart, and his heart seemed to grow. Then it was too large for his chest. He was sure he would burst.

"All that I lack now," said Lebía, "is Voran, to make my joy full."

Mirnían's heart froze at the words. At that moment, seemingly for the first time, he remembered that Lebía was Voran's sister, and hatred for him threatened to drown out every other emotion. Something stabbed him under his left arm, like a pinprick.

"My love?" Lebía's shoulders tensed, as though she had read his thoughts. What was wrong with him? Why did he have to kill his own happiness the moment it was born? He forced Voran out of his mind, though a sliver of hatred still pulsed deep within.

"Burn away the old life, my love. You and I will be everything to each other."

She sighed, but seemed content.

"Wash, wash!" cried the children. "Wash away the old life, bright to life the new!"

At that, Mirnían and Lebía were carried to the opposite sides of the village for their ritual bath.

The village feasted deep into the night on trestles set up in the center of the village under a sky plowed with stars. Mirnían and Lebía sat at the high table that was built on top of a mound of earth, but Otar Svetlomír sat between them. He made sure they hardly had a chance to look at each other.

The food was never-ending. As soon as all the fresh trout was devoured, platefuls of boar magically found their way to the tables, followed by venison. Ale flowed more plentifully than mountain springs.

Mirnían had never seen Lebía so happy.

As the village's smith blew the midnight oxhorn, everyone fell silent.

"Behold, the beauty of the bride!" someone called.

The women all keened—a wild, unfettered sound. It sent pleasant chills down Mirnían's back. Something walked up the road toward the square, something huge. It bobbed up and down like a drunk man.

"What in all the Heights?" Mirnían heard himself say.

It was an effigy of a young woman with a long braid, carried on a stick by a boy with red cheeks. It was the size of a house. Ribbons flew from every conceivable place on the effigy, in all colors ever seen by man. Or so it seemed.

"The beauty! The beauty!" All the women keened again.

"What shall we do with the beauty?" asked Otar Svetlomír from his seat.

"Burn away the old! Make way for the new!" cried the women.

The effigy was now in the midst of the feasting crowd, facing Mirnían.

"Who will burn away the old?" Otar Svetlomír stood from his seat. "Who will make way for the new?"

Mirnían looked around, expecting one of the girls to answer. But no one did. Then he realized, with a sinking feeling, that everyone was looking at him.

Oh no, he thought. These village rites are all quaint enough, but they can't make me actually take part. Can they?

Everyone looked at him. No one moved.

Finally, Mirnían turned to look at Lebía. There it was again—that new look. It commanded.

Mirnían sighed and stood up. The crowd erupted into cheers.

A girl ran up to Mirnían, holding a candle. She gave it to him with hands shaking from excitement and cold. He skirted the table and approached the effigy. He shook his head, and smiled.

"I will burn away the old!" he cried, trying to sound enthusiastic. "I will make way for the new!"

He stayed as long as he could at the table after the effigy had burned away. He wanted to feel everyone's joy, but something pricked like a thin dagger under his arm. At first it throbbed, then jabbed. By the time the sun began to come back up, his skin prickled with the same heat that he had while still leprous.

Excusing himself to Lebía and Otar Svetlomír, he slipped into Lebía's house and examined himself in the polished metal hanging on her wall. Facing him were nothing but eyes, deep gouges in a bony face that challenged him angrily. Were those his eyes? They looked more like Voran's half-mad falcon eyes. He shivered, disgusted that he had allowed himself to descend to such a state. He shrugged off his shirt and probed under his left arm. There it was. He turned to see his side in the metal, and his heart plunged.

There was no mistaking it. It was a sore.

And behold, I will show you wonders in that final day. There shall be a black sun, and the moon shall turn to blood. A column of fire will stand in the midst of the congregation of peoples, and the temple of the abomination will fall, stone by stone. And yet not one of them will know it for the work of the Most High. Such is the work of the prince of lies, the great deluder of human hearts.

From "The Prophecy of Llun"
(The Sayings, Book XXIII, 2:4-7)

CHAPTER 19
SABÍANA'S TEST

Sabíana stood rooted to the ground before Dubían's empty bier, unable to muster the strength of will to move.

The Sirin were real.

Everything was now different, and all possibilities must be considered—the Covenant first among them. If the Sirin were real, the Raven might be real, and they would need the help of the Heights against such an enemy. But how does one go about re-forging forgotten covenants? What did Voran say? We must begin by caring for the downtrodden of the Outer Lands.

Freed by this thought, she hurried out of the room. She must make arrangements to care for the refugees. Now that the Dumar was disbanded, she must convince her father to open the first reach and to lift the quarantine, no matter what the risk.

The door to the Dar's chamber was shut, but she barged in as she always did, heedless of the proper form. She shut the door behind her. It thudded.

The Pilgrim faced her from the other side of her father's bed. His eyes were softer than she remembered. He showed no sign of the wounds on his body suffered in the Temple. He looked into her eyes, and she felt like there was someone behind her, so completely did his glance spear through her.

"Sabíana, you have come. That is good." His voice sounded like it came from a great distance, or even out of the deep past. "Your father sleeps, but he will wake soon. He will not see me again. You must tell him I am well, and that I have gone. He will be worried, as he always is."

Sabíana found it difficult to think, much less speak, in his presence. It was like trying to breathe under a waterfall.

"Sabíana, I know you saw the Sirin take Dubían away. I know that you desire to re-forge the Covenant. But it is too late. The Raven is at the gates."

"But why is it too late?" she whispered, the tears gathering in spite of herself. "Surely Adonais can forgive."

The Pilgrim's face dimmed at the mention of Adonais. "There are so few Vasylli left. The fate of Vasyllia now lies on the edge of a knife. I do not know what will happen, though I fear the worst. It is given to me to offer you a choice. Vasyllia's trials do not have to be your burden if you do not wish it. If you come with me, I will take you to a place called Ghavan. There, the Covenant may be re-forged with the remnant of the faithful."

"Pilgrim, I am afraid."

"Yes, Sabíana. I fear as well. Vasyllia is a place far more important than you can ever imagine. If it falls, much that is good and beautiful in the world will wither. Possibly until the Great Undoing."

"I cannot leave Vasyllia, Pilgrim," said Sabíana. "I cannot leave my father."

The Pilgrim smiled, and his face brightened and he became young, his wrinkles smoothing into the face of a beautiful youth, a face that shone white. His robes were gold like the sun.

"You are indomitable, Sabíana. Perhaps I am wrong. Vasyllia may yet survive, with the Black Sun at her head."

He was gone.

"Sabíana?" said the Dar, waking up. "Oh, thank Adonais! I was so worried for you."

"Father, my poor father." She had not seen him this wasted away. He looked like an old man playing the part of the Dar on one of the market-day spectacles. She wanted with all her heart to cry, to comfort and to be comforted, but she had made the choice. She must be iron and stone.

"Yes, my love." He laughed softly and coughed. "I am at the doorstep, so to speak. I've always wondered if Death was a man or a woman. I suppose I'll find out soon enough."

"Father." Her voice sounded harsh to her ears. "The Pilgrim has gone. He asked to be remembered to you. He leaves us with hope."

"Did he say anything about Voran? About Mirnían?"

Sabíana shook her head.

"I suppose we must continue to hope, even when darkness falls. My dear, you must prepare yourself. Soon you will wear the crown. I do not think I will live out the week. I am so tired."

"Sleep, my dear," she said, feeling strangely motherly toward him. "I am ready. Sleep now. Rest." She did not, could not cry, though it seemed a violation of her nature to prevent it.

Sabíana remained by his bedside all night. She left when the sky was still dark, but a certain tense watchfulness in the air predicted the coming of dawn. Feeling already burdened beyond what was humanly possible, she went outside, hoping against hope that today the fog would lift—though it had choked Vasyllia for weeks—and the sun would rise.

As she left the palace, she stood before the Covenant Tree. It looked cold and pitiful. To think that this had once been a symbol of Vasyllia's dominance over the Other Lands! She recoiled from the view and turned away.

Sabíana closed her eyes and let the mist of the falls soak into her hot cheeks and burning eyelids. She saw, even through closed eyes, two red dots approaching her. She opened her eyes to see two firebirds flying toward one of the basins left especially for them to bathe in. Sabíana always loved to see them wash, rare as that sight was. They alighted on the lip of the basin, but as soon as they touched it, they disappeared in a white light, blinding Sabíana. The light didn't abate, and Sabíana's eyes adjusted slowly. Something many-colored fluttered and cavorted in the basin. The blur resolved, and Sabíana recognized her. She was one of the Sirin at Dubían's bier. The one with the feathers dark as twilight.

The Sirin bathed as a bird would, splashing light around her in defiance of the surrounding murk. The effect was like looking through the window of a dark room at the rising of the sun. Sabíana felt a thin filament weaving between her and the Sirin. The Sirin looked at her with eyes like lightning, opened her mouth, and sang.

The weight of the song crushed Sabíana, as though she were pinned down by the full force of both twin waterfalls. But as it washed over her, it lightened her. The heaviness of her father's sickness, the doubt over Vasyllia's fate, the fear about her own place as future Darina, the pain of losing Voran—all of it fell away from her. She felt re-forged from within, the impurities burned away by the force of the song. The Sirin stopped, and Sabíana felt light enough to fly to the Heights. Barely evident inside her chest was a soft patter, like another heart, and the faint sense of warmth, like a candle flame.

"My name is Feína, my swan. We are now joined until the Undoing."

Sabíana remained silent for utter wonder.

"Sabíana, you chose a difficult path, but I will bear it with you. May it be a lessening of the burden on your heart."

"Feína," she whispered, feeling no bigger than a child. "It is going to be terrible, is it not?"

The Sirin spread out her wings and looked to the horizon. At that moment, the sun came up for the first time in weeks.

❦

Sabíana rushed to the first reach. It had been walled off for quarantine, its only entrance a black iron gate manned by several armed guards. Sabíana stopped for a moment, wondering if what she planned to do was as mad as her rational mind insisted. But reason had no place here, she told herself, and swallowed her revulsion.

"Open the gates," she said.

The guards at the gate hesitated. For a moment, Sabíana was sure they would challenge her. She was in the middle of preparing a withering response when they simply turned, opened the gates, and bowed to her. Sabíana walked in. Immediately, the stench beat her back.

The people were teeming, like rats in a gutter. Dogs and children lay together on the road, covered in sores. Mothers rocked babies that cried for milk from withered breasts. Eyes with no hope looked at her, then looked away again. Flies swarmed. Burial mounds poked up everywhere, like cysts on dry skin. Garbage lay interspersed with the half-rotting carcasses of horses and goats. Some children played near the dead animals, apparently unsupervised.

Many, especially the aged, fell at Sabíana's feet and kissed the hem of her robe. They chattered at her in their own dialect, words interrupted by sobs.

Sabíana's tears gushed, and it took a good deal of self-control to prevent the sobs from shaking her visibly.

What has happened to Vasyllia? How could we have allowed this to happen in our own house?

Just down the lane, a doctor in the pantaloons of the merchant class applied some sort of creamy poultice to the sores of a pregnant woman. His hands were caked with the white cream, and his goat-beard was smeared with all manner of dirt and blood. But he didn't seem to notice. In fact, the dirt only made his hazel eyes shine brighter. They looked like little suns. Sabíana, mesmerized, came to watch what he did. He looked up at her, recognized her, but looked back down at his work without acknowledging her presence. Her momentary wounded pride faded when she saw how pockmarked the young woman was. She was probably no more than twenty, but she looked over fifty.

"What does the poultice do?" Sabíana asked, feeling foolish for having nothing more erudite to say.

"It heals the sores," said the doctor nonchalantly.

"Heals them?" That surprised her. From what she heard of the plague, it had no cure. "But what about the plague?"

"Plague?" He snapped his head at her, his eyes furious. "There is no plague. It is only lack of food, lack of water, and dirt. That is all."

Sabíana's head began to spin. She should have known. The Dumar hadn't quarantined anyone. They had caused "the plague" in the first place.

"Guard!" she called, and four immediately appeared at her side. "You, inform the elders of the warrior seminary that every cohort is to be called to the marketplace this moment. Every merchant table and booth is to be disassembled, and tents for the refugees are to be built from them. You, go to the healers and tell them that the refugees are to be relocated to the second reach, and that they will need care immediately. You, go find the Marshall of the Dumar. He is to be told that there will be a collection of food, living necessities, and medicine from the houses of the third reach, beginning tomorrow morning. You, go to the palace and tell the scribes to await my coming. Warn the criers of city-wide circuits tonight and tomorrow. Why do you still stand here? Go!"

They went, bowing hastily. "Dear Feína," she said silently. "The Pilgrim may have said that remaking the Covenant is beyond our hope, yet I will restore Vasyllia to its honor in spite of it all."

"Highness!" The voice was behind her. She turned to see Rogdai in full armor, save for an uncovered head. "You are summoned to the palace, my lady."

She understood.

"I come," she said, and her voice cracked. As she passed, the soldiers inclined their heads. The whispers accompanied her out of the first reach: "The Black Sun. *Our* Black Sun."

Dar Antomír's eyes blazed with unearthly light as he lay on his deathbed. Sabíana understood it to be the last surge of life before the final dimming. He saw her and smiled, extending a bony hand. She took it—he was still so strong for a dying man—and fought to contain the tears. The light in his eyes was almost blinding.

"Sabíana," he whispered frantically. "Listen to me, listen. I have seen a vision, a final gift. I knew I had few hours left to live, and I begged Adonais as I have never begged before, to tell me something of my sons. For I had no hope left.

"As I lay on my bed in gloom, I was in my chamber no longer. I stood at the edge of a stream fed by a cascade of falls. The river wove into a deep emerald pool, fringed with a dense assortment of birches, osiers, and hollies. Beyond the trees, jagged hills sheltered the pool from all wind. On three sides was the pool thus sheltered, but the fourth was a great tumbling waterfall.

"I walked to the ledge and there was no bottom in sight. I looked once more and saw a different sight—a dry marshlands with many rivers snaking through it. Two men ran across it, pursued by a shapeless darkness. Still a third time I looked, and I saw the Great Sea, interminable to the horizon, and in it lay an island from which grew a white sapling covered in golden leaves.

"Then I stood on the top of the tallest mountain in the world, and the earth was riven at my feet, riven and bleeding. A voice thundered at my right, coming from a pillar of a thousand eyes and a thousand wings, all of fire and light. It spoke these words to me:

"'Behold, this is the place of death and the place of healing. Tell me, Dar of men. Will the water flow?'

"I said to him, 'It will, for without it the world will wither and die.'

"He said, 'It will, but only if the falcon sheds its skin, the swan spreads its wings, the bear forsakes its hunger.'"

At these last words, the fire within Dar Antomír simmered and began to fade.

"Father, not yet, please!"

"Do not grieve for me, my child. Do you not understand?"

"No, father, I do not," her voice subsided to a hoarse whisper.

"The falcon is Voran's blazon, the bear Mirnían's. They are alive. And the swan is you, my love. It is your time now."

His eyes wandered beyond Sabíana, smiling at something he saw there. She looked up to see a dark-haired Sirin, her face wet with tears. Sabíana found her strength returning.

"Taryna," said the dying Dar. "I am ready. Take me with you."

Sabíana walked out of the chamber, hardly conscious of anything except her grief and the need to hold it in, to not give it any quarter. Rogdai stood at the door. One look at her face, and he fell on one knee and took her right hand in his own shaking hands and kissed it. His face was hot to the touch. He looked up at her through his own veil of tears, and said, "Praise be to Darina Sabíana. May your reign be long, and may the holy gaze of Adonais shine upon you."

Kalún had waited in the palace cherry grove for what seemed like hours. He was growing extremely displeased with Yadovír. He had had such high hopes for the young man. But all Yadovír seemed to do was run around, very busy and very solicitous on behalf of the Dar, though with little to show for the work of their conspiracy. With every passing day, the pestilence reached its pox-ridden hand closer to the third reach.

Something rustled in the trees. Yadovír squeezed himself between two trunks and nearly poked his eyes out on the groping branches.

"You do seem flustered, Sudar Yadovír, if I may be allowed the observation."

Yadovír sighed in obvious exasperation.

"Otar, I know you expected me to arrange matters with greater alacrity. But I do have good news. All is in readiness for a meeting with the Ghan himself."

"This Ghan travels with his own army?" Kalún was hardly a strategist, but it seemed a foolish way to conquer future tribute states. Unless the Ghan never intended to return to his capital city of Gumir-atlan.

"So it would seem, yes." Yadovír did not seem perturbed by it. "At great personal danger to myself, I arranged an exchange of information with their camp. They made it clear that they would welcome us tomorrow night."

"How are we supposed to do that? Walk out of the city and stride over to the enemy side? That should go over very well with the door wardens."

Yadovír ignored the sarcasm. "The Raven's escape, Otar Kalún. You know the old story, yes? Well, it seems at least part of it is true. There *is* a way out of the palace through the dungeons. An old passage into the forest below the city. Not many know of it, and those that do, think that it's been blocked for centuries. But I was curious, so I checked. It is mostly blocked, but after some careful manipulation of the fallen rock, I found that one or two people will be able to squeeze through with a little difficulty."

"How convenient. Can you guarantee our safety?"

Yadovír smiled, and there was a kind of madness in his eyes. "Oh, Otar Kalún, I think we have gone too far to think about safety."

Gamayun, the Dayseer, sits in an ivory tower in the sea of times. Does she sing the future into being, or does she only speak of what she sees? No one knows.

From "The Tale of the Black Sirin"
(Old Tales, Book VII)

CHAPTER 20
A NARROW ESCAPE

Tall warriors, robed in grey, faces confined behind black iron helms with no eye-slits, held screaming children over vast fire-pits. The mothers, shrieking in despair, all turned to Voran, asking him that most horrible of questions: "Why?" Tortured forms that once were men—now misshapen freaks with empty eye sockets and bald, bloodied pates where their hair was torn off—huddled around him, reaching for him with blackened nails. The ones without eyes saw him the best.

Tarin laughed, and Voran awoke. Voran's upper lip twitched. He snarled and barked at Tarin. His hands groped for a rock with which to beat the old man to the ground. With a start, Voran awoke again.

They were still in the hag's village, though some distance from the carcass of the dead serpent-hag. Voran's wounds throbbed. The skin around them was yellow and gummy. He tried not to look, afraid he would be sick or faint. Tarin sat by the river, arms hugging his knees, looking at nothing. His lips moved noiselessly, repeating something. He turned at Voran and made a face.

"You should wash," he said. "You're quite filthy, you know. A bath of fire would really be best."

"A bath of...what?"

Tarin turned away and began to mumble to himself again.

"Why?" asked Voran. Tarin's expression was unreadable. "Why did you come to save me from her? What am I to you?"

Tarin huffed. "I knew your father well."

Voran fell silent. It was not what he expected, and he was not sure how he felt about it. For so long he had grown used to avoiding thoughts about Otchigen, or when that failed, to hate him until his heart grew numb like an overused muscle. Now, to think of his father in any positive light was uncomfortable.

"It's a strange thing about words, Raven Son," said Tarin. "We talk and talk and talk and never seem to get anywhere. While if you really meant the word, you could make a tree flower."

"I don't know what that means."

Tarin chuckled and continued mumbling to himself happily, patting his head with his hand. His kestrel flew down from a branch above. Tarin made a show of falling to the ground in fear as the kestrel landed on his head, as though it were a dragon with talons bared. Then he turned over and laughed at himself.

What a strange man, thought Voran.

"That dream you just had," said Tarin, "the warriors holding babies over bonfires. It was not a dream, you know."

Voran's heart tripped and started again.

"Vasyllia has fallen?"

"Not quite. I didn't say it was the *present time* that you saw. Just one of possible futures. It seems Gamayun whispered to you in your sleep. She really can be the most pestilent annoyance."

Gamayun? Who in the Heights was Gamayun? Voran was becoming infuriated with the man's lack of useful answers.

"You come here and rescue me," said Voran. "You helped me kill the hag. Now what?"

"Who said she was dead?" Tarin had an impish smile. "The hag is an intimate of the dead lands. Don't count her out yet."

"Will you help me?" Voran felt like punching the crazy old man.

"Will you help yourself?"

Turning to a stone on his left, Tarin kissed it and blessed it with a strange sign. Then he crouched with his ear to the ground, listening intently, until his eyes closed and he began to snore.

"Tarin!"

Tarin opened his eyes and winked.

"What should I do?" Voran felt no older than ten, called to account before the elders of the seminary. Come to think of it, this man could very well have been an elder in his time, if not for his madness.

"Ah, something useful at last," said Tarin, becoming serious. "I know of your search for the weeping tree. I can take you to it. One condition. You must become my slave."

Voran laughed. "You freed me! Now you want me to put on my shackles again?"

"That is my condition."

"And if I refuse? What is to stop me from going to Vasyllia now? As you said, Sabíana waits for me."

Tarin grimaced like a masked jester. He extended his hand and began to count off his fingers. "First, those wounds will kill you soon. Second, you severed your bond with Lyna when you lay with the hag. You won't stand a chance against anything out in the wild. Third, you are still in the Lows of Aer, and I doubt you will find a way back without me. Fourth, Vasyllia is already under siege by the Raven. Fifth, you are an idiot."

Voran bristled, but managed to keep quiet.

"While I offer you a solution to all of those problems, especially the fifth one. You have the word of a storyteller, and tellers never lie. But you must become my slave."

There was no point in having this conversation. Voran was too tired to think, much less construct a rational argument.

"I am leaving in ten minutes," said Tarin. "Come with me or not. Your choice."

Voran followed Tarin through the village. Beyond a stone hedge marking the edge of the village, the valley continued straight for a day's journey, then crested up into a narrow pass.

Where were they? Were they in the Lows or in the real world? What was the real world, anyway? The thoughts left Voran with bile in the back of his throat.

As they approached the last house of the village, a leaning ruin with a young osier bursting from the roof, Tarin stopped and entered.

"Stay here, slave" he said, leaving Voran no time to come up with any suitable answer.

When Tarin came out, he had a pack in each hand. Tarin laid both packs —one of them felt like it was full of rocks—on Voran's back and took the sword from him.

"You are now my ass," he said, beaming at him proudly. He slapped him on the back, and Voran fell face-first into the mud. Tarin laughed as he walked out of the village. Curses that he didn't even know he knew hissed out of Voran's lips. Tarin seemed not to hear.

It took them most of the day to reach the pass. Beyond, the grayish path switchbacked up into white-capped mountains, taller even than those in Vasyllia.

"We are going there?" Voran pointed at the peaks. "It's the middle of winter. We'll freeze to death, if an avalanche doesn't get us first. And I don't have any clothes other than these rags."

Tarin broke into verse:
"Raven Son, hark now to me.
Twixt faith and mind, what shall it be?
A choice I leave to you to make—
To crawl to doom (a fool, a snake),
Or walk with me. Which shall it be?"

Voran sighed and bowed his head. Tarin clapped him on his shoulder again. This time, Voran stayed on his feet. Tarin seemed pleased by that, judging by the way he hopped in place and hiccupped.

They continued to walk, even after the sun set. Voran expected them to camp for the night, but Tarin kept on walking, head erect and back perfectly straight. Heavy flakes soon swirled around them, but Tarin only sang at them. They seemed to dance to his melody. Voran had always prided himself on his strength, but his endurance was nothing compared to the old warrior's, whose head did not so much as dip during those heavy night hours. Voran soon began to trip over his own feet from fatigue, and once or twice he caught himself falling asleep between steps, only to jerk awake at the pain in his knee as his leg caught the full weight of his body and the two packs.

Just when Voran thought he could go no further, a dark shape loomed directly in front of their path. It was a huge bear, standing on its hind legs. It roared and rushed at them on all fours. Voran cried out in warning, but all that came out was a dry rattle. Tarin didn't seem to see the bear.

At the last possible moment, the bear pulled up short and stood up, waving its arms like a child learning to walk. Tarin raised his own hands and whooped. He chattered and growled at the bear, gesticulating with his hands. The bear...*laughed!*

Tarin embraced the beast and slapped him on the side of the head, and the bear continued on his way. Voran's shuddering limbs refused to listen to him for a time as Tarin—grumbling and whistling all the while—kept walking forward.

This occurred several more times throughout the night, but every time the encounters were never less than horrifying. Finally, the sun inched toward the horizon.

"Well, here we are," said Tarin, stopping in the middle of the road. They had climbed about half the distance up the switchback path hugging the mountain, and the peak loomed above them, still impossibly far. The sounds of the waking forest bubbled up to Voran's awareness—snakes rustling through dry brush, rabbits running from the cover of one shrub to another, groundhogs pushing up against the fresh blanket of snow covering their holes.

Then Voran saw it. Just off the road was a hole in the ground, gaping at them uninvitingly.

"In you go, slave," said Tarin, waving his arm toward the hole.

"Yes, Lord," said Voran, with a hint of sarcasm that earned him a sound blow across one ear.

"You will learn to keep a civil tongue, my ass."

Voran jumped in head-first, then the world turned upside down and he found himself sitting on prickly, yellow marsh grass. For a moment, his mind thought that he should be falling still, and it spun uncontrollably, until he felt his feet sink into a pool of icy water. He cursed and pushed himself up, and the world righted itself. But something was still wrong. It was too quiet, so quiet that the silence buzzed in his ears.

Someone was watching him, but every time he turned around he saw nothing, not even Tarin. Yet the feeling remained. It grew, until he was sure that an invisible army was staring at him. Far away, dim across the endless marshland surrounding him, Voran thought he saw something swirling and dark.

"Hurry," said Tarin, appearing suddenly at his side. "It seems they knew we were coming."

Now the malice coming from that mass of something dark was palpable, as though Tarin's appearance had enraged a great beast.

"What is it?" gasped Voran as they ran across the dry grass and through shallow pools, turning this way and that to avoid the deeper tarns.

"Raven's horde," Tarin said. "Run!"

Voran's sides felt as though one hundred knives pierced them. His vision grew foggy. His wounds oozed and throbbed, and his feet squelched in clammy water. He tottered. Tarin grabbed his arm and threw it around his shoulders, holding his side with a grip like iron pincers.

"I can't..."

"Just a little farther," Tarin said between heavy breaths.

The long marsh-plain suddenly ended. They stood on the edge of a precipice plunging thousands of feet down, with nowhere else to go. Voran turned around, and now the swirling cloud was much closer. He thought he could glimpse indistinct shapes in the mist.

"Do not stop, Voran. Forward!" said Tarin.

"Forward? Are you mad, Tarin? What should we do? Fly?"

"If that is necessary, yes."

Voran felt the fear rise like vomit.

No, he said to himself. Enough.

In his mind, a fog seemed to lift. This was another parting of the ways, similar to the waystone. There was no going back, the way forward led to certain death, and yet there was no other way.

I do this for you, Sabíana, he thought with a stab of guilt. Maybe my death will pay my debts.

He stepped forward into the air, expecting the rush of mad pleasure that accompanies a fall and precedes the terror. Tarin followed, laughing, singing.

They walked on air. As they walked, it was not they who descended, but the land underneath them that ascended, almost as if they were climbing. Before Voran's mind registered it, the thick, wet smell of peat slapped his nostrils. He and Tarin stood in another marshy plain. Mountains sheer as glass rose to their left. Only their extreme tips were white; the rest of the slopes were a lush carpet of green. All around was brown-yellow marshland, veined over with meandering rivers of inky blue. Ahead of them was a sight that made his legs, already throbbing with exhaustion, dance with joy. Twisting hearth-fires. There was a village ahead.

Tarin fell on his knees and raised his arms up to the sky.

"Sing unto him, let your voices exclaim!
Bring unto him all your praises and glory,
Honor his name, by its power exult,
For the voice of the Lord thunders over the waters,
For the voice of the King fills with life all the forests,
For the voice of the Father lifts up the high mountains.
Rejoice in his name, all you fighters of darkness,
For his mercy and glory illumine your passes,
For his love and his power destroy all your weakness
We run with all speed to the Lord of the Realms!"

Voran turned to look back at the cliff from which they had descended, and felt the danger fading away. No swirling darkness followed them. Voran laughed, coming back to life with every twitch of his exhausted legs.

"How did we...?" Voran began.

"Sometimes, the earth itself helps us poor ones," said Tarin in an awed whisper.

All around them, grey branches and dead stumps reached up from the muddy earth, giving the land an agonized look. In the riverbeds, glacial water trickled, carving through the land like a blade through clay.

"It's...beautiful." Voran was surprised to hear himself say.

Before Tarin answered, something struck Voran in the back. Sharp, throbbing pain wove through every inch of his body.

It's like I'm milk being churned into butter, he thought.

He fell, cramped over on the grass, the pain rising in waves. He breathed in, but his chest didn't respond. His heart raced. His mind reeled with panic. There had never been anything else but the pain. He had always suffered. He would always suffer. It would never end.

A firm hand took his clenched fingers and forced them open. The hand was warm. Tarin's face looked like it was in a fog, but he smiled. He whispered, and in spite of the noise in Voran's mind, he heard his master.

"Raven Son. Focus on what I am telling you."

The agony twisted Voran as though he were a dishrag.

"Listen! Repeat in your mind, clearly, this one word. Do it, no matter what doubts creep into you head. 'Saddaí, Saddaí.'"

Voran twisted his lips into the right shape, though even that effort racked him with pain. He repeated the word under his breath, softly. The pain receded and his mind cleared. Into the breach in his mind a thousand thoughts barreled through.

That word! What does it mean? What if it's an evil summoning, and Tarin is no more than a creature of the Raven? What have I done? Look at him, that foul beast with his smirk and detestable face. I want to claw that face open. What a pathetic creature I am. Why could I not stand the pain on my own? Stop saying that word. Stop! *There is awful power in it!*

He continued to repeat it stubbornly—Saddaí, Saddaí—until all thoughts ceased. Warmth suffused his body. He stopped twitching. He noticed the sun was shining.

"Raven Son, you did not yield," said Tarin, tears pouring down his face. "As a reward, look. You are healed."

All Voran's wounds had closed, leaving only purple scars.

"Tarin, what in the Heights was that word?"

Tarin lifted Voran by the hand with no apparent effort.

"Perhaps, someday, I will explain it to you. Don't forget it, Raven Son. It may save you again, and not only once."

He looked suddenly thoughtful and perturbed by something.

"What is it?" asked Voran.

"They overreach themselves," he said. "I did not expect such boldness from them yet. Vasyllia must be on the very brink."

In the year of the covenant 845, Dar Mikahil left no male heirs. His only daughter Albiana and his daughter son's Barhuk both claimed the right of inheritance. Rather than choose between them, the Dumar decided to summon a Council of the Reaches to choose a new Dar. On the day before the announcement, Albiana commanded the warriors to imprison the entire Dumar as traitors to the Monarchia. Soon afterward, Barhuk chose a life of solitude and contemplation in a monastery, and no one challenged the rise of the first Darina in the history of Vasyllia.

From "A Child's History of Vasyllia"
(Old Tales, Book I)

CHAPTER 21
COMPLICATIONS

"Highness," said Sabíana's trembling maid—she trembled constantly these days— "the representative of the Dumar has been waiting to be admitted for the last hour."

"Let him wait," said Sabíana, not raising her eyes from her scribbling. They all think too much of themselves, these third-reachers, she thought.

There had been nothing but complaints from the rich ever since she mandated that every citizen of Vasyllia donate their food and clothing stores to the refugees now camped in the second reach. She knew what this man would say to her. More complaints, more bitterness. More insinuations that had she been a *man*, things would not be so dire.

Her nib cracked under her hand. She cursed. She had no more quills. With a reluctant sigh, she looked at her maid.

"Let him in."

To her surprise, it was not Yadovír, whom she expected. It was Elder Pahomy of the warrior seminary. She stiffened. Battle with the old warrior required tact as well as forcefulness.

Elder Pahomy lumbered in, dressed in the black, flowing robes of a cohort father. The traditional dress did little to diminish his significant belly. He bowed formally. She saw his jawline ripple as he rose.

He is as unsure as I am, she thought.

"I did not expect the Dumar to send you, Elder," she said, standing up and approaching him. She lightly took his forearms and reached up to kiss him thrice on the cheeks. His jawline relaxed a little, and his eyes changed from stormy to merely threatening.

"I do not relish the role of errand-boy, Highness," he said, his jowls quivering in irritation.

"I do understand you, Elder." She kept her left hand light on his arm and continued to look him directly in the eyes. "But I promise not to be cross with you, no matter what their nonsense."

"Sabíana," he said, sighing heavily. "May I sit?"

"Of course." She smiled and led him to a chair, which creaked dangerously when he sat down. She remained standing by him. It gratified her perversely to see how uncomfortable that made him.

"Highness, the third reach is very... *unhappy* about your arrangements concerning the refugees," he began.

She sighed very loudly, and he stopped.

"Get to the point, Pahomy."

He flushed briefly and cleared his throat. "It's been three weeks since the siege began, and the weather is only getting colder. They fear a long winter. If their stores are used on these refugees, many will starve."

"And they think I do not know this?"

"Highness, I think it an admirable thing that you do. I do. But necessity sometimes dictates that we become cruel and hard, for the sake of the many. And treachery is a terrible disease to catch during siege-time."

"I know all this, Elder. But if we cannot extend our compassion to our neighbors in the times when that compassion is most needed, we do not deserve to survive this siege."

"In that case, you leave me no choice."

He stood up ponderously and drew himself to his full height. The room seemed to shrink as he stood.

"Highness, the third reach demands, by its ancient right, to convene a Council of the Reaches."

Sabíana felt the blood drain from her face, and spots began to dance before her eyes. The nobles wanted to elect a new Dar. The nobility of Vasyllia had just committed treason.

"Rogdai!" Sabíana called, and immediately the door flew open and the old swordsman strode in and saluted. He looked slightly perturbed at seeing the elder, but only for a moment.

"Rogdai, Elder Pahomy has just informed me that there are traitors in the third reach. Take a full detachment of the palace guard. The elder will lead you to the houses of the conspirators. You are to arrest all of them. Our dungeons have stood too long unused."

The elder looked at her for a long time, then his eyes creased and twinkled. He bowed low and offered her a hesitant hand. She extended hers, and he kissed the tip of her right forefinger.

"Come, Vohin Rogdai," he said and walked out of the room.

Sabíana stood for a long time, smiling. She had taken a tremendous risk, won an important ally, and removed a dangerous infection from the city in one move of the chessboard. It excited her, far more than she expected.

Kalún and Yadovír each held a torch that smelled unpleasantly of burnt lard. The nether regions of the palace, far below even the dungeons, were hardly more than caves. In some of the rooms stalactites dripped water in a maddening, steady rhythm. Every drop made Yadovír want to jump out of his skin. He knew that there was a significant possibility that they were walking into a trap. He was ready to give up and turn back. The darker the caves became, the more the recent stories of the Gumiren's atrocities bubbled up to his conscious mind.

You think you can reason with blood-drinkers? asked his mind. *What sort of madness possesses you to think you can reason with savages?*

"Not much farther now, Otar," he said, more to distract himself than anything.

And yet he recognized that a kind of madness had bitten and infected him. Yadovír wanted power, absolute power, and he was even willing to speak with the Ghan, to give up his own city on the enemy's terms, if only it meant a chance at that power. It was increasingly becoming an irrational urge. The knowledge that he would sell his own family for it no longer bothered him.

"Yadovír." The priest's voice was insufferably calm. "Tell me again why you waited so long to meet with them?"

Yadovír wanted to scream. They had spoken of this already at least five times.

"Winter deepens, Otar. They are Steppe-people. They do not know *real* winters. I waited for them to feel a truly deep Vasylli freeze. It will make them more amenable to our terms."

"Our terms. Yes. Very good." His voice was soft and absent.

Yadovír wondered if the priest was going senile.

They turned past the last bend, and before them the passage was blocked by fallen boulders and dirt. Here, as Yadovír had already found, was a small hole, barely visible even with the torches, through which they should be able, with some difficulty, to push to the other side.

"I am afraid we must leave our torches behind, Otar."

Kalún grumbled under his breath. They left the torches in an old, rusty brazier that clung to the cave wall and plunged into the dark on the other side. The murk was almost substantial, like a hand that groped for their eyes at every step they took.

"Otar," whispered Yadovír, the echoes running ahead of him. "Follow my voice. I know the way from here well enough."

The priest didn't answer, but Yadovír heard his breathing, so he stepped forward into the void. It was far more frightening this time than the last. Every step he took increased the sense that he was approaching something horrid and irrevocable. Maybe it would be best to go back? To just pretend that the way ahead was hopelessly blocked?

"This way, Otar Kalún, follow me. We should come out not far from the enemy camp. Their soldiers have free rein to wander about in search of food or stragglers. If we are accosted, we must not panic. Even it if seems they will kill us, it will be no more than a show of force. The Ghan has ensured our safe passage." Did he really believe that himself?

Yadovír kept one hand on the walls, feeling for the telltale change. The bare walls needed to give way to scattered roots, and only then could they be sure they were near the exit. But they walked for a long time, and Yadovír felt no change. Had they taken a wrong turn? What if they were going deeper into the mountain, and all that awaited them was a dead end and a stone tomb? His temples began to ache with increased pressure, or was that his imagination? Surely they were going deeper into the earth, not closer to the exit.

Otar Kalún persisted in his silence. Finally, Yadovír felt a moist root.

"Not far now, Otar. I did not tell you this before, but the Ghan is eager to meet the chief cleric of Adonais. He said that he expected an interesting conversation."

Otar Kalún merely grunted.

Soon they came out through a small opening, and the icy wind bit Yadovír's face, freezing even the hairs in his nose. Rare, sharp snowflakes did not so much fall as shoot down from the sky like arrows. Below them the mountain sloped down away from the walls of Vasyllia to their left, only a few hundred feet away. There was no path here through the thickly-growing pines. They climbed down with difficulty, slipping on the icy rocks and roots. Mist lay thick around them.

"What's that?" Yadovír pointed ahead of them.

"Torchlight," said Otar Kalún.

"Sixty-five," said Rogdai.

"Sixty-five?" Sabíana could not believe her ears. She had expected ten, maybe fifteen traitors. Sixty-five? A heavy dread settled into the pit of her stomach. This was obviously just the beginning.

She and Rogdai walked through the dungeons, Rogdai naming every one of the conspirators as they passed their door.

"Lord Rudin, his son Nevida..."

Nevida? She thought, alarmed. *I grew up with him. He was one of my closest friends. You have no friends,* she reminded herself.

"Any clerics, Rogdai?"

"None, my lady. Did you expect any?" He seemed surprised.

She would not speak it aloud, but she feared Otar Kalún had no great love for her. But would he turn traitor?

"I think I have had enough for now. Bring me a written report of their questioning by early tomorrow morning."

Sabíana allowed herself to wander through the lower reaches of the palace on her way back from the dungeons. She found herself in the passage she often walked with Voran whenever they had wanted to be alone. After the bond with Feína, she found it easier to think of him. Her heart did not immediately fold in on itself as though it were trying to hide.

She remembered the moment she first saw Voran as a man, not a boy. He had just successfully finished the Ordeal of Silence, but the only reward he was to receive was the disappearance of his beloved mother, the madness of his father, and the terrible events of the failed Karila embassy.

Voran was only sixteen at the time.

The memory was as clear as though it had happened yesterday.

It was the first sunny morning after nearly a month of rain, and the air was so clear, so washed, that it seemed there was no air at all. Father had relented for once and allowed her to attend the Dar's hours—the one day in the month that the Dar accepted direct petitions from any person in Vasyllia, regardless of reach. Voran was the first to come.

She had not recognized him—he was so serious, so thin. The six months of the Ordeal of Silence lay heavy on him. She knew how much heavier his burden was about to become, and she wanted to leave, to not be forced to endure the pain in his eyes. But she forced herself to stay.

"Voran," her father had said. "I would give my right hand to reward you as you deserve. Instead, I have only pain. The embassy to Karila was attacked. Every single member of the embassy—yes, even the women—were killed. Worse. They were gutted like animals. But…"

Voran's lips were a white line in his face.

"Your father was not among them."

Voran gasped in relief. Then, his face changed. He realized the implication.

"But, Highness," he said, in the voice of a man who had forgotten what is was like to speak. "Surely you don't think…"

Sabíana's heart contracted, but she held still.

"No, Voran. I do not. But others…"

Something happened to Voran's body. It seemed to grow, to become firmer. His face aged before her. His eyes sharpened. They were the eyes of a full-grown warrior on the eve of war.

"Highness, I will do as you command. If it is your desire that I abandon my place at the seminary, I will do so. If you wish me to leave Vasyllia, I will do so. Only I ask one thing. Not for myself. For the memory of the man whom you loved as a brother."

Tears gathered in Sabíana's eyes. She batted her eyes, and the tears fell. She sniffed. Her hands shook.

Dar Antomír wept openly. He nodded. "Ask, Voran."

"Lebía. Make her your ward. I will leave your sight then, and my shame will not reflect on your brightness."

"Scribe!" Dar Antomír cried, and his voice echoed. "Let it be carved in stone."

Voran assumed the military stance.

"From this moment, Vohin Voran and his sister Lebía are declared wards of the Dar. Vohin Voran is relieved from his studies. But he is not to abandon them. Elder Pahomy of the warrior seminary will study with him personally. He will graduate with his cohort in time. Let Dumar confirm the words of the Dar."

In a softer voice, he had said to Voran, "Go, my son. Take whatever time you need to comfort your sister and to arrange your affairs. Our treasuries are at your disposal…"

"No, I must not think of him," she whispered now to the darkness, its cold bringing her back to the present. "Voran must accomplish his quest, or he will never be complete. I do not want half a man as my husband."

A gust of wind blew through the underground passage. The torches flickered and went out, leaving her in complete darkness. Throbbing like a heart, a white light appeared from the depths ahead of her. Strangely drawn by it, Sabíana walked forward. The white light flared, then faded. The torches came back to life.

Her heart pounded with dread.

A bundle lay just ahead of her. Was it her imagination, or did it move?

Terror engulfed her. With shaking hands, she reached down to touch the bundle. It was warm. With a sickening lurch, her heart stopped, then raced with redoubled fury. A body.

She ran back to the dungeons, where Rogdai still paced back and forth, overseeing the questioning of the traitors.

"Rogdai, come with me."

When they reached the bundle, she found it difficult to look at it. She pointed, and watched Rogdai's face, gauging his reaction. Every time she tried to look down at the body, terror crushed her, and she had to close her eyes.

"The face. Uncover it," she said.

He did as he was told. His eyes went round, and he gasped softly. But not with fear. Sabíana forced herself to look down.

A man. So familiar, yet so strange. A face she had never thought to see again. A face so entangled with recent regret, worry, and loss that it was nearly as well known to her as Voran's. But he had changed so much. He was drawn, starved, ashen, his face overgrown with a matted beard, no longer black, but not yet grey. Arms once bristling with the strength of ten men were little more than brown twigs cracked by winter. At her feet lay the erstwhile Voyevoda of Vasyllia, Otchigen. Voran's father.

"Highness," whispered Rogdai. "This is not possible. We are under siege. How does he just *wander* into the palace? There is something very wrong here."

She nodded. "Take him to my chambers, but tell no one. I must think on this."

"Highness, what is there to think about? He *must* have been sent by the enemy."

Thoughts of pity and vengeance tore at her in turn. There was also something else: a sickening unease in the deepest pit of her stomach. She agreed with Rogdai. It was no accident that Otchigen appeared now, of all possible times. So why was she taking him? She had no firm answer herself.

. . .

Rogdai laid him in Sabíana's own bed, and she wrapped him in her costliest furs. His breathing, so ragged and rushed, softened. From sickening green, his face took on the pied hue of the hearth-fire. She washed his hands, arms, and feet, marveling at their brittleness. With rose and lavender water, she gently teased out the brambles in his hair and beard. She undressed him and threw the rags into the hearth. She put a royal robe on him. Soon, a vestige of the former nobility began to reveal itself in subtle shades.

"Highness," said Rogdai. "What do you intend to do with him?"

She bristled at the informality, but their shared confidence softened her. "Double the guard at the door, and be there yourself at all times. If this is some ploy by the enemy, we must be ready. But Otchigen was always a well of information. Now, perhaps, more than ever. I know the risk. But I will get it out of him by any means necessary."

He stood straight and gave her the warrior's salute. In his eyes, she saw something exhilarating. *I am their Black Sun,* she thought. Rogdai is my man, heart and soul.

Two dancing fire-lights resolved into three, then five, then seven. Seven torches, carried by seven burly Gumiren. The biggest made directly for Yadovír, showing no surprise at meeting him there. The other six surrounded them. Yadovír's heart dropped to his ankles. The leader turned around and indicated that they should follow. Soon, they entered a bustling war camp.

Yadovír was so surprised by what he saw that he nearly forgot to be afraid for a few moments. Campfires surrounded them, some with no people around them, which Yadovír found strange. From all sides, he heard the sound of pounding hammers and harsh words. Logs were dragged back and forth, and he noticed a good number of the Gumiren constructing siege towers fitted with rough, wooden wheels. Yadovír was surprised that the Gumiren were intent on storming the city in winter.

Everywhere, he smelled horseflesh and feces and sour milk. Goats and sheep roamed freely among the men. He was momentarily distracted by the loud braying of a bull, and he turned to look. Immediately, he wished he had not, though he found himself fascinated in spite of himself. Five of the Gumiren lay a bull on its back and held it down as it thrashed. One of them slashed its chest and belly open so quickly, even the bull was surprised. Yadovír expected a spray of blood, but saw nothing. They held the bull until it stopped shuddering. Then they turned it over, and all the blood was collected in wooden basins lying in wait underneath.

"For sausages," said one of the torch-bearers in a surprisingly friendly tone.

"Blood sausages?" Yadovír tried not to sound as revolted as he felt.

"Yes, very good!" said the Gumir.

Several men milked horses. Yadovír was disgusted, but then he realized that by bringing mares, the Gumiren had a nearly limitless supply of milk and cheese on the war path. Grudgingly, he admired their intelligence. He continued to look around, trying to understand these strange enemies better. There were few quarrels, to his surprise. Other than the constant barking out of orders, the predominant noise was laughter. Many sat by campfires joking in their rat-a-tat tongue. Some wrestled goodheartedly with each other as the others cheered. They did not seem like the killing force that had razed Nebesta to the ground.

Then he saw the Vasylli prisoners—all of them men. Hundreds of them, mostly tied back to back and thrown in heaps on the edge of the camp, just far enough from the fires not to freeze to death. It chilled him even as it confused him. What was the use of keeping all these prisoners? The possibilities were frightening, and ruefully he admitted that this was no common enemy. These were experts at total war. Several large mounds of earth lay beyond the prisoners, probably burial mounds for the dead Gumiren who fell when the Vasylli took back Dubían's body. It reminded Yadovír that the Gumiren were still human, for all their prowess in war, and the thought gave him strength.

The leader stopped by the prisoners and said something to the six torch-bearers. Two of them seized Yadovír and Kalún and tied them up back to back, pushing them down next to the other prisoners.

"What are you doing?" said Yadovír, heart and mind racing. "We have an arrangement!"

The leader laughed and said something in his tongue. The rest of them laughed and one kicked Yadovír. He fell over and his head landed on a rock.

Otchigen's eyes opened, and their color was Voran's. Sabíana shuddered, but kept quiet. He looked at Sabíana in some confusion, then recognition warmed his eyes.

"You've grown so beautiful, Sabíana," he said, his voice a rasp, nothing like the booming voice that used to be. "But your beauty brings no warmth. How unlike your father you are."

His words were not bitter, but strangely expressionless. It gave no foothold to her anger, which annoyed her.

"What happened to me?" he asked.

"I was going to ask you the same thing, Otchigen. How is it that you appear in the nether regions of the palace in the middle of a siege?"

He struggled to remember, it seemed to her. He shook his head.

"You do not remember?"

He shook his head again. "Did you say Vasyllia is besieged?"

She didn't know what to think. Silence groped from him like heat from a fire, and Sabíana found herself entranced by his still undeniable presence.

"She disappeared," he said, his breath ragged, his eyes glazing over. He seemed half-delirious. "On a day unmatched for brilliance and warmth, she vanished without a trace. My wife, my life-giving spring, my rock. What was I to do? I could not be without her. I left and wandered. Blank, faded years. Memories…bleaker than the wastes of the far downs…"

Sabíana was entranced, drinking in even the silences between his words. No wonder the people loved him, she thought. No wonder my father loves him.

"I never found her," he continued. "Only rumors in lands where untamed forces twist men's minds into shapes of horror. No, I do not want to remember." He panted, and his face was spotted with red. "I heard that she had gone mad, that she was taken by men who would use her for her beauty. I never heard or found anything more. I was half-mad with hunger and grief. I am still mad, I think. Then, nothing. Somehow, I ended up here in your bed. Thank you, Sabíana."

At the unexpected thanks, she felt herself redden. She turned away, eager to be freed of his enticing influence. This was not the playful Otchigen who used to wrestle with her and Mirnían in the tall grass, to the shock of their prim chaperones. This man had suffered, so much was clear, but he was too self-possessed for someone who had descended into madness. There was something indescribably alluring about him. It made Sabíana long to give up her self-control. This man could be an incredible Dar, she thought, then wondered why she had thought it.

She felt nauseous at the thought. He says nothing about the Karila embassy, she reminded herself, forcing herself to be calm. She failed and rushed out of the room in a confusion of scattered thoughts and emotions.

I will come, I will come
I will come to the Dar's City
I will beat down, I will beat down,
With my spears the city's wall!
I will roll out, I will roll out
The barrels from the treasury.
I will gift, I will gift
Them to my father-in-law.
Be kind to me, my father-in-law,,
As is my own dear father...

Vasylli wedding song

CHAPTER 22
THE WEDDING

Nearly two months after the rescue of the pilgrims, the eve of the wedding arrived.

Three aspens stood in the center of the village, alight with lanterns. A life-sized Sirin carved from birchwood adorned the top of the center tree. All of Ghavan Town assembled in a circle around the trees, and steamed breath rose up in tendrils entwining with the smoke from the candles in their hands. The women sang, their joy enough to banish the cold to the outer fringes of the village. But Mirnían shook from miserable cold, and he was ready to fall asleep on his feet from exhaustion.

They had been standing vigil for four hours already, Otar Svetlomír doing his best to keep everyone awake with his dynamic voice and inspired manner of serving. The vigil would last for at least another three hours. Mirnían felt guilty, in spite of all his rational objections to this ancient rite. Every person he looked at was on fire from within. Even the children were still awake, their cheeks pink and their eyes sparkling. As for him, he could barely prevent the snores before they erupted from his throat. He berated himself. *Why can you not stay awake, even for a service performed for the sake of you and your beloved?*

So he stood, and gradually the inner grumbling stilled. Yet he remained apart from the rest, especially Lebía.

Otar Svetlomír approached Lebía and took her by the hand. To the accompaniment of a rhythmical chant in the women's voices, he led her around the trees three times. The children, who had been waiting for this moment for hours, began to ring small handbells handed out before the service. The sound was chaotic and wonderful. Lebía smiled, but tears ran down her cheeks.

Mirnían remained cold, both in body and in heart. He wished with all his strength to include himself in the joy of the village, to foretaste the pleasure of tomorrow's wedding, but his emotions were dull, like a bell cracked from excessive use. The sore under his left arm flared, as though mocking him. Whoever said that all mystical experiences are wishful thinking should be publicly flogged, he thought.

The men erupted into a joyful chant, almost a shout. Lebía returned to her place next to him, and Svetlomír took Mirnían's hand and led him around the trees as well. The bells clanged twice as frantically. One little boy in particular was so red-faced with the exertion of wringing every possible ounce of sound from his bell that Mirnían was afraid he would faint.

Their joy was palpable, obvious. Mirnían could almost smell it, it was so intense. Still it remained outside his reach. He tried to stop himself, but he blamed Voran, as he so often did these days. Surely the hag's curse was still on him in some way, even after Lebía's incredible healing.

"Bless them as you blessed Cassían and Cassiana," intoned Otar Svetlomír, nearly dancing in his ecstasy. "Bless them as you blessed Lassar and Dagana. May their union be a fruitful joining of Heights and earth. May their children bring healing to our land."

"So be it!" exclaimed the women, all of whom were trying to keep a reverently serious expression on their faces, but failing miserably.

"Honor their petitions, Adonais. Hear their requests!"

Lebía gathered her furs and placed them carefully before her, then knelt on them gingerly, trying to avoid the snow with her clothing. She closed her eyes, her mouth moving in quick whispers, her eyebrows trembling. He did not deserve this perfect creature. Mirnían fell on his face before the tree.

"Feel!" he commanded his heart. "Why can you not feel anything?"

Three hours later, he began to feel a slight flutter of longing in his heart. Seven hours, he thought, and only this. It was enough to make him scream in frustration. For the sake of Lebía, he remained silent. The wedding is tomorrow, he reminded himself, you are just nervous. Everything will be well.

Otar Svetlomír raised them up, taking Mirnían's right hand and Lebía's left. He placed a ring of clear quartz on Mirnían's right ring finger. A single pine needle ran the length of the ring. Mirnían realized someone had crafted the ring around the needle. The artistry amazed him. Lebía's ring was smaller, of pink quartz, flecked with pine seeds within like insects captured in amber. It was even more wondrous to behold than his ring.

"The promise of fidelity," said Svetlomír, quiet enough for it to be intended only for the two of them. "Though the temptation be strong, let this night be the pledge of your future faithfulness, for you must wait to perform your duties until after the wedding service."

Lebía blushed, and even Mirnían could not stop a slight smile. Then his sore throbbed, as though the hag stood invisible by his side and prodded him with a white-hot poker.

<hr />

"Careful around the sore," he said to the boy assigned to help him into the ceremonial wedding garb—an absurdly heavy red-gold kaftan whose tall collar chafed his neck even before he put it on. Mirnían suspected the embroidered sunbursts were sewn with actual gold thread on the doubly layered red velvet.

"What sore?" asked the boy, looking directly at it, but apparently not seeing it.

"Never mind," said Mirnían, fumbling for the boy's name. The boy had already repeated it three times, but Mirnían forgot it every time. It bothered him even more than the boy's apparent blindness or idiocy.

As the boy helped him haul the massive garment onto his shoulders, Mirnían almost screamed with pain. The boy had pushed upward onto the open sore, making fire run up and down Mirnían's side.

"I told you to watch the sore, you idiot!"

The boy looked not at all upset at being called an idiot, but he did regard Mirnían with a look that doubted his sanity. Could the boy really not see it?

Confused by the long vigil and the subsequent lack of sleep, and exhausted by his battle with the kaftan, Mirnían sat down on the long bench against the wall of the main room and closed his eyes. Just for a minute.

He opened his eyes, and saw a vision. Some creature of legend stood before him. Her dress also had a high collar and was also red with gold embroidery of crescent moons and stars. It looked even heavier than his kaftan. Her long sleeves opened at the elbow and trailed to the ground. Her hair was intertwined with a latticework of gold wire and gems that looked like the sun rising over a peak.

"Lebía?" He could do little more than whisper.

She smiled, and the sun itself could hardly compare with the light of joy in her eyes.

In a half-dream state, he stood and took her hand, leading her out through the door into the midwinter sun. A carpet lay before them, made of cut flowers. Where had the villagers found flowers in winter?

The air was still, as though all of created Nature took a long breath before the opening chord to a festal hymn. Villagers stood here and there in loose clumps, every face a red sun surrounded by furs like clouds. Mirnían and Lebía walked by the houses of Ghavan, their road a river of red amid white. The gentle ascents and descents of the village brought the aspens ever closer.

They spoke no word to each other, though Mirnían could not tear his eyes from her, and almost fell on his face several times. Every time she looked at him, the rosebuds on her cheeks blossomed. Only when they stood before the trees did she meet his gaze, stopping him with a gentle squeeze of her fingers on his hand.

"Mirnían," she whispered, "whatever Voran may have done to you, forgive him for my sake. That is the only gift I ask of my husband on our wedding day."

Mirnían's chest constricted, his breath rasping with difficulty. The sore prickled, taunting.

"Yes," he whispered and smiled. His face felt like deer-hide being stretched on a rack for the tanning.

She had not seen it.

The lambswool blanket was like butter on his skin. The hearth crackled and smelled pleasantly of apples. A drowsy inactivity suffused through his body slowly, groping toward his fingertips, as though he had drunk just the right amount of Otchigen's famous wine. At the heart of his contentment was a lightness in his chest that he had imagined gone from his life forever. And yet...

She had not seen it.

Lebía slept. In his own bed. In *their* own bed. There was a wonderful dreaminess about seeing her there, a kind of mystery to her sleep that warmed him more than any fire or blanket. He could sit here staring at her sleep for countless ages, and not feel the need to move. And yet...

She had not seen it.

Their lovemaking had been awkward and—he had never expected it—

absurdly comical. He smiled at the memories, embarrassing and warm. No one knew, no one would ever know—though every lover in history were to write a paean to first love—the strange madness of the wedding night, not without experiencing it firsthand. And yet...

She had not seen it.

Was the sore even there? The pain of it, underlying all his thoughts and emotions, seemed all too real. But how was it possible that only he could see it? He had to remind himself that for all the normality of daily life in Ghavan, the boundary between real and legendary was translucent. That left him with the uncomfortable suggestion that no amount of medicine would heal this last sore. No physical medicine, that is.

A Sirin-song sounded outside the house, urging itself on his attention. He dressed quietly and wrapped himself in his thickest furs. He suspected this conversation would be a long one.

Lebía had told him of the soul-bond with Aína on the same day that she had healed him, but he had not fully believed her until Aína herself appeared, her rebuke evident in her hard eyes. He had never imagined eyes could cut so deeply into his very essence.

Now Aína waited for him by the house, looking over the slight descent toward the middle of the village. The houses were all dark, though the paths between them were still visible in the light of the torches kept alight throughout the night. Each of the braziers holding the torches had been made by a member of the village, and even after so many weeks here, the whimsy of each design—a fish, a horse with wings, a many-headed serpent, a six-winged giant with coals for eyes—continued to amaze Mirnían.

"Did you know that the aspen sapling in Vasyllia is no longer on fire?" Aína said, her voice wafting in from some unspeakable depth of antiquity. He never felt fully *there* when she spoke to him. His wife—how extraordinary to think of her as "wife"—tried to explain it by saying that Aína was only really present for her. For all others, it was like speaking through a transparent door.

"Is there no hope that this place can be a rebirth of Old Vasyllia?" he asked her.

"There is a very great hope of that, Mirnían. *You* stand in the way."

Mirnían laughed dourly. "It's always my fault."

"Mirnían, self-pity is the refuge of the weak. You are not weak."

"Tell me then."

She nodded, her eyes half-lidded, assessing him as she spoke. "Among our sisterhood there is one who is apart from us. She is named Gamayun, the Black Sirin. She alone has never felt the fire of soul-bond, for she is set apart, an oracle. Gamayun sings all possible futures, and Gamayun sings invariably of one thing concerning your future. You will meet Voran again, and soon."

"I can't trust myself not to kill him."

"That is why you still have the leprosy on you, though it slumbers, and that is why you alone prevent Ghavan from becoming the hope of Vasyllia."

He knew it, had known it for a long time, but hearing it from a Sirin gave it the kind of finality that a man condemned to death is sure to feel in the long agony of the blade's descent to his exposed neck.

"Mirnían, your father is dead."

He heard the words, and his body involuntarily tensed in anticipation of the inevitable shock, but nothing came.

"Vasyllia?" He asked, his voice hoarse, his throat bone-dry from the cold.

"She still stands, but is besieged. Her fate is no longer yours. At least not for now."

No. His fate was rooted here, in the fertile earth of Ghavan. The remnant of Vasyllia must flourish. He must find a way to forget Voran. Forgive him? He could not.

"Aína, there is some measure of protection against the Raven here, on this island, is there not?"

She half-nodded. He sighed, relieved of tension he hadn't realized was there.

"However," she said, looking back over the town. "You, Mirnían, are outside that protection while you are marked."

Marked. Would he never be free of some kind of mark? Dar's son, Sabíana's brother, heir to Cassían's throne, beloved of the people…it was tiring. When would he ever be able to be merely Mirnían, to do with himself as he pleased?

"What can I do, Aína?" he asked.

But she was no longer there, if she had been there at all.

*"Why do the innocent suffer?" asked Dar Cassían. "Why do the guilty prosper?"
A voice thundered from the heavens.
"When you have given your life to the suffering innocents, then you may ask. Not before."*

From "Dar Cassían and His Daughter"
(Old Tales: Book IV)

CHAPTER 23
TRAINING

A thin brushstroke of gold painted the tips of the pines on the horizon, but the marshes were already the deep purple of twilight. Achingly close were the wood-smells, the fire-lights, the meal-sounds of the village ahead of them, and yet Tarin remained in maddening stillness on his knees, head bowed, leaning on his old sword. His stained mantle wrapped around him, he blended into the darkness like a boulder or a barrow. Only the sibilance of his repeated whisper marked him as living.

The change was uncanny—the lunatic had become an old warrior again, a kind of warrior Voran had never encountered. Tarin continued to repeat the word, or words, under his breath. Voran could not catch the meaning, but whatever it was, it seemed to diffuse a vibrant calm, as though Tarin were a pebble dropped into a pond, and his calm presence rippled outward. Voran found himself sharing the stillness, entering into it bodily. It reminded him of singing in a choir, in the way that seasoned chanters seem to be absorbed into each other's sound, unconsciously wringing their voices into a single, multifaceted music.

They had spent the day on the threshold of the village, just near enough for Voran to imagine the villagers hosting a feast in their honor on trestle tables in the village square. He knew it was mad to expect anything of the sort, but it was so long—how many days? Three?—since his last proper meal. Instead, he had to content himself with hearing the sounds of the evening meal, which echoed in the clear air of the marsh-valley.

"YEEEAAAAAAOOOOOOUUUUUUUUU!!!!"

Voran managed not to jump, but he was sure three grey hairs had sprouted on his head instantaneously from that cry. Tarin crouched to the ground, arms akimbo, neck stretched out. He yowled like a wounded animal. Then he retracted his head into his neck like a rooster, and proceeded to cluck as he waddled back and forth in a figure-eight.

All over the village, storm-shutters slapped back, making the houses look like they opened their eyes. The doors swung open, and the houses yawned. The village stirred from sleep, a wild noise rising toward Voran. The strangeness of it disoriented him. Only when he saw them did he realize what it was—a crowd of children, followed by disapproving parents, many of whom ran after their bare-headed charges, armed with hats.

"Tarin! Tarin!" They all cheered wildly, expectant joy in every face, even in the faces of the disapproving parents.

He clucked and clucked and let himself be enfolded in their mittened hands and arms, until he could no longer contain his own joy. His laugh was so natural, so unforced, that Voran thought he was a completely different man. Despite all Tarin's strange behaviors, this reaction to the children was one Voran never expected.

The wave of children had crested and was about to pull Tarin back into the depths of the village. Voran followed, already tasting meat and mead, his mouth filling with saliva. They had all surged to the edge of the village when Tarin turned, so suddenly that Voran nearly ran into him.

"Ah, Raven Son! I had forgotten about you. You may not enter the village. There is a task I need you to perform. Here."

He pointed to the second pack on Voran's back, the one that felt like it was filled with stones. Voran opened it. The pack *was* filled with stones.

"These are stones imbued with power," Tarin said in his sing-song storyteller voice, more to the children than to Voran. They all approved, tittering. "Raven Son, you must arrange a perfect cairn here, where you stand. Then wait for me. I will come out to you and give you leave to enter the village."

"You cannot be serious," Voran said, before realizing that silence was probably a better strategy.

Tarin stiffened and fixed Voran with a gaze that promised repeated retribution.

"Children," Tarin said in a voice that brooked no opposition, "go on home. I will come to you soon."

Only after the houses had once again fallen asleep did Tarin release Voran from his gaze.

"Have you forgotten your word?" he whispered through gritted teeth.

"You are my slave. My commands are not to be questioned, especially by a well-known lunatic such as you."

Voran breathed deeply, trying not let the sparks come tumbling out of his eyes.

"Cairn," Tarin growled. "Now."

He turned and walked into the village.

It took all of five minutes to construct a cairn of stones. It took all of three quarters of an hour for Tarin to return for his inspection.

"Good. Now put the stones back into the pack."

"But what about their protection?"

Tarin looked genuinely puzzled.

"You had said they were invested with power."

Tarin threw his head back and laughed, his hands on his belly. It was a parody of a laugh. Voran wanted to strike him.

"So I did," Tarin said, wiping his eyes of the tears of laughter. "Well, I lied. Get on with it, then."

***

Tarin only let Voran into the village after midnight, and by that time he was obviously the worse for wear. Voran didn't look at him, hoping the churning annoyance—so thick he was sure it would eat him before he ever had supper again—would be obvious. He wanted Tarin to apologize, or at the very least, to notice his displeasure. Tarin hardly seemed to notice anything.

As a final insult, Tarin let Voran no further than a mudroom that smelled of old furs, wood, and rats. A plate of bread and dried meat sat next to a clean straw pallet. Voran tried to console himself with the blessed warmth of the room, but it did little good. He silently promised himself that he would not sleep all night. That would show Tarin.

Voran was awoken by a laughing Tarin. The door was open and a nearly midday sun streamed into the mudroom.

"Well, you proved your point, Raven Son," said Tarin, and erupted into his lunatic laugh. The crowd of children cheered and jumped and laughed with him. Voran found his resolve to punish Tarin—for what, he had already forgotten—fading at the sight of the children. In the daylight, they looked much worse than last night. Most of them were stick-thin, the whites of their eyes more like yellows. Some had bellies protruding even through the furs. With a rush of shame, Voran realized that Tarin was probably the only joy this village had experienced in months. And all Voran had thought of all night was his own comfort. He swore and promised to curb his pride better next time.

In the center of the village, Tarin climbed a rickety table that shuddered every time he moved, and he moved constantly. Voran was just about to utter a curse about breaking wood and fallen warriors when he remembered his promise. Grumbling, he moved closer to the assembled throng. It seemed the entire village was present.

"In a certain kingdom, in a certain land," declaimed Tarin with a flourish, the table reeling like a drunken man underneath him. The children all hopped up and down, clapping and screaming their delight at the top of their voices. Even Voran, in spite of himself, felt propelled into the energy of Tarin's speech. For all of his madness, the old goat had a way with words.

The Tale of the Cub's Hunger

It was spring, the time for a new-born bear cub to attempt the hunt for the first time. The cub was, as you might expect, excited and full of energy. He left in the morning, sure he would bring something big home—a badger maybe, or even a buck—but the figure he cut when he returned that evening was not what his mother expected. He was bedraggled, wet, and utterly miserable.

"Well, my boy," she said, "did you bring anything to comfort your old mama?"

"Oh, Mama, it was horrible! Even the squirrels laughed at me. I gave them my best roar, but they threw nuts at me. I came to the river; the fish were lazy, sleepy in the summer sun. Easy picking, I thought. I made my attack, and suddenly they were all gone. One fat porker of a salmon actually jumped out and smacked me in the face with his tail. I saw a perfect berry patch—the berries were so perfect, Mama! —glistening and nearly popping with ripeness. But as soon as I came close I was viciously attacked by a stinkbug. It sprayed me! My eyes are still crying from it."

"My poor boy. So much to learn still. You can't conquer the forest in a day. Try again tomorrow. Be patient and careful, but do not let your poor mama go hungry for a second day."

For four days, the cub caught nothing. On the fourth day, he waddled through a birch glade, his stomach grumbling. Suddenly a finch, all yellow and obnoxious—all of their species have that unfortunate deficiency, I'm afraid—took it into its little brain to torment the cub. Around and around his head it flew, screeching always at the moment it passed his ears—for maximum effect, you understand. Finally, the cub had enough, and he swatted the bird with his paw. His swipe was mortally on target, and the bird fell at his feet, its wings awkward and its neck snapped. The cub looked at the bird and felt a savage kind of pleasure. It was the killing itself. He liked it.

That evening, he brought his mother a rabbit. She praised him, but something about his manner—maybe it was his eyes, she could not tell—frightened her.

After that, he killed more and more, starting with small animals like squirrels, and sometimes even bringing down a mountain goat or two. But the more he hunted, the more he began to kill for the mere pleasure of it. Sometimes he even wounded small animals and left them in the forest to die. The kill dominated his thoughts day and night. His mother saw the macabre series of dead creatures from afar, but she was a wise old bear. She bided her time.

One day, the cub came to her, shaking and crying inconsolably.

"Mama, Mama, I'm so miserable!"

"What is it, my sweet cub?"

"I can't stop killing. The desire for blood is huge inside me. It's so big now, it has nowhere else to go. Maybe I should jump off a cliff, so the forest will be rid of me."

She cradled him in her warm embrace, like she did during his first months underground. He cried and he cried, until he could cry no more. Then she looked deep into his eyes, and he felt the pieces of something broken inside him come together again. Drying his eyes, he went out on the hunt again.

Two squirrels were playing in front of their cave, completely oblivious to the bears' living in the vicinity. The cub felt the now-familiar, groping desire to kill them. He was not even hungry, but he could imagine the warmth of their blood and the feeling of power it gave him.

He looked at them for a long time, then sat on his haunches and bellowed. The squirrels nearly left their bushy tails behind them, so far they jumped, and began to chatter at him angrily from the safety of a high branch, though neither was brave enough to throw anything at him. He laughed at them and turned back inside. It was time to sleep.

"They loved it," said Voran as he and Tarin enjoyed a quiet repast, sitting on the ground, leaning on one of the houses. "I didn't think they would understand it, but they seem to have understood more than I did."

"Does that surprise you?" Tarin's voice was only slightly sarcastic. He seemed younger and in better spirits after the telling.

"How much of that story was intended for my ears?"

"You do think much of yourself, don't you, Raven Son?" Tarin shook his head, apparently genuinely disappointed in Voran. "It was a story of the darkness that lives in the heart of every man, not merely the great Voran, son of Otchigen of Vasyllia."

Voran's face grew hot, and he was grateful for the sound of approaching footsteps. It was a little boy, hardly more than four or five. His face was pockmarked, and there was something wrong behind his eyes. The realization pained Voran more than he expected—the little boy's mind was damaged, probably by some kind of disease.

He approached Voran, not Tarin, which surprised Voran, even as a kind of panic began to itch at him. What does one do with a damaged child? His instinct was to ignore the boy or to shoo him away. Actually speaking to him, interacting with him was more frightening than walking off a precipice in the wild. The boy looked at Voran's shoulder, never at his eyes, but still he shuffled nearer. He had no shoes, only rough leather slippers tied together in a slipshod manner. It suggested that the boy had an older sibling, but no parents.

"Is he an orphan?" whispered Voran to Tarin, unwilling to look at the boy, feeling the unwelcome revulsion, yet unable to look away.

"Why do you not ask him?"

"He is not?... You know..."

Tarin did not answer. The boy reached out a hand and touched Voran's knee, then smiled, tucking his chin into his neck and leaning back. He moaned a little and began to chortle. The piercing in Voran's heart was now a torrent of fire. With a trembling hand, he reached out to the boy and curled his fingers in, inviting him closer. The boy closed his eyes and shook his head, moaning gently, but he didn't back away. Voran spread out both arms to the boy.

The boy cocked his head to the side, his eyes still closed, and turned sideways while shuffling forward, like a reticent crab. He tapped Voran's knees, as if appraising them. Before Voran realized it, the boy was curled up in his arms, his head on Voran's chest. The boy's breathing stilled and deepened, and soon a faint snuffle rose and fell with the little shoulders. He was asleep.

Voran wept, afraid that his heaving chest would wake the boy.

"His name is Voran, by the way," said Tarin, looking away. "And yes, he is an orphan."

Voran did not think he could feel any guiltier in his life than he did at that moment.

When the tears were spent—though the wound in his heart still throbbed, as he hoped it would throb forever—Voran turned to Tarin. The old madman looked different now, as though the touch of a damaged little child had transformed the entire world for Voran.

"Tarin, this village. These children. What happened to them?"

"*You* happened to them. Vasyllia happened to them. But that is the difficult answer. The simple one is that they were in the path of the Raven's armies. Many of them are Nebesti outliers living near the Vasyllian border. Their men were foolish enough to raise arms against the invaders."

That was why there were so many women and so few men. Voran let the reality seep into him as it irritated his new heart-wound, like fermented potato-brew poured over infected skin.

"Tarin, I must find the Living Water. Finally, I know why I must."

The old warrior smiled and closed his eyes. The wind shifted, bringing a strange, almost spring-like fragrance of budding snowdrops. Was it really so near the end of winter?

"That is good, Voran. It will help you in your training. As for Living Water, you are not ready yet."

Tarin stood up and wiped the brown grass from his robes. He yawned hugely and stretched like a cat, until something popped loud enough for the entire village to hear. Tarin yelped in pain and grabbed his back.

"It is time we were off, Raven Son," he said, straightening out with a grimace. "Don't want to attract anything that might hurt these children. Your smell is ripe, and there are many hounds still seeking."

Voran looked down at the boy, trying to commit every single pockmark on his face to memory. *This is our son, Sabíana, our little Voran. They are all our children.*

Don't look for evil in the dark shadows. Don't look for evil in the night. Look for it in the middle of the day. Beware the demon that wears the skin of those you love.

From "The Tale of the Raven and the Living Water"
(Old Tales, Book II)

CHAPTER 24

THE RAVEN

Though it seemed like days, the Gumiren kept Yadovír and Kalún tied up for little more than several hours. When the guards came to untie them, they could hardly contain themselves for laughter. It seems this "imprisonment" was intended as little more than a practical joke. Yadovír failed to appreciate the humor.

He and Kalún were led, hands untied, to a flat space cleared of trees, various stumps poking out here and there from the frozen ground. In the center of the clearing lay a long sheet covered in a wooden board. The board was laden with foods of many different shades of brown. Wooden pitchers were filled with some white liquid. A group of Gumiren half-reclined, half-sat around the board, grabbing brown bits of food from common platters with their hands, then wiping them on their long, brown, fur-lined coats. By the designs on their hat-sashes, it seemed these were the elite. The Ghan himself, an enormous man with a rare beard and almost feral cunning hiding behind his eyes, sat at the head. His face creased into a smile, and he looked like he would explode any minute into a torrent of laughter.

The Ghan saw them and half-bowed, still sitting, indicating places on his left. For a moment, Kalún looked unwilling to debase himself at such a table, but to Yadovír's relief he sat down, leaving the seat nearer the Ghan for Yadovír. Yadovír didn't speak at first, thinking perhaps it would be considered rude to speak to the Ghan with no invitation. Kalún stared down at the food with a white face, and seemed intent on saying nothing at all.

"You no offend?" said the Ghan, laughing in his eyes. "Men have little jest at you." He laughed loudly, his rounded belly bouncing up and down. "Eat! We make *horse* for you. Eat."

They were given a plate of brown meat cut into small pieces. Yadovír was sure he would be ill if he ate any of this food, but the Ghan's emphasis on the word "horse" made it clear they were being given a great honor. Yadovír took a large piece and tried to swallow it without chewing. It was not horrible, even faintly seasoned with a spice he didn't quite recognize.

"Saffor, yes?" The Ghan frowned as one of the others corrected him. "Ah, yes. *Saffron*. Your people do not know this, I think."

"It is very good, thank you," said Yadovír, not sure what honorific to use.

"Ghan speak now, yes?" said the Ghan. "My name—Magai. Ghan Magai. You, I know. Priest Kalún and common man Yadovír. You have offer for us, yes?"

Yadovír nodded, pleased things were progressing so quickly.

"Wait," the Ghan laid a meaty hand on Yadovír's shoulder. The reek of body odor was the last thing Yadovír expected of the Ghan, and he blanched from it. "You no tell me yet. I *guess*."

Yadovír inclined his head, hoping no one noticed his fervent desire to vomit.

"You have secret way into city, yes? No need tower and—how say? —*elaborate* attack? Yes?" The Ghan seemed very pleased at his extensive knowledge of the Vasyllian tongue.

"Yes, Ghan, you are right."

The Ghan clapped once and said, "Ha!" All the other Gumiren lifted their small wooden cups in salute. It soon became clear that Yadovír and Kalún were expected to do the same. But no one drank yet, to Yadovír's relief. He could only imagine what sort of abomination these savages drank.

"But I ask you," said the Ghan, a little crease appearing between his eyes, "Why we go your way? Why, when we already destroy all city in this land. Why use secret way, when we can use *our way?*"

Yadovír took a deep breath. This was the moment. The power was within reach now.

"It would be easier for all concerned, great one. You would not have to weather this winter, a winter our wise men predict will be terrible. You will lose fewer men, and Vasyllia—a beautiful city with riches you can scarcely dream of—will be yours with little destruction. Is it not better to have a strong city as tributary, instead of burnt ruins? You have seen how tenacious the Vasylli are when pressed to the wall."

The Ghan did not seem appreciative of that reminder. "Gumiren always destroy city if city no surrender. Always!" He frowned grotesquely, like a mask, and the whole assemblage tensed.

"It is a very wise policy, Ghan Magai. I understand your wisdom. You discourage rebellion, and you reward those willing to submit without a fight. Am I correct?"

The Ghan smiled again. "You clever man. I like you. Yes, you correct understand. But still, you no answer. Why work I with you? Why trust I a traitor to his own people?"

Yadovír's heart raced briefly at that reminder, but he persevered. "It is a time of confusion, Ghan. The Dar is dead."

This provoked an unexpected round of whispers, until the Ghan slapped a grimy hand on his thigh, cutting off the sound instantly. He nodded at Yadovír to continue.

"The future Darina is not yet crowned, and already there are people in the city who would stand against her rule. There are several conspiracies, and the people grow testy. There is no better time for your armies to come in secretly, kill the warriors, and secure the city for the Gumiren."

"What say dark one?" The Ghan nodded at Kalún.

Kalún looked up with a dreamy stare, as though surprised to be called upon. He looked like his mind was addled. Yadovír feared this would be the end of their short conspiracy.

"I am the high priest of Adonais, Ghan Magai," Kalún said with quiet firmness. "It is my belief that you are sent by my god, an instrument for our correction. I humbly beg you to grant us peace under your wisdom."

Yadovír breathed out, amazed at the tact from Kalún. The Ghan was also surprised, but far from pleased, as though he had read some secret intention behind the spoken words.

"Dark one. You—no good. You have—how say?—*deceit* in your heart. Yadovír, we have no agree if dark one remains."

Yadovír's mouth dried up in an instant. If they did not agree soon, neither he nor Kalún would be offered the luxury of returning to the prisoners. There was death in the eyes of all the Gumiren.

Sabíana stopped before entering her chamber, her heart leaping like a fish snatching at flies on the surface of a lake. She tried every exercise she knew to calm the heart and still the breathing, but nothing seemed to work. Worse yet, her complete inability to control her emotions at the mere thought of Otchigen lit a spark of panic deep in her stomach, and if she did nothing, soon it would be a conflagration. She pushed the door and entered.

Otchigen lay in her bed, sleeping as before. Even asleep, his allure caught at her and tried to pull her in, a fish-lure sparkling in the sun just above the surface of the water. *Let him be Dar.* Not quite pushing the thought away, Sabíana poked at the fire in the hearth to give her hands something to do.

Then she sat down in the great chair by the fire, looking at Otchigen. The knife hidden in her palm was a steadying weight.

When Otchigen awoke, his eyes were still watery with sleep. He smiled a little, though now it seemed a hollow mockery of his former joy, which had rivaled the twin waterfalls for its enthrallment with life.

"So. What do you intend to do with me?" he asked, lightly mocking.

"I have not yet decided."

"I don't expect a hero's welcome. There must be much about my disappearance that looks suspicious. I want to explain it to the Dar. Will you let me?"

Sabíana was surprised at the question, not immediately realizing that of course Otchigen could not possibly have known of the Dar's death.

"Dar Antomír is dead."

Something twitched in Otchigen's face, something *underneath* his face.

"You will have to answer to me now," she continued, trying to push down her revulsion. "I should have you put before the judgment of the Martial Voice. That would be the proper thing to do. But we shall see. You can speak to me for the time being."

"Ah, I see. I am being fattened for the slaughter."

"Perhaps. Or perhaps what Vasyllia needs is forgiveness. But you are useful in either case. I can have you executed as a traitor. It would be easy to tie the current invasion to your personal treachery. That would excite the warriors. Or I can publicly pardon you, appealing to the compassion of your fellows. You would then lead them in war against the enemy."

"You want to know what happened in Karila," he said. It wasn't a question.

"Yes. Spare no detail. The full truth, if you please."

He smiled sardonically, as if questioning the existence of truth at all.

"Nothing could be simpler, Sabíana. There was no real reason for a man of my rank to go on a routine embassy to Karila. But the Dar and I both agreed it would be good for me to leave Vasyllia for a time after Aglaia's disappearance. There was not supposed to be any trouble. Before we ever reached Karila, in the lower Downs of Nebesta, we were attacked by a band of marauders. I thought they were Karila, but they were darker of skin and spoke an unknown language. I suppose they were from beyond the Lowlands, maybe even the Steppes."

"Beyond the Steppes," said Sabíana. "Sounds like the Gumiren."

"The ones besieging Vasyllia." Otchigen laughed at the realization. "In that case you could very easily tie my supposed treachery with this invasion." He descended into thought, the light going out of his eyes in a moment.

"Go on, Otchigen."

"Whoever they were, they were the most bloodthirsty warriors I have ever encountered. They drank the blood of their horses instead of water. I saw it with my own eyes. They killed every member of the embassy, expect for me. I was necessary, they said, to warn the others of their coming. I think they intended me as a scare tactic, so they began to do unspeakable things to the ambassadors, even after their deaths. I will not describe it. Suffice it to say that had I not been Voyevoda, had I not seen death and torture firsthand, I would have done as they wanted and run screaming for the hills, whipping up the populace with the nameless fear.

"But I did not. As they left me alive, I considered it an uncommon gift from Adonais. I would go searching for my Aglaia, I thought. She was supposed to have been seen near Karila, so I sought her trail. I should have returned home; I know that now. I could have warned Vasyllia. But I wanted to find her. Instead, they found me again and brought me to their great secret, their true inspiration."

"The Raven."

Otchigen was taken aback at this. His smile was now venomous. "You know much more than I expected," he said with a voice not quite his own. Terror ran up and down her back like mice. She clenched her hidden knife so tightly, she was sure it would draw her own blood.

"Yes, I saw him," continued Otchigen. "Well, not *him*, exactly. His vessel. That is what they called it, I think. It seems the Raven has a habit of possessing human bodies, though this vessel was hardly human by then. The Raven had consumed most of him already."

He stopped, the memory apparently too painful.

"The rest is rather dim. The only other thing you might be interested to hear is that I *did* find one of my family out there. I saw Voran."

Evidently, whatever valiant effort she mustered to prevent her face from reflecting the mad dance of her heart failed miserably. Otchigen's snigger was more than malicious, it was nearly feral.

"Oh, yes. Happily living with a certain red-haired farmer's daughter in the wilds. She was very fetching, if I say so myself."

Sabíana saw it. Voran entwined in lust with another woman. Hatred rose up from her depths with the sudden ferocity of a winter blizzard. She looked at Otchigen and spots danced before her eyes. She nearly fainted.

There was bestial hunger in the face of Otchigen.

"Why, Sabíana, you look upset. You did not set your hopes on Voran, did you?"

All pretense had been dropped. This was not Otchigen, but some *thing* wearing him like a winter coat. And yet, that frightened her less than the visions of pain and blood that danced in her head—all of them variations on the theme of killing Voran.

"Oh, you could kill Voran easily, Sabíana. I know you would like that. For me, it would be a simple thing to arrange. I could do that for you."

Her vision swam; her thoughts moved like stale molasses. Everything about this seemed dream-like in its simultaneous vividness and indistinctness. Small details took on ridiculous clarity—the ashes fell by the hearth in a floral pattern, the blood pumped through Otchigen's temple like a wriggling worm, she had a speck of dirt under her third left fingernail. The room looked like it was underwater.

"All you have to do is desire it with all the force of your will. I will make it happen. Go ahead."

Sabíana tried to look away, but couldn't. Voran lay on the flagstones at her feet. His eyes were closed; he seemed to be in great pain, his skin pasty and splotched with red in several places; his shirt was open just enough to allow for a quick knife-thrust to the heart.

"Imagine that you are plunging that knife you hold in your hand into Voran's heart."

She gasped, sure that he couldn't possibly have seen the concealed knife.

"How did you know?" she began, her voice sounding groggy, half-drunk to her own ears.

"That you were ready to use that thing on me? You are not as subtle as you imagine, Sabíana."

Though her mind recoiled from it, the desire to plunge the knife into Voran's exposed chest uncoiled itself like an adder inside her chest, an adder that had slept her whole life, waiting for this moment. She knew Voran was not actually there, that this was some kind of phantasm conjured by her imagination or by the power that possessed Otchigen's body. But it no longer mattered. She wanted to kill Voran, and the desire was warm and sweet like too much wine.

"Just do it," he whispered. "I offer you your heart's desire. Go ahead.

Take the knife, stab him, plunge the knife in."

An ever-shrinking part of her still felt intense revulsion, but it was too late. Her hand moved up of its own accord, the knife coming out of its concealment like unfolding fangs. Voran's chest moved up and down steadily with his breath. She thought she could see the thumping of his heart through his ribcage.

"Just a little stab. So little effort, but the pleasure is great, I promise you. Go on."

"NO!" She screamed and hurled the blade into the hearth. Immediately, Voran dissolved, and the light in the room went dark. Only a glimmer remained among the smoldering logs. Sabíana faced the savage fear weighing on her and willed herself to stare at Otchigen, though she knew he was Otchigen no longer.

The creature was shadowy and black, all darkness and chaos spread out like huge wings, and its eyes burned darker than the darkest black. It did not speak so much as groan like falling boulders. She did not need anyone to tell her that this was the Raven.

"Too late, Sabíana. You've let me in."

The Raven embraced her with wings of shadow and death, and Sabíana choked under their weight and the pressure of the malice bearing down on her.

The door flew open with a crash, and a winged fury of dark blue feathers and ice-grey eyes flew into the room. Faintly Sabíana heard the music of wind whistling through reeds. Time ceased for Sabíana. All that remained was the song—wailing, keening, bursting with ancient power. Feína sang, and each note was a barrage of fire-arrows, a forest of spears, a field of slashing blades. Her wings were a rushing wind of fire, hurtling the song at the Raven. He shrieked in agony and hatred and released Sabíana. It felt like the snapping of twine, and Sabíana fell back.

But Feína was only one Sirin. Despite her song, despite his pain, his wings moved ever closer, choking her. Feína battled on with voice and talon, trying to gouge out the eyes of black flame, but he repulsed her. Her song faltered, faded, and stopped. Her fire turned into shadow. The Raven growled over his two fallen adversaries. Sabíana closed her eyes, ready for death.

A light brighter than the sun shattered the gloom of the Raven, forcing Sabíana's eyes open. Its edges were red and white flame, curling and twisting like living creatures. The Raven burned from within, and his agony shone out of his eyes like a beacon on a foggy night. A magnificent rose of light and fire swelled and blossomed from inside him, until he was completely engulfed in a writhing pyre that smelled of crushed rose petals. The Raven screamed and dissipated into a foul, swarming mist burned up in the rising fire of the hearth. Soon all that remained was the rose of fire.

"Do not fear, my own Sabíana. Look up."

Sabíana recognized Feína's voice, but it was different. What she saw was impossible. Feína was still a Sirin, but a Sirin of flame that filled the entire room with her warmth and soft fragrance. Her every fraction cascaded with kaleidoscopic light, her eyes so effulgent that Sabíana couldn't look at them directly for more than a few seconds. But somehow Feína seemed more truly a Sirin than ever before.

"Dear Feína, you saved my life! What happened to you?"

"I...Oh, by the Heights! How wonderful!" Her voice was as bracing as the sound of morning trumpets on a cold, clear day of winter. "Sabíana. You saved *me*. I can see...so much. My Lord, how wrong have we all been!"

"What is the matter? What do you see?"

Feína's eyes bored into Sabíana. The flame that she had ignited in Sabíana's heart fluttered and flared. Sabíana wanted to embrace Feína for a mad second, before she remembered Feína was fire. She laughed.

"I cannot put it in words yet, my Sabíana. But know this. What you did by resisting the Raven may have changed the fate of Vasyllia. It may have been a pebble. But sometimes, sometimes pebbles start avalanches."

There is still hope for Vasyllia. Sabíana nearly collapsed into tears before bracing herself again. I am stone. I am steel.

"I will come to you again soon. Soon."

A great wheel of fire began to spin about Feína, faster and faster until Sabíana had to look away. Even with her eyes shut, the wheel danced purple and green before her. When she opened her eyes, she was again alone in her warm room, but the sweetness of Feína's fragrance still wafted in the air, cleansing any vestige of the Raven's presence. It was only then that she noticed the body of Otchigen near the hearth. He was wasted and drawn, nearly a skeleton, but his dead face was once again his own, and it was finally peaceful.

The Ghan was tense, rubbing his hands together, and Yadovír noticed with disgust that they were nearly black with grease. He also noticed that of all the people at the table, the Ghan alone used a knife to cut his own meat. It lay on a plate next to Yadovír, its handle slippery with the grease from the Ghan's hand.

Yadovír grabbed the knife. Falling on Kalún, he plunged the knife right into the cleric's neck, through the silky hairs of his beard. The expression on the priest's face was one of complete surprise. A horrible gurgle seeped from his throat, and he fell over, dead. His eyes were still wide from astonishment. Yadovír crumpled over to the ground and vomited.

All of the Gumiren stood, hands on the defensive, shoulders tense and ready for attack. Only the Ghan remained seated, not having moved an inch. He took Yadovír by the shoulders, and pulled him back to the table. His eyes were cold and inscrutable.

"You no common man, Yadovír. You make good Gumir. Is sad for me."

"Sad?" wheezed Yadovír. His face was still warm with the priest's blood, making him want to retch again and again. "Why sad? I have done a terrible thing for you. I have killed the chief priest of Adonais. Do you not understand what that means?"

"Ghan no fool, Yadovír. I know."

"Ghan Magai." Yadovír collected whatever little was left of his self-control and forced his shuddering body to stay still. "Will you agree to my proposal? Do we have a deal?"

"Yes, *Ghan* agree."

The emphasis on his title was unmistakable and significant, but Yadovír decided to ignore it.

He sighed, and his whole body sagged with relief. He even began to laugh a little, not yet fully aware of what he had done, though that knowledge stood off in the shadows like a silent predator. The Ghan, however, continued to stare at him with hollow eyes. This was not how Yadovír expected them to seal a bargain.

"Should we not drink to our bargain?" Yadovír smiled, but the utter lack of response from any of the Gumiren chilled him. Then he noticed that the Ghan no longer looked at him, but a little behind him. Confused, he turned around.

It was a feathery, shriveled creature that would have been pitiful, if not for the eyes. They were black, but somehow they glowed with fire—not orange-red, but utterly dark. At that moment, Yadovír understood and despaired. With the desperation came a cold kind of acceptance that stopped the hammering of his heart and began to slow the blood flowing through him. So, this was why the Gumiren seemed to know everything in advance, he thought.

"You are the Raven," said Yadovír, his voice husky and not his own.

"Ah, a clever one." The voice was a bestial cackle, something between the wheeze of a sick child and the bark of a dog. "Well, you must have something you wish to tell me if you have gone through all this trouble." The Raven looked with disgust at the corpse of the priest. "But do hurry. You cannot imagine how hungry I am."

The words nearly stopped Yadovír's heart cold, but he forced himself to clear his throat. "I can be useful to you, Raven. I know the ins and outs of the city, and I am well studied in Vasyllian lore. I am an indefatigable worker, and..." As his mind blanked, he felt himself reeling from panic.

"You can be useful, yes. I agree. I do not think it will be conceding too much to tell you that I have been disappointed in a line of attack I was sure would work. No matter. You provide me with a different opportunity. I am sure you will be happy to oblige. Yes, my little rat?"

The Raven extended outward in flame and fury. The eyes turned yellow with a pit of black fire; the back expanded into billows of brown smoke like jagged raven wings. A clawed arm whipped out and picked up Yadovír by the scruff—a bird of prey dangling a rat before swallowing it. A foul stench filled his nose, and he began to dry heave.

"I accept your bargain," said the Raven.

Yadovír fainted into the stench and blood and smoke, pursued into the darkness by the face of Kalún and his surprised eyes.

When Yadovír awoke, he was in his own room back in Vasyllia, shaking in a pool of his own sweat. A rotting stink permeated the room. He tried to find the source of the smell—perhaps a mouse had died in the walls? —then realized that he was the source. The stench came from inside him.

Elder Pahomy chewed his lip; Rogdai shook his head as his eyebrows furrowed deep into his head, threatening to dig into the soft matter underneath. They both avoided looking at her, instead inspecting every possible detail of the map laid out on the table in her private chambers. Sabíana's impatience loomed over them all like a twisting snake's head, poised to strike at the first sign of the prey's lapse in attention.

"Well, my lords? I ask you again? Is it as bad as I think it is?"

Finally, Elder Pahomy answered. "It is worse, my lady. We do not have the force to dislodge this siege, and our stores are already thinning. The imprisonment of the traitors, though necessary, is vastly unpopular among the people with influence in Vasyllia."

"Not merely that," said Rogdai, scratching the back of his head, his eyes wide. "The Gumiren have built siege towers of amazing complexity. They could use them at any moment, even in winter, but now they have stopped.

There is nothing stirring their camp. Silence. Enough to drive us to madness."

"Or they simply wait for us to destroy ourselves from within," said Sabíana and sighed. She had come to rely a great deal on the opinions of only two men. It was a dangerous trust she placed on them. *I have no choice*, she reminded herself through the pain of her ever-clenched jaw.

"There is one option we have not yet considered," said Rogdai, though he did not look confident in his own idea. "Escape."

"Are you mad?" Elder Pahomy looked personally offended at the suggestion.

"Why not? I see two possibilities—one, a spear thrust through the enemies…"

"You would sacrifice most of our fighting force to do that," growled Elder Pahomy, his jowls quivering with anger, "and it may not even work then. We do not know the full number of this enemy."

"Or we may cross over the summit and flee over the back of the mountain."

Sabíana gasped, then felt the blush creep up. There was an ancient, traditional taboo about climbing Mount Vasyllia, though now that she thought of it, she could not call to mind a single good reason for it.

"Why not?" she asked, directing her gaze at Elder Pahomy.

He sighed. "Old superstitions die hard, I suppose."

She smiled at him. "For my part, I think crossing the summit in winter would be inviting disaster. How many of us would survive? And where would we go? For all we know, even Karila is destroyed."

"If that is our people's only chance of survival," said Rogdai, "why not set out farther east, toward the Steppelands? Or West, to the deserts and beyond."

"I do not know why," she said, "but I have a strong feeling that Vasyllia must not be abandoned to this enemy. It is stronger than a mere sense; it is almost a compulsion."

"I agree with you, Highness," said Elder Pahomy, and for the first time she heard respect in his voice.

The door slammed open, and in flew a mass of silver robes billowing about a thin figure hidden somewhere in their midst. It fell at the feet of Sabíana. Rogdai lifted it, none too gently. It was Yadovír.

"Oh, my lady," he finally said. "It's…unspeakable. Otar Kalún's body has been found at the gates of Vasyllia. It's rumored that he was murdered by the Gumiren for trying to strike a deal with them to save his own skin."

A novice came into the monastery. He knocked on the door, begging for admittance. The abbot came to the door, looked at him, and shut the door in his face. The next day, the novice was still there, begging for admittance. The abbot came to the door, looked at him, and shut the door in his face. On the third day, the same happened. And the fourth. And the fifth. On the tenth, the abbot came to the door, looked at him, and opened the door. The novice entered.

From "The Paterikon of the Great Coenobium"
(The Sayings, Book III, 4:8-11)

CHAPTER 25
THE WARRIOR OF THE WORD

A week of traveling the marshes satisfied even Voran's appreciation for their beauties. He and Tarin now seemed to be beyond the knowledge of any people whatsoever. The only inhabitants of these lands were the many animals—rabbits, foxes, wolves, deer, and elk with antlers like young trees. None of these paid Voran any attention, but every one of them met Tarin personally, a friend returned from long travels. The wolves in particular greeted him with high-pitched yelps, no more than friendly dogs to all appearances, though if Voran was foolish enough to extend a hand too close to any of them, the fangs were quick to flash. Tarin enjoyed them immensely, loping on all fours with them, his tongue lolling out absurdly.

They still walked day and night, but Voran grew accustomed to gathering enough strength during their short morning rests to last him the whole day. Despite the poverty of the village, Tarin didn't refuse their gifts of food. It was enough to feed an army. Voran understood: refusing such gifts, given freely, would have been worse than stealing from starving children. Such was the hospitality of Vasyllia as it used to be.

How far have we fallen, thought Voran with a pang.

Though Voran now bore four packs instead of two—*two* were filled with rocks as punishment for his insubordination—Tarin allowed him to carry the sword, and leaning on it provided some support. Secretly, Voran was grateful to Tarin. The hag's ravages had left Voran rail-thin and weak, and though he was not gaining much flesh, his muscles grew wiry like a horse's.

It was a sword like its master—not much to look at, old, tarnished, but impossible to break. Unlike every sword made in Vasyllian smithies these days, it had no fanciful decorations, no etchings on the blade, no jewels on the hilt. Only one strange sign—something between a flame and a feather, or maybe some amalgamation of both—was stamped in the place where the thumb gripped, as though it were a reminder of something.

"Lord Tarin," said Voran as they made an unusual stop in the early evening. "This mark on the hilt. Does it mean anything?"

At first Voran was sure Tarin would answer as the lunatic, but it seemed Tarin had a last-minute change of heart. "Have you heard of the Warriors of the Word?" he asked in a voice remarkable only for its normality.

Something warm and pleasant stirred in Voran's memory. The piney smell of morning fog. The thrill of hiding all night in the burial grounds. The sting of young nettles on hands and ankles, and the white spots on the skin that burned and burned. Morning sprints through dewey fields, the wet rising up the leg with every step.

"Of course," said Voran, smiling in spite of himself. "Every boy pretends to be a Warrior of the Word in childhood. The games are quite elaborate, and the stories are always the most colorful and strange."

"They are not stories," said Tarin.

"You are a Warrior of the Word?" Voran laughed, thinking Tarin was again playing the madman, but Tarin remained still and serious, until Voran's laugh subsided awkwardly. "You can't be. They're legendary, like the sleeping-woods and the..." Voran felt himself turning red.

Tarin smiled, and it was warm, like a father's. "Yes, it does take some time to come to terms with the legendary, I'll grant you that. There are few of us left. None in Vasyllia. We were established by Lassar at the very beginning, you know, but always have we been consigned to the shadows. Those youths who show enough spirit are whisked away for the training at night, and though their parents know, everyone else is told stories of sudden illness and early death. You would be surprised at how many graves in old Vasyllia are empty."

"Why the secrecy?"

"Because of the nature of evil, Voran."

Tarin busied himself about making a fire, and Voran knew now was not the time to continue speaking, though he buzzed with excitement at having a childhood dream come true. He hurried to be useful, gathering dry moss and twigs for the kindling, but Tarin immediately threw out most of it as unsuitable.

"Get me some dry birch-bark," Tarin said as he pulled out an old flint and a char-cloth from a tinderbox of wrought iron, garishly decorated in a flowing script that Voran couldn't read.

After the fire had caught, Tarin began to dig in one of the packs. He pulled out two chipped earthenware bowls and placed them on the ground. Reaching into a pouch on his belt, he pulled out a brown rag, much-used, unrolled it, and took some dried leaves with his thumb and forefingers, rubbing under his nose. Even from across the fire, Voran could smell the earthy smokiness. Tea.

Voran never had a better cup of tea, not for the rest of his life.

"I suppose, since you've gotten me to say so much, you may as well try your luck with more questions, Raven Son." Tarin's eyes smiled, though his face remained serious. He cupped the bowl in dirty hands, resting his elbows on his knees, seeming to absorb the tea's warmth with his whole body. Voran hastened to do the same. It seeped lazy comfort into his aching body.

"You said that the nature of the Warriors of the Word has something to do with the nature of evil."

"Yes." Tarin looked annoyed. "Is that a question?"

"The sign on the sword. What does it mean?" asked Voran, strangely afraid of speaking it aloud.

"Have you heard of transfiguration, Raven Son?"

Voran must have had a remarkably stupid expression, because Tarin winced. "Perhaps that is not a good place to start. We should start with the least important, and work our way inward, like a cockle shell."

Voran had not the faintest idea of what a cockle was, but he knew it would be counterproductive to ask.

"Let me start by asking *you* a question, Raven Son. Why do you think that you were attacked in the marshes after we crossed from the Lows, while nothing happened to me?"

"You obviously have power, Tarin. I do not."

Tarin nodded and chuckled. "Well, that is part of it, yes. But my kind of power never frightened the Raven and his beasts very much. No, you were attacked because you are still stained. What you did with the hag bound you to her. Yes, some of the chains loosened when you killed her, but you are not free of her curse."

"But it felt like every link of that chain burst apart when I spoke that word you gave me." A sudden insight flashed on him, and he felt foolish. "Is *that* the word that your kind is named for?"

"Well, not quite, but if we don't get into the details, yes. When you were attacked in the marshlands, you called a great power to your aid by the invocation of the name. A power even greater than...well, perhaps now's not the time to talk about that."

"Greater than what? The Sirin?"

Tarin had a pained expression, the kind a parent has when their child no longer believes in childish fancies.

"Yes, certainly greater than the Sirin. It was a taste of the power with which the Warriors of the Word are invested. But if you were to neglect yourself, if another ruse of the darkness—like the red-head in the village—were to ensnare you, you would be in great danger. They know your weak point, and now you should expect to see buxom young women throwing themselves at you in every village. I doubt you'll be able to keep chaste for long."

Voran felt disappointed, for he had hoped that his deliverance from the hag had been immediate and complete. Now it seemed it would take a deal of labor to wean himself from her continued influence. He should have known.

"Never mind," said Tarin, eyes closed as he smelled the tea. "I will help you with that. If you are willing to suffer through my training, anything is possible. The power to which we submit is an old power, a wild power, one that makes and harmonizes out of nothing in perpetuity. Not the soft, gentle divinity you Vasylli are used to worshipping in the Temple."

"You speak as the Sirin do—" Voran stopped in mid-thought. "Of course! The Sirin. They also thrive in a similar power, one equally destructive and loving. Do we even know Adonais, whom we claim to worship? Have we become so comfortable with a loving, endearing father figure that we stopped considering his unbridled power?" With chagrin, he realized by Tarin's rapt expression that he had spoken these thoughts aloud. "But what am I saying? What do I know about all this?"

To Voran's increased embarrassment, Tarin laughed out loud, making no effort to conceal his enjoyment.

"Oh, Raven Son. How close you come to wisdom, without even realizing what you are saying. If only you could see the whole truth!"

"Why not tell me?"

"Because you wouldn't believe me. You may even want to do something drastic. You may even want to kill me."

The conversation was not going as Voran had hoped. For the first time since the hag's village, Voran feared Tarin.

"If that is true," countered Voran, "then how can I know whether to trust you?

"Indeed, my falcon," Tarin said, chuckling. "You have hit on it exactly. How indeed?"

What a terrible lack of an answer, thought Voran.

The silence surrounding them deepened, until even the crackling of the bonfire faded. Gently, with no jarring effect, Voran's heart inclined to the calm surrounding Tarin like his own breath. Unbidden came the word to his lips—*Saddai*—and he whispered it, feeling the stillness reach out to him and envelop him, until the very act of questioning seemed spurious. How long they sat thus, minutes or hours, Voran never could recall. It was one of the most wondrous moments of his life.

"You begin to understand, Raven Son. Good. I hoped you would."

"Lord Tarin, it has no words, what I experienced," said Voran, breathless with wonder. "It was as if the most thunderous harmony and piercing silence mingled into one. Time raced and stopped altogether, all at a still point. It was as if I actually experienced truth personally, and yet I know nothing at all. How can I explain it? If the power of the sea could be contained in a drop of water, if the limitless potential of words could be expressed in a single thought. An infinite multiplicity in a single entity. Is it I who even speak? I don't recognize my own voice."

"What you experienced is but a splinter in the Great Tree, so to speak."

Like a sunset, the nameless experience faded, but it left behind a twilight magic.

"What else was it like, Raven Son?" Tarin's eagerness was child-like.

"It was like being on fire."

Tarin slapped his knee loudly, his smile creasing every possible inch of his face.

"Yes! You asked about the sign on the sword? It is the wing of a Sirin that has undergone the baptism of flame. It is said that, to scale the Heights of Aer, one must be baptized in fire seven times…"

Tarin grew thoughtful, and his recent inspiration seemed to run out. There was much Voran did not understand, but it seemed he would have to content himself with waiting for now. Nevertheless, he decided to try one more question.

"Why do you call me Raven Son?"

Tarin, torn from his train of thought, looked irritated. "The question of your name is not mine to answer. You will know soon enough." He stood up and began to pack. "Time we were off. Not so far now."

"Are we so close to the weeping tree?" asked Voran.

Tarin stopped, sighed heavily, and stretched himself to his full height.

"Raven Son. You must give up all thoughts of finding Living Water. You are not ready. You need to be trained. When you are ready, we will both seek it."

An avalanche of fury burst from Voran's chest. "Vasyllia is on the brink. You said it yourself. Why do we dawdle? We do not have the time!"

"You do not direct the flow of events in the world, Voran. There is a greater power than you at work here. If you go now, you will be eaten alive in minutes. Have you heard nothing of what I have said? The hag's curse still stinks on you. Do I need to remind you of the five reasons for your slavery, especially the fifth one?"

The morning sun revealed a change in the landscape. In the distance towered a line of cedars—incongruous amid the bare trees and low shrubs—standing as if sentinels over an ancient borderline.

"That is the extreme end of ancient Vasyllia," said Tarin. He hoisted his single pack and turned toward the cedars.

They reached the treeline by midday. The cedars were even more impressive in proximity, standing so near each other that the other side was barely visible, even through the trunks. There was something shimmery on the other side, as though they looked into a pool of water, not a landscape.

"That is a doorway, yes? We are entering the Lows again?"

Tarin winked at Voran and chattered like a chickadee.

As they passed through the trees, they were plunged into complete darkness. Voran could only see Tarin's outline in the shadows the trees cast. On the other side, to his disappointment, Voran saw nothing but a fallow, brown field. Drab elms, shorn of leaf, surrounded the field. Nestled under a particularly large elm, still within the shadow of the sentinel trees, three greyish wooden shacks slouched.

They appeared hardly standing, almost ready to fall over at a whisper of wind. Sloping thatch roofs, brown and ancient, bleary windows framed in dirty, cracked carvings—these were the only adornments, if they could be called that. They seemed to have been thrown together on a whim, not built according to plan. Voran's heart sank at the thought of living in such a place. Tarin, on the contrary, seemed genuinely excited, and even broke into verse again.

"I know you marvel at this land,
This paradise, my palace grand.
Does not its splendor catch the eye?
Do not its many towers high,

Replete with every earthly need
Surpass all legends that you read?"

He spread his arms out like a child presenting a favorite toy to a new friend. He actually seemed to believe in his own description of this eyesore as a palace.

The inside of Tarin's shack was as the external appearance would suggest—four walls, a rough pallet in the corner, the straw brown and pungent with neglect, a bench, a small table. On the windowsill stood several clay jars with twigs sticking out in odd assortments. Tarin diligently watered the twigs, as if they were exquisite roses. Voran half expected them to sprout on the spot, but nothing happened.

Voran's own shack was much the same, except without the twigs, for which Tarin apologized: "You have no garden, Raven Son. You have yet to earn it."

The brief tour completed, Tarin sighed and seemed to brace himself for something unpleasant. Walking to a sort of courtyard of mud between the three huts, he drove his staff into the soft ground. Turning to Voran, he said, "Raven Son. If you have any idea of what is good for you, you will water this tree"—he indicated the staff—"every morning, until it flowers. Today, since we've traveled long and you are tired, your work will be easy. Come."

He led Voran behind the largest shack, where Voran saw a large metal tool that looked like the lower jaw of some huge animal, with rusted metal teeth pointing up. It had a harness that looked fitted for an ox. Voran's heart sank.

"The land is not fit for sowing," said Tarin, his hands on his hips as he looked over the field with an expression of distaste. "I have not harrowed it in years. Hundreds of rocks in the soil, I'm sure. So. Strap the harrow on your back, since we do not have a proper ox, and you, as we already know, are my ass. Collect all the rocks and pile them up on the left side of the field."

Voran laughed. Tarin's face frosted over, turning white as his eyes grew larger. He drew his sword.

Voran stopped laughing.

"Raven Son," said Tarin calmly. "It would be wise for you to consider even the most ridiculous things that I say as indispensable. May my words be sacred scripture for you."

He turned back to his hut. "Oh, one more thing. You are never to enter my palace without abasing yourself before it, face to the ground, and saying in a loud voice, 'I, who am wretched, beg leave to enter.' Those words, please, slave. You may not rest or enter your own rooms without my permission.

As Tarin turned, Voran tried his best to burn Tarin to the ground with his eyes. But nothing happened.

The sun had crested by the time Voran began. The harrow was old, and its teeth were worn down. Sometimes it didn't pick up stones at all, just nudged them for a few feet, then gave up with a groan. Voran had to work every inch of the field with his hands, digging into the sandy soil until his fingers hit stone, then digging them out, then repeating it all again.

Soon he gave up the harrow entirely, and just crawled up and down the field, digging up stones.

The sweat poured down him and his chest burned from the inside. Worse than the fatigue was the mind-numbing boredom that accompanied such work. He imagined all the different ways he would make Tarin suffer. Soon his irritation extended to stones, trees, shacks, everything. All his thoughts became a long drawn-out grumble.

After digging up all the stones, he carried them to the left side of the field. Some of the stones were almost as large as he was. These he could not raise, but only push inch by inch to the edge of the field. Voran soon realized that he had lost much more strength than he had thought. Maybe Tarin was right. Maybe a stick-thin former warrior with no endurance wasn't the best choice to find the Living Water.

As he placed the last stone on the pile—now taller than he was—he sat on the earth and closed his eyes. A thought flitted through his mind: Tarin told him he could not rest without permission.

"AAAAAASSSSSSSSS!"

Too late.

"Raven Son, you blithering idiot! Why did you put the stones on that side of the field? I expressly told you to put them on the *right* side of the field."

He stood with one arm cocked on his hips, like an irritated mother.

"But...you said..."

Tarin shushed him.

"Did anyone give the idiot leave to speak?" He addressed the shacks directly, then cupped his hands to his ears, as if listening for their response. "No? I didn't think so. Go, fool. Carry the stones across to the other side."

"But Tarin..."

"Don't dare to call me by my name. What? Don't you have an ounce of shame? I am your lord, so call me so. Now take the stones away, and put them in their proper place. You'll never finish at this pace."

Voran sized Tarin up, thinking it was time to teach the old man a lesson. Tarin merely laughed.

"You don't want to try it, boy. Believe me."

For the next few hours, Voran carried all the stones to the other side of the field.

The next day, Tarin told Voran to return the stones back to the left side. The day after that, he told Voran to put the stones back in the soil.

"What?" said Voran, his fists balling up of their own accord.

"You heard me," said Tarin, as calmly as a corpse.

The day after that, Tarin told Voran to dig the stones up again and pile them up on the left side of the field.

"The left?" asked Voran. "You're sure?"

Tarin grinned at him stupidly and crowed.

Voran dug up the stones and piled them up again. Without even realizing it, he fell asleep while placing the last rock on the heap, still standing.

"UPUPUPUPUPUPUPUP!!!!"

Voran jumped in the air, and all the rocks fell on him, nearly burying him alive before he managed to roll aside.

Tarin was dancing around the field, smacking a wooden spoon on a frying pan. Every time he had to take a breath, he stopped and hopped in place three times, as though that would help him inhale more air. Then he danced again, smacking and screaming "UPUPUPUPUPUPUP!!!" at the top of his lungs.

It was pitch black outside. Still night.

"Raven Son! Who sleeps during the day? Get up and working!"

"Day, lord? It's the middle of the night."

"What? Look! There's the sun!"

He pointed at the thinnest moon Voran had ever seen, just rising over the tips of the sentinel trees.

"Oh, yes," said Voran, mustering as much sarcasm as he could. "How foolish of me. There's the sun."

Tarin cocked his head at him like a curious bird. "Sun? You're confused, my dear boy. That's hardly enough sliver even for a moon! I think you've gone a little soft in the head."

Tarin patted Voran on the head as though Voran were a sick dog. His expression was the kind reserved for children who insist to their parents that their imaginary unicorn friend is real.

The next day after that—the fourth day after their arrival—Tarin didn't bother Voran at all. That worried Voran more than any of the other nonsense. He approached Tarin's hut, fearing that he had forgotten something, and that he would be punished with another round of tiring absurdity. Falling on his knees before the door, he spoke through cracked lips, "My lord. I, who am wretched, beg leave to enter."

"You may enter." Tarin's face showed only composed calm. "Raven Son, did I not make myself clear to you? Why did you put all the stones in a heap? What a waste of time. Did you not understand that you had to plant them all and water them?"

That's it. The old goat's gone crazy.

"Raven Son," said Tarin with a face that suggested that the half-wit he was speaking to may have dangerous tendencies. "Do I have to use a stick on you, or will you do as you are told?"

Voran went. Though he was starved and every muscle in his body shuddered with overwork, he did as he was told. The sun rose, bathing even the lifeless tract around him with unexpected colors—hazy purples, dark reds, and oranges in the field, blue tones in the bark of the trees.

Voran had been wrong about this place. It *was* beautiful here.

As he worked, a compulsion to sing tickled at him. Soon he could hold it back no longer. He bellowed all the old sowing songs that his third-reacher education had given him. As he did, he understood them perhaps for the first time in his life. How he wished, at that moment, that he had become friends with Siloán the potter earlier. His first-reacher sowing songs must be even better.

The earth itself seemed to respond to his song, seeming more willing to accept even such lifeless seeds as he was offering it. He began to notice birdsong, tentative at first, then stronger as he worked. Somewhere very far away, he heard the music of wind whistling through reeds. Lyna was close, though still she could not approach him, it seemed.

As Voran worked, a calm seemed to rise up from the earth and hug him. He laughed.

He thought he finally understood what Tarin was doing. It was probably a trial that every young Warrior of the Word had to undergo at the early stages of training. A kind of breaking down of the self, so that the master could rebuild the student in his own image. A true warrior. Voran realized, with something like surprise, that he actually *wanted* Tarin to continue the nonsense. He'd never felt more free, more truly himself, in his life.

"Lyna, wait for me," Voran said to himself. "Sabíana, don't forget me. I will come back, and whatever the cost, I will bring back Living Water."

Eventually, Voran planted all the stones at equal intervals and watered them from a moldy bucket that threatened to fall apart at any moment.

After he finished, Voran walked on stiff legs toward the staff in the middle of their small court of huts. No longer thinking lightly of the absurd task, he diligently watered the "tree," leaving no spot of earth dry. So intent was he on his work, that he didn't notice Tarin standing behind him until he spoke.

"Voran, you may rest now." Tarin's eyes, full of tears, glimmered in the morning sun.

"Thank you, my lord, for a most interesting few days," whispered Voran, hardly able to keep his eyes open as he half-walked, half-dragged himself to his dirty straw pallet, which for one night at least was the most luxurious bed of his life.

Do you never wonder about the power of the earth? Earthquakes, avalanches, lightning strikes, deluges...It is great indeed, is it not? But do not think it is accidental. There is a race of beings that manipulates the power of the earth. And they want to be worshiped.

From "The Wisdom of Lassar the Blessed"
(The Sayings: Book I, 7:4-6)

CHAPTER 26
CONTAGION

Even in winter, life on Ghavan was loud. For Mirnían, it began with the morning bell, whose tongue he could feel beating the inside of his right temple. Lebía never heard it, but in her condition, it was entirely natural—or so he was told—to sleep through anything until ungodly hours of late morning. Then the storm-shutters slapped open, one after the other, as goodwives and their daughters and daughters-in-law traded the latest gossip from house to house. How they could have gathered so much information in the dead of night, Mirnían had no idea. Nor did he particularly wish to find out. Then the call to prayer, nearly as insistent as the morning bell. Then the endless chatter of men and women at work around the village, which was too small to provide any modicum of peace or privacy.

After a month of married life, Mirnían had found that there was really only one place where he could be comfortably alone. This morning, as Lebía lay next to him, one hand instinctively protecting her belly, the other thrown across her eyes in a position Mirnían found uncomfortable even to look at, he felt an especial need of that place.

It was the work of a few minutes to dress and be out of doors. Luckily, not many of the villagers were up yet this morning, so the going was quiet. He gritted his teeth as he passed the house of the baker and his wife—she was always very solicitous about Lebía's health, and the word-for-word repetition of their daily conversation grated beyond endurance—but they were either busy or sleeping in. As soon as he passed, he rushed along an uphill

THE SONG OF THE SIRIN

path, then down an incline to the rocky beach. Every step on the old snow crunched. He was sure that someone would accost him with yet another pointless conversation. But no. Before he knew it, he was in the thickest part of a pine grove.

The pines leaned down a little over his head, as if bowing in greeting. He didn't mind the noise *they* made—as opposed to the women in the village—though here the trees were a little too quiet. Most of all he preferred the noise of the sea, its gentle and constant complaint about something so old it had long forgotten what it was.

Finally, the deaf stillness of the forest gave way to the suggestion, then the echo, then the sea itself—slate-grey near the beach, then deepening to black farther out. He had never imagined water could look so black. There was a mystery and a beauty to it, one he never thought he would appreciate in a color always associated with the darkness in stories. He sat on his knees on the last stone before the water. The water tried to reach him, but lazily, as if it never got enough sleep, despite the endless nights of winter. He agreed with the water, once again wondering how it was possible to constantly want more sleep in a season when ten hours a night was not considered over-much.

Such trifling half-thoughts took up all his time at the sea, doing what they were supposed to. Everything would fade into the soft complaints of the sea and his mind—the disaster of Vasyllia, the unhappiness of Sabíana, the death of Dar Antomír, the fear that gnawed at him as Lebía's paleness daily tried to match the new-fallen snow for whiteness. She was transformed by what she carried within her. The mystery was too deep for him to fathom, and more often than not he felt isolated from that almost sacred reality of the child inside her.

There goes the bell again, he mused as the sound reached him like the sun through a heavy fog. He continued to stare over the water, hoping to glimpse a rare otter, or even a pair of them entwined by their paws, as they did for hours, even as they slept. The ringing continued, still a haze in his mind, until he snapped to attention, like falling out of a dream. That was not merely a bell. Its insistence, it regularity, its color—that was an alarm.

Lebía lay on the floor of the bakery, covered with blankets up to her chin, though her right hand lay atop the covers. It was so pale, it was nearly blue. Her lips *were* blue, and the skin around her eyes was splotchy, though that could have been the light of the fire in the oven. But it was not all this that poured terror like ice water down Mirnían's throat, but the complete lack of expression on her face. She looked dead.

"...knew something like this would happen, I did." The baker's wife had been chattering on for minutes now, but he heard little until that moment. "Weak blood. Nothing to worry yourself about too much, my dear boy. Now, mind you, I don't think we have enough stores of game to toughen her blood back up."

"What? What are you saying?" Mirnían croaked, his throat dry and gummy.

The baker's wife was a round woman just the far side of middle-aged, though her skin was smooth and her quick smile showed the lasting vestiges of a former beauty, of a sort. Bits of grey-flecked hair kept getting entangled in her temple rings. She seemed ashamed of it, and would retie the scarf every few minutes, no matter what the conversation.

"And you, a future Dar? Silly. It's normal when a woman expects a baby. The baby takes all of mother's best blood. Lebía should be all right, my boy. If we can find enough meat, that is."

Mirnían was confused by the constant talk of meat and blood. He was sure that Lebía was in the first stages of leprosy, but he didn't dare speak it aloud.

I've done it, he thought. *Everything I touch gets infected and dies.*

"There isn't enough meat for her in the village," said the baker, who was a passable leech as well, though where a Vasylli first-reacher would learn such things, Mirnían couldn't imagine. They were still talking about meat, to Mirnían's annoyance, but the repetition of the theme began to suggest to his limping mind that perhaps it was important.

"Is that all it is?" he asked, incredulous. "She needs more meat?"

"I see no other reason for concern," said the baker's wife. "She has been overworking herself, yes, but now it seems the baby and her body will force her to rest and sleep. It is well that she lives here, not in some mountain city where no one cares for anyone else." She harrumphed. "The entire village will take care of our swanling."

He had no doubt they would, and it relieved him. But something else—a thought, or the beginnings of a thought—added excitement to the relief, something that he almost felt guilty about.

"Matron," he said to the baker's wife, "will you be kind enough to take charge of Lebía's care for a day or two? I have determined to go hunting."

"But there is no meat to be had on the island. Not after all that feasting," protested the baker.

"I know," he said, hoping the excitement now flaring inside him like the fire-light over the mountains would not show in his face. "I intend to try the mainland."

Mirnían had come so close with a few of the arrows, but the deer escaped him. One of the arrows even had the slightest dab of red gore, tipped with a fluff of downy fur. Always at the last possible moment, it ran, as though it were prescient. A few times Mirnían nearly screamed in frustration, but he must not. No need to scare anything that might not have caught scent of him yet. Though he had been hunting for three days, enough of his original excitement remained to keep him going forward at full-tilt.

It was not merely deer he was after. Seeing Lebía in that state, pale as death, finally suggested to him a horrible truth—if he was still marked by leprosy, however latent, he was a threat to her and to their child. He needed to find healing. He needed to finish the quest for the Living Water, and quickly. How, he had no idea. But a strange kind of sureness was on him; a buzzing excitement that suggested the possibility of merely crossing the next ridge and finding another waystone, this one with a much more helpful direction. In the meantime, he hunted in vain.

He didn't know the part of the world where he hunted. The trees were mossier, somehow more sinister and older than at home or on the island. Even the sounds were foreign. The trees creaked in the wrong tune, the needles of the conifers were the wrong length and far too sharp, the smells were old and dank, as though the trees didn't breathe in this part of the world. Then a creeping certainty—he was being watched—tickled at the back of his neck and needled at the pit of his stomach. Shadows became hidden beasts waiting for the pounce.

Something immensely bright flew over his head and landed in the forest ahead. It was round and burning, like a sun fallen from the sky. He couldn't hear the force of impact, but then he noticed that sound itself seemed to cease. He drew his sword and crouched forward, half-crawling, using his other hand to find the quietest path. Smoke filtered through the trees, but it did not burn his eyes. It was pungent, like the scented resin burned in the Temple, and it seemed to contain flashes of light, like small bolts of lightning, within it.

Mirnían saw that an entire section of forest had been annihilated, though there was no fire except for a few smoldering logs at the edge of the cleared circle. In the middle stood a monolith of stone, or at least so it seemed at first. Then the smoke cleared enough for a full moon to shine milky-blue, illuminating not a stone, but a giant warrior.

He was the height of a tree, the width of a house. His mail was golden-red, reaching down to his knees. His helmet was peaked and open-faced; its horsehair flowed down to mingle with his own hair like molten gold. The ear-covers were gilt serpents of iron that seemed ready to burst out of the iron and bite the giant's neck. His eyes glowed, and his features were smooth like marble and beautiful like an iceberg. He held a tear-drop shield bearing the same twisting serpent as on his helmet, and the sword in his right hand was taller than a full-grown man. Flames of dark red played around his body, and Mirnían was reminded of the circle of fire around the darkened sun he had seen in Vasyllia, what seemed so many years ago.

"Your light has dimmed of late, Mirnían, scion of Vasyllia." The giant's voice was surprisingly gentle, though it echoed. Mirnían had no doubt that this was the giant's whisper, and that he could tear down trees with a shout.

"I have been watching you for some time. This sedate, quiet life you have chosen. It does you no good. When my brother saw you last, you glowed with black fire. Now your sister is alight, and you are in wane."

Mirnían, without realizing it, had cast aside his sword somewhere and stood at the foot of the giant, feeling for all the world like a two-year-old being scolded by his mother.

"Who are you?" he managed to whisper.

"I am the serpent of fire, the old power of the earth, the ancient lore long forgotten. You may call me Zmei."

"What would you have of me, Zmei?"

The giant smiled, though his sun-eyes remained beyond all emotion.

"That is the right question, future Dar. I would have you healed. I would have you empowered. I would have you take your rightful place as Dar of Vasyllia."

Mirnían scoffed. "You must be so old that you do not know of the Raven. Soon there will be no Vasyllia to rule."

The giant laughed, and the earth rose and fell like a wave, throwing Voran down to the scorched grass. "The Raven? Do not make me laugh. A doddering fool who cannot understand that his time to die came centuries ago. A leech whose power derives from the power of others. He is nothing, a mere phantasm."

"If you are so powerful, why is he ascendant?"

The laughter stopped, and the world seemed to hang in the balance, waiting for Zmei to pronounce judgment on it.

"It was not my time yet." He rumbled, his fire dimming a fraction.

Mirnían snickered, then wondered at himself. When had he become so comfortable with the dark and legendary?

"I have never heard of you, Zmei," he said, sneering. "You are not spoken of in the legends."

"I predate the legends, Mirnían," he said. "I was here before any Covenant, before any Adonais, before any Lassar. My power is not like theirs. It is the power of the earth itself."

"You lie, giant. No power existed before Adonais."

The giant's half-smile returned. "Oh, is that so? Tell me, wise one. Why has that sore under your arm not healed, for all the power of the Sirin and their precious Adonais?"

"Are you baiting me? It is leprosy. Leprosy cannot be healed."

In answer, the giant thrust his sword into the ground, shaking the trees as though they were mere bushes, and reached down with his finger. Mirnían wanted to run away screaming, but he held his place and didn't flinch, sensing that this was some sort of test. The fires licking the edge of Zmei's finger touched Mirnían, and his entire body flared with pain for a moment, then it faded. Something was different about him, though his senses were confused about it. He touched the place where his sore had been, and his touch revealed nothing but smooth skin. A wave of exhilaration rose up inside Mirnían.

"Very well, Zmei, you have my attention. But I know how this works. You require something of me in return for your generosity. What must I sacrifice?"

The giant smiled, and there was something fatherly in his expression.

"Ah, you poor child. The world has used you ill. But the *earth* will not. I require nothing. It is enough for me to see you rise in power, and to know that my gift began it."

"I don't believe you."

"Do as you will, Mirnían," said Zmei, chuckling. "Only know that if you seek to use my power, the only power that made you whole, you must always force events to turn in your own favor. Never wait for things to happen. *Forge* events. I happen to know that your steps are directed to a place of great moment. The Sirin was right in one thing—you will face your old enemy, Voran. And he is being trained in another power, a power not as old as mine, a power that revels in weakness and submission. You must exert your control, your will over him. If you do, you will have access to his power, which is not insignificant. That is the road to Vasyllia."

The image of Voran standing on his knees as the hag danced around him flashed in Mirnían's memory. A rush of hatred rose up with his gorge, and he nearly vomited from its fury.

"My pleasure, Zmei," he said, and a savage excitement took him by the throat until he laughed from the sheer thrill of it. "It is the duty of any future Dar to ensure all traitors receive their just reward. Lead on, Zmei. I will follow you to the very edge of the world."

The giant rumbled in laughter. "As a matter of fact, that is exactly where we are going."

The fire licking around his edges consumed him until he was a nearly circular ball of red flames, dark as blood. Something seethed within the circle, and it resolved into a sinuous neck attached to a scaly body with a humped back, the legs long like a horse's and covered in piebald scales. It had horse-like hooves and tufted ears that were too big for its head, a strange amalgam of a lizard and a horse, but not in the least awkward-looking. Its mane and tail were flame, and yet they were solid things that you could hold.

"Mount," said Zmei, "if you have the stomach for it."

The world spun in all directions, with Zmei as the eye in a storm. When Mirnían closed his eyes, he felt no movement, but as soon as he opened them, he felt sick. Mountains formed around him like piles of newly-churned butter, craggy ridges of hard grey-brown rock with hardly any plant life. As they hardened and ceased their strange, undulating dance, Mirnían breathed in, and felt the sparseness of the air. It left him giddy.

The giant stood next to him, looking over the dips and rises of the crags. They stood before a tall conical peak, probably the highest point of the ridge.

"There it is," said Zmei, pointing at the tip of the peak.

Mirnían saw nothing of importance. "What am I looking at?"

Zmei sighed. "I had thought that maybe..." He shook his head. "The weeping tree is on the tip of that conical rock. You cannot see it; neither can I. But it is there. Just not in this Realm; it is in the Mids of Aer. Very soon Voran will find a way to it. We will help him find it."

"Why can you not find it yourself, if your power is so great?" Mirnían was beginning to doubt his strange new friend.

"You have much to learn about the world, young pup," said Zmei, no longer smiling. "Try to pay attention."

With that, he spun into his serpent-horse form again and disappeared in a storm of fire and thunder. Mirnían sat down in the sparse shelter of a twisted pine, and closed his eyes to sleep.

There will come a time when the glory that is Vasyllia will fade. Much knowledge will be lost. Much wisdom. Much beauty. But we, the Warriors of the Word, will preserve it. In time, one will come who will have to restore it all.

A private letter from Vohin Elían to Dar Martinían, year 643 of the Covenant

CHAPTER 27
BLACK TURNIPS

Voran faced Sabíana, but she refused to look at him. For all his desire, he could not approach her. She sat at the edge of a still, oval pool, ringed on all sides by holly trees and osiers, their silver bark luminescent. She sang, and she and the song were somehow one. As her fingers plaited her black hair, they seemed to be plaiting music as well, the melody intertwining in and out of itself. Then she looked at him, and her eyes were all wrong. They were blue and cold, and too narrowly set together. Then her nose shifted slightly in her face, and green sprouted in her hair like fast-growing moss. She smiled, and her canines were long and sharp. The ground gaped at Voran's feet, and he fell awake.

The terror was a foreign thing in his chest, a parasite feeding on him from within. Just a dream, he reminded himself. Just a dream.

This was the third night that the drowned girl, one of the three Alkonist who ruled in his favor against the hag, intruded on his dreams of Sabíana. Now, Voran no longer doubted she had done it intentionally. Every night, she seemed to be digging deeper into him, provoking, and today the unpleasant stir of lust for her was intense, yearning for release.

He threw aside his wool coverlet, stale with sweat, and ran out into the winter night with no shirt or boots. The biting cold, quickly turning to fire on his skin, was effective at purging the desire that she kept feeding him at night.

"You must be dying here, Voran," said a girl's voice, husky in a sultry way. The drowned girl, naked in spite of the cold, sat in the branches of a nearby oak. Her hair still waved as if she were underwater. The darkness did more than enough to hide the details of her nakedness, but Voran still squirmed. The unpleasant stirring was not going away this time.

"Why do you torture me?" he whispered, not wanting to awake his master. "I want no part of your games. I remember very well what you wanted to do with me. Tickling, was it?"

"Oh, it would have been such fun, I promise." Her laugh was lunatic. As if to taunt him, the moon decided to pick that moment to show its nearly full face.

"For you, I have no doubt. But I imagine I know what happens to the men whom you... tickle."

"Really, Voran, you are so morbid. Not everything in the world is out to kill you or eat you, you know. I can't help it if I am desirable to such as you."

He guffawed, though his stomach still churned from the thoughts he was trying to beat back from his conscious mind—images of white flesh and red lips.

"What do you want?" He spat in her direction. The spittle froze before it reached the ground.

"I want what you want. The right thing to happen. I want you to go on your quest, to find the weeping tree, to heal Vasyllia, and to live happily ever after."

"No, you do not. You want something else."

"Why do you men always think every woman desires them? Could I not want something simply because it is the right thing to do?"

She sounded sincere enough, but the moon did not provide enough light to test the truth of her eyes.

"What are you suggesting?" he asked.

"I am a bearer through the levels, like the white stag. I can take you to the weeping tree in a heartbeat."

"How?"

"Well," she looked away like a demure maid, and he thought she blushed, "I am not a beast you can simply ride. I am a creature of love and passion. You would have to bed me, properly. That is my only way of passage."

Voran laughed. "I knew there would be a fee."

She slapped the branch like a petulant three-year-old. "It's not my fault. I'm a rusalka. It's what I am. I merely give you a choice to fulfill your vocation."

"You offer me a way back to my love by taking it from me?"

She tossed her hair back in a parody of an elegant lady's gesture. "I am basically a goddess, anyway, Voran. Your princess can't hold it against you if you are bedded by a goddess."

He shook his head, smiling in spite of himself. He didn't like to admit it, but it was a tempting offer.

"Go away," he said. "If I need you, I will call for you."

"That is really all I wanted from you, dear little thing. Was that so hard?"

She was gone, and the place where she had been was nothing more than an oddly shaped branch illumined by the moon into the semblance of human shape. Had he dreamed it all? He returned to bed and was asleep again in moments, this time dreamless.

"Up, up, you ass!"

The daily wakeup call was more joyful this morning, to Voran's surprise. Gold dust was suspended above his head, caught by the sun's ray, turning softly as if dancing to an unheard tune.

"Come, Raven Son. Look what you've done!"

Normally, Voran would have cringed at his words, expecting a fresh round of pointless work. But the joy in them—a child's undiluted outpouring—was obvious. Voran heard thumping outside. It seemed Tarin was dancing in the snow.

Then Voran saw the reason for Tarin's excitement, and all tiredness fell from him like molting skin. The field—despite the snow, despite the cold, despite the stones—was covered in strong, green shoots reaching up to Tarin's knees. Turnips. Voran laughed, and Tarin laughed with him.

For the first time since they arrived almost a month ago, Voran had a day of rest. Tarin himself harvested the black turnips—each as big as a melon—and stored them in the third shack. He sang and screeched a litany of birdcalls and growls and whines and whistles, as if practicing his varied knowledge of animal languages.

Then he fell silent for hours, a silence almost impossible to bear. Not that it was empty. On the contrary, there was too much uncomfortable presence in the silence, as though Tarin was bracing for something wonderful or terrible that would happen very soon. Voran hoped that meant they would be leaving soon. He had no desire to force the issue with Tarin, especially since his only way of leaving the Lows seemed to be a half-crazy drowned girl with improper designs on him.

That evening, the smoke rising from Tarin's small roof-hole was scented with pine. Voran's heart gamboled like a child. They were having tea again. Perhaps this was a sign of important conversations to come. The invitation came as soon as the sun went down.

Tarin's table was laden with two old radishes and a black turnip, still steaming from the boil—a veritable feast. The same two earthenware bowls were already filled with resin-thick black tea. Voran's mouth watered.

"A good day today, Raven Son. An occasion. And we have been working hard. A bit of a chat will do us both some good. Don't let the bow get too stretched, you know? It might crack, and then what good would all the arrows be?"

Voran chuckled. It was exactly the kind of thing Dar Antomír used to say in the old days.

"But I can answer your first question even before you ask it. No, it is not yet time for us to seek the weeping tree."

Voran's heart sank, along with all the pleasant sensations of the previous moments. The turnip turned hard; the radish was peppery; the tea faded to ash in his mouth. A storm threatened somewhere in the back of his head, but it was still distant enough for him to remain calm. For now.

"There was something that made me wonder," said Voran. "The Alkonist. They are higher beings than both humans and Sirin, yes? But they seem just as susceptible to vice. If they are higher, should they not be also... more virtuous?"

Tarin's expression soured, as though his tea was too tart. "That is a very simple way of imaging the world, Raven Son. It sounds like you see the hierarchy of the world's levels as a great ladder, the earth on the bottom and the Heights of Aer on top, with Adonais's throne somewhere in the clouds."

Voran wisely kept silent, though the invitation to comment was there. Tarin looked pleased.

"The world is not like that, Voran. It is difficult to find a good analogy, but I imagine it is something like this. When you peel an onion, eventually you reach the smallest layer and the golden middle, yes? Well, imagine that instead of getting smaller, the onion gets bigger every time you peal a layer."

"The middle would be infinitely great," said Voran, unable to contain his eagerness. Tarin looked as though he were considering boxing his ears.

"Yes, precisely. The earth is the outer layer of the onion, and only to the external appearance is it the largest layer. Every deeper layer is more complex and greater. But it does not end there. Each layer is not whole, but porous, like a good cheese, and the layers of reality in those places fold in on each other."

"That is why there are doorways to the other levels, such as the Lows, yes?"

Tarin nodded. "As for the Alkonist and the Lows of Aer, although technically speaking the Lows *are* higher up, that only means that there are fewer places for evil to hide. Earth is a realm of shadow. Evil hides better here than in the Lows, but that does not mean there is less evil in the Lows. Does that answer your question?"

Voran nodded. "But inspires new ones, of course." He smiled sheepishly, and Tarin laughed, giving Voran enough encouragement to ask again.

"When I walked with the Pilgrim, I was able to cover great distances of space and, I think, time, by crossing the boundary between the earth and the Lows on the white stag. Is it possible to cross the boundary when the bearer is on the same side as you are?"

"Crossing the layers on a bearer is extremely dangerous, Voran. Effectively, you are ripping a new hole in the barrier between the worlds. Every time you do that, you give access to the evil things that seek the shelter of earth's shadows. Even the most powerful use such means only sparingly. And no, bearing only works if the two are on opposite sides of reality. I do not know why. I think it is a natural defense mechanism, something to discourage easy passage to and fro."

Voran was amazed at his master's volubility. He hurried to press his advantage. Who knew when he would be so chatty again?

"The Raven," said Voran. "I want to know what his power is. Why is he so dangerous?"

Tarin harrumphed with a rueful smile. "If only more would ask that question, Voran. Things would be much better in the world. Recall the story of the bear cub that I told the children. The hunger for killing that seemed to possess it, turning it into a monster? That is an effective illustration of the Raven's power. He is endless, ravenous hunger—for self-ness, for acquisition of power over others, for pleasures. He eats everything in his path. If there were nothing left in the world, he would end up eating himself.

"Do you remember when I mentioned transfiguration?"

Voran nodded.

"I told you only a part of the story. It is true that humans and Sirin can ascend all the way to the Heights of Aer through the seven baptisms of fire. The other orders of creation also have that privilege. Through every baptism, they transfigure, losing more and more of the old, and becoming gradually something new. But true transfiguration is a painful process that can take entire lifetimes."

He stopped, then began to whisper, his eyes screwed up in concentration, as he had a silent conversation with himself. After coming to a decision—punctuated by a vigorous nodding of his head and a hard slap on his knee—he hugged himself, crossed one leg over another, and looked at a point somewhere to the right and above Voran's head.

"Have you heard of the concept of universal harmony? No? No, I don't suppose philosophy is much taught in the seminary these days. Pity. Anyway..." he coughed twice and breathed sharply in through the nose. "The world, as intended by the Lord of the Realms, is like music. Every voice—that is, every reasoning creature—must sing its assigned part for the song to sound well. That may sound limiting, as though the notes that determine the fate of the world have already been written, but that is not quite the truth. There is a great deal of room for improvisation, as long as harmony is maintained throughout. Thus, the low voices must not break the flow of the high, so that each moment is a beautiful chord. Do you understand so far?"

"Yes, and I think I can see where you are going with this."

"I doubt that," said Tarin, grinning widely before assuming his previous faraway expression. "Try to imagine that one of the voices improvised wildly, beyond the scope of the harmony. What would result?"

"The music would be jarring and ugly."

"Precisely. Now, what if not one voice, but many would simultaneously break the harmony to seek their own melodies."

"The noise would be horrible."

"Perhaps. Or, if they were very talented and attuned to each other, they could make a new, strange, different music. Do you see?"

"Yes, I think so."

"Well, something like this happened. Transfiguration is a gift given from the Heights to those who ascend. But some creatures were weary of waiting, and tried to ascend themselves. They found ways of changing their physical form, thereby gaining some of the higher realms by stealth, not by virtue."

"Like the changers of Nebesti lore, yes? The stone I saw turn into a wolf-man in the forest."

"You encountered one of *those* and lived to tell the tale? You are strangely lucky, Voran. Yes, the changers are lower orders of such creatures. Their masters were originally High Beings who willingly combined their natures into a single being, shedding their personal existence to become an amalgamated High Being of tremendous power. This chimaera then stormed the

Heights of Aer with an army of changers, intending to seize control of the Realms."

"The Raven," Voran whispered, his skin prickly and cold.

"Yes, that is one of its names. This abomination appeared lordly and beautiful, and many other beings were tempted to follow him. But the Heights' retribution was swift and terrible. The changers and the Raven were stripped of their original forms, which they had shed so lightly, and they were left as beings of pure will. The now formless ones realized the agony of being formless, the agony of infinite desire, infinite will without the power of fulfilling infinite desire, of bringing that will into action.

"They wandered as their hunger increased. The Raven gathered them to himself, having found a way to allay the hunger temporarily. Whenever a creature of the lower orders—human, Sirin, Alkonist, Mujestva, Vila, Serpent, or many others—was tempted to follow the Raven and his horde, the formless ones found a way to possess their forms. But their hunger was so great that they quickly devoured every form they assumed, and still their hunger grew. That is the Raven's power."

"But what would possibly tempt anyone to follow such a monster?"

"His cunning is old, and he lies very well. He is a master of gathering power to himself, and he often allows his allies the fulfillment of their most cherished desires and dreams before he devours them. And he is a chimaera. He enjoys wearing the form of a creature of Light. It is his most effective weapon. He can afford to give much to his followers, even things that are initially good, because he inevitably devours all his children."

"That is why he seeks the weeping tree, is it not?" asked Voran, the terror growing. "Living Water is a healer. He thinks it will give him a permanent form."

"So the legends say. Permanent and immortal form, yes."

Voran jumped up and threw the cup of tea to the earth, shattering it.

"Then why do you persist in keeping me here? If the Raven finds the Living Water, it is not merely Vasyllia that will fall, it is everything! All the Realms!"

Tarin remained immobile and calm, though his voice sharpened to a knife's edge. "Have you not considered, dear boy, that because of your *association* with the hag, the Raven might be trying to use *you* to find the Living Water?"

All of Voran's bluster evaporated in an instant, as cherished hope after cherished hope collapsed in a heap near the shards of earthenware at his feet.

"You have declared the kind of war that takes no prisoners," said Tarin.

"And you are not ready to fight it. If you were to be found alone by the enemy, you would not be destroyed, no. You would succumb to the Raven. You would become his creature in a heartbeat. If you do not believe me now, I fear you will soon enough. You need a guide, a master, until the moment when you can so guard your thoughts and inner movements of the heart that not even a stray intention will escape that can aid the enemy."

"Is that why you call me Raven Son?" Voran asked, his voice hardly more than a whimper.

Tarin fell on his knees before the standing Voran and extended his arms outward—the traditional gesture of a supplicant. Amazement gripped Voran at the sight.

"Voran, my son," he said, and his voice broke. "Do you not know that when I took you from the hag, I took upon myself your suffering, your pain? I feel everything you do. Every doubt that pains you, every wound that ails you pierces me as though it were my own. I call you Raven Son because that is what you must never become. Raven, the color deeper than black, is a color for the fallen sons, not the sons of light."

Voran couldn't halt his own tears. He leaned down to embrace the old warrior, feeling something he never thought he would feel again—pain and sorrow and joy like fire. He had found another father.

Tarin tensed like a bowstring at its breaking point.

"Voran, did you hear that?"

It was faint, but unmistakable. Something growled outside Tarin's window.

Trust in the Heights with all your heart; lean not on your own understanding.

The wisdom of men is madness with the Heights; the wisdom of the divine is inscrutable to mortals.

Above all things, guard the ways to your heart and sow its pathways with divine seeds, so that the thoughts of your heart sprout the wisdom of faith.

In the vale of the dark shadows, seek the guiding star of trust in the Most High.

From "The Wisdom of Lassar the Blessed"
(The Sayings, Book I, 15:4-9)

CHAPTER 28
THE FUNERAL

Sabíana was swathed in furs and warmed somewhat by the braziers in each corner of the stone gazebo. Built near the altar of the Grove of Mysteries, it was almost completely concealed from the view of the people in the Temple. She had been here, trying to contemplate in peace, for the whole night.

One of the guards hiding behind the redbarks sneezed. Elder Pahomy, standing by her side, sighed in exasperation.

So much for the secret guard, thought Sabíana with a smile.

She had been against it, fearing that any public display of protection, however secretive, would only play into the conspirators' hands. She wanted to show her people that she feared nothing, that there was nothing to fear. But the unexpected treachery of Kalún convinced her to listen to Elder Pahomy's suggestions. Twenty of the best seminary men, fully armed, hid among the trees.

"Elder Pahomy," she said, turning to him. She was sick of trying to concentrate. It was useless. "Tell me. Do *you* think Yadovír was complicit in Kalún's treachery?"

"Yes, I do, Highness."

She sighed.

"You do see what a position I'm in, don't you?"

Elder Pahomy spread his arms out in an apologetic gesture. "I do, Highness."

She was momentarily annoyed by his prescience.

"Speak it out for me," she said curtly.

"Yadovír claims to have tried to save Kalún from the Gumiren. It's made him into a bit of a hero with exactly the kind of people who are most sympathetic with the traitors. If you imprison Yadovír..."

"I could have a full-blown rebellion on my hands." She sighed again, then felt disgusted with herself for it. "He's an odd one, that Yadovír. Do you remember how my father invited him to the palace to witness the execution? Well, I caught him staring at me with the strangest look. Adoration, but contempt also. It unnerved me. Caused me to shudder physically. He noticed, and his face changed so quickly into open malice and hatred that I was afraid for my life, for a second."

"He wouldn't have dared to do anything. Not with all the—"

"Of course not, Elder. That's not what I mean. But I think him capable of exactly the sort of treachery that got Kalún killed. Only he wouldn't die. Too good with words."

Elder Pahomy said nothing. His expression gave nothing away either. To her own surprise, she was grateful for it. She didn't need someone to coddle her. She needed to be decisive. On her own.

"Do you know?" She smiled at him. "I think I need the spectacle of this funeral as much as the people do."

Elder Pahomy smiled. It was a gentle, fatherly smile, a rare gift from the old warrior. She felt warm. *Now I'm ready,* she thought.

Soon the Temple began to fill with people. They were silent, even sullen, though nearly everyone seemed to find comfort in the serene beauty of the redbarks and the whispering intimacy of the aspens, still orange-clad despite full winter.

The great bells exploded in cacophony, all of them ringing at once, the kind of peal usually reserved for weddings and the births of new children to the Dar. She hoped it would raise a dormant half-hope in the hearts of those assembled. The very rocks seemed to sing aloud in welcome to the bodies of the last great men of Vasyllia. Clerics robed in purple trimmed with gold—vestments crafted in the likeness of ancient Vasylli armor—entered the Temple in rows and began to sing. The hymn was fierce and olden, in a dialect not spoken any more save in certain Temple ceremonies. The curious martens and foxes amid the trees stopped and harked to the song, laden with the grace of the ages. Behind them came the coffin-bearers—lightning-white against the profusion of dark furs worn by the people. Then, the singing and the ringing ceased in a single thunderous chord that threatened to topple all the assembled to the ground with its force, just as the two bodies were placed on a bier in the midst of the Temple.

The master bell tolled its velvety call forty times. Sabíana saw the bell in her mind, an ancient relic of old Vasyllia, made in a time when the art of pouring great bells was not lost. It was adorned with reliefs of legendary beasts too old to be named, with deeds of heroes raised to the rank of demigods, some of whom were still remembered in the songs of blind Bayan, Dar Antomír's ancient verse-weaver who still lived in a high chamber in the palace.

The final toll rang, then continued to pass through the crowd like a rising tide. Sabíana followed it, surrounded by her guard, many of whose tears streamed down their beards. She took her place by the bier, and the clerics surrounded her and the bier before beginning the lament. Sabíana felt the blood rush to her face as the bass voices among the priests took the drone, deepening the sound of the singing into eternity. She wanted to weep with the men, but forced her face to remain as stone.

Acolytes lit and scented censers, and the smoke rose to accompany the chant offered on behalf of the fallen Voyevoda of Vasyllia and the greatest Dar of their time. Slowly, with each new hymn sung by the weeping warriors and the priests, the nightmare of Otchigen's fate, though not fading completely from memory, molded itself into a hopeful longing for his eternal rest. If any man deserved to find lasting peace, it was he, for he had suffered the ultimate ignominy and pain.

Soon all the people, their voices cracking in the cold, the steam from their speaking merging with the smoke of the censers, joined in the final lament.

Peace eternal to your servants
In your halls, O Adonais
Grant this.

Sabíana took a torch from one of the warriors and lit the biers herself. She paused, savoring the hunger of the flames, forcing the spectacle to imprint itself on the back of her eyes. This is what will happen to us if we do not prevail, she thought.

She turned to look at the people. Seeing them made her realize how right she had been to burn these two—inseparable in life, as in death—in the same ceremony. It was as she hoped. There was a calm acceptance of the burden of what it meant to live—to carry on the work that others, so much greater than we, have started, but not finished. I can mold this, she said to herself.

"My people, go in peace!" Sabíana said in almost a whisper, but her voice carried well. "Rejoice as is meet for the passing of our father Dar Antomír, but be mindful of our constant danger. Sleep not the sleep of the unprepared. Any day the call to battle will sound, and though it be in the dead of night, may your sword-hands be not found empty."

As if on cue, the bells accompanied her last word with a thunderous ovation. Many eyes glimmered, ever so slightly, with hope that had been dead only hours before.

"Highness," said Rogdai a bit behind her. A loud thump indicated he had fallen on one knee. He was doing that a lot more these days, and every day a more worshipful look came over his face as he watched her. Poor man. She turned and nodded to him, half-smiling the graciousness she didn't feel in her heart.

"There is something I believe you would like to see," he said, his voice slightly tremulous. But it wasn't fear in his voice, not this time.

Yadovír saw Sabíana take Rogdai's arm and walk back to the palace. Even now, there was a fresh pain from the wound she had inflicted on him. A small part of him still wished that he could tell her everything in the hope of seeing her eyes light up with hope. It was only a small part of him, though, and it was drowned out by the hatred that glowed like white metal in his chest. That part of him was disgusted to see how many of the warriors had been moved by the funeral and were now obviously Sabíana's men. Many of them now worshiped the ground she walked on.

"Don't worry, my rat," a slithery voice sounded in his head. "Let them have their moment. It will not be long now."

Rogdai led Sabíana to one of the many open-air cloisters of the upper level of the palace. The snow was eldritch under the nearly full moon. In the center of the cloister, adorned with the remnant of trailing vines and asters still in bloom, stood one of the palace's many small bell towers. It was built over an enclosed pool of spring water blessed by the Sirin, as the tales told. It was also said, Sabíana remembered, that this particular tower's bells quietly rang on their own some mornings, beating melodies that no bell ringer knew any more.

They entered the white chamber of the spring through a low, crumbling doorway. The room was covered in a series of panels, framed in gold. Each panel contained an ancient fresco of a king, a queen, an ascetic, a saint, or a hero. They all wore the flowing robes of Lassar's time, painted in a flat, abstract style with exaggerated poses and over-large eyes. The colors of the robes were still bright. Sabíana realized they must have been made of crushed precious stones--the most expensive kind of paint, used only on the most sacred icons. Some of the panels were so old that the faces looked intentionally rubbed out. Perhaps they had been, it occurred to her. Nothing was impossible any more.

Even in winter, the spring was not frozen. She knelt before the pool and dipped her face in the water three times, then took the silver flagon and drank.

"In here, my lady," said Rogdai, indicating a blank wall behind the pool.

"There is nothing there, Rogdai," she said, confused.

"That is what I thought as well," he said.

She followed. As it turned out, there was a faint outline in the wall—a low doorway hidden by age and cracked mortar. She was sure no one had opened it in generations. Rogdai took a candle from the many stands in the chamber and pushed at the door, which creaked as it lurched open.

Ahead was a stairway leading down into another chamber, apparently hewn from the mountain itself. Rogdai walked in first and raised the candle, and golden light bounced off the walls. Sabíana had the feeling that she breathed gold. The walls were gilded in more panels containing even brighter and more ornate icons. These were all of hermits, notable for their floor-length beards and hair-shirts. Some of them were completely naked—the ultimate sign of renunciation of decadence. Sabíana remembered from her studies that this kind of chapel was common in the outliers. In Vasyllia, icons of kings and queens were preferred to those of ascetic men and women of the wilds.

There was a low table at the end of the semi-circular altar, and the back wall was covered in florid text, the gold paint as bright as though the brush were applied only yesterday.

"This place must be hundreds of years old," Sabíana whispered.

Rogdai was on his knees, his head bent. She began to read the text aloud.

"*Thus saith the Most High King, the Unknown Father, the Artist of the High and the Low. I will make my covenant with Lassar of the Vasylli, to be binding on his children, and his children's children until the final fading. Upon this people I appoint a sacred duty—to protect and ward the Three Cities, with all lands appertaining to them, or to die in their sworn duty.*

"*For duty faithfully rendered, great shall be the measure of my recompense. I shall make this race glorious among men, and the grace of my power shall flow through them as a river of Living Water. For failure in duty bound, terrible shall be the wrath of my reckoning. Their seed shall be wiped from the earth, and they shall be cursed to the darkness eternal.*

"Yet if they endure the war that never ends, they shall have peace in a place of sanctuary beyond the endless ages."

"O Adonais," whispered Sabíana, trembling. "How foolish have we been."

Around the text, smaller icons of great kings of old were rendered in astonishing detail, barely tarnished with age. It struck her that if the figures came out from the walls and spoke to her, she would not be surprised. For the first time in her life, the Covenant, Adonais, and all of the old stories were no longer fairy tales, but had become painful reality.

"You feel it too, do you not, Rogdai? The terrible abyss of time in those words, especially when read aloud. We forget so easily..." A thought struck her. "We must read this aloud at my coronation. We must pledge, as a people, to renew our commitment to the Covenant. We must seek for the last help we have left."

And then she knew what she must do, and she began to weep.

The warrior came to the edge of the forest. There, in a clearing, he saw the hut standing on chicken feet. "Hut, hut! Turn with your back to the forest, with your front to me." It turned. He stepped forward, but stopped in fear. A river of fire appeared between him and the hut. The hag stood at the doorway, leering at him. "I can give you what you want!" she cackled. "But you'll have to brave the baptism of fire."

The warrior jumped in...

"The Tale of Alienna the Wise and the Deathless One"
(Old Tales, Book II)

CHAPTER 29
THE RIVER OF FIRE

The stars were snuffed out like candles. The field was shrouded in black. The other shacks were simply not there. Outside Tarin's window, it was so dark that it looked as though someone had painted the windows black. The growling continued—regular, insistent, ravenous. Voran's hands shook.

"How?" whispered Tarin. "They could not have found this place. It is protected. It is beyond their knowledge."

Voran knew how. Tarin had said it: "You must so guard your thoughts and inner movements of the heart that not even a stray intention will escape that can aid the enemy." Apparently, even considering the drowned girl's offer was enough to open a chink in the ancient protection.

"I did it," Voran said. "The drowned girl, the Alkonist, she offered me a way out of the Lows." Tarin's eyes grew wide. "I did not accept it, but neither did I curse her out of my hearing. I may have even considered the possibility."

Tarin breathed out heavily. "Perhaps. But she is an insignificant power, a thing the other Alkonist endure only because they must. She could not have done this...unless..." Something dawned on him, and he seemed even more afraid, if that were possible. "Oh, my dear Voran, I hope not..."

"What, my lord? Tell me, please."

"There are powers of the earth...strange, shadowy powers with ever-shifting allegiances. They have no love for men. They have long remained dormant, but if they have awoken, it could only mean..."

Tarin took Voran's forearms in his hands—an ancient gesture of kinship in war—and his eyes were frightening. They were the eyes of a man ready to die.

"Listen to me, Voran. The only way that the Raven's horde could have found me is if the boundaries between worlds are tottering. That could only happen if Vasyllia is on the verge of falling to the Raven." Voran must have looked more confused than usual, because Tarin smiled in spite of his fear. "Yes, my boy, Vasyllia is far more important than you realize. It hides a secret that may determine the fate of all the Realms, not just this one. Promise me, my boy. No matter what happens, you must not let Vasyllia perish. Even if it has already fallen, you must win it back. At whatever cost!"

His eyes were on fire now, and Voran was truly afraid for the first time in his life. His restlessness, his desire to quest, his wish to make a name in the world—all that vanished. He knew, with the conviction of someone on the doorstep of death, that he was not ready to face the Raven and his darkness.

"I promise, my lord."

"I am no longer your lord, Voran. You are a free man. Though you are so unprepared, so unprepared."

Once again, Tarin had a mumbled conversation with himself. Something knocked at the door, a soft knock, not threatening at all. It chilled Voran to the marrow. Tarin's eyes were full of tears.

"I have been cruel to you, Voran, but it was done with a pure intention, I hope you realize. And it has not been enough. I am throwing you to the Powers, and I do not know if you will survive. But if you do not, we will all die."

He fell on his knees and began scrabbling at the hard earth of the shack. For a moment, Voran wondered if madness had finally struck Tarin, but the old man looked up after his fingers had grabbed something, and he smiled his usual, impish grin. He scratched out a wooden trap door, pulled on it, and the trap screeched open.

"This place is protected, as I said. The line of sentinel spruces is a line of power, and the rest of my land is encircled by a river of fire—both are a deep magic from the days of Founding. If the Raven's horde has truly passed it or avoided it somehow, then there is no hope. More likely, they are casting illusion at us from the other side. In any case, you must chance it. At the end of this passage, you will come out on the banks of the river of fire. You must not hesitate even a moment—jump in. It will be excruciating, yes. You may be consumed by it. But we have no more time to prepare. The battle has come to us."

Before Voran could say anything, Tarin pushed a sheathed sword, bundled in fresh black fabric and tied with a new belt of black leather, into his hands and nearly threw him into the passage.

"Go, before it is too late."

The knock on the door repeated, still soft and not remotely threatening.

"That is good," said Tarin, smiling. "It suggests they are not actually here yet. You may have time. Run!"

The darkness in the passage was so thick that Voran was sure it would simply eat him before he could pass through. The silence was so complete that it thundered in his ears. His heart did its best to try to jump through his chest. He exhaled until there was no breath left, then inhaled a long, pure breath, and began to repeat the word in his mind.

"Saddaí. Saddaí."

There was no change in light, but suddenly he realized that his hearing was enough to tell him exactly where to go, how long the passage was, and how fast he could run without falling or crashing into anything. This must be how a bat sees, he thought. He wrapped himself in the black fabric—which turned out to be a full cassock with fine bone clasps all the way down the front—strapped on his sword underneath it, and ran forward, the loose edges of the garment flapping behind him.

It seemed a long time, but the air eventually changed, becoming cold and fresh. The passage sloped sharply up, and before he knew it, he stood outside on the banks of a small river that flowed contentedly as though it were the middle of summer. It took him a moment to realize that this must be what Tarin had called the river of fire, but it looked merely river-ish.

"It took you long enough, my sweet," said the drowned girl from above him. She landed on him like a cat, and her claws were just as sharp. Her arms and her hair engulfed him. He tried to push her off, but she was inhumanly strong. As he thrashed, he tripped on something and was on the ground. They rolled back and forth violently, and Voran felt her nails tickling him. They were cold as iron.

At first he laughed, it was so absurd. But it soon grew unpleasant. She laughed and laughed and continued to tickle until the nails dug into his skin, and the pain was searing. He found it harder and harder to breathe. The stars danced before his eyes for a moment, and he felt himself go under, but then she sprang off him.

"That was a foretaste," she said in her girlish voice, dusting off her arms with her fingers, again parodying a typical gesture of a courtly woman. "I can kill you quickly, or I can do it slowly. It depends on my mood. Now you know."

Voran reached for his sword, but it was not there. She held it, still sheathed on its belt, though it seemed to disgust her, like an old cheese gone green.

"None of that, Voran. Last chance. Take my offer, bed me properly, and I will take you to the weeping tree."

"You lie, as I should have known. You are in the Lows of Aer with me. Of that, I have no doubt." He felt the soreness under his arms. His hand came away bloody, and it disgusted him more than the sight of blood ever had before. "You cannot bear me over the barrier unless you are on the other side."

"How clever you are." She looked disappointed. "Never mind. I can still get my pleasure by force." She lunged at him with the speed of a lynx, but he had no desire to stay and fight. He merely stepped a few paces back and fell into the water. The girl recoiled from the splash with a shriek. Voran, not stopping to think, splashed her as hard as he could before she could get away. The water caught fire on her hair, and in a moment, she was a blazing inferno, running away into the darkness. Her wail cut into him almost as painfully as her nails had.

Voran was in pure, clear water, but somehow it was also fire, though nothing like the usual red-orange flame. Each little eddy was also a translucent tongue of fire, and he was covered in them. At first, the flames were dew-like—soft and cooling and thicker than water. Then the pain seeped in as the flames reached through his clothes into his skin. He threw off the new cassock—it somehow remained untouched by the fire—and hurled it to the shore. It landed next to his sword.

He fought down the rush of panic, held his breath, and forced himself to submerge completely. It was excruciating, as Tarin had said. As he washed, he burned. As he took off the thick layers of mud and sweat, layers of skin sloughed off as well. Soon the pain was a scream in his ears, but he forced himself not to come up. He continued washing himself, continued mouthing the word—*Saddai, Saddai*—until even the scars from the serpent-hag came off in purplish clumps.

He stood up, bracing for the cold air, and waded out of the river. The water should have frozen on his skin the moment he broke, but the flames continued to dance over his body, though they no longer hurt very much. With a flash of embarrassed fear, he touched his head and chin. No, his shoulder-length hair was still there, only smoother and silkier, as was his still young beard. He sighed in relief.

He wrapped himself in the new cassock. It was clean. He had last been clean months ago. That moment, a short moment of exhilarated pleasure, was one of the longest of his life, one he would remember again and again for many long years. The fabric was thick and well-woven, excellent for cold weather, though he wished he had his old travel gear from Vasyllia to go atop it. As it was, his training with Tarin had hardened his body against cold in a way he did not think possible. All Vasylli prided themselves on their ability to bear cold, but his capacity to endure it now was far greater than the hardiest Vasylli.

There was something else that was different as well. As he realized what it was, he almost wept for the sheer joy of it—the soft palpitation in his chest, as of another heart.

Lyna had come back, and with her came the dawn. She sat on a low bough of a bent-over oak, its bark green with moss. Behind her head, the sun rose between two distant hills, giving Lyna a halo of gold. At first, he couldn't see her face. When his eyes got accustomed to the light, he saw she was smiling.

"Lyna, how I longed to see you."

"Oh, my falcon. My poor falcon. You cannot imagine the pain I felt when you broke our bond. It can be remade, if you wish it. But it will be painful as nothing else."

Voran laughed dourly. "Today, that seems appropriate."

"First, you must hurry. Tarin has crossed the line of sentinel trees to distract the Raven's creatures, so that you could escape. I do not know how long he has left."

※

As soon as Voran passed the line of spruces, the swirling darkness was on him, and invisible bonds stronger than steel pinned him in place. His senses sharpened, so that every movement of his pinioned arms was a cacophony of pain. At first, he saw nothing but murk, but the shadows resolved like fading smoke around a prostrate figure on his knees, bloodied hands clasping a hoary head, face planted firmly into his thighs. Voran refused to believe this was Tarin. Over him towered a hideous monster—a leonyn over seven feet tall, his head and face a horrible amalgam of feline and human, with only the worst qualities of both. He bared brown fangs and roared as he beat Tarin with a monstrous leather whip, edged with many tails.

Voran could not move. His frustration reached a boil, and he screamed out his defiance at the mass of formless creatures swirling in the darkness around the leonyn and Tarin. The lion-thing turned to look at Voran—its eyes were black shards of the void swirling around them—and smiled.

"Ah. The hag's lover." The leonyn's voice was incongruously gentle. "Well met at last. How typical of your kind to hide in the stinking marshes. Quite a warrior you are."

Tarin looked up. His face was battered, but his eyes still had the old fire. He assessed Voran for a heartbeat and seemed content with what he saw. With a groan, he got up. The leonyn stepped back in surprise.

"The old goat has some strength left," the creature said and hissed, skin stretched back over his gums, revealing all of his fangs in challenge.

Tarin paid him no attention. He assumed the stance of the storyteller and cried out, as if in challenge, "How do you feel, young man?" The leonyn beat him again, but Tarin only flinched at it, as if it hurt no more than a mosquito's bite.

Voran remembered the ordeal with the hag, when Tarin told the story of the healing of the crippled young man by the Sirin. To his amazement, Voran did feel an increase of strength, as though the river of fire had newly forged him.

"I feel the strength of ten men within me," Voran said, echoing the words of the young man in the story.

Tarin laughed with tears in his eyes, and the leonyn stepped back in fear. Into the blackness flew Lyna, her eyes glowing golden fire. She fluttered overhead like a falcon readying to dive. Voran shrugged off the power holding him pinioned as if it were string. He unsheathed his sword. His heart beat like a hammer on new steel, and his sword responded. It turned red with heat, then lightning-white, as if it were itself furious at the attack of the Raven's creatures.

From a deep recess of his heart, something flowed out like fresh wine bursting out of its cask. He began to sing, and to his heart's leaping joy, Lyna sang in harmony with him—a hymn he did not know, yet it flowed unimpeded from his lips.

I arise today
Through the love of the Heights.
Light of sun, radiance of moon,
Splendor of fire, speed of lightning,
Swiftness of wind, depth of sea,
Strength of earth, firmness of rock.
I arise today
Through his strength to protect me
From snares of the darkness,

From tempting of pleasures,
From everyone who wishes me ill,
Both far and near, alone, among many.
I summon today
All these Powers to keep me
Against every cruel and malevolent power,
Against every thought that kills body and soul,
Against poison and burning,
Against drowning and wounding.
I arise today
Through a mighty strength—
The power of the unspeakable word.
May the grace of the Heights
Sustain us forever.

He rushed sword-first in a wild attack, completely careless of life and pain. The leonyn unfurled like a banner into ash and black smoke, though his black eyes still burned in the storm of the formless ones. Voran flew at the seething wall, and his white brand cleaved a furrow in it. The sun's light streamed in like water, and the slit expanded outward, pressing in on the host of creatures until Voran, Tarin, and Lyna stood in the sunny marshland, and before them spun a column of blackness swirling in rage, reaching higher than the clouds.

A flash like a thousand bolts of lightning struck the mass of the Darkness. Voran fell on his face from the force of it, barely able to look up. Something mountainous looked down on him and spoke in a voice like a thousand trumpets in unison.

"I come as summoned, Son of Otchigen."

It was a giant in the form of a man of light and fire. His eyes were suns, his teeth were moons. Six tapered wings of gold, lapis, emerald, ruby, silver, and topaz flickered in constant movement about his body. He had four faces turned in each direction—a man of searing beauty, an eagle, a lion, and a Sirin. As monstrous as such a creature should be, Voran could hardly keep from worshipping him right there on the field of battle, so beautiful he was. In his outstretched right hand, he held a sword of fire that was at once the sharpest metal and the hottest flame. In his left was a war hammer the size of a small mountain.

The giant attacked the column of darkness, and everywhere he walked, the earth opened and fire burst forth. Fissures in the ground yawned open, and winds swirled from every direction, visible winds like molten gold and silver. Voran realized they were not winds at all, but living creatures. They pushed the mass of the Raven's creatures inexorably down into the earth. The formless ones wailed and burned and cursed, but they could not withstand the attack. Voran's entire body shook from fear and exhilaration, and he fell into a stupor.

Voran came to himself as silence once more reigned on the marshlands. He feared to look up, feared the Power he had summoned. He wished he could just crawl under a rock and wait until everything went back to normal again.

"Voran," said Lyna next to him. "It is time."

Groaning within, Voran stood up and faced the giant, who towered over the place where the Raven's horde had been. The great rents in the earth were healed, and the marshes looked as though nothing strange had happened at all.

"I am Athíel of the Palymi," said the Power in a voice that could rip stone apart. "I have heard much of you from my brother. He has hopes for you."

"Brother?" Voran's voice sounded like the squeak of an insect.

Athíel smiled, and it was like lightning. "Yes, the Harbinger. Do you wish to have your bond with Lyna restored?"

"I do," said Voran, with slightly more power in his voice.

"Know this. The Palymi come as summoned by the great hymn of the Powers, but I can help you no more. You have gained much strength from your time with Tarin, but you must never forget that such strength is nothing against the Raven. You can only prevail as the true Vasylli have ever prevailed. Nurture the flame in your heart, cultivate your bond with Lyna. That bond is the lifeblood of good in this world. And take heart, dear one. Your path will be dark, and in the Heart of the World you will face the crumbling of everything you ever believed in. In that time, listen to the song in your heart."

Athíel raised his sword of flame and pierced Voran through the chest. Voran fell, his mind shrieking with the pain. It was as though his body had been unmade completely, then put together again, piece by piece. When his eyes could see again, he saw a foul green-brown vapor seeping out of the wound in his chest. It hissed in the crisp air until it ran out. The wound closed on itself, leaving a hairline scar down the length of his chest bone.

Athíel was gone. The song of the Sirin was inside him again in thunderous harmony, and his inner fire blazed. Lyna flew above him, hovering on her jewel-wings, crying tears that landed on his face and steamed.

281

"When will I see you again, my Lyna?"

"I do not know, my falcon. Gamayun can see no further than this moment. I fear for you and for Vasyllia. I do not know how this will end."

"I will seek you after I find the weeping tree. Much will be determined there, I think. Will you come to me then?"

"I am with you always," she said, and was gone.

The palace of Vasyllia has seven towers. The tallest of them is closed off to all, locked away, the key in the keeping of a select few. For that is the home of the treasure of Vasyllia, the bard of the Dar. Every Dar has had his own chosen bard. The last, and most brilliant of all, was blind Bayan, who outlived two Dars and died on the eve of the great battle for Vasyllia.

"A Child's History of Vasyllia," chapter 21

CHAPTER 30
BAYAN'S LAST SONG

On the morning of the coronation, Rogdai was turned aside from his already mounting responsibilities by a very annoying boy. At first, he could not for the life of him recognize who the boy was and what his position in the household was intended to be. The boy was not particularly illuminating, waiting to be told to speak before offering any useful information on his own.

"Go on, boy," Rogdai said, exasperated, rushing through the halls of the palace as everyone else seemed to be going the other way. "Tell me your charge."

"It is my master. He begs a word with the Lady. He says it is very urgent."

Rogdai almost growled at him. "*Who* is your master, boy?"

The boy's eyes were as big as trenchers. "Bbbb..." he stammered.

"Well?"

"Bayan. The bard."

Oh, by all that is holy in the Heights, he thought. What horrid timing.

"He will have to see me, I'm afraid," Rogdai said. "The Lady has been in the Temple since midnight, preparing for her coronation."

The boy nodded and rushed forward, almost as though he were escaping Rogdai, not leading him. For that speed, Rogdai disliked the boy a little less.

The old bard was dying. It was the smell that made it most obvious—something like stale bread and rotten fruit mixed with sweat. He knew that smell well enough from seeing both his parents die.

"Vohin Rogdai," Bayan croaked, his white eyes uncannily fastened to Rogdai's face. "The Darina will not see me?"

"She is at her coronation, my lord," said Rogdai, his voice soft in spite of his irritation. Bayan commanded respect, even in the worst of times.

"You will have to tell it to her, then. I was visited by a song this morning. It has not happened in decades."

Rogdai understood. Writing a song was one thing, but being visited by one was another. This was an oracle. He bent to his knees and leaned on the deathbed, so the old man did not have to strain.

"I will not play it for you, for my fingers are stiffer than old roots. But I will sing the words."

Rogdai's heart leaped to hear the clarity of the old man's bass, so unexpected after hearing his croaking speech. It was almost as though someone else sang through Bayan's body, using it as an instrument. But as the words sank into his conscious mind, his heart did an about face and plunged into his heels for sheer terror. Bayan sang a prophecy of defeat.

The smoke! It blinds and frightens.
The shouts! They're all around.
The flaming stones are falling,
But the shouts don't lose their sound.

The Lords—impotent, silent—
   Lie crumbled in the smoke.
   The shouts increase their fury
   At Dark's death-dealing stroke.

You cannot see their faces,
   For darkest is that hour
   When skies light up in fury
   At chaos' gath'ring power.

While Raven in his glory
   Declines to show his face,
   The wise hear in the shouting
   His rotting, fallen grace.

. . .

The time for words is over
 For Light hangs by a thread.
 Will no one stop the shouting?
 Will no one stir the dead?

Rogdai walked like a dead man back to the walls of Vasyllia. Bayan's words thundered through Rogdai's consciousness as he joined the throngs headed for the Temple, feeling like a corpse carried by a swift tide. He could not tell Sabíana this prophecy. Not in her hour of glory.

Sabíana closed her eyes and reveled, for the last time, in being merely Sabíana, daughter of the Dar, intended of Voran, sister to Mirnían, Black Swan of her people. She opened her eyes, and now and forever she would be the Black Sun, the Darina of the dark time of Vasyllia. Swathed in a brown fur, Sabíana walked out from her gazebo slowly, with bowed head, not daring to look up yet. She stopped before the throne and turned to the assembled crowds, so full that some were even standing on the lowest boughs of the redbarks. Falling to her knees, she touched her forehead to the bare ground and raised herself up again. She repeated her obeisance three times before turning to the Grove of Mysteries.

The new chief priest, Otar Gleb, stood in front of the grove by the ceremonial throne—an unadorned chair intended to remind the future Darina of the need for humility in the wielding of power. He was a surprisingly young man with a joyful face, if somewhat ugly. His hair was blond and curling at the ends that rested on his shoulders. His eyes were deep and kind, so different from Kalún's wells of contempt. He placed his right hand on Sabíana's forehead as he half-chanted, half-cried in a sharp, high tenor, "Woman! Why do you approach the sacred grove?"

"To abase myself before the mercy of Adonais and to confirm his will in the choice of a new Darina." Her voice sounded weak to her own ears, young and scared.

"Why do you, a humble slave, dare to take this duty upon yourself?"

"By the right of blood..." She paused, hoping she had memorized the words correctly. "...and by the humble desire of my people do I approach. I, a worthless thrall, do myself neither desire nor deserve such honor, such a dreadful duty."

"How do the people answer this claim?" His voice rang out regally, and she was jealous of it. "Are they in one mind and one mouth of accord?"

"Yea!" echoed through the Temple, truly as if it were one, many-faceted voice.

The priest indicated that Sabíana should kneel.

"I confirm, as mouth and warden of the will of Adonais, your claim, slave Sabíana, daughter of Antomír, to the Monarchia of Vasyllia. Forget not that you are a servant of your people, the slave of a higher Dar. Rule in remembrance of the ancient Covenant that our forefathers made with Adonais."

How empty that sounds, she thought. It reminded her of how difficult it would be to awaken in the people any understanding that the Covenant needed to be upheld as a reality, not merely as a beautiful idea.

One of the clerics held a gilded malachite box. The chief priest opened it carefully, pulling out a silver crown of ancient make. It was wrought in the shape of a flowering wreath, rising to a single peak above the forehead, like Mount Vasyllia. In the midst of the silver peak shone an emblazoned red-gold sun. Sabíana stood up, kissed the sun, then sat on the throne, still facing the Grove of Mysteries. He placed it on her head.

"Adonais, with your glory crown her..."

"So be it!" cried the priests.

"...with your invincible grasp wield her scepter..."

"So be it!" cried the clerics and the royal court.

"...with your omniscient providence guide her judgment."

"So be it! So be it! So be it!" cried all the people.

Four of the priests lifted the throne with Sabíana on it to face the people. She felt the emotions they had all held back suddenly overwhelm her. Instead of cringing, her heart held firm, and she took the energy of their worry, their tiredness, their pain, and forged it inside herself into pure joy that streamed out of her to the tips of her fingers. She felt afire, re-forged, new. She smiled.

Everyone prostrated in the snow. Many faces were white with awe, even terror. She raised her hands to bless them, when frightened cries and gasps rose among the people.

"The crown! It flowers!"

Unprompted, many voices began to chant, "So be it! So be it!"

Sabíana threw off her fur, and her cream and gold underdress shone like lightning. Under the fur, she was girt with a sword. She unsheathed it and raised it high.

"Words? What use are they now?" Her voice rang even louder than the priest's, and her heart rang with it. "Hope? What hope can you expect, my people?"

Her eyes teared up from the icy air, but she held her body firm. The steam floated from her body like an aureole. She felt the fire of the flowering crown on her head. She was half-mad with exhilaration.

"Death awaits the sleeping, death spares not the upright. It is death's time, my people."

The fear was everywhere, in every pair of eyes now, but still they hung on her words, hungry for more.

"Come, death, I say! Come, so we can spit on you. We are not your slaves. We serve life, and we defy you! Sword-fisted, helm-crested, we take life and we impose it on you!"

All through the crowd, swords were unsheathed and held aloft. They scattered the feeble light of the sun hidden in fog and the fires of the lanterns.

"We are a high people. We are the hammer of Adonais, the axe of the Heights. We are the wardens of the Three Cities. Arise with me, raise your swords and your hearts, set them alight, blaze forth the anger of the righteous!"

The sea of people seethed. Old men, boys, warriors, even priests raised weapons. Their eyes were alit with the war-wind.

"But dare I say the righteous?" She moderated her voice, allowing it to soften, as though she doubted her own words. "Are we not perhaps become fallen, diminished by long laziness and selfishness? Do we dare to take up arms in the name of Adonais if we have broken Covenant with him?"

Not a single voice, not even a whisper disturbed the silence of the frosty air.

"Hark now to the word of your Darina! I have found proof of the Covenant's existence. I have read words carved by our fathers into the face of the mountain, words that cannot be unsaid. Hearken to the words of Adonais, my people!"

It looked like a wave struck the people's backs, so quickly did they fall down on their faces. All the armed men thrust their swords into the ground before abasing themselves. Sabíana did the same, but she only knelt, her gaze intent on the people she hoped to move to an act of insane heroism.

The herald read out the words that Sabíana had first read only a day before. Even now, after copying it for herself and hearing it reread many times, the words pierced with their power. It was not incantation or magic. The words had the power of making. These kinds of words were spoken by the deity that created them all. Sabíana was either committing terrible blasphemy, or she was re-forging a lost Covenant. She did not know which it was, but she had cast the stones, and it was too late.

After the herald finished, murmurs rose like the first rustling of wind that promised rain. Here and there she heard expressions of agreement. She searched for any sign of defiance, but all she saw was the adoration.

"Now is the time, my people. Now we must renew the Covenant with Adonais. But I cannot do it for you. We must all agree to it; we must all renew the Covenant within our hearts. Vasylli! Pledge yourselves to the will of your Darina, the will of Adonais!"

"So be it! So be it!"

The cries were reluctant at first, hesitant, but the sound rose like a fire. Soon the mountain shook with the repeated cries. Still, even now she saw that some held back. The fire of the flowering crown dimmed, and by the lessened light in the eyes of the people, Sabíana knew that the sign had faded. It left her aching and empty. She gathered the reserves of her strength.

"So be it! We will be his people again, and may he guide our death-stroke against the foul enemy outside the walls!"

The terrible understanding dawned in the eyes of many. They understood.

"Sing with me, my children!" She stood up. "We go to war."

The warriors surrounding her bellowed the opening chords of the ancient call to war, and the women and children in the Temple joined them. Even the clerics sang, tuning into the single harmony like a bag-pipe warming up. Over their combined voices, Sabíana unfettered her own, and it flew above the choir like a hawk catching a warm gust.

The Heights resound with thunder;
The mountains sing aloud.
Our people burn with anger
At the enemies' gathering cloud.

We gird our arms with iron;
   We bind our tongues with prayer.
   Our children and our loved ones
   We leave to Sirin's care.

. . .

O Adonais, hear us,
  Defend us as we cry:
  "Annihilate this Darkness,
  And give us strength to die."
  Lord! Give us strength to die!

The fog outside the city glowed yellow, swirling with loathing, challenging any who would come. Arrayed like rows of candles ready to be lit, Rogdai's men tensed for the charge behind the great doors. A moment before, the gates throbbed with the violence of the drums; now the air echoed with silence. Rogdai held his breath, trying to calm the thump of his heart. Any moment now the call to charge would sound. As mad as he knew it was, and probably fatal, he was infected with war-wind, and his finger itched to feel the cramp of a sword-hand after hours of battle.

All around him, the men stood with jaws set and swords out, so still they could have been statues. His heart burst with pride at their form. Only the banner-bearers betrayed any of their eagerness, but they were all boys still in the seminary. Rogdai recognized Tolnían, the young scout who had started everything with his report about the tree that wept Living Water. He impressed Rogdai more than the other boys. There was no bravado in his manner, only calm determination that belied his tender years.

"Ho there, boy!" called Rogdai at Tolnían. "I believe I see your nanny over there. Hide, or she'll uncover your secret. What are you, ten?"

Tolnían didn't even flinch as he answered. "Vohin Rogdai, before this is over, we *will* be arming ten-year-olds."

Rogdai laughed, because it was necessary, not because he was amused.

Tolnían's hand-woven banner—a Sirin in flight, talons bared—caught even the sickly glare of the foggy sun, sowing light on the warriors. Rogdai felt a semblance of hope rising. He turned to look back at the palace. He imagined he could see Darina Sabíana even at this distance, raising her hand. Something gleamed in the highest turret of the palace, and the braying, glorious cacophony of trumpets exploded around them.

The doors groaned. Rogdai screamed white-steaming anger as his men rushed out into the high fields around the city. All of his brothers strained—he could sense it as his own strain—for that fearful first blow of steel against steel, that entry into the whorl of war. He sang, and his brothers took up his song, an old ballad of death and glory.

They were answered with silence. Out and out they poured through the open doors, but no enemy came to greet them.

Something hissed and crackled around Rogdai. A wall of malice rose up from the very earth, it seemed. The fog swirled, as if some huge, invisible finger was mixing a poison to choke all who approached. The hissing grew louder. Rogdai realized it came from above. Swarms of ravens plunged down in a blinding attack, a black wave of talon and beak. Just ahead of him, the fog suddenly resolved itself into thousands upon thousands of Gumiren. But then they all changed, as though their human forms were cloaks to be cast off before battle. He faced an army of monsters.

Most were chimaeras combining human and animal features in the most grotesque parody of creation—leonyns, wolf-men, bull-men. Huge snakes seethed everywhere. Some walked on short legs, and some were no more than worms with mouths that unfurled outward to reveal rows of dagger fangs. Everywhere, growls replaced the calls of men.

"What in the Heights is going on?" Only decades-long discipline stopped Rogdai from running away, screaming.

"It is the Raven, Vohin Rogdai," said Tolnían next to him. All that was visible of his fear was a slight paleness in his cheeks. "The Darina was right. Only Adonais can help us now."

"Well, I am not going back, crying for my nanny, boy," said Rogdai, punching himself on the chest to knock his sense back into his body. "Vasylli! For our Darina! For the Black Sun!"

"The Black Sun!" The lines caught the chant like a wooden ball and passed it on, until the field rang with it.

There was no time to form ranks: the monsters were among them, biting and clawing. Before charging, Rogdai looked back to see how Tolnían fared, and laughed to see him mumbling some prayer under his breath.

"Careful, boy, it will take steel, not words, to survive today."

"I am not interested in surviving. I am interested in the annihilation of this Darkness." He smiled, but it was a warm smile, a smile of farewell.

Then, Rogdai was in the midst of it, and the war-wind took him. Even through the haze of red, Rogdai saw that the monsters were aiming for the banners, as though the embroidered High Beings were a source of power. The Vasylli would not long survive without the hope that the banners held out to them.

One by one, the ranks of spear-men protecting the banners were mowed down by the rising enemy. One by one, the banners near Rogdai tottered and fell, and with each one the growls of the creatures seemed to grow more vicious. As they fell, the light they scattered faded, and Rogdai felt the terror rising with each downed banner. Some of the boys fled in screaming fear. They were easy prey for the ravens, who wheeled above, ready to swarm on anyone who ran.

A ring of spearmen directly in front of Rogdai disappeared like smoke. Before he realized it, he engaged a reeking lion-thing over seven feet tall, with two or three more at its heels. They pushed Rogdai back into Tolnían, and his strength proved nothing against them. Cursing aloud, he tripped on a rock and felt the sinews of his ankle tear. What a pathetic way to die, he thought.

But the creatures reeled from a new, ferocious attack. Tolnían had thrust the point of the banner into the earth and attacked the enemy like a one-man avalanche. Every stroke was perfectly directed, striking some vital part of the monsters now cringing from him. He hacked and slashed and parried with incredible skill, not a hint of fear in the way he held himself. The creatures shrieked with mad terror at his calm and deadly assault. They ran, falling over friend and foe alike. All around them the Vasylli, embolden by Tolnían's courage, shouted and charged.

The banner-bearers that remained alive—and they were few—labored to raise all the fallen banners by lodging them in earth as Tolnían did. Once again, the images of ancient Powers rose over the battle-scarred slope. Some boys even began to climb the trees to lift the banners higher, to try to catch the sparse rays of sunlight. Rogdai was amazed—the ravens did not touch them, as if their resurgent courage somehow gave them added protection.

The battle raged. More and more creatures rushed at them from the mists below, constantly replenishing their losses. Rogdai saw many men simply crumple to the ground in pain, though they faced no enemy. Snakes hidden by creeping mists were everywhere. Rogdai himself was surrounded by a mass of snake carcasses, since they were the only creatures he could still fight off, unable as he was to stand on his torn ankle.

Then he heard the great bell, and his heart sang. Its velvet peal poured fresh strength into the men around him, and they redoubled their fury, pushing the monsters back into the churning mists. Someone picked Rogdai up and supported his weight. It was Tolnían. Together they pursued the enemy to the churning fog on the edge of the killing field.

Something bright flashed deep within the fog, and the mists dissipated with a breath of wind. Not a single monster remained in sight. All the way down the slopes, beyond the plateau surrounding Vasyllia, boulders and earth and grass were covered in the bodies of fallen Vasylli—many too young to be called men. Their dead faces were bone-white in the sun, expressionless and calm. Rogdai wondered if their spirits had found better habitations in the Heights. As he stared at them, the momentary ardor of victory cooled.

"Where are they?"

Not a single mangled corpse—or any trace at all—remained of the monsters that had appeared from hell and apparently returned there. And there was no sign of any Gumiren anywhere. Rogdai wondered if this was victory, or a prelude to something far worse.

I have seen evil. I have felt it in my blood and in my bones. I have been it. And I survived. But after it all ended, after I paid the ultimate price, the question still remains. Did the Raven control my actions without my will? Or did I willingly let him into my body?

Unsigned note found among the personal effects of the Karila embassy

CHAPTER 31
THE LAST BATTLE

"You are mad!" Yadovír shrieked, sick with nervous excitement. His clerk had just burst in on him, announcing the victory of the Vasylli warriors over the enemy. Yadovír was so shocked, he even forgot to hold the lavender-scented kerchief to his nose, as he did ceaselessly now, only to have the stench of the Raven inundate him again. He raised his now-skeletal white hand back to his nose, and stamped his foot, whining.

"You lie, you gullible fool. How can that be? The day is not even far gone, and already we are victorious? Impossible. You lie! Get out. I do not want to see you anymore. Out!"

Yadovír was aware that to others he now cut a rather pathetic figure, always shuddering, muttering to himself, and holding his scented kerchief to his nose, but his mind was as keen as ever, and he took special pleasure in storing hatred for every slight—perceived or otherwise, it didn't matter—for the right moment.

"Ha! It seems they have done it," he said aloud after the clerk left him. "Now what will you do?"

The appearance of solitude belied the obvious presence—unseen, but sensed by creeping skin, foul stench, and slithering voice that was and was not in Yadovír's head.

"It is unbecoming of such a noble heart to stoop to foolishness, my rat."

The Raven's tone oozed malice and calm. Yadovír's momentary excitement shattered, and the voice laughed, almost in spite of itself.

"My very own fool," he hissed. There was even a kind of unctuous tenderness in the voice. "Your people truly are fools if they think to have won any victory."

"Fools that somehow managed to beat off your creatures."

Yadovír felt a chill of displeasure from the presence.

"Yesss. There was perhaps a moment or two of unexpected bravery there. But no matter. It just makes your part in all this a bit more urgent, nothing more."

"You have c-c-come to d-demand payment, h-have you?" Yadovír's assumed bravado was completely betrayed by the unfamiliar stammer, which had begun to decorate his speech at the most inopportune moments.

"Y-y-yes, I h-h-have," the voice mimicked with half-suppressed laughter.

"Will you leave me alone then, after I have done your dirty work?"

"What? No demands that I install you in a position of power over those you hate? No pathetic attempts to wrest terms from the jaws of the pitiless Raven?"

"I don't n-n-need you for that," Yadovír said.

"Oh, I see. You rely on my munificence to keep you alive as a boon for your treachery, and then you plan to take advantage of the ensuing commotion to murder your enemies in their beds, is that it?"

Yadovír stamped his foot again in frustration. The Raven laughed inside his head.

"Do not worry, you will get all you wish for in that quarter. But you can give up any puerile hope of my ever leaving you alone. You are my favorite plaything."

Yadovír almost gagged at the feathery touch on his arm.

"What do you want of me?" Yadovír nearly screamed.

"What do *I* want? I want you to be happy. I want you to feel the pleasure of vengeance, my rat. Not to wait and wait and wait. When all this is done, you can punish Sabíana in whatever twisted way your strange mind desires. Now go. The Gumiren are waiting for you. They have already cleared the blocked passage. Open the hidden way into the city."

"But how will I protect myself? I don't want to be known as the man who betrayed his people."

"Of course, how noble of you! I have a very special idea on that score. Come, my stupid little one. I will explain everything on the way."

Sabíana rushed into the palace proper, surrounded by her generals. Contrary to her own common sense, she had summoned the Dumar, reinstating their privileges, hoping the victory would rally the representatives to her. Her sense told her that there was little chance of that. She battled a heavy dread, fearing that everything she had just witnessed—all the monsters, the carnage—was all a play, a farce to distract her from something else, something she could sense with every cell of her body, but could not see. She tried to maintain the appearance of confidence.

Her heavy wolf fur chafed at her neck, and she wished she could cast away the heavy curved sword she wore at her side. She had chosen her clothing for a purpose. She needed to be an avatar of victory, as far as the warriors were concerned. She strove to maintain that illusion for as long as possible.

"We must not become drunk over this victory, my lords. True, our men have outdone themselves today. We must reform and defend the city against any further attack. It seems we have the upper hand now, and perhaps we can even send out sorties into the forest to harry the Gumiren." Wherever they are, she thought, but did not say.

"Darina, is it wise to entrust so much of this to the Dumar?" rumbled Elder Pahomy by her side. "They have hardly deserved much trust of late."

"They dare not rebel now, not with this success in the..."

She was cut off by a wheezing intake of her own breath. They had entered the Chamber of Counsel. The room was a lurid mess of bloodied bodies. Every member of the former Dumar lay dead or dying, stabbed many times. The floor glistened with blood. Some still moaned. Only one among them was still lucid—Yadovír, who was also wounded, though not fatally. He wept uncontrollably, his voice like a serrated knife.

"Darina Sabíana, we are undone! Do not believe anything of what you have seen or heard. We have not triumphed. It was all a ruse of the Raven. One of the clerics did this, possessed by our ancient enemy. I barely escaped with my own life before I stopped him."

Yadovír pointed at the body of a young priest holding a long knife, red to the handle. He lay open-eyed in the shocked surprise of death.

"One of our prized clerics," screamed Yadovír.

Sabíana shook like a leaf in a gale and found no voice to answer Yadovír. Her knees no longer supported her; she fell and the shuddering grabbed her violently. Her mind was a protracted scream of pain; her eyes lost their focus, and she felt foam rise to her mouth. Against her will, a moan slithered out of her, and even to her own ears, the sound of her teeth chattering was pitiful and horrifying.

Two of her guards knelt by her, trying to do something to relieve her, but they had no idea what to do. Finally, the convulsion stopped. Her eyes remained cloudy and unfocused, and she couldn't speak except to moan without words.

Yadovír stopped weeping as if he had become another person in the blink of an eye. Cold terror gripped Sabíana; Yadovír seemed to grow in her eyes, as if a shadow spread out behind him like a raven's wings. His eyes were black fire, and he commanded with the power of a legion.

"Come," he said with a voice not his own. "We must see to the order of Vasyllia."

To her shock, everyone did as he commanded, crumbling to a will that seemed to be outside him, yet inside him as well. Her two guards picked her up and dragged her. All she could do was moan.

Rogdai limped back to the city, leaning on Tolnían. By now, most of the warriors had returned, leaving the wounded on the field of battle. An eerie uncertainty hung about the air like smoke, and most of the warriors were intent on the palace, hoping for some word from the Black Sun. Tolnían still clutched the banner as if his life depended on it.

"That was quite a thing, my boy," said Rogdai, shaking his head in disbelief. "I did not know they still made warriors like you."

"I never made it through the first year of warrior seminary," said Tolnían and laughed.

Rogdai struck Tolnían playfully on the back of his head, as if to stop him from becoming too tall in his own estimation.

Rogdai couldn't concentrate his vision through the throbbing pain. Everything slowed down through his eyes, and objects didn't focus unless he looked at them with careful intention. But when he did, they became somehow too real, and he had to look away again. When he heard the marrow-chilling cries coming from the palace, he looked up at one of the turrets to see the pale figure of a skeletal Yadovír holding his hands out. Then the terrible focus came, and the horrifying reality struck him.

Yadovír's hands were covered in blood.

Sabíana was next to him, but she was unrecognizable—white and hardly standing, supported by two of her black-robed guards. They looked like the bringers of death.

"People of Vasyllia," roared Yadovír. "Fell deeds have been done. The Dumar has been infiltrated by treachery. Every last one of your beloved councilors lies in his own blood. I alone escaped by a miracle. Who could

299

have done such a deed? The Gumiren, you say? No. One of our own people has perpetrated this atrocity. One of those sworn to protect us, to minister, care, and watch over our lives with benediction is a traitor. One of our priests has sold himself to the enemy, for I know not what price. His knife it was that brought death's swift bite to our own people. A priest! We are betrayed by one of our own!"

Yadovír foamed at the mouth. A young priest, one of those who had just fought at the wall, stepped forward to protest, but his words stopped short. Silence filled the open courtyard where he stood. The priest, fair as a spring lily, was alone, ringed by warriors who looked at him in disgust. His eyes rolled back, and he rattled at the back of his throat. A sword's point thrust through his chest, and Rogdai, red with fury that he did not realize was there until this moment, held the sword.

"Death to all traitors of Vasyllia!"

Rogdai's cry was taken up all around him. Swords were unsheathed yet again. He was the first among them, charging at any priest he could find. Some were in mail and fought back, but none could withstand his fury. He no longer felt the pain of his ankle, rushing back and forth, stabbing and slashing and hacking. When three bodies lay at his feet, he pursued the fleeing priests. He ran into homes, broke down doors, overturned tables and ripped off curtains to find the cowering traitors. The shock and pain he saw in their eyes only fed his hatred. He spit on them as he skewered them.

When he had run out of priests to kill, he stopped to look around, finally noticing that his right leg could no longer support his weight. The streets were spattered with red, and everywhere the open eyes of the dead clerics stared at him from dead pates. There were even a few dead women—wives, sisters, daughters—who had tried to appeal with their bodies to the mercy of the sword. There was one in particular, a girl hardly out of her childhood. There were tears on her dead face.

It was that detail, not the blood and carnage, that thrust into his mind the realization of what he had done. He tore at his hair and screamed.

Tolnían, still clutching the banner, ran from the scene of carnage back to the gates of Vasyllia. He had tried to fend off Rogdai himself, but he could not, and nearly everyone else had followed in Rogdai's madness. Vaguely, he hoped that some of the still-returning warriors might help him. As he turned a corner, he ran into a wall of men. They were not Vasylli.

The Gumiren surrounded him, silent as hunting cats. They crawled out of every street, every shadow in the city. Tolnían thrust the point of the banner into a crack between two flagstones, drew his sword, and sang a challenge. The banner fluttered slightly, showering Tolnían with dappled sunlight. The enemy advanced.

As they attacked, he lost sense of his own arm. It flailed back and forth, striking everywhere with deadly accuracy. Like being possessed by a High Being, he thought. Two of them were at his feet. Another three came down in two strokes.

When he came to, ten mangled figures lay before him. He stopped to breathe, and iron pierced his left side. He fell and his eyesight began to dim. All he saw was five curved blades above his head, rising with the war-shriek of the Gumiren. They waited for the command to hack him to pieces.

Suddenly, light streamed from his banner, striking them like spear-thrusts. They screamed and retreated from him. Leaving him alone, they walked around him, not daring to approach the image of the Sirin in flight. They passed by and continued toward the palace. Tolnían succumbed and fell unconscious.

※

The despair that followed Rogdai's madness choked him. At that moment, when the last hope shriveled within him, Gumiren warriors—hundreds, thousands of them—entered the courtyard, and with them came smoke and fire.

The war-wind abandoned Rogdai. He hardly tried to ward off the avalanche of curved blades rising high against him. He fell. He saw his brother-warriors around him fall like wheat cut down by a scythe. All of them—dead or wounded.

Within minutes, not a single armed Vasylli stood against the invaders. Rogdai, blood pouring from three wounds, lay on the ground, trying to rise only with a left arm. His right arm lay near him, hacked off by the Gumir who stood over him now with death in his eyes.

A loud retort of an ox-horn stopped the Gumiren, as though they were one man.

Yadovír, white as death, stood next to Sabíana, looking down on Rogdai and the rest of Vasyllia as though he had just given birth to a stillborn child.

I have long wondered what the fate of humanity is. We have a spark inside, fed by our soul-bond with the Sirin. And it leaves us forever restless, searching for something. But for what? I have heard that some holy men have experienced a change, a transfiguration into something higher, something stranger. Perhaps we have to shed this body of flesh for a body of fire. Perhaps the flame in our heart must engulf us whole. Perhaps only afire can we stand before the throne of the Most High and hear our ultimate fate...

From the personal archive of Dar Lassar the Blessed

CHAPTER 32
THE STAFF IN BLOOM

Voran laid Tarin down by the staff that still had not flowered. Tarin's face was white, but his arms were streaked with blood, and his breathing was labored and heavy. Voran could not believe that the man who had projected such physical strength for so long could simply wither like a rose struck by an early frost. It hurt Voran, more than the river of fire, more than the sword of the Palymi. It did not help that after the war-wind had passed, it left Voran exhausted, his strength sapped.

Tarin opened his eyes, and still he did not groan or give any other indication of the pain he must be feeling. His young eyes—still such young eyes—were plaintive.

"Where were you when I suffered?" he exclaimed.

Voran leaned back, shocked and struck dumb. Then he realized Tarin was not speaking to him.

"I am your faithful, loving slave." Tarin's voice was stoic, lacking any hint of self-pity. "Why did you wait so long to send deliverance in my hour of need?"

The silence that followed was immense and terrible. But then, the voice. The ineffable voice.

"I was waiting, Tarin, by your side. I wished to see your greater victory, to grant you the greater reward."

Tarin laughed and wept at the same time.

"Tarin," whispered Voran. "Was that…Adonais?"

The look in Tarin's eyes was strange. Voran didn't understand it. He had never seen it before.

"No, Voran. Not Adonais." He began to cough, and could say no more. The voice spoke again, soft and yet terrifying.

"Come to me, Tarin. I have need of your counsel."

Tarin burst into flame—a bluish, warm flame that consumed his frail body. But it left behind something greater, an ageless warrior with sad eyes and dark hair. Completely alight, the transfigured Tarin stood up and bowed to Voran.

"Voran," said Tarin in a high tenor, without the grating heaviness of his usual intonation. "There is much you must still learn. I fear that when you learn the truth about Vasyllia, about the Raven, and about Adonais, you will find no more strength to go on. In that moment, remember me. I have lived my life in the shadows, never thanked by anyone for what I do. And yet, we Warriors of the Word have buttressed the walls that hold up the worlds."

Voran said nothing. Pain pressed his heart, and his mind refused to think.

"One gift I leave you," said Tarin. "There is a path behind the third shack that leads out into the plains. Follow it. When you reach the end, an old friend will be there. Till we meet again, my friend. Oh, and congratulations on your first three baptisms of fire."

He smiled, and Voran was alone.

The staff was covered in small pink blossoms that smelled of orange. Voran laughed, but his joy was a shard of metal in his heart.

It was as Tarin had said. The path—curiously untouched by snow—was a purple shadow between snowbanks gilded by the early morning. It sloped upward toward a rise, atop which tall grass waved awkwardly, encumbered by the snow at its feet. During his time with Tarin, Voran had never so much as left the enclosure with the three huts, much less ventured to see the view from atop the rise.

It was finally his, as he had dreamed of for so many weeks—freedom. He could go anywhere, do anything—a strangely frightening thought.

He looked around, unwilling to go anywhere. Not yet. For all of the drabness of the huts, this was a beautiful place. In the distance, the mountains peeked out above the line of sentinel trees. All around him, the land rolled up and down like gentle waves, mostly clad in white, but with occasional flashes of color—red berries hanging on for dear life, a sprig of purple heather anticipating spring, the pink flowers of the staff-tree.

I could stay here, he thought. I could weather the storm here. No one would seek to find me.

It was a comforting thought, so unusual for a life filled with ranging, training, weeks on the march. Tarin was right. If Vasyllia was to fall, what could he possibly do to stop it, much less bring some dreamy vision of old Vasyllia back to life?

His conscious mind offered him the traditional riposte—will you stand by while the world burns? Yes, he said. If I learned anything from my master, it is that one man's efforts may avail much, but not everything. It is too late to seek the Living Water, too late to seek pardon from my exile.

But what about Lebía? His stomach lurched in warning, and his heart tugged in rebuke. He had not thought of Lebía in so long. What had happened to her? To the pilgrims? Were they safe?

Then a picture flashed on his mind. Otchigen, with his familiar, thick braid and tightly curling black beard. He lay by the hearth in the sleeping embrace of three hunter-borzoi. Lebía, a newborn child, lay cradled on his thick forearm, her own arms extended at impossible angles, like an archer nocking an arrow, her mouth open, a wheezing half-snore rising up and down with the roll of Otchigen's great body. Aglaia stood in the doorway, wrapped up against the cold, stopping for a moment before going out to pick the last of the rowan berries before winter. Her eyes were filled with tears, in spite of her laughing eyes. He remembered the immensity of the peace, the contentment of the scene, and some of its old grace still remained in his heart.

He ran into his shack to gather the barest of necessities. Somehow, he knew that the journey would not be a long one. Last of all, he took Tarin's old travel cloak and wrapped himself in it. Perhaps, he thought, someday I can find respite in the life of a Pilgrim? He chuckled.

"Not likely," he said aloud, his thumb tracing the comforting outline of his sword-hilt.

Voran reached the top of the rise. The view was a continuation of the same landscape surrounding the three shacks, save for a clear path, which led directly to a trellised doorway covered in green ivy. Voran laughed. Even for the Lows of Aer, this doorway was comically obvious. Maybe this was Tarin's final joke? It was as though his old master were saying, "I know, Raven Son, you are quite the idiot, but I have made it easy for you."

Voran ran forward, not even slowing to pass through the doorway. The already-familiar sensation of displacement and temporary confusion quickly faded. He stood on a wide plain, the thinness of the air indicating high elevation, and just ahead of him was the waystone, and not a stone's throw beyond it—the giant head, still snoring as the flocks of starlings flew up and down, as regular as heartbeats.

Voran was thrown to the ground by something huge. A huge dark thing was atop him, its snout wet against his face. It licked him.

"I'm happy to see you too, Leshaya," spluttered Voran as he labored to find enough space to breathe.

She growled. "You are such an idiot, Voran." Her body quivered with mixed excitement, anger, and joy. He understood her completely.

"Tarin had said I would find a friend. I hoped it would be you."

"That old goat. Do you know how long I waited for the two of you? Where is he?"

It was strange. In the excitement of seeing Leshaya again, he had momentarily forgotten everything. Now the world came crashing through the walls he had put up around himself, and all of a sudden breathing the very air seemed dangerous.

"They found him, Leshaya. He's gone. Transfigured."

Leshaya's ears went back in pure animal fear, and she bared her fangs.

"It is time, then," she growled. "There is something you must know about our friend, the giant head of Buyan. He is the father of a race of giants who wield immense earth-power. They've been asleep for a long time. But they have returned."

Voran nodded, remembering Tarin's warning.

"He wants to make a deal. He says he knows where the weeping tree is, and he is willing to show us the way."

"For a price, naturally."

"I imagine so. Come."

The head was awake, its stillness more unnerving that the bluster it showed the last time they met. It raised its eyebrows ponderously, and Voran took it as the only sign of greeting the land-bound giant could still express.

"Well met, son of Otchigen. It is unfortunate that you did not inform me of your exalted bloodline the last time we met. I may have arranged things a little differently for you."

"We don't have time to play riddles this time, Buyan," said Voran. "To be frank, I have no desire to treat with you. I would much rather seek my own path."

"Are you sure about that, my boy?" asked the giant head, almost growling. "Have you looked at the waystone?"

Voran did. The writing was different.

If left you go, there death awaits

If right you go, there death awaits
If straight you go, there death awaits
If back you go, there death awaits

Voran became aware of a brooding sense of menace bearing down on him from all sides. He had a strong desire to turn around, but his heart told him that if he did, he would be dead in seconds.

"Is this another riddle?" Voran challenged Buyan, his hand on his sword.

The giant head laughed. The sound ripped several shrubs in the vicinity out of the ground with their roots still intact.

"I am quite sick of lying here in the ground, tied by the Powers. It is time for me to come out. My sons are awakening. Zmei is already abroad."

The sun hid behind clouds over Voran's head. He looked up, and it was not a cloud, but a giant in full armor, a spear in his right hand, his teardrop shield taller than the walls of Vasyllia. He inclined his head at Voran, but his face was backlit by the light of the sun surrounding his head like a parody of a halo. It called to mind the omen of the darkened sun.

"Why would I ever want to help you, Buyan? Do you not come from the same fallen line as the Raven?"

"Do not insult us," bellowed the other giant, Zmei. "Our power is not his borrowed power. We are the power of the earth. Ancient, eternal, self-sufficient. We owe allegiance to no one but ourselves."

"Our power is mighty," continued Buyan's head. "But it has been chained, contained for too long. You will restore that power, and in payment, we will give you Vasyllia, for you to refashion in whatever way you see fit."

For a moment, Voran saw the vision of the Pilgrim, the Vasyllia of old where every person was animated by a burning soul-bond. Could they truly have the power to give him Vasyllia? He could restore its ancient splendor. He was sure he could. But at what cost?

"I am but a humble warrior," said Voran. "I don't seek to play a role in the games of the Powers. I only want to find my family. Leave me be."

Buyan raised an eyebrow. "Your family? We can arrange that." He smiled, and his old, rotting teeth stank.

Like a bolt of lightning, Zmei's spear flew over Voran's head. Voran ducked. It hit with a sickening thud, and not into the ground. Voran trembled, not wanting to look at what he knew he would see, but forced his eyes to look at Leshaya.

She was pinned to the ground, so completely that she had no leverage even to push herself up, like a butterfly pinned to a piece of parchment. Something about her began to change, shift, like ripples on water. Her wolf form lessened, faded, turned in on itself, lost its color. Voran became ill and vomited violently. She was not Leshaya. She was his mother.

"You did not know?" said Buyan, all innocence and good humor. "Yes, Aglaia was transformed by my power all those years ago. It was a mercy. She was on the verge of death, were you not, my dear?"

"Why do you do this?!" Voran pulled out his sword and tensed, ready to fling himself at both giants.

"To make a point, you fool," said Zmei, moving just enough to let Voran see his face—beautiful, yet cold as chiseled stone. "We have no love for the Raven, and the Raven fears us. It is time for us to reclaim ownership of the earth. Your supposed master, the Power you call Adonais, has abandoned you. The Covenant, such as it was, is broken. We offer you everything that he gave you, and more. All we need is Living Water."

"*You* need Living Water as well, little man," said Buyan, looking significantly at Aglaia. "Better hurry, or you won't be able to heal her."

Voran looked at Aglaia. Her hair was whiter than he remembered, but otherwise no different than his memory of her, except for the paleness of her face and the look of absolute terror in her eyes. They rolled into the back of her head, and she fainted, though she did not fall, stuck as she was by the spear through her chest. Voran's terror swallowed him, and his hands shook uncontrollably.

But something in his mind nagged him. It was something that he should have noticed a long time ago. The Raven had great power; these ancient giants claimed to have even greater power. But the Raven had not even seemed to make the attempt to seek out Living Water, going straight to Vasyllia, as if that were his only goal. And Buyan claimed to know the location of the weeping tree. So why did the giants not take it for themselves? There were reports of at least one person being healed by the tree. Unless....

"You cannot find the weeping tree without me."

Buyan's face darkened visibly. "It is the nature of our power. A bargain, sealed ages ago with the Powers. We would rule the earth, but we abandoned our right to travel the other realms."

"But you know of a doorway?"

"Yes," said Zmei.

It explained much. People could cross over into the other realms. Some, a few, obviously had, and they were healed by the Living Water. But the giants could not.

Voran looked at Aglaia's limp body, at the blood choking her clothing, and he went on his knees to touch her face. It was still warm.

"I will come back for you, Mother," he whispered.

An icy breeze pushed Voran's hair across his face, coming from the right. Not a bowshot away, Voran saw a hole in the fabric of reality, a shimmering gap. On the other side, mountains stood tall, and atop one of them was a tree, made black by the setting sun behind it. Before stopping to even think, Voran ran to it and jumped through.

O tombs, you tombs,
Our eternal homes!
Long may we live,
But your doors we must face.
Our bodies belong
In our mother, the earth.
To be given to the soil,
To be eaten by worms.
But our souls will wander
Each to his own place...

Old Nebesti funeral dirge

CHAPTER 33
THE RAVEN'S CHOICE

Horrible cries surrounded Sabíana, exploding into her confused consciousness and fading to nothing in strange waves. Dimly she glimpsed blasts of flame and smoke belching from rents in the earth. Not yet fully recovered from her fit, she saw everything with varying focus, through a fog. She couldn't form her thoughts into complete patterns; the words gathered together only to hit an obstruction like a wall inside her head, and she gave up, exhausted from the effort. But through it all, she heard the sound of wind whistling through reeds. Sabíana felt the nearness of Feína, the terror receded a little, and her mind began to clear. But her limbs were still stone-dead.

Feína sang quietly. All the noises of war, the screams, the madness faded away, replaced by the blossoming rose-fire of the Sirin of flame. Sabíana's thoughts gathered in her mind like raindrops falling into each other down a windowpane. The pain was still there, but now it was bearable.

"My Sabíana," said Feína. "I cannot bear to see you like this."

The voice was in Sabíana's mind, as was the vision of the Sirin of fire. In her mind, Sabíana found it possible to answer.

"Feína, I do not know if I can bear my burden much longer. Please, lighten it for me."

"I cannot, my swan. It is beyond my power."

"Dear Feína, I think I could bear it if I understood what is happening. Why do I not just die and leave this pain behind? Why do I linger?"

"If that is what you wish, Sabíana, you can lay down your life right now.

You are given that choice. But if you die, the last spark of light in Vasyllia dies with you. The Raven's victory will be complete."

"So I must remain and suffer on? How can that possibly benefit anyone?"

"Your suffering is not without purpose, my bright swan. Your remaining in Vasyllia is a challenge to the Raven that cannot fail to bear fruit. Ever the Sons of the Swan will be a thorn in his side. And perhaps, if things go as Lyna hopes, you will be the source of his downfall."

Sabíana understood the reference to Voran. He was alive, and he still strove on his quest. His image warmed her heart, and the song of the Sirin rang out, stoking her inner fire until it blazed. She understood.

Her presence in Vasyllia was necessary. The Raven would not touch her; she was Cassían's line, and he needed legitimacy if he was to maintain any sort of power other than the rule of the fist. She must slowly heal, slowly become an image of endurance and hope for true Vasylli. Perhaps Adonais would see her sacrifice and would re-forge the lost Covenant.

Sabíana regained full consciousness at Yadovír's side as the smoke began to clear. Near her, the young chief priest Otar Gleb lay on the stones, bloodied, but still alive. Yadovír seemed to be protecting him, or keeping him for his own use later. Gleb nodded at her once and raised his hand, blessing her. She felt new strength rush into her.

The Gumiren had herded all the people of the city to every open square and courtyard in Vasyllia. The faces she could see seemed barely human; nearly all had succumbed to brutish terror and hatred. Only a few still had the same light in their eyes that she had ignited at the coronation.

Yadovír twitched and his face pulled into a focused expression, listening intently. Looking at Sabíana, he seemed for a moment to lose confidence, as if he noticed some change in her, some addition of power. He must have decided it was nothing, because he turned away from her and faced the crowds. He spoke not in his own voice, but in one augmented by several others, so it seemed a host declaiming from a single mouth.

"High people of Vasyllia! You have fought valiantly, but not to victory. I, the Mouth of the Raven, now declare your doom. The women and children may all live, provided every one of them gives up the worship of Adonais and spits on the Covenant. You warriors must pledge your swords to the Raven and swear to do his bidding in all things. Refuse, and the beasts whom you defeated not an hour ago will gladly feast on your unarmored bodies. Warriors! How say you? If yea, raise your right hands in solemn oath.

It took a long time, but eventually nearly every warrior did so. Sabíana's balance tottered, and her shakes began again. Somehow, she stopped herself and forced herself to watch on.

"Warriors of Adonais you were," said Yadovír, sneering. "Warriors of the Raven you become. But first, a test. Desecrate the Temple of Adonais, and you will live. Refuse, and your women and children will die before your eyes."

Now everyone was frozen in indecision. Sabíana understood them. It was one thing to denounce Adonais with the lips and to secretly worship in one's heart and home. It was another thing to raise a hand against his Temple.

Yadovír leered like an old man of millennial cunning, gesturing to the Gumiren with an arm that was made more terrible by a suggestion of a wing-shadow behind him. The Gumiren built a pyre around the Covenant Tree and lit it. Sabíana felt the terror of the blasphemy like it was a living presence next to her. The Gumiren then gathered all the women and children like cattle and pulled the babies from the arms of their mothers. They held them over the fire. Unmoved by the screams, they stood still as cold stone, ready at Yadovír's command to hurl the shrieking children into the fire, even as they reached for their mothers in uncomprehending terror. Sabíana thought her heart would rip apart from the strain.

None of the warriors hesitated any longer. Given torches and axes by the Gumiren, they rushed through the reaches like a swarm of fire-ants and vented all their fear and frustration on the trees of the Temple. Red-barks were torn asunder, burned, hacked to pieces. The Grove of Mysteries was mutilated, and Sabíana felt the death of each tree as though a child of hers were killed before her eyes. The low wall surrounding the temple was broken stone by stone with meticulous malice. The altar table was hurled off the edge of the cliff. The lanterns were shattered, and with their undying flames the Temple burned, and the conflagration rose up to the Heights, joining the blasphemous sacrifice of the Great Tree. Sabíana closed her eyes and willed the tears to come, to unburden the heaviness of her heart, but they would not.

With an effort, she forced her eyes open again. She needed to see this horror to its end. The warriors who still refused to join the Raven were jostled toward the gates of the city. Many of them bowed before the burning Temple as they passed it, heedless of the sharp points wedged into their backs. At that small act of bravery, Sabíana's tears came—slow and deliberate.

Many women and children followed their men, desiring no other fate than to join their loved ones in death. Most of the others who remained huddled away from them in fear. The crowd of faithful ones stopped at the open doors leading out of Vasyllia, and all turned back to Yadovír to hear the final pronouncement. His voice became impossibly loud, so that Sabíana was sure they heard every word.

"People of the Raven, denounce your allegiance to Adonais!"

Now there was no hesitation.

"We reject him!"

"Behold your queen." He raised Sabíana roughly with a single hand, and she felt no more dignified than a sack of potatoes. Many faces blanched and lost all remaining hope when they saw her. *I must look as bad as I feel,* she thought.

"Behold your Black Sun!" Yadovír screeched. "May her reign be long and blessed!"

"Long live Darina Sabíana!" they all cried. Some of the women wailed and moaned.

Sabíana wanted with all her power to at least raise a hand to them, to acknowledge that she was with them in spirit, but no part of her body moved.

"Death to the traitors!" Yadovír jabbed his right forefinger toward the people at the gates. "Go, and meet your just reward!"

Sabíana watched as the condemned walked out of the city, showing not the slightest sign of fear. At first quietly, then with greater intensity, they all began to sing. Even in the high turret of the palace in the third reach, Sabíana heard them clearly.

O Adonais, hear us,
Defend us, as we cry:
"Annihilate this Darkness,
And give us strength to die."

Lord, give them strength to die, Sabíana thought.

No sooner had all of them left the city than a white light washed over them. A radiant Sirin appeared over each person—a lamentation of thousands of Sirin in flight and full-throated song—bemoaning the fall of Vasyllia with voices that cut Sabíana with their agonizing beauty. Taking each of the faithful by the arms, including the many wounded still lying on the field of battle, the Sirin flew up into the light of the sun. Their song faded, but the song in Sabíana's heart rose to a great fury. She tested her limbs, and to her exhilaration, the smallest finger of her right hand twitched. The iron of her courage poured back into her heart. She could do this. She would be their hope.

Have you seen the hands of a healer?
Are they rough?
No.
Are they dirty?
No.
What are they like?
Like the sun reflected in water...

Karila nursery chant

CHAPTER 34
HEALER

Voran stood at the top of the world. He had crossed more than a single boundary. This was not the Lows of Aer; this was something deeper. Clouds were scattered below him, as though he were set here by a Power of Aer to herd them. Most of the clouds sat barely higher than a great moon-shaped tarn far below his feet, nestled among the crags that divided Vasyllia from Nebesta. The tarn was lined at one end with bunched conifers that looked like bristles on a hair-brush from this distance. Where he stood, there was hardly any vegetation, except for a few pines gnarled by the constant wind. The rest was grey-brown stone and snow, though there was strangely little white for this depth of winter.

Then there was the black hawthorn.

The young hawthorn, frothing with white flowers, stood on the tip of a conical rock, its roots trailing downward along the stone until their tips dug into great cracks. Its thorns were like iron nails, but each dripped opalescent water onto the rock. The drops rolled individually down the stone, slowly, carefully, as though they were looking for the right path down, until they followed the roots through the cracks into the earth. There were no clouds above them, Voran checked. The tree wept.

Though Voran's panic and fear beat at his heart like hammers, he froze in wonder at the sight. The hawthorn sang. It was nothing like the song of the Sirin; it was far more ancient and alien, and it revealed to Voran a depth of natural power that he never could have imagined. He had no doubt this tree was capable of healing the sick, and much more than that.

Something thwacked in the thin air and whistled. Voran's left shoulder jerked back at a violent angle, and when he looked down, it had sprouted an arrow. He tried to move, but the pain was like his shoulder ripping apart. He was pinned to a tree.

Voran turned his head, trying to gather his thoughts in the maelstrom of pain and panic. Mirnían came out of a shelter of a crag, a set expression on his face. Mirnían pulled the bowstring back to his cheek and waited. His hands trembled slightly, and his face had gone white. He shook his head and closed his eyes for a moment, then tensed and loosed. The arrow grazed Voran's left arm, tearing the flesh. Its whistle lingered in the sparse air.

Voran caught Mirnían's eye and nodded, then dropped his head. He waited for the next arrow, sure that this time a marksman as good as Mirnían would not miss. He couldn't help but feel intense sadness that it had come to this, but to his surprise, he didn't blame Mirnían. He breathed out and was strangely calm.

Mirnían's breathing was loud enough for Voran to hear. "No," whispered Mirnían, his breathing turning ragged, "No, it can't be."

Voran looked up to see Mirnían ripping off his tunic with hands shaking so violently that he remained fully clothed despite all his efforts to disrobe. Finally, he managed to pull part of a sleeve off. His chest was leprous, and it stank, even at this distance. Mirnían's eyes were wild. He raised his hands, and they were riddled with sores. He showed them to Voran like a frightened child.

"They are back," he said, his eyes nearly all whites. "They are back."

He ran toward the hawthorn and scrabbled up the rock, but it was slick with the tree's tears, and he kept falling down. Finally, he reached the lowest thorns with one hand as he clung to the stone face with the other. He grabbed and screamed with pain, let go, and fell head over heels to the ground, where he lay, twitching spasmodically and sobbing. His hands were torn where he had grabbed at the weeping thorns. The hawthorn had not healed him.

Voran could no longer bear it. Gritting his teeth, he pulled the arrow out of his shoulder and nearly passed out from the pain. He forced his mind to ignore it, even as his head began to spin and his limbs wanted desperately to give up the fight. Somehow, he made it to Mirnían's side, and dropped to his knees next to him.

Mirnían no longer struggled; he merely sobbed, looking like a wounded animal more than a human being. He raised both hands to his face in a half-hearted gesture of protection. Voran put his good arm under Mirnían's neck and hugged him close to his body. He wept again—he was weeping far too much lately.

"Look at us," he said to Mirnían through the racking sobs. "Is this what we wanted? How did it come to this, my brother?"

Mirnían's eyes were wide with shock. "You will not kill me?" The question was full of disappointment, as though he had given up on life and wished that Voran would be brave enough to end it for him, since he couldn't do it himself.

Voran's body shook from his anger. Not letting go of Mirnían, holding him with the same gentle care as a mother gives to a newborn, he looked up at the cloudless sky and screamed his defiance.

"Where are you, Adonais?!" Voran's voice echoed, broken by the sobs. "Mirnían has served you with his life. He has sacrificed everything to follow my mad lead. How could you have allowed it to come to this? You have all-power. What Vasylli has given more of himself, lost more of himself, gained more of himself in your service? Will you curse your own child?"

"You're asking the wrong questions, my boy," said a familiar voice. Standing under the shadow of the hawthorn was the Pilgrim, even older than Voran remembered him, leaning on his staff now for support, not merely show. The setting sun above his head hung blood red, barely touching the tips of the hawthorn. "Why do you expect the Heights to intervene for you whenever you need saving?"

"How many times has Adonais already intervened?" said Voran, forcing his voice to remain contained, though it trembled from the effort. "How many times have I been guided precisely to the place I need to be, at the appointed time? Even after I turned away from him, he found me a deliverer. Tarin died for me. Why all the extraordinary care for me, and this disregard for Mirnían? I do not deserve any of it!"

The Pilgrim smiled. "No, you do not."

"I do not hold Mirnían responsible for shooting me." said Voran. "I deserve much worse at his hands. I *should* be dead."

Mirnían's expression was unreadable, but he had stopped crying.

"I call on Adonais," cried Voran. "Let him answer. Why do I, the guilty one, enjoy his patronage, while the one who has suffered the most remains cursed by leprosy?"

The Pilgrim raised his arms and grew, larger and larger until the very sky seemed to rest on his head. His grey cloak thrust back, he exploded into the radiance of a thousand suns. His knee-length chainmail was woven of light itself, kaleidoscopic, yet purely and utterly white. His eyes were as twin beacons, and his face was beyond youth or old age. His helmet-plume was a billowing flame; his hair was fluid gold on his massive shoulders. Joy poured out of him, joy like the first cry of a newborn, like the first star after a week-long snowstorm.

"I am the Harbinger, brother to Athíel of the Palymi. I am the mouth of the Most High. I am the light behind the dawn. I am the fire that burns the setting sun. I am the one who witnessed the covenant between Lassar and the Heights. Do not call on Adonais. Speak to me, if you dare."

For a moment, Voran thought that the Harbinger spoke the name Adonais with distaste. But how could that be?

"I am a servant of the Heights," whispered Voran, forcing himself to look at the giant of light. "I am nothing. Yet has not this man, this prince of Vasyllia, done enough to deserve more than this?"

"Do you doubt that all he has suffered is part of a design?"

"Design? What design can there be? Adonais has abandoned us, and old Powers are coming back to take the earth for themselves."

"Voran. Consider the past days. You cannot fail to come to this conclusion. You four—Voran, Mirnían, Lebía, Sabíana—have been *led*. By me and by the white stag and by others, all along paths thorny and painful. You ask why? If I told you the full truth, you would not believe me. You must come to it yourself. The answer to all that your questioning heart desires is at the heart of Vasyllia."

"The one place that I cannot reach."

"You *must* reach it. Do not forget. Vasyllia is *everything*. Even if she falls, you must go back. Search for its heart. At the heart lie all the answers."

The Harbinger's light flared like a huge furnace and spun faster and faster, until the white light was a huge pillar, reaching up far beyond the sun, ending on Voran and Mirnían, blood pouring from both their wounds. The rest of the world was a colorless darkness; only they two were illumined in color and light. Then the Harbinger disappeared, and time seemed to begin anew. The sun descended behind the flowers and thorns of the weeping tree, turning the tears red as blood falling from spear-tips.

"And so it is the two of us at the end, Mirnían," said Voran, smiling. "As it should be."

He stood up awkwardly, nearly fainting again, and unsheathed his sword. His left hand limp and throbbing with fire, he somehow leveraged himself with his right, sword in hand, and clambered up the rock, foot by foot, until he lay under the shadow of the branches. Breathing with difficulty, he rose to his knees and touched the pale flowers, grazed his fingers over the thorns. It was so beautiful. His tears returned, and he spat in disgust at himself.

"No one should have to make this choice," he whispered. "Forgive me, Mother."

He breathed in, braced himself, and hacked at the thin trunk with his sword.

"What are you doing?" shrieked Mirnían.

Voran struck again and again like a man possessed, his eyes blurry with the flow of tears, his hands unsteady from the pain.

"No one should have access to so much power," he said.

He saw Aglaia's stricken body in his mind, and he despaired.

The sword finally broke through the trunk, and Voran pushed the hawthorn down the far side of the cliff. It fell out of sight. A fountain of fragrant water blossomed from the raw, jagged stump and immediately began to ebb. Voran had a sudden compulsion to drink the water before it disappeared completely. He caught a little in his hands. It sparkled in his cupped palms, multifaceted like a fluid diamond. He drank.

The waves of hot pain receded into the back of Mirnían's awareness. He was tired, so tired that he could easily fall asleep on the bare rock. Now that it was over, now that Voran had singlehandedly destroyed Vasyllia and dashed all their hopes, there was little left to do except die. But he remembered Lebía; he remembered their coming child; he remembered the life in Ghavan, and somehow he knew he would press on.

Voran had stopped weeping. He looked at Mirnían with eyes that seemed centuries older, eyes so green that they seemed almost mad. Voran slipped off the top of the rock, holding on to the stone with his left arm and balancing with his right.

His left arm?

"Voran, your arm!"

Voran looked confused for a moment, then looked down at his shoulder. The black fabric was clotted with blood. Voran poked his fingers into the rip made by the two arrows, and his face turned white.

"Mirnían, I am healed."

Mirnían's heart raced. He thought he understood what had happened. He got up, groaned from the pain, and hobbled to Voran, feeling more an old man than a youth of twenty-two years. He took Voran's right hand in both his own.

"No, Voran," he said, strangely elated. "You are not healed. You are the healer."

Mirnían placed Voran's right palm on his own exposed chest, and his entire body felt as though it were burned with hot irons. He screamed, but held on to Voran's wrist as if his life depended on it. It lasted a long time, but then the pain went out, like a fire extinguished by a gust of wind.

Mirnían knew that he was healed—this time completely—but to see that truth reflected in Voran's expression was glorious. Voran looked like a gleeful boy, making his wiry, sparse beard seem a storyteller's disguise. His strong features softened into a smile so full of joy, Mirnían realized he did not know the meaning of the word until he saw it in Voran's face.

"Voran," he said, unsure of the words, "I—"

"No, Mirnían," said Voran, more calm and in control than Mirnían had ever seen him. "All that is past. There is a great deal of work left to be done. A great deal of hardship to be overcome. It would be easier to overcome it all together, as family."

Mirnían felt as though an old version of himself died in that moment, and a new Mirnían arose in his place, a Mirnían who did not merely act the part of the solicitous leader, as he so often used to do in Vasyllia. At that moment, Mirnían felt ready to contain all of Vasyllia in his heart. It occurred to him that his father must have felt the same way every day of his life.

"There is something you should know, Voran. I married Lebía, and we are expecting..."

Voran grabbed him and raised him off the ground. At first, Mirnían thought that finally Voran's temper had the better of him, but there was nothing but warmth in his embrace, and then Voran laughed. It echoed over the mountains.

"My little swanling picked *you?*" He chortled.

Mirnían felt himself blush violently, something he could not remember ever doing in his life. It was very strange for their roles to be so reversed, but there was something liberating in it. He returned Voran's embrace.

"It is time, my brother. We must go," said Voran, staring over Mirnían's shoulder, his eyes illuminated by a golden light. Mirnían turned to see a majestic stag, his fur completely white, his antlers sparkling gold. It wasn't entirely *there*. It shimmered, as though it were in water.

"Will you consent to bear us to the waystone, old friend?" asked Voran.

The white stag lowered its head.

As Voran stood before the waystone, he laughed.

It was the last thing either of the giants expected, and their expressions soured.

Voran turned his back to both of them and ran to Aglaia. Even with his new strength, even with the healing flowing through him, stoked by the Sirin's flame, he was afraid to touch her. The spear point was deep in the ground, passing through her chest completely.

"Mirnían, help me," he said.

Mirnían's face was a fierce shade of green, but he came. Together, they snapped the haft of the spear in two and gently pulled her body up, until she was free of it. She gasped in pain as the blood gushed. Mirnían held his hand to his mouth, looking ready to vomit at any moment.

Voran closed his eyes and began to mouth the word—*Saddaí, Saddaí.* He placed both hands on the gaping wound and breathed out deeply. He reached for Tarin's stillness, deeper and deeper within, then gently nudged at his heart-flame. Aglaia's breathing was ragged, then she moaned. Voran looked down at his hands, and the blood still flowed over them.

"She is not healing," whispered Mirnían.

Voran plunged deeper within, and forced his accelerating heart to still again into the pleasant rhythm and presence of the word. He forced all thoughts to cease. When there was nothing but the word in his heart, he submitted. *Let it be as it must.*

A soft light throbbed from his hands, and Aglaia was bathed in it. Her eyes opened, wide and surprised, and she gently gasped.

"Oh," she sighed and smiled. She looked at Voran chidingly. "I think now you have paid off your debt to me, my son." Not only was there no wound on her, but her clothing was clean and untouched—a rich overdress of gold brocade, covered in jewels, like something out of an ancient tapestry. Mirnían chortled.

"That was a bit much, no?" He raised one eyebrow at Voran, and Voran shrugged his shoulders and shook his head.

Aglaia closed her eyes and fell into a deep sleep instantly, her wrinkles smoothing away to reveal the same face Voran remembered so well. Only her white hair told of her actual age.

"What have you done?" thundered Buyan. Zmei assumed a fighting stance. "Where is the Living Water?"

"It is gone. I destroyed the tree. Whatever power it left me is now gone in the healing."

Zmei roared and charged the three of them. Mirnían reached for his bow.

"No, Mirnían," whispered Voran, unfazed by the giant. "Wait."

Voran raised both his hands. Zmei jerked back in fear, as though someone threw fire at his face. His sword out, he backed away.

"Very fine," he growled. "But do not think that trick will work for longer than a day. You shine with the power now, but it will fade. You think you have come out the winner in this game? You fool. Every darkness, every shadow, every power in this world and all the others will hunt you from this moment forward. You thought the Raven was a problem. You do not know what you have unleashed on yourself. You will see me again, soon enough."

Voran unsheathed his sword and saluted, as he would at the training field in the warrior seminary.

"I look forward to that day, Zmei." He bowed low, to his waist. When he looked up, Buyan snored, and Zmei was nowhere to be seen.

There is one thing you must never forget. No matter how evil the times, no matter how dire the calamity, if there is but one person on earth who makes Covenant with Adonais, then the world will not fall. The dawn will come after the dark night, though it lasts for centuries.

From "The Testament of Cassían, Dar of Vasyllia"
(*The Sayings: Book II, 21:30*)

CHAPTER 35
COVENANT

Lebía stood, as she did every morning, on the banks of the sea, waiting for Mirnían to return. For more than a year, she had seen nothing. After the baby had been born, she came with the little bundle in her arms, that simultaneous source of pain and joy, terror and courage that taught her, for the first time in her life, that she had no idea what it meant to love.

The baby gurgled something profoundly wise, and she found herself enthralled by him. Already he smiled when she looked at him, opening a toothless mouth wide and cackling in joy. *If only he would sleep a little more at night.*

When he had finished his oration, she looked up again and saw something. It was probably nothing; probably yet another trick of the light, another game of the early spring sun. Already all around her Nature was just waking to life; only she remained cold with the winter of her heart.

Then she recognized them—longboat sails. She watched in mute astonishment as two, then five, then ten, then twenty boats came into view, all of them bearing the standard of old Vasyllia—a Sirin in flight enclosed within a fiery sun.

"I will not expect it," she said aloud. "It is not my husband. He is gone from me."

Still, her heart pined and agonized and shuddered in fear. Soon the first boat came close enough for her to see the passengers at the helm. Mirnían and an older woman, hooded, stood together. She looked directly at Lebía.

The wind caught and threw back the hood, revealing a face Lebía never expected to see again in her life. The face of her mother. Lebía burst into tears and lifted little Antomír above her head.

The moments of waiting were each an exuberant eternity. Lebía imagined asking them every question hoarded over months and years, felt every prick of pain and swell of joy she could have ever conceived, all in a few moments. And yet, the boats seemed to do no more than stand on the water.

Now, she was in Mirnían's arms, limp from tears of joy. Aglaia held little Antomír. She seemed a favorite of his already, and he babbled to her with all the seriousness of his three months. Mirnían could not contain himself at the sight; he tried to enclose all of them in his arms at once. Behind Mirnían, the twenty boats were filled with Vasylli.

"Who are they?" Lebía asked in wonder at their tear-streaked faces.

"They are all that remain of the true Vasylli," said Aglaia, "rescued by the Sirin from the Raven."

"We have little room on Ghavan," said Otar Svetlomír behind them, approaching Aglaia with open arms. "But we will make more."

Aglaia embraced him as an old friend, then seemed to recollect herself and fell on her knees, begging for his blessing. He put his hand on her head and pulled her close, and they sobbed together.

All of Ghavan met the refugees with cheering and wonder. Some found brothers, children, friends among them, and the dead eyes of those who had seen the Raven began to flutter with new life. Immediately, Mirnían took control of the situation and ordered that trestles be set in the center of the village, and that a great feast be prepared for the faithful Vasylli. But no sooner did he command than Lebía heard a surge of the song of the Sirin in her heart. Aína whispered to her, and only she could hear.

"Vasyllia!" exclaimed Lebía more loudly than she ever had in her life, feeling foolish and elated all at once. Everyone hushed and looked at her in surprise. "This is not the only joy for Ghavan. Come, my dear family, I must show you Vasyllia's hope."

She rushed out of the square into the woods, pulling Mirnían's hand to follow. Aglaia came, still discussing great things with little Antomír. The villagers, somewhat confused, followed a little hesitantly. They walked for what seemed like hours, but the early spring cold dissipated with their brisk pace. Finally, they reached a spruce grove, stately in silence. Hidden within the trees was a tiny white aspen, gently pulsating with light.

"Is that what I think it is?" Mirnían's eyes wide with wonder. He turned to see Lebía smiling at him proudly. "How did you know?"

"The hope of Vasyllia," whispered Otar Svetlomír. He fell on his knees before the sapling.

"We must replant it in the center of the village," said Mirnían.

"I do not know, my love," said Lebía. "It seems somehow disrespectful, no?"

"I mean to honor it, swanling. Were we not punished enough for hoarding our treasures in Vasyllia? Let us bring the tree to a place where all can see it and be filled with hope."

Filled with sudden inspiration, Mirnían walked up to the sapling and reached for the roots.

"Be gentle with it," whispered Lebía.

"I will be gentle with both of my new treasures, always."

Lebía blushed a little, like a white rose tipped with red.

Mirnían gently took the trunk near the base, and to his amazement the roots disentangled themselves from the ground and wrapped themselves around his hand.

"The blessing of the Heights is on you, Dar Mirnían," said Otar Svetlomír, his eyes brilliant in the white light.

They planted the tree in the center of the village. The roots took the earth by themselves, just as they had taken Mirnían's hand.

Lebía hesitantly touched the quivering branches of the white sapling. They thrummed with life, and she gasped in pleasure, like a child might when touching something unexpectedly cold. Suddenly, the tree grew before their eyes. Within seconds, it was a full tree, adorned with golden leaves still half-folded. The white light rose until it was hard to look at the tree directly.

"Look!" said a girl in the crowd, pointing upward.

The sky above them shimmered with red gold. Hundreds of firebirds circled the tree. A single pin-prick opened in the sky above the firebirds, and a light descended on the tree, until it seemed to burn with fire. Then Lebía realized it was no illusion. The white aspen was on fire.

Mirnían embraced Lebía. She nestled under his chin, that most comfortable of places, where she fit perfectly.

"I have so many questions, my love," she said. "But one will suffice for now. How is Voran?"

Mirnían pulled away from her and put his hands on her shoulders to look intently into her eyes.

"How did you know?" he asked.

She smiled. "We have always been bound unlike other people. I feel him like he is part of me."

Mirnían nodded, understanding. "He is well, as well as can be expected." He huffed, at a loss for words. "I do not even know where to begin."

"Where is he now?"

"He is going to Vasyllia. Sabíana waits for him, you know."

Lebía smiled. "Did he find what he sought?"

"No. He seeks still. I think he will seek always. If things were dangerous before, now they are far worse. Thank the Heights, this place is safe. No other place in the world is safe anymore."

On the next morning, before the sun rose, Lebía came one last time to the shores of the Great Sea, to take leave of that part of her life—the long wait for Mirnían—forever. She was surprised to see Aglaia standing there as well, looking out over the water.

"Mother? You are up early."

"Wolves don't sleep as humans do. They need much less." She grinned. Lebía gasped.

"*You* were the wolf that brought Mirnían? You brought me my happiness. That was you!"

"Yes, my swanling. And now, I must leave you again."

Lebía started to protest, but Aglaia silenced her with a glance, as though no time had passed at all since Lebía was a five-year-old girl. Lebía even giggled nervously.

"My poor boy needs someone," said Aglaia. "Voran has taken the healing of many on himself. But he is still so young, so inexperienced."

"Dear mother," Lebía smiled wryly. "What can an old woman do to help the greatest warrior of our age?"

"Ha!" The grin on Aglaia's face was uncomfortably wolfish. "He is nothing without me." She winked, and suddenly a wolf the size of a bear stood next to Lebía. Lebía laughed in her shock and clapped her hands like a little girl.

"Voran thinks I am a helpless old woman. He will learn to value his mother more in the future."

She leapt into the water without a backward glance. Lebía stood there, watching her turn into a black dot. In an instant that seemed to stop time itself, the rays of the sun streamed out between two distant peaks. Everything the sun touched danced with life. Lebía realized with a start that Antomír would be awake already, and poor Mirnían would have no idea what to do with a screaming baby. She turned around, hiked her skirts up, and ran back to Ghavan.

THE CURSE OF THE RAVEN

Raven Son: Book Two

THE CURSE OF THE RAVEN

(Raven Son: Book Two)

Copyright © Nicholas Kotar 2017

All rights reserved. No part of this book may be reproduced, stored in a retrieval system, or transmitted in any form, or by any means, digital, electronic, mechanical, photocopying, or otherwise, without prior permission of the publisher.

This is a work of fiction. All the characters and events portrayed in this book are either fictitious or are used fictitiously.

Cover Design by Books Covered Ltd.

Published by Waystone Press 2017

ISBN: 9780998847931

LCCN: 2017913721

❀ Created with Vellum

To Adrian and Emilia

In the year of the Covenant 1066, the great city of Vasyllia, the very heart of the known world, was betrayed to an invading army of nomad Gumiren by its own people. What many did not know, but suspected, was that the invading southerners were no more than a tool in the hand of Vasyllia's ancient enemy. He has many names, that demon. The Raven. The Great Changer. The Bringer of Darkness. But as often happens, in the moment of the Raven's ascendance was the seed of his demise planted. All that remained was for at least a few Vasylli to remain true to the Old Ways until the time of reclamation. But when the Healer returns, will he find any true Vasylli left?

From "A New History of the Covenant" by Dar-in-Exile Mirnían II

CHAPTER 1
LLUN THE SMITH

Llun the Smith gazed into the fire. The bellows blew, and the sparks exploded before him like a shower of fireflies. He breathed in. The smell—soot, sweat, dross melting from pure metal. It was as near paradise as anyone could get in Vasyllia. Especially after Vasyllia fell.

"Smith Llun! How much longer?"

It was the fifth time Garmun had asked the same question in the last half hour. The old fool. Llun was continually amazed that the fat man was the most sought-after master builder in Vasyllia. All he ever seemed to do was sit in Llun's smithy, covering most of it with his belly.

"It's coming, it's coming," growled Llun. He didn't mind Garmun sitting around while he worked. But no one...no one was allowed to break the hallowed moments when the fire and the metal fused to become something new, something sacred.

"By the Great Father, Llun, I only asked for nails, not works of art."

Llun twitched at the name. *Great Father, my muscular left bicep. Why is the Raven renaming himself now, of all times? Does he imagine we've forgotten how he took everything from us?*

"What is it about you master builders? What ails you? Too many children?"

Garmun turned purple, opened his mouth to speak, then choked on himself. He had no wife, but his illegitimate progeny filled half of Vasyllia's first reach. Crude people snickered that being so fat was normal after so many pregnancies.

"Peace, Brother Garmun," said Llun. "They're all but done. And I promise you they'll be the hardiest, longest-lasting nails you'll find in all Vasyllia."

And the only ones with a raven etched on the nail's head. May his memory be forever cursed, and may every hammer stroke hasten the time of his demise...

"You mean the most *exquisite* nails in Vasyllia, no doubt," the fat man complained. "I've never seen anyone so taken with his own talent. Don't you know that your little frills and personal touches make no difference? Competence! Competence! That's what the market wants."

"The market, with all its frippery and cheap wares, can burn in the fires of the land of the dead for all I care." It slipped out. Llun hoped the hammer would be distraction enough. But he had never been blessed by fortune.

"Your talk smacks of the Outer Lands, you fool. Be careful no one in the Great Father's good graces overhears you."

"Overhears what?" said a new voice from the doorway.

The stranger who walked in was the antithesis of Garmun—short and wiry like a ratter. Everything about him suggested potential action—his smile, just on the verge of malice, his hands, holding his thick belt as though it were someone's throat, the sharp line of his cheekbones, suggesting some nomad blood. His physicality was so overwhelming that it almost distracted from the dog's scalp hanging from his belt.

So this must be one of that new department that the Gumiren—those filthy nomad invaders from the South—had concocted for collaborators. What was it called? The Consistory, yes. The secret police of the Raven. Dog-men, the commons called them. A kind name for a traitor against his own people.

"I'm not open to new customers," said Llun, trying to keep his tone light.

"That's a relief," the stranger said, with more gentleness than Llun expected. "No one will bother us, then."

He closed the door and dropped the black curtain over the door-window.

"What a pleasant smithy you have here, Brother Llun."

Llun stiffened as the stranger began to look around the smithy. Like a bitch on the scent, the stranger's pointed face bore down on the cluttered left counter of the smithy. He pulled out two interlacing shields of iron leaf-work tracery so fine they almost looked woven. Each held a heraldic icon of a raven in flight.

"Well, that's..." He didn't finish, but to Llun's surprise it sounded like he was about to say "beautiful." What? A Raven's man actually admiring beauty for its own sake?

Llun's stomach churned. It was all wrong: there was genuine admiration in the stranger's eyes. He appreciated the shields as things of beauty, not as objects to buy or sell. That wasn't supposed to happen. The Raven's men followed a script. They were supposed to ask where Llun was going to sell these useless trinkets, and when he hemmed and hawed about beauty and artistry, they would threaten Llun with something horrible.

Llun had seen enough of the Gumiren's work to know that the threats of the collaborators were never idle—weavers with one eye burned out just so their depth perception would no longer be of any use, sword-wrights with their right hands chopped off at the wrist, potters with broken feet.

Damn them all, he thought bitterly.

But this one was admiring decorative shields that had no practical use whatsoever. Llun had made them merely for the sake of beauty.

"What possessed you to make such a thing?"

Llun's hammer stopped in mid-air. It was the choice of words. "Possessed." No, this was no mere inquisitor. This man understood the creative process. What it means to make something, and how it feels to be taken by the hand of the Maker.

"It made itself," said Llun, hesitating. "I was just the instrument."

The stranger gasped with pleasure, as though Llun's words had given him a taste of something he hadn't felt in a very long time. Maybe this was an impostor? A motley fool who put on the dog-scalp to ridicule the Consistory? But such people did not walk the streets for long before their bodies were used as decorations for lamp-posts.

"Llun," said the dog-man, and looked Llun directly in the eyes.

The lack of the "Brother" before Llun's name frightened him more than the direct gaze. This collaborator was something new. Yes, he was likely an artist. An artist of torture and death.

"Llun, you stand there, gawking like a fool, telling me you made something for the sheer pleasure of artistry?"

The stranger's right index finger caressed the outline of the raven, as though he could memorize shapes better with his finger. Could he see it, the *true* picture? The hammer slipped in Llun's hand and almost landed on his thumb. *Careful...*

"Yes." Llun's voice didn't remain as steady as he would have liked. The stranger noticed. His smile was an adder's smile.

"Who taught you to waste your time like this?"

So they had come to it at last. The stranger wanted Llun to be an informer to the collaborators, a friend of the dogs.

Not on my life.

"No one," said Llun, continuing to beat the nails. "Don't think I use my work-time on these things. I give all the Great Father's time to my customers, as anyone, even fat Garmun here, will tell you." The builder looked like he wanted to kill Llun and run away from him at the same time. "I do this...art...in my own time."

The stranger raised his eyebrows slightly, faintly amused. Llun immediately realized his mistake. He shouldn't have said anything about having the luxury of time for himself.

"What a shame," said the Consistory man. "You should *rest* during your free time, Brother Llun. It will help you make better nails and horseshoes and braziers. *Useful* things. Will you accept a gift from the Great Father? A gratis pass to one of the houses of rest?"

The dog-man leered. Llun flushed, embarrassed. Did the dog-man really think that sort of thing appealed to an artisan? How typical. The smith working off his frustrations with a romp in the hay.

Llun struck the nail so hard it cracked in half.

"I don't fraternize with prostitutes," said Llun. His finger bled where the cracked nail had pierced it. *Concentrate!*

The Consistory man smiled, gentle as ever. "I didn't say a thing about *fraternizing*. And why use such a crude word as prostitute? I believe I have heard them better described as purveyors of pleasure."

Garmun chortled, then tried to disappear. For a man of his size, that was not easy.

"Anyway, I don't have time for that nonsense," said Llun.

"Nonsense? It is all sanctioned by our Great Father himself. Are you suggesting that anything his greatness allows is not worthy of your time? I will not say coin, because I have already offered you a gratis pass."

"That is not what I meant to say." Llun stopped hammering, put the hammer down, and wiped his hands on his apron, which only made them dirtier. "I'm sorry, I don't believe I have the honor of your name, Brother?"

That should bring matters to a head, whether or not Llun's head would be the cost.

"Ah, my mistake! My name is Aspidían. You may have heard of me."

Oh, *Heights*. Aspidían? The right hand of Yadovír, the traitor who had opened the gates of Vasyllia to the invading army of Gumiren. Some even insinuated that Aspidían was more than his right hand. By all accounts, he was a monster that had killed over one hundred true Vasylli with his own hands.

"Brother Llun." Aspidían's face no longer showed interest in anything. He leaned against the wall in assumed fatigue, the very picture of a man who had seen too much and wished merely to be left alone. "I would be most honored if you would come to the Consistory's halls on the morrow, perhaps at three hours after sunrise? I would like to employ your skills in a most important matter. Good day to you."

"As you say, Brother Aspidían."

As soon as he left, the forge coughed, the bellows sighed, the anvil begged to be struck again. Everything in the smithy heaved out a relieved breath. Garmun was near to tears of hysteria.

"Brother Llun, Brother Llun," he whispered, as if expecting the inquisitor to be eavesdropping just outside the door. "Do you know what this means?" He threw his hands up above his head. "Who will make things for me now? Don't you know you are the best craftsman in Vasyllia? Have I ever told you that, Brother? Have I?" Both sweaty hands, fleshy and fat, wrung Llun's arm, kneading it like bread, though even his massive hands hardly encircled the width of Llun's arm, hardened by years of the smithy. "Why must it be you? I know the Great Father needs an occasional example for everyone's instruction, but ... why *you*?"

"Calm yourself, you fat fool. Why not take the man at his word? Perhaps there is some manner of work to be done?"

Garmun guffawed. "You madman of an artist! Don't you know what they do to people like you? Have you forgotten Dashun?"

Llun tried to stop the grimace, but failed. Why did Garmun have to mention Dashun of all people? Llun was sure he would never forget the sight of Dashun's mutilated body. But what was worse? The torture, or the way he had publicly recanted all his beliefs and convictions? He had read aloud a text prepared for him by the Raven. Then he had collaborated with them, even uncovered a conspiracy against the Gumiren. And still they killed him horribly.

"You exaggerate," Llun said, coughing to cover the quaver in his voice. "I'm no danger to anyone. I am simply an odd, self-absorbed craftsman."

"Brother Llun, do you know *anything* about Aspidían?" He raised both hands, palms out. The gesture to ward off evil.

"Your nails, Brother Garmun."

"Brother Llun. Oh, my dear friend." Garmun wept, blubbering like a woman. Perversely, Llun remembered the jesting commoners and the purported pregnancies. He couldn't help himself.

"There, there, Garmun. I know it's common enough to cry more than usual when you're pregnant."

Garmun turned purple again. Shoving Llun back so that he nearly flew into the forge itself, he pointed a finger thick as a blood sausage at his nose. "You ... you ..." He huffed out like a passing thunderstorm, taking his bombast with him.

Llun remembered to breathe.

"You can come out now," he whispered. The entire left side of the table heaved. "Did no one teach you discretion, you little idiot?"

"Llun," said the girl of thirteen who finally managed to extricate herself from all the bits of metal. "Did you mean what you said to Garmun? Or did you just make him mad so he wouldn't be associated with you when you're trussed up like a chicken on the spit?"

"Which do you think, Mirodara?"

Mirodara's face went white. "I wasn't serious, Llun."

"Never mind. I'm not that worried. I'm not nearly as important as your father was."

"Dashun is *not* my father. I have no father. Not after he collaborated."

"You can't wash his blood from inside you, girl! Why do you think they've been after you all this time?"

Llun's breath caught as he realized how close the girl had been to death only a few moments ago. Was *that* why Aspidían had come in? Was someone blabbing again?

"Anyway, I don't even look like Dashun. Everyone knows I'm my mother's—"

"Don't!" Llun's voice cracked. The last thing he wanted was to be reminded of Vatrina.

"I'm sorry," said Mirodara, her face switching from red to white and back to red with dizzying speed. "I know you don't like to talk about her. But she was my *mother*, Llun. You're just her brother."

"You don't have any siblings, Mirodara. You don't know. You just don't know. I never knew either of my parents."

"Yes, yes, and now I'm the only one you have left. Blah blah blah. You won't talk me out of it."

"What do you hope to accomplish, anyway, with these...what do they call themselves?"

"The Sons of the Swan. We're going to reclaim Vasyllia for Darina Sabiana, the true queen of all the lands. She's still alive in that palace. I *know* it."

Llun laughed.

"You laugh? You're about to be thrown into the middle of it all. You think they'll let you stay on the side, uninvolved?"

Llun sighed and stretched his aching shoulders. Mirodara, for all her silliness, was older than her years. She had no choice. All the children had grown older the day Vasyllia fell.

"You'll stay here tonight," said Llun, the tone of finality clear in his voice. Mirodara looked like she wanted to argue, but nodded and extended a hand to Llun.

"Peace?"

Llun embraced her, trying hard not to weep. She did look just like her mother, his sister.

Please, Adonais. If you still listen to us who failed you, don't let them take her. Not her. She's just a girl.

On the day of blood, a day when the sun turns black and stars fall as flames from the sky, those walking the streets of the Great City will seem alive. But they are naught but the hordes of the dead. In that day, the swan's wing will be broken, and the falcon will be too far to hear her cries of pain. The earth itself will moan for the Healer. But the Healer is lost in the maze of his own doubts...

From "The Prophecy of Llun"
(The Sayings, Book XXIII 3:1-3)

CHAPTER 2
THE CONSISTORY

The early morning light showed Llun's smithy off at its best. The prevailing colors peeking through the soot-grimed windows were gold and orange. No customer came this early, and as the sun rose, the true, hidden beauty of the place came to life. In the light of the fire, the smithy danced with shadows, but the morning sun, which coddled like a mother and warmed like childhood memory, showed the things Llun made in their true aspect.

He picked up the decorative shields that Aspidían had so admired. Only now could their secret be told, their mystery uncovered. They were not ravens at all in the tracery. The morning rays, coming through the window at a very specific angle, revealed the ravens to be two falcons. The dancing fire-light of any house's interior was intended to trick the casual observer to think they were ravens depicted flying at the observer, head feathers curiously ruffled by the wind. The figure was made so that it shifted in the mind's eye after long contemplation in the light of morning, like a difficult sentence in a book that rewards the slow reader. Then, the ravens transformed into falcons.

Llun wondered if Aspidían had read the riddle in the tracery. Was that why he was so astounded? Or was it true appreciation? It was bad enough not to have any visible representation of the Raven in his smithy, as was required by the so-called Great Father. But to blaspheme him by association with something as unclean as the falcon—the sigil of Voran, the Healer and the great enemy of the Raven—that would be reason enough for a high inquisitor to pay a visit to the first reach of Vasyllia. Or was it simply that someone had reported Llun in hopes of gaining his smithy as a reward? Llun knew of too many such cases to consider it impossible.

Too many thoughts. Like someone banging an iron pan with a wooden spoon inside his head. Llun decided to take the long way to the Consistory.

He looked in on Mirodara sleeping in the back room. She was sprawled on the floor, snoring. As though she had not a care in the world. He couldn't help smiling, though that only brought back the pain of memory. The way her nose bent slightly to the left, giving her mouth a soft quirk, as though she were always on the verge of laughter—that was her mother's most obvious feature. Rubbing his eyes until the stars exploded on the inside of his eyelids, he hurried out into the street.

I will not be maudlin this early in the morning, he thought.

He still thought of his smithy as belonging to the first reach. Only a few houses down, Siloán the potter's home stood, now even smaller-looking than usual after the mead-house had swallowed two neighboring houses to become the largest building in the reach. The roads were as meandering, the refuse as omnipresent. The poor still bickered at street corners, fighting for the rights to an intersection as though their eternal soul depended on it. But it wasn't the first reach any more, he reminded himself. Just a few roads down was the new merchants' quarter—part of the "Great Father's" efforts at equalizing opportunities for all citizens. Or some such unintelligible nonsense.

The walls that had stood between the three reaches of Vasyllia for centuries had been torn down. The stairways joining them together now seemed naked without the walls buttressing them. They were a pitiful sight, and most Vasylli instinctively avoided the stairs, preferring the new, wide gravel roads that joined all reaches in stark, over-straight lines, so counterintuitive to the gentle roll and sway of the mountain's side.

In the other direction from the merchants' quarter was the other great equalizer—the pleasure quarter, as it was officially labeled. Llun flushed with sudden disgust, remembering the dog-man's offer. The air of the first reach had always been redolent with aroma. But it had been good and clean, for all its earthiness. The first reach had had its problems, but people had been principled, keeping to a code that separated them from the corruption of the upper reaches. It had been important before, to keep oneself clean of the base and the vile. Now, worker and noble alike drank sour ale in the wide anterooms of the whore-houses. Equality indeed.

The former second reach was now a shambling mess. Most of Nebesta's refugees still lived there in tottering canvas tents. Every hundred paces or so, a pile of those tents was set apart from the next by a line of spears stuck into the earth, their points directed at the people in the camps. Guards with longbows patrolled the spear-lines constantly. Whenever they passed, silence fell.

Cutting into the silence like a knife into flesh was the sound of children. Two Nebesti boys, dressed in barely anything but loincloths, chased a much smaller boy through the pile of tents, screaming something menacing. The small boy turned directly toward the lines of spears. Llun felt his vision go dim as he saw that none of them were stopping. Two grim Vasylli warriors converged toward them. One of them grabbed a standing spear from the ground and pointed it at the children, shaking it menacingly.

The children tried to stop, but their momentum was considerable. The first one—a ratty-haired boy of about six or seven—managed to dig his heels in at a suitable distance. But his assailants, who were both muscular and seemed large for their age, were not as quick to stop. They scratched and pulled at each other, trying to stop in time. At the very last moment, even the Vasylli guard paled. But he didn't move.

The small boy, pushed toward the spear, managed to twist aside at the last minute. He wasn't impaled.

But his side was slashed open. There was a lot of blood, even from the distance where Llun stood, clutching his chest for horror. A young Nebesti man ran into Llun's field of vision, his hands shaking in those ridiculously expansive gestures that all Nebesti indulge in. Behind him was a young woman. She stopped as soon as she saw the boy. Her sunburned face blanched, and she screamed.

The warriors tensed as the Nebesti man approached them. The warrior who had not hurt the boy stood in front of the one who had. His fists were bunched, and he yelled at the Nebesti to back down. The father did not. His eyes' whites grew, and his hands waved more and more frantically. All the while, he moved toward the spears. The second warrior drew his sword, yelling. Llun couldn't make out the words in the general mayhem of women and children screaming. The stricken boy moaned not at all, which was even more frightening. The father shoved his face into the warrior's face, his raspy torrent of words turning into shouting. The warrior's eyes bulged, and his face grew red. He kept repeating something again and again. Not once did he look at the boy.

Something twanged by Llun's ear. The boy's father twisted back unnaturally and fell to the ground. An arrow shivered in his shoulder.

"Move along!" A rough voice yelled near Llun. A huge Gumir, his face twisted into a grimace, making his already angled eyes disappear in the folds of his dirt-brown face. "Not your concern, Vasylli. Great Father's business. Move along."

Llun looked away and moved along. As he walked, he heard the familiar laugh of the Gumiren as they closed in. Then the thudding began. The sounds of fists on flesh and bone. Gritting his teeth, Llun ran on.

Where the Covenant Tree had once stood, a pile of kindling reached as high as a two-story house. It stood as a dour reminder of that day Vasyllia fell, when the Gumiren had nearly thrown the children of Adonais's faithful into the fire. It had been a cruel joke of the Raven. Deny your divinity, your Adonais, he had said. And I will spare your children. And for what? For an existence of fear and no hope of a brighter future? Perhaps it would have been better for the children to burn.

Above the pile of logs—it obscenely resembled a huge raven's nest—was the Raven's totem: a stone obelisk that branched out into a pair of jagged wings. It was black as obsidian, but without that stone's glass-like sheen. Whatever it was made of, the material seemed to suck light in, making it not so much black as absent—a hole in the fabric of the world shaped like an obelisk.

Llun stood before it, his hatred a hair's edge from boiling. He forced himself to move on toward the third reach.

Of all the former reaches, the third was the one least affected by the Gumiren. Most of the damage of the battle for Vasyllia had been quickly repaired, as the Gumiren took residence in the mansions of the wealthy third-reachers. Many of them had kept the nobles as their servants. More like slaves, in fact, especially the women. Some old noblemen had been quietly dispatched during the now-infamous "night purges" that the Gumiren conducted every so often. Llun had heard that the purges continued, but now it was not the Gumiren, but turncoat Vasylli who would rat out their own brothers for a chance at a better set of table knives.

Seeing the mansions still sparkling like the jewels of great Vasyllia that was—it gave Llun vertigo. For a brief, brilliant moment it seemed that everything—the Gumiren overlords, the horrors of the nightly purges, the baseness to which everything had sunk—was just a dream. After all, wasn't the palace of the Dar still standing, its seven towers like beacons of hope leading toward a glorious future?

Except now the palace was the dwelling place of a demonic Power who had the brazenness to call himself everyone's father.

The gates to the outer courtyard of the palace, which now housed the Consistory, used to be open at all times as a sign of the Dar's closeness to his people. After the fall of Vasyllia, the gates had been shut. So, when they opened to admit Llun, he had the sinking feeling that he was being invited to step into the gullet of a hungry monster.

He had been inside once only, during the matriculation ceremony of the warrior seminary. In the old days. He, as one of the preferred swordsmiths of the seminary, had received a place of honor in a front row of the viewing gallery. It was an impressive sight—the pentagonal courtyard filled with silent, unmoving, black-robed warriors, all with their swords drawn. At the whip-like calls of their cohort elders, the hundreds of warriors had demonstrated, as one man, every step of the sword-forms. It was like a dance, and it had taken his breath away.

Now, he was struck by the emptiness of the square, save for a few scurrying forms of servants. Instead, his eyes were drawn to the huge banners flapping on the walls of the keep—the red raven obelisk on a black field. Like a bad joke, Sabíana's sign of the gold sun on black field flitted small and insignificant from a pole jutting up above the smallest of the seven towers.

Perhaps she is alive, he thought. The thought did little to comfort him. What was a crippled young woman with no army behind her supposed to do to change the fortunes of Vasyllia?

"What, you as well?" Aspidían materialized out of nowhere. "It's the strangest thing, Brother Llun. Whenever one of you old Vasylli come up here (oh, it's rare enough, I grant you) their eye is always drawn to that pitiful banner. I wonder why?"

"Brother Aspidían," said Llun, bowing in greeting. The wiry inquisitor was dressed in simple linen trousers with a billowing linen overshirt—the picture of leisure and relaxation. Only his eyes still smoldered behind his smile.

"Come, Brother Llun. I want you to meet someone."

They took an unobtrusive door in the keep's wall that led to a twisting staircase. It was dusty and disused, and Llun was sure that this was where he would be suddenly attacked from behind and thrown into a dungeon. Instead, at the top of the staircase, Aspidían opened another unobtrusive door. Facing the golden light that streamed into the stairwell was like staring into the sun. When Llun's eyes adjusted, he saw they were in a vaulted chamber covered in frescoes. Every inch of the curved ceilings and walls burst with giant-sized fancies on the theme of flowers and birds. Bumblebees painted with actual gold leaf seemed to buzz on purple and red petals of peonies. Strawberries and blueberries burst from the confines of their green and yellow leaves.

"He likes it. How pleasant."

Llun's stomach lurched at the sound of that voice. It was more than one voice. It was like a voice with a hundred echoes, coming from one mouth. When he saw the speaker, it took a strong effort of will not to cringe.

He was...well, beautiful. Flawless skin, like polished ivory. Soft eyes, almost lavender colored. Long-fingered hands, the nails reflecting the golden candlelight in the room like polished metal. Llun had heard that Yadovír, the Mouth of the Raven, had grown younger and more pleasing to look at in the five years since the fall of Vasyllia. But the beauty was somehow... wrong. As he stared at Yadovír, unable to look away, it seemed to Llun that something shivered in his face. No, *under* his face. Like his entire surface—skin, face, hands—was an elaborate costume for something foul underneath.

Yadovír cocked his head to one side and slitted his eyes, assessing. "You're a bear of a man, aren't you? But my friend here says that you have talent."

"That he does," said Aspidían, coming close to Yadovír. *Too* close. Llun felt sick to his stomach.

Yadovír's eyes wandered over Llun, from head to foot, lingering. He smiled, a predator's smile that was not his own. Llun had the sensation that he was being judged as potential food.

"For all your strength, Brother Llun," said Yadovír, with a hint of a growl. "You are rather soft, aren't you?"

Aspidían chuckled, and they both turned away from Llun and walked to a strange contrivance in the middle of the room. It was so out of character with the general opulence that at first Llun didn't understand what he was looking at. The he realized it was a hole. In the floorboards. In that hole was a hearth, the simple kind that you find in a first-reacher house. There were pillows around the hearth—simple, red pillows of no especial value. A small table stood by the hearth. Three goblets and mead. Mead? Llun couldn't understand what he was seeing. Why, in this palatial room, was there a sliver of commonness more appropriate to Llun's own back room behind the forge?

Aspidían and Yadovír sat on two of the cushions, leaning into one another in a way that bespoke more than casual intimacy. It was unsettling. The whole picture was unsettling. Was this part of an elaborate plan to confuse him so much that he would somehow stumble into revealing some dangerous truth? Did they know about Mirodara?

"Why do you gawk?" Aspidían guffawed. "Sit. That cushion's for you."

Llun did as he was told. Yadovír continued to look at him hungrily as Aspidían poured him the mead. Llun tried to focus his attention on the cup, and once again he lost himself in the quality of the work. The wrought iron tracery woven like ivy around the wooden goblet was exquisite. It nearly rivaled his own abilities. Then he drank the mead and nearly drowned in the pleasure of that taste. He had not had good mead—hearty, first-reacher bread-ale—in years.

Laughter jolted him out of his contemplation.

"You're right, Aspidían," said Yadovír. "He really is…an artist."

Llun felt his face get warm, and suddenly he was angry. Sick of it all. His teeth creaked as he tensed his jaw.

"What do you want of me?" he asked, surprised at the audible growl in his own voice.

"Oh, how disappointing," drawled Yadovír. "No small talk? Cut straight to the heart of the matter, eh? Artists." He sounded faintly disgusted with the idea.

"You never understood us," said Aspidían. "We operate on a different schedule than most. Don't we, Brother Llun?"

Llun refused to be included in the offer of intimacy. He had no desire to be named the kind of artist that Aspidían was. If they wanted something of him, they would have to pry it out of his hands. The thought gave him shivers.

"As you wish," said Yadovír, putting his cup down, then yawning as he stretched against Aspidían, who still seemed amused by everything. "We want you to take on a commission. For the Consistory. In fact, we want it to be the last commission you take."

There was a double meaning there, Llun knew it. But he pretended not to hear it. "You want me to be your exclusive smith? But why?"

"We have a…sudden vacancy." Aspidían's eyebrows came together, shadowing his eyes.

Llun picked up his cup and offered it to them, significantly.

"Yes," said Yadovír. "These cups are his work. As you see, he was very good. But he had an unfortunate slip in judgment. He can no longer help us."

"You killed him?"

Yadovír looked disappointed. "No, of course not. They only took his hand. The Gumiren."

"So…wait, I'm not sure I understand. Are you saying that you and the Gumiren are not…on the same side?"

Aspidían's eyes were no longer smoldering. They burned. "Now *that* is a comment unworthy of you, Brother Llun. What makes you think any Vasylli would willingly collaborate with those animals? No. Compromises were made, yes. Necessary ones. But never think, not for a moment, that we do not anticipate with great joy the moment when we can slaughter them in their beds."

"What about the Raven?" said Llun.

Aspidían tensed, and his hand went to his boot. Something gleamed there.

"Do...not...utter—" he whispered menacingly.

"Oh, don't worry, Aspidían," said Yadovír. "He's brave, for all of his goggling at the fine things in life. Perhaps not as soft as we thought." His smile stretched his face. "Brother Llun, I'll let you say it once. But never again. The *Great Father*, for your information, is well on his way to becoming a figure of speech. Soon the Vasylli will forget about the Raven. Just as he would want it. His desire is not Vasyllia itself. It is something else. He has promised me that, soon, we will have Vasyllia back to ourselves."

"How can you trust him? He seems willing enough to turn on those he needed to get into Vasyllia in the first place."

"I don't trust him, you fool," said Yadovír. Something shimmered in the shadows behind him—a suggestion of huge, jagged wings. Llun's heart plunged to his ankles. "I'm useful to him. And I'm making the Gumiren less so. Soon, their time will be over."

"And high time too," said Aspidían. "They've all become so fat and complacent. The Ghan himself can hardly walk now, he is so round. He must be carried around on a litter."

Llun's curiosity got the better of him. "Is it true, what's been said in the first reach? That there are troubles in the Gumiren ruling council?"

Aspidían put on an entirely new face. Intense concentration, with a hint of anticipation. Llun had a suspicion that was the sincerest Aspidían face yet. "Do tell, Brother Llun. What sort of gossip are the commons bandying about?"

Llun resented the tone, but forced himself to speak evenly. "Well, in the first years of the occupation, the Gumiren were everywhere, weren't they? Patrolling streets, eating at the public houses, propping up the spear lines in the refugee camp. But over the years, fewer and fewer of them were seen in the lower reaches. Then the rumors started that the Gumiren had taken to Vasylli luxuries. Particularly wine and mead. Not surprising, given their nomad bloodlines. And they were willing to give more and more of the ruling responsibilities to the collaborators."

Yadovír smiled again, and Llun realized he had said "collaborators" out loud. *Focus, you idiot!*

"Then there are the rumors of diseases among the Gumiren. Some sort of pox, some say. Others are less...compassionate in their guesses."

"Yes, you could say that," said Aspidían, snickering. "Why are you so afraid to say it out loud, Llun? Your tongue won't be polluted. Say it. 'Venereal diseases.'" He mouthed it, slowly, as if he could taste the syllables.

Llun scowled.

"To answer your question, Brother Llun," said Yadovír, "yes, the Gumiren are growing complacent. And soon, soon the time will come when we will take back Vasyllia for the Vasylli. I ask you now. Will you help us? Will you help your people?"

This was not collaboration with the enemy at all. This was...well, this was exactly what Llun wanted. But not with Yadovír. He was there during the battle for Vasyllia. He remembered what Yadovír had done. Yadovír had orchestrated a pogrom of clerics of the cult of Adonais to cover up his own crimes, his own treachery. The thought propped up his cold hatred, and the words tumbled out of his mouth even as he thought them.

"And what about the Darina? Where is she in all your plans?"

The silence hissed, so complete that Llun heard the squelching sound of Yadovír's feral smile stretching across his gums.

"She is...instrumental."

"She is alive, then?"

"Oh, yes. Very much so."

"I don't believe you."

Aspidían got up, slowly, his muscles so taut that it looked like an invisible hand lifted him up, like a marionette. "You don't seem to understand, Brother Llun. Here we are, extending you a hand of friendship when you know very well that we could be extending a corkscrew to separate your nails from your hands. And you spit on this hand of friendship? Is that wise? Do you not understand who it is that sits before you?"

Llun's breath quickened. His head buzzed. He had had too much of the mead. Or was there something in the mead? Something to make him more...malleable?

"I...forgive me, Brother Aspidían," said Llun, nearly whimpering, and hating himself for it. "I...why me? Why choose me to be your exclusive smith? You have seen my work. It is good, yes. But I do not work fast. And if you need a swordsmith for an uprising against the Gumiren...well, you would not have many swords..."

Aspidían relaxed back into Yadovír's side. "He has a point, you know," he said, conversationally.

"You forget one thing." Yadovír looked at Aspidían. "Who he *is*."

"Ah yes!" Aspidían's eyes sparkled with mischief as he crossed his arms across his chest. "You are related to key members of the Sons of the Swan."

And there it was. The trap snapped shut. Llun almost imagined the sound, like a big bear trap chomping down on his ankle. He nearly panicked then and there.

"Dashun is dead," Llun managed to say, barely containing his fear within. "His infection has been cut out of Vasyllia. I am not of their mind. I do not seek what they seek."

"No, but Mirodara does," said Yadovír.

"She is a *child!*"

"Children will grow to be men and women, a new generation of rot at the heart of Vasyllia. Until every Son of the Swan is killed, no peace will ever last here or anywhere else in the world."

"Unless..." Aspidían cut in, his voice reasonable and kind. "We are prepared to overlook her involvement with the Sons as ... a youthful indiscretion. But only if you take up our offer."

Llun sighed. "Am I expected to give an answer immediately?"

"No, no!" Aspidían waved his hands placatingly. "Take your time. Just ... not too much of it."

The dawn of hope rises. From the dirt of the tree's roots will arise a sleeper of ages. She will be braver than many men, stronger than myriad warriors. Her age is not counted in years, but in the bitter days of pain and loss. Her death will bring forth life. Her sleep will make Living Water flow again in the wasteland...

From "The Prophecy of Llun"
(The Sayings, Book XXIII, 5:8-10)

CHAPTER 3
MIRODARA

Llun hardly remembered the way he took back to his smithy. It didn't help that most of Vasyllia was hidden in fog, dropping the early summer temperatures down to what they had been in late spring. The kind of weather that obscured one's thoughts and deadened one's limbs.

Bacon. The smell shocked him back to awareness. He was nearly home, and the bacon-smell, to his amazement, was not coming from the mead-house, but from his own smithy. He laughed with pleasure. It had been a long time since he had eaten bacon.

Mirodara.

Idiot girl. Is this your idea of being unobtrusive?

He rushed into the smithy, and the smoke attacked his eyes and mouth. He choked as the pleasing smell of fried pig transformed into the sickly-sweet smell of burnt pig.

"If you're going to let the whole neighborhood know you're here, at least don't burn the bacon!" He smiled as he saw Mirodara blowing on a thin, black piece of something that could have once been edible. She breathed out in exasperation and offered him a bite. He shook his head and laughed.

"I wanted to make you something nice," she said, never more like his sister than at that moment.

"If you really want to do something nice for me, you'll sit down and listen."

She straightened at the change in Llun's voice. Nodding slowly, she threw the charred bit of meat back into the pan on the hearth. It sizzled, as though hurtling a final insult at her.

"So ..." she began, "what sort of false promises did they make, the vipers?"

"Stop." He raised his voice just enough for her to curl in on herself a little. "I said listen. Open mind, yes?"

"Fine." He saw that she was working very hard not to sulk.

"They know about you. Not about the Sons in general. About you, Mirodara."

"Then why am I still here?"

Llun sighed and looked away from her. He suddenly, ridiculously, really wanted to eat that bacon.

"Oh, I see," she said, her voice husky. "They're using me to force you to do something. What, exactly?"

"I'm not entirely sure, to be honest. They say they need a swordsmith. But I can't imagine why they'd want me for that. Unless Yadovír wants a family heirloom he can hang over his door."

"Yes, you do take rather a bit more time than necessary on ... well, everything. Even nails!" She chuckled.

"I think there's much that they're not telling me. But one thing I know for sure. If you do not stop your silly association with the Sons of the Swan, it'll be the end of both of us."

Mirodara took Llun's paw of a hand between her own. They were so uncalloused and small. Like a mouse holding on to a lion. Llun's heart felt stretched to a breaking point.

"Llun, let's be honest. They're going to get us, sooner or later. Whether or not you help them. Whether or not I ever so much as speak to a Son of the Swan again. At some point, in the middle of the night, you'll be taken in your sleep. Me too."

"Don't speak like that. I'll—"

"What matters," she said, not listening to him, "is what we manage to do before they stop us. What have either of us done in our lives that is worth remembering? Hm? But now, when our world has already ended, now ... well, every decision of every person can have huge consequences. Don't you understand that? Every person who capitulates to the Gumiren and their collaborators is guilty of treachery before our whole people. But every single child who refuses to bow down...How can I make you understand? Every sacrifice...it matters. Even if it seems pointless. It *matters*."

"When did you grow up, my little cub?" He tried to smile through the tears that now fell. He wiped them off. "But what if I were to tell you..." He lowered his voice to a whisper. "There are rumblings ... that the collaborators are preparing to throw off the Gumiren. To restore Vasyllia to the Vasylli. Even to restore the Darina to her place."

"You believe them? They'll say anything, Llun. Have you forgotten what they did?"

"I haven't, no. *You* were too small to remember, I would have thought."

"I was nothing of the sort. I saw the warriors ... *our* warriors turn into beasts. I saw them attack defenseless women who tried to reason with them, to prevent them from hacking down every priest in sight. You don't forget such a sight. Not ever. And these are the people you entrust the safety of our city to?"

"You're right. I just can't fathom losing you."

"You'll have to fathom a lot more than that. Don't you understand? This isn't the battle for Vasyllia. It's the battle for the soul of Vasyllia."

She breathed deeply, as though considering whether or not to divulge something.

"There's something else," she said. "It's Voran, the son of Otchigen."

"What about him?" Llun couldn't help the bitterness coming through. Voran, Darina Sabíana's intended and the supposed hope of Vasyllia's reclamation, had been exiled years ago. But rumors had trickled into Vasyllia that he had found Living Water and that he was using it to heal those who had fallen to the Gumiren onslaught. Others suggested that he was gathering an army to reclaim Vasyllia. Probably all of it was rubbish.

"The Sons have it on excellent authority that he is finally coming back to Vasyllia. And he has Living Water."

Llun couldn't muster the enthusiasm necessary to believe her. He found he had run out of things to say. She hugged him.

"I want to go out in a blaze of glory. I want to do something so mad that the Heights will have no choice but to bow down again before my act of courage. You'll see. It'll happen soon. Everything is going to change very soon."

How horribly have you grown up, my little one, Llun thought. *Can I expect anything else, when all you've ever known is fear and death?*

The Day of Blood will be dread and awful. But it is not the end of the tribulation. Hear my voice, O faithful of Vasyllia! There will come a time when brother will slaughter father, for he will not recognize his face. Brown-faced Gumir will attack white-faced Vasylli, but he will be stabbed in his back. No one will know the face of his enemy in the darkness and the chaos. Nor will he know the face of his friend.

From "The Prophecy of Llun"
(The Sayings, Book XXIII, 2:4-7)

CHAPTER 4
THE SONS OF THE SWAN

After Mirodara left, Llun could not face his thoughts. He opened the smithy and threw himself into his work with the kind of abandon he had only really felt in the early days, when his body hardly noticed the strain of smithing. It was a surprise to him when he looked at the window to see that it had gone completely dark.

He allowed his forge to sputter and die. The shadows at first faintly resisted their inevitable end, then they lay down to a quiet death. He went to his rest in the back room, bare as always but for the bench lining the back wall. The barrenness was a comfort, clearing the mind, especially in its contrast to the clutter in the smithy itself. Llun lay down on the bench, not bothering to undress. In spite of the buzzing of his mind, he could not keep his eyelids open, and only a few moments later, he was asleep.

When his door tore from its hinges, he woke with a start. There were five men in his room, dressed in black, a shriveled dog's head hanging from the belt of each. In the absurd confusion of the just-awoken, all Llun could think of was how disappointing it was that the promise of bacon had not lived up to the reality. The intruders gave him no time to reflect. They all fell on top of him like the dogs that they were.

He struggled, but it was soon obvious that any sign of resistance meant an excuse for them to inflict unnecessary pain. But pain was an old friend of Llun's. He fought them back as furiously as a cornered rat. They were in *his* smithy. He knew better than they where the most painful weapons were, if only he could get to them.

Two held Llun's arms pinned to his back, while two more demonstratively took off their gloves. Underneath, Llun saw black metal between their fingers. This was not a mere arrest, then. He was to be made an example of.

Not in my smithy.

He made a feint of losing consciousness, forcing the two holding him to lean down to keep him pinned. As he leaned hard against the shin of the man holding his right hand, he twisted into him, catching his foot under him and pushing his knee back. Llun felt it crack, and the man howled. Before the others could restrain him, Llun lifted both his attackers up with his huge body and threw them at the rest of their fellows.

Under his sleeping bench, Llun kept a half-done war hammer. It was too heavy for most men to lift, but in the heat of the struggle he lifted it like a dry twig and swung with all his force at his assailants. Something gave way behind the blow. More wailing. For the briefest of moments, Llun saw a way through the five attackers as they tried to avoid his blows. Dealers of pain were always the worst at bearing it themselves, he knew. Llun rushed past them, through the broken doorway, into the smithy proper. It was still dark, except for the gaping hole where the butchers had broken in. Llun ran through it, but stopped dead in his tracks.

Unaccountably, it had snowed last night. The moon being full, the thin layer of pristine white seemed to give off its own eerie light. In the dark, there were smears of black all over the snow. Blood. A lamentation of swans lay like an unholy sacrifice before Llun's smithy. All their heads were cut off. He understood. Yadovír and Aspidían were not waiting for his answer. He turned around and ran back into the smithy, a red haze before his eyes.

The dog-men must have felt it, because they hung back for the blink of an eye. It was enough. Llun crashed onto them like a wave onto a cliff, and they scattered before him. One swing of the war hammer, and two came down with crushed heads. One tried to lunge under Llun's attack, but Llun had a knife in his left hand, and he plunged it into the man's arm before he could reach his body. With the back hand of his hammer-arm, he crushed the man's shoulder into his backbone. The man screamed.

Only one left.

The last one turned and ran away. Llun put his hammer on the ground and took the knife in his right hand. Balancing it on his fingers, he felt for the center of heaviness, remembering his occasional training from the old days, when he had forged for the warrior seminary. Then he flipped it forward. It landed in the man's neck. He fell, spluttering.

Llun picked up his hammer and rushed toward the nearest of the new roads.

Once in his life, Llun had seen a beehive overturned by a bear. It had been in an outlying village near Vasyllia, where his favorite great-aunt lived with her woodsman husband. The bees, normally sleepy and gentle, had frenzied into a mass of death-dealers that could no longer distinguish their caretaker from a marauding bear. After the bear was done, his aunt had come out—wearing chainmail for good measure. For the first five minutes, they had swarmed her as though she were the bear's consort. Only her stillness and her crooning song had eventually calmed them and allowed his uncle to begin the work of rebuilding the hives.

But she was not here in Vasyllia now to calm the masses that roiled in the streets of the first reach.

Madness seemed to have taken over. It was too dark to make out much except that everyone seemed to be attacking everyone. In brief snatches of focus, Llun saw what looked like Gumiren warriors, judging by their kaftans and silk-sashed caps, attacking and hacking and burning everywhere they went. But there was something wrong about them. Then he heard it. They were speaking Vasylli to each other.

Without another thought, Llun plunged into the swarm, brandishing his war hammer over his head and screaming at the top of his lungs. To his own surprise, he remembered how to use it. It had only been a few lessons with Elder Pahomy of the warrior seminary, years ago now. But he had taken to the weapon like a babe to its mother's teat.

The false Gumiren had not expected any serious resistance. That was clear enough by how they fled from Llun's wrath. But he was fast, in spite of his size. And some kind of war-madness was on him. He had heard a name for it: the war-wind. It was said to make dark gods of men. Well, perhaps Mirodara was right. It was far better to die like this than to continue merely existing in the Vasyllia of the Raven.

The false Gumiren were like sheaves of wheat, and he was the scythe. At fourteen, he lost count of the ones who fell under his war hammer. Before he knew it, the swarming had stopped. Everything was silent, save for the lingering ringing in his ears. Then the sounds of the after-battle began. The crying and the wailing. The wounded. The beloved of the wounded. The war-wind still blew within him. He could not stay here, could not bear to listen to the groans of the weak and fallen.

He ran on, toward the second reach. The Nebesti refugee camps were on fire. Mounted figures rode back and forth, black and demonic against the dancing flames, screaming and whooping. These were not Gumiren. The flopping sacks on their belts—no, they were dogs' heads—revealed them to be warriors of the Consistory. What was going on? Who was attacking whom? Why?

Suddenly, a wave of armed people—they were not warriors, for there were women and children among them—encircled the mounted Consistory men. Banners fluttered among this rag-tag army. In the smoke, it was difficult to make out much, but then the firelight exploded as a tent collapsed, and Llun saw Sirin and other High Beings embroidered on the banners. These were the Sons of the Swan.

His war-wind fled at their sight. So many of them were children! What were they hoping to achieve? Was all this madness of their doing? Is *this* what Mirodara meant when she said that everything was going to change?

Llun was frozen in place, torn between a desire to run and save Mirodara and a gut-deep need to see what was happening in the third reach. Something was going on. Something vital. His hammer could prove important here. But he needed to be near the palace. At the center of everything. He needed to *know*.

With a groan, he wrenched himself away from the sight of the child-army. Running past the Raven's totem, he found time to spit at it. No Gumiren stood guarding it. If he had time, he would have defiled it properly. But no time. Up the gravel roads he ran, the pebbles barely holding him up as he flew with unnatural speed for his bulk. Blasts of fire seemed to be everywhere, exploding even out of bare earth. Then, the rains came. Smoke belched up in black, choking billows. Llun lost all sense of direction, but continued to push upward. Bloodied people ran past him, down into the first reach. Screams burst from in front of him, then behind him, then from the left. Then the screaming was *above* him. He stopped, completely lost, his head spinning, his throat raw from the smoke. He coughed, and it seemed his coughing was adding to the smoke choking everything around them.

The rain fell again in gusting sheets. Then the wind, a gale from the mountain. Everything cleared in Llun's vision suddenly, and he couldn't understand where to look to get his bearing. He fell on the ground, thinking it was the sky.

"There! The smith. Over there!" Vasylli voices. In seconds, black figures surrounded Llun. Dog-men. Llun growled.

"Take care. He's taken many already." The voice was unfamiliar, but unmistakably of the Consistory. It had an emotionless quality about it. Nothing personal, it said. We have to kill you, because it is our business to kill you. Llun raised himself with difficulty, his head still spinning. He tried to orient himself by the tallest tower of the palace, which was directly ahead of him.

He froze. Something was hanging from the turret. A bloody and battered body, hanging on a rope attached to its neck.

Oh, by the Heights. That's... Yadovír!

Something struck him in the back, and searing pain spread across his shoulder blades, hot and prickly. Then something hit his head. Blackness.

<hr />

Water splashed over his face. For a moment, he couldn't breathe. Then he woke up.

Llun was strapped to some sort of metal post, tied down with both chains and leather. He couldn't move anything except his head. His back tingled with nagging pain that seemed to slowly bore into his backbone. The water splashed over his face again, and he gagged.

"Enough!" he bellowed when he managed to shake the water out his mouth and face. Three dog-men surrounded him, swords drawn and pointed at him. Beyond them, Llun saw darkness. The only light in the dim space came from a table directly ahead of Llun. A single candle, barely illumining the cave-like interior. Three thin, weasel-faced men with salt-and-pepper beards sat there. They were second-reacher, merchant class, judging by their mien and the luxurious fur ringing their felt hats. The hats were red. But the rest of their clothing was black. Black kaftan, black shirts of rippling silk, black vests with silver buckles. Very fancy. One of them, the central one, had dead eyes that latched on Llun's face like a leech on an exposed leg.

"You are Smith Llun, yes? Brother of the traitor Dashun?"

"Hrrmph." Llun's mouth was caked with something sticky. Probably blood. Though his tongue was too swollen to taste it. "Brother-in-law."

"Ah, yes. How stupid of me. Brother of the traitor Vatrina. Even better."

"Worse, you mean," said Llun, under his breath. He had the absurd desire to antagonize that man. To really annoy him.

"Yes, I do," said the man, without expression. "Smith Llun, do you understand why you are here?"

"I may have killed some fifteen of your fellow dog-men."

The man looked down at a parchment before him, as though he had not heard the insult. Then he leaned over to another of the dead-faced inquisitors. None of the three, he now saw, had any expression at all, just blank faces. Not even boredom.

"Twenty-two, by our last count. So, you admit to this treachery and murder of your fellow citizens."

Llun laughed. One of the guards slashed his face with a knife. It left a burning gash—not deep enough to cause serious damage, he felt. These men were good at what they did.

"I do no such thing. I charge you, dog-men of the Consistory, collaborators to the invaders, of treachery and murder. I charge you with impersonating Gumiren to start riots in Vasyllia. I charge you with instigation of violence against your own people and against your unlawfully placed ruler. I—"

This time, the guard punched him with the pommel of his sword in his gut. It was studded with blunt nails. Llun couldn't breathe for a minute, and when he coughed, his stomach lurched in a way that suggested something may have been torn.

"No matter. Your admission is not necessary. Are we in agreement, then?" He turned to one dead-faced inquisitor, then the other. They both nodded, and continued to stare into empty space ahead of them.

"Smith Llun, you are found guilty of conspiring against the state and the person of Yadovír, the Mouth of our Great Father. Your sentencing will be held at a later date."

He waved at the guards, as though he were waving off a mosquito. One of the guards put a bag on Llun's head. It smelled rank. He saw nothing, but suddenly the ground was the ceiling, and his hands were his feet, and...

I have always been fascinated by the effect of pain. Not that I found any particular pleasure in dealing pain. No, that sort of fetish is base. Not worthy of an artist. Rather, I explore how the subject's mind and body twist and mold themselves in incredible ways in response to pain. I have also found ways to control that twisting and molding, to make the subject into something that I can use. That is the true art. To create, as the commons call him, a dog-man. The perfect perpetrator of justice, for he has no conscience of his own. Only the need, bone-deep, to be found worthy in the eyes of his handler.

From the personal notebooks of Aspidían, Grand Inquisitor of the Consistory

CHAPTER 5
A DEAL WITH THE DOG-MAN

Llun awoke. His head throbbed as though separated from his body. He couldn't understand his body's position. He did not feel his feet. Rather, they were there, but not solidly established. His arms were wedged behind him, and something cold pressed against his face. Slowly, concentrating through the throbbing pain, Llun made out that he hung inside a metal cage, his face leaning against one of the bars. He opened his eyes. Nothing changed. Total blackness.

Something whispered far above him, like a soft wind rushing through a narrow passage. The temperature plunged. Something licked his face. He recoiled in terror and disgust, but it kept licking him, like tens of small, ridged tongues, like a cat's. But that wasn't right. No. It was...was it possible? Snow? But he was inside, he was sure of it.

Soon there was no mistaking it. Snow pelted his face. Gritting his teeth against the pain, Llun managed to yank one of his arms out from behind him. He groped across the chain, trying to understand its shape and make. Then he reached further out with his hand. It met stone. Cold, dry stone. Not weathered. No, he was not outside. Then how could it be snowing?

He shivered. Every shudder of his muscles sent arrows of pain from the center of his back. Something crunched there, like broken cartilage or a ripped ligament.

The temperature fell again. Now it was ice pelting his face, not snow. Wind howled, just like it did during a blizzard. Was he going mad? No, the cold was very, very real.

Then, an explosion of light and heat burst from above his head. He jerked his head without thinking. It struck the metal grating, and his ears rang.

He sweated, his skin tinging where it was encrusted with ice just seconds ago. It was momentarily pleasant. But the heat kept rising. He forced his eyes open, and through the reddish firelight he saw that he was in a tower with no bottom to be seen. Just above his head was some horrifying kind of chandelier, but the heat from its torches was unbearable. He watched with horrified fascination as the hairs on his arms curled up, thickening into deep black, then smoke rose from them as they singed. The smell was sickening, mixed as it was with his own sweat and something far worse. Something rotten and musty and sickly-sweet.

His skin puckered and twitched. It bubbled. Llun closed his eyes, unwilling to see it through to its end.

The light went out. The darkness was so sudden and complete that Llun thought he had gone blind. Something scraped above him—the sound of metal scraping against metal. Cold wind blew in. Hard, sharp snowflakes followed. On his burnt skin, it felt like fire.

It all happened again—the snow, the wind, the biting cold. Only it was a hundred times worse. Then, just when sleepiness began to pull at his eyelids and he was ready to succumb to it, the strange chandelier returned with its blazing heat. Then again it was replaced with the winter storm inside the tower.

At some point, it all blurred into a monotony of agony. Llun must have lost consciousness for a long time, because when he woke up, he was in the throes of a chest-deep cold with a fever so hot, he could probably fry eggs on his forehead. Everything was hazy, and he was sure he had begun to hallucinate. After all, where did that hole in front of him come from?

It was a monstrous emptiness in the stone wall. The sight outside it was so elaborate a deception that Llun decided it must be real.

He had never seen such a sunrise. The clouds were striated like brushstrokes, each layer a deeper red the closer it was to the horizon. The tips of the trees were gilded, while the shadows underneath were a rich nightshade purple. Llun couldn't help himself. He chuckled. This was the perfect torture for an artist. In this place, at this moment, it did not seem absurd that Aspidían had ordered the sunrise especially for Llun. The beauty of it seared his mind, to remain there forever—far more a torment than a relief.

A strange sound reached Llun's ears. It sounded like ... market day. But surely not! Vasyllia wouldn't go back to its daily routine, not after everything that happened. Or ... how long had he been hanging here? At the thought, a hunger so huge it was like a living creature inside his stomach started to claw at him. A long time, then. But still! Had Vasyllia become so depraved that it could just go to market? After all that happened ...

Something cracked inside his head, and he screamed and shook the cage with all the strength he had left. The bars bent, but did not break. All he got for his pains was bloodied fingertips and a headache that felt like two hot pokers pushing his eyes out of his head.

Llun leaned forward, hard. The cage creaked and moved just enough for him to catch a glimpse of the accursed marketplace. It sprawled over the former Temple to Adonais. The ring of red-barks glittered with hundreds of lanterns, but no longer were the lanterns symbols of the flame in the heart, the inner striving for the Heights. Now, they were a convenience that allowed the market to remain open far into the night. This morning, the clearing seethed with brightly-colored dresses of brocade and silk, tall beaver hats, fur-lined mantles sparkling with golden embroidery. The resplendent walking dead.

How dare they! Their own people were being slaughtered in the streets only days ago. By other Vasylli. But still, the market thrives!

Llun's thoughts were interrupted by the sound of footsteps. Many men in a rush. After endless clanking of old keys in even older locks, a sickly light shone far beneath him. Steps echoed through the tower, which Llun now saw was narrow but immensely tall. The figures below him were no bigger than mice. At the head was Aspidían, gesticulating in a manner suggesting, to Llun's surprise, extreme displeasure, directed at a man to his left, apparently the keeper of the tower cells. The man had the air of a dog expecting a beating.

Suddenly, at a strange signal from Aspidían, three of the dog-men behind him grabbed the jailer, who screamed. They dragged him, though he bit them and flailed with his legs so hard Llun was sure his back would break. Another cage lay unused on the ground. They threw him in, so hard it must have broken some of his bones. His screams of defiance quickly changed to supplication, but Aspidían, busy working a rusty winch, ignored him. The chains all clattered at once, then the man's cage began its slow ascent toward the window. To Llun's amazement, his own cage descended at the same time.

Aspidían's face, as it came into focus, was a study in inscrutability. On the one hand, he had the air of a foreman exasperated with his workers, but on the other, something glinted behind his eyes that suggested bestial enjoyment at pain. He smiled.

"Brother Llun!" He raised his hand, as though they were old acquaintances running into each other at a popular market-stand. "You must forgive me. There has been much confusion after the failed coup. I had no idea you were here."

So there had been a failed coup. Or at least, that was what Aspidían wanted Llun to think.

Aspidían led Llun out of the cage with his own hands, and when his legs failed to support him, he grabbed the huge smith by the waist and forced him to lean on him. Llun was reminded of those snakes from travelers' tales that encircled their prey in a warm embrace before squeezing the life out of them. But he had little strength in his legs, and so he submitted to his torturer.

"Come, my brother," said Aspidían, as cordial as a viper. "Have a drink with me. You look awful."

Llun spat on the ground. But nothing came out. It was like he had been sucked dry.

The long hallways seemed endless. Endless curling staircases, endless rows of black doors. Endless smoking torches jutting out of stone walls that seeped with dark and fetid moisture. The sudden end of the dark was replaced by jagged light. But Llun had grown so accustomed to those changes that he didn't even bother closing his eyes. He just waited for them to adjust.

Aspidían took him to the same room where they had shared mead with Yadovír. Now Llun saw that there were three arched windows looking out directly over the marketplace. He also noticed that the false-commoner hearth had been wiped out of existence. There were new floorboards in the space where it had been. Strange.

Aspidían slumped into one of two extravagant chairs facing the windows and motioned for Llun to do the same. He did, but he nearly fell backward when his muscles failed to hold him. Aspidían laughed.

Between the two chairs stood a short table with a long-necked urn and two squat clay cups.

"I never liked those elaborate goblets," said Aspidían, answering Llun's unspoken question. "And I find clay brings out certain unexpected flavors in the wine."

Llun said nothing, feeling the tension behind Aspidían's words, even through the haze of his burning fever. "Brother Aspidían," whispered Llun. "Who did it? Who killed Yadovír?"

Aspidían turned on him, and for a moment Llun thought that he was going to bite him like a rabid dog. Breathing like a bellows, Aspidían steadied himself.

"You know who," he said.

"The Gumiren?"

Aspidían nodded. "And not only they. The Sons of the Swan. They colluded with the Gumiren. Can you imagine? After all that talk of evil collaborators and traitors to Vasyllia? They did it themselves!"

"That's not possible." It came out before Llun could stop it.

Aspidían smiled, but it was poisonous. "Oh? Enlighten me then."

"There were Vasylli dressed as Gumiren in the first reach, killing and destroying everything in their path. And..." His head spun, and he had to cover his eyes with shaking hands. "It...it was Consistory men who burned down the Nebesta refugee camp."

Aspidían shook his head and sighed. "So much madness. So much confusion. Everyone pretending to be someone else. We need... we need to purge the filth from Vasyllia. For the last time."

"How will you identify friend from foe?"

"Oh, we have ways." He smiled, probably contemplating some especially subtle form of torture. "Shall I demonstrate?"

Aspidían jumped to the windowsill. Llun was surprised to see that the arches were open to the air with not even a thin layer of parchment against the elements, though how no wind or cold blew in, he couldn't understand. Aspidían whistled and nodded. A drum rolled. Easily visible through the arched windows before them, lines of spear-bearing Consistory men surrounded the market from all sides. The bustling people, without even thinking, all stopped their purchasing, haggling, gossiping and stood still, as though they were hoping that they wouldn't be seen if they didn't move.

"Brother Llun, I know you do not think highly of the new way of Vasyllia. But I will show you how effective it can be. It is winnowing time."

Llun stood up from his seat, his head spinning for a moment before his body found its place, and put a hand on the arch to better see. His hand was thinner than he remembered, and the sight of caked blood on it confused him. In the haze of the fever, he had almost forgotten the torture. Had it actually happened? He shook his head, trying to clear the mist from his thoughts. The hot pokers behind his eyes prodded him, and he saw stars. He almost fell, but the wall caught him.

Aspidían braced himself against his side of the arch, looking at Llun. He was done with pretense, it seemed, though his posture was casual, even languid. He even seemed faintly bored. Again, Llun had the sense that he was stuck in a dream where the details were terribly clear but made little sense when put together.

"People of Vasyllia!" Somehow, Aspidían's voice echoed through all

Vasyllia below them, as though the mountains caught his voice like a child's wooden ball and threw it back and forth for their own amusement. Every face in the crowd craned upward, listening intently. "Please forgive the intrusion into your day of rest and pleasure. After what we have all been through, you deserve it. But we now have clear evidence. Yadovír, the man who is so dear to all of us, who has made the transition to the new order as bearable as possible, was betrayed by his own people. Yes, the Gumiren killed him. But we now know that he was delivered to the Gumiren by those vipers, those hawks wearing dove's tail-feathers. It was all an attempted coup. By the Sons of the Swan."

The crowd seethed as people began to whisper to each other and push each other and gesticulate. From this distance, it looked like an anthill disturbed by the stick of a small boy.

"Yes, my people," he shouted over them, arm outstretched for silence. "I know your anger, your frustration with these cowards, these degenerates, these postulants of a retrograde idea. It is time to winnow them from our ranks. I charge you. If any of you know of a friend, a neighbor, or even a family member who is of the Sons, you must come forward. The doors of the Consistory are at your disposal. Come. Let us cleanse the foulness of the Sons from our Vasyllia!"

He turned back to Llun, his face a careful blank. "As soon as I hear of Mirodara's involvement, I will bring her here before you. You will sit there and watch as I kill her. Slowly. Would you like to hear the details of my process? It is quite...artistic."

Llun's hands shook, and his head spun wildly. He was sure he would faint. With an effort of will, he straightened himself and looked down at Aspidían. Such a small man. He would be able to crush his head with a single hand. Yet he had so much power in him.

"I will be your man, Aspidían. But you must promise not to touch Mirodara."

Aspidían looked away from Llun, a slight smile playing at the edges of his lips. Swift as an adder, he backhanded Llun across the face. Hot, wet blood spurted. He had struck him on the place where the dog-man had sliced him during his mock trial. Llun looked at the blood on his hands, and could no longer support his own weight. He fell on his knees, the sobs racking his stomach. He released them, and a blubbering groan came out of his mouth. He hardly recognized it.

"Don't imagine you can haggle with me, vermin. You will do what I say."

Llun breathed deep. His heart slowly calmed, and he looked up at

Aspidían. Deep inside, there was still something left of his strength. He shook his head.

"No, Brother Aspidían. You let too much slip. I don't know why, but you need me. And I will kill myself before I help you, if you so much as scratch Mirodara."

Aspidían held his gaze for an endless minute. Then he collapsed into hearty, chesty laughter.

"Oh, Llun! I'm so glad I met you. It's impossible to be bored with you around."

He snapped his fingers, and two dog-men appeared. They picked Llun up and carried him back the same way they had come.

"No," whispered Llun.

"Oh, yes," said one of the guards, flashing his eyebrows up and down at his companion.

They took Llun back to his cage.

I do not know if this letter will ever reach you, my beloved. I know that you are doing everything you can to come back to me. And I know that the forces arrayed against you must be strong indeed. But Voran, my love, I do not know how much longer I can hold on. I lost my body on the night of the Fall. I can hardly feel it any more. I fear my mind will be next. They say that you have become a Healer. Come to me, my love. Heal me. I need you.

From an unsent letter found in the apartments of Darina Sabíana of Vasyllia

CHAPTER 6
THE DARINA OF VASYLLIA

The first night, the cycle of cold and hot repeated five times. The second night, the cycle repeated six times. By the fifth day, Llun had trouble distinguishing day from night. It may have been a month, it may have been a year. The fever in his body reached some kind of critical point, and there was a period when Llun remembered nothing. He came back to consciousness with a strange sensation of being that he had never before experienced. He felt every fiber of his body separately. He moved individual muscles with a clear understanding of where they began and ended and how they worked. At the same time, every breath was an unbearable agony. It was as if there were two of him.

"There's more to this than mere torture, you know," she said. "There's a foul magic at work here. Not something I understand. But I've seen it at work in others already. They're preparing you. Reforging you, if you like. To be able to withstand the horrors that you will perpetrate on others. And, possibly, for something even worse."

Where did she come from? And how did he suddenly get from his cage to this garret? It looked like an unused attic room, the kind where all the unnecessary bric-a-brac of a great house was placed in piles that were once orderly, but had long ceased to be so. Immense mounds of fabric, bits of metal, broken chairs. But then there was the wooden throne, its every inch carved into shapes of Sirin and wolves and giants and vila that came out of the wood like ripples on water. It was illumined with a dappled fire-light that...yes, it was fragrant. Like roses.

"I will not be like them," he said to the figure on the throne, whom he could not quite see, though he didn't understand why.

"No, I don't believe you will. But there will be a price to pay."

Something about the voice enchanted Llun. It awoke forgotten images of sharp mountain peaks and waterfalls at dawn, images associated with a childhood longing that flared in his heart whenever he listened to his mother sing a ballad of Old Vasyllia.

"I will gladly pay the price of my life," said Llun.

"You do not know what you are saying," said the figure. She shifted in the throne, and the light also changed, so that he could see her more clearly. She was a young, dark-haired woman in chainmail, a heavy wolf fur draping her shoulders. Across her chest flew a black swan embroidered on a snow-white field. Her expression was still, but joyful. It was almost as though she were laughing at Llun, except her eyes were so old, deep as a lake with no visible bottom, that Llun was certain she was incapable of mocking others.

"What if you did give them the gift of your life to save your niece? Mirodara, was it? You would be able to bear it, perhaps, but only because you knew you would die eventually. At some point, all the pain will end. Perhaps you even keep suicide in the back of your mind as an extreme measure."

She sighed and shook her head. Her hair shone in the firelight, mesmerizing Llun with the play of dark red and brown and even purple tints.

"But you don't understand what the Raven is. His eternal quest is for endless life. And if he does find the source of endless life, whether in the form of Living Water or in some other unknown form, then imagine what they can do to their dog-men. Given a few centuries of constant atrocities, a few centuries for the mind to hide their atrocities under a mental scar, they will be capable of any evil. Not just capable, but confirmed in it. Any internal change will become impossible. They will not think twice about murder, rape, torture. They will no longer be men."

"Why are you telling me this? And who are you?"

"Can you not guess who I am?" She smiled mischievously, patting the black swan on her chest with her forefinger, with an expression that said, "Can it be any more obvious?"

"You are Darina Sabíana? But they say you are bed-ridden. Unable to move."

"Yes, that is all true," she said, faintly annoyed, "but you are also in a cage, are you not? And yet you stand here with me."

Llun opened his mouth to retort, but found nothing to say.

"Have you never wondered," she said, "why your name is Llun?"

The name was a rare one, it was true. "I always thought my mother wanted to be unique."

Sabíana rolled her eyes. "Not much imagination, for an artist. No. Have you never considered the importance of names before? Why, for example, there are so few Cassíans and so many Lassars in Vasyllia?"

"Oh," he understood immediately. "It's the old superstition. You need to give your child the name of a person who was successful in life. For good luck. Name a child after a martyr, and ..." He chuckled significantly.

"No, no, no," she waved her hands in frustration. "That's the ... No ... There is something profoundly important about naming. It's not a matter of luck. The name does, in some ineffable way, reflect a person's place in the Universal Harmony. Have you never wondered why in some of the Old Tales, you have different characters with the same name living in vastly different circumstances, yet in all of them, the same events keep happening? It's not an accidental pattern. It's part of the fabric of the creation."

"But Llun. He was a mad prophet, wasn't he? His writings in the *Sayings* are incredibly arcane. More interpretations of his prophecies exist than the prophecies themselves. What does that say about me and my name?"

"Llun wrote of a terribly important event. A time of blood, when the dead would walk as though living, but with no souls to speak of. He said that he, Llun himself, would bring this time about as a punishment for Vasyllia's iniquity. But..."

"Oh, you mean he could have meant that I am the Llun that will bring divine retribution? How?"

"I cannot say for certain. But Aspidían has been studying Llun's prophecies for years. He even comes to me in my bed of misery to speak of it. He finds no one else who believes him. But he seems to think that a smith is necessary. You are to make something. Something rather banal, I think. But with unexpected uses."

Hardly helpful. "Why are you telling me all this, my lady?"

"It's the only thing I have left, you see," she said. "And it is why I linger here in Vasyllia. I am given to help those who are needed at Vasyllia's sticking points. Yours is coming. You may have to make the most difficult choice of all. To abandon everything. Not only your own life, not only your own death, but even Mirodara."

"No. That I will not do."

"And yet, the alternative will be far worse than you can imagine."

"I will not!"

The pain in his back grew and arched and exploded into stars that danced before his eyes, before they pulled him back underneath into the darkness. He felt turned inside out, and once again his legs were clamped in place, his arms hanging useless outside the cage that was too small for him. He closed his eyes and tried to sleep.

And I, Llun of Vasyllia, will bring down the retribution of the Heights on fallen Vasyllia. The stars shall weep blood, the immortal one shall hold the lifeblood of the worlds in the palm of his hand, and the Realms themselves will hold their breath for utter terror. But in that day, the truth will become known at last. And the fire-born will brave the seventh baptism to demand vengeance from the Throne of the Most High himself.

From "The Prophecy of Llun"
(The Sayings, Book XXIII, 10:3-6)

CHAPTER 7
THE CHOICE

When Llun came to himself, he was no longer in the cage, but in a simple prison cell. He lay on a straw pallet on a wooden ledge. A pitcher of water was at his feet. He attacked the pitcher, spilling much of the contents on the ground in his haste. His hands shook, and he was unable to stop them. His hands...they were blackened with soot, thin and brittle-looking. How would he ever again manage to create anything with his hands? Why did they do this to him, if they wanted him to become the exclusive smith of the Consistory? Or had they now abandoned all that?

Still, despite his shaking hands, he felt clear-headed for the first time since the ordeal began. He groped his chest and arms, trying to see how much muscle mass he had lost. It was not as bad as he thought. About as much as he would have expected after not eating for a week. No, they hadn't been torturing him for months or years, then. Only days.

It was then that he realized that, outside, some sort of commotion had been going on ever since he had woken up. He listened, trying to understand. Lots of pushing and jostling, by the sound of it. Scraping metal. Gumiren voices, angry, yet without that note of defiance that usually characterized their speech. These voices sounded...yes, frightened.

So, the pogroms have begun, then.

He was too tired to feel any emotion accompanying that thought.

For the next few days, he was brought heaping plates of chicken and boar meat. It was unseasoned and not very well made, but these were the tastiest meals of Llun's life. Almost in the space of hours, he began to regain his strength. His hands stopped shaking. He found the courage to try to scratch off the scorch marks on his skin. All that came off was a layer of dead skin. Underneath, everything was smooth, almost baby-like. Strange for a man whose skin was more like leather after a lifetime at the forge. But it would harden again, soon enough.

A few days later, Aspidían himself came in the morning, bearing a tray of roasted ribs. Even from a distance, Llun smelled the rosemary. This was a king's meal, not a prisoner's. Behind Aspidían came a host of servants bearing trestles, stands, plates, crockery, spices, and wine. Urns and urns of wine. Llun's mouth watered at the sight, even at the clinking of the cups on the makeshift trestles.

"What are you doing?" asked Llun, his voice hardly more than a croak.

"Your last meal," said Aspidían, smiling. When Llun's jaw clenched, Aspidían laughed. "Your face! Even after all we've put you through, you're still as innocent as a babe in swaddling clothes."

Llun didn't know whether to laugh or cry. Aspidían poured wine for them both. It was blood-red, almost viscous.

"I wasn't lying when I said it was your last meal. It is. From this moment, you will be something else. It will be your choice, what you will be. But not Llun the smith of the former first reach of Vasyllia." He raised his cup. "To the new order."

Llun hesitated a moment, then drank. There was something different about this wine. It burned him on the inside. Llun suspected that there was more than just wine there. But Aspidían drank it with Llun, so it was not poison. At least, not the kind that kills.

"New order, you say?" croaked Llun. "One cleansed of both the Gumiren and the Sons of the Swan?"

"Oh yes," said Aspidían. "You would not believe how willing our Vasylli were to rat out the Sons. So many traitors in our midst!"

"You do realize that people will say anything to keep themselves from being implicated. It proves nothing."

"Yes, yes. But that is well and good. It doesn't matter who remains in the new Vasyllia, really. As long as they understand the new rules. As long as they are the ones who will resist external influence to the last drop of their blood. As for the Gumiren, we've killed most of them already. The Ghan escaped with a small band of his elite warriors, but they have nowhere to go. They'll be found in the mountains soon enough. If not, they'll have a surprise waiting for them at the border with Nebesta." He chuckled. The expression on his face left no doubt that whatever it was, it would be painful and probably fatal.

He snapped his fingers, and the servants began slicing the ribs apart. The meat practically fell off the bone. Llun's hands shook again, and it took all the will he had left not to attack the food. Aspidían watched him the whole time and seemed pleased with what he saw. Finally, all the ribs were separated and placed in a pile in the middle of the table. A servant tossed herbs over it, and another poured sauce that smelled strongly of onion and beer.

Aspidían inhaled deeply, eyes closed in pleasure. He sat there, savoring the smell, for what seemed an eternity.

Llun could wait no longer. "Tell me what I want to know," he said. He knew that he risked losing this meal, possibly the most elaborate and well-made meal of his life. He didn't care anymore.

Aspidían inclined his head and smirked. "Yes, Mirodara was turned in. I've kept her safe, for now. I was waiting to see how you'd do in your ordeal. And you did surprisingly well, considering the ordeal lasted almost two weeks. Do you know how many postulates to the Consistory survive it? Less than half."

"You risked losing your exclusive smith?" Llun said, with a hint of mockery.

"Yes." Aspidían became deadly serious. "Enough games, Llun. The Great Father needs you for a frightfully important work. I know you are squeamish about serving him, but you were never a particularly devout member of the cult of Adonais. You weren't much of anything, really. But we live in a time where half measures have no place. I think you know that now, and not merely with your mind."

Llun nodded. His body would never forget the lesson.

"You are more important than you know, Llun." Aspidían pulled out his table knife and speared three ribs through, then dropped them on Llun's side of the table. "Eat, O important one."

Llun did. Somehow, he managed not to transform into a wolf on the spot, but ate with admirable restraint. Or so it seemed to him. Aspidían shook his head with a smile, again in his faintly amused persona.

"Brother Llun, have you ever read the prophecies of your namesake?"

So she had *been real. The warrior-Darina who spoke to him from her throne.*

"Of course ... when I was a child. Everyone reads *The Sayings* at least once."

"Ah ... you have not *read* them, then. Have you ever heard the idea that names are not accidental? That when one takes on the name of another, especially an illustrious name, he takes up some of the qualities of his namesake?"

"I have not given it much thought, to be honest."

"Well, you would not be the first. But your name. What a name! A rare one. And with good reason. 'The Prophecies of Llun' is the strangest book in *The Sayings*. So many contradictory interpretations. So many phrases with no apparent meaning. Until now."

Llun's back straightened as he listened, unwittingly enchanted by Aspidían's voice. The pain was there, but now no more than an ache. Amazing. Sabíana was right about the body's ability to heal itself. Or was it perhaps something in the wine? Something with the appearance of goodness, but actually dangerous?

"There is a series of images that keeps popping up," continued Aspidían. "Most of them involve fire and a night full of stars in the constellation of the sword. The stars begin to weep. Then the tears turn to blood. By themselves, these images make little sense. But there is a mathematical precision to the prophecies. Certain images appear at regular intervals. Every seven verses, every twelve verses, and every four chapters, these central images repeat. I won't bore you with the calculation, but I have managed to make a cipher of the prophecies. They speak of a moment in Vasyllia's history when the lifeblood of the worlds will come into the hands of an 'immortal one.' At that time, the key to life and death will be revealed, and the dead will walk as though alive."

"*As though* alive? Animate corpses walking around Vasyllia? Sounds horrifying." He thought of the people in the market and realized that part of the prophecy may have already come true. They were no better than animate corpses.

"I do not jest, Llun. I am speaking of something monumental." His eyes widened, his eyebrows shot up, and he spoke in hushed, awed tones. "I have the ear of the Great Father. He has helped me to understand the true meaning of everything that has happened. All the suffering Vasyllia's been through. All the troubles. Nothing more than a cleansing. A time of ordeal. We are about to embark on a new age for Vasyllia. One unmatched in glory in the history of the world. Man will not lord it over man. Everyone will be equal. Opportunities to rise in the world will be given to all. Every person may choose what he or she would like to be. And the might of Vasyllia will become legendary. Then we will be a beacon, a city on a hill, truly. Other nations will seek alliance with us, and we can choose with whom to associate. No more need to pander after the pitiful Nebesti or worse, the Karila.

"At the heart of this new world will be the ultimate gift. Eternal life. Even now, the Raven is at the cusp of finding it. But it will only be given to the chosen. Only to the men of the Raven. They will live for all time."

Sabíana's warning about an eternity of atrocity rang in Llun's ears like a bell. Truly, she was right. If the dog-men had millennia to live, they would be no different than changers or any other evil Power.

And yet...

"Brother Aspidían. I hear you. I am moved by your words. But I am a simple man, not given to theorizing. Tell me, simply, how I am to help in this new age of Vasyllia?"

"You will be one of the Consistory. But not yet. After a time. First, a test. There is a trinket that the Great Father would have you make for him. A simple thing, really. A metal flask that a man can wear on his hip. To hold wine or mead or water, even."

Llun was taken aback. He had expected something elaborate. But a flask? And a metal one, to boot? He had never seen such a thing. Why would anyone want to drink water from a metal flask? What was wrong with leather skins?

"Is there any design the...um...Great Father would prefer? Any details he would like included?"

"He wants you to...be possessed by your inspiration."

Again, Llun shuddered at the use of that particular word. It tainted his enjoyment of the rest of that meal. It didn't help that though his mind registered how superior the cooking was, his heart ached with worry for Mirodara and fear for what he would have to do. Aspidían was content to allow Llun his silence, though he talked the entire time. Llun had only a faint recollection of what he spoke about, but it left a sour taste in Llun's mouth.

To Llun's surprise, Aspidían led him through the Consistory back to the outer courtyard of the palace.

He's not letting me go home, is he?

At the gates, Aspidían embraced Llun and hugged him warmly. Llun stiffened, not sure whether to be afraid or uncomfortable.

"I am giving you this day and night as a gift," said the dog-man. "For you and Mirodara. Use it well. For both your sakes, help her understand the way that is best for all."

It has been the source of some debate—where did the essence of the Raven go when Yadovír was killed? Some survivors of the wars for Vasyllia insist that, a few nights after the death of Yadovír, they saw the presence of the Raven hovering about a smithy in the first reach. Impossible to confirm now, of course, since that smithy no longer stands...

From "A New History of the Covenant" by Dar-in-Exile Mirnían II

CHAPTER 8
THE CREATION

Mirodara lay curled in a ball on the floor of his back room. She did not budge at his call. She shrank from his touch on her shoulder.

"What did they do to you?" he asked, shaking with the suppressed desire to kill everyone who would dare to so much as lay a hand on her.

She uncurled slowly, like a flower opening over the course of a long morning. Her eyes were hollow. Not a sign of tears on her face. Just horror lurking behind her eyes, like a parasite that had invaded her body. She would not look him in the eyes. The closest she managed to get was somewhere near his left eyebrow. He waited for her to sit up, giving her what he hoped was enough space to feel safe, without the distance he feared would clam her up even more. He wanted to enfold her in his arms, to hide her in his bulk, to never let anyone else see her.

"Not much," she said, but it sounded like she had forgotten how to speak. Her own face looked surprised at the sound of her voice. "It's what they did to the others. They made me watch." Her face turned green, and her hands went up to her mouth as she retched. But nothing came out. She dry heaved for almost a minute.

Llun went outside to the well and pulled out a bucketful of water. He nearly threw it on her head in his haste and in his desire to make her better. She had to calm him down by taking his lone wooden cup and dipping it in the cold water. Her eyes closed at the pleasure of the water.

"You must have some bread. I have a little. I think..."

His bread box was nearly empty, and what was there may have been a feast for the mice in the last few weeks, judging by the suspicious looking crumbs in the left corner. Sighing out his exasperation, he took his table knife out of its sheath on his belt—he still couldn't believe the dog-men had given it back to him—and cut a thin outside layer off the crusty, black rye bread. Without much hope, he looked in the apple basket for last year's shriveled apples, few of which had survived the winter. He was shocked to find one tiny, shriveled, but bright red apple hiding in the far corner. He picked it up. It smelled like autumn.

Mirodara took both the bread and the apple and looked at them for a long moment, not understanding what they were, or what she was supposed to do with them. That, more than anything else, cut his heart. How could he go through with it? They'd already damaged Mirodara, possibly beyond repair. She was not strong enough to survive what was coming.

But the food gave her obvious strength. Her breathing slowed and deepened, and a spot of warmth touched her cheeks, though they were still far from a good color. It was as though the blush of healthfulness had gingerly approached her cheek, had even tried to warm it, but ultimately scurried away like a skittish deer. Still, she looked much better for the food and water.

"Why?" she asked as he brought her tea, the last of his precious hoard, probably never to be replenished now.

"Why what, my cub?"

"Why are you and I here, now, speaking to each other? Is this a test? Are they waiting outside, waiting for you to lull me into a sense of security, so I can let slip some vital piece of information about the Sons of the Swan?"

She looked at him with such a strange expression—anger, distrust, defiance, exhaustion. And yet, they had not stamped out the hope, deep within her eyes, no more than a fading ember.

"It is a sort of test, I think," he said. "But not the one you think. This is the last chance you and I have to lead a normal life before everything changes. I am to become one of them. To save your life. And maybe even to save your death."

She stiffened. "Oh, Heights! Has the Raven found it, then? His immortality?"

"No, not that I can tell. But I think he is close. The Consistory wants me to make something for him. I don't understand it, not quite. Aspidían did a very bad job trying to make it sound unimportant. But what the Raven would want with a metal flask, I haven't the faintest idea."

Mirodara's eyebrows gathered in confusion. "That's...unexpected. One of the Sons was deep inside the Consistory, and before the last purge, he managed to find out that the Raven is burrowing *inside* Vasyllia. Inside the mountain, searching for some elixir, like the Living Water, but possibly something else entirely. I know, bad information. It's the best we have."

"It's clearly important. Maybe the flask is intended to hold this elixir. But wouldn't it have to be a magical artifact then, to hold a thing of power?"

"Perhaps you have magical powers you weren't aware of."

It was a joke, though she barely smiled as she said it. It made Llun smile and nearly exclaim in joy.

"Llun, you must do what you think is right. But let me say one thing. I don't know why, but I think that this object will be your last as a smith. Your work is too beautiful to be allowed by the Raven. And I think that you need to be very careful when you make it. It's going to be not a battle, but a war."

He knew what she meant. Every *thing* he made was made with pain, in a process of battle with himself and with forces outside himself that tried to stop him—tiredness, lack of inspiration, a sense that he was incapable of creating beauty. Only after it was complete did the sense of synthesis, the joy intertwined with intense grief, come flooding over him, threatening to overwhelm him. In that moment, he and the Heights were one, until once again the hunger for creation overtook him, and the process began anew.

If, instead of the usual, natural antagonists, the Raven and his dark Powers interfered with his work or tried to subvert it to their own desires, the struggle would be a hundred times more intense. It might even kill him.

But what better way to die, than in the creation of a perfect piece that would never, not over his dead body, belong to them? After all, nothing created through the mediation of the Heights would ever be corrupted. It would simply be. And even if they later used it for their own vile ends, its beauty would be a thorn in their side, a reminder of their eventual failure and end. For nothing evil can last forever, not unless it were already the Unmaking of the world.

"Yes, Mirodara. You will have to help me. There will be times when I will want to stop. Or when my creation will try to wrest itself from my hands. Be my cold water. Be my conscience."

She smiled, and the ember of hope in her eyes lit up.

"Our last hurrah. Yes. It will be glorious."

"I must do it in my forge. And I need Mirodara with me."

Aspidían had come to the first reach with a full honor guard, and he looked a little offended at being thus greeted. But that quickly passed, as understanding crept in. Again, Aspidían surprised Llun. He had expected at least something of a fight.

"I understand," said Aspidían. He looked at Llun, his gaze slowly boring into him as though he were pushing a knife into his eye, waiting for it to come out the other end. He dismissed the guards with a wave of the hand, still looking at Llun.

"Only know this. This is a concession. My final one. After you join us, you will not come back here. In fact, I intend to destroy this smithy. I know about the foulness that you perpetrated here. Those decorative shields. I did not see it at first. But later, after the benefit of some...external aid," for a moment, the mask slipped, and Aspidían's pain shone in his eyes. Was the inquisitor the recipient of the tender mercies of the torturer himself? "I recognized them for what they were. I should take both hands from you for that. And both eyes for good measure."

"I understand you, Brother Aspidían."

He met the inquisitor's gaze. It was terrifying, but already Llun felt the beginning of the inspiration. The process of creation. He could not be gainsaid by anyone when in this state. Aspidían began to smile his adder's smile, but he stopped in mid-smirk. His eyes softened, and a face Llun had yet to see manifested itself. It was terrifyingly, heartbreakingly sad.

"Brother Llun. It is my great regret that we did not know one another before ..." He choked on what he almost said, before his eyes filmed over with their usual expression of assumed boredom. He turned and followed the honor guard back to the Consistory.

For a moment, Llun watched in wonder. Was this last, sincerest version of Aspidían the greatest lie of all?

But the forge called to him like a lover after a long absence. And Mirodara's gaze was burning swirls into his back.

"I'm ready," he said.

"I don't think you are," she said, but she was deadly serious.

A shudder ran up his spine. She was right.

Llun took the piece of iron like a mother taking her child from the midwife. Llun folded the iron gently into a thick block. He cut the block into two billets and placed the two halves on top of each other, with the grains perpendicular to each other. Then, he forged it into a thin sheet, so thin, he was afraid it would crack in multiple places at the smallest stress. But it held.

As soon as the sheet was ready to be shaped, it began. The heaviness in his mind. Usually it was no more than a kind of fog that pushed him to stop, to lay down his tools to wait for a better moment, when his heart would be more into the process. But this time, it was like a voice in his head.

You are weak. Why do you labor? You know that it can never be appreciated for what it truly is. It is going to be twisted out of shape and out of its intention. Better give it up. Come what may.

He was already sweating, but now it poured like rain down his body. His breathing hurried, and the heat on his face was more than just the forge.

"You don't matter," said Mirodara. "*You* don't matter. This thing you make. It matters more than you or I or my mother or anyone else. It may be the last thing of beauty created in Vasyllia."

He breathed a sigh of relief as the enthusiasm caught at the wave of his shame. He began to shape the iron around a rounded wooden block. It felt like butter in his hands, supple and easy. So easy. He could do anything he wanted with this. Would he be remembered for this creation? Would Vasyllia sing the praises of Llun the smith after this final, wondrous thing he made?

A flask?

Truly, an insignificant, pitiful thing to make as one's swan song. Why not change it? He could use this metal to make a weapon so fine, so strong, that it would make even the dullest swordsman brilliant. Why not? Surely such a gift would be acceptable to the Great Father.

Great Father? Have you gone mad?

Something chuckled behind them.

"Don't look," said Mirodara, her voice shaking. "He wants you, Llun. Not as a smith. They've been lying to you the whole time. He doesn't want your flask. He wants *you* as his…" Her voice squelched, like someone were holding a wet towel over her mouth and throttling her by the neck at the same time. Llun nearly turned around. Something kept him firmly in place, working the sheet around the mold.

The presence in the room was unmistakable, its malice so palpable it was akin to a smell of something rotten, like old eggs or a week-old corpse. And yet, there was a kind of energy in that presence. It fueled Llun's manic activity. His hands worked faster than they ever had before, with as much, or more, control than he had had since his early days. Already he saw the decorations of iron he would place on the flask, fine as embroidery.

No! Not for him. Not ever!

There were two Lluns in that room. One was already finished with the creation of the flask—a marvelous thing that sparkled even in darkness, that was light as a feather but virtually unbreakable. A perfect receptacle for an elixir of power. The other Llun was still in his human body, sweating, aching, laboring over the sheet, which every second threatened to break apart into splinters of iron. This Llun was tired. He wanted to give up. The other Llun, the one in his mind—how he wanted to be him already! To rush past the drudgery of the work. To stand at the completed stage, the state of synthesis, to feel the joy of it.

"I can give it to you," said the presence in his mind, "all you have to do is desire it with every fiber of your being."

"Is beauty without suffering possible?" asked a new voice, strong and regal. Sabíana stood before him, half-insubstantial, her eyes dancing in the shower of sparks Llun sent up with each blow of his hammer. "Is it even preferable? You are the last true artist in Vasyllia, Llun. Not because of some talent given by the Heights. You are the last in the tradition of the old masters. The ones who understood that the secret of beauty is pain. Only through birthgiving can the miracle be brought forth."

The presence in his mind laughed. "Yes. Listen to the woman. She is a pitiful creature, chained to her bed. I offer you the way of fulfillment. It is also the path to power. Never again will you be subject to the whims of the Consistory. You will rule them."

"You have no power here, foul thing," Sabíana cried. "This is a place protected by me. It is given to me from above, this protection for my chosen few."

Again, the laughter, only now directed at her. "And what if I told you that everything you think you know about your precious Power, your Adonais, is a lie? What if I told you that your entire existence is a mistake, but one that is mercifully coming to its end? What would you say to that, eh?"

Sabíana's eyes filled with tears and she shimmered for a moment, then faded.

"You see? She cannot protect you. Only you can protect yourself. And Mirodara as well. Save her from what the Consistory will do. Become the Consistory."

Llun breathed deeply and closed his eyes. He stilled his breathing and focused on the beating of his heart. It began to slow. He waited until the beats were regular and unhurried. He breathed again and smiled. Everything hurt. His mind, his body. Everything. And he loved it. He would have it no other way. He would make this thing. This last thing of beauty.

But not for you. Begone, you foulness. You have no place in the creation of the beautiful.

"Llun? Are you well? What happened?"

Mirodara touched his shoulder.

"Is it...Can I turn around now?" He asked.

"Yes. I think it's over."

Llun turned to look at her. She was unharmed. Only a little pale. He nodded at her and turned back to his work, suddenly sure that the time needed to create this thing properly would not be given them. With a speed he never expected from himself, he created something... remarkable.

He puffed like a bellows after it was done, cradling the thing in his hand like a child. It was a flask, but it did not even look metal. It looked like a dark flower enfolded in leaves at midnight. It was the most beautiful thing Llun had ever seen. And he recognized that it was not *he* who had made it. He was but the instrument.

"Mirodara," he said. "Go. Take it. You are its only hope. It must never fall into the hands of the Raven. Find a way. Leave Vasyllia. Seek the true Vasylli out there, in the wild. If you find Voran the Healer, tell him to hurry. There may not be a Vasyllia left if we wait much longer."

The doors to the forge flew open. Aspidían stood there, his gaze expectant. It quickly turned to disappointment, then anger, then horror.

"What...? What have you done, Llun? Where is Mirodara?"

"I am ready," said Llun. "I am ready to be a dog-man."

Aspidían gestured, and the guards behind him swarmed in and seized Llun, pulling him out of the smithy on his knees.

"Turn him around," said Aspidían. "Make him watch."

Ten dog-men with torches stood in a semicircle around Aspidían, their eyes red in the fire-light.

"Burn it," said Aspidían. "The whole block."

And it came to pass that the sacrifice was offered, and it was found acceptable by the Most High. And he deigned to bend down from the throne of his greatness to confirm the sacrifice, and to give a final gift. But his words were terrible. Thus saith the Lord, the Most High: "For the last time I grant the fallen a boon, until the fire-born braves the final baptism and stands before me in his transfigured flesh."

From "The Prophecy of Llun"
(The Sayings, Book XXIII, 4:1-4)

CHAPTER 9
THE ESCAPE

Mirodara dropped the flask into the first canvas pack she found lying in a heap of rubble in Llun's smithy. It tied over her shoulder well enough. She hoped it wouldn't look conspicuous in the first reach. She must do everything possible not to attract too much attention to herself on her way out of Vasyllia.

She stopped at a food stand and bought three breads and some dried meat. Enough, she hoped, to get her into Nebesta, where she would try to find some gainful employment while she searched for Voran. She had nothing more concrete than that as far as plans go. Some very reasonable part of her, deep inside her mind, nagged at her that the lack of a plan was no plan at all, but she was too excited by her forthcoming adventure to listen.

Only when she was halfway to her destination—a side gate in Vasyllia's wall that was usually undermanned and filled with merchant wains entering and exiting—did it fully hit her. She would never see Llun again. She sped up her walking, if only to force the hard cobbles in the streets to rattle her out of her desire to sink to the ground and weep like a baby. It was no use, not any more. Yes, she was an orphan, but she had gotten over that (or so she kept telling herself). Now she had no one left. But the world was ending. What difference did it make if there was no one to share it with?

Focusing on the ground before her feet, she almost didn't notice that she was at the gates, even as she joined the line of people leaving. Her good fortune held strong. Several caravans of merchants were lining up to take the shorter, more difficult routes that skirted the mountains and led out to the lands that used to be taboo to the Vasylli. Magical lands with monstrous creatures with many eyes that spun silk out of their own saliva. If the stories were to be believed. Mirodara certainly believed them.

She tried her best to blend into the gaggle of merchants, some even with their families, as they prepared to take a journey that could last them years. What sort of hopes animated them? How did they survive in the new Vasyllia? Were they not also affected by all the madness? Perhaps they did well to leave, hoping beyond hope that things would be different when they returned?

A little boy of two or three saw Mirodara and started making faces at her. She did the same, and he laughed with pleased surprise.

"What's your name?" she asked him quietly.

"Adarin," he said, sheepishly.

"I'm Mirodara," she said. "Do you want to play a game?"

He nodded, eyes sparkling.

"I'm going to hide under your father's wain, under here. But I have to get there without anyone noticing me. You can help me, right?"

"I want to hide with you, too," he said.

"But then we'll both get in trouble, won't we? I'll tell you what. If you help me hide now, I'll let you come down with me for the rest of the trip. I just need to be under there when we pass the gates. Got it?"

Adarin looked dubious, but he obviously wanted to play. He nodded seriously, then started to scream bloody murder. Every adult within earshot was completely absorbed by his screaming. Mirodara slipped under a wain and held on for dear life. As soon as she did, Adarin stopped, as though it were the most normal thing in the world to scream one second, then stop the next. Mirodara had to bite her lip to keep from laughing aloud.

Just as they approached the gates, Mirodara heard the stomp of booted feet. Many booted feet.

"Stop the wains, stop the wains!" Someone called from behind.

"What's the matter, sir?" asked someone Mirodara assumed to be the warden of the side gate.

"Political prisoner. Escapee. Young girl, thirteen maybe. She has something of value needed by the Consistory."

"We'll keep a watch out for her, sir."

Adarin. Please don't say anything. Please don't say anything.

He didn't. They passed without so much as a peep from the boy. To his credit, he waited until they were well beyond earshot before he crouched down to look for her.

"Well? Can I come down now?"

Mirodara laughed, dropped and rolled out from under the wain. She hopped up and ran away from the merchant caravan. A few surprised merchants reached out to catch her, but she had always been fast. She managed to squeeze past them. She ran down into the deepwood without stopping or looking back.

This part of the Vasylli mountain woods she knew like the back of her hand. Even as a child, her—she almost thought "father," then realized she *had* no father—"treacherous person who raised her" took her often into the woods for days at a time while he would find the best kind of wood for his carpentry. So, finding the backwoods paths that eventually joined the Dar's Way to Nebesta was easy enough.

She ran with inhuman speed all the way to the border of Nebesta. Three days and three nights of nearly constant running and walking, with only short naps for rest whenever she felt like she couldn't go on any more. The rough mountain tracks she followed were well-worn, though strenuous. But she found unexpected reserves of strength inside herself. She ate less than she had expected, and she traveled farther, faster than she had thought possible.

When she joined the Dar's Way, she was sure some sort of alarm would blare the moment she stepped onto the pavement. Nothing happened. At least, nothing she could detect. But there did seem to be some kind of unseen energy that hummed on the level of emotion, just beyond sound. She was unsure if she had caused it, or if it was some devilry of the Raven. It left her stomach queasy. But she resumed her easy pace without any hindrance.

She knew that just before the Way crossed over into Nebesta, it would rise up onto a ridge, then fall away steeply into a shallow valley walled by two tree-covered hills. If there was going to be an ambush anywhere, it would be there. So, she took her time cresting it, listening for the slightest sound of pursuit or ambush. But she heard nothing at all. Not even the sounds of animals. That frightened her, and as she crested the ridge, her breathing became shallow and spots danced before her eyes.

On the downslope, a wall blocked the Dar's Way. It was not very tall yet, clearly in the process of being built, though it was dark and imposing. Menacing, even.

The moment she stopped to stare at the wall, she heard it. Horses behind her.

She ran to the wall and tried to find a handhold to launch herself over into Nebesta and safety, but her hand shot back in pain as though there were tiny barbs all along the wall. She looked at her palm, and it was bloody. Her arm pulsed with pain. Had she just poisoned herself?

She turned around to face whatever it was that was coming after her. Three horsemen. Gumiren. They were bloodied and their eyes were wild and hungry. She would get no quarter from these. They looked like they had just escaped one of the latest pogroms.

"Why you out here, Vasylli girl-child?" asked the central of the three, the youngest.

She said nothing.

He talked to his neighbor in their rat-a-tat tongue. They quickly came to a consensus.

"Your hand." He pointed. "It bloody."

"Yes?" she said. "The wall. It's..."

"Pricked...yes? Keep you in. Keep others out. We guard the wall. All who touch it are for to be executed. You not know this?"

She gulped hard and shook her head. These Gumiren had death in their eyes. She supposed she should be grateful it was only death she saw in their eyes.

"Well, it sad for you. But law is law."

He nodded at the Gumir at his left. In a smooth motion, he pulled a knife from his belt and threw it at Mirodara. It struck her in the chest, the blade going in all the way to the hilt. She stared at it in fascination, before the spots began to dance in her eyes and her knees wobbled. The ground reached up and grabbed her. No, it was the Gumiren. They hoisted her above their heads, she thought. Then, the sensation of weightlessness, followed by the earth falling on her body. No, it was she who fell on the earth. Why was it so hard to concentrate? Everything hurt, especially her left leg. Strange. Why her left leg? She felt at the thing that tugged at her chest. It was knobby. That didn't belong there. She wrenched it out, and a fountain of red poured up and out of her. It was mesmerizing.

Then she realized it was her blood. She seemed to be drowning in it. But no. It wasn't just blood. There was a great deal of water. And it smelled... like...roses.

Voran and Aglaia—he still had trouble thinking of her as Aglaia when she was in her wolf form—had been traveling toward Vasyllia in a straight line for a week. It was the first time they had done that since the fall of Vasyllia, almost ten years before. At every step, Voran expected that the road would fade, that he would fall into a different realm, or that reality would shift around him, and he would find himself where he had started a week before.

Returning to Vasyllia was impossible. He had tried it. Hundreds of times. But someone—whether Zmei and his brothers or the Raven, Voran didn't know—had made the lands before Vasyllia a warren of hidden doorways and traps. Time and time again, Voran took a step toward Vasyllia, only to find himself in the Lows of Aer, or displaced hundreds of miles farther away from Vasyllia. Something was doing everything in its power to prevent anyone from approaching Vasyllia.

It also didn't help that he hardly had a day when he wasn't running away from Zmei or his giant brothers. It didn't take him long to realize that they had noses like hounds, and they were nearly always three steps ahead of him every time he made his way toward Vasyllia. A few times the encounters had been close to fatal. When his mother Aglaia had joined him in her wolf form, it had actually gotten worse. The giants had bound her to her wolf form in the first place, and somehow her presence made them seek him out ever more ferociously. But she had refused to leave him. She still bristled if he so much as mentioned it.

There were other reasons Voran didn't come back to Vasyllia earlier. One was that Voran had been healing everyone he could find. As Zmei had predicted, the power of the Living Water only lasted for some time. Voran learned to supplement its lack with a thorough study of herbs and medicines from every leech he could find, in whatever village he happened to be at the time. Those travels had taken him as far as Karila, even to the edge of the Steppelands border. He had become a competent enough healer with his hands alone. But sometimes, rarely and never according to his own desire, an echo of the old power came out of his hands, and people were healed by his touch. That alone had been enough to make his legend travel ahead of him. He hoped that it had reached Vasyllia by now.

A year ago, something had happened that made him seek Vasyllia with renewed energy. Lyna stopped coming to him. He realized in the pit of his gut that she was upset with him for not managing to return to Vasyllia. For not accomplishing his calling, so to speak. He felt he had had little choice in the matter, but her lack was like a knife slowly cutting a hole in his chest. He needed her like he needed to breathe. So, he and Aglaia had braved the most obscure paths, some of them nothing more than pure deepwood, with little more than pressed-down grass from the passage of some wild animal.

It took much longer than it normally would. Finding food was a problem, even for Aglaia. But they had done it without even a whiff of giant-stink anywhere near them. Somehow, either the traps had faded in power, or they had managed to evade them. Finally, they came to a sharp ridge of mountains. In them was a narrow pass, hardly noticeable to the naked eye, beyond which lay a hunter's track that connected with the Dar's Way near the border between Nebesta and Vasyllia.

The trek over the pass was difficult—it was late spring, and the cold and ice were omnipresent—but they made it over with only scrapes and bruises, not broken bones. Voran was continually astounded by the unseen grace that protected him in the wild. Sometimes it was just a whisper of a thought that kept him from falling into a crevasse in the night. Sometimes, it was more obvious, like the gust of wind that had actually lifted and carried him and Aglaia over a gap in the mountains that a mountain goat couldn't have jumped. Voran was sure it was no wind, but possibly even a Majestva, one of the higher Powers of Adonais. But he kept his thoughts to himself, and Aglaia had not commented.

Finally, they were within visual range of the border.

A wall towered between Nebesta and Vasyllia, uncommonly high. Higher than the red-barks in Vasyllia, without a doubt. Voran didn't think human beings could build such things. Perhaps it was the giants?

As usual, it was as though his mother had read his thoughts: "No, that doesn't smell of giants, Voran. Very clearly Raven-made."

"Not Gumiren?"

She sniffed the air for a long time, her head bobbing up and down hypnotically. She did this for more than a minute. Then she huffed and sneezed.

"Some Gumiren. But I think it's an old smell. Very little human smell at all, actually."

They approached it carefully. Voran unsheathed his sword, and Aglaia's hackles rose in concert. Her low growl made the ground shake. It gave Voran the needed push of courage.

Nothing stopped them as they approached, their eyes fixed on the wall. Voran could see no way in or out. He could see precious little at all, as though this were not a wall, but a single, strangely-shaped piece of stone that snaked along the border. It stank of dark magic, even to him. Aglaia's nose wrinkled more and more with distaste the closer they came.

Then, sudden as a sunrise in the middle of winter, the smell. Tube-rose and lavender. Even a hint of orange.

"Is that...?" Aglaia ventured, her tail out straight behind her.

"Yes, it has to be," said Voran. "Only Living Water smells like that."

The road bent leftward, just before rising toward the first ridge of the

Vasylli mountains. As they turned the corner, Voran saw the strangest thing he had ever seen. And he had seen some very strange things.

It was a dome-topped square building, similar to the kind of chapel to Adonais that rich merchants liked to build on crossroads in the wild. But it was built entirely of thick vines with vaguely heart-shaped leaves. Tiny purple-blue flowers exploded from the vines at regular intervals. The dome was an interweaving of some fibrous, root-like material that from a distance looked like an oversized onion. It was tipped with a single white blossom with eight petals, larger than any flower he had ever seen.

"What in the Heights...?" Voran said.

"The smell..." said Aglaia, "it's not coming from that edifice. It's from *inside it*."

Voran's hands shook. But it wasn't fear. It was the overawing sense of presence that he used to feel in the Temple in Vasyllia in the old days. A sense he had not had in the wild for many years. It almost physically pushed him down. He felt the need to approach it on his knees.

The vines moved with the slight breeze, revealing a chamber within the strange edifice.

"There's something inside," said Voran, a little lamely.

Aglaia chuckled. "You always become so painfully obvious when you're in the presence of the grace of the Heights."

Voran smiled.

He pushed aside the vines, and a light shone from within—warm and yellow, like a firelight. He climbed in.

A girl lay on a bed of moss and leaves. Her hair—wavy and strawberry blond—reached to her ankles. Her hands were crossed on her chest, where they barely covered a wound from a very wide knife-thrust.

"She's alive! Look at her nails," said Aglaia.

She was right. Her nails were long and curled, as though they had been growing for years.

"But how? That wound would kill a warrior, much less a girl like that."

"I think she's been here for years," said Aglaia, ignoring him. "This place smells strange. Fresh and old at the same time. Only one other place has ever smelled like this. The barrier between the worlds."

Voran reached for the girl's clothes, and realized they were wet through. Her hair remained strangely dry. What sort of place was this?

A compulsion came upon him. He recognized it. It was the same as the push he had felt the night he first heard the Sirin in the forest. He turned the girl over to reach at her back.

She wore a pack made of old canvas, from which the ivy that made the walls grew. This was the source of everything. He opened it gently, and the smell of tuberose inundated him. His hand touched something metal. He pulled it out and gasped.

"That is gorgeous," said Aglaia. She had turned human again, her eyes filling with tears.

The object shimmered in the strange light inside the room. It looked like a budding flower erupting from a nest of leaves. Only it was metal. As he turned it over, he saw that one side was smeared with blood. He tried to wipe it off, but it seemed to have welded to the metal itself. Suddenly, the flask grew heavy in his hand, as though filling with water.

"What in the Heights?" Voran dropped the flask, and it fell down on the girl, overturning its contents of what looked like, and smelled like, Living Water. He picked it up again, and it was once again full.

The girl gasped and sat up, eyes wide.

"I died," she said. "You brought me back." She looked at Voran, then at the flask. "I think I understand."

"I don't," said Voran, crouching down to the girl, examining her chest to see that there was nothing, not even a scratch, left from a wound that was surely fatal.

"A final gift," she said, her voice not quite her own. "for the Healer. It is the final sacrifice of Llun the smith for the sake of the reclamation of Vasyllia."

A song like wind whistling through reeds sounded all around them. Lyna the Sirin showered them with her song. The ivy burst apart in flames that were warm, but not burning. The sun streamed down on them, far too warm for this time of year. The girl's eyes opened wide and she laughed.

"You are real!" she said. "The Sirin. You are real!"

"You came back," said Voran, his voice shaking with the joy-pierced sorrow that he had not sensed for what seemed an eternity. "Thank you. I can breathe again."

"Yes, my Voran. I come to confirm this blessing. But it is one laden with pain."

"Is it ever not, Lyna?" Voran laughed ruefully.

"This flask contains Living Water. An inexhaustible source. But it will only remain as long as the Healer heals. If you leave your path, your chosen calling, it will empty and not fill again. And your path does not lead to Vasyllia. Not yet."

And so, Voran walked away from the wall, away from Vasyllia, away from his beloved Sabíana. His heart was a stone inside him, the flask was a burden on his hip. He turned back to the wall a final time.

When will I see you again, my Sabíana? Voran thought.

The girl stopped next to him, staring up at him with eyes that had not yet returned to the mundane.

"What will you do now?" she asked.

"I will do what I'm supposed to do," he said. "Ready the rest of the lands for the return of Vasyllia. Stop the internecine war that's raging among the city-states. Prepare the soil of people's hearts for the bond-fire of the Sirin."

"You will do all that? You're only one man."

He laughed bitterly. "Sometimes, there is only one man left who is willing to do what must be done." He sighed. "Where will you go, little thing?"

Her expression clouded, like she was trying to remember something important.

"She's coming with me," said Aglaia. "We're going to find her a place to rest and heal. Maybe Nebesta, maybe farther away."

"So, you're finally letting me out on my own?" he asked, smiling.

The wolf sniffed loudly through her nose. "You have to grow up someday. Might as well be today."

THE HEART OF THE WORLD

Raven Son: Book Three

THE HEART OF THE WORLD

(Raven Son: Book Three)

Copyright © Nicholas Kotar 2018

All rights reserved. No part of this book may be reproduced, stored in a retrieval system, or transmitted in any form, or by any means, digital, electronic, mechanical, photocopying, or otherwise, without prior permission of the publisher.

This is a work of fiction. All the characters and events portrayed in this book are either fictitious or are used fictitiously.

Cover Design by Books Covered Ltd.

Published by Waystone Press 2018

ISBN: 9780998847948

LCCN: 2018902622

✿ Created with Vellum

To the children that we couldn't save

CHAPTER 1
KHAIDU

Khaidu had not always wished for death. She still remembered when the sky's endless abyss spoke to her in hushed tones. She used to prance like a goat on the mountains while her ten brothers laughed at her. Now that she couldn't walk, now that her face was a broken ruin, now that she could hardly speak two words without the pain in her head turning white-hot, they no longer laughed at all. Not in her presence.

Her family, the last true nomads of the Gumiren, had a saying. *The Steppe is a hard mother.* The Steppe provided food and grass for the herds. The Steppe gave water and firm land, comfortable for the feet of the horses. The Steppe's endless sky and limitless grass—it was a home as great as the earth itself. But the Steppe was cold. The Steppe was wind and driving snow. The Steppe was dearth and labor and, sometimes, death.

Khaidu often wished her hard mother, the Steppe, would end her.

"You need something to distract you, my little wolfling," said Etchigu one day as he came into her yurt with two steaming cups of salty tea. He was the only brother who still spoke to Khaidu. She suspected that he did it only because it was his duty as eldest.

"I've spoken to Mamai," he continued. "She is willing, this once, to let you come on the hunt."

Khaidu laughed, though through her crooked mouth it sounded more like hissing. She made the sign that meant "horses will fly before that day comes."

Etchigu smiled. "Yes, I know it isn't proper for a girl to come. But Mamai can make an exception."

"Hhhoold...f-f-fasttt."

"To tradition? Yes, we must. You needn't remind me. I know we're all that's left of the Gumiren in the Steppe. But you need this, little one. And I know you want it."

"Y-y-yes..." A little ember of delight lit up somewhere deep inside her.

A rumbling sound, like the soft growl of a bear, rose up outside the yurt. It was echoed by the rhythmic strumming on a three-string *tobashur*. Then someone started to play the bowed two-string *kabukar*. To Khaidu, it sounded like a river breaking free of ice in spring. Her ember of delight flared into the beginning of joy.

Etchigu must have caught her expression, because his eyes lit up with more than the light of her dim hearth-fire.

"Yes," he said. "I asked the boys to sing the one about the wolf cub who couldn't hunt."

"D-d-did...y-y-ou...hm-hm-hm..." She was too tired to go on, but Etchigu caught her drift.

"Yes, I asked them to sing it in 'mother-bear.'"

It was Khaidu's favorite. There were three kinds of overtone singing, some more piercing than others. But the rumble of the mother-bear—it had a quality that sweetened even the worst pain for Khaidu, though it was laced with wistfulness and loss.

Etchigu carried her out of the yurt. Four of her brothers sat around a large fire. Three of them were playing their homemade *tobashuri* and *kabukar*, and the fourth was searching for the overtone, his eyes closed. All the muscles of his face were slack, except for his eyebrows, which threatened to bore into the bones of his head, they were so tight. Then they relaxed, and the overtone poured out just as the logs of the fire cracked and fell in on each other. A shower of sparks rose, then faded into the heavy fog encircling them.

As soon as the singing started, children materialized out of the fog. The evening song called to them, and they were always preternaturally quiet when "mother-bear" was used. It soothed Khaidu, for whom their physical games were a constant reminder of her loss. Then one of them, probably some distant cousin of Khaidu's that she could never remember—there were so many of them, after all—moved into a dancing-pattern that mirrored the words of the song.

"A cub there was, who howled with hunger ..."

All the faces turned toward the fire were calm, but smiling. This was *right*. At such moments, the painful reality of being a people in exile faded into the larger tapestry of their Gumiren history—so rich, so ancient, and so pure. At least until the recent time of darkness.

"*Her legs were weak; her teeth were cracked...*"

A masked figure with trailing sleeves of bright red emerged from the darkness. Khaidu's heart leaped. It was a rare thing for the old shaman's daughter, a dancer of the spirits, to come out for the evening song, to transform it into more than a simple remembrance. Her movements, inspired by mystical currents in the eternal expanse of the sky, gathered all the threads of their individual worries, desires, aspirations, and intertwined them into a single petition to the silence of the Heights. To the Unknown Father whom all true Gumiren have sought for hundreds, perhaps thousands, of years.

"*Many were the years of hunger, many the days of pain...*"

The spirit-dancer spun on one foot, then seemed to fall, until she caught herself at the final moment. It looked as though someone had lifted her by an invisible string attached at her shoulder. Back and forth she swayed, softly humming along as her fingers, arms, and legs painted pictures that spoke in a silent language of supplication.

Until she shed her downy fur and tasted her first kill..."

Khaidu's eyes hurt from the firelight. She closed them. With something like surprise, she felt wet drops fall on her hands, lying upturned on legs like matchsticks. Was she crying?

Will I ever shed my downy fur? she wondered. Then the bitterness rose up again. *No. More likely I will be the first kill, not taste it...*

Three days later came the Red Day, named for the unbearable fire of the first sunset of spring. It was the first wolf-hunt of the year, fraught with special significance. In the misty morning, all the hunters bantered, eager for the start of the hunting season. They fell silent as Etchigu carried Khaidu out of her yurt. He strapped her into the special saddle designed for her lifeless legs and too-strong arms. The silence grew to murmurs, all of them unfriendly. Khaidu heard them all:

"What is Etchigu doing? This is not allowed..."

"A bad omen, especially for Red Day..."

"Has Mamai gone soft in the head?"

Only Batuk (Khaidu's personal torturer) had the courage to walk up to Etchigu and openly remonstrate. Etchigu took him aside and spoke in angry whispers. Khaidu tried not to listen, but she heard enough.

"How much longer does she have? Have some pity," whispered Etchigu. That was especially painful to hear, but it seemed to work. Batuk subsided, though the look he gave Khaidu promised no respite from future pain.

Khaidu tried not to care, though the tears were already threatening to come. Not an auspicious beginning for the hunt.

It took them most of the day to approach the hunting fields. As they rode, the beauty of the landscape pushed aside all Khaidu's other thoughts. This Red Day seemed created by the Powers especially for her. As the sun set, the horse-clan's hunters—twenty picked men, ten of whom were Khaidu's brothers—stilled their horses on the tips of the Teeth, the last ridges before the mountain flowed wave-like down into the Steppe. The setting sun gilded their furry-eared hats and the plumed heads of their hunting eagles. They stood in a rough semicircle, each hunter the prescribed ten paces away from his neighbor, just close enough to hear the raised voice of the hunt leader. The horses stamped and tossed their heads in frustration, their breath clouding around them. The eagles shrugged—first one shoulder, then another—anxious to begin. Khaidu thought her heart would explode from the beauty of it all.

Yeeeeeeeaaaaaaaaaaaauuuuuuuuuuuu!!!

Khaidu's heart caught in her throat at the sound of Etchigu's hunt-shriek. The horses flew over the lip of the Teeth, and their breath mingled with the fresh powder thrown up by eighty hooves in concert. Etchigu launched into an old ballad, and Batuk backed him, adding his own improvised harmony to Etchigu's raspy tenor. Then all the men joined in, and the river of song grew to a torrent. For a moment, Khaidu thought the eagles sang with them as well, their wings half-unfurled, their darting tongues visible in their open beaks.

The single wolf in the valley below looked up, as though curious. Arelat, Etchigu's eagle, screamed. At that sound, the wolf turned and fled. The sons of Mamai jani-Beg, the greatest matriarch of the Gumiren, shouted the final chord of the ballad and threw their arms up. Gold-flecked in the evening light, the eagles leaped up, awkwardly catching the air as though they were out of practice. All together as one, they caught a thermal and spun around each other, dancing, then each wheeled out and plunged down toward the fleeing wolf. For a moment, Khaidu felt a pang for the poor creature. No wolf, no matter how big, could come away unscathed from a Gumiren eagle attack.

Suddenly, Arelat the eagle banked left, nearly crashing into the other eagles in mid-air. Khaidu forgot to breathe in surprised shock. An eagle twice the size of Arelat materialized seemingly out of nowhere. It was black as a raven, except for the head and tail, which were whiter than new snow. Incensed at the challenge, Arelat dove at the intruder. At the last possible moment, the great white-headed beast maneuvered out of the way. Arelat missed.

Khaidu gasped. This could be the end of Arelat as chief hunter's eagle.

But the white-headed monster seemed to have no interest in dominating the rest of the eagles. Its behavior was unlike anything Khaidu had ever seen. It wheeled back and forth, toward the other eagles, then toward the riders, then back up into the expanse of sky, seemingly for the joy of flight alone.

Khaidu slowed her horse to a complete stop. The black and white eagle compelled her with a yearning stronger than thought. She wanted the eagle for herself, to bind it to herself as all hunting eagles were bound to Gumiren hunters. She wanted to show them all she was worth something. No, it was more than that. She ached to have her own purpose within the rule-bound world of the Gumiren nomads, the world that had no place for a cripple.

Etchigu had taught her the song of binding; would her body cooperate?

Khaidu raised her gloved right hand, palm up, toward the eagle. She keened that peculiar call that so enticed all eagles. The inside of her head convulsed with pain. The eagle shuddered and stopped in mid-soar. Her tongue cramped and her throat burned with the effort, but Khaidu gritted her teeth and kept on. She wrapped her awkward lips around the words of the binding.

The eagle trembled, battling with what Khaidu could only imagine was an ecstasy like nothing a human being could bear. It broke free for a moment and managed to fly up a few feet, then again seemed chained in place, shuddering in midair. The other eagles circled it now, and Arelat was primed to strike at the now helpless creature.

Now, thought Khaidu. *To me!*

The eagle plunged toward her, and the rest of the eagles followed in single file like the tail of a spirit-banner snapping in wind. Khaidu focused her song to a higher pitch, then reached deep within her throat to find the elusive overtone. When she found it, the sound pushed through her broken body like a spear-thrust, and she almost lost the thread of the music in the ecstasy that erased all her pain. That was the final blow. The eagle veered, then alighted clumsily on Khaidu's gloved hand. Khaidu fell silent, and the eagle remained in place. It worked.

Up close, she saw that it was not quite twice the size of a normal Steppe-eagle, but even with her strong arms, Khaidu had to strain to keep it steady. It looked at her with eyes nearly human and clicked its beak. For a terrifying moment, Khaidu thought it would peck her eyes out. Then it squawked and preened like a sparrow.

With her other hand, Khaidu grasped the thick mane of her pony and whistled. The pony cantered down toward the ragged line of hunters who had stopped in the middle of the slope. They all looked at her as though she had grown a second head. She smiled internally. Far away, barely more than a speck of dust, the grey wolf ran like the wind. If wolves could speak, he would have a story to tell that would make him a legend. The only wolf ever to escape a Gumiren hunt.

Etchigu clicked his tongue, and his horse pushed uphill toward Khaidu. He smiled broadly, his eyes lost in the folds above his high cheekbones.

"Well, well, wolfling," he said. "Trying to take my place as head hunter?" His laugh was raspy—a sure sign of real enjoyment. He regarded the eagle, the whites of his eyes stark against the winter-burn red of his face. "What a beast! Poor Arelat. He'll never live it down."

Khaidu gathered every ounce of physical strength left to speak. "Gh..hh...ank you....f-f-for t-t-take...mmme."

"You're welcome," he said. He raised his arm and whistled. Arelat came, but with bowed head. It avoided looking at Khaidu. Her eagle completely ignored Arelat, intent on Khaidu's face. She felt the heat of the gaze, as if it were human. It gave her a perverse kind of enjoyment. But the best was the embarrassment on Batuk's face.

⁂

The hunting party's return journey was interminable. Eagle, pony, and hunter alike rode with heads half-bowed. Khaidu alone rejoiced as she contemplated her eagle circling overhead, never too far away from its new master. Lost in her thoughts, Khaidu did not realize that she had fallen behind the rest, with only Batuk still behind her. Panic pushed out joy in an instant.

Batuk trotted up to her. Etchigu was too far for her to cry out. She willed her pony to canter. She was too late. Batuk rode alongside, matching her pace. His eyes were like two prods on her left cheek. I will not panic, she said to herself. Her heart refused to listen. Already the cramping in her hands presaged one of her fits. Batuk did it on purpose. He wanted her to have a fit and fall off. She was so far behind the rest that it would take a long time for anyone to realize that something was amiss.

She knew what she had to do. "Breathe long, extend your fingers, turn the rocks in your neck into water," said Mamai's voice in her head, but Khaidu only felt herself curling inward like a poppy closing at night.

"You shouldn't have come," said Batuk, wolfish. "You ruined the hunt for us."

It seemed Batuk was not content with waiting for her fit. He struck her on the back of the head, in the place that hurt more than any other, as he knew well enough. A light flashed behind her eyes, a moan bubbled up from deep inside her, and she fell to the ground, screaming like an animal being butchered.

But no. That was not her screaming. Batuk screamed. The white-headed eagle was on top of him, scraping his face with its talons. Even in the tangle of hands and black feathers, the telltale red splashed.

The rest of the party rushed back, but they were far away. By the time they arrived, Batuk's face was a ruin.

Khaidu retched on the ground, barely managing to avoid fouling herself with the sickness. Her body throbbed with pain, her mouth was fuzzy and tasted of metal. With an effort, she moved her tongue over the inside of her cheek—it was thick as felt and ragged. She suspected she had bitten through her tongue. Something sharp and insistent pounded at her left hip. She sobbed. To her own ears, she sounded like little more than a wounded animal. Something reptilian and repulsive, worse than a lamed horse or a sick dog.

Etchigu picked her up. His expression was difficult to read.

"Khaidu, did Batuk attack you?" he asked quietly.

She shook all over but managed to force her head up and down. Etchigu sighed.

"Then he deserved what he got. But Mamai will be furious. There's something you must understand, little wolf. You are responsible for that eagle now. If it attacks anyone else, you will have to put it down. You do not know the pain of killing your own eagle. It is worse than losing a prize stallion."

The hunters stopped soon afterward, warding the four corners of their makeshift camp with the ragged spirit-banners. The pain from her fit was now a dull throb. Etchigu helped her set up a stoop for her eagle inside her travel tent, as was traditional for a full-fledged hunter. Khaidu nearly burst with pride, looking at her eagle. But the eagle ignored her, staring into space for a long time, still as a statue. Khaidu fell asleep.

She woke up to someone shaking her hard. A woman. In panic, Khaidu looked at the stoop. It was empty.

"What have you done to my—?" Khaidu cried out but was struck dumb at the sight of the woman.

She was dark-haired, slim, her skin the color of olive-meat, reddening at the cheeks. But it was her dress that stopped Khaidu—heavy wine-red brocade embroidered with gold suns and moons—a dress of greater worth than the entire horse-clan of Mamai jani-Beg.

"What have you done to me?" the woman said. "Who are you? Are you a wielder of power?"

"I don't know what you—?" Khaidu fell silent. She was talking. Like a normal person.

Khaidu looked down at herself, and her legs were rounded with muscle. They moved when she willed them to. With trembling hands, she traced the too-familiar path of the scars running down her face, but they were gone. Her face was whole, intact, symmetrical. The drooping, scarred half was as firm as a ripe pear. She was herself again.

"I am Sabíana, Darina of the Vasylli," whispered the woman fiercely. "I am also, as you so rudely suggested, *your* eagle. I demand that you tell me who you are, and how you bound me to yourself."

CHAPTER 2
THE SIRIN OF FIRE

The morning fog, dripping wet on the spruces ringing the oval pool, was doing its best to stop the sun from rising. The sun fought half-heartedly, its light a sickly yellow. The grass, inundated with dew just on the verge of hoarfrost, shivered from the breeze as though it had lost its patience with the long winter. Voran shook with the grass and tried to remember what a beautiful sunrise felt like.

This same sort of fog had marred his last morning with Sabíana, what seemed like twenty lifetimes, not years, ago. Then, they had been young, their hearts bursting with fire. Voran had just been exiled for life by Sabíana's father, but neither of them had expected that separation to last long. He would find the Weeping Tree. He would bring the healing power of the Living Water back to Vasyllia. He would bring the Covenant Tree back to life, restore the Covenant with Adonais, and Vasyllia would embark on a second golden age. And they would marry and live out their lives with ten children tussling by the hearth-fire.

Instead, he had hacked down the Weeping Tree, unwilling to take responsibility for its power. Vasyllia had fallen to an army of Gumiren nomads who had allied themselves with the demonic power of the Raven. And Voran had not so much as seen Vasyllia in twenty years. At first, he had tried repeatedly to return home. But the Raven had set strange traps for him. Everywhere along the way into Vasyllia, he had placed hidden doorways into other realms. It could be anything—a low tree branch leaning over a mountain path or a pool of rainwater under a tree. All Voran had to do was touch one of them by accident, and he would suddenly find himself lost in the Lows of Aer or in a different place entirely. How the Raven could manipulate the doorways so effectively, Voran had no idea. But no matter how many roads he tried, they were all impassable.

To add insult to injury, now a wall stood between Gumiren-occupied Vasyllia and the rest of the world. Voran had traveled the length and breadth of that wall, as far as humanly possible. It extended all around Vasyllia in a semicircle that ended only where the Vasyllia Mountains became virtually impassable, where the peaks were almost indistinguishable from the clouds. The peaks that the first-reachers often called "the Footstools of Adonais." Beyond them, no Vasylli had ever ventured, and not merely because they were so tall. They were taboo. No self-respecting Three-lander would dare cross over into the unknown country on the other side, on pain of eternal damnation.

The sun exploded into life, so quickly that it took Voran by surprise. Then came the music—a soft whisper of wind whistling through reeds. So, it was not the sun after all.

A Sirin of fire materialized before Voran, her woman's face brighter than the sun, every feather of her eagle body a golden-red flame that pulsated with light.

"You are Voran, soul-bond of Lyna, the eldest of my sisters."

The Sirin were often prey to bouts of painful obviousness. There was a time when it had amused Voran, but in the absence of Lyna, it only irritated him.

"You are *not* Lyna, so-called soul-bond of Voran. I do not know you."

She didn't answer, though he felt the heat of her disapproval, even more intense that the light cascading from her feathers. Her feathers. They were like the flame-feather etched on his sword, given to him by Tarin the mad warrior-storyteller. The sword that he had abandoned years ago, swearing never to use it again.

"I can practically hear you saying it," he grumbled. "Go ahead. Say it. No one has for so long. Clear the air."

"It is your fault that Lyna avoids you."

"And there it is!" Voran struck the trunk of a tree with an open palm. It did *not* make him feel better, and now his hand throbbed. "Always the same. Always the fault of the human. And what about Lyna? Where was she when I failed to heal the hundred children in Negoda? Where was she when I had no strength left to move, much less heal all those hacked down by the Internecine War? Where was she when I needed her? I became the Healer, the bearer of the only Living Water left in the Three Lands. The only person capable of stemming the blood of the wars. All those lives. All those deaths. All on my back. And do you know how heavy the water is? How it weighs on my very soul?"

Her glance was incorrigible.

"Where were you when she needed *you*?" she whispered.

"Do the Sirin even need us pitiful humans?"

Her fire flared, and now her eyes—they shone green in the midst of the red and orange tongues of flame—bored into him. He thought they might actually leave smoking scars on his face.

"You have seen so much, Healer. And yet you persist in your stupidity. To give love without expecting return is not the gift of the Sirin. It is the *torture* of the Sirin. We need your love even more than you need ours. But we are the stronger, so we can endure more neglect. You of all people should know that."

Only then did he notice that it wasn't disapproval emanating from her like steam from hot springs. It was pain.

"You also have a soul-bond?"

"I did. But I broke our bond as a final gift to my beloved."

"Who?" As soon as he asked, his heart gave him the answer.

"You know who."

Voran's heart tried to flip over in his chest.

"Is Sabíana..." He had to stop to catch his breath, it came in such ragged bursts. "I can't even ask it."

"I do not know where she is. She flew away from Vasyllia, choosing the form of the eagle."

"Choosing...I don't understand."

Ox-horns blared to their right, no more than a league away. Another battle. Who would it be this time? How many brothers would shed more fraternal blood?

"Voran, I do not have much time. Listen. Do you know of our dark sister, Gamayun?"

"The bird of prophecy. She who sings the futures."

"She has disappeared. All the Heights are in an uproar searching for her. All she left was a final prophecy."

Voran scoffed. "Words, words, words. What do they mean anymore?"

The Sirin of fire grew into a conflagration. Voran flew back into a tree. It knocked his breath clean out of his chest.

"Silence! Believe what you will. Only listen. The infection in Vasyllia is nearing the heart. Only the lame horse, the flightless eagle, the sword-less warrior can stop it in time. Look to the East!"

The ox-horns blared again from the West. The Sirin of fire was gone.

"They speak words that make no sense. And then they leave. It's always the same."

Voran scraped himself off the earth. His hip throbbed. The flask of Living Water was a stone on his hip and his heart. He picked it up. It looked like a dark flower bursting from vines. He had thought it so beautiful five years ago, when he found it at the walls of Vasyllia in the hands of a dead Vasylli girl that had come back to life. What had she called it? The final sacrifice of Llun the smith.

Will his sacrifice ever bear fruit, I wonder?

He bent his back toward the ox-horns. The Healer had work to do.

CHAPTER 3
THE STRANGE QUEEN

Sabíana, the beautiful queen of that faraway kingdom that Khaidu had already forgotten the name of, paced back and forth in the small yurt. A caged animal in everything but appearance. Every three or four rounds, she stopped by the flap, seeming to assess the possibility of leaving the yurt and testing Khaidu's binding.

Khaidu ignored her. She was too busy pushing her thumbs into the full muscle of her thighs. She couldn't even feel the bone that usually jutted out through sickly-thin skin.

"Now that you know I am not just an eagle," said Sabíana, "free me from that hold you placed on me!"

Khaidu shook her head, agog at the feel of her body, whole.

"I order you to release me!"

Khaidu laughed. "Command all you like. Won't do you any good. I have no idea how to undo the binding. I've never read the story where the eagle comes to life as a person and asks to be released. Have you?"

"It's not enough that I saved you from that brute who attacked you?"

"You're bound to me," said Khaidu, smiling at the thought. "You had no choice in the matter."

Sabíana narrowed her eyes, her words frosty, "Even if you *did* know how to, you still wouldn't release me. Am I right?"

"Look at me!" Khaidu wiggled her toes and nearly exploded in laughter. "I am whole again."

Sabíana stopped pacing.

"Child, don't you realize…"

"What?"

The lady's fury seemed to soften—a change from red to pink in her cheeks. She looked at Khaidu with pity.

"No, you couldn't possibly know. You're not Vasylli. I can walk the nether-region of dream and weave images around me. I can also invite others into the images. In Vasyllia, I did it to soften the despair of those who lost everything. It's…well, almost second nature by now, really."

Khaidu's heart fell. She should have known it was too good to be true.

"You mean that this body…it's an illusion?" Khaidu asked, not even recognizing her own voice. "But how? Is it somehow connected to your transformation?"

Sabíana's eyes were full of remembered pain. "No. It's an old gift that was given to me."

"So… I'll wake up as a cripple again. But at least…Even one night…" Khaidu felt the self-pity creeping in on cat-like feet. It enraged her. "What could you possibly understand about it? You who are so perfect."

Sabíana flushed violently.

"I do understand…" Sabíana tried to continue, but it was visibly difficult. "I was on my way to die."

Khaidu was astounded by the strangeness of her. Everything about the lady spoke of wealth and health and beauty and comfort and joy. What business had she to speak of dying before her time? She was not a slithering half-broken thing.

"You should be ashamed of yourself," Khaidu said.

"What are you, some Gumiren runt, that you speak to the Darina of the Three Lands thus?"

"Well, as a matter of fact, yes. I am Gumira. Didn't you know? And we are nowhere near your Three Lands."

That shocked the lady.

"Have I come so far then? Where is this place?"

"In the heart of the Steppelands, lady. My name is Khaidu. I am daughter to Mamai jani-Beg."

"Is that supposed to mean something to me?"

"Mamai's is the lost horse-clan of the Gumiren. She leads all the ones who did not follow the Dark Father into the West. I think you've met our cousins who did follow him."

Realization softened the lady's eyes. She sank to the bare ground, her skirts like ripples of water around her. She sat there, thinking, for a long time.

"I am just as broken in body as you are, Khaidu," she said, and even the pitch of her voice was lower, as if burdened by the weight of the truth. "You at least have strong arms. I cannot even move a finger. What you see is not me, no more than your wholeness is real. In Vasyllia, I am an animated corpse."

Khaidu felt herself going red and hot with shame. She did not answer.

Pain crossed the lady's face as vividly as though someone had painted it with a brush. "I chose to take the form of the eagle. I could not bear the pain anymore."

Khaidu intuited something, and it made her angry. "Wait... Are you saying that you left your body behind willingly? That the eagle form is a new set of clothes for your spirit?"

Sabíana nodded.

"You coward!"

Sabíana snapped out of her thoughts, surprise obvious in her face.

"Would you not do the same, if you had the chance?"

Khaidu's nails bit into her palms, and her jaw ached with the clenching. "If? We mere mortals do not have the chance. We must live in our broken bodies. We must submit to taunts and kicks and jabs. But you! You ruled a nation. You had the responsibility of thousands under your care. A little discomfort, and you lose all patience and become a bird. Flee the golden cage. What about your people? What about the sacred duty of a queen? You are disgusting!"

"Idiot," whispered Sabíana, her face white with fury. "You have no idea what I suffered."

Khaidu was so angry that she was unable to continue speaking. She turned over, wrapped herself in her furs, and wiggled her toes again until they cramped. Even such a cramp was pleasant compared to the usual deadness. The lady said no more, and Khaidu soon fell asleep.

When she woke, she was her broken self again.

CHAPTER 4
A MASSACRE OF GUMIREN

There was a time when Parfyon Krivoshey of Nebesta would have been exhilarated at seeing an enemy army march straight at him. But no more. All he could think of now was the inevitable outcome: the bodies of pale-faced boys strewn around the field of battle. A sowing that would never reap a harvest.

That enemy army from the city-state of Negoda must have known the outcome as soon as it saw Nebesta's warriors blocking their way across the valley. The fools. They had come in force down the nearly sheer walls of a natural amphitheater, never stopping for a moment. Down and down they came, an ever-increasing mass of men, until there was a roiling cauldron of spear-tips in the glen. Behind them—a wall of rock. Ahead of them, hidden among the trees—all of Nebesta's strength in muster, the most disciplined army left in the Three Lands, seasoned by five years of uninterrupted victory. They had no chance.

Parfyon used to feel the deep thrill of that kind of desperate valor, the sense of longing that only men with bared swords in their hands can feel. But what was valorous in this? Two armies, set for slaughter, yet both sides had the same skin, the same pale eyes, the same flaxen hair. Both sides bore the same ancient, tattered banners of the same deities, whose protection was nothing short of a fantasy now. Perhaps there were even brothers on opposite sides. And for what? To satisfy the power-lust of rival princelings? There was no one left who could unite the cities and stop the bloodshed.

"Parfyon, a moment." The voice was raspy, quiet, but commanded like the crack of a whip.

"Yes, sir," said Parfyon. "Nothing wrong with my men, I hope?"

Yarpolk Dolgoruk was the most powerful man in Nebesta. The Dolgoruki had done much to keep together what remained of Nebesta's people after the Gumiren invasion. More importantly, he was father to the most beautiful woman in the world.

"Well, I'm not entirely sure about your decision to place the spearmen at the front," Yarpolk said, "but no matter. This is not a seasoned foe we're facing. Only Negodi would be foolish enough to ignore such an obvious trap."

Parfyon saw no reason to answer. Yarpolk would make it clear soon enough what he wanted from him.

"Parfyon," he said, his voice almost gentle, though the broken vulture-nose made any gentleness in the voice a caricature. "You know I have not looked favorably upon your suit for my Alienne. It is not merely that she is my only daughter." He looked at Parfyon in a way calculated to remind him that the fair Alienne was as far above his kind as an eagle is above a mosquito. "Neither is it your bloodline, though it is hardly as ancient or pure as ours."

He was mocking Parfyon. All the Dolgoruki knew well enough that the Krivosheys had been no more than drudges for generations. "Sir, you doubt my valor, is that it?"

Yarpolk smiled crookedly and scratched the thick red beard growing in a tuft from under his chin. "Well, since you put it so bluntly, yes, I do."

"What must I do to change your mind? I tell you now that it will take much more than your disapproval to prevent my marrying your daughter. I intend to have her."

"Ha! If boldness in words meant prowess in war..." He looked out over the ranks, brows furrowed in concentration. "Very well. I will give you the chance."

Parfyon had not expected him to agree so readily. It deflated him, knocking him off course like a river-ship whose mainsail drooped for lack of wind. Yarpolk grabbed Parfyon's arm by the elbow and led him—none too gently—to the cover of a circle of aspens. They stood outside of earshot of anyone in the camp, but he still lowered his voice like a conspirator in a parley.

How I hate the Dolgoruk stink of politics. It was more suited to the Veche than to the battlefield. Still, he would have to learn to stomach it for the sake of the fair Alienne.

"Not many know this yet," Yarpolk rasped, "but Nebesta's reconstruction is complete."

That could not be possible. "Sir, do you take me for a child?"

Yarpolk squinted in irritation. "Parfyon, I speak to you as an equal, though you may consider yourself on probation. There are Powers in the world willing to aid Nebesta. They have done much to earn our trust already. One of their preliminary gifts has been a rebuilt New Nebesta. There is to be a Veche of Choosing very soon. Do you understand? We will be choosing, for the first time in hundreds of years, our own ruler. I intend to be there to see it."

So, you mean to grab the reins of power, leaving your army behind? Foolish. "That is good news, sir."

Yarpolk scowled, obviously hearing how little Parfyon believed him. "You think you deserve Alienne?" he said. "Prove it. I leave the command of the entire Nebesti army to you. My generals will not mutter too much. After all, it's only the Negodi we're fighting."

Parfyon's own command. The exhilaration was swift and unexpected, though something intangible left a shadow over the enjoyment. Yarpolk's smile revealed more than he intended, perhaps. Some insinuation poisoned the space between his words. Did he suggest that fighting the pitiful Negodi would be more difficult than expected, or was there something else?

"You will be expected to minimize our casualties, of course. Considering the advantage we have in ground, they should not be significant in any case. What shall we say? Limit the deaths to a hundred, and the fair Alienne is yours."

Was this the trading-block? He spoke of his only daughter as one does of horseflesh.

"Sir, you overestimate the Negodi. We will have no more than fifty deaths." Parfyon hoped Yarpolk wouldn't sense the bravado behind the words.

Yarpolk smiled, but the smile stopped at the corners of his mouth, not reflecting in the eyes. The skin curdled at the back of Parfyon's neck.

"Good. Make it so," he said.

An hour later, all the generals had assembled in Yarpolk's tent, which was raised on a slight incline, giving a good view of the lines. Parfyon stood outside until such time as he would be presented to them as their new commander. The ranks of soldiers were pristine, barely moving, even though the call to battle would not sound for a while yet. It was a perfect chessboard before Parfyon. The black squares were commoner-spearmen, their spear-tips smaller versions of their peaked helmets. The white squares were either bowmen, their bows taller than their short, squat bodies, or sword-and-shielders, faces hidden behind faceplates wrought in the shapes of monsters from the darkest of legends. The mounted elite, the Sheloma—what few remained after the Gumiren's ravages—held heavy hammers and maces. Their ragged line formed the rear of the chessboard, but their nonchalance was a ruse—these would be the warriors to strike the death-blow to the enemy.

Though Parfyon had initially regretted the battle, now that the pieces were at his disposal, his mind entered a new awareness. Already in his inner eye he saw every unit in precise moves across the enemy's side of the board. Bowmen should go here, directing their arrow-fire across at the vulnerable spots of the enemy's flank—over there. Spears moving ever forward, impassive as pawns, but far deadlier. Sword-and-shielders maneuvering the board in strange patterns, a rook and a knight combined, wreaking havoc wherever the enemy expected them least, their face-guards as much a weapon as their teardrop shields, sharpened at the point, and their double-edged steel. Then the queen—the elite mounted Sheloma—waiting until the board was in seeming chaos, no side the clear winner, to begin picking off the enemy, one square after another. It could all be done in less than two hours.

All the fatigue, all the reticence was gone. Had he felt regret for the coming deaths of the Negodi? Had he seen similarities in their appearance to Nebesti? How foolish of him. No, their features were angled, a clear sign of inbreeding with wandering nomad tribes. Their hair was straw to Nebesti flowing gold. And their banners, he now saw, had images of dark deities of whom it was not fitting to speak: mermaids and vila and changers. It would be a pleasure to see them burn.

"Parfyon, they are at your disposal," said Yarpolk, as he bent down to exit the tent.

"I will not fail you, or them, sir."

Yarpolk's look was queer. There was an inordinate amount of genuine emotion there, completely unfitting to his face or his person. Was it regret?

"See that you do not, Parfyon," he said. "I need hardly tell you how failure will be rewarded by the new knyaz of Nebesta." His smile was too smug. Parfyon had a sudden desire to spit in his face, but he contained himself.

Yarpolk's horse already twitched with the excitement of the coming ride. As he mounted, he turned the horse sharply to face Parfyon, just close enough that Parfyon had to jump back to avoid being struck by bucking hooves. Yarpolk rode off without saying another word, not looking back.

At that moment, Parfyon swore that he would make them all pay, all the old guard who thought they controlled the strings that pulled the world into action, striding on the backs of better men who died in the field of battle for their sakes. Parfyon bent down to enter the council of war, his thoughts as dark as the inside of the tent.

The men facing Parfyon were, to a man, furious. Most of them were grey-beards, men seasoned in war, bearing scars as proudly as ancient family swords. The only two young men were already famed for their deeds in the last war. Sviatopluk the Bold was a commoner who had killed twenty Gumiren in a skirmish, saving two hundred women and children from certain slaughter. His hatred of all non-Nebesti was legendary. Ulik was Yarpolk's only surviving son and was already more respected than his father after he endured unspeakable tortures at the hands of a Tiverna princeling. He had managed to kill his torturer and still escape alive. For a reason Parfyon never understood, Ulik hated Parfyon even more than Sviatopluk hated all non-Nebesti.

Parfyon realized the battle against Negoda was nothing—the more serious hurdle must be faced before the battle even began. A particular glint in Ulik's eye suggested Parfyon might not survive the war council, much less the battle.

They all stood silent, tense, waiting to pounce on the first error in Parfyon's words or actions. How was he supposed to command the respect of these warriors?

"Well," said Parfyon, failing miserably to sound older than his mere twenty years, "How like the Nebesti to assign a pup to lead the wolf pack, eh?"

It worked better than Parfyon expected. The atmosphere in the room lifted, like the release of rain on a humid day, though no one laughed yet. Sviatopluk rolled his eyes but held his peace. Reluctantly, Parfyon forced himself to look at Ulik, knowing he would be the deciding factor in this game. Parfyon decided to be bold, hoping to put the much larger man on the defensive.

"Ulik, my soon-to-be brother, you will lead the Sheloma."

"No. I will lead your proud ass to the nearest pile of cow dung." He said it without a hint of mockery, as though he were reciting a scouting report to a superior. Parfyon had once been struck in the gut by a kicking horse as a child. This was worse. His face must have reflected his shock, because Sviatopluk grimaced unnaturally, mimicking Parfyon, before spitting at his feet. Parfyon clenched his fists, trying to retain some measure of decorum.

"I think *horse* dung would be more appropriate for a Sheloma, my friend," Parfyon said with measured, calm tone, belying his inner desire to rip Ulik's long braid from above his absurdly shaved temples.

A few of the old men laughed, relaxing more of the tension. Ulik bristled and charged at Parfyon like an enraged bear, stopping a mere foot-span from impact. He was a full head taller than Parfyon. Only by sheer force of will did Parfyon's hands not go up in self-defense. Ulik still guffawed.

"It makes no difference to me," he said, baring his teeth. The canines were sharper than Parfyon had ever seen in a man. "Cow or horse—they both smell as foul as your lineage, you low-born son of a bitch. Should make you feel right at home, seeing how your mother birthed you in that filth."

Everything went silent. Parfyon's heart beat like a series of thunderclaps. Hatred spread through his body as fast as strong wine. His right hand shot out, almost outside of his control, and grabbed Ulik by the throat, so that Parfyon could feel the sinews twitching underneath. With his left, he grabbed Ulik's belt and lifted him off the ground. He hurtled Ulik against the tent wall.

The entire tent collapsed under Ulik's weight, but Parfyon had anticipated that. His knife was in his hand as the canvas came down, and he sliced it open and jumped out. Ulik's form struggled under the canvas. Jumping on him, Parfyon pummeled him with his fist and the butt end of his knife until the canvas grew red underneath. Someone knocked Parfyon on his back, and a black shape, so fast it was a blur, proceeded to beat the pulp out of him.

Somehow, Parfyon managed to keep hold of his knife and turn it point-down. Just as he thought the world would spin out of control, he jabbed through unimpeded into his attacker's side. The man grunted, annoyed. It was Sviatopluk. Parfyon rolled out from under Sviatopluk and stabbed at him just as he was about to strike again. Parfyon caught Sviatopluk's fist with his knife, and he bellowed like a pig being butchered.

Parfyon's left eye could see nothing, and he could put no weight on his right foot. He pushed himself up with his left hand, still tense in anticipation of the next attack. The old men encircled him, half of them with swords bared, the other half still trying to pull themselves out of the ripped canvas. Ulik staggered up, a bloody hunk of meat on two legs. He pulled out his greatsword and lifted it to come at Parfyon, but he had little control over his body. Parfyon deflected the blow with a knife alone, held in his left, and pushed him aside. Ulik landed on a pile of dung next to his own horse.

Turning around, ready to take on the entire armed old guard, Parfyon stopped dead in his tracks. They were laughing. Two of them stood over Sviatopluk, pinning him down and taking away his weapons. Parfyon had won.

"I am Nebesti. I lead the Nebesti way," Parfyon said, spitting. Blood came out, mingled with the phlegm. As his fury subsided, the pain came rolling in like a fresh tide. Dark spots danced before his eyes, and he felt sick to his stomach. Gritting his teeth, he grabbed his right shoulder and shoved it back in place, hearing a loud pop. Relief flooded him, just enough to gather his wits.

"Tie up these brawlers," he waved at the two bloody warriors. "We'll let the Veche deal with them."

Eyes widened all around Parfyon. They had not known about the calling of the Veche of Choosing. Good.

Two or three of the old guard immediately responded to Parfyon's command. He had done it; they were following his lead. The exhilaration was almost enough to soften the pain, but it kept coming over him in fiercer and fiercer waves. His left eye seemed sewed shut, and now his right leg was having difficulty supporting his full weight. Something crunched in his ankle, shooting knives of pain upward toward his back. He almost retched.

The humming in his head pounded more loudly. *Not now*, he thought, *not when I have won everything. At all costs, I must stay alert.*

But the humming was not in his head. It was coming from the lines. To Parfyon's horror, Nebesta's perfect lines were wavering. The front was already rushing ahead blindly, engaging the Negodi head-on.

"What in all the Heights," he cried. "Baryan!" he pointed at a thin voyevoda. "Find out what is happening! Go, all of you! Reform the lines. We can't attack blindly like this, not even if they're Negodi."

Before they could respond, ox-horns blared, but not from the field before Parfyon. It was behind the army. All the old guard cried out in dismay.

He could hardly see anything, even with his one good eye, but it seemed that behind the lines, appearing out of thin air, another army was rushing straight at the Nebesti flank. They were hemmed in, as were the pitiful Negodi.

"Who is that?" Parfyon yelled above the commotion. "By all that is holy in this world! Do we not have lookouts covering our flank? What is this madness?"

No one answered, though many would not look Parfyon in the eye. He shook his head and sighed.

"I cannot make out their banners. Taverni? Bskavi? Someone, tell me what is going on!"

"You fool," muttered Ulik, still on the ground. "You have no understanding of what is about to happen to you. Run. If you have any sense left, run away!" He laughed like a madman. Gooseflesh crept up the back of Parfyon's neck.

"They're Gumiren," said one of the generals. "Powers help and keep us. Gumiren!"

The news was no less incredible than the dead walking among the living. Vasyllia, once Mother of all Cities, had closed itself off from the rest of the cities after the Gumiren invasion. No one had seen so much as a Vasylli scout or a Gumir bowman in the last five years. In that span, rumor transformed Vasyllia into the walking nightmare, an abyss of every possible human depravity and evil. Could Yarpolk have made a pact with the denizens of hell?

"To me!" Parfyon shouted, trying to throw back the waves of pain buffeting him. "Hear me, Nebesta, for I have news wondrous to your ears! Our city is rebuilt, and a Veche of Choosing has been announced. If you win today, you will live to see a Nebesti knyaz chosen! Who knows? Maybe it will be one of you dogs!"

Everyone laughed.

At that balm of a sound, Parfyon turned to look at the unexpected charge of Gumiren. He only had a few minutes to make his plans, for they were all mounted and bearing down on the Nebesti with frantic speed. But it didn't take an expert eye to see that these were not the disciplined troops that had destroyed Nebesta and ravaged the Three Lands twenty years ago. These were ragged refugees, their banners no more than fluttering shreds, and even from this distance, he saw emptiness in their eyes.

They are fleeing Vasyllia, Parfyon realized with wonder. Why?

"Baryan, Tarmund, take your divisions and wheel them out and about those Gumiren. Engage carefully but seek to outflank. They'll charge the center, hoping to break through. Look at them. They're not angling for a fight. They're running *away* from Vasyllia."

Baryan smiled, and his eyes seemed tinged with red. "It'll be like culling salmon against a waterfall."

"I'll take the brunt of their attack here in the center," said Parfyon, baring his sword. "Go."

The mass of Gumiren fell on the center of the Nebesti lines like a swarm of ants escaping a house on fire. Many of the Gumiren had no shields, and some were even bereft of swords. For a moment, Parfyon even felt pity for them. But only for a moment.

A quiet calm descended on him. No pain, no chaotic rush of warriors, no thoughts of strategy, only a thin, high scream—the sound of his sisters burning alive on the fateful day that Nebesta the Old had been burned to the ground by these same Gumiren twenty years ago. Parfyon looked up beyond the line of attackers and saw, far above them in the valley wall, a circle of fire-tipped cherry trees growing on what seemed to be the bare cliff-side of the valley. But that was impossible. Above the pink blossoms, suspended in mid-air as though nailed to the sky, an eagle hovered, waiting to plunge to earth. Parfyon's pain receded, his mind cleared, and his foot held his weight again. He was surprised to find his cheeks wet with tears.

Then—chaos. Utter, brilliant chaos, like the music of a thousand ox-horns without a hand to direct them. It was glorious for a few minutes, then a kind of under-consciousness took over—the mind of sword and shield. Sounds faded. Still images replaced smoothly-flowing reality—a splash of red, the empty stare of death in a fallen soldier. In the rare respite, when the mind stilled, Parfyon saw that his men were cutting through the Gumiren lines like fresh butter. If butter could bleed, that is. Parfyon was drenched in red. The pincer movement of the Nebesti Sheloma had reached the far end of the Gumiren lines, ready to encircle them in a grip of sure death. Parfyon lost himself again in the chaos as he hurled a spear, pinning two Gumiren to the ground in a single throw.

When Parfyon's mind stilled, he stood in the midst of fallen Gumiren. The battle raged around him, but it was silent where he stood: the eye of the storm. Parfyon turned to see the front attacking the Negodi. His men had nearly reached the wall of the amphitheater of stone. They were slaughtering the Negodi like lambs.

He turned back to see three men surrounded him. They were neither Negodi nor Gumiren.

Ulik rushed at Parfyon, his greatsword raised in a killing stroke. Behind Parfyon, Sviatopluk rushed in to stab him in the back. A third warrior hung back to finish the job. Parfyon choked back the anger but had no time for anything but the parry and counter-thrust. All three were wounded, but the war-wind made gods of them all. Exhilaration filled Parfyon as he rained blows backward and forward like fire-tipped hailstones. He retreated step by step until he slipped on a fallen Gumir. As he slipped, one of his attackers' swords caught at his hand. When he looked to find it, there was nothing but a spray of blood. Both of his attackers jumped on him like famished lynxes, and the third was not far behind. Parfyon feinted, and Ulik overextended. With a vicious backhand of the shortsword in his left hand, he hacked at the man's neck. The sword lodged between his neck and shoulder. Ulik's eyes rolled into the back of his head as he fell. Sviatopluk stopped, disgust plain in his face. The third warrior ran away.

Parfyon pushed himself up, trying to ignore the pain. He looked at Sviatopluk. "Are you a dog or a man, Sviatopluk? Choose for yourself. Don't let those noble sons of whores dictate anything to you."

Sviatopluk took a step back, still looking at Ulik. Parfyon quickly glanced down and wished he hadn't.

"You're an animal," hissed Sviatopluk. He had tears in his eyes. Before Parfyon realized what he was doing, Sviatopluk turned the blade of his own sword upward and leaned it down against the earth. With a final look of despair at the body of Ulik, he fell on his own sword.

Then the pain in his hand reared itself up like a wyrm breathing fire, and Parfyon collapsed. The darkness took him.

CHAPTER 5
NEBESTA'S FINEST

Voran surveyed the slaughter-fields from a promontory. Bodies twisted out of recognition. Two buzzards fighting over a corpse. A banner of gold and purple streaked with mud, trampled into the green of young grass. A cracked shield pillowing a head with no lower jaw.

It should leave some impression on him. Something. At least revulsion. But Voran felt nothing. Seeing years' worth of battlefields on a weekly basis did that to a person's soul. If he even had a soul left in that cold, barely-beating heart of his.

In the middle of the field of the dead, strangely separate from the rest, lay a youth barely out of his childhood. His was a faint smile in a face white as milk. His mail was barely tarnished from use, set like a jewel in a casing of spotless clothing in the bright colors favored by noble families. A pendant hung around his neck, bearing the mark of a Sirin or some other Power. A single arrow flowered from his chest. There was almost no blood visible on him.

That enraged Voran. So many years of warfare among the city-states left abandoned by Vasyllia's loss to the Gumiren. The youngest and best men cut down, sometimes by their own fathers. Why did they not take the enormous energy needed to kill their own, and direct it to where it would be useful? Why, in the many years of his wandering through battlefields, had hardly a single battle-lord so much as listened to his call for peace?

What was the point, anymore? Why should he labor in the fields, searching for the dying and the wounded, wasting precious days trying to convince the great of this world to follow a cause that he no longer believed in?

But what else was there for him?

As habitual as a nervous tic, his left hand fondled the flask at his hip. The Living Water was still there. Still so heavy. Still draining him of his life and his energy.

More to silence his mind than anything else, Voran ran down the hill toward the pavilions of the victors.

"I've heard of you, sir," said the young warrior, sitting uncomfortably in a chair too big for him. *Not the commander, then*, thought Voran. "They say you do everything, save raise the dead."

"Then you also know of my conditions." Voran said it by rote, already groaning inside at what he knew would be only polite attention on the part of the young warrior.

"Ah, I had heard of it. Well, get on with it then."

"Should I not speak to your superior, young man?"

The warrior, a sub-voyevoda probably only a few battles away from a command of his own, flushed. "I did not say? Forgive me. Parfyon Krivoshey, the commander of this force, is badly wounded. I was assigned to take care of the administrative details while we wait for official word from Lord Yarpolk Dolgoruk."

Ah, so these are Nebesta's finest. What are they doing so close to Vasyllia? Last I heard they were fighting off Karilan bandits.

They were geographically closer to his home than the Dar-in-exile Mirnían, still hiding on Ghavan Isle. The thought gave him a strange sense of urgency.

"I will want to see Parfyon first, to heal him. Then I can make the necessary arrangements with him." Voran made to get up from the rough camp stool they had provided him, but the young man stiffened. Voran stayed seated.

"That will not be possible," said the young man, apologetic in word only. "Parfyon is to be remanded to the Veche's judgment. He killed two of his own during the battle."

"Ah. So you are to be the unfortunate recipient of my sermonizing?"

Voran tried to deliver it with levity, but the words thudded on the ground as soon as they left his lips. The youth looked embarrassed, more for Voran than for himself.

"You would not have seen many battles, I think, young man," said Voran.

"Enough." He smiled.

"May I ask you why you do it? Is it for glory?"

The young man laughed. "Glory? Certainly not. It is what I do best. Killing. I do not pretend to have lofty ideals, healer. I was born in a world of war. I deal in it, because it is what I know."

"But why do you wage war against your own blood?"

The young man's face darkened. "Negodi are not our blood..." There was a hint of a growl in the voice.

"No? You don't know, then, that Negoda, only a hundred years ago, was a district in Old Nebesta? That a group of Nebesti woodsman and their families founded a small village for the sake of adventure, and that it grew into its own city?"

"That's not possible, healer. What is next? Will you suggest that we are brothers with the accursed Vasylli?"

Voran's heart dropped. It was worse than he had thought.

"Vasylli and Nebesti have been brothers for a thousand years. How can you have forgotten this in less than a generation?"

"So it is true, then," said the youth, dismissively, "all they say about your drivel. You wish to restore the ancient monarchy of Vasyllia, yes?"

Voran nodded, a half-hearted gesture.

"Why? It was because of Vasyllia that Nebesta the Old was razed to the ground. Where were our brothers when the armies of the Gumiren nomads came to burn our cities and wipe out our people? Vasyllia would not even harbor our refugees. They left them in camps outside the city walls, for the Raven's sake! How many of them were then slaughtered when the Gumiren came unexpectedly and besieged the so-called Mother of Cities?"

Voran forged ahead as he had done so many times, though he came up against the same arguments again and again. Not once had he convinced a single person. Not yet.

"Vasyllia is not blameless for what happened, I agree. But it has paid a heavy price. And what good has come of the end of the monarchy? Has there been anything but bloodshed since then?"

"No, but the answer to the bloodshed is not to go back to a repressive old order. I will never bow my neck to a Vasylli dog."

"You don't understand, do you? Vasyllia is not merely a city-state. To be Vasylli is to subscribe to an ideal above allegiance to a city or even a bloodline. To be Vasylli means to protect the weak, to set aside personal desires for the good of the Dar and the people. To be a Vasylli warrior is to be a man of peace, a farmer, a scholar. The sword is the least-used of his tools. It is an ideal that bends down the Heights of Aer to the level of earth. Sirin sang in Vasyllia's trees; Powers walked its cobbled streets."

"Quite the fanatic, you are," said the young man, smiling crookedly.

"It's not a matter of faith alone. I saw the ideal. I tried to live it. *I* am Vasylli."

"Enough!" The sub-voyevoda's face was flushed. "I have listened. For the sake of my men, I will not throw you out, though I dearly wish I could. But no more. Will you heal my wounded?"

Voran sighed as the flask at his hip grew heavier, filling with the necessary Living Water to heal them all. He nodded.

"Healer," said the young man, a bit repentant for his outburst, "would you allow me to come with you? I may not be a devotee of the cult of Adonais, but I believe in my own way. I would be honored to see the Living Water at work."

Voran was more gratified by this than he expected. "Thank you. That would be pleasant for me as well."

The youth stood up and proffered an ungloved hand. "My name is Novvik, sir."

Voran took him by the forearm in the traditional warrior's grasp, prompting a surprised smile from Novvik.

"Vohin Novvik, my name is Voran."

There were only about twenty wounded. Far too few for a battle with so many dead. Perhaps the rumors were true. Perhaps Nebesta was on the cusp of taking the high hand in the never-ending Internecine War.

The first had an arrow in his chest. His breathing was labored. Voran tied him to the cot and placed a leather strip in his mouth. He caressed the man—dark-haired and blue-eyed, a typical Nebesti—on the head, whispering consoling words so habitual that he himself didn't attend to them. He pulled the arrowhead out quickly and heard the collarbone break. The warrior convulsed in pain and grunted and sweat sprouted on his forehead. But he subsided quickly.

"Your men are strong, Novvik. My compliments to Lord Yarpolk."

After Voran had stuffed the gushing hole with clean rags, he prepared the poultice, made of bitter birch bark, lavender, and clover root. The pleasant aroma lightened the heaviness of the tent, and the wounded man's shoulders relaxed a little.

Voran concentrated his scattered thoughts into himself. It took longer than usual, but finally all he sensed in his mind was the warm throbbing of his own heart. Calm at last, he took the flask from his hip and poured several drops on a fresh rag. In a swift, practiced motion, he pulled the bloody wad from the arrow-wound and wiped it with the Living Water.

Novvik's eyes were large, the whites striking in his war-tanned face.

"You...wiped it away! As if there never were a wound. Remarkable. How do you do it?"

"I don't know how it's done, Novvik. Sometimes it heals outright, like this. Other times, it provides relief, but not healing. My own hands do little but provide physical relief with herbs and manipulations."

Novvik stood in thought, as though he were having a difficult time coming to terms with what he had seen. It was a typical enough reaction, though this youth's battle with his logical mind took longer than it did with most. Most simply chose to disbelieve the evidence of their eyes. Voran imagined that it was easier that way.

Novvik looked at Voran with something very near admiration. "Why do you not choose a side, Vohin Voran?" Voran noticed that he used the warrior's honorific. Novvik had just admitted Voran to be a fellow-soldier, an equal. "You do realize that with that power of yours, you could end the war in weeks? And I don't doubt the legends of your fighting ability, either. You are of larger build than most of our best warriors."

"I did choose a side once," said Voran. "It... didn't end well."

Novvik seemed to wrestle with his courtesy for a moment, but his youthful energy would not be bridled. "Would you not reconsider now? I will even let you in on a secret. Nebesta is on the verge of something great. There are new alliances with certain great Powers that...well, I would even venture to say guarantee our place as the new Mother of Cities. You believe in a higher ideal? Why not be there, at the inception, to see it come about in Nebesta? Such an ideal need not be bound by physical place. Why can Nebesta not be the new monarchy?"

This sort of response was not typical, not in Voran's experience. It was a tempting proposition, but only for a moment. He remembered his first passage through the realms of the world, led by the mysterious Pilgrim. The details of that day were still vivid in his mind—the rustle of dry leaves underfoot, the wet smell of birches in the morning, the Pilgrim's mischievous eyes. And his words, branded on Voran's memory: "Whatever happens, my falcon, do not forget this. Vasyllia is everything. You must never let Vasyllia fall. She is everything."

Voran had not been able to prevent Vasyllia's fall. But he would never stop his work until Vasyllia the Old stood anew.

"Forgive me, Novvik. I cannot."

There was something else that churned his stomach. *What are these great Powers he speaks of?*

Someone screamed outside. It was not the scream of a wounded man. This was a sound Voran knew far too well.

"You are not..." he turned on Novvik, his body tense.

"It's not what you think," said the young man, his hands palm-out, placating. "There was more to this battle than a tussle between cities. Come, I will show you. You of all people should be pleased."

Voran wondered what he meant.

Behind the tents of wounded was a clearing with a single old oak in the center. Someone was tied to the trunk. No, nailed. His hands were nailed to the trunk, and his feet were barely above ground, unable to support his hanging body. His torso was chained to the tree, the links biting into his exposed skin. Two arrows shuddered in his right leg and his left arm. Another had missed but took a bit of an ear off. All that was not as horrifying as the realization—brown skin, flat face, angled eyes—this was a Gumir.

Voran felt his breath grow ragged. The Gumiren were more hateful to him than all the powers of darkness. If not for the Gumiren, he would not have been separated from his beloved Sabíana for twenty years. The Gumiren were the reason a wall stood between Vasyllia and the rest of the city-states. This hateful race was the source of everything that had gone wrong in the world.

Now, looking at the face of this tortured man, Voran felt only pity. Not merely for his physical pain. The Gumiren, he knew, were trained to endure uncommon levels of pain. It was his eyes. They were mindless with fear, a different fear than the fear of torture. This man had seen something so horrifying that it had robbed him of his mind. *What is going on in Vasyllia?*

"Why are you having your way with him?" asked Voran, his voice cold. "This man is a broken vessel. He was so, even before you began toying with him."

Novvik's eyes widened. "You can tell, just by looking at him? Remarkable... But what does it matter? This is a Gumir. I would prefer the Ghan himself, but he will do. We will not kill him. Just disfigure him enough to make a point. Then he will go back into Vasyllia."

"NO!" screamed the man, his eyes clearing for a moment. "You not make me go back there. Not..." His eyes filmed over with the madness again, and he began to babble in Gumir.

"Novvik, let me heal this man. You are above such bestial cruelty."

Novvik's expression was like a door shutting in Voran's face. The hatred there was staggering.

"Captain," he said to the man who had been shooting arrows at the Gumir. "Throw this charlatan out of the camp. If I so much as see his face again, I will string *you* up to be shot at."

Outside the camp, Voran washed his hands in a fetid pool of rainwater. It stank, seeming to only add to the grime on his body and to his general sense of heaviness, even old age. The sun cleared a bank of clouds, making the water sparkle for half a second. In that instance, he saw his face. There was no trace of age. He looked younger than ever, nowhere near his forty some years. He had looked exactly like that when it all began, when *he* had been the one pinned to a tree with arrows. Though then, it was no enemy, but his own future brother-in-law who had attacked him. Mirnían, now husband to Voran's sister Lebía.

Where was he now? Why had the remnant of Vasyllia not entered the fray in the Internecine War? What were they waiting for?

CHAPTER 6
LIVING WATER

Antomír, the young son of Mirnían, the Dar-in-exile of Vasyllia, watched the flights of firebirds from the branches of an old beech tree. They rose from the center of Ghavan Town in waves of two and three, their red-gold tail-feathers trailing behind them like tongues of fire, as the children released them from gilded cages. Even from this distance, Antomír clearly heard the call-and-response songs that ushered in spring. Today was the ceremonial birthday of nature, only days away from Antomír's twentieth birthday. All month, the migrating firebirds had been returning, and all week the boys had been losing sleep to capture them at night. This year, they had caught thirteen. An omen for a warm and fruitful growing season.

"*Kulik-kulik! Birds of fire!*
Bring to me my heart's desire
Bring nine locks from over-sea
Lock up winter's gates for me."

Antomír couldn't help it. He hummed along the response:

"*Kulik-kulik! Birds of fire!*
Bring to me my heart's desire.
Bring nine keys from over-sea
Unlock the doors of spring-to-be."

"Hhrmgh!" rumbled something huge under the tree.

Antomír sighed. Would he never be left alone? "Veles! I told you that I would go alone this time."

The looming shadow resolved into the familiar—far too familiar—stone-shouldered form of Veles, the royal bodyguard. What a ridiculous title for him, thought Antomír, not for the first time. The royal bull was more like it.

"Bah. You want me to beg forgiveness. Keep dreaming your rose-scented fantasies. The anointed one must never walk alone."

Antomír shook his head. Always that mystical brooding with Veles, ever since he had appeared in Ghavan ten years ago, unexpected as snowfall in July. All these years in the safest place in all the Realms, and still nothing would ever dissuade him from it.

"What could possibly harm me in Ghavan, Veles? Does it never occur to your thick head that the protection we enjoy is a little more effective than you?" *Even if your arms do look like smoked hams.*

Veles extended his head forward in that curious way of his. His shoulders were so huge that he probably couldn't lean his head back at all—too much muscular obstruction. His arms hung in beefy half-moons framing his almost comical torso, giving him a simian appearance. But all that hid a quick intelligence that few appreciated, seeing only the bulk and hearing only the platitudes of the fanatic.

"Anointed one." This time, there was a twinkle of sarcasm in Veles's tone. "You give yourself too much credit. Remember what happened last time you ventured out alone? Hm?"

Antomír jumped down from the tree, ready for a proper argument.

"Shush!" Veles stopped him before he could even start. "Useless to argue with me. You remember, yes? A broken shinbone. And the time before that? The gash across your knee? The one that was so deep you couldn't walk for a week? You may be twenty years old, but you're a child, and you need a nanny."

The idea of this lion-haired bull-man as a nanny was enough to make Antomír break out in laughter. Veles did not appreciate the levity. He picked Antomír up by the scruff of the neck and shook him as though he *were* a child.

"Stop acting like a two-year old, anointed one!"

"Stop calling me that!"

"I will not, anointed one. Vasyllia needs a proper Dar, not an over-pampered lily-handed milk-sucker!"

It had the desired effect. Antomír could come up with no witty response.

Veles dropped Antomír unceremoniously onto his royal buttocks. Briefly, the youth thought about attacking Veles with his sword. As usual, it was as if he could read Antomír's mind. Veles cocked his head and laughed. If you could call it a laugh. It sounded more like coughing.

"Go ahead, Antomír. Try me. How long was it last time? Thirty seconds?"

And, as it always happened, Antomír found himself overcome with sudden affection for the walking monolith. The son of the exiled Dar of Vasyllia had few friends. But even if he had a hundred, no one would be as devoted as Veles.

"You may as well be useful then," said Antomír. "I know you have the nose of a hound. Find me lavender."

"This early in the year?" Veles pursed his lips and shook his head. The brown curls danced on his shoulders. "Unlikely."

"But necessary. For my mother."

The single massive eyebrow of Veles rose knowingly. His eyes softened.

"Then we must."

Truth be told, Antomír didn't expect to find any. He had tried to explain it to Mama Lebía; how it was still early spring, how the cold nights would kill the young blossoms, how…

It didn't matter. Her headaches had gotten worse, and her willingness to remain in the realm of the reasonable was waning. She had said that she needed lavender, and that was that.

"You can find it for me, my love," she had said, her nearly translucent right hand clutching at her temples. "You always manage to find it for me."

"But Mama, could we not just crush some of last year's dried blossoms into hot water and make a compress for you?"

"It's not the same, you know that," she said. She still spoke to him as though he were ten. "Living blossoms…they have something to them, something of Vasyllia. Please, Antomír…"

It was all she ever had to do. That terrible "please" that held in it the thing he feared most—losing her, and what that would do to his father.

"Well now," growled Veles in the same voice he used when he spied a deer on a hunt.

Was that lavender-smell? A strong, pungent stream, as though someone had placed a bundle of it under his nose. He could see nothing but the trees and the slanting bars of golden morning sun, and the more he focused on his sight, the less he could smell or hear. So, he closed his eyes, and the smell flooded him. How strange…

Veles, his head forward, his arms bent slightly backward like strung bows, was already on the scent. Antomír followed.

The smell drew them toward a bend in the river not far from Ghavan

Town. The town was situated in between and among a series of rolling hills, but here, the forest floor neither fell nor rose, going straight toward the beach on the other side of the island some twenty miles away. At the bend, the trees parted to reveal two of the town's hills, a long bow-shot away. Each had a large stone house on the crest—one was Antomír's father's house, the other the chapel to Adonais, built on the place where his parents had been married. He had loved to hear stories of the feasting after the wedding, which had gone on for three days and three nights, or so the old women claimed. Now, he turned away from it, his heart heavy.

Veles froze in the hunting stance like a pointer, his expression confused. Antomír leaned forward and looked down to a place where the river fell over a ledge into a shallow pool, perfect for swimming. A copse of birches grew on the bank, their roots dipping into the edges of the water. Sunlight hung in sheets between the trunks, shimmering with the swaying of the trees. Something moved in the trees, undulating like ripples in water.

Antomír couldn't understand what he was looking at. He had the sense that he was supposed to see something clearly, but the details—intricate in their separateness—refused to come together to create a picture in his mind.

"Oh, by all the songs of the Heights," whispered Veles.

And then the details shifted in Antomír's perception, and he saw the whole. Dancing through the shafts of light were maidens made of rain. They were barely there, coming in and out of sight as clouds passed across the sun's face. When the sun shone directly on them, they looked no different from Ghavanite maidens in red sarafans and bare feet, but as the clouds passed, they dissolved into sheets of rainwater with only the hazy outlines of young girls.

Antomír was long used to the supernatural. Mama's Sirin, Aína, still came to him in dreams sometimes, though not as often as before. But this was different. More dangerous, edged like a blade.

Veles began to chant.

"When walls that stood for centuries strong
Begin to fade and disappear,
Hark to the day-seer's tragic song,
Look to the East, the lame horse nears..."

"I haven't heard that one. Is it one of the ones that my father would prefer I *not* hear?"

Veles smiled. "I have told the Dar many times. You can muzzle a dog, but if you do, the trees will sing the truth instead."

Antomír chuckled. Sometimes Veles came up with real pearls. He turned back to the dancing maidens of rain.

Now they were more substantial, their long shirtsleeves wispy like fog. They danced in a circle around the clump of birches, waving their hands in, then out. Every time they swung their hands out, they dropped what looked like dew onto the earth. Everywhere the dew fell, tiny blossoms of lavender sprouted up.

"Look, Veles. Lavender…"

Antomír tried to jump forward, but Veles grabbed his shoulder.

"Sire, be careful." Antomír's blood ran a little colder at the use of that word. Sire. Veles had only called him that once. An evening, not long before. They had been drinking ale deep into the night, talking of the mysteries of the Heights and the delusive abilities of some great Powers who put on visages of light and beauty to fool men into trust. Vila, mermaids, likhi—Powers who occasionally tried to break the borders of Ghavan, attracted by the power within it.

Veles was right. This lavender was too convenient, too good to be true.

"I suppose we should turn back," Antomír said.

The rain-maidens broke the circle of the dance and lined the riverbank across from Antomír, their extended hands full of fragrant lavender. For a brief moment, Antomír thought that he glimpsed fangs behind their smiles. A cloud partially obscured them into half-incorporeal ripples of falling rain. When the sun returned, there could be no mistaking their feral expressions.

"I don't think they mean you well, anointed one," said Veles in one of his usual bursts of obviousness.

"Well. You'll have to beat them off if they come for me then. I am sure you can handle a few vila."

Veles grimaced. "You think they are vila? Good Powers above, watch over your humble servant as he enters the eternal battle against the churning powers of evil…"

Antomír drew his sword, thrilling at the chance to actually put the many hours Veles spent training him to use.

As he mumbled his prayer, Veles reached over his back to take the iron-studded tree stump that he used as a mace. The piety in his eyes melted, filling instead with the angry fire of the berserker warrior. He was even more terrifying than the creatures on the other side of the bank. His knuckles were white on the mace, and his entire body tensed, ready to make the leap ahead of Antomír across the water. What could he hope to accomplish against the vila? They were not even fully corporeal. What could a tree branch do to hurt rainfall?

A screech tore through Antomír's head, so loud that he crumpled over, dropping his sword. A dark shadow passed overhead and fell on the rain maidens like lighting. Antomír could barely see through the pain of the scream, but he saw enough to understand that the vila were being ripped apart by the sound. The dark shadow had wings and taloned feet and…was that a woman's face? A Sirin? If so, it was no Sirin he knew. She was hideous —yellow-pale, like someone suffering from a mortal illness, and her black hair only served to accentuate her ugliness. This was no Sirin.

Just as suddenly as she had arrived, she disappeared, leaving behind a faint smell of rot and no rain maidens.

"What in the Heights was that?" said Antomír. His hands shook.

To Antomír's surprise, Veles was still as a stone, his face hard, but calm. It was not a good calm.

"Tell me, Veles. You *know*."

"I do not. I suspect. But if it is how I suspect, then things are much worse than I thought. The walls between the worlds are cracking."

Antomír was shaken by the strange vision of the vila and the dark non-Sirin. With Veles trailing behind him like a loyal dog, he turned away from the river and plunged into the deep wood in the opposite direction from Ghavan Town. He made straight for *his* place—the tallest hill on Ghavan, near the central point of the island. From there, he could watch the sea undisturbed, except for the occasional squirrel or marmot that came to him and sat on his lap and shoulders.

He never made it as far as the hill. Deep in a birch wood, the impossible smell of lavender inundated him again, so strong that Antomír was forced to stop. He and Veles stood at the mouth of a cave overhung with young, translucent ivy. The sound of dripping water came from within, echoing. Just within sat a little bush of lavender with three frail blossoms.

"Now *that's* interesting," said Antomír and came closer to the cave. He had never seen this place before, despite his constant wandering over the island. The smell of peat and earth was like a wet slap across the face. The cave was flush with lavender, laid out like a carpet leading deeper into the cave. Antomír saw much farther than he expected, as though the lavender gave off soft light. Intrigued, he lifted the ivy and walked in, careful to gather a few of the largest blossoms and to tuck them into the ready pouch at his belt.

"You won't stop me now, Veles?" Antomír teased over his shoulder.

Veles didn't answer, remaining still at the mouth of the cave.

Antomír didn't wait to hear the big man's rejoinder. Unexpectedly excited, he rushed forward, tugging at the biggest blossoms, ripe like blackberries, as he passed further into the cave. The sound of dripping water grew more and more intense.

Something shuffled by him in the darkness, grazing his leg. He nearly jumped in fright, but the creature passed by and continued on into the cave ahead of him. It clopped on tiny hooves on the stones, the rhythm of its walk uneven. A fawn, still in its spots. It limped, favoring one of its spindly legs. He felt sorry for the creature. Why had it come into this cave? Why did it seem to have no fear of him at all?

Antomír followed it, his curiosity piqued. The fawn remained barely illumined by a half-light that seemed to come from nowhere. They walked for what seemed a very long time, though time and distance were both hard to measure in this place. It seemed to be another Realm entirely. Then the fawn turned sharply out of his vision, and Antomír heard a clear sound of splashing water. He hurried to see what had happened to it.

He almost fell into it himself—a pool in a cavern roughly circular in shape. Water dripped into the pool from stalactites. But no, they were not stalactites. They were tree roots. The fawn swam a circle in the water, then came back to where Antomír stood. It hopped out of the water and trotted back out toward the cave opening. It no longer limped.

"I should have known," Antomír said aloud as his heart raced with hope and fear. He had found Living Water on Ghavan. He was sure of it. Now Mama would be well. Now everything would be well again.

Antomír rushed out, his soul singing with the early spring.

CHAPTER 7
THE QUEEN WHO WALKS THE SKIES

Khaidu rose before the sun and was already on horseback by the time the dawn sketched a line of mountains to her right. She and the rest of the hunters rode alongside the mountains for much of the day, but soon Khaidu sensed the peaks pulling them closer. Her backside hurt, and her hips felt like someone was pinching them at the place where her legs met her body. She would have given anything to be able to stretch at that moment. She could move her arms, but her hands felt fuzzy. When she flexed her fingers, a hailstorm of pricks and needles ran up and down her arm. She watched, fascinated, as she began to feel her hands again, one twitching finger at a time.

She should be sick with despair at being a cripple again. She should want the Steppe-death a hundred times over. But to her surprise, a reserve of quiet joy still simmered inside her.

The lady-eagle dipped close to her right shoulder. Beyond her, a half-day's ride away, two promontories jutted out from the sea of undulating rock.

The guardians must look strange to you, Khaidu thought at the lady-eagle.

Two immense statues—a Sirin and a firebird, both in flight—were carved out of each promontory, facing each other. Even from this distance, Khaidu could see the Sirin's half-open mouth, as if she were just about to sing her legendary song. The firebird's tongue was frozen in mid-dart. How such colossi could have been carved in the wilds of the Steppelands, Khaidu did not know, though it was one of her favorite pastimes to imagine possible origins. Her latest and favorite theory was that a race of giants fashioned the colossi long ago, and now they slept under the earth, waiting for the hand of time to wake them.

Etchigu was far ahead of her, and Batuk, though cowed by his injury, still lingered near her. She could sense his enmity like the heat from a fire pit on the side of her face. He would not forgive her for what her eagle did. She would have to deal with him somehow.

He avoided hurting her when Etchigu could see. Whenever she would cry out in pain, prompting Etchigu to step in for her, Batuk had always punished her for it afterward, twice as severely. He had a talent to inflict pain in covered places of her body—her back and stomach especially. Eventually, she had learned to endure him as well as she could. She had tried, once, to complain to Mamai, but Mamai had not had enough patience to parse out Khaidu's labored, garbled speech. That was more painful than any of Batuk's insults. Khaidu had been Mamai's favorite once, an only daughter in a storm of sons. But after Mamai's brother, the Ghan Magai, had beaten Khaidu to within an inch of her life, Mamai shied away from contact with her only daughter.

That evening, they passed under the guardians and into the massive city beyond. Even though it had been her home for years now, it still took her breath away—the log towers that seemed piled on top of each other from this distance, each gable painted a different color and design. Then the huge faces painted on the walls took shape—here a bearded ancient with a red and gold band across his forehead, there a maiden with plaited hair elaborately pinned atop her head. The bright colors belied the age of the place, its terrible ancientness. Their pale faces and flaxen hair always bothered Khaidu. They seemed unnatural. Impossible to think that such pale-skinned people actually walked under the burning sun. Even Sabíana, though lighter-skinned that the Gumiren, was much darker than these pale-faced monstrosities.

Among the towers, in a wide space that could have been a town square for a city of giants, the horse-clan of Mamai jani-Beg lay sprawled. Hundreds of yurts winked among bonfires. Thousands of Gumiren of all ages sat, slept, cavorted, wrestled, sang, and feasted, their every action given epic proportion by the light of the fires. Mamai's yurt—small for someone who was effectively the leader of a nation—was in the exact center of the camp. She alone seemed carved of stone as she sat by her fire, while her people lived their lives at a fever pitch around her.

The hunters rode up to her in two perfect rows. Etchigu sang the song of greeting after a hunt, and the rest of the hunters hummed the accompaniment behind him. Usually, they couldn't quite manage the overtone, but today, it sounded just like it was supposed to—like a wolf growling. They raised their right arms with their eagles perched on them. Then they dismounted as one and fell to their knees, bowing their heads. Khaidu was breathless with pleasure at how perfectly Etchigu had managed the ritual of return, but then her eagle flew up and landed on both her shoulders, to her annoyance. Even through the thick leather, the talons bit hard.

"No success, then," Mamai said, in her unexpectedly quiet voice. Her long black hair rippled over her bosoms that were huge like maces.

Etchigu shook his head.

"But you lie, Etchigu," said Mamai, looking at Khaidu. "Little Khaidu has come back with a bird of her own."

"A monster, not a bird," whined Batuk in the back of the company, his face a riot of bandages.

Mamai only then saw him, and her face changed. As usual, Khaidu could not read the exact emotion. Mamai waddled up to Khaidu and looked into her eyes, unblinking.

"Yes, there's something new in your eyes, my little one," she whispered, only for her to hear.

Khaidu felt a stab of panic. Would she take the eagle away from her?

"It was your eagle that did this." This she said louder, for the benefit of the hunters. "Doubtless for good reason." In the churning noise of blood rushing through her ears, Khaidu thought she misheard. "Batuk had it long coming. You are a jester, not a hunter." This she hurled at Batuk, whose face flushed red to match his bloodied bandages. "What? Did you expect me to cry over you and pat you on the head? Weak, pitiful idiot. You have been bested by the eagle of a half-broken girl ten years your junior. Shame be upon you."

Mamai took Khaidu's pony's reins in her own hand and began to untie the harness that kept Khaidu a-horse. Khaidu started to melt into pitiful emotion at the unexpected kindness. She had to remain firm, though, or Batuk would punish her later. The eagle nibbled her ear. It brought Khaidu back to herself.

"T-t-ank you," she said. Mamai smiled, but didn't look at her. She lifted Khaidu and placed her by the fire, her back propped against a bundle of clothes.

"Boys, let us give thanks that you came back alive." She turned to the totem standing near her tent—a wooden carving of a cliff jutting out of seawater, with a three-tongued flame on the top. The strange symbol of the Unknown Father whom the Gumiren had sought for thousands of years.

As the men performed the ritual, Khaidu remembered the story of how, twenty-five years ago, most of their people had thought that they found the Unknown Father in the creature that they later called the Dark Father. What joy there was in the finding! All the Gumiren, of the many horse-clans, had feasted for twenty days without stopping. But then the tale told how quickly her child-like and carefree brothers and sisters were twisted into beings of careless cruelty, torturing small animals for amusement as a prelude to the slaughter of entire villages and cities. How had they been so easily led astray?

Next to the totem stood the ceremonial mound covered in a blanket studded with silver suns and moons. The symbol of the Queen Who Walks the Skies. The one who would lead them to the Unknown Father. As the chant of thanksgiving ended, Khaidu realized that she had seen something very much like that blanket only recently. But where?

Of course! The dress of Lady Sabíana. It was the same design as the symbol of the Queen Who Walks the Skies.

"You!" Khaidu said to the lady when she woke her again in the middle of the night. "You are the one to bring us to Him, aren't you?"

Sabíana, who seemed on the verge of plunging back into the argument of the previous night, sputtered into confused silence.

"The Queen Who Walks the Skies! That's you!"

Sabíana rolled her eyes. "Typical." She practically snorted. "One evening among the savages, and already I'm the chosen one destined to lead the people to greatness."

"No, you over-pampered good-for-nothing!" Khaidu was a little shocked at her own vehemence. She had never been this quick to anger before, not even with Batuk. "No wonder your Three Lands fell as quickly as they did. You know very little."

Sabíana colored, giving her olive skin a pleasing bloom. For a moment, the lady revealed some of the queenliness that must have attracted so many to her in former times.

"Very well, Khaidu of the horse-clan of Mamai jani-Beg." With her strange accent, it sounded much more pompous than it should have. "Enlighten me."

"We Gumiren are not the marauding savages you think us. We are an ancient, nomadic people. So ancient that we cannot even remember when or where we began." Sabíana's lips began to curl sarcastically, but a look from Khaidu was enough to force the curl in the other direction. "No, we do not have *written records*." Khaidu spit. "Why would we let a few people who scrawl on stones with pointy sticks rewrite things that can be handed down from mother to daughter unchanged for centuries?"

Sabíana was about to counter, but Khaidu had no intention of giving her a chance.

"We do not choose the wandering life because it suits us, lady. We do it because we search. We have searched. For centuries. For an Unknown Father who will teach us the way to live properly. The way to live permanently."

Sabíana's eyes were inscrutable.

"He is Unknown," continued Khaidu, "because he is incapable of being known. Not without help. That help will come from a woman, a great queen. A queen who..." She stopped, suddenly embarrassed.

"...who walks the skies," murmured Sabíana.

"Yes."

The silence hissed around them, and Khaidu had a premonition that the next words would be important. She tensed and waited, hoping that the lady would be the first to break the silence.

"Khaidu. This Unknown Father. Do your stories tell where he can be found?"

"No. But the Queen Who Walks the Skies will take us to a city in the mountains, within which is the Garden in the Heart of the World. There, the way to the Unknown Father will be made known."

"I have not heard of this place," said Sabíana, though the sudden paleness and confused expression suggested otherwise. "Khaidu, your people seem to have abandoned the nomadic life. You still live in tents, but you've holed yourself up in this city of giants. Why?"

It was still a matter of pain for Khaidu, this departure from the ways of their fathers. "About twenty-five years ago, before I was born, the Steppe was filled with horse-clans. There were many of us Gumiren then. My uncle, the Ghan Magai jani-Beg, had the greatest horse-clan. One night, a man came to him. Claimed to be a messenger of the Unknown Father. He had powers, incredible powers. Able to change his physical shape and create fire from nothing and other such things. Ghan Magai and many others were sure that he was the real thing. They followed him and made him the leader of many horse-clans.

"Over the next several years, he gathered nearly all the Gumiren under himself. You have to understand. That's unheard-of. We nomads don't unify for anyone. Then things started to change. He began to force people to do petty, cruel things. To ... desensitize them to pain and meanness. Steadily, it got worse. Eventually—I was still a baby then, so I heard all this later—we began to attack peaceful merchant caravans and slaughter them for no reason.

"He said that all the people that we slaughtered were not human, because they did not seek the Unknown Father. He said that all who did not seek him should be slaughtered. And we believed him. Only Mamai and a small group refused to follow him. They called him by his true name—Dark Father. They escaped under cover of night, a thousand-strong horse-clan, and did not stop until they came to this place with the colossi. We had a shaman then, and he sensed that this place was powerful. That we might be safe.

"We were. No one came. But eight years ago—I was eight years old then—the Ghan Magai came back. He was a shell of himself. Told horror stories of the invasion, of coming to Vasyllia, of the terrible things that happened there. There were purges. The Gumiren apparently had the tables turned on them, and they were killed in mass numbers—"

"Yes," said Sabíana. "I was there. It was the final lie of the one you call the Dark Father. The Raven, we call him. He gave Vasyllia back to the Vasylli who pledged themselves to him. The first thing they did was slaughter all your people, who had been getting fat and complacent for years."

Khaidu shuddered. "Magai said something of the sort, yes. Mamai felt sorry for him and took him in. But he was lying. The Dark Father had sent him back to find us. To punish us. The Dark Father knew that Mamai had a single daughter—me—and he wanted to punish her by hurting me. He'd tortured Magai until my uncle lost his mind. He was not a man anymore. All that was left was his need to kill me. He tried. He came close. Batuk stopped him. Batuk and Etchigu killed him."

Sabíana's face was ashen. "I had no idea the Raven's darkness reached so far."

She wrapped the silence around herself like a shawl and rocked in place, biting the tip of her thumbnail insistently. Khaidu sensed her desire to be alone. She was exhausted by the telling and the memory of pain and fear, and she lay down and wrapped herself tightly in her blankets. She was cold and her heart was heavy. It took her a long time to fall asleep.

CHAPTER 8
FAIREST OF THEM ALL

Foggy forms dressed in black loomed over Parfyon. Some had leering faces, some had no heads, some had war chests instead of heads. They had more hands than they should have. Horses with wings, bearing the black forms down a waterfall. He floated down a river, cold and swift. Rocks reared up where he couldn't see them and he hit them with his head, repeatedly. Torches bobbed up and down as though they had legs and were running alongside him. Were they racing? Tall beaver hats, long brocade coats, rows of sharp teeth. Or were they spears? Winged monsters with bodies of vultures and heads of... he couldn't remember. A flock of ravens. Three cherry trees in bloom standing in the middle of a river of fire. Quivering, quivering leaves in wind.

Something jolted, and Parfyon jerked awake. Everything hurt. He groaned, trying his best to descend back into sleep. But no. He had no desire to go back to those nightmares.

"He's awake," barked a voice behind Parfyon. As his body's pain became more specific, Parfyon realized that he was lying in a rough cart with other wounded, though his vision was still hazy. Their nearly constant moaning filtered into his awareness, making him feel nauseous. As though on purpose, his sense of smell returned at that moment, inundating him with the smell of fecal matter, sickness, blood, sweat. He nearly passed out again. He tried to sit up, but his hands only felt cold, clammy flesh around him. He screamed.

The cart stopped. Four hands dragged him off the rest of the bodies as though he were a cow carcass.

"Can you stand?" It was a second voice, less grating than the first.

"I think so," said Parfyon.

The hands disappeared, and Parfyon fell.

"That went well," quipped the first voice.

"Yes, very well," the second voice said, sarcastic, "especially if you have no especial desire to keep your head attached to your shoulders."

The sniggerer stopped abruptly. Four hands again lifted Parfyon, this time onto the driver's seat. His swimming vision had begun to clear by now. They stood in the middle of a single-file caravan of carts bearing wounded. Woodland, evergreen mostly. By the look and smell of the trees, they should be close to New Nebesta. Two armed Sheloma rode on either side of them.

"Why the honor guard?" asked Parfyon.

The second speaker, a young tradesman whom Parfyon did not know, looked surprised.

"You ask me? Strange man."

Parfyon decided that he had not quite come back from his nightmares.

The ride was pleasant enough. He let his thoughts wander through torturous labyrinths, not trying to make sense of anything yet. Only when they approached New Nebesta did he come awake fully.

"By all the Powers," whispered Parfyon. His mouth remained agape. "Is that?...What happened to New Nebesta?"

The first speaker, a leather-faced old man almost as round as he was tall, croaked a bitter laugh.

"Wonders and miracles, my lord. The kind of thing that makes decent people's skin crawl."

He was right. Something not entirely natural hummed in the air, just beyond perception. Only a few months ago, the Nebesti army had left behind it a lowly collection of log huts and hovels, barely standing up to the incursion of trees and thickets and tall grasses.

Now, half the forest seemed to have been cleared, the felled trees sharpened into a tall, pitch-soaked wall. It looked like the jawline of a monstrous predator. A terraced bridge led over the Nebestaala River to an arched gate that was not merely tall and sturdy—it was tiled and painted red. Under the tiled roof, over the gateway, glittered a vibrant fresco—two spears crossed above the sun rising over the Nebestaala. It was breathtaking, even from this distance. Inside the wall, the trees seemed practically domesticated in comparison with the tiered wooden towers, all of them gabled and tiled and even—Parfyon could hardly believe his eyes— *gilded*! This was truly a New Nebesta.

The gates opened. A mounted guard of twenty warriors, bristling with more armor than Parfyon had seen in his life, rode straight at the caravan. Their helms were new, and the faceplates were unlike anything Parfyon had ever seen. They were a strange amalgam of the maw of a serpent and the elongated nose of a horse.

"Parfyon Krivoshey!" barked their leader—a man twice as tall as the rest. "You are under detainment by order of the Veche of New Nebesta."

"On what charge?" Parfyon shouted in surprise.

"The murder of Ulik Dolgoruk."

The oak door slammed. Five locks thundered shut. Parfyon was bemused at the idea of being a guest at the Hall of Veche, the quarters of high-rank prisoners awaiting trial. His drudge-laborer father would have been amused at this choice of prison for his common-born son.

The room was comfortable, lit by an austere hearth. The logs were frosted with white ash, only a faint red strip glowing underneath. By now, it was evening, and he was tired and confused. Falling onto a surprisingly soft coverlet, Parfyon fell asleep instantly.

When he awoke, his left eye felt less leaden; still, he saw nothing but a grayish darkness with it. Raising his right hand proved to be impossible, the pain too searing. Something stirred on the other side of the room, distracting him from his pain. It was a hunched-over figure in layered clothing, seated.

It resolved like a flower blooming into a tall, dark-haired young woman with sharp eyebrows. Her hair was yanked back into a black headscarf. A grey wool headband bore two heavy iron temple-rings. Her dress was a mass of grey and dark navy, though the cross stitching was in pure gold. The fair Alienne did not smile, but everything about her quickened Parfyon's pulse and cleared his head. A pleasant tickling sensation deep inside: it happened every time he saw her.

"I hear you performed great deeds in my name," she said, her tone neutral.

She would not look Parfyon in the eyes. He wanted her to look at him, willing it with all the remaining energy of his mind. If her amber eyes would not turn at him, the substance of his inner self would rip apart. At last, they flicked over him, but only for a moment. It was enough for floods of warmth to pour over him.

"Ulik," Parfyon said.

"Ulik," she repeated, nodding once. Her eyebrows twitched toward each other. "He's dead," she said, more loudly. "You killed him."

"I did not kill him."

She curled the first three fingers of her right hand inward, a gesture of questioning unique to the fair Alienne. "The presence of your knife in the side of his neck suggests otherwise."

"I did not kill Ulik, Alienne," Parfyon repeated. "I killed his dark shade. I think Ulik died a long time ago. I think you know when he died."

She froze, her mouth parted a little. "What sort of—?" she said, when speech returned. "Dark shade? Do you lack the manhood to accept responsibility for your actions?"

"Alienne," he said, "why would I kill your brother? I love you."

"So you often claim, and yet you do your best to antagonize my father, and now..." She threw her arms up, then dropped them to her sides. They slapped loudly on the silvered brocade. "Ulik's dead. You do amaze me with your courting, murderer!" Her face was inches from Parfyon's. She jabbed the last word as though it could pierce him through.

He struck her face with the back of his left hand.

The shock on her face flared, but quickly faded. She began to laugh.

"I didn't expect that," she said, her tongue teasing the small cut on the side of her lip. "Not from a worthless, crippled thing."

"You'll get more of that if you act like a child again."

She shook her head and smiled, stroking the place he had struck, already an angry red welt. It would leave a mark for a few days, one Parfyon guessed she would even boast of. Such was the grim reality of courting in a ravaged world of perpetual war.

"Fair enough," she said, and turned to face Parfyon, allowing the light of the fading hearth to illuminate her face for his benefit. "But you speak first."

He was not confident that he had enough strength to match the fair Alienne in such a parley, but she was worth the battle.

"I think you Dolgoruki are hiding something. I know the official story: your father sent Ulik on a scouting mission to try to subvert Tiverna's army without a fight. The prince of Tiverna found out, was less than impressed with Yarpolk's offer, and decided to test his latest torture techniques on Ulik. But that's not what actually happened, is it?"

Something dark seemed to descend on her shoulders. They slumped the slightest fraction.

"No." She said no more, her eyes challenging him to guess further.

Parfyon tried his first tricky move in this game of chess. It required a leap of faith in his own intuition. "It was Vasyllia, wasn't it? He was imprisoned and tortured in Vasyllia."

She tried to remain impassive, but her eyes widening a mere fraction gave her away. Parfyon had guessed it. By the Heights! What could have possessed Ulik to go searching for trouble in Vasyllia, whose very name had become associated with the horrors of the land of the dead?

"That would explain why he was acting so strange." It also suggested something sinister about Yarpolk's political motives. "Let me see if I understand this. Your father is interested in the legendary riches of the Mother of Cities, Vasyllia. So he sent his only son into a land possessed by some sort of legendary terror to ascertain the danger to Nebesta. How am I doing so far?"

Her mouth had curled, but it was not quite a smile. Too unpleasant.

"He must have found an unguarded entrance through the wall of Vasyllia. Somewhere off the beaten path"

"Not exactly, Parfyon." She had *named* him. Another point in his favor, a concession that she was speaking with an equal now. "There *are* ways into Vasyllia. Only the old families know them, of course."

It was a cheap shot, but still a point in her favor.

"So Ulik got himself captured and tortured by whatever horror rules in Vasyllia. Then they...what? Just let him go?"

"He claimed to have escaped."

Parfyon didn't believe that for a moment.

"He was in a lot of pain when he came back," said Alienne, for the first time warming to the idea of Parfyon as a confidant, "but it was physical pain. He didn't seem to have been changed by the torture. He still had the same sense of humor, the same impulsiveness. The change happened later. No apparent reason. He just came to the table one supper—it was the night before this latest campaign began—and his eyes were different. He was somehow...empty."

Parfyon nodded for her to continue.

"He began to laugh at all the wrong times. He started to use foul, ugly words. Things I've never heard anyone in Nebesta speak. The laugh was the worst. It was not his. As though... as though someone else had put on his skin like clothing, and that someone found it very funny that we couldn't see him."

She had led Parfyon to it. He smiled. "You said it yourself. Someone else. I repeat. I did not kill Ulik."

She sighed in frustration, though not without flashing a quick smile. Parfyon pressed his advantage. "I win this round. Concede?"

"Yes, yes. You'll want a reward, I suppose," she said and turned her head away, teasing.

Parfyon reached out with both arms to grab her and pulled her to himself. He pressed her lips to his, but she was able to extricate herself easily. Too easily. His right hand tingled strangely. He pushed the sensation aside. Alienne flushed with pleasure, though there was a tinge of distaste in her look that she tried to hide by turning away. Parfyon ignored it.

"Alienne, what happened to New Nebesta? The sudden rebuilding?"

The room became wintry cold as the last ember fizzled out. An ashen sun peeked through the cross-bar window.

"I've made some new friends while you men were out chopping limbs."

"For your father?"

She scoffed, and the look on her face was one he expected to be reserved for enemies, not fathers. It confirmed something he had suspected and hoped for a long time—that Alienne had little love for her father.

Parfyon lifted his right hand to wipe the sweat clinging to his mustache, but no hand came up to his mind's summons.

Seeing Parfyon's confusion, Alienne put her hand on his shoulder. Her eyes were still veiled with distaste, but something else as well. Was it pity? Why did she not take his hand? Parfyon looked down and saw that he had no right hand. At first, he thought it must be a mistake. His hand must still be under the coverlet. He willed it to move, as fiercely as he had ever willed anything, but nothing budged, because nothing was there.

"Alienne, what's wrong with me?" The panic rose up to choke Parfyon as he realized the extent of his injuries. "How badly was I wounded?"

"You've lost your left eye. And they had to cut off your right arm at the elbow."

Oh, Powers of Aer. A cripple. A left-hander, someone not worthy to lead. Not a fitting suitor, not a fitting warrior, not a fitting Nebesti. A man better killed for mercy than left alive to be the laughingstock of women and a practice dummy for spears.

"It seems I've paid handsomely to prove my worth to your father," Parfyon growled.

She laughed at him.

It was the medicine he needed.

He grabbed her shoulder with his one good hand, and she cried out from the unexpected force. Shocked for a moment at his own vehemence, he let go, but she fell down hard. This was no longer the playful courtship of a

463

warlord and his future bride. He had hurt her, and the ease with which he had done it frightened him. More to distract himself than anything, he spoke quickly and loudly.

"You Dolgoruki have a great deal to learn about strength and valor. I will make you my wife, Alienne, whether you prefer a man whole or not. You and I are made to be one. Your father will not stand in my way. I will destroy him. And do you know where I will destroy him? On the stage of the Veche. I will turn the Veche to myself, and it will be your father who shares the hospitality of this room after me. When I am knyaz."

She raised herself with an effort. He had hurt her more than he intended, but to his joy he saw how truly Nebesti she was: no pain showed in her eyes, only determination, sharp as the short-sword every Nebesti woman wielded with pride. She approached Parfyon and pushed him back against the bed with both arms, holding him down to assert her control. It excited him more than he expected.

"Do it, Parfyon," she whispered, her eyes nearly all furious whites. "The day that my father takes your place in this room, I will be your wife." She pushed off his chest and stalked to the door, slapping it three times with her open palm. The five locks groaned in unison, and a heavy chain retracted from the other side. The door swung open. Two armored guards escorted her out. The door slammed behind her, and they barred it again.

CHAPTER 9
THE BUKAVACH

Voran stood at the place where it had all begun, between the two drum-hills—one crowned in aspen, the other in birch. Here, Voran had first met Lyna, had first walked the perilous nether-space of the Lows of Aer, had first felt the fire of love for the Heights that he thought would last forever. Here, he hoped to see a door, an intersection of worlds, a way to speak to Lyna the Sirin, his soul-bond. But the Lows of Aer were shut to him. There was nothing, not the slightest note of the ineffable music of the other realms.

An ache rose inside him, inscribing a fire-rimmed hole in his chest. Lyna's crying face occluded all other memories. He had neglected that love; he had not spoken to Lyna in years. Would she ever speak to him again? He had to try to reach her, now especially. He had not upheld his end of their love. He had been so foolish and ungrateful, expecting Lyna to do nothing but give, give, give from her eternal stores of love. Only now, he realized the hard truth. Whatever overflowing love he had felt for Lyna, for the Heights, even for Adonais at the beginning—all that was a mere seed. It was for him to nurture the seed, to plant it, to protect it. That he had not done.

Now, he reaped no harvest.

It *is* my fault, he thought, thinking of the Sirin of fire and her strange prophecy. There was little compunction in the thought. There was hardly any emotion at all in the thought. It was a mere reflection of reality.

He kept walking, passing through the shadow between the hills onto the slight dip in the road before it began to climb sharply into the Vasyllian ranges. Here, five years ago, he had first seen the stone wall between Vasyllia and the rest of the world.

It stood before him now, looking like a discarded snakeskin. There didn't seem to be anyone guarding it. The lone turret was unlit by torches. Voran suspected that the silence was deceptive. Surely there would be anxious eyes watching for any breech of the wall. He had heard of terrible things happening to people who tried. But there had to be a way in.

Voran assumed that the wall was intended as much to keep the Vasylli and Gumiren *in* as keep everyone else *out*. Perhaps it followed that if the Gumir soldier who was tortured by Novvik had gotten out, maybe there was a way in?

Something in Voran's peripheral vision caught his attention. He turned to the right. A tall aspen just off the side of the road bent awkwardly in its middle. The twisted branches in the upper half of the tree had only just sprouted with the translucent green of early spring. The middle branches were bare, either because they lagged behind the ones above them, or...

As he approached, a chill passed down Voran's back. There was something wrong with the aspen. Its lowest branches were not brown, but black. They glimmered, as though they were covered with slime. He touched the black stuff and a shock of pain ran up and down his arm like a lightning strike. That was nothing natural. The tree was cursed.

He looked deeper into the grove of aspens. The black slime was in patches on all the trees. Even the dead stumps of old, collapsed trees were polluted with the stuff. This was the Raven's work, Voran was sure of it.

He unstoppered his flask and let a few drops of Living Water fall on the blackened branches. Nothing happened. Seized with a sense of dread, Voran poured a few more. Was it his imagination, or did the slime pull back a little, leaving only the brown of old wood? He poured a few more, then a few more. Yes, surely the tree was getting better.

He tipped the flask over again, and... nothing came out. He was out of Living Water.

It was always like this. Every time he approached Vasyllia, the Living Water stopped flowing. Only when he walked away, back into the horrors of war, did it fill up again. Voran sighed, his exhaustion so deep it creaked inside his bones.

There was nothing else he could do today. He found a tree moderately free of the slime, and sat down at its roots, leaning against the trunk. Now, all he could do was wait for nightfall and blessed sleep.

He woke up to a world shrouded in fog. It slithered by him like an engorged snake, churning over the top of the wall like a slow waterfall. Voran shuddered from both cold and unease.

Voran walked along the wall as it rose into the Nebesti side of the Vasylli Mountains. Soon the pine wood gave way to shorter shrubs. The deciduous trees disappeared entirely. The higher he went, the shorter the trees, until he reached a point where loose rock replaced greenery entirely. It had taken most of the morning to reach this height.

He looked back the way he had come. The wall—a mass of dun rock twice the height of the tallest conifers—curved downward and into the woods. Its surface was as smooth as metal. Either it was coated with something or filed down somehow—or even magicked—but not a single individual stone was visible. Now, it looked like a whole snake, not merely its skin. In the midst of the fog, it seemed to move down the mountain, crushing the earth as it slithered over it.

The sight left him with a queasy feeling in the pit of his stomach. He turned away from it and followed the valley's incline toward a peak about an hour's walk ahead. Before he reached it, he stopped, crouched to the rocky floor, and lowered his head only inches away from a small pile of rocks. It was darker than the surrounding scree. Voran smelled it.

Scent markings. A large cat, maybe even a snow leopard. Strange. The elusive cats rarely came this far down from the peaks where they lived.

The rest of that day, he climbed steadily up toward the peak. He saw no more signs of any animals. At the point where there was nowhere else to go but straight up, Voran turned back again and examined the valley, now extending far below him. Back at the place where he had left the woods, something twitched.

It was large, possibly a bear, though it moved strangely for a bear. It was white. A white bear? Impossible. No white bears lived anywhere near Vasyllia. They were far Steppeland creatures. Then it moved again. It was definitely a white bear, though now it walked on its hind legs. Voran's curiosity got the better of him. This he had to see. An old hunger nagged at him— the joy of the hunt. Killing a white bear—that would be something. Food for days, at the very least. He had heard from travelers that the meat of the white bear was unusually dense and rich, giving lasting endurance to a man ranging the wilds.

He went back the way he had come, cursing the open ground that wouldn't hide him from the animals. As soon as he entered the cover of the fir trees, he saw it—a fresh patty of bear dung. He ran faster, careful to avoid branches and fallen pinecones. His nose itched as the mist tickled it.

He was wet through, but not cold. The idea of hunting such quarry warmed him, as did the run.

A swamp-scented breeze met him head-on. He stopped. That was wrong. There was no swamp in this part of the mountain range. The nearest was at least ten miles away.

He crested a ridge and stopped in his tracks. A pool of water, fetid and black, lay in a place where there should have been an aspen grove. The aspens had been torn to shreds, as though a giant child had had a tantrum. Their ruin ringed the edge of the pool. For some reason, the sight made Voran's heart race with terror.

Then he understood why. Aspens and birches were Adonais's trees. There was something...premeditated in the manner of their destruction. As though their death were being offered as a sacrifice to a dark Power.

Sacrifice. *Wait. Is that blood?*

The ruined aspens were spattered in regular intervals. The blood was very fresh. His eyes followed it around the pool until they hit white. Fur. More red. What had been the white bear was now a twisted carcass. *That was quick*, he thought. What can kill a white bear that fast?

A noise exploded around him. It was like a hundred mallets striking wood. It fell silent again. Did the black waters shift? And what were those two strange, twisted rocks in the middle of the pool?

They moved. They were not rocks. They were *horns*.

Voran exclaimed aloud. A Bukavach.

"What let *you* in?" he cried. Bukavachei were creatures that haunted the outer reaches of the Lows of Aer, not the level of Earth. So either someone had sent it into earth to wreak havoc, or... Were the walls between the world starting to fade? The thought terrified him even more than the Bukavach.

Two lizard-like eyes focused on him, and he felt a sucking sensation in the pit of his stomach. *Don't look at the eyes.* He had forgotten. The last time he saw a Bukavach, it had almost eaten him. That was fifteen years ago, at least.

The Bukavach's scaly head swayed right and left on its snaky neck. It continued to rise up out of the water, rearing on its two hind legs. The four forelegs were tipped with jagged claws. Its mouth was ringed with three layers of teeth that cut like knives at every facet. It looked like a sickening amalgam of a chameleon, an ibex, and a pike. Its horns were gnarled, like old tree roots, and now their black points stared at him like eyes. The Bukavach jumped at Voran and made that mallet-noise again.

Voran slipped under its massive body as it tried to land on him. As it fell, Voran twisted to the side and pushed himself onto already running feet.

There was no way of beating a Bukavach. Especially not without a sword. He ran.

It ran after him. Entire trees splintered and glanced off the ridges on its back as though they were no more than stalks of wheat. He had forgotten how fast they were. Its swamp-smell inundated him again, and he ducked just as its horn lunged forward. He grabbed the trunk of an oak, and spun around, switching direction in mid-stride. It ran past him, its surprise evident in the ruckus of mallet-noises and exploding trees.

I'm not going to make it this time, he thought. Last time, the landscape was in his favor. He had ducked into a cave and hidden in a passageway that was only large enough for small animals. But here, there was nothing but mountain forest for miles. Voran knew this land. He had no chance.

The Bukavach's pant grew louder behind him. It was gaining fast. Voran stopped, and turned to face it, pulling out his hunting-knife. He may as well meet his death face-on. *By the Heights.* It was a very ugly face.

An arrow flicked past his left ear, barely making a sound. Voran fell on the ground and rolled over his shoulder. As he came up on his knees, he froze in place. Three more arrows flicked past him. Each one hit the Bukavach exactly where it needed—one in each eye, one in the ridge above the eyes, and one between the clavicle and the neck. Five more arrows followed, with deadly precision. The monster rattled and collapsed on the ground, thrashing about and shredding swathes of forest in its death throes. Behind it, a path of destruction stretched nearly all the way back to the wall.

It took the monster at least fifteen minutes to die. Voran watched it from behind a downed oak that had been pulled up by its roots. The old wood smelled of fresh earth and wet leaves. A pleasant alternative to the swamp-smell of the Bukavach.

As its thrashing was reduced to occasional twitches, Voran put his knife in his left hand and reached for his sword, forgetting for a moment that it was not there. That he had not carried it for years.

Focus! What's wrong with you?

Breathing out fully, he stilled himself, waiting for his heart to slow before breathing in again. It sharpened his hearing. He heard them padding behind him. Four sets of feet, very quiet. Excellent woodsmen. Definitely human.

They came out from behind the trees. For a moment, Voran thought that they were half-man, half-beast changers. Two of them looked like bears walking upright, two of them wolves. Then he realized they were men wearing full-sized furs. The heads of the dead animals reached over their heads like hoods, so that the hunters' faces were partially obscured by fangs.

One of them had matted black hair and an untrimmed beard reaching to a dull iron belt buckle. Two others had shaved their chins, but left the mustaches to grow long, dropping down past oversized Adam's apples. The fourth's face was barely visible in the shadows. Three of them held nocked bows. The fourth...With a surge of interest, Voran realized she was a woman. They all had dark skin, darker even than Gumiren, but her skin was so dark, it could almost be black. She held a long, curving knife.

"Did you summon it? Are you a mage?" asked one of the men. His accent was strange. Tiverni? Bskavi? Or was that Karila?

Voran shook his head. "I am a hunter. The white bear, over there." He pointed back toward the black pool, where the carcass of the white bear lay. "The Bukavach got there first."

The dark-skinned woman scoffed. "A hunter? Where is your bow?"

Voran showed her his knife. She laughed. "A mad hunter, then."

The three archers pulled back their strings tighter. Voran raised his other hand.

"Let me explain."

"Later," said the largest of the men, the one with the beard. "Hunter or no hunter, you're a big one, aren't you? You'll do just fine. Come quietly or come loudly, your choice. Be grateful you still have a choice."

Slavers. Of all the rotten luck... The realization curdled his stomach. Still, something about them didn't quite smell right. They looked and carried themselves nothing like slavers. Something tugged in the corner of his memory. There was something familiar about these slavers.

"I will come quietly," Voran said.

CHAPTER 10
THE CHILDREN OF THE PRIEST-KING

Antomír rushed back to town from the cavern with the Living Water, Veles barely keeping up behind him. It was already passing high noon, and the spring festivities were reaching a boiling point. Antomír joined the main path to Ghavan Town from a dirt road that ran through tall alders and birches. By now, hundreds of bird-shaped breads hung from every tree. Some of them even had small bells attached to the wings, and Ghavan's frequent sea-gusts made the path ring with chimes of different timbres. The breads almost looked like living birds. Of course, that was the point. The more breads the women baked—and the more realistic they were—the faster spring would come. Or so said the old Vasylli tradition.

No sooner had Antomír entered the village proper than he was pelted from all sides. First, it was the heckling—

"Antomír, Antomír! Tell us, are your undergarments truly stitched with gold?"

"Boy! Is that a bull following you, or a man? Not strong enough to take care of yourself, eh?"

"I've heard that all you eat is fine goat livers spiced with saffron! Is that true? What's wrong with good rye bread?"

—Then he was pelted with rye bread, some of which was bird-shaped.

Antomír sensed Veles simmering behind him like a pot about to boil, but he only laughed. It was traditional, after all. The only day in the year that Ghavanites allowed themselves the luxury of insulting the family of their Dar. They would have willingly heckled the Dar himself. But Mirnían had hardly left Lebía's side these past weeks. The thought left a bitter taste in Antomír's mouth, especially as he realized that he had just named his own father "Mirnían" in his thoughts, not "Father."

But he was not going to let his thoughts carry him there. Catching a particularly large hunk of rye with a single hand, he threw it back at the old fisherman who had hurled it, and it landed square on the man's chest, knocking his breath out. The crowd—mostly men at this point of the day, the women still at work baking the pies for the evening feast to be held under the shade of the Covenant Tree—roared their approval. Veles subsided, and Antomír walked on.

The songs continued to pulse in his memory even after he walked through the silent wall of cypress trees that marked the beginning of the Dar's estate. Their wild music buoyed him forward, though the closer he came to the white stone house, the more dread pushed back at him, encouraging him to return to the comforting unruliness of the people in the village. But he pushed on, fingering the fresh bunches of lavender at his hip. Their smell reminded him of his mother in better days, when her face was not so flushed, when her voice was not so languid.

Inside, all sound died. His every step was muffled, as though even the rushes on the ground were taking care not to disturb Lebía. The air had long ceased moving, the windows being boarded up for fear of moving air and its insidious effect on the already sick. Secretly, Antomír thought that a bit of fresh air would do Mama a world of good, but there was no arguing against Ghavanite superstitions concerning the fatality of moving air. The door to her room looked black in the light of the two candles—only two lit, out of twenty! *I'll have to have a word with the servants about that.* He hated how everything seemed to presage Mama's death even before it happened. Why had Father taken this approach? Why would he not embrace the possibility of her improvement?

In his mind's eye, he saw the healed fawn cavorting in the cave. If Father had no hope left, Antomír would provide it. She would be better, now that the Living Water was found. He pushed the door open with a shaking hand.

The smell struck him like a slap in the face. Stale air, sickness, sweat. The smell of impending death. He nearly retched.

"Is that you, Antomír?" Lebía lifted her head slightly. Her face was white except for two livid spots on each cheek.

"I've brought you lavender, Mama," he said, trying to make his voice light. It cracked instead.

"I knew you would," she whispered and fell back against the cushions, apparently exhausted even by such an exertion.

He tied the over-sleeves of his kaftan behind his back and rolled up the sleeves of his undershirt. The rest was so automatic as to require no thought at all. His hands poured the water boiling on the hearth into a clay pot, crushed the lavender, stirred in the necessary herbs and oils, soaked the liquid into long strips of muslin. His mind invented visions of his mother, cheeks pink (not red), sitting on a flower-strewn blanket on the pebbled beach of their private cove, eating strawberries that he had picked himself.

"I have some wonderful news, Mama," he said as he applied the warm rags to her forehead, her upper arms, and her ankles. "Veles and I wandered into some of the densest forests, downslope of the central hillock. You know, where the blackberries grow the fattest."

"I don't remember, dear one." A week ago, there would have been such wistfulness in her voice for blackberries! But now, her tone was flat and uninflected.

"Well, never mind. I'll take you there soon. Especially after you've heard what I found."

"You shouldn't burden your mother with your enthusiasm, Antomír," said another voice, behind him. At the first moment, Antomír didn't recognize his own father's voice, it was so frigid with regret, fear, and pain.

"Father, I did not hear you come in." Antomír approached his father and fell to one knee, as was customary. His father did *not* place his hand on Antomír's head.

"Antomír. Whatever you think you found, you should not bother your mother about it. Tell me, instead." Mirnían pulled Antomír by his arm with more insistence than he had shown in any action for the last several years. Antomír was annoyed, but a sliver of fear occluded his irritation. Something was very wrong. Father never used physical force against him, not even when he was a child.

By now, the entire village feasted in the center of town under the Covenant Tree. All the houses were eerily calm. Not quiet, exactly. Much of the surrounding nature, finally free of the boisterous festiveness of the humans, was beginning to venture out. Antomír saw two foxes run between the houses, followed by a pup no larger than a day-old kitten. Dragonflies cavorted by the hundreds, filtering the fading daylight through their wings to make a dazzling display of shimmering colors. A soft rustling filled the gaps of silence between the occasional muffled cheers coming in waves from the feast. Antomír imagined that the rustling might be the sound of plants growing.

Everywhere, life was boisterous. And why shouldn't it be? Now he knew—this isle was fed by a source of Living Water. The very soil must be saturated with it. The animals' food must be laced with it. The strange healthfulness of Ghavan's population must be entirely due to it.

Except for Mama.

Now that Antomír thought of it, he couldn't recall anyone falling to her kind of sickness. When people died—there were precious few deaths on Ghavan, as it was—they simply faded into their sleep. There were no physicians on Ghavan. So what was wrong with Mama Lebía?

For the first time, Antomír had a nagging doubt: would Living Water be able to save her, if it was already present in their drink, their food, the very air they breathed? With a shudder, he remembered his own family history, how Aglaia, his grandmother, fell into a strange, fading kind of illness that no physician could understand, let alone cure. Was there something wrong with their bloodline?

Mirnían led Antomír through a grove of young cherries. Most were still bare of blossoms, but several had exploded in clouds of pink and seemed to taunt the nakedness of their slower brothers.

"I want you to tell me what you saw, Antomír," said Mirnían as they walked through the trees.

"Father, is this some kind of a test? Why do I think you already know what I'm going to say?"

Mirnían's smile was rueful, but genuine.

"It's hard for young people to understand the intuition of their parents. Intuition is a very powerful thing."

"Then why are you taking me so far away from home? Couldn't you just scold me at home and sent me on to the feast?"

"I want you to say aloud what you wanted to tell your mother, but to Otar Yustav. I think the conversation will be…illuminating. Though I have an inkling that you will not like the way it goes."

Otar Yustav? Why? Antomír had never felt comfortable around the new priest. Otar Svetlomír he had loved, but not his replacement. What was it about him? Was it his small size? He was very strong, no doubt about it. No, it was his almost martial eagerness. Like he was waiting for the first opportunity to rush into battle against anyone and everyone. It didn't fit the Ghavanite way of life.

"You need not worry that anything you say will be spread about,

Antomír," said Mirnían. Antomír, who had been lost in his thoughts, was surprised to see the intense and sorrowful expression on his father's face.

"You will find this place even more secret than my house, young prince." Otar Yustav materialized as though out of nowhere. He pointed at two recently sawed-off tree trunks, perfect for resting and looking up at the cherry blossoms. "I come here myself often, and the favored of my heart-children know to find me here when they are especially pained or lonely or afraid."

Antomír awkwardly took the priest's blessing. He was happy for the opportunity to do something definite with his hands. They always felt big and fuzzy in uncomfortable situations.

"No, Father," said Antomír, not even sure whether he should address his father or the priest. "I would never imagine that you would betray my confidence."

"Sit, young Antomír," said Otar Yustav. It was kindly said, but the edge of a military commander's bark was palpable. Antomír sat, as did Mirnían, but Otar Yustav remained standing, back straight as a riverboat's mast. Antomír began to feel hemmed in. He shrugged his shoulders, trying to shake off the discomfort.

"Otar." Antomír cleared his throat loudly, still not sure whom to address. "I found a cave in the hills. There's a pool of Living Water there. You can imagine my joy at the discovery. Now we can save Mama." The enthusiasm he had felt then, now sapped of energy, sounded childish to his own ears.

Otar Yustav looked at Mirnían, the worry evident in the sharp angle of his eyebrows. Mirnían nodded, encouraging.

"Antomír, how did... how did you find this cave? Was there anything strange about it? Any odd circumstances that preceded your finding it?"

How did he know?

"Well, yes. There were vila in the forest immediately before." He wanted to continue, explaining to them about the strange dark Sirin who had saved him, but something stopped him.

"Vila?" Mirnían scoffed. "Impossible. The walls protecting Ghavan Isle—"

"Are cracking." Otar Yustav interrupted him.

"What?" said father and son together.

"I've seen it in small ways here and there. A rose blooming in the middle of a snowdrift a month ago. The smell of Bukavach on the air, so faint I thought it was simply my imagination..." He trailed off, thinking. "But that is a larger problem than we can solve now." He looked at Mirnían with significance, and to Antomír's shock, his father actually blushed. *What was that about?*

"Antomír," Otar Yustav continued. "The cave you speak of has been hidden behind the same wall of protection that guards the rest of Ghavan. And I think you can guess why. You cannot use the Living Water in the way that you want, to heal your mother."

Antomír's cheeks grew warmer. Why was Father not standing up for him? There was also something else, and its implication made Antomír simmer.

"Why not?" asked Antomír, his inflection rising. "If it is part of Adonais's gift to us on Ghavan, why can't we use it?" Antomír tried to reel himself back in, but he felt like a snowball gathering speed as it fell down a mountain.

"Highness, I will not insult you with platitudes, but I will tell you the truth. We do not fully understand the nature of Living Water. All we know is that wherever Adonais's blessing abides, the Water is present. We also know—and you may trust me on this, I have made extensive study—that taking it for selfish use is far worse than not using it at all."

"Selfish?" was all that Antomír could manage. He felt like a child being held accountable for something he did not do. He felt as though they considered him guilty for his mother's illness.

"I know you are only considering her benefit. But there is much you do not know. I ask you to listen with an open mind."

Antomír forced himself to take a deep breath, though he could not look at Otar Yustav's face. He stared at the ground instead. There was a fascinating bit of dirt that he proceeded to examine as Otar Yustav began, in his "sermon voice."

"There are only two examples in known history where a land or a people were openly protected by a Power of the Heights. Vasyllia is the obvious one, the one everyone knows. But there was another. Of all the legends to come from the far Eastern lands, only one persists through all the known ages of our own Three Lands. It concerns a mythical kingdom established by a brother of Lassar of Blessed Memory, a man foolish enough to try to usurp his brother's throne. He was banished not only by powers of men, but by the Sirin themselves, sent into a desert country beyond the Steppes to die alone. There he was taken in by a strange people. Black as pitch was their skin, it is said, and they were the height of two men standing on each other's shoulders. Some say they rode white bears, some say they transformed into bears when angry. It is not very clear…"

"Please, Otar. The moral of the story." Mirnían said. Yustav inclined his head.

"The important thing is this. This brother of Lassar (his name is lost, but he is known in the legends as the Priest-King) found that these people were the protectors of a fountain of youth whose water, if drunk thrice at specific intervals and accompanied with certain rites and sacrifices, gave a person the continuation of young life for hundreds of years. But there were strict conditions to the drinking of the water, kept scrupulously by these people, for which reason their memory-history reached far beyond what any other people could boast.

"The brother of Lassar married a high lady of theirs, and they made him their king after some kind of divine revelation (the details are hazy at best). He had three sons, two of whom married local girls. The third son was a sickly thing, barely alive when born. He was his mother's favorite, as the Heights would have it.

"This lady was a warrior, a leader, respected by all for her merits, not her birth (rights of inheritance were unknown among these people). But her sickly infant took the life-joy from her, and she faded along with the child. Finally, she could not stop herself. She took the boy and bathed him in the fountain of youth at an unprescribed time, in a forbidden way. The baby died instantly, and the lady was struck mad."

Antomír was so enthralled by the tale, that for a moment, he forgot to be angry at Otar Yustav. Then he remembered his mother, and his mood darkened again.

"An interesting story," Antomír said, keeping his tone light. "But there are no such restrictions placed on this Living Water, are there?"

"Oh, but there are, Antomír." It was not Yustav speaking. It was another voice, distant and shimmering. It sounded like rain illumined by a sudden burst of sun. Antomír knew that voice, and his heart unwillingly jumped at the unexpectedness of it.

"Otar Svetlomír?" It could not be. He was dead these three years.

The voice came from a spring about ten steps away from where they sat. Antomír ran toward it, not knowing what he should be looking for.

"Young Antomír, it is here," said Otar Yustav, pointing at a round stone at the fountainhead of the spring bubbling from beneath the ground, joyfully foaming. In the midst of the churn, Mirnían could just barely glimpse the shape of a beard, two eyes, and a beak-nose, immediately recognizable.

"Otar, you are dead!"

"Quite," said Otar Svetlomír, his smile still visible, even in the bubbling spring. "But death is not what I thought. It is more a change of place than an end of life. The land of the dead—at least, this part of it—is an unexpectedly beautiful place. And the walls between Ghavan and this land are thin at all times. Especially now. But that is not material. What you must know is that we Ghavanites were bound by the hands of the Pilgrim himself. He foretold that the Living Water would flow here. He also made it clear that it was not to be touched. Not by human hands. At the cost of losing the protection of Covenant."

"What, again?" Antomír exploded in anger. "Do not, do not! Why must it always be so? Why cannot Adonais be a reasonable god?"

"Peace, Antomír," said Mirnían, but his eyes were full of tears. "I used to think as you do. I used to be so full of anger, so ready to rail against the unjust Powers who refuse to fix all our problems for us. It does not do, my boy."

"You ask the wrong questions," said Otar Svetlomír. "They distract you from the more pressing question. Are we intended to remain in Ghavan forever? Or is it a resting-place for us to gather strength before the great ordeal?"

Antomír had often asked himself the same question.

"You saw the vila, did you not?" said Otar Svetlomír. "For those evil creatures to come so close to Ghavan... The walls between the Realms are shaking. The Raven must have accessed some source of great power in Vasyllia. Something that, I fear, will lead to a war the likes of which we have never seen in these Three Lands. There will be cataclysmic changes, even on Ghavan. The Living Water was given us for our time of preparation. But soon, it will be time to act."

"So no matter what, I must trust in the word of a Pilgrim I have never seen, and not try to use the Living Water to save my own dying Mama?" Antomír's voice came out as barely a croak. There was bile in his mouth.

No one answered.

CHAPTER 11
A PROPHECY OF GIANTS

In a tribe of eagle hunters legendary for their skill at killing wolves, Khaidu became the best. Arelat and Etchigu were still chief hunters, but the greatest number of kills belonged to the white-headed eagle and the idiot girl. Etchigu, Mamai, and nearly all Khaidu's brothers were overjoyed at her successes. She could hardly believe it herself.

On an especially clear day, when the wind was only a caress on the cheek, not a slap in the face, she even thought that she could feel her legs a little more than usual.

The now nightly conversations with Sabíana were an even greater source of joy. After so much time of enforced silence, it was a drink of cold water through a parched throat. Khaidu began to live only for the hunt and for the night. When she remembered her desire for the hard death of the Steppe, it almost seemed comical. Sabíana was still cantankerous, but Khaidu found it easier by the night to incline her to conversation. She told Khaidu many things of the world she had abandoned. Of Voran, the beloved warrior she had not seen in twenty years. Of Vasyllia, its mountains and forests. Of the singular beauty of a city carved out of the mountains.

Even during the day, Khaidu relived these conversations so clearly that she sometimes forgot that she was still a half-broken creature that had no place in the horse-clan of Mamai jani-Beg.

A morning about two weeks after she had caught the eagle, Khaidu sat on the hard ground near Mamai's yurt while everyone else rushed by her, living their lives at the feverish pace of horse-breeders. She was just about to fall asleep when a knocking sound jarred her out of her torpor. She had almost forgotten what time of day it was.

A grey, hooded figure danced in and out of the yurts. His features were shadowed, and in any case, he moved so frenetically, jutting back and forth in an almost unnatural motion, that she couldn't have seen his face if she tried. In his left hand, he held a well-worn wooden board—more grey than brown—while his right flailed about with a short stick that sometimes struck the board in a regular rhythm, and sometimes seemed to float in the air, as though drawing esoteric charms in the Steppe-air.

Everyone in the vicinity stopped. Some even fell on their knees, with a select few prostrating themselves with their faces to the grass, whispering ancient words of enchantment into the earth of Steppe-mother. For a few minutes, there were no sounds other than the rat-a-tat...rat-a-tat of the stick and the hiss of the wind through the grass. Khaidu closed her eyes in pleasure at the spectacle.

"Poor old Guyuk," said Etchigu beside her. He and his two salty teas had materialized by her side more and more rarely the last few days. Khaidu thought about being resentful for a moment, but the buttery smell was too much. She turned her face to him. He was framed by the morning sun, his features inscrutable. She squinted, and he laughed.

"I love that face that you make," he said, sitting down next to her. The grey figure had moved far away enough that his sound was only the distant knocking of a woodpecker. "Not only when you look in the sun, you know. Whenever you're deep in thought, you have that face. Very *you*."

He sighed and looked at her intently, as though trying to gauge her thoughts. She smiled, as though daring him to try. He shook his head wryly.

"You're very thoughtful lately, you know. Is it the eagle? Has she bewitched you?"

Khaidu said nothing, but she took the tea when he offered it. It was even better than usual.

"T-t-tchigu," she said. "Y-y-u know th-th-the st-t-try of Kw-kw-kw..." She gave up in a huff, the effort leaving her breathless.

He sat staring at his tea in silence. She knew that expression. He was piecing together what she was trying to say. He was the only one who ever did that.

"Kw...Wait... do you mean the old story of the Queen Who Walks the Skies?"

How was he always so exact in his guesses? She smiled and nodded.

"Why do you want to hear that old story? It's a sad one."

"B-b-but-t-t... Un-un-nnnown..."

"Oh, yes. She leads us to the Unknown Father. But that's the only good part of the story."

She cocked her head at him, feeling her face twist into that same expression that he apparently liked so much, even before she could stop it.

"No, I'm not surprised you don't remember that part. It's not often spoken of. The coming of the Queen is a dark time. Yes, she leads us to the one we seek, but that way is a twisty one, thorny and rocky. Many die. It starts, apparently, with the earth opening up in great rents, and giants made of rock coming up from the depths to destroy all in their path."

"H-h-horrible."

"Yes. Although I often think about how it would be quite a thing to see the day when we find the Unknown Father, I'm content to wait. After the Dark Father, I don't want any more divine monsters wreaking havoc in my world."

You may not have much of a choice, dear brother, she thought, thinking of Sabíana and wondering if her coming would bring calamity down on them. But she said nothing.

※

"Tell me, Khaidu," said Sabíana that night. "Why does that old man in the grey robes beat a board with a stick three times a day? And why does everyone stop and listen to him?"

"We're not listening to *him*," Khaidu said, laughing. "It's a moment of remembrance. Surely you have those."

Sabíana's look was enough to prove the opposite.

"Well, the morning call is to remember the creation of the world from the dark waters. The midday call is a reminder to always seek the Unknown Father. The evening call is a remembrance of death, which will come to claim us all, until we find Him."

"He will deliver you from death?"

Khaidu nodded.

"The ritual dancing, the songs before and after meals—is that part of the same remembrance?"

"You don't know much, do you? No, the dancing is to ward off dark spirits. The songs are blessings."

"You do have a very regimented life, don't you?" Sabíana said it with detachment, like a boy might observe an anthill. The now usual anger came bubbling back up inside Khaidu.

"That's not it at all! I'm just a girl, I can't explain it well. It's just. Life is hard, you know? There are things out there that are always trying to kill us. All these things we do—it's a way of putting some order into the world. So every Gumir, every Gumira knows what their particular place and duty is. To shirk duty is to invite death. And we don't like shirkers."

This she said darkly, thinking again of Sabíana's abandonment of Vasyllia. Judging by the heightened color in Sabíana's cheek, she understood, but did not rise to the bait.

"So what is *your* place in such a structured world?" asked Sabíana.

Khaidu felt as though Sabíana had struck her in the gut. Sabíana stared at her intently, not backing down from the question.

"I... without you..." Khaidu felt the shame hot and red, smudging over her face. Sabíana had the sense to look abashed at that.

"I'm sorry. That was cruel. But maybe now you'll understand, at least a little, why I wanted to escape."

"NO!" Khaidu exploded, her shame now fueling her anger. "It is not the same. I have no place...*had* no place until now. Gumiren usually kill those who have no place. Only Mamai... But you! You had a place. You had thousands depending on you. And you abandoned them all. If I had a real purpose, I would do it until it killed me. And the place of the queen is sacred. Everyone knows that. To abandon a sacred duty... there are no words for that abomination."

Sabíana was white, but not with anger. She looked genuinely afraid.

"What are you?" she said, speaking somehow beyond Khaidu. "Can you read my thoughts? Stop echoing the pain that jabs at me with every continued second of existence."

"I'm sorry, I didn't..."

Something tingled in the air, a sense of potential, possibility. Khaidu suddenly was overflowing with love for Sabíana, so much that she wanted to cradle her in her arms and rock her to sleep.

"My lady," she said, in a tone foreign to her own ears. "You have a chance to change all that now. I don't think it's an accident that you are here. I believe you are the Queen Who Walks the Skies. I believe that your flight— yes, though it was a cowardly thing to do—is the first chance you've had in years to take charge of your fate. You've been pushed around too long. Accept it. Do what you were called to do. Guide *us*." *Even if the giants come, and the world tears itself apart. I am ready.*

Sabíana's breath slowed, and she looked at Khaidu for a long time.

"I don't know what to do, Khaidu. I don't think you do, either."
"No, I don't. But I can help you."
"No one can help me. I've died, don't you see?"
"What? What do you mean you've died?"
But she could get no more out of Sabíana that night.

CHAPTER 12
THE VECHE BELL TOLLS

For weeks, Parfyon battled with dreams as though they were living enemies. Every morning he would wake with no memory of any images, only vague emotions, like echoes, but sleeping exhausted him even more than staying awake. In his waking hours, the physical pain nagged him constantly. But the reality of his crippled state being permanent was far worse.

Still, he waited patiently. Nothing happened for weeks. In the early mornings, he thought the single bell in the center of the Veche square softly chimed from the wind, but it was probably his imagination. The clapper was far too heavy to be moved by a breeze.

Most of the time, he wiled away the hours by listening to the prattle of the people milling about Veche Square. He heard an endless litany of woes concerning a lack of edible fish. Men grumbled about weather, girls about the lack of *real* men, children about the unfairness of their parents. No one seemed to even whisper about the preternaturally quick rise of New Nebesta. Parfyon found that disturbing.

He had decided on a course of action. Ulik's strange behavior over the last months before his death had been generally noticed by the warriors. He thought he might be able to convince a few other warriors that Ulik had been captured, not by Tiverna, but Vasyllia. If he could do that, the lie would be easy: Yarpolk had sold Nebesta out to save his only son, and now if Yarpolk became knyaz, he would ally with Vasyllia as payment. It was not entirely implausible, but he would have to be very convincing.

In the meantime, Parfyon rotted away in prison, unable to try out his lies on anyone. The guards posted at his door were taciturn types. They were changed once a day, and they were never the same twice. Yarpolk was taking no chances.

One morning, Parfyon finally heard what he had been dreading—the insistent clanging of the Veche bell. The city was soon awash in streams of conversation, the noise a rising flood as more and more rivulets of rumor and gossip flowed in, all of them paling compared to the insistent, angry clang of the Veche bell. Each strike of the great clapper beat into Parfyon's head, taunting him with his impotence. He climbed up on the one small table in the room to look through the barred window, which looked out directly onto Veche Square, giving him an excellent, almost bird's eye view of the proceedings.

Veche Square seemed filled with every conceivable Nebesti social rank crowding the trampled red clay. To Parfyon's left, the rich merchants' hats rivaled the towers of the largest building in Veche square—the old wooden temple to Adonais with its five domes. To Parfyon's right, tight-knit pockets of nobles shone in the sunlight, the gold of their earrings and the jewels sewed into their kaftans a fitting rival to the gilding and red tiles of the new towers marking the four corners of the square.

Even the blacksmiths, tanners, and carpenters, who rarely came out for the nonsense of politics, stood together at the far end of the square, leaning against Nebesta's pitch-soaked new wooden wall, directly across from Parfyon. They were like a range of mountain-men garbed in the artisanal black, faces smeared in unwashed beards. In them, Parfyon hoped to have allies. They hated landed gentry, considering them lily-handed milksops. But how was Parfyon supposed to inspire anyone to side with him if all he could do was stew in his own frustration inside a luxurious prison cell?

He ran to the door and pounded on it, shouting. The chain pulled back, the locks unbolted, and a young warrior, face red with murder, lunged at Parfyon with a knife.

"Down, dog!" He growled, trying to kick him for good measure.

Parfyon spit in his face. It distracted the young warrior long enough to give Parfyon the time he needed. Before the guard knew what had happened, Parfyon twisted the knife from his grip, kicked his knee inward and pushed him down. Then he jumped on him, pinning him down with his body. The tip of the knife barely pricked the space between the bones of the guard's neck.

"Didn't expect that from a one-handed man, did you?" he hissed in the guard's ear.

The other guards rushed in, swords-first.

"If you move," Parfyon shouted, "I'll butcher him like a pig."

Though armed and tense, they stood their ground. This was his one chance. He would have to weave his words carefully.

"You are true Nebesti," he said, breathing heavily. "You are loyal to the sword and to the office of knyaz. But you are being betrayed to Vasyllia."

Their expressions did not so much as flinch. Parfyon cursed silently.

"Are you that stupid? Didn't you wonder at how strange Ulik was acting during the campaign? Yarpolk has lied to you. Ulik was tortured not by a Tiverna princeling. I had it from the lips of the fair Alienne herself. Ulik was tortured by the Gumiren in Vasyllia. Yarpolk bought him back from them by promising an alliance with Vasyllia. Why do you think he is calling Veche now? He is to be made knyaz, of course. As soon as he takes the oath, he will cement alliance between great Nebesta and that filth, those traitors who burned our cities. And you're just going to sit back and take it, aren't you?"

One of the guards sheathed his sword and yanked off his Kolontari helmet with its monstrous facemask. Underneath, Parfyon recognized one of his own division, a young commoner-soldier named Bragadun. Hope flickered in his mind.

"Talk fast and to the point," Bragadun growled. "What's this about a Vasylli alliance?"

Parfyon laughed, feigning incredulity. "Why did the Powers give you brains if you don't use them? Why do you think I killed Ulik? He was bought by Vasyllia, already sowing discontent with Nebesti autonomy from within."

There was a palpable change in the room. The guards were angry, but no longer at Parfyon. He had touched a sore nerve. Somewhere in the tangles of his lies, he had found a knot of truth, a string that might unravel Yarpolk's plans. It was time for another roll of the dice.

"Aren't you all tired to death with the tricks of the nobility?" he asked.

Bragadun went red. Parfyon's lunge had been straight to the heart.

"You filthy traitor—" Bragadun hissed through his teeth.

"*I* am the traitor? I have no interest in alliance with Gumiren. But think about it. What would stop someone like Yarpolk Dolgoruk from allying with the Raven himself if it suited his personal ambition?"

Grudgingly, all of them nodded. Parfyon was close.

"Let me tell you the rest, and you can decide for yourself if I am lying. Yarpolk orders the army into battle with Negoda. Why? Who has ever found honor in battling the pitiful Negodi? Because he staked all his family's honor and future on a devil's bargain with Vasyllia. He needs the Veche's support for an alliance. So he left his army to fight a sham battle with the Negodi, while he rushed home to prepare the ground for the Veche. To canvass support to make himself the new knyaz. Once he is knyaz, who will stop him?"

Bragadun didn't seem convinced.

"Do you want a Vasylli puppet as your knyaz?" Parfyon cried, pushing the tip of his knife deeper in the neck of the guard under his knee. The young soldier winced, audibly. Bragadun, every muscle rigid, looked as though he wished more than anything to slice Parfyon's head off. "Or do you want one of your own? Someone who will water the earth with the blood of Vasylli traitors."

Bragadun laughed. "What, are you suggesting yourself? You're a useless cripple. You can't even fight off one man with that stump."

Parfyon wanted to prove him wrong then and there, but even with both hands intact, that would have been suicide. He calmed his breath, looked Bragadun deep into the eyes until he began to flinch.

"Perhaps so. But I saw through Yarpolk's machinations even from this prison cell. Make me knyaz, and you will see a truly New Nebesta, one that will be raised on the skulls of Vasylli. Bragadun, my brother. You saw the Gumiren—the Gumiren!—fall like wheat before our swords. Vasyllia is a pear ripe for the picking. Make me knyaz, and I will decorate our walls with Vasylli heads, and Nebesta will be more feared and loved than Vasyllia ever was in the days of yore. You have the power to make history, Bragadun. Make me knyaz!"

"Shut him up, Bragadun," said one of the other two guards.

To Parfyon's surprise, Bragadun turned and struck the man with a ferocious back-hand of his mailed fist. A streak of blood splatted across the floor.

"If you want your idiot teeth to stay in your snake-mouth, then shut up!" Bragadun glared at the other of the two, daring him to challenge his authority. The other backed down.

Bragadun turned to Parfyon, and for an interminable second Parfyon was sure he would kill him and take the Veche stage himself.

"You're a bastard," Bragadun said. "But you stuck it to Ulik and Sviatopluk, those bootlickers. I'd never been so proud to be Nebesti as when you showed all the old guard what a real Nebesti *man* can do."

He turned to face his fellow guards.

"I'm sick of kissing the hairy asses of the rich. What about you?"

"He's a cripple, Bragadun!" complained one of the others.

"And he's managed to take control of this situation pretty well, I'd say. One hand, against four swords? And we're the ones on our heels?"

He looked at Parfyon and smiled. It gave Parfyon goosebumps.

"I'd much rather have a *ragger* be knyaz, than one of those milksops from the big houses. Parfyon, I'm with you."

And Parfyon almost gasped as Bragadun offered him his sword. For a frightening moment, he thought this was a final trap, but he dropped his knife, let the trembling guard go, and gripped Bragadun's sword. It felt awkward and heavy in his left hand.

"So. Now what?" said Bragadun.

"Get me out of here in one piece, and bring me to the center of Veche square, to the barrels."

Bragadun nodded, understanding. It was insane, Parfyon knew. He intended to take the ceremonial opposition stage—nothing more than a pile of broken barrels in the center of the square—a place that had seen few men become knyaz. Many more had been pulled down to be trampled by eager brawlers.

"Risky," Bragadun said, "but probably your only chance."

"What do you think, Bragadun? How many of the warriors will follow me?"

"If you play this right, all the sword-and-shielders will follow you without question, as will the bows and spears, I think. The elite Sheloma are a problem, as are the old guard. But even they are angry with Yarpolk for his high hand."

Parfyon breathed deeply as he took in the scene—four soldiers, two of whom had faces turning a sickly combination of grey and green. Bragadun, red-faced and excited. The fourth, sitting on the ground and grasping his injured leg. He had an expression of rueful respect as he met Parfyon's gaze.

For a moment, the vision of the burning trees flashed on his memory again, so bright it was almost blinding. Parfyon was weighed down with a heavy sense of impending...something. A sense of significance that sang on the air, like the whistling of wind through bulrushes. A thought—*Am I in control of these events, or are they controlling me?*—then, he snapped back to himself, his head slightly groggy. None of the others seemed to have noticed anything.

"This is it, boys," said Parfyon. "Last chance to reconsider."

Bragadun broke into easy laughter, drawing Parfyon and the others into easy intimacy with him. "Parfyon, you don't get it, do you? The young warriors, they were thrilled by how you battered Ulik and Sviatopluk. You won many hearts that day. Plenty of us are still fuming over your imprisonment. If you play your pawns right, you could checkmate the Dolgoruki with only a few moves."

Parfyon liked him. He knew how to speak in a way Parfyon understood. He would do well, both in battle and in the political arena, if they survived this day.

"Now listen to me," Parfyon said. "Give me your helmet, Bragadun. We will leave our wounded brother in my bed—don't worry, brother, I will send for the healers as soon as I may—and wait for the moment of highest commotion to take the high ground. For now, we wait."

Not only did Bragadun hide Parfyon's face with his helmet, but he ingeniously tied one of his own mailed gloves to Parfyon's stump of an arm and tucked the false hand into Parfyon's belt. It gave Parfyon a bit of an air of nonchalance—a young warrior slightly bored with politics.

Parfyon knew they had no more than a half-hour at most, but every minute had the weight of days.

CHAPTER 13
THE MIDS OF AER

Voran's four captors took positions—two before, two behind him—that bespoke their efficiency at capturing human flesh. They took off at a steady trot through the trees, at a right angle to the main road. Voran saw no discernible path, but they moved with such sureness that Voran suspected they had a kind of invisible path of memorized landmarks. The ground they crossed was nearly always grassy or covered in short shrubs.

Very effective at hiding tracks, Voran realized.

So these were more than simple brigands. The furs were another hint. They were of superlative quality, well preserved, and coming from healthy, young beasts. Probably each beast was a pack leader when alive. The pelt of the white bear in particular was a thing of beauty. Voran suspected it could fetch a king's ransom on the black market. That the leader wore it into battle suggested either that these were sanctioned unofficially by a very rich family (or city), or that they traded in much more than furs and slaves.

They continued up the contour of the hill, traveling at a slight angle away from Vasyllia. Deeper into Nebesta. Voran suspected they were making for the river Ulna, just on the other side of this ridge. It was a major tributary of the Nebestaala, which would suggest that these slavers were working for Nebesta. Perhaps they were sent by that young commander, Novvik, to intercept Voran and punish him for his interference with the Gumir prisoner.

As they reached the top and continued down the other side of the hill,

Voran saw the river. By now, it was late evening, and the reflected half-moon danced on the shallow rapids of the Ulna directly below them. An unusual boat bobbed along the shore—long like a blade of grass, with a square sail and oars running down the length of the ship. A fast ship, Voran realized.

Next to the ship was a small hillock that looked unnatural in the landscape. Then it moved. Voran's heart plunged. *Giants.*

Voran flung himself to the side, exactly between two closely-growing birches, and rolled over his right shoulder. His tied hands made it awkward, but he landed on his feet and almost managed to continue his momentum at a run. He leaned hard on his right leg to propel himself forward. It collapsed under him. He fell. Pain shot up from his foot, and his entire leg froze in a spasm. He rolled over, but now his other leg cramped.

Two of the slavers—a dark grey wolf and a red-brown bear—crouched over him, their sharp knives pricking both his jugulars. He froze, thinking frantically. The woman approached from behind, her short bow bent with a fresh arrow nocked. The first was lodged in his calf.

"Are you insane?" she asked, calmer than he expected.

"I can't be seen by the giants," whispered Voran, huffing air. "They're... I'm...let's just say that if they find out I'm here, there won't be much of me left to sell."

Grey Wolf chuckled. "Well, your little performance just now is exactly the kind of thing to attract that giant's attention. You're lucky this is one of the idiot brothers. Tie him up and carry him. Gag him for good measure."

Voran tried to fight them off, but Red-brown Bear slapped him across the face. It was like a branding iron on his cheek.

The memory of Zmei, the prince of giants, was like a white-hot prod at his back on even the best of days. He had promised to pay Voran back fourfold for not giving him Living Water for his own dubious use. Voran had successfully evaded them for years, but they were never far behind. Some seasons he had had to go underground for weeks at a time, living like prey, cowering in caves and dense groves.

As they approached the giant, Voran saw that it was not Zmei. The half-light of the moon revealed a much smaller giant, unarmed. He seemed to be inspecting a group of men and women standing on the bank of the river, facing him. Their hands were tied behind their backs. Were the giants now trading in human flesh as well as objects of power? Two of the older-looking men were shaking with fear, barely standing on their shuddering legs. The giant, huffing with disgust, kicked them into the water.

Voran gasped audibly, but Grey Wolf elbowed him in the stomach.

"Dung-brained *meryn*," swore White Bear ahead of Voran. "When will those dirt-magickers understand that they're not the only power in the Realms?"

The woman by his side—she wore a light grey wolf pelt—said something quietly. White Bear nodded and the tension seemed to ease. Even in his panic, Voran made a mental note of that. The woman was the one with the real power in the group.

"Hey! You castrated son of a moon-born nag!" White Bear cried, still running forward at an even pace. "Tell your idiot brothers that we've had enough business with giants to last us a lifetime. Get out before I really get mad."

To Voran's surprise, the giant actually retreated a step behind the barrage of insults. It swore at them but continued to retreat.

"Zmei knows that this is not our day for trade with you walking boulders," said White Bear. "Are you acting on your own, or is he pushing his luck with us?"

The giant fingered a knife on his belt, which looked big enough to cut a grown man in half.

"Don't even think of threatening me," said White Bear, his voice dangerously quiet. "Consider our arrangement at an end. You can explain to Zmei that it was your fault. I had plans for those you just killed."

The giant turned without a word and ran away. Voran remembered to breathe again.

Two more raiders rounded up the men and women and pushed them efficiently onto the long craft, seating them in tidy rows by the time Voran was carried onboard. He was lashed down onto a rough bench at the nose of the boat, directly behind a carved and wildly painted figurehead at the prow of the ship—the head of a roaring bear.

As the panic of his near-encounter with the giants faded, Voran was amazed to see how the slavers worked without any pushing or intimidation. They were so quick and good at what they did that everyone fell in line automatically. Voran suspected there could also be some kind of subtle magic at work here. The involvement of a Power?

Before he had time to fully think it through, the boat was on the water, flying down the Ulna faster than a galloping horse. It was exhilarating at first. But it was too tidy, too effective. Even the speed of the boat seemed beyond natural. Who were these raiders? And more importantly, who was backing them?

They rowed at an even, but punishing, pace for the whole night. The enslaved men and boys were forced to row for a time, but Voran sensed it was not to torture or misuse them, but to gauge their strength and ability to work under pressure. After tending to his wounded calf, they left Voran alone, though he caught all of them casting furtive glances at the flask on his left hip. Despite his fears, they did not so much as ask to touch it.

White Bear (as Voran thought of him) was clearly deferred to as leader by Dark-grey Wolf and Red-brown Bear. But the more Voran watched all of the raiders, the more he was sure of his first impression. The woman—Light-grey wolf—was the emotional core of the group, if not the one actually holding the reins. Of all the raiders, she avoided his gaze the most. When Voran did catch her eye, she immediately turned away, and he had the distinct impression that she was not simply angry with him, but furious. He wondered if he had encountered her before in any place. Was she somehow involved in the disasters of his early years as healer?

In the very beginning of the Internecine War, about ten years after the Gumiren invasion, Voran had actively championed the cause of a lesser Karila prince named Rogned. Rogned was an anomaly. Despite being in a family that had been wiped out by the Gumiren, he staunchly championed the cause of the Vasyllian Monarchia. With Voran's help, he began gathering a small army of well-trained guerrillas. Voran planned to take them to Ghavan Isle and present them to Dar Mirnían, with the intention of beginning the reclamation of Vasyllia from the Raven and his Gumiren.

Voran had thrown himself completely into this project, so completely that he ignored certain clear signs that Rogned was not entirely right in the head. He had fits that would leave him physically ill and barely able to speak, usually around the time of the full moon. Voran was sure that there was some physical reason for this, but the Karila—if possible, a more superstitious people even than the Vasylli—believed him to be moon-touched. He was not merely removed from power, but he was publicly hanged.

Voran was away at the time, unable to protect Rogned. Later, he found out that a conspiracy planned the execution for the exact time of Voran's absence. A conspiracy led by Lord Yarpolk Dolgoruk of Nebesta, whom Voran had personally healed during one of the early battles between Karila and Nebesta.

After that, Voran had refused to do so much as wear a sword.

Voran's reverie was interrupted by the approach of the dark-skinned woman. She still did not look at him, but her intent to speak was clear.

"Your leg?" she asked.

"Your men are good with healing. It should close up in no time." In truth, she had hit him exactly in the meatiest part of the leg. It was painful, but the leg was healing remarkably fast. "You run a very tight ship."

She smiled at the cliché, but Voran noted that she didn't dispute his underlying suggestion that she, not White Bear, was the actual leader.

"You shouldn't speak so openly about the things you see. The things that other men miss." Her accent was pure Vasylli. Voran was amazed. He didn't think that any Vasylli lived free of the Raven's bondage. And he had never met a Vasylli with such dark skin.

"I can't help myself," he said, grinning ruefully. "I must uncover the things that others hide."

"Ah, so you *are* that Healer everyone is going on about."

Voran sighed and resisted the temptation to roll his eyes.

"Am I allowed a question?" he asked. She looked at him sharply but gave a quick nod. "You are not really slavers, are you?"

She half-smiled, looking him in the eyes for the first time. Her expression was quizzical. There was a notch in her slightly crooked nose. It was unexpectedly attractive. He noticed something of Aglaia in her: something wolfish.

"I mean," Voran continued, "you are doing everything possible to make it seem like you're slavers. You know, the usual. Furs and human flesh."

Her expression soured, as though she wanted him to get on with it already.

"But actually, you trade in power."

She smiled again—a grudging acknowledgement.

"You took me," continued Voran in the silence she left for him, "because you have some way of perceiving that I am...well... a *bearer* of power. That's why you didn't waste me at the oars. I think you work for some lower Powers, maybe Alkonist. In any case, someone who shouldn't be meddling in the affairs of men, and so...chooses to remain hidden while you do the dirty work."

"You...*could* say that." There was more she was not telling. Voran suspected he hadn't hit the mark. He tried a different approach.

"What will you do with me?"

"You are not in any position to ask so many questions," she said, the jagged edge returning to her glance and voice. "But I am. Tell me. How do you carry the Living Water without it consuming you?"

Voran was struck dumb for a moment. "How did you—"

"We have done business with the giants. They've long asked us to find you for them."

And yet, you didn't sell me to them, he thought, but did not say aloud.

"I don't know why the Living Water doesn't consume me," he said. "Every time I see my reflection in water, I expect to see a white-haired face staring back at me. The heaviness of it. It is more than anyone should have to bear. But somehow, I seem to be getting younger. I don't understand it."

Her eyebrows shot up. "You shouldn't lie about such things."

"I'm not lying," he said, a bit offended. "Perhaps it's because I use the water to wash away the physical suffering of others, not to gather power to myself."

"No," she said. "You have not *used* the Living Water at all."

Voran was confused. "I just told you..."

He stopped, aware that he was missing something important between the lines. Their entire conversation, he now realized, had been occurring on two levels. He had missed the subtext, bantering on the surface about trifles. He felt as stupid as a child.

"Should I be jealous, wife?" rumbled White Bear with comic ferocity. Voran cursed him silently for barging in at the most interesting moment.

"No," she said, and the fierce hatred was back in her eyes as she assessed Voran. A she-wolf assessing her future meal.

"There they are!" called Red-brown Bear at the mast.

Voran turned around. Ten giants stood in a line across the Ulna, all of them in full chain mail, with swords unsheathed. In the very center, standing knee-deep in the river, was Zmei, the prince of the giants. He looked directly at Voran and smiled. Voran's skin curdled.

"Will we make it?" asked White Bear, looking at his wife. "They're awfully close."

"We will make it, my love," she said, and kissed him on the lips.

Voran watched them walk toward the back of the boat before turning around again. The sight that met his eyes shouldn't have been possible. There was a translucent wall of water standing before the giants—a waterfall with no source, a screen of iridescent mist, opal-bright in the rising sun. Then he knew, by the familiar, warm resonance in his heart. It was a doorway to another Realm.

The giants didn't seem to see it, not judging by their demeanor. The boat was not thirty feet away from them, and gaining speed, when Zmei raised his sword. Voran's heart froze for a beat as the sword came down toward the top of the mast, but then they passed through the screen of water, and the sword never fell.

Somehow, they didn't get wet. It was as though the water wasn't there, but in another place entirely. Voran turned back to look at the giants. They were gone. Nor was the waterfall made of water at all. It was hair, flowing down from the head of a translucent maiden as tall as a red-bark. She was like mist and rain and sun all in one. Her eyes were stars, and her lips were wisps of cloud, reddened by the sun behind them. She stood over the Ulna, her left foot on the right bank, her right foot on the left. Fern fronds curled upward at the place where her toes touched the earth. Her robe was a translucent dress of clouds.

Voran was physically pressed down with the energy in the air. It was as if all of Nature's processes that normally occurred in the invisible realm were suddenly obvious to every human sense. He saw the whirring essence of water. He heard the voices of air. He felt the vibrations of earth, the slow movement of rock and soil and loam. It was almost too much to bear.

"We greet you, Dawn most Golden!" the dark-skinned woman intoned in a half-chant. "Allow us entry into the place and time of our ascendance, so that we may better serve the Father Unknown."

The goddess spread out her arms to them, and sun-rays streamed through her fingertips. The four slavers fell on their knees and bowed. Voran felt a strong need—not a compulsion, but a yearning that seemed to come from his own heart—to do the same. He did. Every single person in the boat did the same.

A sense of intense peace descended on Voran at that moment. For the first time in over twenty years, he felt the same way he used to feel in the Temple at Vasyllia. A sense of many people becoming a single heart, a single cry directed upward. It sent chills up and down his spine as he experienced what he had forgotten, what he used to crave on a weekly basis at home.

In a burst of clarity, he realized he had stopped believing his own sermons. Whenever he spoke to a warlord about the ideal of Vasyllia, he spoke exactly of this kind of unity. A sense of wonder before an ineffable absolute, experienced by many people together in a single place—this could easily become the basis for a community of people who shared a common reality that made them like family to each other. No, not family. More like members of a single body. This is what Vasyllia had been built on. That is what he hoped to restore in Vasyllia the New.

How strange that he should experience it on a boat of slavers on the way to a flesh market.

As the wonder wore off, Voran took in his surroundings. The landscape had changed drastically from what it was before the doorway to this new Realm. Where before they sailed through wooded hill country, now they were surrounded by tundra. The sun looked uncommonly large with nothing but grass and hill-slopes to offer any contrast. Or perhaps the sun was actually larger than normal. Anything was possible in his experience of traveling the Realms.

But it was the smell that made Voran wonder. He could distinguish the smell of every individual blade of grass. Each had its own distinctive palette, and taken together it was a symphony of fragrance like he had never experienced. Unbidden, a thought occurred to him: this is an earlier *time*, not a different *place*.

"We are in the Mids of Aer, aren't we?" Voran asked, inadvertently aloud.

White Bear laughed behind him. "You are unusually perceptive. Have you been in the Mids of Aer before?"

He had, though he had not realized it at the time. After twenty years of trap doors and slips into the layers of the endlessly-unfurling onion of the Realms, Voran thought he understood their structure a little better. If the Lows of Aer was a kind of interweaving of places, then the Mids of Aer was a braiding of times. They were still on the Ulna, still traveling toward Vasyllia. But it was a different time, an ancient time. Yet another example of how wrong people's conception of the world was. There was no ladder leading upward to the Heights of Aer. No, all the levels of the world, all the Realms, from the highest to the lowest, were intertwined on a single plane. It was dizzying to consider.

Then another thought intruded, and joy mingled with fear inside Voran.

"You are taking this boat to Vasyllia," he said, turning to White Bear.

"Yes."

Of course, it made perfect sense. What better way to cross the Wall of Vasyllia than to travel to a time when there was no wall? But that sort of ability to come in and out of the Mids of Aer should be beyond the knowledge of human beings. There could be no doubt now that these slavers were, if not themselves Powers in human form, then agents of someone with frightening power. But good or evil? Voran still had no idea.

CHAPTER 14
GAMAYUN

Two weeks after Antomír was commanded not to use the Living Water, he woke to a morning with no wind. On a small island like Ghavan, where the sea winds never end, it meant a day of rest for the villagers. In past years, windless mornings were Antomír's time to roam in nature. The storytellers sometimes sang about talking trees. Antomír knew that to be more than mere embellishment for fairy tales. He had heard the trees with his own ears.

But that was when Mama was well. Now, it was as if the trees were afraid to speak to him, lest their speech remind him of her love for all things that grow, nibble, gnaw, and chirp. Was the natural world already mourning for her loss?

Antomír left the house before Veles had a chance to check on him. The village was still asleep, but just in case, he avoided the public paths, choosing his favorite route—the back yards, tilled fields, the hillocks separating larger houses from each other. He wanted to see the open water.

The sea peeked out through the quivering leaves of the aspens that stood in rows like sentinels around the central, tallest, hill of Ghavan. The waters looked like the gold-flecked hide of some mythical creature, perhaps the great serpent that was said to encircle the world, slowly choking it to death. He felt trapped. The water—usually a spectacle of limitlessness—was a wall holding him in.

As he reached the top, breathless more with his heart-pain than the effort of climbing, he tried to still himself down to his very center, the way Mama had taught him. At first, he could hear only his own breath, the insistent beating of his heart. No trees. He tried for a little patience, but it was no use. He knew that to hear even the whisper of an alder would be balm to his heart.

The trees' whispers soon took shape from the sound of the sea, gaining strength with each passing second. At first, Antomír melted into the pleasure of the sound, but something was wrong. The whispers were jagged, harried, as though the trees feared to be overheard by someone. But to the eye, everything seemed normal. The leaves on the branches shone in their translucent spring-soft green, the sea-creature still slept its millennial sleep, and the Covenant Tree still towered over the village center, its branches heavy with white flowers, ripe as grapes.

"You are brave, walking the open hills. Now that the vila are about." The voice was from that dark place in fairy tales, the place that all storytellers always try to gloss over.

Antomír looked right and left but saw nothing. Then it struck him: the placement of the voice was wrong. It came from above.

"Or maybe you're just arrogant. Of course, a Dar's son will always be rescued from danger." A bird-woman perched on one of the thicker aspen boughs, no more than a few feet away. Her voice was cold, sarcastic, but enticing.

"Yes. Definitely arrogant." Both eyebrows, thick as overgrown moss, shot upward.

She was the same creature that had scared off the vila. Looking at her face—so sad it would take a desert sun to dry off her tears—Antomír felt no more significant than a small animal. It irked him, but at that moment, for some reason, he wanted to do something—*anything!*—to please her.

"Thank you for saving me," he said, lamely.

She shook her head, the black hair shimmering like silk curtains. The effect was exquisite, but she was not beautiful. Her eyes were too close to the hawk-nose to be beautiful.

"You owe me nothing," the bird-woman said, "What I did, I did for myself. You should do the same."

There was a hidden imperative in her words. Antomír resented it. He did not want to be told what to do, especially not now. "Who are you? Are you a Sirin?"

She looked nothing like the few Sirin he had seen, or even the stylized versions of the Sirin on the chapel wall frescoes. Those were always joyful, even in solemnity, and always beautiful. This one was disfigured—her eyebrows grew askew and her bird body didn't seem to fit her woman's head, somehow.

"I am Gamayun."

It was supposed to mean something important. Antomír sensed that she was playing a game of manipulation, forcing him to be abashed at not knowing a fact that, judging by her tone, anyone who is anyone should know.

"And?"

"You haven't heard of me," she said. Gamayun turned to gaze at the sea, as though Antomír were not standing there at all.

"*Should* I have heard of you?" he asked.

"I thought everyone knew of Gamayun. I sing the futures."

Then he remembered. Gamayun. The black Sirin-sister, sometimes called the Dayseer. The singer of all futures: those that would be, those that could be, and those that never would. A shadowy figure of legend. Good, evil? He couldn't remember. Or maybe it didn't matter. Some of the stories were nebulous about moral absolutes.

"Are you here to sing Ghavan's future?" he asked, not really knowing what he asked. As he said it, the air palpitated with the power of incantation. The trees stopped their whispers to hearken to him. A cold tremor ran up and down his back.

"No, Antomír," Gamayun whispered. "*You* are."

Antomír laughed. Gamayun's ugly face grew uglier with blotches of irritated red.

"I thought your bull-man nanny was the foolish one. I was wrong."

"I never expected Sirin to be so petty."

"I am not a Sirin," she said, and there was venom in her tone.

Antomír wanted no part in this conversation with an emotionally troubled non-Sirin. He turned to go back to the village.

"Your father and the priest," she said, her voice still quiet. "They lied to you about the Living Water."

He froze.

"The only reason they don't want you to use it for your mother is that they're afraid."

"Afraid? Of what?"

"Of you."

Antomír laughed aloud.

"You give yourself too little credit," she said. "That is good. Foolish, but good. Dar Mirnían is a fading man. You have seen it yourself."

Grudgingly, Antomír turned back to face her. He had often been bothered by the same thoughts.

"If he were ever to leave Ghavan to reclaim his throne in Vasyllia—Adonais knows when *that* will be—he would be a divisive figure, not a unifier. He knows this, knows that he is a weak-willed man, not made for times of war. That is why he tarries in Ghavan for so many years."

"Even if that's true," he shook his head, which was getting foggy with too many interesting thoughts, "all that is hardly reason for a priest and a Dar to lie to me."

"Think what you like," she said, now seeming bored by the exchange. "I only offer you the truth. It is in your hands—to save your mother's life, or to end it."

"How dare you! I am not the reason—"

"No, but you have the power to heal her. It would be a simple thing. Take a cupful of Living Water and give it to your mother to drink. All that mystical nonsense about the taboos and the priest-kings and their mad wives. That's all it is... nonsense."

"Interesting. One legend calling another legend nonsense. You are quite the charmer."

"I offer you a way to make yourself useful, Antomír, for the first time in your pitiful, pampered life. Do you know the horrors that are unfolding out there, in the world, while you Ghavanites sit in your safety and wait for everyone else to kill each other off?"

"I didn't...It's all rumor anyway."

"I am Gamayun," she screeched, and grew with the spreading of her wings to monstrous proportions. "I see. I do not guess."

She raised her black wings, too long for her body, and flew up like a parody of a vulture. Antomír stood tense, fists balled at his side, and whispered curses in her wake. But in the darker corners of his mind, the thought flickered. She may be right.

CHAPTER 15
SYMPATHY WITH THE BEASTS

At the next hunt, Khaidu and her eagle reached the crowning glory of their hunting together. The eagle managed to catch a baby mountain goat. To find it, they had to ride away from the main body of hunters, something that Etchigu did not like, but tolerated. Anything that broke with the proper order of the hunt was frowned upon by all Gumiren, but no one knew what to do with Khaidu, who did not fit into any existing category of hunters, for she could not descend from her horse to make the ritual killing blow with her knife.

This distressed Khaidu more than she was willing to admit. She treasured the comfort of being within a duty-bound category for the first time since her injuries, but it was a tenuous thing that could crack at any moment.

Today, she was willing to risk it, just for the joy of being the best.

The baby goat lay on its side, its white haunches streaked with blood, huffing painfully. Its eyes were nearly all whites. The white-headed eagle loomed over it, waiting for Khaidu's permission to take its allotted portion. Khaidu stopped to drink in the moment. She had done something that even Khaidu and Arelat had not managed this year.

Something twisted inside Khaidu—an almost physical sensation. A confusing jumble of thoughts raced through her mind, more a series of images tinctured with jagged emotions—the wide, tall Steppe: home; the rocks of the cliff: playtime; the occlusion of the sun by huge wings: curiosity; the flash of white amidst black as it fell from above: terror. Was she seeing through the goat's eyes?

Khaidu's stomach roiled, and a wave of nausea rose from the pit of her stomach to her throat. She held it down, but it caused stars to dance before her eyes.

She shook her head and clicked her tongue at the eagle. *Time to go.* The eagle seemed almost to frown at her, then quivered.

I know you want to eat, thought Khaidu. *Just not this poor creature.*

She clicked her tongue again and began to hum—the warning sign for the bound eagle. It flapped twice and flew within an inch of Khaidu's head, then keened with anger.

Khaidu watched her fly, her heart ripping apart between their shared bond and this strange new sympathy with the baby goat. The poor creature was heaving, as though stuck between death and life. *Get up!* she thought. *You must not die.*

It looked straight at her, and the flash of whites punched her breath out from her chest. They held each other's gaze until something softened in the white of the goat's eyes. It blinked with a curiously surprised expression and got up. Shaking itself off, it pranced away on three good legs.

Two days later, Khaidu asked Etchigu to take a ride out to the nearest river. It took longer than usual for him to tie her to her harness. Her pony was restive and snapped at Etchigu a few times. By the end of it, both she and Etchigu were huffing and puffing. When Khaidu tried to coax the eagle onto her hand, the eagle bit her. She felt it, sharp and surprising, even through the leather. The eagle's eyes challenged with the same intensity as the human Sabíana. Squaring her shoulders, Khaidu reached for the overtone in the back of her throat. It came out as a growl, a fitting warning to the eagle. It bowed its head with an almost human gesture of annoyance, then flopped onto her back, holding on to her shoulders hard, almost as though she were gripping them on purpose to hurt her.

Khaidu sighed and shook her head but gritted her teeth against the pressure on her back. She and Etchigu clicked their tongues and cantered off.

The river was at the foothills of the mountains that bulwarked the back of the giant city, an ever-present looming shadow at night, an almost living presence during the day. The day was warm and breezy, and Khaidu couldn't help but smile when she smelled the pine-flecked scent of the river. It came from the mountains, and even tasted of them, somehow.

As they approached a bend in the river, where it was broken by several boulders jutting from the river floor, the eagle launched from her shoulders, pushing her down onto the pony's neck. It screamed defiantly. A hunter's scream.

Khaidu rejoiced at that sound. She watched with amazement as the eagle swooped down toward the water, barely touching the surface of the water with her talons. Suddenly, a pike the size of a large dog flopped about in her claws. Khaidu gasped in surprise at the dance-like beauty of the attack, but the surprise ... twisted inside her. It sharpened at the edges. She tasted blood, sharp like metal against her cheek. She gasped for air, unable to breathe.

"Khaidu? What's the matter?" asked Etchigu.

"S-s-s-top! N-n-n-o!" She screamed at the eagle, who seemed as surprised as Etchigu. So surprised, that the pike's lurch freed it from the eagle's claws. The fish landed on a flat stone on the bank of the river. It thrashed about but was unable to push itself back into the water.

Not again. She had seen the world through the eyes of the pike for a moment, just as she had seen the world as the baby mountain goat.

This is ridiculous. A hunter must not feel sympathy with the hunted.

The eagle landed next to the pike, its head cocked at Khaidu. She could almost hear the question in Sabíana's own voice: "Can I eat it, *please?*"

"No," she whispered. "No k-k-k-ill."

The eagle almost seemed to sigh in exasperation. She launched into the air and flew back toward the city.

Etchigu came up to the pike and bent down to look at it. He cocked his head back at Khaidu with an unreadable expression.

Khaidu nodded, confident he would understand her.

Etchigu shrugged and threw the pike back into the water. With a flourish of its tail, it propelled itself into the rapids.

At the next hunt a week later, Khaidu could not bring herself to allow the death of a long-tailed pica. She felt as if the eagle's talons had raked her own side, not the silly oversized rat's. It was so real that she had to touch her side to make sure. There was nothing there, but she had lost her appetite for the hunt.

That entire day, the eagle avoided her gaze as stubbornly as a woman scorned by a lover. Batuk, like a wolf smelling blood, took to lurking in her peripheral vision, or so Khaidu imagined. In her mind, he was sharpening his fangs, sensing that the eagle was unlikely to protect Khaidu today. Not being able to turn her head fast enough to see his expression made the butterflies in her stomach more like bats. Mamai was more distant than usual, and Etchigu was nowhere to be found. Probably on some special errand for Mamai.

For the first time in a very long time, Khaidu was afraid to fall asleep.

She kept herself awake for a long time by tensing the muscles in her legs (the ones that still listened) until they cramped into clumps. A painful way of avoiding sleep, but very effective. The eagle sat on her perch, her tail feathers facing Khaidu, unwilling to acknowledge anything other than her disgust with the world. As the hours passed, Khaidu's pain and frustration focused in the backs of her eyes, until she felt that boulders were pushing the lids down and the eyeballs out of their sockets. Finally, she collapsed into sleep.

In the dream-woven world of Sabíana, the lady sat with her back to Khaidu. Khaidu tried not to care. Rather than look at Sabíana, Khaidu looked around to the far reaches of this dream-recreated version of her yurt. It seemed to get more insubstantial the farther it got from Sabíana, as though it might simply stop existing if Khaidu went far enough. What would happen then? Would she melt back into a puddle of broken flesh as soon as she left the protective girdle of the tent?

Khaidu felt she had nothing to lose, not tonight. Not with the two joys of her new life in danger of being snuffed out as quickly as they had appeared. Something about Sabíana's pose suggested their bond had suffered serious damage. The joy of the hunt, an always present thing, was now darkened by Khaidu's strange new sympathy with the beasts she was supposed to hunt and kill.

The faint sun danced through the crack between the flaps of her tent. At that moment, all of her fears, desires, hopes, and despair coalesced into an intense need.

I must see the sun rise.

She left her yurt. Outside, everything looked as it did in the world of day, though dimmer somehow, as though the air were full of smoke. The Steppe stretched in rippling waves of green-brown, as far as the eye could see. The sun was a pool of molten gold in a sea of soft, morning blue. The few bands of clouds were pink nearest the sun, transforming into orange, blue, then purple farther away from the horizon. Immediately above Khaidu's head, the sky was still dark, almost black—a casting mold waiting for the sun to be poured in. Nothing moved on the sea of brown gold, only ripples of wind, like sidestepping snakes.

The tears came, but they brought no relief. What was the point of all this heart-punching beauty? If all her joys—rich as they might be in the moment of experience—were so brittle that a breath of wind could break them, why have them at all? Wouldn't it be better to be a beast in the Steppe, to worry about nothing but finding food, sleeping at night, and avoiding predators? There would be few joys, yes. But at least her place in such a hierarchy would be ensured. No hierarchy was as unbending as the food chain.

She walked as far as she dared away from everyone else, outside the bounds of the giant city, to sit down in the undulating grass. The stalks were high enough to reach her shoulders, hugging her with every breath of wind. She did not notice that she fell asleep.

"So," hissed the voice of the predator, jarring her awake. She had only a split second to register that she was back in her yurt. "You're dumber than you look, little one. No one to protect you here."

A quick mind was always Khaidu's curse. In the second before utter panic overcame her, she appreciated the irony of being thrust into the bottom of the food chain, just as she had wished.

Batuk loomed over her, his scarred face red in the light of her yurt, the patch over his damaged eye like a hole in his face. One of his hands was behind his back, the other held a club. He pushed it down on her chest, pinning her to the ground. For a moment, she was confused when her legs didn't listen to her. Then she realized she had woken up to the daylight world.

"I never liked you, Khaidu. It was bearable before, but after Ghan Magai broke you... He took with him the only strong men we had. All who were left were women and weaklings. That is not the Gumir way. It's as if we forgot all our history. What if another tribe comes from the dark East? We can't withstand anyone. We sit here, hunting and hiding and hoping nothing attacks us. We are dead men, even though we walk upright."

Khaidu's terror pinned her down even more than his club. Her heart tried its best to flee without her, to leave her broken body behind.

"And then you...you broken thing, you shouldn't be let anywhere near the hunt. It's not... not right! We've left the Gumir way. Maybe we should've followed the Dark Father into the West."

Khaidu tried not to breathe, not to move, to disappear, to make him forget she was there. Let him talk himself into a stupor. He wasn't speaking to her anyway, not really.

"And now, you manage to bind such an eagle to yourself. Was it witchcraft? How else could you have attracted it? Well, I've taken care of that."

He pulled out two scorched feathers from behind his back. Eagle feathers. Khaidu's vision blurred, her mind reeling. She sought that deep place in her heart, that seat of the link between her and the eagle. It was blocked. She couldn't feel anything. Khaidu almost screamed, but somehow managed to keep it in.

"If you have any sense about you, dog-filth, you'll follow your monster bird away from here. You know that without it, you have no place here. Go. Don't burden your family with your care anymore."

There was pain in his voice now. Her shrieking panic faded, as though wiped away. She looked at Batuk's one good eye, and she did not want to look away. There was such regret, such doubt in his eyes. Batuk was not the person she had imagined him to be.

Again, the twisting sensation inside her stomach. She felt shame, so sharp that it caught at her breath. Pain smoldering beneath a veneer of anger and violence. Nagging, moaning pain in the back of her neck, so still it hardly moved.

Khaidu gasped as she came to herself. She looked at Batuk with her own eyes, but he was different. Now she saw beneath the petty brutality. It was still there, but beneath it was the pain. The loss. The lack of a proper direction or purpose. To her shock, tears gathered in her eyes.

Batuk was something she had never expected. He was the other half to Khaidu's coin—a true Gumir. He understood, as well as she did, how the life-commandments of the Gumiren ensured their survival, both in this brutal world and in the hopeful, unknown world to come. He was right. Their clan, Mamai herself—they were all drifting in a sea of grass. Ever since the coming of the Dark Father, they had lost their bearings, wandering about, doing little more than eating and sleeping. This was not a right life. Batuk felt it most. Well, he was a man of action, not a man of contemplation. Understandable...

"Batttk." Khaidu tried with all her might to speak. "You...rrrright. I... g-g-go."

Batuk sneered and spit in her fire. "Good." Surprisingly, there was no venom in his voice. In their moment of sympathy, he was no longer a predator. He turned his back to her and stalked out of her yurt.

The sun was already midway up its morning path. Khaidu felt emptied. Exhausted. A dry stalk of wheat.

Forcing herself with more intensity than she ever had, she pulled herself out of her yurt, dragging her body behind her like a hamstrung cat. Tears of pity rose up, but she pushed them down. It was still early morning, and so one was out and about yet. Pushing against the ground as though it were her deadly enemy, she slowly propelled herself away from the camp, the city, her people. The tears burst out in between her awkward lunges. She closed her eyes to keep the tears from gathering, though that did little to stop them. Still, she pushed and pulled and grabbed and dragged.

Finally, Khaidu stopped on a tuft of dry grass. The wind shifted, moving the high, tufted crests of the grasses over her body, covering it. No one would find her here, she hoped. She could die in peace.

There was no comfort in that thought.

CHAPTER 16
THE VECHE OF CHOOSING

The roar in the Veche Square crested as the Dolgoruki took the stage. The crowd swelled back and forth like waves on a sea before a storm. Piles of swords, spears, teardrop shields like burial mounds marked the four corners of Veche Square (no one was allowed to enter armed). Yarpolk and his ilk were in fur-edged hats and vests, blood-red boots, gold rings on fingers and in ears. The soot-grimed smiths and brown-faced farmers shook their heads at the finery stomping on the stage. With evident pleasure, they rubbed calloused hands together, foretasting the pain of bone crunching against bone in the inevitable fist-war to decide the new knyaz.

Parfyon watched all this from behind a window, surrounded by a conspiracy of three men. He wanted to rush in, to challenge Yarpolk or just kill him on the spot. But it was not time yet. If he mismanaged the time, they would all die.

The harsh bark of Yarpolk's voice cut through the noise, and the entire city hushed to listen to him.

"Peace to the soul of our departed lord and knyaz, Glebis Kharitonuk. May his memory be eternal in our hearts!"

Hundreds of knees smacked the hard clay, followed by silence, utter and beautiful silence. Someone began to sing:

"Peace eternal to your slave, in the halls of endless feast. Grant this, O Powers of the Silent Heights!"

Unexpectedly, a heave of emotion rose to Parfyon's eyes. He remembered the Veche that chose Glebis, who had been a mere wandering merchant of dubious parentage. But he had swayed an entire city to his will with a few words. Not a single head was broken in that legendary Veche, an unheard-of phenomenon. Then Parfyon remembered the barrenness of his own father's funeral. No one had attended the funeral of a lowly rag-factory hand. Parfyon had been ready to curse all mankind, when a massive form wrapped in furs joined him at the bier. Knyaz Glebis himself. He had wept with Parfyon then, and he had bound Parfyon's heart and sword-arm to him forever. Now Parfyon wept for his old knyaz.

For a moment, Parfyon saw a strange trio of cherry trees with fruits that burned with gold fire growing in the center of the Veche square. It was the same vision that he had seen on the battlefield. Annoyed, Parfyon blinked the vision away.

"As commander of Nebesta's armies"—Yarpolk's voice was like a sacrilege—"I convoke the Veche of Choosing."

The square surged again, and the shouts began anew.

"As you all know, I have the ancient right to declare myself as knyaz-elect, for the consideration of the Veche. But I do not!"

"Did he just say that, or have I gone mad?" asked Bragadun. His whisper sounded like thunder in Nebesta's shocked silence. Parfyon raised his hand for silence and craned his head to hear the rest.

"Nebesta," Yarpolk said. "We have been at war with brother cities for almost twenty years. Is it not time to end the bloodshed? Can you imagine what it would be like to grow crops without fear of looting and burning? Can you imagine living outside the city walls, near rivers, on open ground, never a care for the marauder who takes your wife and your daughter in the night? Is it not time for this?"

"Who are you to offer us this peace, Dolgoruk?" asked someone in the crowd, to a buzz of approval. "We did not start the war."

"No, we did not," Yarpolk agreed. "Vasyllia did."

The buzz grew to an angry roar. Interspersed curses and taunts. A gobbet or two of red clay thrown at the stage, for good measure.

"Vasyllia did," he repeated firmly. Once again, his voice hushed the Veche. How he did it, Parfyon could not begin to imagine, though he had the passing thought that if he ever wanted a lesson in how to sway men to himself, here it stood before him on two purple-breeched legs. "But what if I were to tell you that Vasyllia wants peace? What if I were to tell you that Vasyllia offers us a hand of friendship, yes, even kinship!" The jeers rose again, but he overwhelmed them with a mere finger. "Nebesta, you are known for your hospitality, even to the enemy who comes to your door asking for bread in the night. Extend it now to our guest from Vasyllia. I present to you Novomir, high ambassador for the Ruling Council of Vasyllia."

"You are right, Parfyon," whispered Bragadun. "How in the Changer's name did you know?"

Parfyon was just as surprised as Bragadun. He had thought it a good lie to sway enough warriors until he could grab for power, but this was almost too perfect. Yarpolk was falling into his lap.

"I must see this firsthand, brothers," Parfyon said. "Now. Into the Veche. No one will notice a few warriors when all are staring at the ambassador."

They took off their helms and laid them in a row by the wall, next to their swords. Bragadun took care to arrange them crosswise, apologizing with his eyes for the superstitious gesture. *The silent Heights know we need all the help we can get, real or imagined,* thought Parfyon.

Bragadun, half a head taller than Parfyon, took the lead. Parfyon followed with the other two behind him. The prison cell was on the top story of the Hall of Veche, and as they walked, the walls gave way to an open-air gallery with a plank roof held up by undressed oak timbers. This was the knyaz's family's private walkway between the Hall of Veche and the palace (such as it was, being no more palace than any other four walls in Nebesta). That was wise of Bragadun. They would enter the square behind the crowd.

They entered the palace. It was empty and cold. Someone stood at the far end of the hall, black against the light streaming through the open door. Bragadun hesitated for a fraction of a second. Not someone he expected, then. Striding into the room, he turned right abruptly, indicating to Parfyon that they should fan out in case this was a challenge to passage. Parfyon indicated with a flick of the finger to the other two. They advanced on the figure in darkness.

"Fine men!" It was the fair Alienne, resolving out of the shadows, "but are they enough to sway a city?"

Parfyon laughed, showing more confidence than he felt. "No man can fail to succeed, if the most beautiful woman in Nebesta stands with him."

They stood face to face, the sunlight behind her obscuring the fine details of her expressions.

She took his left hand and laid it on her right breast. "You have this heart," she said, indicating with her eyes that she did not mean her *heart*. She lowered her voice so only he could hear her. "You will have the rest of me by tonight if you take the Veche."

Parfyon took her in his arms and kissed her. Her lips were scalding, and she trembled as though she had a fever. A woman of such strength, but such softness as well. His arousal was deepened by a fierce desire to protect, to nurture. Alienne was worth a city. Alienne was worth a Brotherhood of Cities.

Bragadun cleared his throat.

Without another word, the warriors walked into the blinding sun. The cold air was an unexpected relief, and for a moment Parfyon wanted to stop. It had been a long time since had breathed fresh, free air. But they moved on, through the knyaz's small courtyard and out into the streets of Nebesta. Not a single person stood in the cobbled road, not a single woman leaned out of the windows. Nebesta here was dead, a chilling mimicry of the Nebesta that had been defeated in war twenty years ago. To their right, a muffled roar crescendoed. They ran.

Two wooden turrets flanked the entrance to the Veche square from this side. Parfyon had forgotten about them and looked up nervously, only to see the bowmen leaning in the other direction, intent on the proceedings. He slipped unnoticed into the heaving mass of people.

Bragadun half-shoved, half wriggled a path through the throng. Not far in space, but an endless league away in time, stood the unkempt pile of barrels. Two boys sat on top of them, raising their fists and screaming something. That was Parfyon's stage, and for a moment his heart froze in panic. If an entrenched power such as the Dolgoruki were to be rooted out of their centuries-strong ground, he would need more than the support of his brother warriors. It was an inconvenient truth that warriors were not always the best bet in an old-fashioned fist-war. Parfyon needed the smiths and the farmers, who were often the tide-turners in the brawl that decided nearly every Veche of Choosing.

Yarpolk's voice intruded on Parfyon's thoughts. "Yes, my friends, you heard it. I pledge all the lands and moneys of my ancient family to this bargain. All you must do is give me your blessing."

His posture was loose, confident, both hands resting rakishly on his hips. Yarpolk's wiry red beard stuck out from his chin. Parfyon wanted to grab it, to pull it out hair by hair. Next to him stood a man of middling height with a beard tucked in his belt in the old Vasylli style so common in all the picture-books. Novomir, the ambassador of great Vasyllia. His face left hardly an impression on Parfyon, except to note that his left eyebrow was crooked, giving him an air of disapproval. Such a face would be effective at a negotiating table.

"Give *me* your lands, instead, Dolgoruk," blurted a fat innkeeper to

Parfyon's right. "I'll keep them in good care for you!" Laughter erupted around him.

"As good care as you provide for your sons, Tolstun?" barked Yarpolk back at him. "When have I ever seen them doing anything but drink?"

The barrels were still an eternity away.

"Vasylli dog!" shrieked a one-eyed geezer leaning on a stick as twisted as his back. "Your lot has stayed safely behind your wall for years! First you start the Internecine War, then you sit back and watch as the rest of the cities devour each other? If we listen to you, we are no more than hens squatting to lay eggs in an eagle's nest!"

Approval rang through the square. Novomir, the ambassador, raised one hand, placating.

"Brother Nebesti, if we could bring back your dead, raise up your burned crops, replenish your stores—we would. But you know the nature of the enemy that took Vasyllia. Be grateful that the Gumiren did not choose *your* city as their home."

"Can you believe this moron?" the guard behind Parfyon said in his ear. "He's using *that* old excuse. As though the Gumiren nomads didn't raze Nebesta to the ground on their way to Vasyllia."

Parfyon nodded. It didn't make much sense.

"Don't insult our intelligence, dog! You Vasylli always looked down on us!"

"Forgive us, if we have," said Novomir. "But let it be known now throughout the Three Lands. We Vasylli have purged the Gumiren. Ask your own warriors. They routed the remainder of the Gumiren on the battlefield, only a few weeks ago. Now is not the time to remember past grievances. Now is the time to end all wars. With Nebesta and Vasyllia as sister cities, the rest of the world will cower and bow."

"We do not need Vasyllia!" A woman's voice rang loudly. Alienne, backed by a personal guard of five elite Sheloma, stomped onto the stage. "Have you forgotten, Yarpolk? Look at the wonder of this New Nebesta, this gift from new friends, far more powerful than Vasyllia. We have no need of old encumbrances now."

The sea heaved and half the men lunged forward toward the stage, hands bunched into fists. Another swarm pushed back against them from the stage area, obviously placed there by Yarpolk. The two waves met and crested as the crowd roared on. Several men fell, their shrieks muffled by the shouting. Parfyon's men had been pushed away from the barrels even farther than when they began. Bragadun looked back at Parfyon with an expression of rising distress. It was now or never.

"Now!" Parfyon pushed Bragadun hard. Beautiful Alienne! She set the stage perfectly for him. They lunged forward, ignoring the complaints of the men they shoved aside, until Bragadun stumbled, nearly bringing them all down. Parfyon walked over a body, a man crushed by the mob. He no longer looked human. The barrels were tantalizing, just out of reach.

"We've all suffered, brothers!" Novomir's voice cracked like a whip, unexpected in its command. Even Parfyon flinched. There was something twisted in his intonation, as though it were not merely one man talking, but several. The man was loathsome. He was not even a man; he was a disease on the cusp of infecting Parfyon's city. Just a few more steps to the barrels.

"What Vasyllia offers is brotherhood, not merely alliance. We are one people, bound by the blood of Lassar and Cassían of Blessed Memory. Though we have had our differences, the Ruling Council of Vasyllia counts them as nothing, if it means true kinship."

"What's in it for us?" asked a young warrior, near the front. The tide was turning. Parfyon was losing his chance.

"Everything remains the same for Nebesta," said Novomir. "You choose your own knyaz. It need not even be a Dolgoruk." He grinned, and some in the crown laughed. "You will then be offered exclusive access to the trade routes and markets of Vasyllia. While we were walled off, we explored extensive trade opportunities on the far side of Vasyllia. Peoples you have never encountered, goods you have never dreamed of. Gold, silk, pepper, saffron. Even a new kind of drink, a bittersweet elixir called coffee. It is time to unify the cities."

"Under whose final authority, you great goat of Vasyllia?" Parfyon cried out, as loud as he had ever screamed. He stood atop the barrels. The entire mass of people turned. Some laughed. As they realized where Parfyon stood, and as more and more recognized him, a murmur rose and passed over Veche square like a rising storm. "I say death to all Vasylli dogs. Let Nebesta be Mother of Cities!"

The warriors cheered as one. Yarpolk's shoulders sagged. He looked Parfyon straight in the eyes and shook his head in a quick jerk. Fear flooded Parfyon. Yarpolk was trying to tell him something, but not what he expected. *You are being played for a fool,* his eyes seemed to be saying.

By now, churning whirlpools of human flesh had formed all over the square, and the telltale sound of bone against bone began to punctuate the general roar. Parfyon smiled at Yarpolk and showed him a rude gesture.

"Nebesta!" Parfyon called over shouts. "Look at my wounds! I was cut down by Ulik, son of Yarpolk. Yarpolk kills Nebesti at the command of Vasyllia! But I did not die. I rose as from the dead to wreak Nebesti vengeance on the traitors. I swear to you! I will raise you to lordship over all cities. I will sweep Vasyllia off the face of this blighted earth. I swear to mix the ashes of Vasylli with the fertilizer of Great Nebesta. Make me knyaz, Nebesta!"

Bragadun and the other two raised Parfyon up on their shoulders as a wave of Yarpolk's men hurled themselves at them. They were pushed back for a moment, but a counter-wall of men buttressed his back. They inched forward slowly. From either side, the reddened fists of smiths and farmers and warriors flowed around Parfyon like a stream hugging a boulder, pushing on and on toward the stage. He had won.

The rest was a blur. Cries of men beaten to the ground. Warriors lifting old men and throwing them. Young boys clutching the backs of farmers and pelting them with fists. The glorious Nebesti madness.

Someone began to sing an old drinking song, and Bragadun and half the Veche took its refrain up, to the laughter of the other half. The storm was settling, and Parfyon was inches away from the stage. With a final lurch, Bragadun threw him to the stage. Somehow, Parfyon landed on his feet, not his head, to a general cheer. There were now many female voices in the crowd. The Veche of Choosing was complete.

The ambassador of Vasyllia was gone. Then Parfyon saw his head on a spear, being passed down the ranks of the warriors. Everyone began to fling mud at it. Parfyon turned away. Let the people have their bloodlust, he thought.

Yarpolk stood in the center of the stage, proud in his defeat. He stared at Parfyon coldly for a long moment, then smiled wryly and shook his head.

"You don't know what you've started, my son. I pray Adonais keeps you safe."

"You never struck me as a religious man, Yarpolk."

"Desperate times," he said.

Then the impossible sight again entranced Parfyon. The fire-flowered cherry trees, the same as he saw clinging to the cliffs by the battlefield, seemed to grow out of the left tower guarding Veche Square. Parfyon had the presence of mind not to dismiss the vision this time. He saw three fruits hanging from one of the branches, too big to be cherries. They glowed from within, gold-vermillion in the autumn light.

"You see them as well?" asked Yarpolk, his voice unexpectedly gentle. "Perhaps I misjudged you, Parfyon."

Two warriors pushed Yarpolk down on his knees and pinned his hands behind his back. Parfyon almost stopped them, but he was knyaz now. No displays of weakness, especially for a man with one eye and a stump for a right arm. Questions would have to wait.

"Take our guest to his quarters in the Hall," Parfyon said, trying to sound gentle. "You will find one of your brothers wounded in bed there. Bring him to a healer. Leave Lord Dolgoruk there to await our pleasure. Make him comfortable. Meat and ale." It was strange how easily the formal "we" came to Parfyon's lips.

The warriors obeyed.

CHAPTER 17
RETURN TO VASYLLIA

The boat made the last turn of the Ulna before it joined the Nebestaala. At that point, they should have been able to catch a glimpse of Vasyllia. But there was no city of Vasyllia on Vasyllia Mountain.

We have traveled far back in time, thought Voran. *Farther even than the time of Lassar of Blessed Memory.*

Voran looked intently, knowing that if he focused long enough, his eyes would notice details that most people would discount. A movement, a blur of color, a flash of light, after years of bearing the Living Water, for him these could become clear vision of animals, houses, beacons of fire. Then he did see something. Light flickered between the many trees in the spot where Vasyllia should stand—or rather, *would* stand in some future time. It was not torchlight. This was something he had never before seen. It looked more like sunlight, but coming from within the mountain. Something told him it was not a reflection of the sun.

Voran felt the dark-skinned woman's gaze hot on the side of his face. He turned to her, surprised that now she looked sad, not angry.

"What is that light?" he asked.

"It is the reason for everything. Have you ever heard of the Garden in the Heart of the World?"

The quality of the air seemed to transform at those words. Silence descended, the kind of silence that presaged thunder.

"No, you Vasylli wouldn't remember it, naturally." There was more than a hint of bitterness in her voice. "So proud of your bloodlines, and yet how much of your old wisdom have you lost! Have you never wondered why no Vasylli ever crossed over the peak of Vasyllia to the other side of the mountains?"

It was an old question, a popular debating point in the philosophy classes at the warrior seminary.

"Most simply agree that there is a taboo, and leave it at that," said Voran.

She harrumphed. "Most people don't even think about it, you mean. There are reasons. For one, the lands on the other side are foreign, unpredictable. They worship strange and dark gods. The land itself gets more and more rugged, even unlivable. Truly, the exact point of Vasyllia City is one of the best places to settle in this part of the world. Perfectly defensible, constant flowing water, soil of uncommon fertility... and...there was already a city there, when the Vasylli came."

Her words rang true with the assurance of conviction. He remembered seeing Vasyllia with new eyes after his first meeting with the Pilgrim, after first hearing the song of the Sirin. The glory of the mountain city had seemed, for a moment, to be like a mask laid on top of a true face. Now he knew why.

"The city is an ancient creation of lower Powers—similar to the Alkonist that you've encountered—whose entire purpose was the protection of the mountain. For the mountain is itself a mask, or rather, a cover for something deeper. It holds the only known entrance and exit to a place known as the Heart of the World. It is the source of the intertwining of the Realms, the place of origin. In this place is a garden. The garden holds the source of all life, as appropriate for a heart."

Voran considered. The name "heart," he felt, was no accident, no mere symbol. It was a practical name, one with direct meaning. So was the fact that there was a garden.

"Is the source of Living Water in the garden?" he asked with bated breath.

"Yes. There is a place within the heart where all the Realms—the human and the divine—intertwine at a single point. In that place flows a river. In the center of that river stands a monolith with three fruits trees crowning it. These trees are not of any Realm. They are from a place beyond all realms, from the country of the Most High. The trees are aflame, but they are not consumed.

"The fruits from these trees grow and ripen on branches that overhang the river in the garden. At a certain moment, the fruits burst and scatter their seeds into the river. They are seeds of divine essence. The source of life in all the realms. When they fall into the water of the river, it transmutes, becoming—"

"Living Water."

"The lifeblood of the Realms. Yes."

A thought nagged at Voran.

"The fruits themselves. What happens if... you eat them?"

"I think you can imagine what will happen. A human being will gain eternal life. A Power that consumes it may even challenge the might of the Most High Himself. If the fruit is picked before it spreads its seed, it gives the lifeblood of the worlds to the eater, but the tree itself will die. Its life cycle is dependent on the fruit coming to complete ripeness and bursting."

"Oh, by the Powers!" Voran exclaimed, heedless of the shocked stares around him. "That is why he came to Vasyllia. That was his purpose all along. Not to destroy Vasyllia. But to gain access to the Heart of the World. He doesn't just want immortality. He wants to challenge Adonais."

The dark-skinned woman laughed. It was bitter and hard, and it chilled Voran to hear it.

"You poor fool," she said, and her eyes were full of pain.

A flash of light surrounded them for a moment, as though a ball of fire had engulfed them out of nowhere. All the women slaves screamed, and more than one of the men looked close to losing their wits. Then it collapsed in on itself, and they all saw Vasyllia directly ahead of them. The Vasyllia of their own time. It seemed insubstantial at this distance, shimmering in sunlight filtering through the tendrils of mist that rose here and there along the wide river. Voran looked back and saw the wall, with a vicious-looking iron gate straddling the banks of the Nebestaala at the point of the wall. The Raven had been nothing if not efficient in walling off Vasyllia from the rest of the world.

They sailed for most of the day, with Vasyllia growing always larger before them. The oarsmen were released from their duties and allowed to rest, though the slowing of the boat was torture for Voran. He had no idea what he could do to counter the Raven, now that he was so close to the unattainable goal that had occupied him for decades. The inconvenient reminder that he was in the hands of slavers with supernatural powers did little to calm him, nor did the throbbing in his wounded leg help much, either.

The lands surrounding Vasyllia City were verdant beyond belief. The greens he saw here were richer and more varied than he ever remembered during his days in Vasyllia. Each homestead already had fields covered in small shoots and even flowers.

It's early spring, thought Voran. *No one in Vasyllia should be able to grow anything for at least another month. What about the overnight freezes, the spring snows?*

Voran nearly jumped out of his skin in frustration at the slowness of the boat. But something new caught his eye. A massive pier stood about two bowshots away from them on the right bank of the Vasyllia River (as the Nebestaala is called as soon as it crosses into Vasyllia proper). It began with a tower on the bank, like a hideous head. It had an open mouth and a long wooden tongue extending into the river. Every inch of the platform rippled with spears like porcupine quills, seething in constant movement. Voran's heart dropped to his ankles. This was the slave market.

Two skin-covered dinghies skimmed over the water toward them. They also bristled with spears. Though the warriors inside them were armed from their feet to the faceplate of their helms, the boats moved easily across the water like water striders. More devilry, Voran grumbled inwardly.

Accompanied by the small boats, the slaver longboat pulled into a narrow space in a gap of the tongue-pier. Voran saw that his initial comparison was not spurious. The massive thing was a log tower actually built in the likeness of a grinning head, complete with painted teeth and two narrow arrow-slits where the eyes would have been. It looked like the lopped-off head of a Gumir. Nothing so ugly had ever befouled Vasyllian soil before.

Two lordly-looking men, dressed in white tunics and fur-lined kaftans bigger than they were, stood at the edge of the pier. They had no hats. Strange, considering the still-present chill in the air. There was something else that nagged Voran about it. He couldn't place their social standing, which was often determined by the size of one's hat. It annoyed Voran, not only because he was unable to determine the proper way of relating to them, but also because, even after all these years, he was still stuck in the old manner of Vasylli thinking.

The two men also had strange belts with odd-looking pouches hanging from them at uneven angles. Voran's realized with a lurch in his stomach what they were. They were not pouches. They were dogs' heads.

White Bear came up to the prow. "Brothers of the Consistory, I greet you! Have you the item we bargained for?"

The one on the left, a short man with a weasel face, answered in a surprisingly sweet-sounding voice, "We have. Have you the goods?"

"We have," said Light-grey Wolf, behind Voran.

He turned to see her eyes boring into him. *Do they mean me?*

Dark-grey Wolf and Red-brown Bear took Voran's arms gently, but with no doubt of their purpose. They led Voran toward the gangplank. His muscles tensed as fear occluded his judgment and as his leg could barely support his weight, but it took no more than a second to calm himself. He decided to go willingly, though his mind raced, trying to find some manner of escape, some mistake in the planning of this sale. The second of the two Vasylli lords looked familiar to Voran. He was probably minor nobility during Dar Antomír's time. Someone insignificant, until the opportunity came to become important, at the cost of his soul. He gave no indication of recognizing Voran.

Voran was pushed to his knees before the two white-robed lords of Vasyllia. The weasel-faced lord smiled at Voran with genuine warmth. Voran's skin crawled.

"So, this is the healer everyone has been so anxious to find. Impressive. Probably not too bad with a sword, either."

"This one?" said Light-grey Wolf. She spat. "He's a famous pacifist."

"In a time of war? Interesting...What about these others?" said the weasel, pointing at the slaves manning the oars. "Will you consider selling them to me? I recognize many Vasylli among them, some of whom I would be happy to reintroduce to the Consistory's tender embraces."

A ripple of fear passed through the slaves, but Light-grey Wolf answered without hesitation, "No, Brother Aspidían. These are for our personal use."

Aspidían shrugged, looking bored. "As you will. Here is your promised payment. He pulled a small linen-wrapped object from a side pocket in his kaftan. As he held it out, the linen opened slightly, and a bright light shone out, red-gold and flame-like.

"How could you!" said Voran, rising up and facing the slavers. "I thought *you* at least understood...Will you stoop so low as to bargain with—"

Something hard struck him on the back of the head, and he lost his footing.

"Bad beginning, Voran, son of Otchigen," said Aspidían, smiling with genuine enjoyment. "You are not expected to speak. If you will speak out of turn, I have no qualms about cutting your tongue out. Your hands are all we need. And that flask on your hip."

Voran reached for it instinctively, but before he could touch it, something hard smacked his head. His legs melted under him, and he fell.

CHAPTER 18
THE WOLF-WOMAN

Khaidu woke up with an acrid taste in her mouth.
Did I bite myself again in my sleep?
She breathed in, but immediately wished she hadn't. A cough grabbed her by her ribcage and shook her until she was exhausted.

Smoke. Not blood. The taste in her mouth was smoke. Lots of it.

With an audible groan, she pushed herself up from the ground. At first, she didn't understand what she was seeing. It seemed like all the pale faces painted onto the giant buildings of the city had come to life and were walking around. She gasped. That's exactly what it *was*, not what it seemed.

Five hulking shapes walked through the burning wreckage of the giant city. Three of them were in full armor, with peaked helms that caught the morning sun and nearly blinded her. Two of the shapes were hard to make out in the smoke at first. But they seemed to slither.

A gust of wind blew the Steppe-grass down, as though the blades were worshipping the giant shapes. For a moment, the smoke cleared, and Khaidu saw that the two shapes next to the giant warriors were serpents—larger than any living things she had ever seen. They walked on gangly legs, like a horse's, but their reptilian heads danced on elongated necks, and smoke and ash spewed forth from their maws. The giant warriors walked behind them, farther into the city, away from Khaidu, swords and war hammers raised for attack.

Suddenly, a wave of hunting eagles struck the giants like lightning bolts.

The great Steppe-eagles looked like biting flies next to the giants, not the majestic creatures that they were. A red-tinged cloud of fire obliterated half of them in a breath.

"No!" Khaidu screamed, but she couldn't hear herself. The fires now reached the tops of the log towers, and each time a flame reached another log, it seemed to roar. Khaidu had never heard anything so loud or horrifying. Then there was another sound, something more familiar. But hardly comforting.

She threw herself back to the ground, ear to the earth. There could be no mistaking it. Thunder of hooves. Moving away, deep into the mountains.

The horse-clan of Mamai jani-Beg was fleeing without her.

Something rustled in the grass behind her. Trying to ignore the searing pain in her back, she craned her head upward to see. A black wolf, the size of a bear, stood only a few feet away. It bared its teeth and crouched. Its growl was deep in the throat—the warning sign of imminent attack. Khaidu could have done nothing, even if she had working legs. Panic was the logical reaction, but Khaidu surprised herself with total calm.

There was a kind of rightness to it all. She had made as much peace with Batuk as she ever would. She understood him, at least. No small thing. She had lost Sabíana, and she had lost, after a short time of glory, her desire for the hunt. For all she knew, she had just lost her entire horse-clan to a rampage of giants. For a brief, but bright, moment, she had had a place in the world. It was enough. Time now to die.

She looked at the monstrous black wolf, and realized it was no monster at all. It was a creature of beauty. Its rippling muscles, its glistening coat, the pearl-whites of its eyes, even the razor perfection of its fangs—this was a creature made for a clear purpose, and it accomplished that purpose with grace and power.

What an honor it would be to help it fulfill its purpose, she thought with no hint of sarcasm. The thought—strange as it might seem—was joyful. Khaidu even smiled, though it still hurt a little to do so.

The wolf stopped growling, and its tail shot straight out, its ears up in surprise. It began to quiver all over. It whimpered.

Poor thing, Khaidu thought. She could see now that it was an old animal, and that it was probably in its last days. Gritting her teeth, she pulled herself forward toward the beast. It was more painful than usual; the stress of the last day had left its mark. Still, she labored on.

I will make it easy for you. I will not even struggle.

Then, it hit her again. The twisting in the stomach, and a sense of vertigo. A jagged series of images, too confusing to understand. A giant head, disembodied, lying on the ground, yet speaking riddles. A tree crowning a dry mountain peak, frothing with white flowers. A man with dark hair and sad, green eyes. Khaidu had never seen such green eyes before.

Khaidu gasped as she returned into her own self. The wolf was in evident distress. It backed away from Khaidu on shuddering legs until they seemed unable to bear their weight any more. Its rump plopped down onto the ground, and it raised both its front paws up at Khaidu, as though pleading. Khaidu was entranced. The huge wolf-head came up and over its back, farther than seemed possible. The wolf's back bent. The paws...transformed.

Khaidu's eyes grew almost beyond their sockets in surprise. The wolf was...changing. The spectacle was grotesque, but somehow intimate too, and Khaidu was strangely embarrassed to be witnessing it. She closed her eyes. Though her curiosity was intense, she waited.

The sound was like two Gumir boys, aged twelve or so, having a tussle in the tall grass. It was so familiar a sound that Khaidu wanted to open her eyes to see if all the preceding day and night had not just been a dream. Maybe now she would wake up again, back in the horse-clan among her family. But she kept her eyelids firmly shut.

Then, all sound ceased, except for rapid breathing. Not animal breathing. Definitely human. No longer able to contain herself, Khaidu opened her eyes. She found herself staring directly into the eyes of a crouching woman wrapped in a dirty black pelt. Her grey, curling hair hung about her head like river-weeds. An old woman. But her eyes were quick, darting. Young eyes.

"How did you do it?" She asked, speaking passable Gumir, in a similar accent to Sabíana's. "How did you bring me back?"

The giants continued toward the mountains, leaving a trail of carnage. For the rest of the day, the woman cowered in her pelt, her whole body shaking as though she were in shock. By the evening, the flaming city was nothing but embers, and there was no sign of the giants anywhere. Silence—still and dangerous—descended on the Steppe as the sun neared the horizon. By then, the woman's chattering teeth had stilled. She looked like she was only now starting to grow comfortable with being human again.

It was a difficult thing for Khaidu to explain her limitations, but the woman seemed to understand intuitively. As the evening chill descended to the ground, she transformed into a blur of movement—gathering dried grass and dung, making a fire, and propping Khaidu up against something that was at once solid and comfortable. The more human she became, the more she talked. Khaidu was relieved when she seemed to require no response.

"So, what sort of Gumira are you, then? Far away from the rest of your people, that's for sure! And a large horse-clan, if the trampled mess you've all left is any indication. Your family left you behind, because you're a burden to them, yes? Typical of the Gumiren, that."

Khaidu grunted disapprovingly.

"Well, I'm sorry, dear, but what else would you call it? Charity? I think we'll have to take you to a place where people act more like people, not like animals."

And she went on like this, without stopping, for what seemed like hours. The entire time, Khaidu tried to find enough of a silence in which to say something. Finally, it was too much to bear, and she exerted her lips as she had not done in months.

"Stttop!"

It was such an unexpected sound in the babble of the wolf-woman's words, that she actually stopped dead in her tracks and looked at Khaidu with mouth agape.

"You *do* talk."

"Yyyyes. L-l-l-l...llw--isten! Kh..Kh..ooo—"

"Who am I? I am Aglaia." She blurred into movement again. "Though I hardly think that means anything to you."

Actually, it did. Sabíana had spoken of her beloved Voran's mother Aglaia many times. Her disappearance in Voran's youth was his great tragedy, the event that forged him into the man he became.

"I... nnnno...y-y-y-yuuu."

"You do?" The whirlwind with a voice stopped. "How?"

Khaidu sighed. This would require more speaking than she had successfully accomplished in a long time. But she forced herself. And, somehow, she managed to convey to Aglaia—she tried to ignore the growing impatience in the wolf-woman's eyes and posture—that Sabíana had also been transformed into animal form, and that they had been together now for some weeks.

"Transfiguration, eh? I had thought it only possible as a gift of the Powers. My own change was a curse. I wonder if hers was as well..."

"No..." Khaidu said, "Shhe... ssaid...twas a lllast gggift ... S-s-sii—"

"Her Sirin? Really? That would suggest that their bond is broken, and that the Sirin gave her a parting gift. It also suggests that she is... No, it can't be...She can't be dead. She's needed. For Vasyllia."

Khaidu felt enormously vindicated. "Y-y-yes! I tttell her itt-t-t-too."

"You are smarter than you look, little wolf," said Aglaia, her eyes warm with compassion. "Now, see if you can eat something."

She had gathered scraps of food left over from the horse-clan's quick departure—a few that were no more than a charred mess—and, somehow, she had also found a pot. The mixture simmering inside actually smelled palatable. Khaidu ate and realized she could eat a horse. She immediately felt guilty for that thought. For Gumiren, eating a horse was almost as bad as cannibalism.

As she ate, Aglaia watched her. Her head shook occasionally side to side, and she bit the lower side of her lip with surprisingly sharp teeth. Her eyes were distant, contemplative.

Only after Khaidu had finished eating did she again begin to speak. It was a different voice now, lower, calmer, more motherly.

"It is hard for you to speak. So I will do it for you. I have tried to piece together what I know and make a coherent story of it. You nod or shake your head as needed to help me along."

"Y-yes."

"Your family left you behind after being attacked by the giants. But you don't seem too upset by it, because you seemed willing enough to be eaten by me." Khaidu nodded. "And I was willing enough to eat you, little one. The Heights know I was hungry. I haven't been that hungry since a certain young man...Never mind.

"You were... how did you express it? *Bound* with an eagle?" Khaidu nodded.

"Who is also Sabíana, and for some time you hunted with her, until something happened to break your bond. A hunt gone wrong?" Khaidu shook her head. "Or was it one of your own? Maybe someone was jealous of your success as a hunter?" Khaidu merely opened her eyes wider, surprised at the old woman's perspicacity. "Yes, well, I would expect Sabíana to be the best at whatever she was. If a bird, then an eagle. If an eagle, then the best hunting-eagle to ever live." She chuckled. "Then the giants came—those cowardly bog-bastards—and you were left behind."

Khaidu felt that it was a very dry account of the events of the last month. Surely there was more to it than that?

"Would you like to hear my story?" asked Aglaia.

Khaidu nodded.

Aglaia wrung her hands briefly, then forced them flat on her thighs. They trembled.

"A very long time ago, I was cursed for some very foolish mistakes by these same giants that just destroyed your city. They are wielders of earth-power, a foul kind of magic. For all time, I was forced to wear two skins, hardly better than a changer." She spit, then seemed to think better of it, coloring with embarrassment. It made Khaidu warm on the inside. She was beginning to like this strange old woman. "Then I was saved by my son Voran. Twice. He healed me, and my ability to change form became a gift, not a curse.

"For years, we traveled the wilds together, healing the wounded of the Internecine War. Eventually I left him and took another charge. A girl, a little younger than you. Her name was Mirodara. Poor thing. She was very lost after...well, you wouldn't believe me if I told you. Anyway, all that's neither here nor there. It's enough to say that the giants found me again and bound me to my wolf self. I lost my humanity in the wolf. I am here now because I hunted with them. I came with them to find your people. I don't know why."

She got up with surprising agility and began to pace. How old was she? She was unexpectedly limber for an old woman. She stopped as though struck by a sudden thought and stared through Khaidu.

"You, little broken wolf-child, have some kind of power. Do you even realize that you broke the earth-magic of the giants?"

"I... dddo...n-n-otting."

"Well, not that you know of, maybe. But I have heard of a strange thing in some of the old tales. It is often the weakest or the stupidest creature that triumphs over the wise and the powerful in the end. I've always thought it nothing more than wishful thinking. But..."

She chewed on her lower lip as her eyebrows hooded her eyes.

"I think you are a very important person, little wolf."

Khaidu guffawed but couldn't suppress a smile. As crazy as the woman was, she was pleasant company.

"What do you plan to do next?" asked Aglaia.

Khaidu had made peace with her death. She didn't think she'd have to make decisions about life again, especially now that everything she ever knew was taken from her. But as soon as she considered it, the answer came.

"F-f-find...S-s-sabbb—"

"I was hoping you'd say that," interrupted Aglaia, her eyes dancing. "You see...I think I know where she may have gone."

"B-b-but...kh-kh-ow w-w-w-e...gh-gh-gho—"

"Oh, *that*. Haven't you been listening, little wolf?"

In a blur of motion, the woman became the wolf again, though the transformation this time was fluid and natural, with nothing of the grotesque in it. She picked up Khaidu by the scruff of her kaftan and lifted her onto her wolf-back. It was as if that muscled back was made especially for Khaidu, so well did she fit on it. She nestled in comfortably, as though it were a bed, not the back of a huge beast. The muscles in the wolf's back tensed, and they flew forward like an arrow released from a bow.

CHAPTER 19
THE FALL OF GHAVAN

One morning, a week after his encounter with Gamayun, Antomír worked alongside the other young men at the shipyard. Shipwright Siloán had decided that this year, he would make three new "branches" for the village. That was the humorous name he gave to the small one-man boats carved out of ash. Ghavan Town had at least twenty branches, but several of them were crumbling at the edges, and Siloán was restless for spring work after the winter, short though it was.

Otar Yustav, knowing the backbreaking nature of the work, had asked the young men to come and donate their time to the shipwright. Antomír had been the first to agree. It had been several years since he had helped at this work. He could use the practice. Next year, he would try to do one himself, he decided.

Even with the ten strong young men present, it was long, tiring work. Each of them had one of Siloán's special adzes. They were sharper than Siloán's tongue—this was saying much! But still, the hollowing out of the body of the boat from the solid ash would take most of the day. By lunch, when Siloán's five buxom daughters brought the ale, the young men barely stood on their feet. Antomír suspected that Siloán worked the young men harder than anyone else because he knew they would have no energy to spare to hunt after his girls, the beauties of the village.

"Antomír, you dim-wit!" called Siloán with eyebrows threatening rain. "A dog walking upright could do better than this." He pointed at Antomír's work.

Antomír smiled, recognizing the warmth behind the bluster. "Enough for today," he said. Verina, his eldest—just over twenty, with red hair and gooseberry eyes that no man could avoid staring at—gave him his tankard and curtsied at him comically, her eyes dancing. He shook his head, smiling.

Siloán took him by the shoulder and pointed at a particularly egregious gouge in the branch.

"Now listen to me," he whispered, unexpectedly conspiratorial. "I've just got a message. The Darina, your mother. She's not well. Turn for the worse. Go to her, but do it discreetly. No need to let rumors fly rampant before their time."

Antomír's heart tried to run away from him. His breath tried to run after his heart. He flushed, then blanched, then flushed again. Siloán nudged him toward the village.

"Go on."

Mama Lebía lay on her bed like a corpse. Her hair was plastered against her head with sweat, and her mouth hung limply open. The ragged snorting was a pitiful excuse for breathing. She had not woken up this morning, remaining in a stupor since the previous night. All efforts to wake her had proven useless. She would probably die before the day was done.

Mirnían had not even noticed Antomír's entrance. He was sitting on the bed, shaking with sobs, his face and hands and hair wet with tears.

It wasn't sorrow that Antomír felt. It was anger. Fury at his father and at Otar Yustav for their proscriptions. Finally, his anger reached to hatred of Adonais. *You are all-powerful. And you will do nothing?*

It was too much. Antomír trudged away from his house, allowing his feet to take him wherever they pleased. He passed the last house in the village without seeing its carved window-lattices. He walked through the newly-tilled fields without registering the mud that caked his boots in layers. He did not even flinch when he walked too close to a hawthorn, ripping his left sleeve. When the blood finally flowed all the way down to his hand, he looked at it with surprise, not understanding what it was.

He found that his legs had taken him to the one place he should have avoided. He stood before the ivy-covered cave entrance. Deep inside the cave, he could hear the Living Water dripping, inviting him in. He turned away, disgusted with himself.

"This is your last chance," said Gamayun, appearing out of nowhere on a branch over his head. "But you already knew that."

"Leave me alone, you...you... *creature*." He turned on her. "Isn't it enough that I have to endure not just my mother's death, but its effect on my father? To see him become diminished, no longer a full man? Do you enjoy rubbing salt into wounds?"

"Oh, my poor boy," Gamayun mocked.

Antomír couldn't hold it anymore. He hugged himself, sat on a boulder, and wept.

His thoughts swirled around him, so vivid he could almost see them as visions. His father, an old, doddering man with white hair and a crooked back, leaning on a stick and wandering through the wilds. His clothes were tattered and his boots full of holes. Ghavan was peopled only with the old, too rickety to follow their children and grandchildren out back into the wide world, away from the tragedy of Lebía's death and their Dar's early descent into decrepitude. Antomír himself walked the long road to Vasyllia, everywhere beset by hunger, dangers, and the threat of an evil that hid in plain sight, ready to devour him at a moment's notice.

"There is more," whispered Gamayun, close to his ear.

His thoughts shifted, envisioning fields full of dead bodies, most of whom were too young or too old to be called warriors. Cities gutted by fire, women and children huddling in dark corners, waiting for their deaths. Huge giant men felling trees with their boots alone, building siege towers the size of cities. Monsters shrieking and cawing and yowling as they were being butchered, their blood taken from them to be used in dark magic to reveal the deep secrets of the earth.

But these were not his thoughts. He was *seeing* them. These were visions.

"Yes," said Gamayun. "I am willing to share my vision with you, Antomír. Look at the devastation being wrought out there, in the world abandoned by Adonais. This is what I must see all the time. I can see no other futures."

"It's horrible. Horrible." Antomír's tears had dried up. He found breathing difficult.

"I don't ask you to do much, Antomír," said Gamayun. "I don't ask you to take up your sword and sacrifice yourself in battle to right these terrible wrongs. No. You couldn't do that. No one can anymore. All I ask is that you brave the displeasure of a few old men and make this small corner of the world a place of joy. At least in Ghavan, let there be feasting at the healing of a woman beloved by everyone."

"But the Pilgrim..."

His thoughts were again vivid in his mind. Lebía cradling him as a toddler, tickling him when all he wanted was to cuddle against her warmth. Splashing water at her on a hot summer day. Reading to her in the evenings.

Just looking at her as she gazed with adoration at Mirnían near the family hearth. She could be like this again.

"Can it be so bad? I will not use it for myself," he whispered. Gamayun said nothing. "Adonais is loving. He will understand why I do this. I take the sin on myself. I will bear the burden of it. But let her live."

The rightness of his decision was like a jolt of heat passing through him, from his heart to his extremities. He had to do this. It was the right thing to do.

I will save you, Mama.

As though Adonais himself had smiled on Antomír, he found his mother's room empty of anyone save herself. He had no idea where Veles had gone. Father was probably drowning in his own misery somewhere outside. Everything was exactly as Antomír wanted. He pulled the flask filled with Living Water off his belt and tiptoed to his mother. She looked a little better in the light, her eyes closed and her breathing steady. She even looked peaceful. Antomír shook her gently.

"Mama," he whispered. She stirred, and to his joy, her eyelids fluttered open. "Mama, it's Antomír."

"My baby," she croaked through a dry throat. "I...thirsty. Water."

"Yes, Mama," he said, smiling broadly. He upended the flask of Living Water into her mouth. It was not much, enough for two swallows. The effect was immediate.

Color flooded her cheeks, and her eyes opened wide. "Oh," she said, surprised, with more vigor in her voice than he had heard in months. "What...good Heights above, Antomír, that is *good!*"

"I'm sorry I don't have more. But you should probably not have too much."

She raised herself up on her pillows, surprised at her own returned strength. "What did you give me?" She looked with clear, healthy eyes at Antomír. He nearly dissolved into tears again.

"Do you promise not to be mad at me?"

"Of course, my dear. What is it?"

"Living Water."

Her face froze in an expression of fear and dread. Her breath caught and seemed unable to release.

"What, Mama, what?"

"Antomír, tell me you're joking. Do you realize what you've done?"

Shouts outside the house, rising every minute in pitch.

"Antomír, you don't think a place like Ghavan, where the protection of Adonais is physically present, is just *left alone* by the Raven?"

She got up, apparently completely healthy, except for the pallor of fear on her face. The shouts were frantic. He began to hear words.

"Changers! Changers!"

Antomír's blood froze inside him. Gamayun had lied to him.

He rushed outside, his sword already drawn. There was no sky above them. There was a swirling mass of blackness, in which he could see the faint outlines of faces. Horrible faces, amalgams of human and bestial, as large as cloud formations. They descended on the village. The firebirds bumped into trees as though they were blind, the moonbirds hid their heads under their long silver wings. Animals ran wild through the streets of the village as Antomír ran toward the Tree. The white flowers of the Tree of Covenant, only yesterday ripe like grapes, shivered and began to shrivel before his eyes.

"No!" he screamed, running through the frantic crowd, intent on the Tree.

Aína and two other Sirin flew a circuit around the tree, singing a lament. The flowers stopped shriveling, but they were pitiful things, barely hanging on the branches. The Sirin continued to lament, their song like a sword hot off the ironworker's forge piercing him in the chest again and again and again. He ran up to the Tree and fell on his knees. Dark, foul water dripped from the mass of changers blotting out the sky. He wiped his face with his sleeve and looked up at the Sirin. Aína stopped and alighted on the tree. The other two continued their circuit and lament.

"Aína. Ghavan is not at fault for this. I am. I am a fool. I listened to Gamayun and I took the Living Water. I admit it! But I did it for my mother!"

Aína's sigh was like the world ending. "Gamayun? Has she been here the whole time?"

"It doesn't matter. *I* have done this to Ghavan. But you can save it, I know. Tell me what price I must pay. I will do it. Anything."

Aína began to weep.

"You cannot stay in Ghavan, Antomír. If you want to save it, you must leave. Now. Before it is too late."

He did not stop to think. He ran to the ship dock. Siloán and the young men were gathering tools and weapons for the coming battle, though they must have known that no steel can do much damage against such enemies.

"Siloán!" Antomír screamed over the rising thunder and boom of the very earth creaking under the onslaught of the dark ones descending. "I need a branch. Give me a branch!"

The old shipwright looked ready to argue, but he must have seen something to dissuade him in Antomír's eyes. He nodded.

"What about him?" he asked, nodding to a place behind Antomír.

Antomír turned to see Veles running not two steps behind him, silent as a cat.

"I am going with the anointed one," he growled, his eyes challenging Antomír to contradict him.

Antomír sighed with joy. "Come on, we must hurry!"

They jumped into the small boat and rowed away from the island. Antomír had not maneuvered a branch in a long time, and his first oar-thrust spun them around several times. But a few more strokes, and he had remembered the rhythm of it.

"Sire, look!" Veles whispered, terror heavy on his words.

Antomír looked back and stifled a cry. Ghavan Isle was sinking under the waters, slowly, but visibly. A churning whirlpool appeared at the edges of the isle, and the entire island began to twist as it descended into the vortex.

Antomír's heart ripped inside him. *What have I done?*

The whirlpool pulled them in, toward the sinking island. The cloud of changers was dissipating, the creatures within it howling their frustration as their quarry slid underwater. They didn't seem to notice the branch with its two occupants.

As soon as the sea covered the last trees on the highest hillock of Ghavan Isle, the whirlpool stopped. The changers disappeared with a bang and the stink of rotten fruit. The skies cleared, the sun shining down on a sea with no island in it. The branch, still propelled forward, shot over the place where the island once stood. Antomír looked over the edge into the depths. He saw the Tree of Covenant, the square, the houses, the people walking back and forth as though they were on dry ground. They were not drowning. It was as though the water did not even touch them.

Next to the tree, he saw his mother, growing ever smaller by the second. Her hands were reaching for him, reaching...

CHAPTER 20
NEBESTA'S TRUE POWER

On the evening of his victory, Knyaz Parfyon of Nebesta rested. His new room didn't have a hearth, but instead half the wall was a stove decorated in blue-and-white tile. In the next room, a steam-room was being prepared for him. Already the enticing aromas of oak and birch leaves teased his aching body. He had not had a proper steam in many months, and his head throbbed in anticipation of the cleansing heat. A host of desires and questions crowded him—visions of Alienne's body first among them—but he willed them all away. First, a bath, then everything else.

A delicate knock on the door. "Enter," Parfyon said. Alienne Dolgoruk, in muted blues and greys, flowed in. Parfyon was not decent, with only a coarse linen cloth wrapped around him.

"Ah, I see this is the wrong time. Forgive me, love," she said, though her glance was an open invitation.

"I will not be long, Alienne," Parfyon said, standing up carefully to keep the linen from revealing anything. "But even the most beautiful woman in Nebesta cannot entice me away from that steam-room."

"I would not dream of depriving you. I await your pleasure." She smiled and bowed. Her neckline was dangerously low.

Parfyon turned away before she could have her way with him.

The wall of steam hit him when he entered the room. The sap already dribbled from the undressed logs, hot to the touch. Parfyon's whole body ached with the anticipation of the initial itch, then the relief of cleansing sweat. His left eye began to burn fiercely, as did his still-bloody right stump. It would have to be a short steam.

When he came out in that perfect languor that one only feels on the other side of a steam-room, Parfyon was surprised to see a table fully set with more food than a family of ten could eat in a week. The ale frothing over a tankard as large as his head caught his eye and danced before it in a foggy haze. He was more exhausted than he realized.

Already tasting the ale in anticipation, he sat and reached out to take the tankard. The handle was slippery, in a chilling, slimy kind of way that had nothing to do with spilled beer. His hand came away red. A bloody dagger lay across Parfyon's plate. The food was sprinkled with blood, a clear trail of it leaving no doubt that the ale was befouled as well as the food.

"What, too squeamish for statecraft, my lord?"

He didn't recognize her at first. She sounded like an old woman.

Alienne's dress was spattered with blood. Her hands were dark red and still wet, judging by the light of the few candles lit at this late hour.

"Alienne? What—?" His eyes had reached her feet.

Yarpolk Dolgoruk lay there, eyes open, face white. His neck was sliced open.

"It's time you knew the truth, Parfyon." Her voice was husky. "Yarpolk was not my father. He adopted me, but only after he had had his way with me…I was *twelve* years old." Her voice shook, but she clamped her jaw shut and breathed out in frustration. "The adoption was his way of atoning. He had violated me in a drunken stupor, you see, and then felt bad about it. He thought that raising me in luxury and marrying me to the best of Nebesta would wash it all away."

Little by little, the layers of realization revealed themselves to Parfyon. He had been a complete fool. He had misjudged Alienne. *Her* power was not Dolgoruk power, with its stink of politics. Her power was one that would wipe everything off the blighted earth to see it grow anew. It thrilled him to share in that power.

"A few months ago," she continued, "I tried to kill myself. You had just applied for my hand, and Yarpolk refused it. I saw you as my best way out, and I could no longer wait. But someone stopped me. His name is Zmei. He is a great power of the world, and he offered me his friendship and alliance. He made it possible to rebuild New Nebesta so quickly."

Parfyon said nothing.

"Yarpolk was at the wars. I took matters into my own hands, as soon as Knyaz Glebis fell ill. It was necessary. You know how Nebesta abhors a power vacuum." Her hands shuddered, and she stopped to look at them, the look of horror growing in the whites of her eyes.

"Yes, my love, I know. Go on," he said, trying to keep his voice level.

She looked confused at that term of endearment and looked at the corpse at her feet.

"I agreed to Zmei's alliance. When Yarpolk came back, he was shocked at the transformation of Nebesta. I explained what had happened, and he was horrified. Apparently, Zmei is aligned against Vasyllia, and Yarpolk had great hopes in a future alliance between the city-states. Then you offered to take him off the game board. I took your offer gladly. Removing Yarpolk was all I needed, and you did it brilliantly. Zmei prefers to work in the background still, and the condition of our friendship was the removal of Yarpolk. As a last effort, Yarpolk tried to push the alliance through at the Veche. But you were incredible."

She smiled, warm and loving, completely oblivious to the carnage around her. Parfyon came around to her and took her bloody hands. He wiped them on his linen shirt until they were clean.

"You need not worry any more, Alienne. He is gone. Together, we will take Nebesta to unheard-of heights. Will you take me to meet this Zmei?"

"Yes," she said and walked out to the balcony. Parfyon followed her but stopped dead in his tracks as soon as he came outside. He stood facing a giant the size of a palace, armed and helmed like a warrior from some ancient tapestry. The giant bowed to Parfyon.

"An honor, Lord Parfyon." His voice was like the hissing of fire and the breaking of rock. "I look forward to burning Vasyllia to the ground together with you."

CHAPTER 21
AN UNEXPECTED POWER

Khaidu and Aglaia stood at the edge of the great sea of grass. Ahead of them were rolling, golden mountains, soft like the breasts of mother earth. Beyond them, something sharp and black grazed the heights of the sky—a mountain range too far and too huge to be real. Khaidu had not known there to be anything but the Northern Mountains and the Steppe. Now she stood at the end of her world. To say she was terrified would not do her emotions justice.

The yellow hills ahead were dotted with scrubby trees. They were fragrant, like rosemary. The yellow grass—thicker and shorter than the Steppe-grass—hid short purple flowers that appeared only when a wind blew. Whenever it blew toward Khaidu, the pungent smell of rosemary was sweetened with something she couldn't describe. Something like fruit, but subtler. She remembered that once she ate a strange berry—all red and made up of small, round balls. She couldn't remember the name. Someone had brought it from a raid on a merchant caravan. It was sweet and sour and tangy at all once. This smell was something like that.

The smell, even more than the sight, made Khaidu tense with fear. The back of her neck throbbed arhythmically. *Please, not one of my fits. Not now.*

"Be still, wolf-child," said Aglaia, her human voice sounding unnatural coming from the maw of a black she-wolf the size of a bear. "Nothing to be afraid of, not yet. That's just the border of Karila up ahead. There won't be any people for miles yet. This is a no man's—"

A high-pitched whistle—a bird call perhaps—interrupted Aglaia. Khaidu looked up at the sky and saw four faint shapes circling the sun. As soon as she saw them, she felt something serrated and fierce—a smell of blood and a flashing image of talons tearing living flesh. She twitched back into her normal awareness.

"Ea-ea-g-gles!" She blurted. "H-h-hunters!"

"Impossible," said Aglaia. "Not unless we've caught up with your people."

"N-n-o. D-d-diff—"

"Well, you would know," Aglaia interrupted. She was trying to learn patience to hear out Khaidu's stuttering, but it was still sporadic.

Just ahead, two of the trees on the left hill began to move. No, not trees. Horsemen.

"I see them," said Aglaia as Khaidu tried to speak. "This smells rotten."

She crouched a little in the grass, though even the scrub-trees would have a hard time hiding her massive form. Khaidu's mind kept wandering up to the eagles. Something was wrong with them. They felt somehow...broken. Or...insane? But how did she know that? She shook her head, trying to clear it.

The whistle became a screech. Two more horsemen appeared on a different hill. They kicked their horses and cantered downslope toward Aglaia and Khaidu, slowly coming together as they approached. The screeching continued. Khaidu looked up. The eagles were closer. Much closer.

When the riders were within hailing range, Khaidu saw that they were dressed in absurdly bright colors with no clear sense of matching. Wide cerulean pants worn with crimson boots, with a forest-green tunic embroidered in purple along the open collar and wide shirt-sleeves. They wore hats with long tails that bounced up and down with their horses. Their hair and beards were braided. They looked wilder than some beasts she had encountered in the Steppe.

"Karila brigands." Aglaia growled. "In my day, these sorts would be safely locked in the deepest of Vasyllia's dungeons."

They stopped at a respectful distance from Aglaia, whose low growl was a rumble that rattled Khaidu's bones. Khaidu was glad to be on her side. Still, those hunting eagles weighed on her mind. They were definitely aiming for Aglaia, but there was something else. What was it? Khaidu grasped for it with her mind, like a word that lay just beyond the tip of her tongue.

"Young lady," said one of them in passable, but very formal, Gumir. It took a moment for Khaidu to realize that he addressed her. Of course. They didn't know Aglaia was more than a wolf.

Khaidu answered nothing, but the back of her neck itched. She could sense the eagles spinning in closing circles over her head.

"You stand on the border of our lands," the brigand continued. "We merely ask—as a courtesy, of course—that you consider giving something to these poor men you see here. We have large families, and the earth in Karila has been struck with blight. We have no food. Our waters have turned bitter. Have compassion and share what you have with us."

Talkative brigand, thought Khaidu with a wry smile. She raised her hands, palms out, then twisted her hands back and forth. The Gumir gesture for "I have nothing to give." The brigand's dark face—he had some Gumir in him, judging by the high cheeks—turned a shade darker. "That is unfortunate. I would not want to deprive you of what seems to be your mount...though who is mad enough to ride a wolf, I don't know. Someone dark and magicked, I would say."

Two of the horsemen began to make a slow circuit around Aglaia, still at a respectful distance. The fur around Aglaia's neck bristled under Khaidu's hand, sending a chill up her spine. She looked up, and the eagles were close enough for her to see the mottled gold, brown, and white of their feathers. They were large eagles, possibly Gumiren Steppe-kind. Again, the images came—incomplete and unfocused. The smell of blood filled Khaidu's nose. They were hungry. Not only that...they had been starved. Khaidu's blood boiled. These birds had been tortured into submission, not united in a common bond as the Gumiren had with their eagles.

Khaidu's chest swelled with pity for the poor beasts. They had nothing in their limited thoughts except killing and eating. This was not natural, not right. In a flash of pain, she thought of Sabíana, remembered the warmth of the bond they shared—now no more than a hole in her chest. Her heart's pain expanded and threatened to burst. She felt the tears, hot on her cheek, streaming down her nose. She began to sob and tremble.

You are noble creatures, she thought. *You do not deserve this.*

One of the eagles struck her shoulders with its talons and grazed her neck. It was like the touch of fire, and she felt the wet blood splash on her shoulder. She touched it. Her hand came back sticky and red. Two other eagles dove for Aglaia's face.

No!

Khaidu fell on Aglaia's neck, covered the wolf-head with her own, the wolf's mouth and neck with her hands and arms. She felt the scrape of talons and screamed. But through the pain, she still felt pity for the eagles like an iron brand searing her heart. No creature, no matter how feral, should ever be reduced to such a condition. The talons continued to scrape at her. Her vision dimmed. Her hands felt fuzzy, too large. She slipped a foot off Aglaia's back, stopped, slipped again. Just before she landed on the hard ground, a thought filled her completely:

You are more than killers. You are more than slaves. You are noble. You are worthy. Remember what you—

She fell, and the impact drove the breath from her body. Her back arched under her. Her strong hands scrabbled at the dry grass, as though she could force her breath into her chest by ripping at blades of grass. Something dimmed the sunlight above her, and she closed her eyes, ready for the impact of talons on face, unable to raise her hands, which had hardened into stone-hard cramps.

But nothing touched her.

Feathers. A burst of feathers tossed in the wind playfully, like a flock of starlings in early spring. Then they...burned. No...melted, coming together into long strands of fiery, semi-translucent...something. Khaidu didn't understand what she was looking at. It was swirling and joyful, and her heart leapt to see it. Was that her emotion? That angry joy, that fierce pleasure...it was too much to bear.

Just as her eyes dimmed, she had a glimpse of a creature of wings and eyes and fire, so large it could swallow a horse. It... *sang.*

CHAPTER 22
A FORCED BOND

Veles hacked at the young fir tree four times in fluid strokes. Four strokes, and four perfectly spaced notches, one above the other. The tree, weakened by the notches, could not withstand his fifth blow. What was left was an exact half of a trunk. The sixth blow was a sideways chop, felling the tree at its middle. Antomír had seen him do it more than ten times already over the last few weeks. It took him a long time to realize that Veles was making a large animal trap, set between the felled stumps of young trees. Then Veles, in three easy-looking strokes, made a U-shaped notch in the stump where the sharp stake would fit perfectly for the trap. He threw the axe to Antomír.

"Your turn."

Antomír looked at his hands. They were half blue, half red from bruises and gashes. The axe felt no more comfortable in his hands than a struggling bird trying to fly away. He began to feel sorry for himself. With that mere inkling of a thought, a storm threatened to rage from inside his memory—all the horrors of that day, still unprocessed, still un-suffered. He grabbed the haft and attached the upper part of the felled tree, the half that would become the sharp stake of the trap, hacking off the branches like they were the reason for all his loss.

"Anointed one," said Veles, laying a hand like a frying pan on Antomír's axe-hand. "An angry axeman is a snake that bites itself. I have a hunch that you will still need those fingers."

THE HEART OF THE WORLD

Antomír sighed and forced his entire body to relax. It was not easy, but he tried Veles's method. First, the toes. Then, the calves. Then, the thighs. Then, the stomach. Then, the chest. Then the neck, the arms, all the way to the tips of the fingers. Last, the face.

It worked, though there was a viper in his stomach, uncurling, threatening to strike. He breathed slowly and tried again. His axe seemed to grow into his hand, the strokes becoming natural and smooth. In a matter of minutes, he had dressed the log. Then Veles, who had been preparing the wedges, applied them to the center of the log, and struck hard with the haft. The tree split like a twig. The work of a few more minutes, and he had prepared the top half of the animal trap.

"Now, go and collect the pine needles and cones, and we'll set this thing."

Antomír did as he was told, forcibly maintaining his calm, though it was already fraying at the edges. The world around him was beginning to blur, as it often did in the evenings, and he felt like he was dissolving into nothing, a speck in a vast, cold world that didn't care for him, or even have an opinion about him at all.

When he returned, Veles had set the trap, and he asked Antomír to dress it. He could have done it himself, Antomír knew, but he was clumsy with the fine work. And it gave Antomír something to do that required intense concentration, or else he would lose a finger, or even an arm.

"There," said Veles, surveying his work like an artist in front of a canvas. He even cocked his head, delighted, something of the small child in his weathered, ugly face. He looked at Antomír, and his pain was suddenly reflected in the bull-man's eyes.

"We are done, anointed one." He took Antomír by both shoulders. "Now, you can weep."

Antomír breathed out, but immediately wished he hadn't. His breath caught and stuck in his throat. He was drowning, drowning in images. He fell into a whirlpool, twisting black waters threatening to choke the life from him. He heard howling somewhere far away, screaming. The sound of a bear cub without its mother. No. That wasn't a cub. It was him. He sagged onto the forest floor and howled again.

Antomír never remembered those hours in detail afterward. Only foggy images tinged with pain like repeated knife-thrusts to the heart. The only clear memory that clung to his conscious mind like a leech on an exposed leg was his mother reaching, reaching for him as she sank deeper into the water. Sometimes he could even hear her say his name. Sometimes she said nothing, but the despair in her eyes was always eloquent.

When Antomír retreated from the darkness of his thoughts, he saw that it was night. He lay under an open sky pierced through with stars. The sparks of a log-fire looked like they hoped to take their places among the stars, before they faded into the misty cold. Antomír felt his fingers come back to him, his hands, his feet. They throbbed with cold. He huddled closer to the fire.

As Veles hung some newly caught fish to dry out overnight, Antomír returned into full awareness of his body. Its shaking was so fierce that his teeth chattered loud enough to hear. The cold seeped into the marrow of his bones. When he closed his eyes, he felt himself expanding, his heart as though pushing against his ribs. He was sure he would burst, so he opened his eyes. He tried to take comfort in the calm, determined movements of the bull-man who was all that was left of his world.

Finally, the shaking subsided. Antomír remembered his name. Then his stomach lurched. He was famished. Then came confusion—how long had they been here? He realized, shocked, that he had little memory of what he and Veles had done since the disappearance of Ghavan. Or rather, he didn't understand what the significance of it all was. Felling trees, setting up animal traps, putting nets into the cove, carving duck effigies out of wood. Antomír realized that he had not said a single word to Veles since...

"Veles," he tried to say, but nothing came out except a croak. He cleared his throat and coughed from all the build-up of his weeks of silence. "Veles!" He managed to expel it like a cat purges a hairball. Veles turned around, his face like a sunrise.

"Well, well. You are strong, anointed one."

Antomír begged to differ. "Veles. What are we doing?"

It was intentionally a question with several levels of significance, but Veles didn't bat an eyelash at it. "I serve you, anointed one. Right now, I will feed you. When you have rested some more, you will know what must be done."

Antomír nodded, strangely calmed by the thought. "How long can we manage out here before we have to...do something?"

Veles shrugged and frowned. "Oh, I think we should be comfortable until mid-spring at least. Some weeks more."

Antomír sighed, and some of his darkness flowed out with his breath. He was inhabiting himself again, slowly.

"Veles, did you see what happened to the isle?"

"It did *not* drown," Veles answered.

"Good, I thought so as well. They are underwater, but the water does not touch them."

He tried to make sense of this event that couldn't be explained in any known terms.

"They will continue to live on Ghavan as they have. The soil will give fruit. They will have access to water. The Living Water will continue to flow." He was sure of this, remembering Aína's face. It shamed him now to think of it. "What do you think? That they have entered another Realm, or that we have been expelled from the Lows of Aer back to Earth?"

"The latter, I think. It will be difficult to find them, in any case, since that particular door has been shut for all times. But they will await your return, anointed one. Or...Or Mirnían will have to find his own way out for his people." Veles said. His eyes were intent on Antomír's face. He was dissolving into his fanatical mysticism again. For once, it was appropriate.

Antomír did not answer for a long time. He still found it hard to feel, much less think, anything. "So what is my purpose, Veles?"

"Far be it for a dog to speak to the master about such things," he said, laughing at himself. His curls bounced on his shoulders. "You will tell me what it is."

Would he? "We don't have many options, do we? We can't stay here."

"I would have thought there is only one place you *can* go, anointed one."

Then it hit Antomír. His father was gone, unreachable, in some other place. Antomír was no longer the Dar-in-waiting. He was now the Dar-in-exile.

"Veles, what do you expect me to do, knock on the doors of Vasyllia? 'Hello, my children! Your Dar is back from exile! Rejoice and be glad!' That will go over well with the Raven and his flunkeys."

"No, anointed one. Not Vasyllia. Not yet. But there is a place—I would have thought your father told you of it—a monastery of warriors who have been gathering men and strength in preparation for the return to Vasyllia. Surely you know of it?"

He did remember something. Something from his childhood—a grey-bearded monk, whose long charcoal robes did little to hide immense physical strength, coming to Lebía to ask permission to take Antomír as a ward. To prepare him to be a Dar that could defeat the Raven. His request, he remembered now, had been politely declined. It was so long ago.

"The monastery is called Raven's Bane by the locals. It is a stronghold, difficult to find, but I've been there once." Veles's brow darkened at some remembrance. "It is a dangerous road, anointed one. We must not go yet. You and I both need to gather our strength. When the lilac blooms, it will be time."

That night, Antomír slept deeply. So deeply that when he awoke in the early dawn, he forgot where he was. Veles was lying asleep at his feet, one hand behind his head, snoring with his mouth open. Antomír, the fog in his mind perfectly complementing the tendrils of mist slithering around their camp, left him in peace.

He trudged, falling over his feet in his drowsiness, down to the shore of the lake. The beach was pebbly, crunching under his feet and massaging them. He rocked back and forth on the balls of his feet as he looked out over the misty water to the place where Ghavan Isle once stood. He could no longer remember the exact place. There was no way of telling—the lake that the Vasylli used to call the "Great Sea" was vast, with no end in sight. Still, he imagined that the place where the fog was especially thick on the water might be Ghavan. He stared so long that he began to imagine seeing the tall hill at the center of Ghavan and the tree with its four-season blooms through the sifting mist.

"Do you blame me, Antomír?" The voice was right next to him. He jumped.

Gamayun sat on the ground, a surprisingly small and pitiful creature now that she was not perched in a tree. He felt that it would be the work of a moment to pull out his sword and end her once and for all.

"What do *you* think?" he said, looking away from her back over the water.

"But did I lie to you? Did I not promise you that your mother would be healed? Do you not feel the joy of that healing?"

Strangely enough, he did. At her words, he felt a surge of emotion, a remembrance without pain, that soothed him and made him smile.

"Yes, I knew that if you did it, you would break the gates of protection. But the changers were coming as it is. The vila had already breached some of the walls. What you did, though you did not know it, was ensure Ghavan's safety. At the cost of your own, of course. I call that a true deed of valor. A manly deed."

"Are you incapable of being silent?" he asked, not looking at her. "What makes you think I would ever want to see you again? Whatever your purpose was in Ghavan, I've doubtless helped you achieve it. Now leave me alone."

"Look at me, Antomír," she said it with such sadness, such pain in her voice that Antomír could not help feeling sorry for her. He turned, not just with his head, but with his whole body. He hated her, but she was clearly suffering. He must do what he could to help her.

Her eyes locked with his, and he found that he could not look away. Something shivered inside him, then began to move, palpitating. Like another heart. His gorge rose and sweat poured down his temples. He almost saw a filigree golden thread being spun from the middle of her vulture body, reaching like a grabbing hand toward his chest. It wove inside him, and he saw visions blurring his eyesight—horrifying things. War, carnage, rape, death, blood, blood, blood.

"You will understand... you will understand." She was intoning, like a chant to some foul, dark deity. He tried to pull away, but he was chained to her with invisible bonds stronger than steel. He tried to scream, but nothing came out. All he could do was look and look and look at the horrors. He was being ripped apart inside. Was this what the soul-bond with the Sirin was like? No, no! This was the foulness of the other side of that coin. A blasphemy, a parody of that love.

"Get away from him, you filth!" bellowed Veles, running with head down and shoulders up. He clutched his tree-root mace in his right hand and swung it at Gamayun, who was momentarily stuck in the ecstasy of her forced bond with Antomír. Antomír watched in slow motion as the mace made a wide arc toward Gamayun, but she was too quick, flapping and flying away with dizzying agility. The mace struck stone.

"He is not yours to take!" He stood before Antomír. The veins in his arms and neck throbbed. Every muscle rippled, ready to be sprung.

"I do not want to *take* him, you fool," she hissed. "He is needed for the world. I am helping him."

"If I ever see you again—and you know I will be watching—I will take you with me to the land of the dead. I do not fear death. I know that *you* do."

She did look afraid. With a last glance at Antomír that burned deep inside his chest, she flew up into the dawn sky and vanished. Veles ran to Antomír and held him at arm's length, looking at his eyes, his face, his torso like a worried physician. Or like a mother.

"Did she do anything to you?"

"She tried to bind herself to me forcefully. Like a Sirin-bond, only horrible. I don't think she managed it in time."

Veles sighed, his shoulders relaxing, making it look like his head was coming up from his back, like a turtle. He turned and stalked back to the camp, mumbling under his breath, gesticulating to himself. Antomír smiled. He did not have the heart to tell his only friend in the world the truth. Inside him, as palpable as his own, a second heartbeat. Gamayun had bound him to herself.

CHAPTER 23
THE CONSISTORY'S MAN

The Gumiren village was a smoking ruin, overrun by Vasylli warriors in little more than half an hour. Not a single man, woman, or child was left alive.

Voran sat on a boulder next to the head man's former house. There was nothing left but the outline of the house's foundation of stone. Voran smelled char and more terrible things he did not want to imagine, but he could not move. He was chained by his bad leg to the rock, left there to watch as the dogs finished their work.

He could not call them Vasylli. He couldn't even call them human beings, these hand-picked warriors of the Consistory with the shriveled dog-heads on their belts. They didn't even kill for the pleasure of it. That would have made them at least like some of the larger predators who like to toy with their prey before eating it. But these were worse than beasts. They killed as a matter of course. Just because it needed to be done. With no more interest in the matter than a scullery girl scrubbing dirt off a pot.

How could this happen to Vasyllia? Voran had expected there to be a reign of terror here, the Vasylli laboring under the yoke of the Raven and his hired Gumiren. But there was no sign of the Raven, no sign of his skin-changers, no sign of anything supernatural at all. Only Vasylli. But Vasylli of such depravity that Voran was surprised they didn't change into monsters before him.

"You think that's it?" asked one of them. He nudged one of the bodies with his toe, examining it. He reminded Voran of a scavenger bird looking for the leavings on an old skeleton. "Have we finally cleaned them out?"

"I certainly hope so," said another, a young man, lazily swatting a mosquito off his arm. He had had the same languid expression when he had butchered the children in the settlement.

Voran had heard this sort of banter all the way to this makeshift settlement. Apparently, this was the last band of Gumiren left in Vasyllia. "A slippery group," one of the dog-men had said. They never remained in one place for more than a few days, always on the move, always looking for that fabled "way out" through the wall somewhere along the border with Nebesta. For twenty years they had managed to survive like this. Voran didn't know how they had managed it. Perhaps it was a last gift of their erstwhile ally, the Raven. But their time had come, as it had come for all Gumiren within Vasyllia.

Still, Voran couldn't quite sympathize with the Gumiren. He *did* feel the desperation of their situation. They had been the consummate invaders, warriors without peer. They had built an impenetrable wall, and now they were hemmed in behind it, butchered by the people they had invaded and ravaged twenty years ago. Nowhere to escape. Finally, the Consistory's purpose—total annihilation of the Gumiren, to the last man, woman, and child—had been accomplished.

Even in his disgust with it all, Voran could not help but feel a sense of poetic justice about the way things turned out for the Gumiren. That is, until he saw the first dead child. That woke something inside him that he had forgotten about for years. Even Vasylli could become demons when left to their own devices, without an ideal to aspire to in faith or civic duty, without a reason to curb their bestial instincts.

Now, after all these years, Voran believed his own sermons. Only a restored monarchy in Vasyllia could put everything to rights. He had a sickening thought that he had not yet witnessed even a tenth of what was actually happening. But who could restore Vasyllia? Sabíana, who bore the sufferings of so many for so long? Mirnían, hiding behind the veil of divine protection on Ghavan? His son? Voran didn't know his nephew, Antomír, except as a precocious, sheltered child. Who could lead Vasyllia out of the mire?

"Healer," barked one of the Consistory men. "Now. You'd better show us something this time."

"I have told you," said Voran, looking down at his empty hands upturned on his knees. "I cannot heal without Living Water, and your masters took it from me."

The warrior struck off the metal spur connecting him to the rock and spit in Voran's face. "Why they keep you alive..." He let it float away, pregnant with meaning.

Voran had never felt so powerless, not even under his bondage to the hag so many years ago, when she had deprived him of speech and forced him to clean her chamber pots. The hard hand of Tarin, who had helped him become a warrior of legendary strength, who had helped him find the Living Water, had never left him in despair. Even visiting battlefields for a living still left a spark of something near hope inside him. But now, he had no Living Water. Without it, his physical strength diminished, and he began to feel, for the first time in his life, his actual age. It didn't help that they fed him worse than they fed their dogs. And he had lost the love of the Sirin. He no longer had anything tying him to the Heights. No sense of transcendence. No perception of Adonais's power flowing through him. Not even a sense of Lyna as a living creature. He was alone, beaten down. And he could heal no one.

"Get on!" The spear at his back pierced skin. The blood oozed out even before the spearhead came out. "We are not at your disposal, O great one."

There was only one wounded man. Voran's heart fell. This was the end. They would have no more use for him, and they would kill him.

The wounded Consistory man had a gash across the left shoulder. It was seeping dark brown blood. A poisoned blade—the last gift of the fallen Gumiren.

Voran scrounged on the scorched earth, hoping to find something that might pull the poison out, or at least force the man to purge it himself.

"What, do you think if you forage like a dog, you can become one of us?" said someone behind him. Two swift kicks in the ribs accompanied the taunt. Voran turned to respond, but the answer died on his lips. What was the point of talking to them? They were not human. He continued to scrabble the hard ground, but the search was useless. There was nothing in the burnt campsite that would help him treat the wounded dog-man.

He stood up. "If I am to heal him, I'll need to go back into the woods to look for a purgative root. This man is poisoned. He won't live long otherwise."

The Consistory man narrowed his eyes, then shrugged his shoulders. He turned away from Voran and waved at the rest of the Consistory men. They converged on him. Voran's stomach lurched. They were going to beat him to death, his mind told him coolly.

They began, without a hint of anything in their actions other than dry practicality. Nothing personal, slave, they seemed to say with their fists. You've just outlived your usefulness.

Voran knew that he was still strong enough to face all of them, if he wanted to. But he did not want to. He had nothing left to live for. So he just accepted it, until the blows dulled from the excess of pain, and the light around him dimmed. But he didn't pass out. He felt every bone break, every bruise burst inside him.

They stopped, but only when they grew tired. Then they got on their horses and left him to die.

Voran lay in place. He couldn't fall asleep. The pain, sharp at first, had descended deep inside him, where it seemed to settle in for a long stay. If he moved, his head throbbed so hard, he thought his temples might burst the blood out.

A night blacker than the moonless darkness descended on him. He had no energy for words, not even for thoughts. If he could have moved his mouth enough to whisper the words, they would have sounded something like this: "Now for the end of all things." He remembered, dimly, that there had been an idea in his heart, a very long time ago. An idea called Vasyllia. Another idea, called Adonais. They were somehow connected. There was someone else there, too, though her face was blurry, like a painting left next to an open window during a downpour. He did not remember her name.

He did remember someone. A boy. His name was Voran. Was it himself, as a child? No. A pockmarked, damaged child. A child who could not speak for the horrors done to him. Voran's first healing. The eyes of that boy, the joy of that inner certitude—he would be well again. And the feeling—like a sunrise inside Voran's heart. How long ago had he last felt that way about a healing?

Someone else—a bear of a man, weeping like a professional wailing-woman. He held a child who fit in the palm of his hand. She was a girl-child named Nadzeia, and she was dying. But her name. It meant "hope." Voran had just touched her, and the Living Water had flown through him with a charge like lightning. The color had rushed into her cheeks, and the baby girl had screamed—a loud, healthy noise that changed the tenor of her father's weeping. Voran remembered his own tears, the prickly feeling on his skin. The thought that he had done nothing, yet the knowledge that if he were to die in the next moment, his would have been a life worthily lived.

An old man, dying after a hard life of toil, had begged only for relief from bed sores. They had grown so fetid, his entire hovel reeked. No one had wanted to help the old man. Voran had tried to heal the man, but he had laughed at him. No, he had said. Not healing. Just a quiet, comfortable death. He had died in Voran's arms with a laugh in his eyes. He was making jokes almost to the end, that old man whom everyone forgot. Voran had wept for almost an hour, holding the luminous dead man.

All the warriors Voran had healed now stood before his mind's eye, uncovering the places where their wounds had been. No more wounds, only baby-skin. And yet, their eyes rebuked him.

Why were they rebuking him? Had he not given his life to them?

The answer came from inside him, empathic and hard: No! He had not. He had skirted around the edge of his duty, never fully committing himself to the healing of the lands, always seeking the easy way out. He never made it back into Vasyllia, though his beloved waited for him for years and years on end.

Light began to flow out of him. Light thick like water, painting the edges of the charred settlement silver, gilding the bones of the dead.

Voran's heart shone. The light revealed all the dark corners of his mind, all the places he had refused to look into for years. What he saw there was terrifying. He saw himself.

He saw his hatred of the Gumiren, his inability to think of them as fully human. He saw his anger with all the sides of the Internecine War. He saw his arrogance before all the puny men who ran around the world, thinking they were shaping events of history. He saw his fear of returning to Sabíana and failing. He saw his endless waffling, excusing himself as not ready, while the Raven grew stronger and stronger in Vasyllia.

Voran knew, with the knowledge that bit deeper than a sword-thrust through the chest—*he had not even begun his real work of healing.*

The light grew inside him, and now the trees around him shone with it. A firebird came, drawn to the light. Two moonbirds followed. Another firebird, joining the first in a rare dance where their trailing tail-feathers, like fire, intertwined and made music out of physical shapes.

To Voran's immense surprise, he probed his heart and found a faint ember of peace. With every breath, someone's invisible hand caressed him like a lover. Someone still loved him. Voran was beloved.

He writhed on the ground as the pain of his body slithered back into his agonized mind. His chest heaved. He had to fight to breathe. And yet...

He was beloved. Sabíana loved him. Lyna loved him. All those he healed had a chance at life because of him.

In that knowledge came a single thought.

Be worthy of their love. Heal!

How? he thought. *I have no Living Water.*

The answer, like a whisper at his ear. "You have never needed the Living Water to heal them. The Living Water was necessary to heal *you*."

He understood what the voice said. He remembered the words of the dark-skinned slaver woman, when she rebuked him for not using the Living Water properly. She had meant that he had to do more than lessen the pain of others. He had to take their pain onto himself. With a lurch of pain that made his head swim, Voran raised himself onto his broken legs and feet. They held him.

He had no more questions. He knew how to do it. He could do it. He would take their inner and outer wounds and lay them, physically, onto his own body.

In a flash, he realized that he had already begun to do it. He remembered the face of one of the Consistory men who beat him. A large man, almost as big as Voran. His last glance was confused, full of pain. The only one with any sort of emotion. It had been beginning of healing. His face rose up again before Voran in his memory...

...Except it was not memory. The man stood before him, bathed in the light, his eyes wide with fear. He looked ready to either fall over or run away. Voran looked him deep in the eyes and did not allow himself to look away. The man seemed to melt before him.

"What is your name, brother?" Voran managed, though it hurt to say it.

"My name?" It was no more than a croak. His eyes were fogged with confusion. Did he really not know his own name? Then, a spark in his expression. "My name...Llun. I was a smith, once." The pain in his eyes flared as he remembered. "Then I was turned. I became one of them... a dog-man. I thought I did it to protect...to prevent greater evils. But I was turned." He shook, fell on his knees and began to wail. "I did it to save the future of Vasyllia. They were going to kill ... my family... Instead, I killed the children of the Gumiren. I...I..."

It attacked Voran like the thrust of a wave. The man's pain. Voran felt it physically inside himself. *This is more than any man should ever have to bear.* But Voran's joy rose to overcome all that pain. For the first time in what seemed like many years, he had the exact remedy for this man's heart-sickness.

"Llun...Mirodara. She's safe. She's well. She did what she set out to do."

The man jerked in surprise. "Mirodara?" His face went white, then flushed as he struggled to breathe. "I was told she was dead. I was shown proof."

"She did die. But she came back to life. The flask you made...it poured forth Living Water. It brought her back."

Llun laughed through his tears, which fell so profusely it almost looked comical. Voran couldn't stop himself from laughing with the big man, then groaned from the effort as his body reminded him of his recent beating. Even so, there was a lightness in Voran, even in the pain.

"But Voran," said Llun. "The flask?"

"They took it," said Voran.

Llun's face fell, wiping away his recent joy.

"Don't worry, brother," said Voran. "I believe it has done all it was intended to do. It no longer carried any Living Water. Not for the last few weeks."

"So," said Llun, after a few moments of calm silence. "What do we do now?"

Voran smiled. "It's time to go home, Llun. We have work to do."

CHAPTER 24
THE WEDDING

Alienne lay beside Parfyon in bed, fitting perfectly against his chest and under his arm, as though she were created to inhabit that place forever. She breathed softly on his neck, tickling him pleasantly. Her eyelids fluttered occasionally against his skin. It was at once unbearable and wonderful. Parfyon still couldn't believe his fortune. Yes, she had used him, but she seemed to genuinely like him. Besides, she kept her part of their bargain with much more than mere willingness. She was beautiful, passionate, even a little wild; but she had a quiet grace about her. It was so unexpected that sometimes he didn't recognize her.

"Why are you not sleeping?" she mumbled, caressing the almost healed stump of his right arm. It never seemed to disgust her, to his amazement.

"Buzzing thoughts," he said, staring at the pavilion above him. The blue cloth was an exercise in excess, adorned in geometric and floral patterns of actual gold and silver thread. He would have made a show of getting rid of it, had it not also been light, sturdy, and very good at muffling sound.

"What is there to think about?" Alienne asked. "You've had nothing but victory after victory for the past three weeks, with hardly a man lost. In your place, I'd be sleeping the sleep of the contented. Or did you have other ideas?" She cuddled up to him, rubbing against him sensuously.

"No, love." He pressed her closer to himself. "It's just. I want to marry you."

She leaned on her elbow to look at him from above, blocking the patterns with her hair. He had thought her made of iron, jagged like a blade.

But he had been wrong. She was strong, no doubt, but in intimacy she was gentle and soft. "We talked about this. We *are* married. We gave word."

"I want something more...I don't know...binding."

She flushed, offended. He hurried to cover his blunder. "No, no. I don't mean that I distrust your word. It's just... it's said that in the old days, the rites of marriage had latent power in them. It was not merely a symbol. The wife and husband were bound at a deep, metaphysical level. They became one flesh. I want that kind of... I don't know... blessing."

She looked at him with an expression that said, "You're getting spoiled by your good fortune." She was right. In the space of a mere three weeks, after the campaign against Vasyllia had been officially announced and mustered, they had already successfully put down Tiverna, Bskavi, and, today, Vanadía. There was hardly any town left between them and the wall. The only contrary news was reports of a coalition of Karila cities that was on its way to attack them from the South. But they were days away, and he was not worried.

"If it's power you want, then I suggest we let Zmei preside over our nuptials," she said, teasing.

"Why not?"

Her eyebrows rose in surprise.

"I imagine Zmei knows the oldest of the rites," Parfyon continued. "It can be a kind of initiation, a further way to bind our alliance with the giants. I think it's a wonderful idea."

He lifted his arm from underneath her, forcing her to roll off him.

"What, *now?*" She looked as though she would much prefer to stay in bed.

"Do you like me because I *wait* to get what I want?" he asked.

She guffawed and threw herself into his arms with a laugh. "Zmei is going to laugh at you."

Zmei did not laugh in the least.

"I would have thought you frivolous, Parfyon, for asking, except that you seem to understand exactly what you are asking. You want power to bind you two, power that you can sense, power that can sustain you. Nourish you. I can do that for you."

Luckily for them, it was a full moon, the best time for gathering the power of the earth. Silver light was better than gold light for weddings, Zmei explained. Gold light was better for funerals. He instructed both of them to wear nothing but their linen underclothes. Their heads were to be wreathed with rowan branches intertwined with asters. At midnight, they were to come to a clearing in the forest about a ten-minute walk from the army camp, wreathed with asters intertwined in thin rowan branches. He would be waiting for them there.

That night, they stole out of Parfyon's pavilion on bare feet. The lingering cold of early spring tore right through them. Their breath was foggy, turning silver-white in the light of the moon. They ran, giggling like children from the madness of it all. It was not hard to find the place, for it beckoned to them softly, as though they heard music and were drawn to find its source. There was no one in the clearing when they arrived.

"I suppose we're early," she said, and hugged him, trying to siphon off his warmth.

No sooner had she spoken than a red light appeared next to the moon, spherical, growing larger by the second. Its edges licked with fire. Parfyon held Alienne close to him, though when he looked at her, she was not afraid, her expression full of fierce enjoyment. The ball of flame was now the size of the moon, then bigger than the sun. Now it filled the entire sky with its fire. It landed near them and uncoiled into a long neck attached to a scaly body. It was hump-backed, its legs long like a horse's and covered in piebald scales. Its tufted ears were too big for a head that at first glance looked reptilian but had something of the horse in it as well. It was repulsive, yet it thrummed with power.

It opened its mouth and licked out a tongue of flame.

"Are you ready?"

Parfyon recognized the voice of Zmei, though it was more guttural and deep, ancient and terrifying. He nodded.

"Take off your wreaths and toss them into the middle of the clearing." They did so. "Get on your knees before them. Now, extend your hands with your palms cupped." Water appeared in their hands, icy cold. "Look into the water. Now, sing."

Parfyon felt like laughing. Sing? He had never sung anything in his life. He wouldn't know where to start. And Alienne, for all her charms, was as tone-deaf as a post. Then Alienne began to wail and keen next to him, uttering words in some unknown language. It raised bumps on his skin, thrilling him with something between arousal and intense fear. She tossed her head back and forth, a thin froth at her mouth. Something stirred inside Parfyon, a compulsion to open up, to let go, to abandon all his fist-tight inner control. He fought, resisted it with all the strength he had.

"Let GO!" commanded Zmei, spouting flame. It singed the grass all around them.

With a last whimper of his older self, Parfyon let go. Pleasure poured into him, so heady that it seemed to dissolve him into pure sensation. He was no longer Parfyon. He was pulsing, rich, drunken pleasure.

The water in his cupped hands was now fire, greenish and smelling faintly of musk.

"Lay the fire on your wreaths," boomed Zmei.

Parfyon and Alienne opened their cupped hands at the same time. The fire poured through their fingers, sticky like sap. Parfyon's anger, pain, his many frustrations seemed to siphon off him and add fuel to the fire. The squalor of his childhood, the hunger, the constant desire for warmth. The simmering rage at being excluded by other children. The hatred of all finery. The long, slow strengthening of his body and mind after a childhood of sickness. The triumph over the Dolgoruki.

The wreath-fires rose above their heads and dissolved into a shower of sparks, dancing like fireflies.

Parfyon turned to his wife, and there was fire behind her. The trees edging the clearing had burst into flame. She was crowned with red-gold flames. A true queen, worthy to sit on the ultimate throne next to him.

Alienne smiled at Parfyon, and his desire for her was frantic and strong. She took his hand. It shook. Her eyes burned with lust, brighter than the flames surrounding them.

"Good. Do you feel it?" boomed Zmei.

Parfyon could no longer distinguish himself from Alienne. They were not merely joined; they were one person with two faces, two bodies. It was terrifying and glorious.

"Now you are joined," said Zmei, his voice like the cracking open of a fissure in the earth. "The power is hovering between you, waiting to be born. You must make it yours. You must take it for each other and from each other. You are of the earth, and its power will flow into you. But you must take. Take, Parfyon. Take!"

Parfyon took.

Parfyon awoke to a world bathed in faint golden light. The sun had just risen above the line of Vasyllia's mountains, gilding the peaks and making the snows blinding. The nearest slopes curved down like a mother's embrace toward a lake that had not been there last night. Pristine waters reflected a mountain range that looked somehow more real than the actual mountains. All around him, bluebells shivered in the breeze. As the breeze gusted, they bent low as though in homage, their purplish tint stark against the white of Alienne's skin. The green of each blade of grass was so vivid that it seemed painted into existence only moments before.

Was this the same clearing that had burned with Zmei's fire all night?

He remembered. The night. Their coupling. The power of the earth that had pulsed waves of ecstasy through Parfyon's body, far richer than any animal pleasure of their merely physical union.

"We created this," he whispered aloud. The breeze turned to him and caressed his body. It was moist with the last tendrils of morning mist. Smells of pine and cedar tickled his nose. His fingertips tingled as the tallest of the grasses grazed his body. He closed his eyes, and the sounds took over—wind whistling through clover, dew dripping from cones into still pools between tree-roots, the buzz of a sleepy fly growing into the humming music of a bumblebee still trying to find its morning wings. Parfyon was one with this nature. It *was* him. This state of being was pure ecstasy, more intoxicating than a hundred bottles of mead.

He opened his eyes, and the picture faded before his eyes, like water dripping on a canvas. Drops of grey and brown filled out and took over the green, like a spreading disease. The burn marks reasserted themselves in the grasses. The lake shriveled into a pile of dust and ashes.

This is what dying must feel like, Parfyon thought as the pain bit into his chest. Where the pleasure was, now a void remained. Only regret and hatred flowed into it, trying to fill it unsuccessfully.

Alienne murmured and turned over.

He had been wrong! Alienne was the decay. Parfyon was life, and she was death. He was the power; she was the drain.

He snapped into himself again, as though thrust awake out of a dream. He shook his head and laughed. What had come over him just then?

"Is it what you wanted?" asked Alienne.

What was wrong with her voice? It was dull, lifeless, lacking in color. And what was wrong with her hair? Was it always that mouse-brown?

"What's wrong?" she asked, reflexively covering herself from his gaze, as though he were a stranger.

Everything. Everything about her was wrong. The way she pulled at her right forelock. Her slightly wider left thumb. That brown spot on her left shoulder. It was disgusting. *She* was disgusting.

Again, he snapped back into himself as though waking from a dream.

His head throbbed with pain, his lips were fuzzy, his mouth tasted of stale bread.

"I'm sorry..." he began, though he did not look her in the eyes. "I..."

It was the power. It had left. It had taken with it a layer of enchantment from the surface of things. Now, they all lay bare before his eyes in their actual colors, their true essence. No. This could not be borne.

"You feel it too?" she said in her ugly voice, the one he had once thought was tinged with wind chimes. "The peeling away of the skin of the world."

That was exactly what it was.

"I want it back," he said. "The skin. Bring it back. The world is disgusting without it." *Even you are disgusting without it*, something whispered into his head. He shook it out.

Alienne sat shaking in the burnt grass like an abandoned child. Parfyon blinked, and things reasserted themselves into their proper order. The world was back to normal.

He picked her up in his arms. She nestled into that comfortable place between his shoulder and neck. The world put on another layer of its beauty again. She kissed his neck, gently. Invisible fingers seemed to run up and down his back. She was beautiful. She was the fair Alienne again.

He breathed out in relief. "Are you alright?" He whispered into her hair, matted with dead leaves and brown grass.

She nodded and sniffed. His shoulder was wet with her tears.

"Please, Parfyon. Let's never do that again. That power. Let Zmei keep it for himself."

"Yes, Alienne. Yes, you're right."

Something slithered inside his head, whispered, *You will not rest until you feel the power inside you again.*

CHAPTER 25
HEALING FROM A HAG

Khaidu wandered through something like fog and water mixed into one. She kept trying to get out, or up, or underneath—she couldn't quite understand which. In rare moments when she seemed to awaken, everything hurt, and she willingly plunged back underneath, into the comfortable murk. Sometimes she sensed that she was not moving, and it jarred her back into the real world. These moments were nearly always at night.

At night, she had longer periods of lucidity. She saw Aglaia as the wolf sleeping by her on the forest floor, and she knew her. But the rest of what she saw disturbed her. Khaidu had never in her life seen a tree grow higher than her head. And now she was surrounded by dark giants that loomed over her and seemed to reach for her whenever she turned away. The vaulted sky that was every nomad's joy was obscured in these forests. She felt claustrophobic, insignificant. An ant surrounded by people with stomping feet.

Sometimes, in the midst of the fog, the supernatural irrupted into her world. In the mornings, just before the sun appeared, a huge warrior in red on a horse of fire passed across the distant horizon, so big that he dwarfed the trees, even though he must have been hundreds of miles away. As soon as he passed, the sun rose, as though chasing him. In the evening, during that hour of twilight when the sun is not quite gone, a somber, black-robed rider on a horse of shadow rode across the opposite way of the horizon, and the sun hid from him.

The visions confused Khaidu, but, in an ineffable way, seeing those giant riders grounded her. They reminded her of the great song of the world's harmony, of her people's constant search for the Unknown Father who would teach them how to live. The fact that such supernatural things not only existed, but showed themselves to her, gave her hope that she was not entirely on the wrong path any longer.

But these realizations were more amorphous than concrete. They were intimations, suggestions that came to her in waves, waxing and waning, never fully present.

Khaidu came back to full realization in front of a crooked hut. At first, she thought there must be something wrong with her eyes. But no, the hut at the end of the clearing was definitely crooked. It stood on two rickety piles of stones, which, from a distance, looked like legs. One of its windows was shuttered, the other not—the house winked at her, it seemed. The open door creaked in a cross-breeze.

Khaidu lost consciousness again. When she awoke, she lay on the grass, facedown, and two voices were trying, without success, to be quiet.

"You should have seen it!" This was Aglaia. "One moment, they were attacking us from the skies. Just like those Gumiren hunting eagles, you know? Then, the wolf-child fell off me, and something seemed to rise up from her body, like steam, but barely visible. The eagles transformed. They were not eagles at all."

"What were they?" asked the other voice, a sarcastic and bored mumble. "Flying hogs?"

Aglaia continued as though she didn't hear. "They were...I don't even know. They were like...Have you ever seen the old tapestries in Vasyllia Palace? No? The way they used to represent wind. Almost like birds, but with huge wings, like oversized butterflies or war banners. And eyes. So many eyes."

"Pfft...don't be ridiculous. What you're describing sounds like...Majestva. But they're mid-level Powers. If you trap mid-level Powers inside eagle forms, you're insane...Wait. You're *not* lying?"

"Hag, if you didn't spend all your time tormenting questing warriors and eating some of them, you'd actually smell what's on the wind. It stinks."

"The Raven was always a stinker." The one called "hag" had a sudden coughing fit so fierce, it sounded like she would fall over and expire on the spot.

"Are you done?" said Aglaia. "Was I not giving you enough attention?"

"Well, you do talk an awful lot."

"Are you listening to anything I'm saying?"

The hag whimpered. "You would think being banished to the armpit of the Three Lands would be enough. But no. You have to come here and demand atonement from me."

"It is only fair." Aglaia's voice had an edge to it.

"What do *you* know? You're his mother. What did I do that was so bad? Hm? Voran ended up pretty solid, if you ask me. And I played a part in that."

Aglaia growled.

Khaidu had grown sick of not seeing this interesting conversation. She tried to turn herself over. It was like a hailstorm of arrows all over her back. She stifled a scream, but something like a gurgle did come out.

"Oh, my, you were right," said the hag. "She's a mess." She ground her teeth audibly. "It'll be a lot of work. A heavy price."

"Don't be absurd. She's a girl, and a good one. She isn't some over-stuffed and under-baked Ivan. She's a Gumira. Iron in her bones."

The hag made an interested sound and bent down to look at Khaidu. "A talent *and* a Gumira. You've done it now, wolfie. I can't help myself. Still, I'm not sure even I can fully heal her."

She did something with her fingers—they were knobby like wood carved by a small child—and Khaidu was hit with a wave of sleep so strong, it thrust her under. Her last thought as she fell was an earnest desire that she would finally stop falling unconscious.

Khaidu woke up. Her mind was clear, as though she had slept for days. She touched her face. Scarred and droopy, but no more than usual. No talon marks in the neck. Her hands were calloused, dark, and rough, but hers. She breathed; it did not hurt. She pushed herself up from the grass. That hurt, but in a familiar way. It seemed the hag had done something to heal her after the eagle attack. Or whatever those eagles were.

She remembered in a flash—the eagles' feathers molting in bunches like autumn leaves falling, and the silvery-blue...Whatever it was. Wings? Bodies? Four majestic creatures made of wind and ice and fog and fire and... eyes...thousands and thousands of eyes. She had freed them. The thought was ridiculous. But it was true. What had the hag called them? *Majestva*...

Something crashed, and the house seemed to jump awake. The closed shutter flew up, a dim fire came alight, and an old woman with three hairs, a nose that met her chin, and a face sprouting warts stumbled out. One eye was still closed, and she tripped over a branch that lay in front of her door.

"Stupid mice ... *every* time." She stopped in place and began to sniff. "Eh? Something smells funny here." She peered in Khaidu's direction, as though she was nearsighted. "Is that...a dog?"

"N-n-n-o!" Khaidu couldn't help laughing aloud.

The hag jumped at the sound, then winced as she grabbed her back. "Ow. That was not nice. Don't you know about old backs, you little beastie? And what are you, anyway? Are you good to eat? I haven't eaten in a long time."

She rummaged around in her filthy rags. She found what she wanted deep inside her skirts-a circular piece of glass on a wooden stick. Trying it from different angles, she finally stuck it in front of her eye. The eye grew to monstrous proportions. Khaidu recoiled.

"What...a boy? Good. Boys I'll eat with pleasure."

"N-n-n-ot boy!" Khaidu was starting to get annoyed.

"You don't look like a girl," the hag insisted.

"G-g-g-irl!!" Khaidu countered.

The hag deflated with disappointment. "I don't like to eat girls. Solidarity, you know. Though don't imagine *I* was ever a girl!" She pointed a finger that curled like a talon.

Khaidu nodded, not knowing what to answer.

Seemingly content with that, the hag stretched, but her back cracked and she yelped in pain. She proceeded to hop on one foot, spinning around like a creaky top. On the last hop, something loud popped back into place, and she sighed with delighted relief. She was just about to walk down the steps and past Khaidu when she seemed to notice her again.

"Who are you?" She asked, as though she were seeing Khaidu for the first time.

"Kh-kh-kh-aidu!"

"What?"

Khaidu tried again.

"What?"

Khaidu tried a third time.

"Wait. Let me get..." The hag went back into the house, from which came a commotion like falling pots. She came out again holding a strange contraption. It was like a set of rabbit ears attached to a metal band that fit over her mostly-bald head.

"Say it again, would you?"

Khaidu was boiling with irritation. "Kh-kh-khaidu!"

The hag jumped from the increase in volume. "No need to shout! I can understand you well enough. Yes, I am doing very well, thank you much. What was it you wanted?"

"H-h-h-elp!!!"

"Oh, you need my help? How refreshing." She sniffed and threw off the rabbit ears. "It's been ages since a girl has come to ask me for help. Only boys do, these days. They're all useless, not like the big, strapping ones from ages ago, the beefy ones with pea-brains. They were lovely. But these new ones? They don't even make for good aspic!"

Khaidu groaned and lay down. She was too tired of holding herself up for this idiot woman.

"Well, come on now. You probably know the drill, yes?" The hag pranced into the house, leaving the door open. Khaidu did not follow her. Where was Aglaia? Was this some sort of absurd test?

After about five minutes, the hag's head peeked out. "Aren't you coming?"

"C-c-c-an't," Khaidu managed. Then, finally, she vented the full force of her exhaustion and began to wail.

"Oooooh! Nonononono! Crying I can't abide. Not womanly, that. Only snotty boys cry. Stop that!" She came up to Khaidu and picked her up with arms like tempered steel. Khaidu found herself too close to those eyes for comfort. They were cunning like a fox's, and just as predatory, but at the moment, mischief seemed to be winning over anything too ravenous. "You little thing. No legs on you at all."

She carried her up to the porch and deposited her on a rocking chair that seemed to move of its own accord. It was surprisingly pleasant to sit on something that wasn't Aglaia's back.

"Now, I have...let me see..." The hag bit her lower lip, screwed her eyes up, and began to count, tapping her one good tooth with her fingers. "... three hundred fifty-nine potatoes that need to be peeled. Show me your hands. Good. Arms? Ooh! Look at those muscles! Are you sure you're not a boy? No? Pity..."

She hopped back into the hut and came out with a vat full of potatoes in water. She pulled out a dirty old knife from behind her back, looked at it, grimaced, spit on it, and rubbed it with even dirtier hands. That seemed to satisfy her.

"Well." She sniffed again. "I have some... business to attend to. You take care of these potatoes, and maybe I'll give you a bite to eat. If anyone comes by, especially boys, just tell them to come right into the hut. The hut will take care of the rest." Her expression turned into a hungry mountain cat's. Khaidu swallowed hard.

The hag hopped and limped across the clearing into the trees, where something very like a huge mortar stood. She climbed into it, pulled out an enormous pestle, struck it against the ground, and flew away faster than a sparrow pursued by a hawk.

It took Khaidu a good three hours to finish the potatoes. Her fingers froze, and the inside of her palms cramped every time she tried to grab the knife. The hag appeared just as she finished peeling the last one, as if she had been watching from afar. Then she took Khaidu into the house and gave her two troughs, one filled with clean water, the other with dirty dishes. These she washed. Then she had to clear out the dirt from inside the old stove, which was difficult without a set of working legs, but Khaidu wedged herself against the wall and managed to find a good angle for her strong arms to work. Then it was scrubbing the floor— "Don't forget the bugs under the table, dearie"—then strewing clean rushes over it. While she was doing all this, the hag busied about the hearth and table, cooking up a storm. It smelled amazing.

"That's good, my boy...I mean, girl—sorry, wishful thinking. I haven't had man-soup in so long, and my eyes and memory are not what they used to be. Now, come and eat."

Khaidu gasped. There was not an empty space on the table. The sauces alone—cherry, gooseberry, blueberry—took up half of it. There was dried fish and roast fowl and smoked eel. Fanciful concoctions of dough rose like towers from beds of cabbage, fringed with radishes. The hag cut one of these open, and Khaidu counted ten—no, twelve!—layers of filling. It was enough to feed half the horse-clan of Mamai jani-Beg.

"Eat, dearie, eat! I certainly will." And she did, with such fierce aplomb that Khaidu had to hurry, lest the hag eat everything in a matter of minutes. The experience was even better than riding a horse for the first time. Khaidu nearly wept at every bite.

"Now dearie, you must sleep. The morning is wiser than the evening."

To Khaidu's horror, the hag was dissolving into mawkish affection. She was obviously very dependent on eating well.

For a moment, Khaidu thought the hag might turn into something monstrous in the middle of the night, but she was tired, tired as she had not been in her life. She fell asleep in the hag's arms, even before the hag had a chance to put her down on the little straw pallet in the corner of the hut.

"You want to go *where?*" said the hag the next morning, with the pastry halfway to her mouth. It stayed there, hovering.

"N-n-n-neb-besta."

"You're crazy. There are giants there, running rampant. And all kinds of other nastiness. And it's close to Vasyllia. Do you even *know* what's in Vasyllia?"

Khaidu stared at her firmly, not letting the hag's glance go. The hag crumpled over in a sigh.

"And to think...I actually liked you. First time in—" She began counting again, tapping her one good tooth. "Four hundred and thirty-nine years. Not since dear old Elena. I wonder where she is now?"

Khaidu cleared her throat so loudly that the hag jumped. "Did I say *like*? No, no. Don't like you one bit. Annoying, stubborn girl."

A pastry flew into the hag's mouth, and she softened immediately, smiling blissfully as she masticated. Bits of dough flew out of her mouth, as though trying to escape the inevitable. Getting up from the table, the hag waddled to an old chest, humming. The lid creaked when she opened it. She rummaged in it, mumbling to herself, throwing rags, old twisted bits of metal, a skein of light blue thread, and other bits of flotsam all over the hut.

"It's like I told that infernal wolf-woman," she said, coming up from the chest for air, "I couldn't heal you from the old damage. Only the new hurts." She plunged back into the chest like a diver seeking pearls. "But I have a few presents to give you."

Khaidu had to stop herself from laughing at the bobbing of the hag's head as it came up and down, mumbling all the while.

"Ah! There it is." She pulled out a silver tray and a golden apple. These she presented to Khaidu, seemed to think better of it, then grudgingly pressed them into Khaidu's hands. "Take these. They're not much. But if you are in a very dark place, with very little hope, just take the golden apple and roll it around the silver dish...No, don't do it now! The dish will then show you your heart's desire. But it only works once, so use it at the right time."

She was dissolving into mawkishness again. Khaidu was afraid she would actually hug and kiss her. Khaidu had heard of such barbarous rites among the pale-skins. She stiffened and bowed a quick thanks. The hag hugged her anyway. Khaidu closed her eyes, hoping it would end soon. She couldn't hold it anymore. Through the smelly folds of the hag's clothes, she managed to chirrup like a blackbird.

Aglaia burst through the doors, teeth bared. "What did she do?" She growled, then stopped, confused by the scene of domesticity.

"Khaidu, I told you to use that call only in the most extreme case!" grumbled Aglaia.

Khaidu shrugged noncommittally.

The hag laughed. "Well, since you're here, you might as well eat."

They all sat to finish the leavings of the hag's feast of the previous night. If possible, the pastries were even more delicious on the second day.

"I see you didn't quite manage it," complained Aglaia, now in her human form.

The hag screwed up her face as it turned pink. She looked like she might burst. "You...ungrateful..."

"What?" said Aglaia. "I see no visible difference. Other than the wounds from the eagles."

Khaidu found she didn't appreciate being spoken about as though she were not quite there.

"I'm h-here, you know," she said.

Aglaia's eyes widened as her mouth formed a slight "O".

The hag laughed, and a fountain of pastry spewed all over the table. "See? She's already taking to it. It'll take some time, and there will be relapses... But I'm pretty sure that you won't thank me, Aglaia. That wolf-child's got a razor-tongue there, you'll see! Still time to change your mind?"

She raised her talon-fingers, but Khaidu grabbed them and pushed them back down. The hag smiled grudgingly.

"See what I mean?" she said to Aglaia. "Good thing I could only heal her tongue, and only gradually. If I healed her legs, then watch out, Three Lands! You'd all have to bow down before a new Gumira queen, the Ghanima Khaidu jani-Beg!"

The name sang on the air, thrumming like a perfect chord played together with the deepest overtone ever sung by a master of the storytelling arts. Khaidu forgot to breathe for a second as she saw visions of herself standing before a crowd of thousands who chanted her name with adoration in their eyes... but wait. No. She had never wanted anything of the sort. She was Khaidu, the broken daughter of a lost horse-clan. She would never amount to much.

"No, perhaps you wouldn't," said the hag, answering her unspoken thought with a strange expression of pity mixed with something like laughter. "And don't expect to be able to speak all at once. Your tongue was very, very stuck. It'll take some time for it to come back to normal. But it will. No need to thank me."

Then Khaidu realized what had been nagging at her. They had all been speaking... what was it? Not Gumir, for certain.

"W-w-wait...How can I sp-p-eak...what is it? V-v-vasylli?"

"Oh, that." said the hag, shrugging it off. "I don't like Gumir. Ugly language. Too much throat. With *my* phlegm problem? Not pretty. So yes, I gave you Vasylli. So what?"

Aglaia laughed, but it was forced. When no one joined her, she subsided into an awkward silence.

A stone-weight descended on Khaidu's chest. To be so close to healing... It was almost worse to have partial healing than none at all. If the hag wasn't lying, of course.

"W-what...will it t-t-take..." Khaidu began, then stopped herself in angry embarrassment.

"To heal you?" The hag was uncharacteristically serious. "Living Water, I think. And on this Realm..."

Aglaia finished her sentence. "There is no more flowing Living Water."

Something huge flew past the window of the hut, obscuring the light of the sun. Khaidu only saw it with the corner of her eye. But it was enough to stop her heart for a full second.

"Ag-g-laia," she croaked, losing the lightness of her tongue. "Th-that... w-w-was th-that...?"

Understanding flooded Aglaia's face as it lost its color. She rushed to the open door, still creaking like a snoring old woman. The sun blanched her face of all its remaining color as she looked up toward the tower-high elms surrounding the hag's clearing. She gasped, barely audibly. But in that sound, Khaidu's heart plunged. Every muscle in her body clenched as she fought her tears with every inch of her strength. They still came. Sabíana had been so close. And to lose her now?...

"It's not too late, Khaidu," said Aglaia, already changing into the form of the wolf. "No eagle is too fast for Aglaia to track, not even Sabíana. Hurry, we can still find her."

CHAPTER 26
THE BEAR-RIDERS

"**V**eles," whispered Antomír. "Bears!"

Veles rolled over in his bed pallet, and already his mace was in his hand. His eyes were clear, as though he only played at sleep. Perhaps he did.

Veles sniffed, and his eyes grew wide. "By the fruitful mother of the five kings! Not just any bears, either. Grizzlies."

"This far west?" Antomír had never seen anything other than a black bear, but grizzlies were supposed to be five times larger. Impossible to outrun. Very, very hungry for human flesh. "I thought they only lived near the northern mountains of the Steppe. Maybe a few in Karila."

Veles didn't answer. He had a strange, faraway look in his eyes, like he was thinking of home. Antomír realized he didn't actually know what *was* home for the giant man. He felt a stab of guilt. How little he knew about the one person who was willing to give up everything for him.

"Anointed one," said Veles. "Do you trust me?"

"With my life," said Antomír.

"Then listen. You must not run. When the bears come, stand up straight and look at the pack leader in the eyes."

Packs? *Of bears?* "Look at it? Are you mad? The first thing any woodsman tells you is never to look in the eyes of a hungry predator."

Veles let out the air from his nose like a bellows. An annoyed bellows. Antomír sighed and nodded. "I trust you. I'll do it."

Something rustled in the bushes just outside the firelight. Bears on three sides, the ice-cold sea behind them. Shapes lurched just beyond, in the darkness of the woods. Hulking shapes on rippling legs. They were trapped.

Antomír looked back to Veles, anxious for some sort of direction. Veles was gone. Antomír immediately cursed him for a coward. But no. He had promised to trust. Veles would not abandon him. Veles knew what he was doing.

The rustling turned into the snapping of branches. Four huge shapes lumbered out of the darkness and stopped at the edge of the camp. Their eyes glowed red in the firelight. Or maybe that was just the way their eyes naturally were. Nothing was impossible anymore in Antomír's world.

They all jumped forward at the same time, their speed almost too great to see with the eyes. One moment, they were vague shapes, the next, they were only inches away from Antomír. They froze in place. The one that faced Antomír directly was the largest, so big it looked down on Antomír. Its muzzle quivered, and saliva dripped from the side of its mouth. The lips rippled up, and it growled so low, the sound resonated inside Antomír's bones.

Veles? Where are you?

The bears to either side of Antomír shuffled closer, and one of them tried to outflank him. Antomír inched backward to keep the water at his back, but the lead bear snapped its jaws at him, and its nape rose, almost like a lion's mane. Its legs crouched slightly. The killing stance.

Antomír grabbed his shuddering left leg with his arm, forcing it to remain still. He gritted his teeth until he was sure they would break from the strain. He breathed out, hard, then inhaled slowly. He looked directly into the eyes of the beast that was preparing to kill him.

Antomír gasped, then smiled. The eyes. They were not wild in the least. There was something intelligent in them. He continued looking at them, so incongruous above a snarling muzzle. He extended his hand, slowly, to the open jaws. He clenched his hips, and his left leg relaxed. He stopped shaking. He put a finger on the beast's snout. It was pleasantly wet.

"You are a mystery, aren't you?" whispered Antomír, in awe.

The bear laughed. Or so it seemed, its snort was so sudden and short. It backed away from Antomír and bowed. The others retreated as well. He breathed, and the stars danced in his eyes. He had been holding every muscle in his body to painful tautness. As he relaxed, his left shoulder flared in pain, complaining.

"As are you, anointed one." It was not Veles. Antomír stiffened again, wary. The voice continued. "Untested, yet full of potential. I wonder what the rest will make of you?"

A man walked out of the darkness. He was as tall as Veles was wide. Rope-like muscle moved just under the skin of his arms and chest, uncovered by the loose linen shirt, open at the collar and with wide sleeves. His skin was the color of a cherry tree's wood. Against the shocking white of his mustaches—they drooped to either side of his mouth, halfway down his chest—and the single thin braid growing from the top of his otherwise shaved head, he looked half a beast himself.

"I am Severuk," he said. "Of the children of the Priest-King."

Antomír remembered the legend of the Priest-King and the fountain of youth. Even now, even after all he had lost, he still felt childish joy at finding out that the legend was true.

Severuk mounted the lead bear. There was no saddle that he could see. "Come," he said, and extended his hand to Antomír.

Riding a bear was not what Antomír expected. The black bears of his home were awkward creatures who did little better than waddle. These grizzlies ran more smoothly than a cantering horse, and they were comfortable in darkness that no horse would ever attempt. More than once, Antomír was sure they would crash into one of the trees. Often they seemed to run straight at it, only to avoid it at a hair's breadth at the last moment.

"Where are we going?" he yelled above the whistle of wind.

"Home," Severuk said.

The appearance of fire-lights out of the darkness was like a passage from dream into waking. It was as though they were in one world in one moment, and in a different world in the next. Even the form of the trees changed. They were mostly deciduous here—beeches and alders and birches—and the air was much warmer. But something was wrong with the trees. Most of them had no leaves, even though it was mid-spring. The leaves that were present were shriveled, pitiful things. Antomír felt it would be a kindness to knock them off the branches. Much of the bark of the trees glinted in the firelight. Some sort of black mold or rot. Then the smell—fetid and warm—infiltrated his senses. The trees were dying.

They crossed the border of the fires and were suddenly in a churn of bear-riders. Antomír had never seen so many people in one place, much less warriors. They all had variations of Severuk's strange, drooping mustaches and shaved heads. Some had the fountain-like burst of hair erupting from the top of their pates, others were shaved bald. Each had two swords, a round shield, and a quiver with arrows hanging from a special holster at the hip. None of the bears wore saddles. Veles was nowhere to be seen.

They congregated around Severuk as he dismounted. Severuk helped Antomír jump down, and he almost fell. He had not noticed that his legs had fallen asleep astride the bear. One of the four bears that had cornered Antomír—it had reddish fur and amber eyes that were like pools of water with deceptive depths—nudged him and made a sound between a grumble and a laugh.

"She likes you," said Severuk, smiling. *She?* "Perhaps you will ride her, once you are found worthy."

The bears acted like no bears Antomír had ever seen. They were comfortable with their riders, though not slavish like dogs. Each animal had its own character, he could see even at a glance. One of them kept trying to wrestle with his rider playfully. Another rested his (her?) head on the rider's shoulder. Some riders leaned on their beasts, some embraced them. Some fed them. One thing was clear—the animals were intelligent enough to have a mutual relationship with their riders. They were not beasts of burden or pack animals. They were... friends.

There was something else Antomír sensed. Intense camaraderie between man and man, between man and beast, between beast and beast. A community so strong, so intrinsic, that Antomír immediately felt excluded, though many of the men greeted him with bold eyes and short bows. A desire to belong to them rose up inside Antomír. It was intense, stronger even than what his youthful heart had previously imagined love to feel like. This was a need, almost physical in its intensity. He yearned to feel the hard embrace of these men, to see kinship in their smiling eyes.

For now, there was no kinship in their eyes, but neither did they ignore him. All—man and beast—regarded Antomír with unconcealed curiosity.

"Come, anointed one," said Severuk. Antomír flushed in embarrassment at the exalted title and looked down on the ground. "Sit and eat." He sat on a log by one of the larger fires, over which a large pot boiled. The smell—beef, onion, and...cloves?—washed over him invitingly. He almost ran to sit by Severuk, almost clinging to him in this sea of unfamiliar men.

Severuk smiled at him as he handed him a bowl, and there may have been a hint of a bow there as well. Antomír thought he would never stop blushing again. Luckily it was dark, and the fire was warm, so some red in his cheek wouldn't give him away. He hoped.

For the rest of the night, Antomír watched, absorbed in every movement of these strange warriors. Soon after he finished eating, flasks of some alcoholic spirit were passed around, and the subdued conversations bubbled into ever louder bursts of laughter, jovial argument, and song.

Soon the entire camp sang the same songs. They didn't seem to end. As soon as one song seemed to come to its natural conclusion, another would form itself out of the last words and notes of the dying song, so that the whole night, it seemed that they sang a single, unending song. Antomír didn't understand the words, but the meaning was clear enough. There was war in it, loss, love, a wistful desire to see loved ones lost in war or living in far-off lands. Notes of joy intertwined with plaintive keening. On the edges of his hearing, Antomír thought he heard women's voices interweaving with the strong, tremulous singing of the warriors.

Every once in a while, when the song became too boisterous, some of the warriors began to dance—flailing about with their fists and their feet in ways that seemed random, even frantic, until Antomír saw the intense concentration, the restrained power of those movements. Swords came out of their scabbards in mock sword-forms that danced in the firelight. Figures of eight, curls, flips—they could do nearly anything they set their mind to with their weapons. *What fighters these men must be*, he thought.

Drowsiness stole over him without him even noticing. One moment, he was watching, agape, as three men took one of their fellows and threw him into the air, where he flipped over and twisted impossibly, landing on his knee as though it were the easiest thing in the world. The next moment, Antomír awoke to find the fire nothing but embers. He lay wrapped in a warm blanket, one form amid a sown field of sleeping warriors. For a moment, Antomír was content.

Antomír quickly assimilated to the camp life, with its daily weapons training, feasting, drinking, and singing. Repetition of rote activities, tempered with fierce joy in the evenings—it was enough for his heart-wound to begin scabbing over.

Every morning they rose with the sun. It was always the same. One of the warriors sang a greeting to the dawn, and as the rest of his brothers awoke, they joined the song in their own voices, with their own harmonies. By the time the entire camp was awake, the song was a torrent of sound, dissonant, yet alluring. Soon afterward, the training began, and did not abate until a short break to eat and rest, while the sun traversed its highest point. Afternoons were for the bears. Some practiced riding, some fought with swords and shields while mounted, some raced each other. Some simply wrestled or lounged about with their friend-bears. Then, another song—this a lament so piercing that Antomír battled his tears every night—accompanied the sun to its nightly repose. Finally, the feasting and singing and dancing, until they would simply collapse from tiredness wherever they stood.

At first, the warriors simply accepted Antomír. They trained with him, shared food and drink with him, but their eyes did not include him in their manly intimacies, reserved for dear friends, brothers, and bears. But as the days turned into weeks, as his skill with the sword began to approach their own mastery, as his body lost every vestige of fat it ever had, some looked on him with interest. With a few, that soon became camaraderie. Severuk alone showed him genuine respect.

Every day, Antomír wondered what could have happened with Veles. But as soon as resentment or doubt began to creep in, he forced himself to recall his promise. He trusted Veles with his life. Veles knew what he was doing.

One mid-morning, in the middle of a particularly difficult sword-form, Severuk whistled so loud that it echoed. All the warriors snapped to attention. Antomír's ears rang from the sound. Like one of the bears he rode, Severuk climbed a pine in three easy movements, so that everyone could see him, no matter where they were in the camp. The bear riders all turned to him.

"My brothers!" he called, his voice full of strong emotion. "One of our long-lost brothers has come back to us. Veles has come! And not only he, but some of our sisters have come as well!"

At first, murmurs and whispers of surprise, but they quickly grew into a wave of cheering. Antomír strained to see his old friend and the women that Severuk had called sisters. His heart was full, so much that he thought it might burst.

And there Veles was, as though he had never left, materializing next to Antomír.

"Anointed one," he said, then fell on his knees. "Can you forgive me?"

Antomír laughed and embraced Veles, pulling him up, though it felt as useless as trying to budge a monolith.

"I said I trusted you," he said. "I'm sure you had good reason to leave me."

Veles, his eyes full of tears, nodded, then turned to Severuk, who still clung to a branch like an oversized squirrel. A wave of excitement seized Antomír. Something important was about to happen.

"The serpents are uncoiling, riders!" Severuk called in a song-voice. "Veles has seen them and come back to tell the tale. You know what that means!"

All movement ceased. Even the bears stood still, no longer leaning back and forth as bears do, not even drooping their heads. As though they too listened. Everyone's anticipation was palpable.

"Who wills to be hanged, impaled on a spike, or boiled in tar?" Severuk intoned.

Gooseflesh tingled Antomír as he realized. The manner, the half-chant: these were words of ritual, binding to death.

Fifteen men came forward with their bears. The tallest one, a youth named Cassián who was not much older than Antomír, though almost a head taller, faced the ones who had not come forward.

"Who will take my orphans and widow as his own?" He had a low voice, much older sounding than his face suggested.

A mounted rider unsheathed a sword and screamed, "I will take them as my own!"

Each of the other fourteen volunteers then repeated the words. Fourteen of those who remained repeated their words.

Antomír's heart sang as it pumped hot blood through his body. He could almost hear it rushing through his head.

"I have no family," Antomír raised his voice about the hubbub, and everyone stilled, looking at him with deadly seriousness. "But I also will to be hanged, impaled on a spike, or boiled in tar!"

Silence stretched over the trees.

"Are you worthy?" It was a woman's voice. The riders parted to reveal a woman dressed from head to foot in embroidered linen. Her head was wrapped in a red sheet, trimmed in gold, from which gold temple rings jingled as they caught the light of the sun and seemed to juggle it. Her skin was as black as tar. Every rider bowed as she passed. The air almost hummed with the respect they had for her.

"I am not," he said, and stood up straighter. "I am not worthy to die in the company of such as you. I deserve a slave's death. But grant me this one kindness. Let me die nobly, as I have not lived."

"This is not a request to be made lightly. The death you will face may be slow and painful beyond anything you have encountered. You are so young. Not much more than a child."

"A child who has caused the loss of the Dar of Vasyllia. A child who has erased the last haven of Adonais from the face of this world. I have never been much in my life, done much in my life. I would give it, such as it is, for the sake of this brotherhood."

"You do not even know us," said the woman, still serious as death.

"I know that you are good. I have put my trust in the people I love, and that has led me to you. It is my turn to give."

"This is what I was saying, Elmira." Veles said. "His greatness of spirit. Only waiting for the stonemason's pick to hack off the rough bits. And that is why I insist he does *not* go."

"You cannot command the will of the Dar-in-waiting," said the woman he called Elmira.

"You would put the fate of the Realms at risk?" Veles growled. His eyes seemed to glow red.

"Veles, my friend," said Antomír, placing an arm on his massive shoulder. "My father is not dead. He is Dar still. He will find his way out of Ghavan, I know it. But I must risk this. Adonais blesses those who willfully give their life's blood for their brothers. I want to be blood brother to you, to your people."

Veles eyes welled with tears. But there was no sorrow in his expression. No, it was pride.

"A Dar risking his life for a dying world. It is fitting," he said. He bowed to Antomír.

"Worthy!" shouted Severuk.

"Worthy!" shouted Elmira.

"Worthy!" shouted the entire mass of warriors.

Three young women in white linen dresses with red cross stitching on their neckline, hem, and sleeves approached Antomír from the mass of men and bears. They were also dark-skinned. All of them were, Antomír realized. It had not really occurred to his conscious mind before, but they were much darker than the Vasylli. Even Veles's skin was bronze—Antomír had always assumed it was a heavy tan, though it never faded in winter. At that moment, Antomír realized another thing that he had simply accepted, without giving it any thought. All of them, the warriors and these "sisters," as Severuk called them—they were all roughly the same age. Late twenties, early thirties, no older. Even Severuk, whose hair was white, had a young face and body.

Of course. The fountain of youth. These people were not young at all. They were incredibly old.

The three women joined hands and walked around Antomír, singing. The words were in that same language of the warrior-songs.

They raised their hands above their heads and closed their eyes. Light rose up from the earth around him like a mist of fire, golden and fragrant. Elmira approached Antomír with a short dagger in her hand. It glinted in the golden light. She took his shoulder length hair and cut off four locks from it, then threw them on the nearest of the fire pits. Severuk and Veles approached with clay jugs of water. Veles had two, and he gave one to Elmira.

"Kneel," said Veles, his voice breaking. Antomír did.

They poured the water on his head. It splashed in sparks of opal as it passed through the golden light, smelling of lilac. As each of the three jugs was poured over him, Antomír felt a weight in his chest fade away. He had not known it was there. Still, he felt the soft palpitation of Gamayun's bond. It had not broken. Perversely, that was the moment he heard her voice in his head, whining like a child:

"Why do you want to get rid of me? I will raise you to heights unheard of. You don't need these people."

He gagged from the intrusion of another's thoughts in his head but kept himself still. He would rid himself of her somehow, if it was the last thing he did.

"Stand, brother of the children!" Elmira chanted.

Antomír stood, and a red-furred bear approached him on her own—one of those who had cornered him on that first day. She nudged him in the chest and nearly pushed him over. He laughed. She nodded her head up and down. He sensed, clearly, her sharing his enjoyment. He could not understand how. There was no bond here, not like the foul thing that Gamayun had done. Only a shared empathy. An understanding. With rising excitement, he realized how useful such an understanding could be in the madness of battle.

The elation continued to bubble up inside him. It was rich, pungent. Did it have to end so quickly? Would he really die with these men? The thought, to his shock, was not frightening. He was ready to die with them. No, he wanted to die with them.

"Anointed one," said Severuk. "You were born to lead. Lead, then. These men are yours to command."

All fifteen of his personal death squad fell on their knees before him. Their upturned gaze had nothing of disdain as he had expected. No, only of determination, cold as the steel glinting in their gloved hands. How could they expect him to lead? He was just a boy.

Something, a song from childhood, taken from a story Lebía used to tell him, came to his mind. The words seemed perfect for the moment. His skin prickled as he remembered the words:

"*The child-king stood on battlefield bare*
Arrayed against a myriad strong.
Alone he battled while the day waxed fair,
Until he heard death's final song."

CHAPTER 27
THE SLAVE PLANTATION

For five days, Voran and Llun remained near the destroyed Gumir camp, just far enough not to smell or see the horror. Close enough for Voran not to forget his new-found purpose. He felt reborn, even though his body could hardly move without a creaking kind of pain he associated with old age. The inability to move was draining, but he knew, through the weight of experience, that the excitation of a new purpose could wear off quickly. It was wiser to keep it in check, to feed it with contemplation, to assess it and make something real of it, even if only in his mind. He also yearned to hear what was happening in Vasyllia.

Llun avoided looking at him. The former blacksmith spent much of the first three days hunting, or so he said. He had enough food in his saddlebags to feed both of them. Though he never brought anything back from his "hunts," every evening he stood a fraction taller, and his eyes were a fraction less leaden. They were both coming to terms with a new reality.

By the fourth day, Llun himself spoke to Voran as they shared the last of Llun's dried meat, drinking it down with very sour ale.

"So which reach do you hail from?"

"You wouldn't believe me if I told you," said Voran.

"Ah, a third-reacher, then. I thought as much. Your kind didn't do so well after the invasion, did they? How did you get out?"

"I was exiled. Before the invasion."

"That's right. I had forgotten. So much I have forgotten these years."

There was still so much guilt in his voice. Voran hoped it would drain away with time.

"Tell me," said Voran. "What position does Yadovír now hold?" Voran was careful not to mention the Raven, not yet. Too dangerous even to name him in his own domain.

Llun laughed—a grating, bitter sound. "You *have* been gone long, haven't you? Yadovír was killed by the Gumiren more than ten years ago."

Voran nearly choked on the ale. That he never expected. In fact, he had expected Yadovír to be the vessel of the Raven to last the longest. If he was gone, whose body did the Raven take? How would he know him?

"Then who rules in Vasyllia?" he asked, his mind spinning.

"Ostensibly, the representative council of the people."

The Dumar? That made no sense at all! Where was the reign of terror, the tyranny of the Raven?

"Ostensibly? Who rules in reality, then?"

"The Consistory. We dog-men, led by our great lord and master."

"The weasel-faced man that bought me?"

"Yes. Aspidían."

Voran filed away all the questions about him for another time. He was pitifully out of touch with the Vasyllian reality.

"Llun, I don't know if you realize how effectively Vasyllia was closed off from the rest of the world. I need to know what happened in Vasyllia after its fall. How did the power change?"

"It's not clear, really, not even to us in Vasyllia." Llun leaned against a nearby pine tree and sighed with relief. His cheeks were ruddy for the first time since Voran had seen him. "I was a youth when it all started. The Gumiren were in total control for about five years. But they grew…soft. More and more of the Vasylli collaborators began to accrue power to themselves. Aspidían the first of them. But there was also a counter-movement.

"The Sons of the Swan, they called themselves—fanatic followers of Darina Sabíana. Mirodara flirted with joining them. But they all got ratted out by their own neighbors. Most were killed. Mirodara was spared, but only so they could use her to force me to do their bidding…

"Anyway, when the Gumiren killed Yadovír, the Consistory charged the Sons of the Swan with collaboration. Aspidían used the chaos of the attempted coup to reveal his own army of dog-men that had been training in secret. They turned on the Sons and the Gumiren alike. It's said that the Ghan escaped, but the rest of the Gumiren in the city were purged. All the Gumiren throughout Vasyllia have been hunted down and destroyed over the last five years. Then came the turn of the Sons of the Swan."

A glimmer of understanding teased Voran. The dog-men could be the next step in the Raven's plans. Give Vasyllia a sense of self-governance, of triumph, before crushing it altogether.

"Soon, Aspidían declared the official end of the monarchia, saying that the true enemy was not the Gumiren, but the old order of Vasyllia. The Consistory then turned to cleansing Vasyllia of the Sons of the Swan. Some they killed publicly, some they sold into slavery to the outside lands. It was quick and bloody, and it ended sooner than you'd think."

"No one defended these Sons?"

"Aspidían is cunning, Voran. He had prepared his coup a long time ago. I don't know how, but he won trade concessions from outer Karila and even some of the lands beyond the Vasyllian taboo. Places we've never even heard of. Vasyllia's market began to explode with luxuries the Vasylli had never imagined. And the prices were cheap. Market day became a weekly, not monthly, occurrence, a high holy day for the new Vasyllia. And so, the Vasylli themselves rounded up the Sons, convinced that they were a threat to the new mercantile order, to their newfound luxuries. To consolidate public support, Aspidían arranged that the Dumar take political control of Vasyllia, at least superficially. He then dedicated the Consistory's warriors to the continued cleansing of Vasyllia of all outsiders."

Voran was flabbergasted. The Raven's plan was even more cunning than he had imagined. He gave Vasyllia back to the defeated, but in a form that he could control. All he had to do was regulate the market, and Vasyllia would dance to his tune. This was the new Vasyllia—a populace craving the ephemeral pleasures of luxury. When Voran returned, he would not encounter a Vasyllia craving a healer or a return to the old ways. He would only find resistance. Probably violent resistance. One question remained in Voran's mind.

"Is Aspidían the new vessel of the Raven?"

Llun took a long look at Voran, then shook his head.

"Very soon after the invasion, the Vasylli were trained to think of the Raven as 'the Great Father.' After Yadovír's death, the Raven seems to have faded into the background, not showing himself to anyone. Nowadays, many prefer to forget about his existence entirely."

Voran laughed. It was all so well executed. *How foolish I've been. I've wasted so much time!*

"Where is the Darina Sabíana in all this?" Voran said. He was breathless and his face flushed as his heart blew hot blood through his face.

"She's probably dead. Some of the dog-men claim that Aspidían killed her. Others whisper that *she* is the real power behind the scenes. I think she lives, but only at Aspidían's pleasure."

His stomach was a stone pushing upward at his chest. But what had he expected? That she was lounging in her room, waiting for him to come have tea in the afternoon? As he forced his breath to still, he considered what Llun had said about Aspidían keeping her alive. It would make sense. A hostage from the royal family. She could become necessary in case the Sons of the Swan reappeared. Even the suggestion of the thought of her being alive was enough to make him dizzy.

"Who ordered the wall built?" asked Voran.

"That is another strange thing. The Gumiren did it. Why? Not the slightest idea. It makes no sense. Why would anyone cut themselves off from the rest of the world like that? It's a suicide move."

"They didn't do it willingly, surely. The Raven probably forced them." But why would the Raven build a wall around Vasyllia? To give himself uninterrupted time to reach the Garden in the Heart of the World? Perhaps he had not found it yet?

One bright morning about a week later, when the smells wafting on the breeze were full of the promise of summer's coming, Voran felt strong enough to travel again. They set out that very morning—trudging, not walking. The slow pace gave Voran ample opportunity to examine the landscape of his long-lost homeland. It was unbelievably green. At first, Voran thought it was the contrast with Nebesta and Karila's dying nature—the drying out of the soil, the droughts, the insistent spread of the tree-rot. But no. He remembered Vasyllia well enough. It had always been a land of spectacular green, but only for four or five months of the year. The winters were too long and harsh for anything else. Usually, this early in the year, the trees would barely be budding. But now, every tree was bursting with verdure.

But the smells were what confused Voran the most. Lilac already dominated, but he also smelled lily of the valley. Too much of it all, so intense as to verge on the unbearable. He should smell nothing but pine for the next month and a half at least. There were also more birds than ever before. But not a single firebird or moonbird.

None of it made any sense. This was certainly Raven's work. But why? All to keep the Vasylli lulled into their luxurious sleep, while he burrowed into the earth, seeking the lifeblood of the worlds?

They saw their first slave plantation on the next morning. They had come down a steep decline into a small dale, watered by about twenty waterfalls created by the melting summit-ice. An azure lake shimmered in the center of the dale. Every inch of land in the dale was plowed and sowed. Most of it was already in bloom. The small shoots were unknown to Voran.

"It's hemp," said Llun, with a look of amused disdain. "Rather, a very specific kind of hemp. It makes excellent fibers for rope. But it can also be smoked. They say it produces a pleasant sort of euphoria."

Voran felt nauseous. It wasn't enough for the Raven to stupefy Vasyllia with luxuries? He had to dull their senses as well?

There were hundreds of people laboring in the fields of all ages—old men to infants strapped to their mothers' backs. The workers all hunched over, weeding and clearing out the soil. They wore light grey felt, but most of it was closer to brown because of the dirt.

"Slaves?" he asked Llun. Llun nodded, his mouth a tense line.

"Come on, then," Voran said and pointed at the two armed guards sitting and drinking in the shade of a shoddily-built stone shack. The guards reached for their swords when they saw Voran approach, but Llun's dog-belt seemed to calm them. Consistory business, their shared glance suggested.

"Vohini," said Voran, in a commanding voice. "I come bearing the word of Aspidían. To tend to your sick and dying."

"Heh. Plenty of those today," said one of them. "None worth saving, though. Not anymore. The slave trade's all dried up, I heard."

"That's not for you to judge, Vohin," barked Llun in his Consistory voice. Both of the guards stood up. They straightened their helmets and brushed down their leather jerkins, filthy with grease.

"No, sir. The sick are in the outhouse, sir."

The stench slapped Voran far before he saw the reed-woven hovel that must have served as an outhouse. Two young women and an old man lay inside, unmoving, flies crawling all over them. The women did not so much as lift a finger to disturb the flies.

Voran picked up two of them and hoisted one over each shoulder. Llun took the third. They walked back toward the guardhouse, intent on coming within. The guards laughed and blocked their entrance.

"No animals here, healer. You can do your work outside. You're a slave too, judging by your garb."

Everything grew still in that moment for Voran, almost as though he were looking at himself from the side. He had sworn off violence a long time ago. It had seemed wise to him then. He had thought to lead by example, not only by word. But it had not come to anything. He had no followers, no disciples. And now, he was in the enemy's camp. It was no longer time to stand aside as the evil plowed over the innocent.

He gently laid the sick women against the wall, near the guards. They watched him, bemused, mocking with their slack stance. He got up slowly, stretching his shoulders until they cracked. His shoulders and back popped with relief.

How refreshing it will be to use my strength again, in the way it was meant to be used, he thought.

He grabbed the guards' sword-hands. Then, he squeezed. They yelped like kicked dogs and fell on their knees. He lifted them up by their crushed hands and crashed them together like two blocks of wood. They clattered at his feet in a heap.

"Why not just kill them?" Llun asked.

"No more senseless deaths, Llun. Tie them up. We have work to do."

CHAPTER 28
THE POWER OF BLOOD

"Zmei summons us," Parfyon said to Alienne. She had just sat down to a full breakfast of fried quail eggs mixed with something dark and unpleasantly pungent. She had taken to eating very strange foods lately.

"Now?" That newly-acquired pitch of annoyance in her voice grew more strident by the hour. Complaints about cooking. About mending his clothes after a battle. The blood everywhere. Just a few days before, she had gotten physically ill at a single look at a dead Bskavi scout. She had lain down for the rest of the day with a wet rag on her face. The dead man wasn't even mangled, or anything like that. What had happened to the woman of iron?

"Alienne, what's come over you? Zmei is not the sort of...person... you ask to reschedule."

She pursed her lips and practically growled, "I know that." She bit her lip, petulant like a child. "Come on then. I've lost my appetite." She looked as though she would happily eat Parfyon instead.

Zmei stood at the gate of a hastily-built animal pen near the camp. It was packed to the edges with dark-skinned children with flat, round faces. Gumiren. Their eyes were wide with fear. As soon as they saw Alienne, they reached out to her with hands red with cold. Parfyon heard their teeth chattering even from this distance.

Alienne froze in place as soon as she saw them. Her hand on Parfyon's forearm shook. He felt the heat of her gaze on the side of his face. He ignored her and strode up to Zmei.

"It is the nature of the power you felt on your wedding night," said Zmei without preamble, "to dissipate, just as it is the nature of this Realm of Earth to fade and die. The power must be fed, just as a predator must eat. The most effective source of power—"

"Blood," interrupted Parfyon, as sickening realization flooded him. Zmei wanted human sacrifice. Parfyon almost lost his breakfast.

"We've had enough of your power, Zmei," said Alienne, with more posturing than actual boldness. "It is too strong, too dangerous."

Zmei smiled a rictus smile.

"Is that what you think as well, Parfyon?"

"Yes!" Alienne answered for Parfyon.

"Don't you dare answer for me!" Parfyon said through gritted teeth. Alienne recoiled at the venom in the words and seemed to forget what she wanted to say. "I am not your dog, woman." The irritation had simmered too long to be held back now. "I will answer for myself. And for you. I am your husband."

She laughed, but without mirth. Parfyon turned away from her.

"Even if I wanted that power again," he said, "these are Gumiren. Their blood is weak." His voice shook like a thirsty alcoholic faced with a frothing tankard of ale.

Zmei laughed. Parfyon suspected that the giant laughed not at his words, but at the loss of his resolve. "You are quick, Parfyon, but you lack vital information. These Gumiren are a special race. They were chosen by a great power of the Heights, a shape-changer the Vasylli like to call the Raven, to be his chosen people. These children have the power of other Realms flowing through their blood. If you use it properly, you can feed your own power for a long time."

"How?" It came out before he could stop it.

"No, Parfyon, you will not," Alienne whispered. "The Heights know I have no love for Gumiren, but you cannot kill children! You are not an animal."

No, he was not. But she would not remind him of that. She had to be put back into her place.

"Me? Where's your iron will, woman? Are those the hands that killed Yarpolk Dolgoruk in cold blood? Do not lecture me."

Her eyes filled with pain that cut Parfyon with quick remorse.

"I have to live with that pain, Parfyon. A pain you will never be able to take from me, though you do not seem to want to any more. Yes, I killed Yarpolk for what he did to me. But it did nothing to wash away the pain. If anything, I hurt even more now than I did before."

He wanted to take her into his arms. He wanted to fall at her feet, to kiss her shoes, to beg forgiveness. Anything, just to douse the fire of pain in her eyes.

"And you!" She turned on Parfyon, pain transmuted into fury. "You say you love me? You lie. I was just a means to satisfy the hunger that keeps driving you. The hunger that eats everything. You will never be still, Parfyon. You will never be content."

"No, I will not, Alienne! Content? I will throw down Vasyllia's throne and build a new one for you. I will sow salt in Vasyllia's fields. I will crown you queen of a new Mother of Cities. You will have the whole world at your feet. Who could ask for a finer gift?"

Alienne cackled. "A world burned down to its bones? A fine gift you offer a lady!"

Zmei's shadow grew, seeming to engulf them like a beast eating its prey. "Alienne, the power I offer is a power of creation. You can build a new world on the bones of the old. A world that you will design. A world of your own choosing."

"One that fades the second you turn away?" The words were flung out together with the spittle. "That ... landscape that Parfyon and I made on our wedding night? It was a false mask. A phantom."

"That was your first attempt. You will grow stronger. Eventually, your phantasms will be more real than Adonais's creation."

"I would rather live in a ravaged world with glimmers of beauty than in a beautiful dream that only hides a spreading rot. You are not a maker, Zmei. You only mock."

Zmei began to shake, and the earth with him.

"Enough!" said Parfyon. "I will discuss this with Zmei, Alienne. You are overwrought."

Alienne nodded, but her face was ashen, her expression empty. She seemed to float above the ground as she waded through the knee-high creeping fog.

"I will do it," said Parfyon, releasing the tension inside him into glorious relief. "They are Gumiren."

He forced himself to remember his home burning, the screams of his sister and mother in the fire, the faces of Gumiren invaders, hellish in the light of the torches they hurled at the houses of old Nebesta. They deserved to die. Their children deserved to die.

"This night," said Zmei, his features sharp and beautiful, the angles of his face augmented by the rising sun, "You will bring them in sacrifice to the fire. I will take of their power and share it with you."

When Parfyon came to the enclosure that night, alone, there were no children there. The gate creaked in the night breeze. He knew at once. Alienne had helped them escape.

Parfyon breathed a quiet sigh of relief, though it was quickly replaced by anger. How dare she do this without even consulting him?

Zmei's steps thundered in the darkness of the forest. The waning moon silvered his ancient mail and blond hair, like liquid gold flowing down his shoulders and dissipating into the darkness around him. The hairs on the nape of Parfyon's neck prickled at the sight.

"Alienne had her usefulness, Parfyon," Zmei said. "Perhaps you can wring some use from her yet. But you must bring her to heel."

"It's not just the softheartedness of it," Parfyon said. "I can understand a woman's desire to protect children. But this world has been wallowing in blood for a generation. You and I will stop it. She knows this. But her weakness...I can't have my own wife be a stumbling stone."

"No, you cannot. But she may have... other uses." There was a veiled threat in the tone.

"What do you mean?"

Shouts erupted in the middle of camp. Then, steel against steel and... was that...the roaring of bears?

Zmei cursed, and the ground shook under him. "I cannot show myself, Parfyon. My brothers and I have not yet gathered the strength needed to break the wall of Vasyllia. You must deal with this yourself." He disappeared.

Typical. Giant warriors who prefer the shadows.

Parfyon ran back to camp, trying not to dwell on it. In camp, everything was pandemonium. At first glance, he counted ten of his own dead on the ground. One looked like half his face was raked off with a claw. Arrows fell like hailstones.

Parfyon ran to his tent. Not bothering to buckle on armor, he threw on his helmet and strapped the shield to his right stump. He took his sword in his left. With passing annoyance, he remembered how it was still awkward to fight with his wrong hand.

Never mind, he thought, now's the time to get some practice. The smoky blackness outside his tent struck his eyes. He saw no enemy, only heard them—whoops and screeches and roars and even a few snatches of song. His own men screamed in fear all around him. One brave idiot ran outside the camp. He was eaten by the darkness and spit back into the circle of fires, now more porcupine than human. This was ridiculous. Were these Nebesti warriors, or untrained children?

"Idiots! Stop going out into the forest! Bragadun! Trumpet call. Assemble. Center of camp."

CHAPTER 29
THE DAR'S FIRST COMMAND

It began with a song. Though the bear-riders' language was still unknown to Antomír, the words painted ever more vivid pictures in his mind. Rolling hills of golden grass. Wheat shivering from the caress of early morning wind. Cold river water washing off the sweat of a day's labor under the sun. A fountain on a mountaintop, its water like translucent fire.

This particular song was familiar to Antomír. It had a similar melody to some he used to sing in Vasyllia, the kinds of songs that reached deep into his gut and twisted until he wanted to cry from the pain. Still, nothing in Vasyllia was as beautiful as this pain, this longing, this yearning for glories that are not found in this world. How could a war song be so uplifting?

They sang it as long as they were still within earshot of their own camp. Then, silence descended with the nightfall.

Antomír still had the faint sense that he was in a dream, though the dry, precise instruction Elmira gave to his band of fifteen rattled in his head like dry peas in a bladder.

Scout the location of Nebesta's army.
Count the number of giants with them.
Assess the best ground for an ambush.
Do not let yourselves be seen, much less caught, until the time is right for battle.

As the dawn bled above the distant peaks of Vasyllia, the bear riders slowed for the first time. Something in the air had changed. The footfalls of

THE HEART OF THE WORLD

their bears sounded odd, becoming wooly and flat, as though the air itself had been gagged with cheesecloth. They had entered enemy territory.

The forests they had covered overnight opened up before them into a shallow bowl of scrub grass and the occasional thistle. A river ran across it, its water black and thick with mud. On the other side of the river, facing the riders, was a hideous creature—some unholy mix of horse and serpent that stomped on four ungainly, spindly legs, but with a slithering, long neck and a reptilian head.

They stopped, still in the shelter of the last trees before the clearing. Antomír found himself strangely fascinated by the creature. He couldn't quite understand what it was doing. At first, he thought it was bathing, but no. Its head bobbed up and down, into the water, then out, down, then up. Again, and again. A strangely lulling motion. With it came a soft, barely-audible groan. Almost a song, but too low for a human voice. Something from the depths of time, haunting and compelling.

"Cassían," Antomír said. "Take your half and ride around that thing. We have to see what it's protecting."

The young warrior nodded, and with hardly a sound, half the warriors were gone.

Antomír turned to the warrior at his left. "Over there." He pointed to the left of the sprawling beast. A ford, partially obscured by a stand of weeping willows. "We cross over there."

The bear-riders nodded. The warmth of their approval went to Antomír's head like strong wine. He tried to shake the sensation off himself.

Suddenly, something screeched a call that was half dog barking, half baby wheezing. Antomír looked at the beast, and it was starting right at him. Gamayun's heart palpitated within him. Had she betrayed him to the serpents?

"Turn back!" cried someone to Antomír's left. "We've been seen. Turn back, before they can catch us."

"And leave Cassían and his men behind?" Antomír spit at the ground. "No." He dug his heels into his bear. She flew forward like an arrow. Cassían was under his command. He would put it all to rights. His bear understood and rushed into the brackish water of the river. As they crossed, the beast suddenly sprouted arrows and fell to the earth, thrashing. His brothers had not let him down. Antomír unsheathed his sword smoothly, and, without stopping the movement, came around again in a perfect arc and took half the thrashing beast's head off. A kind of madness was on him, and faster than he thought possible, he hacked and hacked until the reptilian head hung by a thread.

Black blood erupted from the stump. More surprising was the smoke that came out of the severed neck in billows, snaking around Antomír and into the trees ahead. Out of the smoke, two reptilian heads grew into the place where Antomír's sword had hacked. Antomír leaned back and out of the way of the biting heads, just in time.

"The heart! You need to reach the heart!" He heard one of the riders behind him. "It's not in its chest. Do you see that clover-shaped spot on his back? There!"

He used his knees to move the bear closer to the river, then to rush back at the serpent-horse-thing as it pranced about him, surprisingly agile. It waited, looking for an error in his defense.

Then he saw it: the spot where the heart was supposed to be. Feinting with his sword hand, he pulled out his hunting knife in a smooth gesture, hurtling it at the spot with speed that even he had not expected. It lodged in the right place, and the creature fell back, screaming. It dissolved into a swarming mass of black liquid that ran back along the grass into the darkness of the trees.

Antomír cheered and turned to face his fellows. They did not share his joy.

He looked around. The banks of the river, both sides, swarmed with Nebesti warriors. He had failed his brothers. They were all going to die. And for what?

The war-wind filled him, and a screaming rage gurgled up from his stomach and out his mouth. Screaming, he raised his sword and charged into the mass of warriors.

Before he reached them, three of his fellow bear-riders outpaced Antomír and rushed into the fray. Within seconds, the Nebesti were screaming with fear and pain. Antomír turned and saw Cassían and his group join the fray from the trees behind the Nebesti. With fierce joy, Antomír laughed as his hand seemed to work on its own. His blade met the faces of men still bleary with sleep. Within a few seconds, five men lay dead around him. Two were his own work, three—the work of his bear. Without waiting for his instructions, she turned and flew like an arrow deeper into the mass of warriors. After no more than five minutes, all fifteen of his bear riders stood in a group, their swords bared and bloody. They had barely broken a sweat.

Mounds of the dead surrounded them. They had not lost a single man.

What sort of warriors are these bear-riders? Are they even human?

"The rest will start coming out now, wild and drunk on bloodlust," said a bear rider to Antomír. "What we do depends on you now, Antomír."

Antomír flushed, and for a moment he felt stupid and small. How could he have ever thought to be a leader of men?

But there was a wild kind of light behind his fellow warriors' eyes. They did not blame him for failing to keep their scouting expedition secret. No. Their oaths were spoken with pure hearts. They were ready to die.

"We can't fulfill our mission all together," said Antomír. "But one of us can, as long as we keep the enemy busy. Fifteen of us will engage the enemy. Give them hell. Cassían, do you see that hill?" Cassían nodded. "Go back that way. Crest the hill and watch the Nebesti as we engage. Assess the enemy's numbers and abilities. Hopefully we can flush out the serpents as well. Count them. Then back to camp. Leave us to do the fighting." And the dying, he thought, but didn't need to say.

Cassían looked crestfallen. "I want to die with you, brothers."

"You will have your time," said one of the older riders, his smile lit up with the war-wind.

"Go!" said Antomír.

A nasal oxhorn blast came from beyond the line of elms that shielded the Nebesti camp.

"Now!" screamed Antomír. "We have to hit them before they've formed ranks."

The bear riders burst into their war song, and it seemed to push them faster and faster into the enemy camp.

Here it comes. Antomír could hardly feel his body for the excitement. His hand shook from the jarring blows of blade on bone, but he shrugged it off, clutching his leather-bound sword-grip. It was smooth. Too smooth.

With his thumb, he made five notches on the leather just under the cross-guard. My first kills, he thought. Somewhere, deep inside, a voice warned that he would have to mourn the loss of something precious inside himself. *Not if I die first.* He saw the face of his mother as she had looked right after he had healed her. *I die for you, Mama. May my blood water the soil of a new world.*

The inner voice faded. Just in time. Marching ranks of mounted warriors filed out of the enemy camp. Antomír rode the sudden wave of panic, crested it, and took a long, cleansing breath. The simple pleasure of breathing was so unexpected, so intense that he laughed.

The bear riders rode over the front lines of the enemy, who had not had time to place their spears in line. The screaming began…

Antomír could not feel his right arm any more. His head thundered; his ears rang. His left arm refused to move, its shoulder pouring blood from a jagged slash along the collarbone. The battle had been brief, but bloody. In the moments of clarity (they were rare), Antomír's mind reeled at the number of fallen enemies. The Nebesti were fierce, disciplined warriors, but the bear riders fought like Powers. If every other blow of a Nebesti wounded one of the bear riders, a single bear rider killed a Nebesti with every swing of a sword. And each had two swords.

Before he had realized it, Antomír had nearly passed clean through the enemy camp. For a moment, he imagined their whole group might be able to get away. But the last line of enemy warriors was the elite. Mounted on huge chargers, mace-bearing, and deathly effective with their blows, they were nearly the match of the bear riders. After several minutes of carnage, most of the bear riders were down, but so were most of the Nebesti elite. In a moment where he seemed to be looking at himself from above, Antomír broke through into the thick forest beyond the enemy camp. He turned back to throw himself into the thick of the battle. He saw none of his brothers still standing. All was confusion, dust clouds flying high. Some of the Nebesti were engaging their own in the mad confusion.

He didn't even realize he had made the decision, before he was already down a wooded slope. He realized he wanted to live. He looked back, and to his shock, no one pursued him.

The guilt poured over him then, a cold shower that stuck to him like treacle.

"Are you proud of yourself?" hissed Gamayun in his head. "You are now a butcher. I would have offered you a kingdom that you could have taken with hands untainted with blood."

"You would have me use others to kill for me," he said aloud. "I will do my own dirty work, Gamayun."

"That's right. Don't thank me. I just saved your life. Do you think your bear could outrun one of those chargers?"

Antomír felt her displeasure like roiling heartburn, but he said nothing.

He and his bear rode until they were both exhausted. In a narrow gorge with a mostly dried-up river, he espied a narrow cave in a rock wall, just wide enough for him and his bear to squeeze into. They stopped, and he nearly fell off his bear's back in exhaustion. Antomír leaned against her and hugged her. "It has been an honor," he said. "We need to rest. If they find us, let's make it count."

The bear seemed reluctant to stop riding now, but Antomír placed both hands on her head and kissed her nose. She sniffed in displeasure but turned toward the cave opening. Antomír followed.

Night seemed to fall earlier than it should have. The fog that churned outside the cave entrance was dark and malevolent. It seemed that despite her displeasure, Gamayun was still intent on protecting him. Muffled sounds reached Antomír in waves. Shouts, hoof beats, screams, dogs barking. Antomír drifted in and out of sleep, warmed by the soft rise and fall of his bear's stomach where he leaned against it. He was awakened by voices.

"...you don't understand...not morale." A rough voice that commanded obedience merely by its cadence. "I can beat them into shape, I know it. But how could they have been so stupid?"

"They attacked in surprise, didn't they?" This was a woman speaking.

"Yes, but...Did you see how they fought? Like gods. Or demons." The man speaking groaned. "What a day. First you betray my trust, then this! Alienne, Alienne." He sighed. "I understand why you let the children go. But this is *war*. If we are not bloody and ruthless, we will only prolong the Internecine War."

"I am beginning to think that we have it all wrong, Parfyon," she said. "The early victories were easy. Too easy. At some point, you will have to pay. I will as well. What if the price is too high?"

"What if I am willing to pay it? Look me in the eye and tell me that you do not crave the power we felt on our wedding night as much as I do."

"I do crave it. But that scares me."

"If we have to, we will become greater than merely human, Alienne. Maybe that's what's needed. Maybe we have to become Powers to throw down the walls of Vasyllia and pound its stones to dust."

Antomír perked up. He crept closer to the edge of the cave to hear better. Outside, the man was still speaking, but was now moving toward the cave.

"The giants have their own plans, I know it. But let them have what they want. We will have Vasyllia. Vasyllia, my love! The heart of the world!"

"They will turn on you," said the woman.

"Probably. But it's worth the risk." he said, "For a chance at holding the world in the palm of my hand? Even for a moment? It is worth it."

The woman didn't answer.

"Think on it, Alienne. We are brief sparks, and the afterlife offers nothing but darkness and uneasy sleep. In the space of eternity, what is the time of our life? Nothing. Better to shine like lightning, if only for a moment."

"Where are you going?" asked the woman.

"I need to relieve myself," he said.

Gamayun materialized next to Antomír.

"Listen to me, Antomír," she said, and her eyes compelled him to look at her. "This is a chance that I have bent for you out of a thousand possible fates. You cannot imagine the pain I suffer to bend time thus. This man, Parfyon, is the heart of the Nebesti resurgence. They are allied with Powers that can chew up the world and spit it out. They go to destroy Vasyllia. Your home. Nothing can stop them. Except you."

Antomír gasped at the pain in his chest. It was as if she had his heart in her talons, slowly squeezing.

"I deliver him into your hands," she whispered. "He does not know you are here. Kill him. Kill him. Kill him."

She disappeared, but her words echoed in his mind. His hands moved to his belt without his mind stopping them. His sword was already in his right hand.

The man called Parfyon walked into the cave and stopped for a moment at the entrance, thinking. He cocked his head to the side. He sniffed. Antomír saw his face clearly, though it was dark. A hard face, with eyes like coals. A face made of straight lines, not a curve to be seen. He looked like the whole world was arrayed against him in arms, and he couldn't wait to fight them all off.

Antomír imagined, for a moment, a man who didn't have all the same advantages Antomír had in life. A man who, perhaps, had to scrabble for every scrap of bread. A man who earned every advancement in the warrior ranks. With pain in his heart, Antomír realized that in other, better days, this man named Parfyon would be his mentor, not his enemy.

But he was a child of war. His city had been destroyed, while Antomír had been raised in comfort, safely far away from any danger. He lived under the constant threat of death or slavery. What had Antomír known about any of that?

Who am I to take this man's life?

Parfyon walked into the cave, stopping only at arm's length from Antomír. He didn't see Antomír.

"Do it!" screamed Gamayun in his head.

Antomír raised his sword, silent as a night-cat. He stopped, sword-tip poised before the fall. In a swift motion, he cut. A piece of Parfyon's cloak came off without a sound. Parfyon didn't even notice. He finished what he had come to do and walked out of the cave. He hadn't noticed the bear, which, Antomír now realized, had gone as still as a huntsman in the woods.

Gamayun's scream in Antomír's head deafened him. He gritted his teeth and pressed his fists into his temples. His heart threatened to tear into a thousand pieces.

"You had him at your mercy!" Her voice echoed in his mind.

The voices of Parfyon and Alienne receded into the distance.

"I will not do your bidding. I will kill Parfyon honorably. Face to face in the field of battle. You will not control me."

"I will break you, my prince," she hissed in his head, her voice thick with pain. "If you defy me again."

CHAPTER 30
EARTH MAGIC

For all of Aglaia's promises to the contrary, she couldn't follow the great eagle for very long. After half a day of useless pursuit, Khaidu even began to doubt that it was Sabíana after all. Not a hint of their bond remained in her awareness. She felt nothing when looking at the distant speck that faded every farther into the sun's kingdom. Perhaps it was just a very large eagle.

Finally, they had stopped from total exhaustion, not far from a grotto with a quiet pool at its bottom. Khaidu watched as Aglaia dipped her (human) feet into the pool. The old woman tensed from the cold for a moment, then her entire body seemed to dissolve into pure ecstasy. Khaidu was less sure of the pleasures of icy water. She had tried to wash in a mountain stream once, as a child. She still remembered the feeling of needles in her legs. Of course, she would gladly exchange those needles for the deadness in her legs now.

Khaidu shook the thought out of her head. She focused on the grotto instead. The walls of rock were green with moss. They looked furry. Everything was green—the water, the rocks, the moss on the rocks, the trees. It had never been a color she favored. There was not much green in the Steppes. But this was calming and beautiful, in its own way. For the first time since coming to this barbarous country, she liked it.

Of course, that was just this grotto. Most of the trees outside the grotto were diseased. They smelled like dead horse. They were black where they should be green. They were brown where they should be yellow-gold. Even without Aglaia's unease, Khaidu sensed that it was not a natural thing. It seemed to be everywhere.

Aglaia's cooing of pleasure was getting annoying.

"G-g-laia! T-tell me. W-what is a M-m-ajestva?" Her clear speech came and went, and sometimes she was still unable to frame so much as a single syllable. But she was getting better, so much was obvious.

"You heard?" Aglaia had changed from her fur pelt into some of the hag's not-so-filthy things. She looked like a sparrow having a dust bath. "Do you know about Aer? That there are many levels of the world?"

Khaidu shook her head. She was unsure whether or not Aglaia were joking.

"The Dark Father. He is, as you probably know, not human. He is a great Power, used to be one of the greatest. Basically, a god."

Khaidu stiffened at the blasphemy. There was only one god, and he was unknown.

"Well, a lesser god. Godling," said Aglaia, placating. "Anyway. The world was created with many layers. Doors. Windows. Tunnels. It's confusing."

She screwed her face into a prune-like expression. Her right hand began to caress her right cheek, to pick at the stray hairs at her temples.

"Let's make it simple. There's the world. Our world. But it's only a small part of the full world. Our eyes are limited. They can only see that small part. But some people know how to open up doors, windows that allow them to encounter more. In those deeper layers, there are other creatures. Not human. More powerful than human. Much more powerful."

"Good?"

"Some. Some not so good. Some really, really not good. Your Dark Father being one of the worst."

"Not *my* Dark Father!"

"I'm sorry, wolfling. Of course not. One of the creatures that lives in these other realms is the Majestva. They are like...spirits. Do you understand?"

Spirits Khaidu understood well enough. Old Gumiren lore taught that all things had their own spirit-lives. Khaidu didn't think that was quite true (it was a bit old-Gumir for her, a bit backward), but certainly things that seemed to have no life to them often surprised her with signs of life.

"Yes, well. The Majestva are very powerful creatures. They are like wind, like air moving. But not between places. Between times. If you are friends with a Majestva, you can cross times and places both. They are fiercely independent and very loyal to the Heights.

"To enslave Majestva and use them for evil...that would take more than simple power. It would take an insane kind of boldness. You saw what happened to the hunters."

Khaidu winced at the memory. There was not much left of them after the former-eagles had finished with their erstwhile masters.

"It also means, I think, that the Dark Father is very confident in his plans, whatever they are. It means, in short, that we have to hurry to find Sabíana. She is more necessary by the moment."

"I t-told her as much," Khaidu said.

"Yes. Sabíana is of the blood of the Dars. While she lives, she is a deterrent against the final overthrow of Vasyllia. But if she really is dying or dead, that is very, very bad."

Aglaia looked at Khaidu with a strange expression, as if she had just had an unexpected thought.

"But you...you have this strange power about you. You freed me of my enchantment to the giants. You freed the Majestva. You have this sympathy with beasts and with people. I think it no coincidence that Sabíana was bound to you. You will, I think, play an important part in convincing Sabíana to take her place in Vasyllia, even if..." The thought didn't need to be finished. Khaidu had never seen Sabíana's paralyzed human body lying in a locked chamber in the depths of Vasyllia, but she could imagine it easily enough.

Khaidu wondered, and not for the first time, how it would be possible to coax Sabíana's eagle-spirit back into a paralyzed body. If they ever found her, that is.

"That is why, my dear little wolf child, I think you should try washing in this water. It's really very exquisite. And we have to fly like the wind to the place where Sabíana hides."

"You still th-think you know where sh-she's g-going?"

"I suspect. Not the same thing, dearie."

"W-w-where?"

"The last place where people still prepare for the war against the Raven. It's a place called Raven's Bane. A monastery."

"A....?"

"A place where men go to separate themselves from the world. To train, to study, to contemplate. To become perfect warriors. The most well-protected and well-hidden place in this level of the world."

It did sound like the best place for Sabíana to hide.

"D-do y-you know where it is?"

"I have a general idea."

The farther they traveled into Nebesta, the more a strange heaviness settled on Khaidu's chest. At first, she thought it was losing Sabíana a second time, but it had been there even before they lost her trace. Nothing specific seemed to instigate it; nothing consoled it. It was just...there. But as their way took them past trees that grew twisted, slime-ridden, blackened; as the grass shriveled in on itself; as the chirping of birds grew quieter until it stopped completely, Khaidu thought she understood. Her sympathy with living creatures was not limited to animals. Even the pain of the blades of grass was now her pain.

On the sixth day after they lost Sabíana, the pain changed. It became a wordless agony that physically pushed her down onto Aglaia's wolf-back.

"Are you alright? Khaidu?"

Khaidu couldn't find the strength to answer. She could hardly breathe. She felt sharp stabs of pain in her arms, her legs, her groin. Her temples burned like they were being scraped off with a hot iron.

Through the pain, she sensed a direction. A place. A source. She did something she had never done before. She took Aglaia's ears and pulled them in the direction she wanted to go.

"Ow! Have you gone batty? You can't touch my ears!"

Khaidu only pulled harder.

"Very well, very well. I understand. Just point with your hand. I'll follow."

Khaidu pointed a finger—it was shuddering—to the left. Aglaia followed.

The pain guided her through the trees, which were thickening, blocking off more of the light. Trailing lianas reached for them, and the straight, tall trees turned into twisted, angry, old creatures. Khaidu sensed the path through them as though it were marked for her with golden paint. Finally, the pain was too much for her to endure. She screamed, and Aglaia stopped.

"Oh, my sweet Adonais," whispered Aglaia in horror.

Khaidu thought she had a millstone tied around her neck. It took all the strength she had left to look up at what she feared to see: the source of the pain.

Three ancient trees with drooping branches and leaves like trailing tears stood apart from the others. Their roots stuck out of the ground and interlaced with each other. In the central point where all three sets of roots met was a wide bowl, seemingly grown out of the tree roots themselves. It was filled with what looked like blood.

Something moaned quietly near the trees. No, *on* the trees. Each tree had a...a child. No more than ten years old. Three children. Each child was... part of the tree. No, it was tied into the tree, bound *by* the tree. Thin tendrils pierced the flesh of their arms and legs, and a branch seemed to have grown across each of their midsections, holding them fast. The tendrils were bloated with blood. The children's blood, leading to the bowl.

Oh, Unknown Father. Strength. I need strength.

The bowl. It was filled with their blood. And they were...they were Gumiren.

"Aglaia!" Khaidu screamed, her lips completely free and able to articulate. "Save them. I will help you."

Carefully, Aglaia padded to the closest child, a girl. Her eyes were open, but she seemed to see nothing. Sitting on Aglaia's back, Khaidu was at a good angle to reach the hanging child. Khaidu unsheathed her paring knife from her belt. Working more on instinct that with any knowledge, she cut off each tendril, leaving a splinter in the skin. She felt, more than knew, that it would be better to prevent all the girl's blood from pouring out immediately. As she cut the tendril, it recoiled from her, as though it were a snake. Khaidu fought down her revulsion and continued to hack at them. Soon, all the tendrils were waving about, trying to grab something, looking like fish suffocating on dry land.

Khaidu thought she would have more trouble with the branch binding the girl to the tree, but the child was so thin, that she just slipped out as soon as Khaidu maneuvered her properly. She fell into Khaidu's arms. The pain in Khaidu's head flashed, then faded slightly.

She spoke to the girl. "Your name, my dear. Your name?" To know it was the difference between life and death. She needed to know her name.

The girl directed her empty eyes at Khaidu but seemed to see nothing. Her eyes began to roll back into her head. Khaidu's chest heaved with sobs.

"No," she whispered, hugging the girl to herself tightly. "No. You will not die. I will not let you die."

The girl shuddered, then stilled. Her breathing grew regular. Khaidu felt a hand on her cheek.

"You... poor thing..." said the girl. "Your face."

Khaidu felt something crack inside her. The tears flowed down her face and dripped on the face of the little girl.

"My name is Yesukai," said the girl, wiping away Khaidu's tears with a nearly transparent hand.

"I am Khaidu," she barely managed through the sobs. "You are safe now."

"Giants," said Yesukai. "Lots of them. They bought us from Vasyllia as slaves."

Yesukai sat wrapped in Aglaia's wolf pelt, her shuddering hands extended to a tiny fire. The other two children—a boy and a girl probably no older than seven—lay clasped in each other's arms, asleep under a makeshift blanket of moss and brush. Yesukai had explained that they were twins.

"At first, the white-faces treated us well. Lots of food. Good, tasty food. We were fat." She puffed up her cheeks. It would have been comical, had her face not been hardly more than a skeleton's. "Later, they took us over the wall and to a place with many warriors."

"A military camp?" offered Aglaia, unable to tear her eyes off Yesukai.

"Yes," Yesukai coughed. It sounded as though the effort of a single cough could break her in half. "There, the giants bought us. We were to be...sacrificed in fire. But a woman released us. All of us. We are many." She stopped to drink from the hot water that Khaidu offered her. Her eyes lit up at the taste. "We tried to flee, but the giants caught some of us. They took us and...."

"W-w-when?" asked Khaidu.

Yesukai closed her eyes, mumbling to herself. She was counting, Khaidu realized. But she soon gave it up. "A day...a week? A year? I don't know."

"Why did they want your blood?" asked Aglaia.

"They said that we are...a chosen people of the Dark Father. They say our blood has power."

Khaidu could no longer hold herself in check. She leaned to the side and retched. When she looked up again, Yesukai looked worried. *How can she worry about me?*

"Yesukai," said Aglaia tentatively, "I need you to help me. I think you are strong. Can you tell me? What were the giants going to do with your blood?"

Yesukai did not even hesitate. "They are trying to break the wall of Vasyllia down. Their army wants to destroy the city of Vasyllia. There is also...something there. Something they want."

CHAPTER 31
SABÍANA'S CHOICE

Sabíana perched on the crown of a spruce tree. Not far underneath, in the shelter of a stand of alders, Khaidu sat by a fire-pit. In the sharp angles of eagle-vision, Sabíana noticed details that she would have never seen as a human. Khaidu's head cocked slightly to the side, revealing the long scar that reached from temple to neck. She usually tried to hide that scar, but not now. Another detail: her left eyebrow slightly raised, matching the curl of her lip on the opposite side of her face. Sabíana the human would not have known those specific details to mean much, but she would have intuited, better than the eagle, that taken together, they constituted the purest expression of Khaidu's enjoyment of a moment in time.

Khaidu looked at the little girl whom she had rescued, and she was at peace. Sabíana felt something break in her human self. The eagle nature in Sabíana regarded the human sorrow with detachment for a moment, then it descended back into her human awareness. For a brief, brilliant moment, Sabíana the eagle and Sabíana the woman were one.

In that moment—that last, brilliant moment—their broken bond reasserted itself for a moment. But it faded, this time finally. Whatever shadow had remained of that bond had forced Sabíana the eagle to keep coming back to Khaidu, though always at a distance, for the eagle in her feared the bond as much as the human in her craved it. But now, there was nothing left of it, only tatters. Sabíana the human wept, somewhere deep inside the eagle's mind.

For Khaidu had been, she now realized, her last connection to her love for Voran. Voran, who had promised to come back to her. Voran, who had abandoned her to suffer the pain of hundreds by herself. Voran, who had not so much as sent a letter to her in all these twenty years.

And yet, she loved him still. Khaidu had reminded her of that. The strength of their bond, the intensity of Khaidu's need for her dreamscapes and the conversations they had nightly—they were a reflection of Sabíana's own need. In their joyful communion, Sabíana remembered the last days in Vasyllia, when for a brief day, Voran had been hers without a care in the world. Twenty years had passed, and yet, even in the form of the eagle, she felt his hand on the back of her head, caressing. She smelled him, she melted into his embrace. So long, and yet...

There it was again... that strange breeze coming from beyond this world. Sabíana the eagle raised her wings, drawn toward that scented wind with a force that rivaled Khaidu's binding song. In her eagle gaze, she saw the breeze even clearer than she smelled it. It was a deep, throbbing purple color, and it danced like a firebird through the many other breezes that were only limited to earth. For she understood that this breeze was not of this Realm. It was a breath of the Heights of Aer, and it reached for her.

With a final human gaze at Khaidu, Sabíana the eagle flew into the stream of that scented breeze for the first time. As soon as she did, everything changed. Before, when she flew in the cathedral on the sky, it was like a distant limit to her experience. She was equally tied to earth and to the sky. But within the scented breeze, she saw the sky open before her gaze. Mountains crowned with verdure reached upward far beyond the limits of the sun. Waterfalls that were stars wept golden tears. Crystal plains, dotted with gem-like lakes, revealed Sirin washing in waters that were also flames. Greater beings than Sirin reached from one realm to another on legs like columns. Shifting mists revealed ever-changing vistas, some of Earth, some of the many Realms of Aer. Beyond them all, in an opal-flecked sea, stood a solitary ivory tower that sang a lament of abandonment.

Sabíana was lost for a time in the contemplation of all the Realms, revealed to her in the divine breath of the Heights of Aer. Then she spun around in flight and looked back down to earth. It seethed with darkness like a fog, but it felt like a living thing, seeking to devour whatever stood in its path. She followed it back to the source, and saw a glittering, translucent dome sitting astride a black footstool that pulsated with suppressed energy. No, it wasn't a footstool, it was a wall. Sabíana realized she looked at the wall of Raven, encircling all of Vasyllia in a dome of his black power. As she stared at it, she saw it flare up in red flame, then subside back into translucence, behind which was a churn of black.

As the red flame rose, some of the columns holding the Realms apart from each other cracked. She flew up and saw one of the great beasts of Aer—a winged lion of gold-flecked crystal that filled half the sky—totter from his place. The great wings burst into a flower of rose-scented flame, and then they were no more. Its eyes closed, and for a moment, the Realms wept with terror. Then, the great lion shattered into a million shards of fiery crystal, which faded into a white mist before giving way to another vision, another glimpse of a Realm beyond knowledge.

Sabíana understood. The wall of Vasyllia was a magic of such power that it was undermining the foundations of all the Realms. The membranes between them were folding, the walls were cracking, their denizens were dying. The Raven was consuming all the Realms in his quest for the eternal form that had been denied him.

The fear rose up, and she wanted to flee. It was not rational; it was the response of a hunter who has just realized that she is now the hunted. To fly away, to hide, to seek new vistas, untroubled by the darkness that sought to eat her...

But with that thought, she remembered her own, small role in this cosmic drama. Intense urgency drove her deeper into the scented breeze that had led her to this place. She plunged into it, and drove through Realms, folding through times and places, into the very sun itself. As she breached its red-orange fire, she reappeared in the Realm of Earth. Before her lay a range of blue-green mountains that looked like the frozen ripples of a giant pool. A single jewel adorned the green dress of the tallest mountain. It clung to a sheer wall, though it felt as though the mountain clung to *it*. A many-chambered, many-towered complex of yellow stone buildings awash in dozens of streams of water bursting from the heart of the mountain. Behind her, the sun seemed to turn about to face her again, and the many falls glittered like diamonds.

"You are welcome, Darina of Vasyllia," rumbled a voice in Sabíana's head. "Though this is not, I fear, a place for you to rest long."

Then Sabíana saw *through* the walls, into the depth of the mountain, into a chamber within the heart of the rock. The scented breeze seized her, and pulled her through...

She sat on a cushion, her back leaning against hard rock. The room was warm, and her hands pricked as they remembered how to feel. She gasped through her nose, remembering the odd, tickling sensation of breathing through nostrils. Her legs cramped, and she laughed.

This must be what Khaidu felt like every night.

For this was not her own manipulation of the dream-region. This was someone else's formation of another realm entirely. Something akin to dream, but closer to death than life. A dangerous place.

A white-haired, long-bearded elder sat across from her on a rough stool. She knew how he was. Abbot Makarían of the monastery called Raven's Bane. But how did she know that?

"Don't trouble yourself with the details, my Darina. After all, we don't have much time."

He pointed to a round table that stood between them. There was a flagon of red wine and two goblets that seemed forged from living flame, dancing in an out of concrete form.

"Is it safe?" she asked.

"No, of course not. Nothing worthy is ever safe."

She poured the wine, and it was also a flame. They drank, and it was very good.

"What you saw," said the abbot, "the breaking down of the Realms, the battle beyond. It is far worse than you can imagine. The Raven is very close to his objective. I do not know if we can stop him."

Sabíana heard him, but a weight of heaviness was obscuring her thoughts. She wanted to sleep, to rest, to fade away.

"My lord," she said. "Is it my task any more, to prevent this fate? Have I not done enough?"

His eyes danced with mirth. "Oh, my little one. You are young yet! There is still the promise of life and love, yes, even for you."

"I do not see it. I have done more than any human being has ever done. And yet, even in death, I have not found peace."

"I cannot grant it to you, my dear one. It is for you to find it."

"Where? Tell me where I can go."

He sighed, but only shook his head.

"You will not?"

"I cannot. No one can, save you. The gift of the Sirin of fire is still upon you. And it has had unexpected consequences, I think. I don't think you are quite as dead as you think."

"One thing I fear above all others," she said. "That if I do what I must, that if I return to my body that lies in Vasyllia, that I will return to a body that is corrupted and rotted from the lack of its spirit."

He would not look at her.

She poured the rest of the fire-wine into her goblet and downed it. As she did, she saw her old chamber in the palace in Vasyllia. It was bare, save for a dais like an altar, upon which lay a coffin of crystal. In the coffin lay a young woman, her face white as new snow. She gasped as she recognized herself.

"Is that? Is that real?"

Makarían's voice came as though from a profound distance. "I see it as well. Perhaps it is the final gift of Feína, the Sirin of fire. Or it may be an illusion of the dark one. I cannot give you certainty. All I can say for certain is that if you choose another path, you may join the formless ones in their eternal quest for what they lost. You may become a creature like the changers of the Raven.

"Will I never find peace?" she whispered.

But she was not in the abbot's presence any longer. She hovered over the crystal coffin, looking at the impossibly young face of the dead form lying there. No, not dead. Her eyelids fluttered. The young woman opened her eyes.

CHAPTER 32
THE PRICE OF AMBITION

Five bonfires, each as tall as Parfyon's war pavilion, banished the stars from the night sky.

"We should have burned them on pyres," said Alienne, hugging herself next to Parfyon. "Each one separately. Not piled up like dog carcasses."

Parfyon laughed bitterly. He would have preferred to fill his mouth with the worst oath he could find and hurl it on the sons of bastards who died like flies in the raid.

"They deserve this," he hissed. This. Being burned like piled garbage.

"It's almost as though you're punishing their dead bodies," she said. She looked ready to be sick.

"Someone must pay for the disgrace. They will do for a start. But I'm not finished."

"Parfyon, I know you're hardly in a mood to listen to my advice..."

"Alienne, I..."

"No, listen to me," she said, cold in her firmness. She placed a clammy hand on his good arm. What was a caress only a few days ago was now something else, cold and distant. What had happened to their ardor? Where was the real Alienne? "Parfyon, you won their hearts, but these are Nebesti. They are not Gumiren. We are not, have not ever been, a cruel people. We have been reduced to very little by the Internecine War, but do not force these good men to go down the path of cruelty. You are angry, I know. But know this too. They will follow you anywhere. Be careful where you lead them."

Will they follow? Truly? He was not so sure anymore. Some of the glances that had refused to meet his were cold and angry. Men who sought his eyes before were now retreating before him, bowing their heads. When he passed, he was sure he heard whispers and even a few sniggers. He suspected he was losing them fast.

"This is a stain, Alienne. A blot on Nebesta's good luck. War is not won only with prowess in battle. War is won with heart. With that fire in the heart of men who will give anything to win an extra inch of ground from their enemies. Men who will not flinch at losing arms, legs, even their life, if it means glory for their brothers and their city."

She turned to him, assessing him.

"What happened today will eat away at the hearts of these men," he continued. "They have been fighting for so long. Will they swallow the defeat and use it to push forward, to fight on even harder? Or will they crumble under the weight of the shame?"

"Like you, you mean?" Cold, precise, her words were like an assassin's dagger. She sneered at him and turned away. "You're losing the game, Parfyon. And losing me. You've already lost your men."

He wandered the rest of the night. He knew he was losing Alienne, but to hear it, stark, from her own lips...

Only a week ago, when restlessness like this kept his sleep at bay, he would have milled about with the men. He was one of them, after all, a commoner, the "barrel-rider," as they had taken to calling him. He knew all the punch lines of their jokes even before they finished them. He could outdrink all but a few of them. He recited the best bawdies, some of which even the old sword-and-shielders had never heard of.

But tonight...

It was not his imagination. They were turning away from him, even before he approached. Laughter died at his coming. Flasks hid under cloaks at his passing. As though he would begrudge them their moonshine! Parfyon nearly lost it at one of the meal-fires. He saw Ulik's smiling, mad face staring at him from across the fire. No, it was only his imagination. But it was enough to shake him even more than Alienne's words. She was a woman, and she belonged to him. She could be brought to heel. Ulik come back from the dead—that would be a foe beyond his abilities.

He forced himself to sit at the meal-fire of the bowmen. They were always ready to mock him in the half-serious way he liked. He had always felt kinship with them, with their cynical, yet cheerful, way of viewing the madness of the world.

"Mead?" offered one of the older ones. Parfyon couldn't remember his name. How could he not remember? He was supposed to be the man of the people. Was he becoming like the Dolgoruki? Too preoccupied with the ways of power to do what's necessary, to drink with the men, to feel the sharp enjoyment of their intimate company?

Parfyon shook his head at the mead, too ashamed to speak.

"Those bear bastards," said another one. "Slinking in the shadows like that. They were afraid of our arrows, see? If they had declared themselves open and clear like..." He made a quick slicing motion across his throat. "Even bear riders fear the archers of Nebesta," he concluded with a triumphant flair of his hand.

"You idiot," said Parfyon, unable to stop himself. The archer recoiled, going white with shock at being thus addressed by Parfyon. He had been right; they *had* considered him one of their own. Well, not any more. "We've just been trampled underfoot. We were the ant hill, and those bear riders were the boot. Don't you get it?"

"Sir," the older archer intervened, "it was a hard fight, but they had the element of surprise..."

"Will anyone give me anything but excuses? Or the truth?" Parfyon spit into the fire. The archers' faces grew redder than the glow of the fire. He had insulted their honor. Worse still, he had done it deliberately. "Why can't you be men, and admit that we lost today in a way that no Nebesti can allow himself to lose ever again? If we were honest with ourselves, we could learn from our mistakes and do better next time."

"And so we shall. But we have our pride, lord. Extend us the courtesy of keeping at least a piece of it." The older archer's voice had a dangerous edge of formality. Parfyon was losing them. He had not lost them yet, it seems, but now he was trying his hardest to dig his own grave. And yet, he couldn't stop himself.

"That's what you've been given. For twenty years. Plenty that's gained you! Do you want to slip back into the endless wars? Or do you want to win the world?"

All eyes fell to earth at those words. Good. They still had some dignity left.

"Brothers... I drive you harshly. Yes. But I want you to be remembered as gods, not men."

The archer snickered and locked gazes with Parfyon. Parfyon's stomach dropped. The archer would not back down. Parfyon's hand inched toward his belt. Well, he had said that someone would have to pay.

"Lord Parfyon!" Bragadun's voice rang through the camp. "Lord Parfyon! We found him!"

Parfyon jumped up. "Where?"

Bragadun, possibly the last Nebesti who would still speak to him, came into the circle of firelight. "I should say... He came to *us*."

"What?" The older archer stood up. He was tense, his fingers already in the position of nocking, ready to loose at a second's notice.

"He...wants to speak to you, Lord Parfyon. He calls himself the Dar of Vasyllia."

The men chuckled uneasily.

"*This* I have to see," said Parfyon under his breath.

❦

Antomír, the self-proclaimed Dar of Vasyllia, was obscenely young. Not just in age, though the blond fuzz on his lip and chin could hardly be called a beard. It was in his pale-grey eyes, and an innocence behind them so obvious that Parfyon wanted to laugh. But he couldn't laugh. This was the leader of a ragged rabble that had made mincemeat out of the best warriors in the Three Lands.

"Are you mad or just very stupid?" He asked Antomír as he tried to tuck his right hand into his belt, then remembered that he had no right hand. It irritated him like a wasp's sting. He thought he heard another snicker among the archers. He would rake them over the coals later. Literally, if necessary.

All the boy did was raise his hand. Something fluttered in it. Cloth?

"Is this some sort of ancient Vasylli greeting ritual?" A few of the men laughed at that. Too few.

Antomír seemed to steel himself for something. He breathed in and spoke. A voice calm and lovely, like running water. Parfyon hated him for that voice.

"Lord Parfyon. Permit me. Your cloak?"

He pointed at the fringe of Parfyon's cloak. Parfyon looked down but didn't understand. What was this lack-mind going on about? Then he saw, and his heart stopped for a long moment.

Parfyon picked up the fringe. It was irregular. Not jagged, exactly, but no longer the perfectly straight line that Alienne had always insisted on. It had a clean cut running along its edge.

Parfyon took another look at the boy. He tried to look past the baby-ringlets, the cream-white skin, the lack of any lines in the forehead or around the mouth (except for that offensive dimple in his chin). No. He had been wrong. This was no innocent stripling. This baby boy had seen horrors, and recently.

"Why did you spare me?" asked Parfyon. Around him, the rising whispers told him that the men were slow to understand what was plain to see.

"Vasylli do not kill in cold blood. Nor do Nebesti, I think."

Guilt savaged Parfyon's heart. In his mind, the Gumiren children reached out to him, imploring...

"No, we do not," said Parfyon. "You have not answered my question."

Antomír's eyes softened into...what? Pity?

"Lord Parfyon, my men have all died. All save me. I am dishonored by running from the field of battle. I have returned to face your justice."

The laughter was louder now. Parfyon sensed it—the rising emotion around him. A chance to avenge their loss. A chance to win back some of their lost dignity. If Parfyon gave this baby boy to them, the Nebesti would be his again. No more mistakes.

But...These Nebesti were dogs, not men. They had fallen like moths willingly flying into a fire. They were not worth this gift. But this Antomír, on the other hand...

Parfyon laughed and found that he could not stop. There were tears in his eyes, and his cheeks hurt from the unusual exertion by the time he finished.

"Antomír, Dar of Vasyllia, or whoever you are. You must be mad. But you are brave. I have never seen such bravery. I honor it. Nebesta honors it. As knyaz of Nebesta, I grant you safe passage through these lands for the space of twelve hours. No one will follow you for that space, at the pain of death. Go. Before my men decide that I am too lenient."

The aftermath was worse than Parfyon expected. Now, there was open hatred in his men's eyes. The whispers were no longer phantoms of his imagination. He heard, clearly, the words "new knyaz" and "Veche" more than once.

But it didn't anger him. Not really. He was beyond anger. First Alienne had abandoned him, now all of Nebesta. Well, to the dogs with them all. He would show them. They would cower at his feet before he was done with them.

Zmei was in the clearing, as Parfyon hoped. It was almost like he was expecting Parfyon.

"I want it," said Parfyon. "The power. I will give whatever you require for it."

Zmei seemed to grow in size as he answered. "It is nearer to your grasp that you think. More of it even than I can satiate myself with. More than all my brothers can gorge themselves on. The wall of Vasyllia. It is held by the dark power of the Raven. If we break it, you will have reserves of power that will last you lifetimes. You will become a god among men."

"Tell me what I have to do!"

"Bring me Alienne. Her death, for your new life."

No. No. No. I cannot do this. I will not do this. She is my...

"Done," said Parfyon, and he did not recognize his own voice.

CHAPTER 33
LLUN'S LAST SWORD

All the slaves of the plantation stood before Voran. It had taken nearly an hour for them to gather. They filled the fields, their eyes turned up to him with something like a glimmer of hope, though he could see how fragile it was. Many of them were wary. A few had faces grown hard and sharp with despair.

Voran surveyed them, and fear rose in his heart. Had he gone mad? What was he going to do? Lead an army of pariahs to retake the most well-fortified city in the world? As though Vasyllia itself heard him, the clouds parted before his eyes, and in the distance, between two peaks, he saw the mountain city in a burst of sunlight. Voran found it hard to take a steady breath but forced himself to continue looking. Remember, he said to himself. Vasyllia is everything. Not because of the city, but because of what lies underneath. The Heart of the World.

His fear didn't fade away, but it no longer paralyzed him. He looked at the slaves again. They had trampled all the hemp plants in their march toward the guard house. To his own surprise, he burst out in laughter at that detail. Many of the former slaves smiled, though some looked like they wondered if their deliverer were a madman.

"Vasylli!" Voran raised his hands as he cried out. His voice echoed. "You are free. I do not ask for anything in return. The time has come for our land's healing. But the purging must come first. It will be painful. Many may die in the process. You have women, children here. Go! Leave Vasyllia.

617

Brother Llun will show you secret ways to evade the Consistory, to circumvent the wall."

No one moved a muscle. Llun took a step forward and added his own resonant cry.

"Don't imagine that what has happened here will long remain a secret in Vasyllia. A few days more of freedom. That is all we have. Soon all the dog-men will be on you. If you wish some measure of safety, though there is hardly a safe place left in this world, then come with me."

No one even looked at Llun. They all stared at Voran.

Two men, both scarred and limping, approached Voran. Their glances bore a challenge, not gratitude.

"Vohin, you are unknown to us," said the older of the two. "Will you tell us your name?"

"I am called the Healer in the outside lands…"

"Your name, Vohin," said the other, and there was a note of command in his voice. Voran marveled at the inner strength of these slaves.

"My name is Vohin Voran, son of Otchigen, former voyevoda of Vasyllia under the illustrious Dar Antomír of the line of Cassían the Great."

A wind seemed to pass through the ranks as his name was whispered. The wind grew louder and louder as eyes sparked with light, as hands raised, as voices cheered.

The elder of the two had tears in his eyes. "We have waited for you, Voran, for twenty years. Our Swan, the Darina Sabíana, promised you would return."

"She, however, did not specify the length of your absence," said the other man, bitterly. "Though I see you have seen your share of pain."

"Vohin Voran," said the elder. "Allow me to speak. These are my people, placed in my care by the Lady Sabíana herself."

Voran's heart did a flip at the sound of her name being spoken aloud. He swallowed rather louder than he would have liked but managed a nod.

The elder turned to the former slaves and raised his hands. The murmur of the crowd stilled.

"You have heard it, Vasylli. The name. The name we have waited for. It is time. Go! Fulfill your tasks."

The still crowd turned into a churning whirlpool of people.

"Vohin Voran," said the younger. "Come. The muster has begun. As you have already said, there is not much time."

The two former slaves led Voran and Llun on a half-day's march toward an old mill built at the confluence of two outflows of the Vasyllia River. It was situated on high ground that had good sight lines in all directions and could be easily defended. As soon as their little group was visible, the miller had come out to the porch, head uncovered. He now knelt before his mill, waiting for them to approach.

As they approached the miller, he bowed even lower and held out his right hand. His hat was crumpled in his fist. A sign of self-abasement, utmost wretchedness.

"What do you have to repent of, old man?" asked Voran, keeping his tone light.

The old man looked up with eyes grateful for Voran's tone. "I was a Son of the Swan, once. But I was not strong."

"He is not one of the bad ones," said the elder of the slave leaders, whose name was Ladomir, "are you, old man?"

"I abandoned you all when you took up arms."

"But you didn't betray any of your brothers."

"I did nothing to stop the slave trade," said the old miller, bowing to earth again. "I didn't even take my share of the road-tax." He sounded as though he would burst into tears at any moment. "Though that was common practice enough, and Adonais knows you all could have used the money!"

"Give us your service, your food, and the comfort of your hospitality, and all is forgiven," said Voran, raising him by the hand.

The old man looked at Voran with wide eyes. They sparked with recognition, then wonder. He kissed Voran's hand, then kissed his shoulder, then his hand again. A pledge of service.

"I knew your father, Vohin Voran," said the miller. "I didn't believe what all the gossips said. He was always kind to me."

Voran felt the tears rise. There were still some true Vasylli left.

The miller sat them at his little table and brought them ale in overflowing tankards. Immediately, he bowed and began crashing about in the adjoining kitchen. Soon afterward, smells of roast fowl and apples began to waft in. Voran's mouth watered.

"Vohin Voran," said the younger of the slave leaders, named Lubomir. "I think it's best to get the bad news out of the way. The Darina. She is dead."

"What?!" Blood rushed in his ears, threatening to drown everything else out. "How? What happened?"

Lubomir looked at Ladomir, who nodded at him to continue.

"Do you remember a warrior named Rogdai?" asked Lubomir. Voran nodded. "During the battle for Vasyllia, he took part in a purge of Vasyllia's priests. He and most of the other warriors. It was the Raven's trap, but he never forgave himself for it. He gave his life afterward to the personal service of the Darina. He became her personal bodyguard.

"Vohin Voran, I can't describe how she suffered. Not just the physical paralysis. She was forced to watch as everything she loved about Vasyllia shriveled and died before her. She was powerless to do anything about it. She confided many of her hidden thoughts, her pains to Rogdai. But Rogdai was a man damaged in mind. And our Lady confided in him with too much innocent trust."

Ladomir continued, "She let slip, in an especially painful moment, how she hoped someone would kill Yadovír. If the vessel of the Raven were to die, there would be a respite. A breathing space. A chance for her to do something. Rogdai took her words to heart."

Voran sighed audibly. "So the Gumiren didn't kill Yadovír."

"No. Rogdai did."

"Sabíana would never have forgiven herself for that," said Voran. He was going to say more, but he had to stop. It was painful to breathe, much less speak.

"She faded from that moment more and more. Soon, she was no more than barely living relics. She died a long time ago."

Worse and worse!

"For whom do we fight, then?" asked Llun.

"We fight for you, Vohin Voran," said Ladomir. Lubomir looked away at that.

"We fight for the monarchia, my friend. The Dar is yet alive."

Lubomir turned at that, eyes intense. "Dar Mirnían? Impossible."

"There is a remnant of old Vasyllia, protected by Adonais's covenant, living on an island in the Great Sea. They yearn for the reclamation of Vasyllia as fervently as we do."

"But where are they?" Lubomir's words were bitter. "Why are they not with you? Why is there no army at your back? Are we supposed to give our lives in taking Vasyllia, then give the crown to an exile who lives in comfort far from the war? What is this?" He slammed his open palm on the table. "I won't fight for some exiled prince I don't know. I will fight for you, Vohin Voran. No one else."

"I am a servant of the Dar, Lubomir. I will never take his place."

"You *will*," said Lubomir firmly, "if the Council of the Reaches makes you the new Dar. And believe me, they will."

That whole night, Voran couldn't sleep. The guilt bored into his chest. Llun's rhythmical pounding on the anvil of the forge next door didn't help. The discovery of the old forge had caused paroxysms of conflicted joy in Llun's face that had astounded Voran. It seemed the former smith wouldn't sleep a wink either tonight.

When Llun woke Voran the next morning, Voran was surprised that he had managed to fall asleep at all. His surprise was multiplied by what Llun held in his blackened, shaking hands.

"Take it," he said, placing the newly-forged sword into Voran's grasp. "You have given me purpose again. I was dead." There were tears in Llun's eyes. "I don't know if I will ever truly live again, but having this purpose is enough. I can bear the pain now."

Voran thrilled at the touch of cold steel. It was without any kind of adornment. But its balance was ideal, its weight just right. And there was more meaning in this one piece of metal than in hundreds of jewel-encrusted heirlooms of ancient warrior families.

"You have a talent," said Voran, his voice cracking.

"I haven't touched the forge for years. Aspidían took it from me. But … it all seemed to come back as soon as my hand touched the hammer." His face flushed with embarrassment. "I'm not an eloquent man …"

A sudden wave of emotion engulfed Voran, sweet and painful. He placed the sword on the table by his bed and locked his gaze with Llun. He grabbed his forearm in the warrior's greeting, the brothers' greeting.

"Llun, you are brother to me. Until the day I die."

Llun smiled, and Voran noticed for the first time that his eyes were pale blue and brilliant, jewel-like. In his tanned face and set against the black of his hair and beard, they practically shone.

"Brothers," whispered Llun, his smile infectious.

Voran took the sword again to test it. He sliced across the lone tallow candle on the table. The disk that flew off the top was perfectly shaped. Without a second's hesitation, he sliced in a backhand, then again a third time across. Three perfectly equal disks lay on the table. The sword moved like a swimmer through water. Voran whistled his admiration. Llun turned even redder, if that was possible.

"Llun," Voran said, pulling up a chair for Llun. "Do you want to hear about Mirodara?"

Llun's face flushed. He breathed deeply, then nodded.

"When she came back to life, she was very confused for a time. Hardly remembered anything other than her mission. That she completed it made her feel empty for a time."

"Poor Mirodara. She never had a normal life. She was wanted by the Consistory ever since she was a child."

"My mother took her to Nebesta, then to far Karila. She found a place in the court of a young prince of Karila named Rogned. He fell in love with her, but she never really came back to herself. Always in a different place, somehow. Eventually, she ran away. I found her a year later. She was apprenticed to a hermit living in the wilderness."

"An apprentice? To what trade? Loneliness?"

Voran laughed. "No. Contemplation. Self-knowledge. She called it a 'descent into the self to find the self.' I don't know. But she was happy."

"Knowing her, she'll become a hermit-saint with her icon painted in some crossroads chapel a hundred years from now. If there are still such things left standing by then."

"Yes..."

Voran remembered how Mirodara looked the last time he saw her. Older than her twenty years, yet somehow younger as well. She lived on a platform in a tree, where she sat in silence, staring at the mountain ranges for hours at a time. What he didn't tell Llun was that she was a practitioner of the word, as Voran used to be. The name she whispered—*Saddai, Saddai*—had saved Voran more times than he cared to count. But he had not practiced the stillness of the word for more than a year now. Yet another source for his never-ending guilt. He needed to distract himself with something else.

"Llun, you know the Consistory. How they act. Tell me what you think."

"I'm sure they already know about us. They're probably just waiting for the right moment. To be honest, Voran, I don't see what a slave revolt can do. There is still the problem of Vasyllia's people. They will be on Aspidian's side."

"I know. But choice do we have?"

"Leave Vasyllia. Go to the exiled Dar. Gather strength. Build anew. Let Vasyllia rot inside its wall. It will soon collapse in on itself."

If only that were possible. If only Vasylli were not the key to everything.

"Llun, have you never felt that Vasyllia was different than other places? Somehow...special?"

Llun nodded vigorously.

"There's a reason for that."

As Voran told Llun of the Garden in the Heart of the World, the former blacksmith's expression played a scale of conflicting emotions, ranging from amused disbelief to grudging acceptance. Finally, a calmness to his expression suggested that he had accepted Voran's unlikely tale.

"If what you say is true, then what hope do we have? We are grappling with gods."

"Only the hope that any good man must have when faced with the suffering of innocents, I suppose," said Voran, though his heart still accused him of his failures in that department. "Don't you see? We have no other choice, no other hope. We have to go to Vasyllia before the Raven reaches his heart's desire."

"As always, time is the great enemy," said Llun. He guffawed. "Time and ignorance. What I wouldn't give to know whether the Raven is close to the Garden. If we had the time…"

With a lurch in his stomach, Voran remembered the quick glimpse of the golden fruit—the price for his slavery. If that was one of the fruits from the tree, then they were already too late. The Raven had already found the Garden and was probably gorging himself on the fruit of the trees.

An oxhorn blared outside their window.

"Is that?" asked Llun, tense. "Already?"

Voran looked outside the window. Horsemen. Hundreds of them. Dark banners fluttered among spear-tips. A black obelisk with raven's wings on a field of red.

"They're here," said Voran.

Lubomir and Ladomir burst into the room. Both of them were excited as children. Voran's confusion must have shown in his face, because the always serious Lubomir actually cackled.

"You aren't worried about the host outside?" asked Llun.

Ladomir slapped Llun's shoulder and beckoned to the window.

"Look," he said. "They have brought less than one hundred men. We had counted on them bringing at least two hundred and fifty."

"There are still far too many for us to defeat," said Voran.

"Defeat?" Lubomir scoffed. "We don't want to defeat them!"

Voran's heart fell as he began to understand. "You are going to sacrifice yourselves. Why? What does that accomplish?"

"Simple," said Ladomir. "One hundred of us have made our final farewells with the Sons. You will lead us, Vohin Voran, in an attack against the dog-men. It will be bloody and short. We will lose. But the Sons will have victory."

"I don't understand," said Llun.

"There is an underground passage out of this mill. One of several that the Sons have been working on for years. Most of us will escape that way, then take concealed forest paths back toward the city. There is another passageway that leads under the wall of the city directly into the house of Siloán the potter."

"Siloán is alive?" Voran couldn't believe his ears.

Ladomir's face paled as he seemed to remember something. "No. He did not survive the purge. His house did, and it is a hidden center for the few Sons who remain in Vasyllia. A place for the armed resistance to gather in the quiet of night. It is already happening. Soon we will have enough armed men, even in Vasyllia, to rise up again. You, Llun, will lead the remainder of us slaves back to Vasyllia—"

"No," said Llun. "I must be with Voran. If I am not among the killed or captured, it will raise suspicion."

"He's right, Ladomir. You will lead them."

Ladomir's eyebrows went up, and he was about to protest, when Lubomir interrupted. "Yes, Ladomir. You must do this. I will be the one to die today, not you."

"What's to prevent the dog-men from finding the secret passage?" asked Voran.

Lubomir spit. "It is well hidden. And believe me, they will not bother counting. They will get their one hundred killed or captured and be pleased with it. You will have noticed that Aspidían did not come. These are not even his best warriors."

Voran nodded. The escape could work. As for another armed resistance, he had his doubts. But even the possibility of it filled him with excitement. His sword-hand twitched in anticipation of the feel of the blade as it connected with iron and bone.

※

Voran and Llun came out with blades bared into the cold night air. Their breaths came out in ragged clouds, giving the tableau ahead of them a half-dreamy sheen. Ranks upon ranks of dog-men stood, swords and war hammers in hand, still as stone. Only their own cloudlets of breath steaming out of their dog-shaped faceplates gave any indication that they were not statues. It was a picture out of nightmares. Voran's heart skipped as he felt the easy weight of Llun's last sword.

How good it will be to use a sword once again. He smiled.

As though his smile was a signal, the dog-men all crouched into a fighting stance at the same time, like a series of bristling marionettes. Voran heard Llun's breath catch for a moment, then speed up. It was a chilling sight, yes, but it focused Voran's mind. All the sword forms came back to his muscles, and he imagined exactly which attacks he would use, anticipating all the possible moves of his enemy in advance. How fast it came back to him, even after so many years.

Truly, the Old Vasylli ways were strong. Old, strong, and resilient. We will *rise up. We* will *prevail.*

But first, the purge. And the pain.

Gritting his teeth, Voran felt the war-wind take him with the tingling of his body, the beating of his heart like Llun's great hammer on anvil, and the remembered sound of Lyna's first song. He raised his sword and called.

"VASYLLIA!!!!!!"

He ran at the dog-men. Their line wavered for a split second before he charged into them. It was enough. Two men screamed as Voran feinted then slashed a vicious uppercut underneath their guards. Voran felt, more than saw, Llun's massive war hammer make mincemeat of the dogs that now turned from him in shrieking fear. He parried a blow from his left, then used his body strength to push off. His attacker tripped, and as he did, a Vasylli slave pounced on him, plunging a knife into his faceplate.

Voran killed four more before anyone so much as parried one of his blows. Llun had a mound of men, ever growing, around him. But the slaves were dropping like flies.

Do not indulge yourself, Warrior of the Word. Your death will serve no one.

He snapped out of his berserker rage. A quick glance around him showed that more than half the slaves were already down, and the rest were only seconds away from being hacked down. Llun bled from several gaping wounds.

It was enough. They had given the Sons enough time to escape. And they had killed a good number of dog-men into the bargain.

"Llun!" He called.

Llun turned to him, his eyes bloodshot and his face a feral mask. Then, his humanity softened his gaze. His shoulders relaxed, and he nodded. He threw his war hammer down and raised his hands. Two of his assailants used the pommels of their swords to knock him to the ground, then began to kick him until they were sure he was unconscious.

Voran raised his hands, sword blade-down. Then he went down on his knees. Four dog-men surrounded him, but they did not attack him.

One of them raised a war-horn and blew three quick blasts. All the dog-men stopped what they were doing and filed back into perfect ranks, as though they were in fact nothing more than puppets. Voran's blood froze at that display of power.

The wounded were gathered together, their hands and feet bound, but with enough slack to be able to walk on their own. None of the slaves had escaped unharmed. Only thirty-seven had remained alive, but most of them were wounded fatally, Voran saw. They would not survive any journey.

Voran, still on his knees, closed his eyes and descended with his mind into the quiet, throbbing place of his heart where, years ago, he had mastered the stillness of the word. He was out of practice, but there was no time for halting efforts now. He breathed out and whispered the name. *Saddaí.* It echoed within him, the sound bouncing throughout his body before his seemed to burst out from him through his skin.

Needle-pain pierced Voran from a hundred different places. Blood flowed down every inch of his body. He looked at his arms. They were pockmarked with slashes, punctures, and contusions. His face was a throbbing lump. He couldn't feel his tongue, it was so swollen.

All around him, the Sons of the Swan gasped as their wounds were erased from their bodies only to reappear on Voran's body. Even the dog-men reeled from it.

"The Healer," said one of the slaves. "He has come. And he will heal Vasyllia."

To Voran's surprise, the dog-men didn't react. They didn't beat the slave down. They didn't stab him. They merely stood there, as though enchanted.

Voran still stared at his arms. His jaw ached as he ground his teeth against the pain that buffeted. Then, the wounds began to close, and a new sensation—intense itching and a healthy ache replaced the flow of blood-pain. With it came a wave of exhaustion. For a moment, he fought it, then he could no longer. He closed his eyes.

CHAPTER 34
A DEBT REPAID

Khaidu and Aglaia found more than a hundred children, all told, among the trees. The trees themselves were like nothing Khaidu had every encountered. They were half-alive, their branches almost like the tentacles of some water-beast. *Earth-magic,* Aglaia had said with distaste. *Giant-magic.*

They freed them all and lost none of them. That was the lesser miracle. The greater was that they encountered nothing—no giants, no armed warriors, no nameless spirits of darkness—to stop them in the forests. Khaidu's unease at this was no more than vague, but Aglaia's tenseness never abated, her ears constantly pricked forward, her tail twitching.

All the children had taken to Aglaia like she was an oversized toy. Khaidu had expected them to fear her transformation, or at least to have trouble understanding that she was one being in two forms, but they merely accepted it as "how it must be." Amazing, she thought, how quickly your perspective changes after you've suffered unspeakable pain.

The horde of children that came with them was louder than a spring flock of starlings, and even rowdier. As good Gumiren, they frolicked and wrestled each other at the slightest opportunity. The boys arranged themselves into packs, headed usually by the biggest, but sometimes by the wiliest, boys. Bruises were ubiquitous, but bruised souls were completely healed.

"You have yourself to thank for that," Aglaia had said, noticing how quickly the children had come back to normal. "They see what you're capable of, even with your injuries, and it gives them quiet strength."

Khaidu was less sure. She knew how resilient the Gumiren children were. Not all Gumiren babies survived the first winters of their lives, when the winds of the Steppe turned snowfalls into hurled spears. The ones that did had a surprising capacity for quick joy underneath their physical and emotional strength. How else had Khaidu remained alive until now, her sixteenth year, as a broken creature in a society that had no place, no patience for the crippled?

Coming out of the twisted, dark part of that forest was like remembering to breathe again. Khaidu greeted the thin, light-allowing trees like they were long-lost family. The children, if possible, became even rowdier. The sun filtered through the branches, dappling the scarred skin of the children, changing the signs of torture into reminders of summer's coming. Khaidu had forgotten that there was such a thing as warmth in the constant damp of this horrid, wooded country.

You're getting soft, she grumbled at herself. *Have you forgotten the winters in the Steppe?*

"H-h-ow will we take all these ch-ch-ildren to Raven's B-ban?"

"Bane." Aglaia smiled wolfishly. "I was rather hoping you'd be the one to suggest a way."

"Me?"

"You're friends with the Majestva, after all."

Khaidu chortled. Of course. Who better to help than a legendary creature capable of crossing space and time simultaneously?

The twins they had rescued on the first night ran toward Khaidu—hand in hand, as they had been since they were released from the trees. Ignoring everyone, they had eyes only for Khaidu (they had already taken to calling her "Mama").

"Mama, more of them," they said, nearly in unison.

Khaidu made the Gumiren hand sign that asked for clarification: the thumb and the first two fingers out and extended, with an upward motion.

"Children," said the boy. "Not Gumiren," added the girl.

"Who?" asked Aglaia.

"Vasylli," they said together.

"L-let's go," said Khaidu, already reaching for Aglaia.

Aglaia's powerful jaws lifted Khaidu by her collar up onto her back, and they were off like a black arrow in the direction indicated by the children.

The morning had been fine and sunny. But now the fog came rolling in, ominous and frigid, as though Nature itself had heard the news of more children being sold into slavery. Through the shifting mist, Khaidu glimpsed the ever-closer peaks of Vasyllia stacked against each other like loaves of bread on a table. They were making directly for a wooded peak, one of the higher vantage points of the area.

Khaidu knew it well—it was a place she had asked Aglaia to bring her several times in the past few mornings. A place to gather her thoughts and think, something she had precious little time to do these days.

It was one of the more picturesque places in this Northern wasteland of wood. Just across the Ulna, the hills made a shallow bowl between two toothy ridges. On mornings after rainy days, a single, fine stream of rainwater fell over the edge of the bowl into the Ulna. Khaidu could watch the steady rushing of that stream for hours. It always left her humming inside, as though she had somehow pierced through to the music of water and joined in spirit to it.

Now, the rivulet was a torrent, more brown than white. Again, Khaidu felt that Nature, so long held in the disease that was killing it, was wakening. *Perhaps I had some small part in that*, she thought with a twinge of pride.

Just underneath the falls, a flat barge littered with children bobbed up and down on the unruly current of the Ulna. Most of them were lying in heaps. Only a few seemed able to do as much as sit up. Even from such a distance, Khaidu heard their soft moans and saw enough red amid the pasty white of their skin to make her sick again.

Standing knee-deep in the Ulna was a moving hill, or so Khaidu thought at first. Then it turned toward them, and amid the grey and brown (she had assumed it to be moss and lichen, but it was hair and a beard), she saw a face. Larger than a yurt—the face alone. She covered her mouth with both her hands and let herself groan into her hands. Aglaia dropped on her haunches and stilled.

"Giants." Aglaia's expelled breath sounded like a sneeze. Khaidu had learned that in wolfish that was tantamount to spitting on someone. "Looks like Yesukai was telling the truth."

Aglaia's haunches quivered, eager to pounce, to ravage, to tear out throats. Khaidu heartily agreed.

"Not yet," Khaidu whispered, marveling at the wonder of her gradually loosening tongue. She even found a moment to silently thank the hag. "L-look, down near the barge." She pointed to the riverbank.

Near the barge bobbed a dingy with a triangular sail. Four oarsmen and a lord, judging by the profusion of gold thread in the belt adorning his abundant midsection. Two banners fluttered on the mast—a gold sun on black field, and a black winged obelisk on a red field.

"That obelisk I've never seen. But the other is Vasyllia. Of that, I am sure." Aglaia's quivering had turned spasmodic. "But it doesn't make sense... If the giants are planning to break down the wall, why are they still trading with Vasylli?"

"Maybe the giants need the blood of Vasylli children to take the wall? But how can Vasylli sell their own children?"

"I think this is a purge. Those children must be children of loyalists. Those who refused to follow the Dark Father."

"L-l-listen," said Khaidu. "Wait ... t-t-till those slavers leave."

"Too late," said a voice like glass over gravel. It was accompanied by a whimpering laugh, or more a wheeze. They were just behind Khaidu.

Khaidu felt steel boring into the back of her head. Whoever they were, they weren't interested in giving her any sort of clean death.

"Don't even think of moving, wolf," said the first. "We know all about your kind. I have five of my best archers in the trees. Two of them can get you in a second. Then, they can all take turns picking off the kids one by one."

Khaidu felt, more than saw, Aglaia stiffen. They had no way of knowing if what the man said was true.

"We'll come," Khaidu heard Aglaia say.

Without letting them turn around, the men pushed them down the slope toward the waiting barge and the giant standing there still, inspecting his wares. The dingy bobbed an easy bowshot away. The lord standing in the prow had his hands crossed across his chest, his expression mocking.

"Well, well," he cackled. Khaidu immediately hated the look of him, and her opinion was not improved by the thing hanging from his belt. A shriveled dog's head? What sort of a deranged madman was this? And a lord, to boot... "The legends themselves come alive and grace us with their presence," he continued, clearly enamored with his own voice. "I'm sure all the lands will sleep easier when they know that the wolf-woman no longer prowls the woods." He nodded down at one of the oarsmen, who pulled a short bow from inside the boat.

"Wolf-woman, I want to introduce you to someone." He pointed at the oarsman. "His father was once at the receiving end of your husband's spear-butt. For no good reason, I might add."

"That I very much doubt," mumbled Aglaia into her snout.

"He also happens to be a decent shot with the short bow. I'm going to let him play a game. He has one shot. One shot only. If he hits you, I'll let the Gumira runt go free. If not, I'll let you go free, and take the Gumira for myself. But here's the most important rule of the game. You can't move. If you do, I'll burn the barge with the children."

"You'll do no such thing," said the giant, taking a single step that rocked the dingy so high, it nearly capsized.

As he took a step, several things happened at once. The water underneath the giant seethed, as though boiling. His face turned first red, then white, then a greenish tinge. He opened a massive maw filled with crooked, broken teeth, and bellowed like he was being eaten. The water around his legs foamed red. Right next to him, the barge rose to the top of a roiling wave in which the forms of hundreds of fish could be seen. Not just fish. Pike. Huge, toothy pike.

From the sky, a cloud of white and brown suddenly descended, twisting like a water spout. Khaidu gasped at the beauty of these birds—in forms like hawks, though with ash-white eyes and speckled feathers. They were lissome and flew with grace, as though they were swimming through air.

"Ospreys," whispered Aglaia, her surprise so great it was evident in her wolf-form. "Heights above, Khaidu! It seems everyone is paying their debts to you today."

Khaidu remembered the pike she had not allowed Sabíana the eagle to kill. Could the Majestva come as well?

Just as she thought it, the ospreys all melted into air and turned into swirling, fiery masses of wings and eyes. Hundreds of eyes of every shape, color—cat's eyes, blue baby's eyes, snake eyes, even something that might have been the eyes of a sea monster. They took the children into their wings, embracing each child like mothers swaddling newborns.

"Ooof!" said the man behind Aglaia. The man behind Khaidu gurgled expressively. Khaidu turned herself over and saw him clutching at his neck. A thin metal arrowhead stuck out under his left ear.

"Did he hurt you?" Yesukai ran to Khaidu. She held a short bow. A quiver dangled at her hip. Two bodies lay behind her, each with a knife growing out of the back of their necks.

"N-n-n-o, I'm...fine." Khaidu grabbed Yesukai by the shoulder and used her as leverage to twist herself back onto her knees, to see what the Majestva had done with the Vasylli children. Each child lay on its back on the opposite bank. Each head was pillowed with what looked from this side like moss. Rows and rows of children peacefully asleep.

Khaidu was again distracted by the cry of the giant. But there was no giant any more. Just huge brown coils, serpentine but slimy, like a worm, intertwined in each other, trying to avoid the frenzy of biting pike. A head occasionally poked out of the coils, long and ugly, like the head of a horse, but with scales and tufted ears. Hideous. A stench like rotting flesh rose from the beast. A defense mechanism, Khaidu realized. Those serpent-giants really are nothing more than large, intelligent animals.

Now the Majestva joined the pike. Talons appeared from the masses of wings—long and sharp like spear heads, but with razor edges to go along with the piercing point. The serpent had no chance. It was ripped apart in a gush of blood and bile. The sight finally made Khaidu turn away.

Something licked Khaidu's face. Khaidu turned her face toward it, groggy, only to nearly lose her skin in alarm. It was a lynx, larger than she had ever seen. And not only one. At least twenty lynx, all intent on the pieces of serpent now washing ashore. They looked ravenous with hunger. From above them, hordes of ravens came plunging down, intent on the cats' leavings. Wolverines exploded from undergrowth. Badgers ran alongside, as though they were the wolverines' lesser cousins.

All of nature came to claim the abomination, to cleanse it from the face of the earth. Khaidu found herself a still point in a maelstrom. In the rush of animals, there was unexpected peace. She found it easy to settle into the earth, to relax her back, which immediately responded by sending shooting pains all through her arms and down her spine. Then the pain crested, and the wave of relief flowed in its wake.

With it came a bone-deep thrill. All these tremendous events, these magical creatures, the revelations of other worlds. There was only one possible reason for all of it—the Unknown Father was making himself known to her. She had never thought to be alive to see it. She had seen plenty of her Gumiren brothers and sisters lose their hope, especially after it was shattered to shards by the lies of the Dark Father. She had never ceased to hope, though she never expected to see it.

A small, nagging doubt cut into the thrill. Would the Unknown Father have a place for her? For the broken thing that she was? Would he see through to her intention, her desire to be united with something greater than herself?

"Khaidu!" It was Aglaia. She was flanked by three Majestva flittering with their countless wings of gold and topaz and lapis and malachite-green. A soft music flowed from their impossible forms—part air, part wind, part fire, part feathers. They hid their eyes from before her. Then it hit her. They were...in their way...*bowing*. To her?

The music of the Majestva had words in it, subtle as the whisper of wind. It sounded something like this:

"*To those broken by evil, the grace comes thick and fast*

*To those firm amid doubts, it flows like a torrent
To those who seek, the end beckons at last
The lifeblood of the worlds will wash you in its current."*

She didn't understand what they were saying, but it was—how could this be possible?—directed at her. They were all looking at her.

And the tears dried up, and joy came up like a sunrise. She had found her place. These were her horse-clan: these beasts, these children, these majestic creatures of a heavenly otherworld. She was one of them.

Then, as though all the creatures had never been there, the woods were empty, except for Yesukai, a few of the other children, and Aglaia.

"Khaidu," said Aglaia, deeply moved. "Look around. I'll help you."

The Majestva, now barely visible except for swirls of dead leaves and grass, were doing something to the Vasylli children on the other side of the river. Whatever it was that they did, there was now something different about the children. They were still wounded, still stick-thin, still pitiful. But as they were waking up, they showed no weakness, no fear. Instead, they seemed intent on the bank where Aglaia and Khaidu watched them. More and more began to awake, whispering to each other and pointing at Khaidu, though she was hidden by the trees. Then, they all stood up and...walked on water...

...Or so it seemed at first. It was the pike. They continued to churn and seethe, but now their scaly bodies made a clearly visible bridge over the river. All the children ran across it. As soon as the last one passed, the pike dissolved into the current.

The children labored up the incline, directly to the place where Khaidu and Aglaia waited for them. Aglaia's haunches were twitching again, and she whined in expectation. Khaidu understood. She wanted to help them but feared to scare them. But the first children who came into the shelter of the trees did not even flinch at seeing Aglaia's giant body. They ran to her, most of them breaking into smiles of recognition. She knew these children? Yes, she did! Khaidu had never heard her laugh like that. Aglaia flipped over to her back and raised her paws, just like a house-dog, her tongue lolling out of the side of her mouth. Four of the children immediately started tickling her belly. She yelped, and jumped back up on her legs so quickly, some of the children fell over in a heap. Khaidu laughed, and they laughed with her.

The trickle of pale-faced children soon became a torrent, more and more boisterous. When they saw the Gumiren children, they hurried to them, at first curious, like puppies intrigued by their first encounter with wolf cubs. But it took hardly any time for the nonsense of child-speak to unify them into knots of giggles and shoves, pushes and hugs. The forest—

covered in tree-rot around them—came back to life in the sound of rescued children, Vasylli and Gumiren together, oblivious to the blood and anguish that had separated their peoples for the last twenty years.

"Khaidu, you did this," whispered Aglaia, close to Khaidu.

"No. The Unknown Father did."

CHAPTER 35
THE DAR OF THE HERETICS

Knyaz Parfyon of Nebesta was true to his word. Nothing, not even a stray mosquito, bothered Antomír on his way back to the bear riders' camp. But someone, or something, was not happy. The rain that began on the day of his return seemed to follow him. Ahead and behind him, close enough to see with the naked eye, the sun streamed down in sheets of light, just beyond the black rain. But no matter how fast his bear ran, the sun was always out of reach.

An almost physical weight pushed Antomír's head in from all sides. A headache that only got worse during the course of the day. His mind was groggy, like a drunken man's, while trying to run a race. All the elation, the energy of their wild battle had disappeared so completely that the reality of it seemed no more than a dream he had years ago.

Now, his body paid the price. Bruises in every part of his body, aches in muscles he didn't know existed. Even lifting an eyebrow was painful. But he had no choice, except to ignore it all and carry on.

He was the only one to survive, other than Cassían, whom he had sent away. What sort of leader allows all his men to die, and dares to remain alive himself? But he always knew he would never make a good leader. He was raised too innocent, too closed off from the world. The haven of Ghavan was no crucible to harden the iron of future kings. No. He couldn't even die properly, much less live well. He had hardly a wound on him, after all. Only the cut across his collarbone.

He remembered the mild surprise on the face of the first Nebesti warrior he killed. His first kill. The face had belonged to a young man. A man who looked hardly different from Antomír himself. Fuzz on the chin, no proper beard. Hair so blond it was almost white. Grey eyes that, in the moment of death, lit up from within as the soul departed to calmer pastures than these killing fields. He could have been a cousin to Antomír, for all he knew. And Antomír had *ended* him.

The grief gathered inside Antomír, fermenting, boiling over, ready to burst. But no. It was still too early to give in. Antomír breathed out all the foul air inside him, then breathed in pure, new air, pushing out all remnants of the past two days. Whatever the bear riders decided to do with him, he would accept it. If they told him to kneel and bow his own head willingly under the executioner's blade, he would do it.

Somehow calmed by the thought and consoled by the warmth of the air blowing in his face, he put his arm around his bear's neck. She turned her head to look at him. Antomír leaned down and touched his forehead to the broad, furry space between her eyes. She sniffed and purred, almost like a cat. Then he mounted, and they were off. In the distance, Antomír could already see the smoke of campfires.

Silent lines of men greeted Antomír, arrayed in military splendor. Cassían was in the front ranks, his face inscrutable. Lines upon lines of warriors stood behind him, next to their bears. All the men had swords unsheathed and raised, while their left hands held long, lit candles. In the twilit, early darkness, their faces glowed like phantoms. The lines continued in perfect order all the way up a short hill, cleared of trees. They left a narrow passageway between the ranks, enough for a warrior to walk through, but not to ride on his bear. It was as if they knew Antomír would be returning alone.

Antomír dismounted and stood before his bear to say goodbye. As he embraced her shaggy head, she nuzzled his shoulder until she found the armpit, and she sniffed into it loudly. It tickled, and Antomír barely stifled a laugh.

"You're such a jester," he whispered into her ear. "It's been an honor, friend." He entered the mass of warriors. As he passed every rank, the warriors turned to follow him with their eyes. Halfway up the hill, Veles barred his path.

"Have you come through death itself to reach the sacred mount?" he said, intoning. Antomír felt naked in his ignorance of the rite. Were there proper words to answer?

"I have not, brother," he said, trusting in his instinct. "I have failed. My brother warriors paid the ultimate price, but I remain, to bear the guilt of the living for the rest of my days."

"It is well said." Veles bowed to his waist and touched his right hand to the ground. "Never forget that burden, for it will only grow in the coming war. May the Heights keep you alive, but may your burden never feel less than it is."

Antomír shuddered from the strange tingling in his chest. It was like a flame had ignited inside him. It did not lessen the burden of killing and his new brothers' deaths, but the burden felt somehow more necessary, as though he would not be quite himself without it.

Veles took him by the left elbow and led him onward.

Three quarters of the way up the hill, Severuk came from the right side and blocked Antomír's path.

"Antomír, son of Mirnían and Lebía. You are a sower of death. Everything you touch withers. All who ride with you die. Yet you remain. You are a blight on the face of the earth. You should be struck down here and now, before you cause more sorrow in these lands, already so ravaged by the Internecine War."

The change of tone from ritual to accusation bewildered Antomír. Instinctively, he turned to Veles, for had it not always been Veles who had saved him from such situations? But Veles looked at Antomír with the same air of challenge as Severuk. Antomír swallowed hard and breathed deep, trying to still his heart enough to prevent his voice from cracking at the most important moment. He didn't want the last emotion of his life to be embarrassment.

"I am unworthy of further life," said Antomír. His voice took on a bell-like quality he hardly recognized. "I have, indeed, become a sower of death. Ever seeking the family I lost, I only spread the same contagion. Therefore, I submit to the wisdom of your words. I bow my neck to your blade."

He fell on his knees and lowered his head. The exposed skin tingled from the evening chill. Antomír closed his eyes. At that moment, he had no doubt that this was the end. A deserved end, yet a noble one. He had had his elation of battle; he had had his moment of something like triumph. He had been brother to the dead; he would join them in the halls of Adonais. This was right and good. He was ready.

A firm hand raised him by the right elbow. Severuk's. Veles's own familiar grip doubled down on his left elbow.

"A sower of death you are," said Severuk in a soft voice. "I charge you to sow death to all who stand in your way. Let every man, beast, or Power quail before the coming of your sword."

Images flowed into his mind—the effigy of a dead king grasping a longsword, a tree with a gold-red fruit ripe to bursting, and black water churning in a cavern—making little sense. But he understood with his heart that if he survived the coming war, he would never have a moment for himself or his own wants. Today was the day he died, in a sense. After today, the Antomír that used to be would no longer exist. The new Antomír would be a slave, not a prince.

They almost carried him up the last quarter of the way in their enthusiasm, past four pairs of torches. At the top, dimly lit by torchlight, stood three birches growing from a single root. Elmira stood in front of it, but he hardly recognized her now. She was taller, for one, and her dark skin seemed to glow. Another light was coming from behind her. He couldn't understand what he was seeing at first. Then he saw, and he gasped aloud. Elmira had wings of fire. Antomír fell on his face, terrified.

"Antomír," she said, and her voice cut through his body like a sword thrust. "You are the last true Dar of Vasyllia left in the Realm of earth. Are you prepared to do your duty and reclaim the ancient seat of your fathers?"

What?

Everyone was looking at him, tense with expectation. Was she serious? Were they planning to take back Vasyllia now? Veles and Severuk joined her in a line before him. They also had wings of fire.

Antomír wanted to say that he was not worthy. He wanted to beg them to take him on as a slave, a camp cook, or something like that. But he stopped himself. This was serious. Deadly serious. This was no formality. What he said now would not merely affect the course of his life, but it would affect the history of Vasyllia and the rest of the Three Lands.

He saw his mother's face as she reached for him, falling ever deeper into the dark waters. But her face was different in this memory. Now, it was calm. She smiled, and her eyes crinkled in slight mockery, so rare for her. Antomír realized he was smiling at the memory, like a village idiot.

"I am prepared to do my duty," he said, "though I do not know the way. Will you teach me, children of the Priest-King?"

"We will," said Elmira, and her wings blazed out from her back, five times greater than before. Veles and Severuk's wings also grew, until they illumined the hilltop, catching the glint of mail and sword-edge. Everyone—man and beast—looked like they were on fire.

Elmira, Severuk, and Veles stood in a loose triangular formation, facing each other. Their wings drew together, meeting at a point above their heads. In the exact center point of the three sets of wings, a circlet of fire coalesced into red gold bands intertwining, with five-petaled ruby flowers (or were they flames?) decorating the peaked front. Elmira caught it in her hands, which did not seem to mind the heat of the metal. She approached Antomír, who was still on his knees, and lowered it on his head. It was warm and surprisingly heavy for its size.

Veles and Severuk took his elbows again and turned him to face the warriors. Antomír gasped. He could not see the end of them, there were so many. Women and children in the front, fifteen rows deep. The rest were men and bears, as far as the eye could see. Antomír did not even realize there were so many people in the entire world. And they all fell on their knees in a single motion, with a single thud that echoed through the trees. They were bowing to *him!*

❦

"Enjoy it, anointed one," said Veles in his old half-mocking tone, staring with longing at the hot springs. "Oh, for the pleasures of hot water and foaming soap on my own dirty hide! But such is not the lot of mere slaves, I suppose."

"Balderdash, Veles," Antomír said. "I know well enough that this is the last time in my life I will ever be allowed to have any sort of time for myself, any luxury away from the prying eyes of the world."

Veles shook his head and clucked, so much the disapproving motherly type that Antomír couldn't help but laugh. "I'll leave you alone then, shall I?"

"No, you won't. You'll be lurking behind that rock, and it's not even big enough to cover you up to the shoulder, you overgrown potato!" It was so pleasant to banter with Veles again, as in the old times. "No, you'd better sit here like you're supposed to. You can explain it all to me as I take my last bath."

"Now, don't be morbid. Who knows? Maybe there'll be bathhouses underneath every tree in Vasyllia."

Antomír looked over the rocky edge of the steaming pool. They were alone inside the cave, and the air in it had a faintly sulfurous smell. The color of the water in the pool was unnaturally blue, and it frothed on its own. But he could feel the warmth of it, even as he and Veles had entered the cave. His body ached for the comfort of warm water, no matter how foul-smelling.

He took his clothes off carefully, as Mama had taught him, folding them neatly on the rock, but only after having brushed aside the pebbles and coal-like fragments of the black rock of the cave. Veles laughed his cackle laugh. "Anointed one, you don't actually think I'd ever let you wear those clothes again? They're disgusting, for one. For another, you'll be wearing king's clothing from now on. My own personal choice from ancient kingly stores, I might add. I think you'll love it."

He reached down to the sack at his feet and pulled out a horrifying, frilly dress of a sickly coral-salmon color. Antomír must not have done as good a job as he thought concealing his disgust, because Veles doubled over in laughter, his eyes tearing up.

"You should see your face, anointed one! Forgive your old servant. A joke. This is a Karila dressing gown, belonging to one of the oldest families of that venerable city-state. To the oldest matriarch of that venerable city-state, I might add."

Antomír jumped into the pool, but he made sure to tuck his feet up to his chest, for the largest possible splash he could manage. It worked like a charm—Veles was drenched from head to foot, the dregs of his laughter dripping with the water from his beard and mustache.

It was Antomír's turn to laugh.

"You don't dispose one to speak about anything, with that sort of childishness," grumbled Veles as he tried to wring the water out of his curls.

"Ah, but you forget, dear Veles. I can command you now, and you'd have to do everything I say."

Veles mumbled something into his beard about pompous children, heretic Dars, and the tragedy of the monarchia of the last days. He arranged himself against the rock wall, sitting in the posture he usually reserved for light afternoon dozes. Antomír knew that this was when he was at his sharpest, in spite of appearances.

"So, my dear Veles," said Antomír, melting into the ecstasy of the hot water. "I think it's time you explained who you really are. Those wings of fire?"

"Take your thoughts back to Ghavan, if you can," Veles began, his voice already following a cadence of half-chant. "Otar Yustav once told you the legend of the Priest-King, yes? The brother of Lassar the Blessed who tried to take his throne and was exiled to a land so far east, it was off the map? His name was Askoldír. I am one of his sons. Severuk is as well. Elmira is our sister, though from another mother, his second wife. Do you remember how our mother went mad, trying to save our youngest brother by giving him water from the fountain of life?

"She was something like a Dar to our people. Her death ripped our society apart. Most of our people saw the coming of Askoldír the Priest-King (he was neither priest, nor king, by the way), as an abomination before the face of the Heights. You see, our people had a very direct experience of the Heights. We conversed with Powers directly, face to face. This was all because of the fountain of life, the purest form of Living Water this earth has ever seen. As Otar Yustav told you, the rituals governing the use of the fountain were extremely strict. No one dared, under penalty of death, to even consider using it for personal gain. When our mother tried to force it to heal our sick brother, the fountain went dry.

"Many of our people began to die, something unheard of in our society. That was the final straw for my father's enemies. A group of them tried to kill him. It did not work. Worse, that act led to the complete closure of the Heights against all of us, a curse on us all. We lost all contact with the Powers. Our people, the ones who didn't die—some of us had drunk so much of the fountain of life that we couldn't die—were cursed to wander the Eastern lands. Before, the doors to all the Realms were open to us. We could freely travel to the Lows and Mids of Aer, and to other places that have no name in your tongue. But now we were imprisoned to walk the lowest Realm of earth.

"So Severuk, Elmira, her husband, and I undertook an impossible mission. We had heard of a long, impossible way to the very throne of Heights. It went through the world of the underground, the land of the dead. It was difficult, but we found the way. It was in some ways worse than death, especially for us who had been given the gift of nearly endless life. The hardships I will not describe. They are impossible to describe. But we made it. All the way to the footstool of the Most High. To the Unknown Father's throne.

"If the terrors of the night's kingdom cannot properly be described, then you, my Dar, should understand that I cannot even begin to find the words to describe the wonder and glory of the Heights of Aer. It was surpassing beautiful, but it was terrible as well. The higher Powers subjected us to trials of fire such as no living human has ever undergone. Lassar of Vasyllia later described these trials as the seven baptisms of fire. He was right, though his information was anecdotal. When we endured and passed them all, we were no longer fully human. We had ... transfigured. We had much of the Heights about us, much of the Powers. In this form, the Unknown Father himself heard our plea for the resurrection of the fountain of life, for the restoration of peace among our people. He did not grant our request.

"Instead, he appointed us the protectors of the four ends of the Realm of earth, and we were given the blessing to cross through all the Realms again, in our efforts to protect earth. We have not always succeeded. Men are stubborn creatures, and we have no right to suborn human wills. But we have done what we could, even in the Internecine War. But as the Raven's power leeches at the buttresses of the Realms, so we come to the limit of our protection. The Unknown Father told us that our service as protectors would only last until the time of a great war that would either join the races of the Three Lands for all time or leave this Realms of earth itself a charred ruin, a world forgotten by all, bewailed by none."

During the telling of Veles's tale, an uncomfortable feeling nagged at Antomír. At first, he was so entranced by the story that he couldn't quite put his finger on it. But toward the end of the story, he realized what it was.

"Veles, why do you keep referring to an Unknown Father in the Heights? Not once did you mention Adonais. Is this just another way of speaking about him?"

Veles turned to look at Antomír. His eyes were inscrutable. Hard, flinty. Nothing of the usual softness.

"Sire. Have you ever read the original covenant, as written down by Lassar's scribes? Who were the signatories of the bond?"

"Lassar and the Harbinger, I think."

"Yes. But so many people have forgotten the full wording. *Lassar and the Harbinger, on behalf of the Great Father in the Heights, who is unknown.* Go over your *Sayings*. It's there. The first mention of Adonais is during a renewal of Covenant in the reign of Cassían. Only after that new covenant did Adonais become the object of worship in Vasyllia and the rest of the city-states."

"Veles, what are you saying?"

Veles breathed out long, so long, that it sounded like he would never breathe in again.

"I do not know who Adonais is. We, the children of the Priest-King, do not worship or serve him."

How had Antomír not noticed it before? Veles was fanatical in his mysticism, but he never came to the sacrifices dedicated to Adonais. Never came for the great days of feast. Only to the more esoteric services to the various powers and earthly saints.

"But who do you think Adonais is, then? One of the Powers? A brother to the Harbinger?"

Veles turned away and didn't answer. Antomír realized he was cold, and not just from the rising cold of the night. They remained silent until Antomír had had enough of the water. All through that silence, Antomír tried to quiet his mind, tried not to think. But the possibility was frightening: What if these children of the Priest-King were enemies of Adonais? Had Antomír just walked into a trap of the Raven?

CHAPTER 36
THE TRIAL OF LLUN THE SMITH

Llun sat in his cell with no windows and waited. Any moment now, some contraption would open up above him. Some new form of torture devised by the artist of death, Aspidían, himself, would be tested on him. He would be torn or beaten or dragged to the very limit of human life, then left there to dangle on the precipice between life and death. It had happened twice before to him, before he had been initiated into the dog-men. Both times, he had been a hair's breadth from going mad. Both times, Aspidían had come to rescue him at the last minute. The only man, he was prone to saying, who could provide justice and salvation in equal measure.

But nothing happened. No sham trial. No public humiliation. Not even a private humiliation. Llun was simply abandoned in a cell. Once every two days, someone left him old bread and water. It wasn't even that bad, certainly no worse than some of the slop they served at the refectory of the Consistory.

The strangeness of it, the uncertainty would have been enough to terrify his younger self. But he was Consistory-trained. He was a dog-man, no matter how much he hoped that Voran had given him new life. No. Llun knew death would come. He knew it would be unpleasant. He grieved that Voran would likely share in it. But that was that. He had rolled his dice for the last time. As always, he lost in the most spectacular manner.

In the darkest moments in that window-less cell, Llun allowed himself one small comfort. Mirodara would not see him. Mirodara was beyond the rot in Vasyllia. She was peaceful and happy. It was enough.

One thing was different during this particular imprisonment. Llun didn't lose track of time. He knew exactly how many days and nights passed. How exactly, he couldn't tell, since day and night didn't exist in a cell with no windows. But whether it was the rigorous daily routine of the Consistory or something more mystical, he knew that it was exactly four and a half days from the moment he was brought in, blindfolded, to the moment he was taken out again, equally blindfolded.

Judging by the stomp of booted feet accompanying him, his guard was three men. Not many for Llun, who had kept rigorous control of his body's strength and stamina in his time at the Consistory. But he had no desire left to fight back. He just let them bring him to a room.

The door slammed behind him, but he felt a draft on his face. A window must be open somewhere. That meant they weren't in the dungeon section. *Interesting.* They didn't take the blindfold off.

"This extraordinary session of the special committee, meeting on the fourth of the month of Nasser, comes to order." Llun recognized the voice as belonging to a certain lower noble named Puzyran. A flunkey, no more. So this was not a trial, but a reading of a prepared verdict. It was just as well. It would all be over soon.

"Llun, sub-voyevoda of the inner circle of our exalted Brother Aspidían of the Consistory. You have been found guilty of treason against your brotherhood, your city, and your people. You are remanded to the special judgment of the upper rooms."

Now *that* was surprising, and Llun's curiosity got the better of him. "Upper rooms" was Consistory jargon for a verdict from the mouth of the so-called Great Father himself. Llun hadn't heard of anyone being given such an important death in well over three years. It gave him a perverse sense of self-importance.

A cool touch on his neck, quickly flaring icy-hot. He flinched but forced himself to stay in place. The sickly-sweet smell of burning flesh punched him in the stomach. For a moment, he didn't realize it was his own flesh. As his body shook from the pain, he focused on the thought, trying to hitch his body to it, to stabilize it: *The hot brand is applied to the neck of all whores, catamites, and traitors.* The words of the Great Father himself.

Llun's skin screamed and oozed. His vision blurred, and he almost fell. Before that humiliation, he was hustled by a larger group out of the room and down a series of stairs at dizzying speed. They all stopped soon afterward in a room so filled with light that even Llun's blindfold registered it. He thought he knew where they brought him. They took off the blindfold.

Despite the pain in his neck, he still chuckled when he saw it. Llun stood in the doorway of Aspidían's personal chambers, where once before Yadovír himself had offered him the prime position of chief smith for the Consistory, over ten years ago. Little had changed. The walls were still garish in their many-colored floral motifs. There were still two elaborate chairs facing the three arched windows, with a short table between them. Again, a tall flagon of wine and two clay cups waited for Aspidían's pleasure. Aspidían himself sat in one of the chairs, facing the windows. The perfect picture of domesticity.

"No, I do not taunt you, former brother," Aspidían said, still not looking at Llun. "Leave us."

The armed guard disappeared, and the door closed behind them.

"I am not insensitive, you know that," continued Aspidían. "I wanted you to remember the pleasant moments, few though they were."

"How magnanimous of you," said Llun in a sarcastic drawl.

"You know, I prefer you like this. You took too well to the character reformation. I didn't like you as a dog-man. In fact, in my deep heart, I hoped Voran would be able to turn you back to yourself."

"Of course," said Llun, walking up and sitting by Aspidían. "You had it all planned out."

"Well, perhaps not." Aspidían laughed and blushed slightly. "But it did work out very well. It's been too long since we had a traitor. I've been itching to try out the latest punishments. Our Great Father indulges me in my art. In him I always have an appreciative audience. Or at least I did." The last sentence was full venom, throwing Llun off kilter. "I don't suppose you knew that even I have not so much as dreamed of the Raven in the last three years."

That did surprise Llun. He thought it was a good move for the Raven to stop showing himself to the masses, but he was sure that the puppet master still pulled Aspidían's strings. If he didn't...

"But I am going to force the issue," continued Aspidían. "Not only has Voran brought us nothing in the bargain with those slavers, but the flask itself—*your* flask, I might add—is useless. It does nothing. It's just a flask. Oh, a very fine one, no doubt, my sensitive artist friend. But as for the rumors... No, it contains no Living Water at all."

Llun remained silent. Voran had mentioned his suspicion that the flask couldn't function in the Raven's rotting atmosphere of Vasyllia. To hear that suspicion confirmed was balm to his ears.

"I'm beginning to think we have all been the butt of a terrible, cosmic joke." Aspidían smiled mirthlessly. "I think it's time, dear Llun, to take Vasyllia back for the Vasylli. Please tell me you will come of your own volition."

Llun understood. The time for his execution had come.

"Yes. I've never had much honor in life. Perhaps an honorable death will do."

Aspidían sneered. "Wouldn't count on it, my dear one."

They stopped before a tall, narrow door in an otherwise unremarkable wall, a heavy iron ring fixed into the door's center. Aspidían raised the ring and struck the door three times. It opened on its own. Beyond was a staircase leading up. But that was impossible. Judging by what Llun knew of the former palace of Vasyllia repurposed into a headquarters of the Consistory, there was nothing higher than this level, not that the eye could see from the outside.

At the top of the staircase was another door, carved from top to bottom in a bas-relief of a willow tree with a flock of ravens on its drooping boughs. A sense of heavy malice emanated from the carving, or from whatever lay behind it, Llun couldn't tell. It was so overpowering that Llun's stomach lurched.

"Yes, that door," said Aspidían, his green-tinged face a perfect reflection of how Llun felt. "Silly trickery. Come in."

Beyond the door was a dusty attic-room. There was no furniture, no decorative hangings, nothing. A single, high window and three bare walls. On the fourth wall was a circular, dark smudge. Blood, probably. But it was very old. Aspidían put his hand on the smudge and winced from sudden pain. He pulled his hand back, and it came away bloody. The wall dissipated into dust before him.

"I didn't think..." Aspidían looked genuinely afraid, now. It seemed he hadn't expected even this little of the Raven's presence to remain.

"Last chance, Aspidían," said Llun with a half-smile.

Aspidían turned back, annoyed, but when he saw Llun's expression, his face broke into a warm smile.

"I've missed you, Llun the smith. I haven't had a worthy antagonist in such a long time." He turned and entered into the dark chamber beyond.

It was a tower chamber, round and tall. It stank horribly of excrement and sweat. In the exact center stood a high-backed chair. There were iron rings and chains to restrain a person by the neck, the hands, and the feet. Llun thought he understood.

"You...summon him to take a body?"

"No one summons the Great Father," Aspidían recited as from a manual. "But yes, that's what it is. He's always hungry, so we choose disposable ones. Don't worry. He'll eat most of you, but still leave enough for me to try out my latest work of art. Come, Llun. Sit down."

Llun froze in place. To die by being possessed, then eaten, by the Raven... He hadn't even thought that possible. He inched back toward the door.

Aspidían sighed in bored weariness. "So much for honor, eh?" He flicked a quick gesture with his hand, and two guards with drawn swords walked out of the shadows. They pushed Llun with their sword points toward the chair. Llun, surprised by their sudden appearance, hesitated. Then Aspidían grabbed him by the hair and pulled him toward the chair.

"Enough already, you idiot. What, did you think I'd forgiven you for betraying me?"

They chained him into the chair. It happened so fast, he didn't even have time to be afraid. Until Aspidían started to chant something in a language that Llun had never heard. It raised the hairs on the back of his neck. He gritted his teeth and closed his eyes, waiting for the inevitable.

Nothing happened. Llun sat there until this jaw started to ache with the clenching. He refused to open his eyes.

Aspidían started to laugh.

"I knew it! I knew it!" His laugh turned manic, rising in volume and intensity until Llun was sure he had finally cracked. "Oh, Llun! Finally! How long have I waited for this day!"

He unchained Llun with his own hands. "Well, consider yourself pardoned by the Great Father himself, who couldn't be bothered to come attend to his one true and faithful servant."

Llun tried to stand, but his legs wouldn't hold him. Aspidían, still laughing, held him up.

"Don't you understand, you overgrown child? The Raven is finally gone. He's done with Vasyllia. Now, now is the time to build. You are no longer worthy of building it with me. But you will see it. Oh, you will see it. And that will give me great pleasure, to see all your silly dreams of a restored Vasyllian Monarchia burn again and again."

A commotion at the bottom of the staircase distracted Llun from Aspidían's ravings. A guard ran into the room, his face red with the exertion of running.

"Lord Aspidían," he said. "Sir ... I don't know how best to tell you this ..."

"Spit it out before I pull it out with your tongue," said Aspidían, his eyes slitted.

"Sabíana ... She's alive. She's ... come back to life."

CHAPTER 37
RAVEN'S BANE

A morning several days after the rescue of the Vasyllia children, Khaidu awoke to an exposed, naked world. All the trees had shed their leaves overnight. Khaidu shuddered at the sight of green leaves carpeting the forest floor. It was unnatural, even to someone who didn't usually see a many-colored autumn. The added warmth of the morning—a clear harbinger of summer—only made it more disturbing. As if that were not enough, the clouds obscured even the hint of a sunrise. There was no sky to speak of at all—only a slate-grey wall of churning fog. It came from Vasyllia.

None of the children spoke that morning, upset by the sight of the fog and the dead trees. Only Aglaia seemed strangely encouraged by it.

"I had been wondering when there would be some sign of life from the black hole," she said as she had breakfast in her human form. "Vasyllia has been playing dumb for too long; I was beginning to think the Raven really had gone somewhere else."

Khaidu chuckled. Even if she often didn't understand what Aglaia was talking about, she appreciated the comfort of her never-ending chatter.

"Khaidu, are you sure we're doing the right thing?"

Khaidu was surprised to hear the doubt in Aglaia's voice. But she was sure. These children needed protection. What better way to protect them than take them to Raven's Bane?

"It's just…I haven't been there in a very long time. I'm not entirely sure about the road."

Now you tell me. "Well, you'd better be sure," said Khaidu. "Or the death of all these children will be on your head."

Aglaia's brows knit together. "Maybe the hag was right. I prefer you with a little less salt on your tongue."

Khaidu laughed.

※

For the first time since hearing about it, Khaidu finally saw the war zone.

It was on the next morning. The bare trees hid nothing—as Aglaia so helpfully mentioned at least five times since they awoke—and they saw their first battlefield from a distance. Even before they saw it, the hordes of buzzards fighting ravens in mid-air made it clear enough that they were nearing a killing field.

The worst was that none of the slain had been given the spurious honor of being piled up. They were just left where they were slaughtered. By now, many of them were little more than charred bones under random bits of tattered clothing and rusting mail. The stunted remnants of a burnt town lay on the other side of the battlefield.

They saw the same horror on the next day, and the next. The farther they went, the more the tang of burning wood filled their nostrils at every gust of wind. On very early mornings, Khaidu thought she could hear the sound of steel on steel, but it was so faint that it could have been her imagination. Finally, there could be no mistaking it. The ground thudded ahead of them. They were not one day's march from an army moving toward Vasyllia at running speed.

They waited all that day, not daring to move any further. Aglaia spent the entire day standing on a tall rock, smelling the air. That evening, she looked pleased with herself.

"You found the way?" asked Khaidu.

Aglaia smiled and gave a non-committal shrug.

The tension in the air had begun to lessen, and the fog occasionally let in a glimpse of sun. It was enough for many of the children to begin laughing again.

A few days later, Aglaia led them off the road into a gorge with no river running through it. A natural staircase appeared beneath their feet, almost by magic, and they descended single file into the gorge through a fissure in the rock wall. The river bed was strewn with boulders, making it hard to find a clear road. Everyone was looking down at their feet, trying not to fall. Khaidu alone felt sure of her mount, as Aglaia never so much as tripped. She looked around at the children as some of them decided that now would be a good time to practice their mountain goat impressions. All of them ended with yelps of pain. But no more crying, thank the Heights.

Khaidu was intent on one of the larger Gumir boys, who thought to make a good impression with his leap. He fell spectacularly instead. She laughed so hard, that she didn't see the transition. The girls on her left did, and they were so shocked that they started blabbering in Gumir to their new Vasylli mates (who only giggled in incomprehension). It was the trees. They had all turned green again.

Two days of travel in this impossibly green land, and they stood at the foot of a blue-green range of mountains.

"Well, that I never thought possible," said Aglaia staring upward.

The monastery. It was impossible—suspended, almost in mid-air, hanging on the side of an otherwise sheer mountain wall ahead of them. Not only was it sheer, but it was completely covered in fir trees. There was not a road, a stair, anything in sight.

"How d-d-did they build it?" Khaidu asked in shock. Around her, all two hundred of the children had exactly the same expression, their jaws hanging open as far as they could without breaking.

"Stone by stone?" Aglaia suggested, with mock seriousness. Khaidu slapped her on the head, laughing.

"Seriously, w-wolf-woman!" Khaidu tried on her most fearsome voice. "How do we get up?"

"Fly, I suppose?"

Khaidu rolled her eyes.

"Khaidu!" It was Yesukai, running from the back lines of children, where she had been guarding their rear. "Warriors! All around us!"

Yesukai and a few of the older children managed to wrangle the rest within minutes. All of the kids stopped being children as soon as they heard of the danger. It was in that moment of transformation from carefree to experienced that Khaidu saw how completely their suffering had changed them. It made her angry, and she felt the accompanying rage in the rippling of Aglaia's haunches.

How dare they come now, now, when I am so close to finding my Sabiana? she thought. She grasped both her hunting knives in her hands.

They saw nothing at first. They had been so intent on the road ahead, they had not noticed the fog creeping up on the ground behind them. Now, it was like milk soup, and only when the wind stirred it did it so much as move. Khaidu felt the wall of mountain behind them, trapping them, and wondered how long they would last before they were all killed.

Someone moved through the fog, and it parted ahead of them, like a curtain being lifted by a hand. Three riders. On bears.

"Hello, grandmother," said the first—a young man with sad eyes, grey like a gyrfalcon's wing. He had a circlet of red gold on his pale wave-hair. It looked like actual fire. Aglaia quivered, and Khaidu saw her thoughts for a moment—the shores of a great sea, two longboats bobbing on anchor. A baby in her arms, sleeping.

Tens of monks appeared out of nowhere to show them ways that Khaidu would never have found on her own. The entrance to the walled monastery was an ornate wooden gate crowned by a bas-relief of a singing Sirin, carved from cherry wood. The Sirin's eyes were so realistic that they seemed to follow Khaidu as she moved. The monkish welcomers in their grey robes washed the feet of every single one of the children, who all thought it was great fun.

After the washing of the feet, a veritable army of monks, hooded and robed, began to cluck and fuss like mother hens about the children. Khaidu stood with mouth agape, watching a miracle happen. If she had thought that her children were uncountably many, that was nothing compared to the number of monks. Every cranny, every alleyway, every doorway sprouted a new pair of hooded figures as soon as she passed. Gently, but firmly, the children were organized into groups of ten, with two monks watching over each group. They were given loaves of bread and cheese, and several more monks walked from group to group with a pitcher of milk and a cup. As each group finished drinking, they were herded down the narrow corridors, up the twisting staircases, into the cavernous hallways. Khaidu watched it all with a twinge of regret. She was happy the children were accounted for. But she herself had done so little. The thought reminded her of Sabíana's possible presence here, and something inside her heart flared.

Within a half-hour, all the groups of children were gone. The natural silence of the place reasserted itself. As the last child faded like a morning mist, Khaidu and Aglaia followed their own monkish guide into a low-roofed building near the gate. A single long table dominated the space. Simple long benches stood on either side. The light streamed in lazily through stained glass of a dark blue color, giving the room an ethereal feeling. Khaidu had only experienced such light on rare winter mornings an hour before sunrise, when the clear sky looked like a sheet of metal heating

653

up slowly. The memory warmed her even more than the reception of the monks.

The feast-hall was filled with the warriors of Antomír, the young man who called himself Dar of Vasyllia. Khaidu had never seen such men—they were like action personified. Every look, every movement was economical, as though they were saving their energy for battle. Another thing about them entranced her—they seemed to have no definable age. Those who looked younger were not quite young, while those who looked old had young eyes. She found herself caught staring more than once at several of them. Whenever they saw her staring, they smiled, but there was much of the bear in that smile. No warmth at all.

It was simple food, but nourishing. There were cakes of grain, dried fish, and bread-based ale that was as filling as a loaf of good rye. They ate in silence at first.

Aglaia (in her human form) broke the silence.

"So, I see you've crowned a new Dar while his father still lives. Is it because he's willing to listen to your heresies about Adonais?"

The air seemed to chill in the room. Antomír looked particularly uncomfortable.

The one called Veles answered, "The Sirin placed Ghavan Isle under their protection. None of us—not Elmira, not her husband, not I—could find any way of reaching them. I believe Mirnían himself needs to find a way out. But while he is gone, what must we do? And time is not on our side."

"You seem to have forgotten that Sabíana is still in Vasyllia. Has she not the stronger claim?"

"There are rumors that Sabíana is no longer living," said Severuk.

"Have you subscribed to their heresy, grandson?" Aglaia's voice was sharp, too loud.

"No, grandmother," said Antomír. "I hope to convert my brothers to the truth by the time we return to Vasyllia."

Severuk laughed.

"We are all friends here, and with a common purpose, I believe," continued Antomír. "There's been enough fighting amongst brothers already."

"What is it they say?" persisted Aglaia. "Keep your enemies close, but new friends even closer?"

"My Lady," said Veles. "We all have questions. Doubts. You've heard of the abbot of Raven's Bane. He will answer all questions."

Soon after, a dour-faced monk who seemed incapable of looking up from the ground called them to the abbot's quarter. Aglaia, Antomír and his living monolith-friend Veles joined Khaidu to drink tea with Abbot Makarían.

The path they took was nothing more than a thin bit of rock over a chasm, joining the front part of the monastery to the main complex—a large building like a beehive carved out of the mountainside. Veles, after conferring with Aglaia quietly, put Khaidu on his back. He did not seem to even notice her weight.

They climbed two sets of stairs, nearly vertical, to a chamber set off the main building by a rope bridge. As they crossed it, the sun came out of the clouds, and Khaidu's head spun from the view. They hung over a waterfall, and the mist-filtered sunlight exploded into hundreds of small rainbows through which they climbed. Drenched in mist, laughing from the gorgeous absurdity of such a place, they entered the abbot's rooms.

They were in pitch dark, at first. Gradually, the dim light of red-glass oil lamps colored the darkness. There were no windows.

They walked through a low archway of stone into a larger room. Three walls were covered from floor to ceiling in paneled paintings of men and women in stylized poses of worship. All of them faced the same direction—the fourth, back wall of the room, which was dotted with more than twenty oil lamps of different sizes. All of them illumined, through different colors of glass, a wall-sized fresco. Three cherry trees, aflame, growing on the top of a cliff that jutted out of sea water.

Khaidu stopped, dumbstruck. It was a variation of the Gumir symbol of the Unknown Father. If she could have fallen on her face at that moment, she would have. But being strapped to Veles's back made that slightly difficult.

"Welcome, welcome," said the abbot, rising from a cushion on the floor.

Khaidu had never seen such an old man in her life. The Steppe did not allow for long lives, and most Gumir elders took the final journey into the Steppe-heart on their own before their sixtieth year (it was the proper way to die, after all). But this abbot looked like he could be older than a hundred years, for all Khaidu knew.

He was white-skinned like all Vasylli, his hair like an avalanche falling down his shoulders and down all the way to his hips. His beard, almost as wide as it was long, was also white, though some yellow still clung to his chin and the edges of his mouth. He was bent over double, with a hump like a camel's sticking out under his left shoulder blade. His eyes were a steady river of laughter.

Khaidu liked him immediately.

Everyone around her was bursting with questions (she most of all), but the abbot's presence was like cold water pouring over her head after a day in the sun. It drained her of the immediate necessity of doing anything, except drinking tea. Veles placed her down on a cushion of her own, while the rest of them shared the remaining ones.

"This is real Karila tea," he said as he poured. "Not the usual Vasylli stock that people subsist on these days. Not much left of real Karila tea in the world."

It was very good, if a little too sweet. Khaidu had heard of the pale-faces' predilection for sweet teas, and for a second, she longed for the salty, buttery taste of Etchigu's tea. Dear Etchigu. Where in the world was he? She hoped they were all prospering. Even Batuk.

"No, we were not entirely surprised at your coming." It seemed they had been talking while Khaidu ruminated on teas and family. "If we had not expected you, there would have been...well, a somewhat different reception, shall we say?" He chuckled, though the longswords hanging on the wall behind him gave the chuckle an edge. "You did quite well, Aglaia, in bringing the children here. Poor things. They have suffered much."

"It was not *my* idea." Aglaia's tone had stiffened to match with her high, embroidered collar. Khaidu didn't know whether or not to take this well-dressed, official version of the wolf-woman seriously. Personally, she much preferred the wolf. "This young Gumir girl, our wolfling Khaidu. She has been moving mountains."

"So I have heard." The abbot's eyes creaked, adding playfulness to the already present joy. "A little broken thing, or so I had heard. The reality is... more complicated, is it not?"

Khaidu felt the heavy stare of Antomír on the side of her face—the mostly unscarred side, thank the Queen Who Walks the Skies—and she wanted to disappear. Instead, she turned to look at the young man. He did not look away. Nor did she. A strange thing, like milk curdling into cheese, happened inside her. It was surprisingly pleasant.

Veles cleared his throat expressively. Antomír melted into a quick smile and looked back at the abbot. Khaidu realized the abbot was still looking at her. She blushed.

"I have bad news for you, Steppe-wolf," he said, his quick smile absent. "She whom you seek is not here."

Khaidu sighed, and in the release of the tension she had not realized was there, stars began to dance before her eyes. She would not be whole without Sabíana.

"Sabíana did visit us here," continued the abbot, "but she did not stay. I would like to tell you that I know where she is now. But I cannot say. I will tell you something that may bring you pain, little Gumira, but it is the truth. The truth is often painful." Though he said it to Khaidu, his eyes included both Antomír and Aglaia

"The former Darina, the Lady Sabíana, died. Overwhelmed with her long wait and her long pain, she accepted a final gift from Feína, the Sirin of fire. She left her body behind but clothed her spirit in the form of an eagle, to find a place of rest at the end of the world.

"When Sabíana came here, she was a pitiful thing. Her soul was in tatters from two bond-breaks, one with her Sirin, and one with you, Khaidu. To be honest, I was surprised that her soul was still intact. She asked me if I would help her to find a place of rest. I could not, for I am still of the living, and know not the way to that place. I told her she had but two ways before her—the same choice that Feína gave her. Either to return to Vasyllia and inhabit her body again, to await justice over Vasyllia, or to seek the place of rest on her own. I warned her that the second choice was the more dangerous, for if she lost her way again, she would risk an eternity of wandering the nether regions, an echo of a living soul seeking a place to inhabit. That way lies the abomination of the formless ones of the Raven."

Khaidu caught her breath, in spite of herself. All the possible fates for Sabíana were painful, but this last one was unbearable.

"There is another aspect to her death that we must consider. She left the throne of Vasyllia without an heir of Cassían. By an ancient, forgotten promise of the Heights, the mere presence of an heir of Cassían had continued to give some measure of protection to Vasyllia and her faithful children, even after the loss of the Covenant Tree. With her gone, the Raven has nothing to bar him from his intentions for Vasyllia.

"I admit that our work would be much easier if we knew where she was, and whether she was willing to resume her place as protector of Vasyllia."

Khaidu laughed, and everyone stared at her. She had remembered the gift of the hag. She cursed herself silently for a dim-witted donkey of a fool.

"B-b-but...I c-c-can...f-f-ind her!"

"How?" asked Antomír, his eyes clouded with an inner pain that Khaidu did not understand.

Aglaia slapped herself on the forehead and laughed, lapsing again into her wolf-manners. "Of course! The apple and dish!" She blushed, then awkwardly tried to reassert her queenly bearing.

"You have *that*?" asked Veles, and the walls shuddered a little from his raspy bass. For a moment, his shadow, thrown back against the wall from the dancing hearth-fire, seemed to have wings. So, the mountain-man was more than he seemed.

"The hag gave it to us," explained Aglaia, "She owed me a...particular favor."

Antomír guffawed, his eyes wide. "The hag? Is this the same hag that enslaved Voran and cursed my father with leprosy?"

"Yes," said Aglaia, a little sheepishly. "Well, she was very repentant!"

Before anyone could answer, Aglaia stood up and walked to Khaidu's saddle bag, which had been placed with the other packs in a corner of the spacious room. Wrapped in oilskin paper, the bundle looked insubstantial, but as Aglaia unwrapped it, the room filled with a light like early morning. The apple was the sun, and the silver dish was the sun's aureole.

"You've always been full of surprises, dear Aglaia," said Abbot Makarían.

Aglaia placed the dish into Khaidu's waiting hands. It thrummed in her hands, like a plucked string on a knee-viol. It seemed eager to begin, almost child-like in its enthusiasm to reveal its secrets.

"An-n-tomír," Khaidu said, trying to stutter less, and naturally failing. "You place it. P-p-l-lease."

He bowed his head and stood up. Raising the apple, he admired it without any artifice, clearly astonished by its beauty. As he did, the circlet on his head sparkled in its light. For a moment, his golden hair looked white, and the sharp angles of his face looked lined with premature age. Khaidu now saw that the pale-faced boy had seen his own share of suffering.

Gingerly, Antomír placed the apple on the edge of the plate. It spun about itself and began a slow, deliberate circuit around the edge of the plate, coming closer to the center with every turn. It reached the exact center of the plate and continued to spin. Outward from it, like ripples from a pebble dropped in a still pool, darkness spread toward the edge of the plate. The apple fell down into the darkness...

...It was not darkness. It was a hole, a window between two places. A window in the middle of the air. On the other side, Khaidu saw a dark room, its walls overhung with heavy drapery. In the corner of the room, in the middle of piles of rubbish, stood a... something like a bed, but broken in the middle and barely standing on rickety legs. It had a pile of dirty rags on it. Except... no! Not rags. A body. There was a face there. A face somewhat familiar. Then a ray of sun revealed the face, and the eyes opened. Khaidu knew those eyes.

"Khaidu?" whispered Sabíana from the bed, in a voice Khaidu only barely recognized.

"I know that place," said Aglaia, though her voice sounded distant to Khaidu. "It's one of the turret rooms in the palace of Vasyllia. Sabíana is alive, and in Vasyllia!"

Khaidu's cheeks were wet. Leaning into the darkness with her whole body, hardly thinking about what she was doing, she reached for Sabíana and fell into the hole. She landed on a pile of stinking garbage. Above her, something hissed as a light as bright as the sun sparked in the middle of the room, then faded and disappeared. She was left in complete gloom.

CHAPTER 38
THE SEVEN SLEEPERS

"We have to go after her!" Antomír stood next to the window between places that had blinked out of existence. He had been ready to jump in after Khaidu, but it all happened so fast, that by the time he moved, the hole had vanished. "How could she? She's a cripple! How will she move around? It's...by the Heights...she's in *Vasyllia*."

No one seemed to appreciate the urgency of the matter. They would not even meet his eyes. Veles especially seemed anxious to avoid Antomír's gaze. Only Abbot Makarían seemed to understand the import of helping Khaidu, though he was so much like an old tree that not even a burning building would have forced him to hurry.

"Why is no one moving?!"

"Antomír," said Aglaia in her most grandmotherly tone. "Don't you think I would have done something already, if there was anything to be done? She saved my life!"

Makarían chuckled, a sound that was like ice water slapping across Antomír's face.

"My young Dar," he said. "Do not underestimate the quiet work of the Powers in the fates of man. I think there is no person better suited to help Sabíana in Vasyllia than the little Steppe-wolf."

Antomír felt foolish, chided by the calm tone and stolid presence of the old monk-warrior. He sat down and picked up his tea. Not to drink it, but only to have something to do with his too-big hands. The warmth of the perfectly round clay cup soothed him somewhat. He sipped, and nearly dissolved into the peaty, smoky taste of it. Ghavanite tea was water compared to this elixir.

"Well," said Makarían, speaking now to all. "We know now that Darina Sabíana is alive and once again in Vasyllia. I had indeed hoped that it would happen. Now we have proof. So that changes the tenor of your campaign, somewhat." This last sentence was intended for Antomír.

He could no longer claim to be Dar of Vasyllia. He was more upset about that than he thought. With shaking hands, he reached for the circlet on his head, ready to take it off.

"Just a moment," growled Veles. "Sabíana ruled in Mirnían's absence. But Mirnían's heir is come. Never has the Dar's sister taken precedence over his son."

"That's for the Council of the Reaches to decide, once we've taken back Vasyllia," said Aglaia, her growl matching Veles's.

"Already divvying up the spoils, are we?" Makarían's cheerful tone had an edge of anger to it. "We are far from taking Vasyllia. Have you forgotten about the wall?"

Antomír, feeling the weight of the moment, took off his circlet and lay it on the ground next to him. It flared for a moment, brighter than a hearth-fire, then faded into simple metal. A hollow seemed to have opened up in his chest, filling with regret. He swallowed hard, pushing against the compulsion to pick up the crown again.

"I will not wear it until we take Vasyllia. That is my solemn vow."

Aglaia beamed at him, and Veles bowed to him grudgingly. They all turned back to Makarían.

"What has been unknown for a long time," said Makarían, "is why the Raven built the wall. Thanks to the recent information brought by young Veles here—" Antomír couldn't help noticing how Veles smiled at that, being by far the oldest person in the room, "we now know the Raven's endgame. The wall was his way of buying time.

"We all believed that the Raven's objective was to take Vasyllia as a first step before finding the tree that wept Living Water. Voran thwarted him in that. His new objective, or indeed, perhaps it was his main objective all along, is what is *under* Vasyllia—the only gateway into the Garden in the Heart of the World, the place where the lifeblood of the Realms is born. He is the great Formless One, the one who seeks a form that will never die. A human body, with which he will seize for himself the deathlessness of the Powers. And so, he seeks the fruits from the trees of life. But that is not all. He has already reached the garden."

"Then we're too late?" Antomír couldn't believe his ears.

"No," said Veles. "Yadovír was the last human vessel he took. He has not taken another."

"Why?"

Veles looked at him intently, and Antomír withered under that stare.

"Surely not..."

"Yes," said Makarían. "If he were to possess the body of a Dar of the line of Cassían..."

"That old grudge?" said Antomír, shivering suddenly, though it wasn't in the least cold. "Because Cassían imprisoned him in Vasyllia?"

"Yes," continued Makarían, nodding. "This is conjecture, but it would explain why he has not consumed all the fruit. That he has been eating the fruits is, I think, not merely a conjecture. He needs their power to sustain the magic of the wall. But he also waits for the Dar to come to Vasyllia. When he ensnares you, Antomír, he will consume the final fruit and become deathless. But what is worse is what follows, should he possess a human body. It is my opinion that he will storm the Heights of Aer. I believe he will attempt to recreate the Realms, but in his own image. An eternal Dar of an eternal Vasyllia that would rule over a new world."

The enormity of that horror was so great that Antomír almost started to laugh, for lack of a better response. One question remained. How did they know that the Raven reached the garden? And how did they know that he hadn't eaten all the fruit? But Veles interrupted his thought.

"The Raven's wall around Vasyllia will not stand for long, not with the giants' intention to break it down. Before we consider what to do about the giants..." He turned to Makarían, who nodded.

"What I tell you now," said the abbot, "No one knows except a few warriors of this monastery. Voran the Healer entered Vasyllia several weeks ago, not entirely of his own volition."

Aglaia gasped, and her hands came up to her cheeks, which had turned bright red.

"He has not come out again. And now, the dark fog has come from Vasyllia. Whether that is a sign of Voran's success or failure, I do not know."

"What did Voran intend to do?" asked Antomír.

"To raise up a resistance against the Raven in Vasyllia. Voran is the last known Warrior of the Word, an order of warriors even more extreme in their training than we at Raven's Bane. They are the oldest enemies of the Raven. The only ones who have ever been able to give him any sort of challenge. Even we have not been able to reach their level of prowess. But he was alone. To tell the truth, I am very worried for Voran. It may be that he is close to capture by the Raven."

"More and more reasons to go to Vasyllia immediately. But what about the giants?"

Makarían, for the first time, seemed to hesitate before answering.

"We don't know. The giants are no friends to us. Theirs is a noxious kind of earth power. It consumes constantly, needing to be filled with blood sacrifice. But...this is my own thought, mind. Some in Raven's Bane don't agree with me..."

"Go on, Father Makarían," said Veles, visibly eager for the first time this evening.

"I believe they want to stop the Raven as much as we do. If he consumes the fruit of life, the earth will die, as will the giants. But I do not think we can trust them. They have allied themselves with a resurgent Nebesti army. And the Nebesti want nothing more than to raze Vasyllia to the ground."

"Why?" Antomír, more than ever, felt weak, hamstrung by his father's decision to remain hidden in Ghavan for so long, ignorant of everything happening in the outer lands.

"They blame Vasyllia for the Gumiren invasion and for the Internecine War," said Makarían.

"I do not think we need to worry about the Nebesti," said Veles. "Dar Antomír and our bear riders have revealed them to be inferior fighters."

"You embarrassed them, you mean," said Makarían. "Never underestimate an enemy that has been embarrassed. But...All that may be immaterial, my friends. There may be a course of action we have not yet considered."

Veles stood up from his half-crouch on the floor and walked to the door. Opening it, he stepped aside to let in Elmira, dressed in gold-colored pantaloons and a purple tunic—a walking fresco of the elder days.

Elmira bowed to everyone but did not take the offered seat by the hearth-fire. Instead, she did something with her hands—it reminded Antomír of a dancer's gesture—and in her right hand, a golden fruit lay. It made the hag's apple look like a dull brown rock. This fruit was an ever-changing kaleidoscope of gold and red and silver, moving in and out of itself, yet remaining completely still. In its light, everyone looked youthful and quietly joyful.

"This is one of the fruits of life, taken from the Garden in the Heart of the World," said Elmira. "We bartered for it with the Raven. With Voran's life."

Aglaia bared her teeth, as though she had forgotten that she was still in her human form. "You did *what*? That's what you meant by Voran's 'not entirely voluntary' entry into Vasyllia?"

"Aglaia," said Elmira. "We *helped* Voran."

Aglaia was shocked into silence.

"For years he had attempted to enter Vasyllia. But the Raven's magic was directed with singular focus against Voran. Every time he approached, new traps were set off. The Raven is a trickster, a manipulator of doorways in and out of realms. He had made a habit of catching Voran unawares and hurling him throughout the Realms. Anywhere, so long as he did not breach the wall.

"This is a very long game we have played. We engaged in the slave trade with Vasyllia for years. They give us the Sons of the Swan, the only true Vasylli who are left. We give the Raven's people magical artifacts, some of them real, some only trinkets that shine. When we suspected that the Raven had reached the garden, we needed to act fast. We thought Voran's flask would have been enough. But no. The Raven was willing to give a single fruit, but his price was both Voran and the flask."

"Why did you not *tell* Voran about your plan? Was the slaver fiction so necessary?" The air around Aglaia began to shimmer and spark. Makarían, his eyes angry for the first time that evening, actually slapped Aglaia on the side of her head.

"You will contain yourself." The calmness of his voice belied the power behind them. "This is not a place for your passions to run amok. Do you not yet understand who Elmira is? If she found it necessary to give Voran to the Raven, then it is not only for the good of Vasyllia, but it is also for the good of Voran."

"The Raven will grind him into powder." Aglaia's bluster was undercut by the whimper behind her words. Antomír felt the raw emotion like a knife across the chest. "He has already suffered so much."

"Voran is strong," said Elmira. "But if he knew about us, and if the Raven found out about us... He would never have given us the fruit, and we would never have left Vasyllia alive. We are not without power, but his is infinitely greater than ours, especially behind the wall."

A new voice sounded in the room, a brazen voice, like a trumpet in the early morning. "And who had more right to give Voran over, if not I?" The man who entered the room had Veles's bronze skin. He wore the fur of a white bear. Like Veles, he wore a long beard and hair that he had tucked into the inside of his bear-fur. "I am the guardian of the North, Vasyllia's protector. For Vasyllia's sake, my wife, Severuk, Veles, and I threw Voran into the fire. He will either be consumed or come out as strong as tempered steel."

The stranger approached Elmira and embraced her. She melted into his embrace like a girl in love. So, this was her husband. The fourth of the guardians of the four ends of the earth.

Aglaia subsided. Perhaps she recognized the truth of the stranger's words. Or perhaps she was in too much pain to do anything more.

"I greet you, sire," said Antomír, standing and bowing to Elmira's husband. "It is my honor to meet you. But I don't see how this fruit changes anything. We have a piece of the Garden here. Yes, it's a great gift, and we must treasure it, but..."

"No, Antomír," said Elmira's husband, his voice heavy. "We are suggesting a different path. What if Voran has already failed? What if the black fog is a sign that the Raven has become the Deathless One? If that is so, then we waste our armies in war against him and his changers in Vasyllia."

"But this place," Elmira continued, "is uniquely situated between the Realms. Easy to defend, much like Vasyllia itself in the grand scheme of things. Why not make this the new Vasyllia? Plant a new garden of life. Weather the initial storm and fight the Raven with everything that we and the Powers can muster. The fruit is life-giving. We could fight him and not lose a single man..."

"You are talking not about a great war, but an eternal war," said Antomír. His face felt cold, drained of blood. "That is a horrifying proposition."

Under Antomír's words was the silent reality they all refused to speak aloud. If the Raven had succeeded in becoming the Deathless, would they be able to survive, even in such a fortress as this?

"Come, young Dar," said Makarían. "There is one more thing you must see before you can make your choice. We don't simply train warriors here."

The monastery was like a series of swallows' nests enmeshed inside each other. Terraces led to platforms that led to staircases that led back into mountain caverns that doubled back on themselves and out into turrets sticking out of the mountain like the prows of a longboat. In between the buildings, which were all made of the same earth-colored bricks, small gardens glistened like gems.

The more Antomír looked at the small details, not the wider picture, the more he understood how improbable this place's existence was. It simply should not be able to sustain itself.

"It does *not* sustain itself," explained Makarían, leading Antomír along a twisting staircase that seemed to lead directly to the Heights. "It truly is an impossible place. If we were to lessen our efforts for even a moment, if any of our warrior-monks, no matter how insignificant in the rankings, were to give in to sloth, we would simply fall off the mountain, like an old wasps' nest washed away by the summer rains. But if we labor, the Heights always provide."

Antomír didn't fail to notice that Makarían also avoided mentioning Adonais. It would have bothered him more if Makarían did not exude goodness from his every pore.

He moved quickly for such an old man. When they reached the top of the staircase, Antomír saw a simple platform at one of the highest points of the monastery, with a short viewing terrace to prevent anyone from falling while entranced with the view of the mountains all around.

Makarían led Antomír to a cave in the mountain wall. "In there…" said Makarían, finally showing some of his age in his slightly labored breathing, "is one of the mysteries of this place between the Realms. I show it to you with the confidence that you will not abuse what you see, though I couldn't stop you if you wished it. You are a future Dar, after all."

Antomír's heart skipped a beat at Makarían's endorsement.

They entered into complete darkness. It didn't dissipate, not even after Antomír's eyes did their best to acclimate. There was no light at all.

"Take my hand. I know the way."

Antomír did. Impossibly, he soon began to sense the way they were taking. It snaked deep into the mountain. The air grew warmer, though an occasional cool breeze blew into their faces (where was a breeze coming from inside a mountain?), smelling of tuberose and lavender. It even tasted sweet: a light touch on the tongue, barely there. Then the sounds began—distant dripping of water, something like wind chimes, both surrounded by the muffled hiss that fire makes in an enclosed space.

Antomír was so entranced by the smells and sounds that he hardly noticed that he could see once again, and that he was no longer holding Makarían's hand. The light was like faintly-glowing golden mist. The narrow passage they followed widened into a cavern where stalactites hung from the ceiling like clusters of grapes. Crystals were embedded in the rock wall, and they seemed to give off their own light, but then Antomír realized his eyes were confusing him. They were not crystals. The walls were on fire.

In the midst of the golden flames that danced on the walls were seven sources of golden light, roughly at eye-level, equally spaced in the circular cavern. At first, Antomír thought they were lanterns hanging from the rock wall, though the light they gave was so driving that they seemed like small suns. When he approached one of them, he saw that the light was pouring through holes in the wall. So, the sources of light must be *inside*.

"Go ahead, look inside," said Makarían. "The light is strong, but soft as well. It will not blind you."

Antomír peeked into one of the windows with a strange sense of expectation. At first, he saw nothing. Then he looked down and saw a small cell, large enough for a man to sit in, but not to lie down. There was a man kneeling there, on the floor. He was on fire with the same golden fire that lit the walls and poured through the window like water, though flowing upward, instead of down. The flames were warm, not burning, and the man was not consumed by the tongues. He simply sat on his knees, his head resting on his chest, his hands in his lap, his eyes closed.

"Is he dead?" asked Antomír.

"Only to a lazy eye." Makarían chuckled, as though he had said something pithy. "No, no, he's very much alive. Very hard at work, too, though I don't doubt he would call me crude for saying it so." Makarían's voice was thick with wistful remembrance.

"He was your friend?"

"*Is* my friend, Antomír. He...all seven of them...they are all great friends of mine. Perhaps, one day, we will speak again over tea, as we did before. But now, they are engaged in the most violent warfare."

"Warfare?" Antomír smiled, not knowing whether or not Makarían was jesting.

"Indeed. They are gathering Living Water."

Then Antomír realized why he had been hearing dripping in the passageway. All the stalactites were dripping water into a pool in the center of the cavern. The smell of tuberose and lavender—it came from the pool. Living Water.

"But how? How can one gather it?"

"Have you ever woken up from a dream that seemed more real than waking?" Antomír nodded. "In a sense, it *is* more real. The space between dreaming and waking—it is another Realm of the world. A very mysterious, dangerous place. It does not have a name in the Vasylli tongue.

"Humans do not walk there willingly, for it is the domain of very dangerous Powers that have little love for men. The menace you sometimes feel right before you wake up? It is real enough. If you were to remain too long in such half-dreams, you would not return. These seven sleepers...they willingly walk the world between dreaming and waking."

"I think I understand," said Antomír. "It is a kind of ... ordeal, is it not?"

"Yes, in a way. Every human being fights the eternal war between his dark self and his light self. But that warfare is in the heart, and it is subtle and slow. Many are the years needed for a man to rise to greatness in that arena. But there are those who fight the same warfare, but in the realm of the nether-space between dreaming and waking. Sabíana was one of them, perhaps still is. An uncommonly strong warrior of that region. There, the enemies of the human race fight men openly. There, defeat can lead to things worse than physical death, and victories are so great that they call down Living Water like rain from heaven."

"Call it down? They can constrain the will of Adonais in this?"

Makarían laughed. "Oh, how well you put it, though I doubt you understand what you say! Yes, indeed. Though you see them in body, here in these rooms, their inner man walks the nether places and battles as surely as a warrior in a field of battle."

Makarían raised his thick-jointed fingers up at the stalactites. There were seven of them. Something about them did not look quite real. Like a shimmer, or a refraction of light. Antomír squinted to try to see better. It was...*Heights!* The stalactites were made of fire, but it was also like water.

"They're not stalactites at all!" exclaimed Antomír, his voice bouncing thorough the cavern. The stalactites were more like half-solid columns of flame flickering down to a point, from which opal-brilliant drops fell infrequently into the common pool. Antomír looked into the pool and could see no bottom to it.

"Astonishing," said Antomír, almost to himself. "Tell me, if these sleepers fail at their war, does it affect the monastery?"

"The Living Water recedes, disappears completely sometimes. That is a sign that some, or all, are not faring well in their battles. If they fail completely, it can have catastrophic results not merely for the monastery, but for the Realms."

"*Do* any of them? Fail, I mean."

"Yes. I am one of them."

"You?"

Makarían sighed. "I was too proud. I fought against an adversary I had no hope of defeating."

Antomír had a sudden intuition. "You found the Raven in the nether-space, and you tried to defeat him there?"

Makarían nodded, then smiled grimly. "The other sleepers saved me. I was only moments away from becoming the new vessel to the Raven. He nearly infiltrated this place, this Raven's Bane."

"It can happen, then. I wondered. If that is so, Father Makarían, then we would be mad to try to plant a new garden for the Heart of the World here. It is too obvious a place."

Makarían said nothing.

"Come," said Antomír, no longer doubtful about his choice. "Let us leave these warriors to their battles."

CHAPTER 39
FED TO THE FIRE

Pushed forward by the hope of reclaiming the earth-power of the giants, Parfyon drove his men, lest anyone have time to even think of betraying him. The march was punishing—twenty-five miles a day over rough terrain. By the end of each evening, most of the men would be in that half-sleeping trance-state that often overcomes tired armies. Some slept while still marching, their legs moving automatically, their eyes propped open by will alone.

Parfyon never tired; he only grew hungrier. Alienne had not even looked at him for days. So, he dedicated all his energy to self-discipline, training, and driving his men even harder. Some, looking at his unflagging, even manic, intensity, began to gravitate toward him once again. But most shrank further away. He could only guess at their thoughts, and his guesses were not pleasant. He imagined many now saw him more as a kind of inhuman abomination than a knyaz worthy of their loyalty. And yet, they followed him.

One last band of Gumiren encountered them only a day's march from the wall. Parfyon's army trampled them underfoot. Half of his Nebesti did not even have to unsheathe their swords. His army was like a slow-moving wall of water that churned everything in its path. None of the Gumiren survived. The Nebesti did not stop to celebrate this latest of their victories. Parfyon would not hear of it. He wanted to reach the wall by midnight.

After all, the moon was full that night. Parfyon understood the importance of such things now, and he wanted to present the spectacle of

Alienne's sacrifice to the whole of the Nebesti army under the ghostly light of the late spring moon.

The front lines reached the limit of Nebesta by evening. The setting sun, screened through low-hanging clouds, painted the wall of Vasyllia a bloody red. Fitting, thought Parfyon grimly as they approached. He ordered Bragadun and those warriors who still remained loyal and close to him to pitch his pavilion and walked alone toward the wall.

Everyone else seemed to shrink from it, especially as the darkness of evening seemed to rise up from the ground along the wall, until it was a screen of black emptiness before them, a maw waiting to devour them. Parfyon snickered at their weakness, hurrying instead to find the best place to build the sacrificial pyre. It would have to be a high place, but also a place easily accessible to the ranks, so that files of four or five could walk past Alienne as she burned. If all of them could see the sacrifice at such a proximity, no one would dare oppose him any longer.

He found the place almost at once—a slight rise surrounded by thin and sparse spruces. A large crowd could assemble at the foot of the rise, and the trees would allow his men to pass through without the need to slow down excessively. Yes, it would do very well.

"Parfyon," said a woman's voice. At first, Parfyon didn't recognize Alienne in the dirt-streaked face that addressed him. She had changed over the last few days. "I want to speak to you."

She came closer, and the moon poured its enchanted light on her face. Parfyon had to restrain a sharp intake of breath at the changes he saw there. She was like a rose that had withered to brown after a hot day. This is what you have done, he reminded himself silently.

All the pain he had kept at bay, during all the days after she and the Nebesti had lost their faith in him, came flooding into him. Regret and sorrow buffeted him, such as he had not felt since seeing his father lying dead on a burning pyre, so many long years ago. And now, he was contemplating putting the only creature in the world he had ever loved on the same pyre of death? Was he insane?

"Alienne, you...what happened?"

"I have not slept since the bear-rider attack. I was so angry at you. Afraid for you. You thirst for so much of the giants' power. I fear that it will eat you alive. That you will no longer be yourself, but someone... some *thing* else."

"Alienne." His irritation with her again bubbled up from deep within. "Let's not start this argument again. It will not end well for me or for you."

"Forgive me, my love." Suddenly, she was on her knees at his feet, hugging him, shuddering with sobs. "It's all my fault. I have pushed and pushed you to greater and greater power over your enemies, over my enemies, over Nebesta's enemies. But I've started an avalanche, I see that now. I think I've lost you. And it's my own fault."

Parfyon thought he would be ripped apart from the inside. He hugged her, pulled her hard against him, and his own tears dripped on her head, but his remorse struggled to drown the dryness, the thirst inside him. He tried, though he had failed a thousand times, to stop thinking, to stop analyzing. Just to be in her presence. Just to drink in the fullness of her. She had come back to him. It was she who painted his world with colors, making the greys into brilliant golds and reds and purples. It was she whose glance made the woods ring with music. It was she who had made him everything that he was.

But she abandoned me. She doubted me at the first sign of trouble.

"I have been miserable," she said. "I see you eating yourself from within. All the while, I wanted to come to you, to hold you in my arms, to shush you to sleep as I did only a short time ago. But I was proud. So proud. Forgive me. I am nothing without you. Please, forgive me."

He pulled her trembling body to her feet. She had to lean against him, she was shaking so hard. She was so cold. He would make her warm again. His own Alienne. She had come back to him.

"Alienne—"

Oxhorns blasted all around Parfyon, so loud that he couldn't even hear his own voice. Out of the shadows, one, two...how many were there? *Fifteen* giants came to the bottom of the shallow hill where Parfyon stood with Alienne. In the middle, towering above the rest, stood Zmei. Every inch of his mountainous frame was covered in chainmail and scale-mail. His helmet was coal-black in the moonlight, but the rest of his armor shone blue like ice. His eyes, barely visible under a nose-guard shaped like a serpent's head, seemed to glow red underneath. The other giants were equally well armed.

"It is time, Parfyon," Zmei said quietly, though his voice still echoed through the woods. "Time for your Nebesti to know whose help they have enjoyed. Time for all to understand the price that must be paid for ultimate victory."

Called like moths to a flame, the Nebesti came without prompting, already teeming in the woods behind the giants. Like one man, the giants turned and faced the Nebesti. Their ice-silver armor caught red fire, and all of them, save for Zmei, began to burn. As they were consumed by the flames, their man-shapes melted and reformed into horrifying beasts— serpents on spindly, jointed legs, some with wings like billowing smoke, some with several intertwining heads. Zmei remained still human-shaped in the light of the moon. None of the red of the flames even reflected on him, as though he were a mirage or a phantom. Or an idol.

Parfyon saw that some of the Nebesti were on their knees, and some already worshiped, their faces in the dirt. Fear flared inside him, but he pushed it down. It was too late to go back.

"Alienne," he tried again, desperate to tell her that he...But what would he tell her? Did an executioner ever have anything of substance to say to the head on the chopping block? Whom was he fooling? He had committed himself to these monsters. Going back on his word would be suicide.

"Nebesti! I am Zmei, and these are my brothers. We are the hidden friends of Nebesta. We arranged for the rebuilding of your city; we ensured the success of this army in the field of battle. We now reveal our power openly to aid you in your invasion and the overthrow of the darkness that resides in Vasyllia, in the heart of the world as you know it. You will reign in the Mother of Cities, and we will be your allies."

No one cheered or so much as moved. The implicit "but" that hung at the end of the phrase was too loud, too overwhelming.

"But...you must now pay your share of the bargain. Your knyaz has chosen a fitting sacrifice to prove his willingness to work with us. It is a powerful sacrifice and will serve as a good omen for the start of the real war. He, as your chosen representative, will give the greatest treasure of his heart to the creative element of fire. The power of that gift, the abandonment of what he loves the most, will unlock power that you have not dreamed of. The wall of Vasyllia comes down today."

"What does he mean, Parfyon?" asked Alienne, her lips a thin, straight line.

He tried not to look at her. But he couldn't help it. As soon as he glanced at her, her face turned ashen. Her eyes darted away, as if his glance were the touch of fire.

"Oh, my love," she wheezed through a throat suddenly dry. "You... had I really? ..." She fell silent and swallowed hard. But instead of shrinking from him, she melted into a deeper embrace. He looked at her with amazement, but when she looked back at him, she was no longer Alienne. There was nothing there but despair wearing a human skin, and wearing it badly.

"Alienne, I..."

"Don't speak," she whispered. "It's not your fault. I created this monster. I *should* die for it."

"We are ready," Zmei bellowed, a little louder, "to raise you Nebesti to the summit of what humankind is capable. I say to you: some of you will walk as gods. It takes a leader of great strength to make such a sacrifice. You are not worthy of him! If you do not seek to become worthy, you will not defeat that which infects your former brothers in Vasyllia."

"Please, Alienne, listen to me—"

"No, Parfyon. You can say nothing to me now. It is fitting..."

"Behold!" Zmei's voice shook the earth with each rising inflection. "A knyaz who will sacrifice his own wife, his own love, on the fires of the earth. A knyaz who knows that to be a vessel of power, he has to first abandon everything he has. To be a vessel of greatness, he must first empty himself of all that is nonessential. Behold!"

Flames rose from a fissure that opened up near Alienne's feet. Pushing Parfyon away, she stood at the edge of the pit of fire. Already, her hair and clothing were catching fire. Parfyon reached for her, grabbed at her, but she pushed him away. His sleeve caught fire and he recoiled like a hunted animal, his body no longer listening to his mind.

"I go to my rest now," she said and began to weep, though no tears fell into that fire. Parfyon, despair ripping at him as though a rat were trying to eat its way through his rib cage, fell on his knees before her. He screamed. No one heard him in the booming of Zmei's voice.

"Behold! The sacrifice brings its fruits already!" A crack rose from beneath Alienne and snaked its way up the wall. "Nothing can stand in the way of the giants and their allies, Nebesti! Look! Victory lies just beyond that wall!" The crack branched out into five cracks, each seeking in a different direction. The middle one was mere feet from the top. "Vasyllia will not stand before us, my friends!"

"Oh, my love!" Alienne's voice rang out, louder even than Zmei. "Look! Look at it! It's beautiful!" Her eyes were wide, but her expression was calm. The flames licked around her but seemed reticent to consume her. "How wrong we were..." she said in a whisper meant for Parfyon alone. She smiled at him and turned away. She fell into the earth.

Something broke in Parfyon's mind. He cackled and beat the earth with his open palm. Foam dripped from his mouth.

The cracks in the wall exploded all at once, raining shards all over Parfyon's body. Some stuck in him, but he hardly felt pain, only a faint curiosity. As he looked at the blood seeping from the embedded shards of rock, the blood suddenly turned back in on itself. The shards melted into the skin, disappearing with a hiss through the pores. Parfyon's gorge rose, but he was so curious, he managed to hold himself in check. Then, something like a lightning strike went through his body, and agony seared him. He fell on the ground, his arms and legs splayed out. His entire body twitched uncontrollably, as though he were an insect pinned to a scrap of parchment while still alive. He couldn't even open his mouth to scream, only moan like an idiot child without its mother.

Then, it all released and lifted off him like a wave rising, instead of falling. He saw...

...tiny structures that made up individual leaves of grass; he smelled the unique sweat of every single one of his warriors, and he could name them all by their smell alone. He heard steps, hundreds of them—tentative, bare feet close to the wall on the Vasylli side, and thirty-seven booted marchers behind them. They were armed, judging by the way the ground shifted under their feet.

He pushed himself up and walked to the edge of the fire pit, the fire almost gone. He saw ashes and smolder, but no bones. The sacrificial fire had taken all of Alienne. He regretted it, but now the regret was a mental thing. A calculation of loss, an understanding of an error in calculation. He probed mentally for the place where his heart should be, but it was somehow far away, not immediately accessible.

"Lord Parfyon, are you alright?" asked Bragadun at his side. Parfyon found himself surrounded by his personal guard, and the perfect ranks of Nebesti stood arrayed behind them. They were armed, and their eyes were intent at what lay beyond the wall. How had they arranged themselves so quickly? Parfyon felt an inordinate amount of pride for these men. They were *his* men now, he knew without a doubt. No one would ever question a man who was willing to put his own wife in the fire.

"Lord, look!"

Beyond the wall, not half a bow shot away, a ragged line of refugees—feet bare, clothing ripped, brown blood in patches all over—walked toward the Nebesti ranks. They were unarmed.

Parfyon turned and raised his sword arm...His right arm...It was whole. Then he realized that both eyes saw as well. Exhilaration surged through him.

"Nebesti!" He called, and the ranks stilled to hear him, perfect in their silence. Not a single clink of scabbard on mail was heard. "We have no fight with these refugees. These are victims of the same filth we come to expunge. Let them pass through our ranks. There are thirty-seven warriors beyond them, hoping we will content ourselves will the slaughter of innocents. No! Let these pass. As for the thirty-seven Vasylli warriors beyond..." He stopped, waited, then laughed. The laugh spread through the ranks like fire.

Parfyon approached the breach in the wall and stood before it. No turning back.

As Parfyon allowed the refugees to pass through his ranks, he had a brief thought. *These poor creatures are fodder for the serpents.* But that thought faded, like a spark dropping into a river. He stepped into Vasyllia.

CHAPTER 40
THOSE WILLING TO BE HEALED

Voran had known pain in his twenty years living in the wild. But nothing prepared him for the tender mercies of the Consistory. Throughout all the horrors, Voran managed to keep his mind mostly separate from the pain of his body. But one thing he could not ignore. It cut his heart constantly. His torturers apparently felt nothing while torturing him. If they had shown pleasure at it, at least he could understand it with his reason, even if such perversions were beyond him. But they seemed to have neither pleasure nor distaste in their work. Truly, they were men for a new time in a new Vasyllia.

After every session of torture, Voran fell into uneasy half-sleep. In that sleep, he felt the vestiges of the Living Water knitting together his broken bones, weaving together his torn skin faster than humanly possible. When he woke up, he saw the healing process, and it almost unmade his mind. What was the point of the healing power that still flowed through him, that yearned to take up the suffering of others, if all he could do was provide a blank canvas for ever more elaborate tortures every day?

Almost a week after he had been brought back to Vasyllia, he was visited by the weasel-faced man who bought him. Aspidían. Behind him walked Llun, an ugly, not-quite-healed brand on his neck. At first Voran didn't understand what it was, then realized it was the same raven-obelisk that now defaced the center of Vasyllia. It made Voran sick to see it.

At first, Aspidían didn't speak to Voran, only examined him as a man might inspect his hunting hound. He shook his head, but beckoned to the guards, who brought in a table and three stools. They decorated it with a clay pot of mead and three rough cups.

Aspidían poured the mead with a look of distaste. "I don't like mead myself. Much prefer wine. But I haven't yet come to a place where I will agree to share wine with our Great Father's great enemy."

Aspidían's face was such a clash of competing desires and thoughts that Voran understood him not at all. This game would need caution, not a frontal attack.

"I thank you, Brother Aspidían," said Voran. "For even such a small mercy. Is it the final gift to a man condemned, or do I detect something more hopeful for myself?"

"That depends entirely on you," said Aspidían and looked Voran in the eye without blinking. It was a dead stare, so expressionless that Voran unwillingly lurched back. That prompted a smile from Aspidían, but it was a smile that lit the eyes with malice, not enjoyment.

An adder's smile, thought Voran.

"My brother Llun and I wanted to speak to you. The time of the Raven is at an end. He has left Vasyllia to its own devices. Now, you are no friend to the Consistory, but you are not without influence, even after the purges. I urge you to consider an alliance. Llun's life will be the seal of that bargain."

Interesting, thought Voran. *He's lying through his teeth.*

"What sort of a bond can we have, Brother Aspidían? You are a creature of the Raven. And even if the Raven has abandoned you to your own devices, surely you know that I have dedicated my life to a different ideal for Vasyllia. Not this sham rule of the people that you seem to be advocating."

"Sham it may be. But it need not be for long. Only for long enough for the poison to leech out of our common organism."

"And you and your dog-men will... what? *Nurture* the people until they are ready to take matters into their own hands."

"Something like that," said Llun under his breath. Voran was surprised by the complete lack of hope in his voice. Surely he hadn't given up so quickly?

"You are a healer," said Aspidían. "Use your power to heal the divisions that have ripped apart Vasyllia over these twenty years. Or rot in a prison for the rest of your life, while that healing power goes unused."

Something of Voran's twinge of fear must have shown in his face, because Aspidían's smile intensified.

"Abandon the dream of monarchia. Your Sabíana is dead. There is no heir of Cassían's line in Vasyllia. All that mystical idiocy is for a different age. Forget your Sirin, your high beings. Help me create a place where every person can choose to be his own man or woman. A place not defined by reaches, but by opportunities. Help me build a future for this world."

"A future without transcendence?" Voran warmed to the topic against his better judgment. "Without any interest in divinity? What would be the purpose of life, then? An endless, soul-sucking pursuit of personal happiness. A lure at the end of death's fishing rod? I will have none of it."

Llun looked up at Voran with surprise. Some of his old fire rekindled in the eyes. He gave Voran a curt nod.

Aspidían sighed heavily and downed his mead. He grimaced.

"Foul stuff," he said. "But no worse than this conversation. Why I listened to you, Llun, is beyond me."

He started to get up. Voran grabbed his hand from across the table.

"Sit down, Brother Aspidían." Aspidían looked with surprise at Voran's hand, as though it were a never-before-seen species of animal. With a bemused smile on his face, he sat.

Voran had seen something fleeting in Aspidían's manner as he had spoken. A brief flash of sincerity. And he had him.

Voran reached out with his thought toward Aspidían, and clutched at what he knew must be there... *There it was*. A sliver of the real Aspidían, untouched by the Raven. A genuine enjoyment of the chase, a game, a wager.

"I will offer you a challenge. I believe you are a man in need of an antagonist. A foil. Your best work is done in opposition, not in *building* something. Your own constructions—you want to burn them down as soon as they're up."

Aspidían's mouth opened ever so slightly in alarm. Voran's heart danced. He had hit on it. Not only that, but Voran had healed some old wound in his memory. He could see it clearly. For a few moments, this ruler of men could be influenced.

"You will allow me and Llun the freedom to live in what used to be the first reach. We will not leave it. We will simply live our lives there, away from the great events of your reconstruction. I will heal all who come to me. Even you, if you ever need it. That is all I will do. Heal. Llun will help me. You will leave us alone. Anyway, you will be too busy building your new world."

Aspidían exhaled gently, then shook his head with a rueful smile.

"You are a marvel, Vohin Voran, son of Otchigen. And yes, a worthy opponent."

He flicked his fingers. The guards reappeared.

"I will play your game for a short time. I know you intend more than you say. Know this. Every move will be scrutinized by my dog-men. You will have no freedom to do anything but sleep, eat, and defecate. And no one will come to you for healing."

He turned to one of the guards.

"Brand him."

***

After they had branded Voran with the same mark that Llun bore, Aspidían led the two of them through the courtyard of the old palace. Voran's heart bled with the wound on his neck as he remembered countless moments with his fellow warriors in the warrior seminary. So many years ago! All of them dead. All of them moldering under the earth.

But even as he remembered, he felt the brand already healing on his neck. *Perhaps there are some left in Vasyllia with the same spirit as the old warriors.*

"You do realize that he is using you as bait to flush out all the remnants of the Sons in Vasyllia," whispered Llun as they walked.

"Yes," said Voran. "It can't be helped. We must be very, very careful."

They approached the place where the fiery sapling once stood. In its place was an abomination—a black obelisk with raven's wings. The courtyard around the obelisk was filled with people, reminding him of the fateful storytelling of the Pilgrim, the event that had started the great tragedy of Vasyllia. It was almost too much for Voran to remember—the remembered images crowded on him like a crowd of those willing to be healed.

Aspidían walked up to the oversized raven's nest that cradled the obelisk and climbed on it. As he approached it, he spit on it. The crowd gasped, and whispers ran rampant.

"It is time, Vasyllia!" he roared. "No more need for Great Fathers, for gods, for Powers of imagined Realms. We take our city, our fate, into our own hands today. There is an army of Nebesti approaching the city. They think they can take our city from us. They cannot! We are Vasylli. We survived the Gumiren. We survived Adonais. We survived the Raven. And now, we protect our own!"

Cheers rose from the crowd. Voran's heart plunged at the overwhelming sense of hatred he felt rising off the crowd like steam from a lake in winter.

"No more monarchia! The Dumar, forever. The people's will, forever!"

Aspidían was screaming, his eyes bulging out unnaturally. His veins visibly throbbed in his neck. "Wipe this filth off the face of our city!"

He reached out a hand to one of his dog-men, who held a war hammer. Aspidían swung it at the obelisk, and a piece chipped off. For a moment, the crowd recoiled, but nothing happened. No thunderbolt from heaven, no fresh onrush of monstrous changers from the depths of the earth. And then, like a rising tide, the Vasylli swarmed the obelisk of the Raven and tore it from its place.

Aspidían, his eyes bloodshot, came back to Voran, who had been forgotten in the pandemonium.

"You see?" he said. "We don't need you, *healer*. We take care of our own."

To Voran's shock, Aspidían pulled off a key from his belt and unshackled Voran.

"I accept your wager. But I think you will find no welcome here. Not with that brand on your neck. I think I'll see you again in the Consistory soon. And I do not expect our next meeting to be as pleasant as our first."

Voran gripped Aspidían's forearm in the warrior's grip. He felt an almost electric pulse of pain coursing through him. Gently, he siphoned some of it off and into his own body. Aspidían gasped, then recoiled from him.

"Go," he said quietly and turned away.

For a brief moment, Voran felt with the man's own heart, but the darkness he sensed there was almost without end. Llun took his elbow and pulled Voran away and toward the first reach.

When they had entered it, Voran turned to a narrow alley between taverns. It stank, and the noise of the drunk was deafening, but it suited his purpose well enough. He turned to Llun and embraced him.

"Llun, my brother. We part here. You must seek out Ladomir and the rest of the Sons. Stay quiet and out of sight. Gather your strength for the coming fight. Do not let them catch you."

"What will you do?"

"I will heal. One by one. Until the Vasylli remember who they were, who they must still become."

Llun's expression mirrored Voran's own doubts.

"Llun, if I have learned anything, it is this. We are weak. The odds are impossible. But it is precisely then, when the night is darkest, when hope flickers, that something... some*one* aids us. We do not fight this battle alone."

Voran spoke the word. The brand on Llun's neck faded away.

There were tears on Llun's face as Voran walked away from him. Voran smiled, though he had no joy left inside him. Only the word, bubbling. Only the healing, itching to pour out of his hands.

Saddaí...Saddaí...

Voran wrapped himself in his dirty cloak and closed his eyes, willing his feet to take them where they willed. Into the rotting heart of his home.

CHAPTER 41
THE SEAS OF TIME

The one large open square of the monastery barely contained the assembled bear-riders. They stood in rows, facing Antomír. He felt a bit foolish, because the only raised place in this square was the platform from which the abbot traditionally read the *Sayings* aloud during common prayer. He may be Dar-in-waiting, but he was not an anointed cleric. The expressions on the faces of the four guardians (wings hidden), one huge she-wolf, and two Gumiren children that stood with the bear-riders were also verging on adulation. He tried, unsuccessfully, to ignore them.

At the other end of the square, in the windows of the monks' common building, about twenty monks stood as still as statues in their dark grey and green flowing robes. Their hoods were lowered over their heads, and he only saw the long beards, most of them red or blond. Like all of their movements, even the rustle of their beards in the wind was deliberate and subtle.

Their calm made Antomír fidget, and as usual his hands seemed to grow large and unwieldy. But then, the stillness extended out from them like ripples in a pool. He could almost see it coming at him like a rising mist. He forced himself to at least pretend to be still. It overcame him, and his heart slowed. Breathing in deeply, he waited. The stillness continued to fill out the entire square, visible in the gradual calming of the eyes of his listeners. When he could count his heartbeats without losing concentration, he began.

"All of us have lost something important in these last months." His voice sounded too small to his own ears, but he fought down the urge to clear his throat. "Perhaps we thought that these personal calamities were fated. Perhaps we were crushed for a time by the weight of them. I certainly was." He stopped, feeling himself gasp for air at the memory of his mother. "But now we know. They were all part of a larger tapestry of events that are still being woven as we speak. Now we can all be sure that we all have our singular parts to play."

Antomír sighed, waited, then continued.

"Our Darina, Sabíana of Vasyllia, is in need of our help. She alone holds back the darkness of the Raven. I have considered the guardians' suggestion to make this monastery the new Vasyllia, to plant the fruit from the Garden in the Heart of the World here, where there is a steady source of Living Water. It is a wise suggestion.

"But it is a wrong one. No place, in any of the Realms, is safe from a Deathless Raven. And make no mistake, my friends, the Raven has been willing to sacrifice entire nations—" he bowed his head slightly toward little Yesukai, who looked nearer thirty than thirteen, "—for his long game. Now we know that he is ready to suck the life of the earth itself dry. All for the chance to find his form and his immortality. He must know that if he is to sustain this perversion of eternal life, he will have to slowly kill everything that lives, leaving himself finally alone to face the Heights. I do not think he will stop even then but will even dare to take the Heights for himself."

"It seems wiser to me to attack the Raven now, daring to hope for the assistance of the Heights. Perhaps we cannot hope for much, since every Covenant ever made between man and Adonais has been broken time and time again. We, all of us, are witnesses of those separate breaches."

Elmira, her husband, Veles, and Severuk nodded, though hesitantly.

"Still, we must labor with the faith and hope that our intention will not fail to bring about unlooked-for help, even in the darkest hour."

Aglaia, in her wolf form, shed human tears, no doubt thinking of her lost son Voran.

"The children will remain here with the monks. The fruit from the Garden will be kept here, in case of our ultimate failure. In that day, this bastion will be the last hope for all the Realms. With the blessing of Abbot Makarían, some of you monks will come with our armies. We are not a large army. But now, more than ever, I am convinced that Adonais's power is made strongest in the weak. I do not know why, but I see it too clearly in myself and in others to doubt it."

At Antomír's side, Makarían sighed into his beard, a slight smile playing at the corners of his eyes. He looked very tired. *We all look tired*, Antomír thought. Well, it should all be over soon, for better or for worse.

Antomír turned to Makarían and kneeled before the abbot. "Father, I ask your blessing for myself and for these people who follow me, though the way is sure to be dark, and there is little hope, once we arrive in Vasyllia."

"Grace is given where you least expect," said Makarían, "and sometimes the weak do prevail over the strong. Into these vessels of weakness, may the strength of the Heights flow unimpeded. Lead with humility, my boy. Lead by example, and never forget the ultimate hope of every true Vasylli. May Covenant be restored, may the Tree flower, and may the Sirin sing in Vasyllia's streets once more."

A soft whoosh passed over their heads, growing into a sound like rushing water. Antomír turned just in time to see water burst out of the side of the mountain. There were seven streams of it, and it broke into rainbows as it fell on their heads. All the people in the square were drenched in seconds. It continued to fall, its mist rising up to cover the entire monastery. The sand-colored rock turned into the dark brown of fertile soil, and the smell of freshly turned earth rose up from the rocks beneath them. Intertwined with it was the smell of tuberose and lavender, and the faint hint of strawberries on the tongue.

A lightness—both in the sense of a weight falling off and a radiance lighting up inside his heart—suffused Antomír, and he saw the same effect reflected in the astonished eyes of the onlookers. The monks across the square had lifted their hoods and were staring into the waterfalls with mingled fear and hope in their eyes.

"Poor Khaidu," said Aglaia near him. "To be so close to Living Water, and not have a chance to be healed."

That snapped Antomír back to reality. They were being drenched in Living Water. Had the reservoir somehow been broken?

Antomír looked at Makarían beside him, ready to see the same fear in his face. But Makarían was laughing.

"Young man," he said, taking Antomír by the arm, "come with me. You have received a blessing indeed, though I do not think you have my impoverished prayers to thank for this."

"Veles, Aglaia, please come with me," said Antomír, following the sprightly old man back up to the turret.

At the cave mouth leading into the mountain, an old man stood up to his calves in running water. He was soaked to the roots of his hair, yet still on fire with golden flames that danced in the breeze. Makarían, seeing him, laughed aloud, but now there were tears in his eyes.

"Sarafían! It is a balm on this tired old soul to see your face again."

"Makarían, you give yourself too much credit," said Sarafían, who, if possible, had an even more joyful face than Makarían. "You are not in the least bit as old as you look. You will probably live another two hundred years. Don't forget I was greying when you were a mewling babe in swaddling clothes."

Makarían dissolved into incoherent tears as he fell at Sarafían's knees and embraced them, kissing the flames that began to dance over his own beard and hair.

"My friends," said Sarafían, looking, Antomír noted with interest, directly at Veles, "something completely unexpected…a new presence in the battlefield. Someone… so filled with light and power that it obliterated most of the dark powers residing there. This Someone has caused the sources of Living Water to overflow, as you no doubt see."

"A blessing," said Aglaia. "Now we will have little difficulty getting into Vasyllia, wall or no wall. I can sense it!"

"Who?" asked Antomír.

"A woman, all afire. I have never seen anything like it. She has torn apart the wall of Vasyllia as well, my friends," said Sarafían. "You will have no obstruction—physical or otherwise—on your entry. Though there is already an invading army in Vasyllia, and you will have some difficulty with them, I think."

"You can see into Vasyllia, my friend?" asked Makarían

"Yes. Partially. It is still very dark there. One thing I do see clearly. I see Voran the Healer."

Aglaia's ears perked up, and her tail went straight out like a sword. "What do you see?"

Sarafían's expression clouded over. "I see an emaciated madman begging for food on the streets of Vasyllia. I cannot say what that means."

Aglaia's ruff rose on her neck. "My Dar, I beg leave to go ahead. I must help my son. Please, let me help my son."

Antomír looked at her for a long time, as his desires and fears pummeled each other in his mind. But he was never really in doubt of his answer. "Go, grandmother, go! I would love to see my uncle again."

One minute she was there, the next, a blur on the edge of the mountain, flowing like water down the slopes toward Vasyllia.

A sucking sound turned Antomír's attention back to Sarafían. They were again standing on stone, the waters receding back into the tunnel. Sarafían's flames were dimming visibly. Makarían was still weeping, wrapped around Sarafían's knees like a python.

"You know it must be, my child," Sarafían said, caressing Makarían on the head. "The sleepers are seven. If awoken, they must not tarry. That is the way."

"I am not ready. I will fail again."

"You will not. Go. The battle awaits."

Sarafían fell on the ground, the flames dissipating, leaving barely more than a husk of a body. Makarían was now covered in the flames. Weeping opal tears that caught fire as they fell, he embraced Antomír, but jerked away, as if it hurt him. He looked at Antomír with renewed respect in his eyes. There was something like shared pain there.

"Oh, my boy. Your burden. I see your burden. I had not known...How hard your way will yet be..."

All that day, Antomír was haunted by Makarían's last words. His army traveled thirteen miles of rough, stony road, but he hardly noticed any of it. The thought nagged him: Makarían must have somehow seen Gamayun inside him. And yet, he had done nothing to expose Antomír. Nor had he done anything to help him. It confused Antomír, even as it gave him hope that perhaps there was a way to undo the binding between himself and the day-seer.

She had not so much as whispered in his head the entire time he was in the monastery.

That evening, he refused to pitch the royal pavilion, preferring instead to sleep in a simple canvas tent. The same as any common soldier. He fell asleep as soon as his head hit bare earth.

"Wake up!" said the voice in his head.

Antomír awoke, his head as heavy as after a night of drinking. Everything ached from the ride. But all that was a shadow thrown back by the real pain—the clear sense of Gamayun's heart beating inside his own chest. All the lightness, all the strength he had gathered in the monastery was gone.

"How could you?" she said, behind him.

He turned, and realized he was not in his tent at all, but at the bank of a pool that reflected the starry night so clearly, it seemed to *be* the sky. In the distance stood Vasyllia's mountains, white as ghosts. They seemed to call to

Mirnían, almost drawing him physically closer, even as he sat in one place by a weeping Gamayun.

"Why are you crying?" he asked, unexpectedly touched by her ugly face, smeared with tears.

"I want only for you to be happy, don't you understand? Why can't you act in a way that makes us both happy?"

"What do you want me to do, Gamayun? I have never understood you."

"You've never tried." She looked up, and her eyes were darker than the star-strewn pool.

"I'm sorry," he said, feeling guilty, but not knowing why.

Her face twisted, her eyelids half-closed, and rage washed over her face. "You are nothing of the sort," she said, almost growling. He felt a hot ring of fire around his heart, cinching it closer and closer. "You don't care for anyone but yourself."

"How can I care for you if all you've ever done is lie to me and manipulate me? How can you pretend that our bond is anything but a parody of a Sirin's soul-bond? You give me nothing but pain! How can you expect me to reciprocate with love?"

"If not you, then who? You don't understand..." She trailed off, then sobbed like a child. One half of his mind wanted to embrace her, comfort her, but the other recoiled from so much as the thought of it. He did nothing, though he sensed, clearly, that she was waiting for him to do...*something*. To act, to change the dynamic of their relationship. To instigate, to transform it.

He would not do it.

When she looked back at him, her eyes were red-rimmed, but cold. Whatever sorrow had been there was gone, replaced with something worse than hatred.

"I think it's time you knew the truth," she said, her voice devoid of any emotion. His heart stopped beating for a full breath, then redoubled with twice the intensity. He had never felt fear in her presence until now. "Why I came to you. Why I've made your quiet moments a foretaste of the darkest regions of the land of the dead.

"I am no Sirin. You must know that by now. I am something created afterward, for a different purpose. I was never meant to have any sort of bond with any other living creature."

"That must be a horrible existence," said Antomír.

"You know nothing, Antomír. Time is a sea, far above all the firmaments, dripping down as rain or falling down as torrents on the skies and lands below. I am the only creature in all the worlds who can swim in the sea of

THE HEART OF THE WORLD

times. I live in an island in those seas, on a tower of white, where I sit and contemplate the tides of the aeons. I see all times as in a single sea.

"Some events are clear, like a line of warm aquamarine in the lapis waters. Others hinge on the subtlest choices made by individuals who can shape eras: these currents of time ebb and flow, and I rarely see where they go until shortly before the event actually happens.

"But I always see the future that must be. Sometimes I sing it into being; other times I sing of possible eventualities. Sometimes I remain silent. Rarely do I sing of the past, for it also is a current that those in the present cannot see, no matter how well they think they know their histories.

"But there came a time when all the currents ceased to speak to me. The waters of time grew turbid, dark and without form, churning chaotically in shapes unfamiliar to me. Only far away from my sight, at the limit of my knowledge, I thought I saw something familiar—a future that I had glimpsed once. A terrible future, one in which all the worlds will dry up. Nothing will remain, save a beast that consumes everything, and in the final hunger, devours itself.

"That future could not be, I told myself. It is a mirage, I told myself. But it itched at my consciousness, tugging at me, calling at me. And in the formless chaos of times that surrounded me, I thirsted for something clear, even if it were the only future that must never be. I followed it, doing something I must never do. I left my tower and plunged into the waters of time.

"It was a trap. The Raven had somehow gathered enough strength to be able to pierce through the firmaments and to cast an illusion on the waters of time. As I entered them, he caught me and dragged me into the timeline that he intended for the worlds—the nightmare that I saw from my tower. And so I was ensnared in the lowest of the Realms, caught in the nightmare time that must never be.

"I have no right to intervene in the events of any time—that is the price of being the day-seer, the teller of all futures. To be *inside* time, unable to see its ebb and flow—that is worse than any torture you can imagine. Much worse than any pain you think you feel at our forced bond."

Antomír was about to disagree with her, but he found that he couldn't move. She was determined to finish before he could say anything.

"The Raven made me a promise. He said he would return me to my place, to the tower in the midst of the waters of time. But I had to bring him the Dar of Vasyllia. I could not make Mirnían listen to me. He was too old, too canny in the ways of the Heights to be fooled by my pathetic lies. But you... you were impressionable, thirsting for purpose. You were clay in my talons, little Dar."

Antomír ground his teeth until his jaw flashed in pain, but he still couldn't move, nor say a single word.

"So I will do that. I will bring you to the Raven. And there is nothing you can do to stop me."

His chest exploded in pain. It was like a blizzard of fire. He curled up, trying to breathe, but his chest muscles and jaw were locked in pain.

"That is nothing," she continued. "I will hurt you a hundred times more. I will move your limbs for you, if it comes to that."

"I will fight you to the end," he managed to whisper through his clenched teeth.

"Think, boy!" She lowered her head, watching him as he writhed on the ground like a curious predator. "If even a shower of Living Water could not destroy the tie I have over you, then do you think your own will can manage?"

She loosened his pain, and he gasped for air as the stars before his eyes danced with the stars reflected in the still pool beside him.

"Don't you... understand what he is... doing?" Antomír's breath came in heaves. "He wants my body as his vessel. I am of the line of Cassian, his greatest enemy. It would be his final triumph. Gamayun, listen to me! When he has taken possession of me, he will eat the last fruits from the trees of life in the Heart of the World. He will live forever, and he will become that beast that you saw. I will as well, but as a shell of myself. If you do this, you will ensure the future that you fear so much."

"No. When he returns me to my tower, I will un-sing this future. I will change it all."

"You don't actually believe you can..."

"I *can*!" It wasn't certainty in her tone, it was the last gasp of a dying hope. "And I want you to do it with me. Accept your fate. Let me guide your steps. Together, we can destroy the Raven."

Perversely, Antomír felt like laughing. But Gamayun was serious as death.

"I would sooner kill myself." said Antomír.

Gamayun laughed, but it sounded like a metal spoon hitting a cast iron pot.

"I did not lie when I said I would move your limbs for you, Antomír. I will paralyze you, if needed. You will do no willing damage to your body."

"Gamayun!" Antomír wanted to tear the ground apart at his feet, so it would swallow Gamayun, to poke her eyes out, to do her some irreparable injury. "How can you do this? Every battle we fight, ever victory we win, ever bit of hope my people gather on this road to Vasyllia—I will know it is all a lie!"

"Oh, no. You won't remember any of this when you wake up, my sweet. I'm not *that* cruel."

Antomír awoke in his own tent, shivering from the dew that had soaked his clothes to the skin. He had a nagging feeling that he had dreamt something very important. But other than a nebulous image of a white tower in a sea with currents of many different colors, he remembered nothing.

CHAPTER 42
THE WOLFLING

"Khaidu, is that really you?" asked Sabíana. She looked little like the Sabíana of Khaidu's nights, except for her face, which was still young. But her body, though covered in fine fabric, was thin and wasted. Khaidu's first, absurd thought was that someone needed to feed her.

"Yes," said Khaidu. "I have come to help you."

Sabíana laughed. "And how will a leg-less cripple help a paralyzed queen?"

"I am not leg-less. Just... limited."

But Sabíana was right. What seemed to be an act of devotion now felt like the delusion of a madman.

"My arms are strong," said Khaidu. "And how do you think I survived back at home? I wasn't always carried around or strapped to horses. Maybe...I don't know..." For now, there was not much she could do, except drag herself closer to Sabíana. "Who takes care of you here?"

"I do," hissed a husky voice behind Khaidu. It took her a moment to realize that the voice spoke Gumir.

The door opened, and light streamed into the dark room. Against the light, the woman was nothing more than a black shadow looming over her. By now, Khaidu's eyes had become accustomed to the light, and she saw her face. A wrinkled, angry face belonging to an old Gumira.

"Who are you?" asked Khaidu.

"I'm Kipchak. Who are you?"

"Khaidu."

The woman's lip curled in disgust. "I know you. You're Mamai's girl."

Khaidu nodded. The woman cleared her throat and proceeded to ignore Khaidu completely.

"I've brought you food, lady," she said.

"Not for me, Kipchak. Thank you. I have already eaten today."

"But...a hunk of dried bread is hardly—"

"It's more than enough for me. But you must feed my friend here. Khaidu, Kipchak is the only person in Vasyllia who still serves me."

A Gumira serving the lady of the Vasylli? There was probably an interesting story there.

"Lady, please—"

"No, Kipchak. Feed Khaidu."

Kipchak clutched at her fingers like a beggar grabbing a rich man's hand. Sabíana's own hand didn't answer her clutches. It seemed she could only move her head, and even that with great difficulty. Kipchak looked at Khaidu with a strange expression. There was a kind of obsessive protectiveness there. She recognized that Khaidu meant something to Sabíana, and she was jealous.

"What a group we are," said Sabíana, her laugh bringing a tinge of light and color into the dark room. "How morbid! If my young self saw me now, she would chide me most violently. Come. Let us all be friends. Khaidu, you can do little for me here with your body, but your heart of fire—that I welcome. Kipchak will be our legs."

Kipchak's expression suggested otherwise.

"Sabíana," said Khaidu, "why are you lying here in this... pile of garbage? What happened after you left me?"

"Khaidu, you infuriating Steppe-wolf," Sabíana chided, growing, at least in her voice, more and more the Sabíana Khaidu knew before, "how I've missed you."

Khaidu flushed in embarrassment and looked away.

"You were right, you know," continued Sabíana. "I should never have left my post, my place as Darina of my people. But since I left, everything has changed. There is no longer a place for Dar or Darina in this Vasyllia. I used to be able to help the few remaining true Vasylli hold on to the old ways. Llun the smith. Dashun the tinker. Sioán the potter. Gleb the priest. But they're all dead or turned. All the people that are left labor under the delusion that they rule themselves."

"Well, we'll just tell them the truth!" said Khaidu and tried to walk out of the room, only managing to fall over her legs, which, of course, did not respond to her enthusiasm.

"No, we must wait, my dear Khaidu. Kipchak is my eyes and ears. She tells me all that happens out in the world. I will remain here, out of mind of those madmen who think they rule Vasyllia. It is the safest place to be, for now."

"But we can't stay here. Haven't you heard? Your nephew, Antomír, is leading an army to retake Vasyllia."

"Khaidu, tell me everything that has happened since you and I saw each other last."

The telling was so unlabored and easy, that Khaidu had to actually slow herself for Sabíana's benefit. After repeating a few points—including the presence of two rival armies, both intent on Vasyllia—Khaidu managed to tell it all. Kipchak looked like she wasn't listening to a word of it.

"Well, that is certainly refreshing," said Sabíana. "So much activity after twenty years of silence. What I would not give for an active body now. Even with the Consistory in power, I think I could do something. My young self surely could."

"Is there anything we *can* do?" Khaidu asked.

"Actually, yes." Sabíana's eyes widened and seemed to light up from within. "Kipchak, summon Aspidían to me."

Kipchak's jaw actually dropped.

"Aspidían, my lady? Why do you think I, a Gumira, can approach the chief inquisitor of the—"

"You think I don't know you spy for him?"

Kipchak's face grew as white as a Vasylli. She backed out through the open door, her eyes downcast.

"Why do you keep her around if she's a spy?" asked Khaidu.

"She's a tortured creature," said Sabíana. "Just trying to stay alive. She may be the last living Gumira in Vasyllia. And she is devoted to me, in her own strange way."

For a long time, nothing happened. Then, faint at first, then unmistakable—booted feet. Many booted feet, walking with a purpose that seemed ominous. Sabíana's slight frown confirmed that she had not expected quite so many.

The man who walked into the room was short, but muscular. He had a sparse beard and flowing hair that he obviously took great care with. His eyes darted back and forth like a hunter seeking prey. A kind of smile danced at the edge of his lips, but it was a venomous smile. An adder's smile.

"Highness." The man had a languid way of speaking that clashed with pent-up energy in his body. "You chose an inconvenient time to...summon me. And what is this?" He looked at Khaidu with the interest of a python before its meal. "Have you made this room a refuge for Gumiren, Sabíana?"

"Sudar Aspidían," said Sabíana, "the convenience of a second-reacher makes little difference to me." Khaidu had never heard her use that tone. She was not sure she liked it.

The man's smile shed off his face like a snakeskin. If he was dangerous before, now he was lethal.

"You do not want to do this now. This is not a good time," he whispered.

"Aspidían," said Sabíana, loudly, so that every one of the armed warriors standing in the hallway behind him would hear. "I order you, as Darina of Vasyllia, to return me to the hall of kings. I will assume my place as Darina today. My people have waited long enough."

"What? Will you lie before them in a litter?" He cackled, then spread out his hands, as though he were a reasonable parent speaking to a petulant child. "We can arrange visiting hours, so that your doting people can take turns cleaning your bed pan, eh? If you wanted more than this...disgusting room, you only needed to ask. I've been willing to give you better quarters. You insisted, remember?"

"Are you deaf, or are you stupid, Sudar?" Sabíana said.

His face reddened, and Khaidu realized that some of the warriors behind him were snickering. Aspidían approached Sabíana, and his smooth tone frayed at the edges. "I could have you publicly flayed, you third-reacher whore, but out of the goodness of my heart, I keep you alive. Is this how you repay me?"

"We both know you keep me alive so that you can use my death to better advantage in the coming war," said Sabíana loudly. He flinched, and Khaidu realized that he had not wanted his men to hear that. *Dangerous, my lady*, she thought. *Now, the predator has no need to crouch in the high grasses anymore.*

"Ah, my lady." He sniggered. "I forgot about your famous wit. No need to pretend, in that case. Guards, take the Gumiren bitch and give her to the hunting hounds. As for the Lady Sabíana..."

"Aspidían," said Sabíana, and there was a hint of plaintiveness in her voice. "Leave me my one consolation. Let this young girl come with me. She is a cripple, as I am. No threat to anyone. If I'm going to die anyway, then let me die with the few who still love me."

He looked at her for a very long time. His eyes went slightly unfocused for a moment, as though he were having trouble seeing them. He tottered for a moment. His feet tripped over themselves. Khaidu looked at Sabíana, and saw the beaded sweat gathering on her upper lip.

She's trying to pull him into one of her dream-illusions, she thought. But he wasn't asleep! And surely his mind was too strong for that.

He slapped himself across the face, hard.

"Stop," he whispered intensely. "You think your tricks work on me? My Darina." The knife-edge returned to his voice.

Sabíana's face went white with fear. She had failed. Aspidían grinned with pleasure.

"You shouldn't play by the Consistory's rules, *Darina*. You don't have the wits for it. Take them all down. A public execution, I think, for the last Darina of Cassían's line. And especially for the last Gumiren whores left in Vasyllia."

<hr />

All three of them were hung inside separate metal cages, strung up on creaking chains to the very top of a narrow and tall chamber. Two slits in the wall hardly let in any light at all. Whether it was night, or whether the windows were false, Khaidu did not know. She felt disgusted with herself, useless and tired and very hungry. Sabíana was wedged face-first against the grate, unable to move to relieve her position. It was horrifying to look at. She seemed not to feel it, but that was no consolation for Khaidu. Kipchak moaned and whined without stopping.

"Sabíana," Khaidu whispered as soon as the footsteps of the departing guards stopped echoing over the walls. "I'm sorry. I failed you."

Sabíana said nothing, but all hope seemed expunged from her face.

CHAPTER 43
A BITTER HOMECOMING

Aglaia sped like a black arrow through Nebesta toward the wall of Vasyllia. Fly faster, she kept telling herself, but she needed to stop far too often. She didn't recognize the countryside any longer. The lands that had been her extended home, the roads she had traveled countless times over her long years—everything was marred, pockmarked, or destroyed outright. In some places, it looked like someone had broken off the summits of mountains here and there. As for the greenery, there was none. The grass was brown; the shriveled stumps of trees were black, the air itself seemed to choke on the smoke-fog that swirled everywhere. The rare splashes of color—a fox running for its life, a red-winged blackbird trying to find something to eat in the parched earth, a blue-grey rabbit so thin that every push of its legs looked enough to break its own back—were negated by the slate grey of the overcast sky.

How are we to save Vasyllia, if nature itself seems to be dying?

As soon as the wall of Vasyllia came into view, she saw a different harvest of death. At first, they blended so well into the grey-brown of the earth that Aglaia hardly noticed them. When she was no more than a few feet from the first, the realization stopped her in mid-stride. Three bodies dressed in course grey fabric, tossed to the side of the road like refuse. They were only partially eaten by the carrion-feeders. Then a wave of crows flew up behind them, and Aglaia saw the mounds. Three of them—hills of dead bodies. She could see no weapon marks on any of the bodies. They looked like seed husks emptied of their meats.

The hole in the wall of Vasyllia looked like a mouth ringed with broken teeth.

Inside Vasyllia, things were different. In the area closest to the wall, the disease in nature was sparser than in Nebesta, but Aglaia saw that it was steadily moving toward the city, and soon even the lush greenery of the areas nearest her beloved home would fade and die. It hurried her all the more, even as her doubts began to gnaw at her more insistently.

How would she find Voran?

And now, not far ahead of her—judging by the stomp of men and the plume of rising dust—another army was approaching her beloved city, and they had serpent-giants. Soon she saw the undulating wave of men marching through the night, the moonlight sparkling on their helmets. They were slow and tired, and she easily overtook them without being noticed. Or so she hoped.

There was one moment when she was just passing the vanguard of that army, when she felt a tug of some kind at her mind, a probing push, as though someone were tapping at her skull with a metal instrument. She buried herself deep inside the wolf, allowing the blood-tinged thoughts and desires to come over her for a moment, though not enough to lose herself in the beast again. The tapping ceased, and she went on without any further harassment.

Vasyllia was locked, bolted, and chained against the invasion. All the fields before it had already been burned. The freshness of the fires was acrid in her nostrils. She skirted the wall, looking for the joint between Mount Vasyllia and the wall of the city, where once, long ago, she had found a chink in the ageless armor of the great city.

It was still there, but she could not fit in her wolf form. Cursing her bad luck, she changed into the old woman. Bowed as though by age, wrapping her wolf-pelt about her as the beggar women do, she slinked into the first reach of Vasyllia.

When she was inside, the air changed. Outside, pine and the peat scented the air, but here all she smelled was vomit and sour beer and … She almost reeled when she realized that she was standing in front of a brothel.

"In Vasyllia?" she hissed under her breath, but a little too loudly, attracting the attention of some of the girls hanging out the windows.

"Wrong part of town, granny," one of them cackled at her. "We don't like beggars in this part of the reach. Bad for business. Get out before I call the brawlers."

Aglaia pretended that she had a bad left knee and hobbled off in the general direction of the woman's forefinger. Ahead, the cobbled streets forked. To the left, the stench and the carcasses of dogs declared the proximity of the beggars' quarter. To the right, the sounds of a brawl. That way, there was a profusion of hanging lanterns. The smoke billowed along the ground so thick it could be a snake. Judging by the kind of men coming from this direction toward the place Aglaia had just abandoned, the brawl was probably a violent one.

Aglaia itched to transform back into the wolf, to teach these so-called Vasylli a lesson they would never forget. But she was sure the Raven had eyes and ears everywhere, and even a drunk man would not soon forget a black wolf the size of a bear.

The commotion continued, and now she heard taunts and thudding blows. No, it was not a brawl. Someone was being beaten to within an inch of his life, judging by the sound. She should really keep going. Finding Voran was of prime importance. But a sense of significance drew her to the fight, and she tiptoed forward, keeping to the shadows of the tall, narrow buildings. In an open space between two dimly-lit taverns that faced each other, two men held a beggar, while the third beat him. The beggar, though a large man, was already limp in their arms. His bare feet scrabbled at the cobbles. They kept slipping on his own blood.

The beater was breathing heavily, already tired out by his exertions. "Will you say it again, or have I instructed you enough in Vasylli manners?"

"Don't befoul the air by calling yourself Vasylli," said the beggar in an accent that was unexpectedly third-reacher. "That dead dog down the street is more Vasylli than you."

The brute sighed and continued his beating. Finally, something cracked, and the man collapsed like a rag doll. The two who held him dropped him. As soon as they did, he moaned, but still managed to speak, "Your vices will be your end. Do not let them. Please, listen. You can change your—"

A final, savage kick to the head silenced him. The three brawlers walked away with shoulders bowed. Their manner showed nothing of the usual blood-lusty euphoria of the victorious in a street brawl. The sparse, smoky light showed their faces to be pensive as they passed Aglaia without seeing her.

She approached the man, not knowing what she could do for him, but feeling a need to provide him with some comfort before he died. There was no chance he would survive long. He probably would not even come back to consciousness. His face was hardly human-looking any more. Heedless of the blood, she knelt beside him and cradled his head in her lap, wiping off as much of the blood as she could with the rough edge of her coat. He twitched in her lap, then one of his eyes opened. It widened in recognition.

"Mother?" said Voran, in a voice Aglaia hardly recognized. "What are you doing here?"

She gasped as the tears flung themselves down from her eyes to wash the blood off his face. "I ca-m-me to f-find you, my boy."

Voran chuckled, then groaned from the pain of it. "What a strange place to meet, Mother. I'm sorry it's been so long since I've sought you out."

"Shh! Now is not the time for apologies."

"I think it very well may be."

"Voran, tell me what happened to you. Tell me, so I can exact revenge." The growl at the back of her throat tickled, and she had an absurd desire to cough.

"I've done all I can to heal Vasyllia. But it's useless. The only true Vasylli, the Sons of the Swan, I failed them. Everywhere, everyone spurned me. I begged in the first reach. Even here, I healed. I sow the seeds of Old Vasyllia everywhere I go. But the soil is rocky, so rocky..."

He coughed blood and nearly choked on it. Aglaia lifted his head, barely able to keep her hands steady as her entire body shook in between sobs.

"I will not die, not yet," he rasped. There was no anger in his voice. "But I am so tired. Mother, every day is like this. Every night, I beg Adonais to feed my reserve of strength. My Vasylli are not ready. I need more time. Ask it for me. He hears the prayers of mothers more than any others."

Aglaia groaned.

"Please, mother. So much work still to do."

Aglaia couldn't speak, she was shaking too fiercely. But she thought the prayer, tracing them with words of blood on her memory. Above the din of cutlery, the laughter of drunk men, the barking of dogs, she heard a whisper of wind whistling through reeds. Voran gasped and sat up. Both eyes were open wide, and he seemed to smile, underneath the bruising and the blood.

"Not for me!" he called to the darkness. "For Vasyllia, my Lyna. I ask nothing for myself. Only a little hope."

The whisper blossomed into a song. It was the birth of a waterfall in the spring. It was the fire of the earth erupting through the cone of a mountain. It was the flowering of primroses in the midst of a garden burnt by fire. Lyna the Sirin, her gem-toned wings alight with colored fire, flew down in a blaze from the darkness above them. She hovered over Voran's body, and her tears fell onto his face. To Aglaia's surprise, the wounds were knitting together. He sat up and laughed as he raised both hands to Lyna, like a child in a crib reaching for his mother.

"Have you returned to me?" he asked. "Will you offer me your bond, as before?"

"Our bond is not yet broken, my falcon. Only a little strained." She smiled wanly. "Come. You have done what you can for Vasyllia. There is a final healing you must accomplish, the most dangerous one yet. I will show you the way to the Garden in the Heart of the World."

CHAPTER 44

SKIRMISH

"Will we never see sky anymore?" complained Bragadun at Parfyon's side. He, of all the warriors, had never left his side. His first follower, and his most loyal one. "I'm beginning to forget what it looks like. Or what the sun's rays feel like."

He stood at the edge of the Pass of Ardovían, the highest pass of the main range of Vasyllia Mountains. In front of him, the vanguard of his army had already come through the pass and was already descending along the road gradually meandering downward into the long valley of the Vasyllia River. Standing on a tall rock at the Pass itself, Parfyon should be able to see Vasyllia.

He saw nothing but clouds in the place where Vasyllia should be. The clouds churned and bubbled like the inside of a cauldron. Black interlaced with grey and even dark purple, ever moving and shifting, only to reveal more and more layers of clouds. The hole in Parfyon's chest yawned at the sight, the clouds a mirror to the jumble of his emotions and thoughts. Alienne in the fire, the beauty she spoke of before she died, the disappearance of her body in the all-consuming fire...He still did not know what to make of it all.

"Lord Parfyon, look!"

Even before he saw it, Parfyon felt the sun. It was like a steam room and a bath after a month of lying in the muck. Then, the sky opened, or rather, some invisible power sliced a sliver out of the cloud, and there it was. Vasyllia, the Mother of Cities, the jewel of the earth.

Parfyon forgot how to breathe.

It was not a city. It was a miracle. Stone towers taller than the giants, some clearly not built, but carved out of the mountain. Domes, arches, spindly bridges that jumped over chasms thousands of feet deep. It was impossible! Amid the stone building grew groves of trees in bloom. Some were taller even than the towers. Terraces hung between the layers of the city, built as it was along the ascending wall of the tallest mountain Parfyon had ever seen. The terraces glistened like emeralds, but there were splashes of other colors, too, visible to Parfyon's new senses, enhanced by the giants' magic, even from such a distance. Flowers, probably, and fruit trees and herbs and gardens. But most spectacular of all—the two waterfalls falling down either side of the great city. Each of them was gathered into—*by the Heights! Those are giant chalices!*

Alienne would have wept to see this, he thought, and the hole in his chest grew, and the ever-present saw cut deeper and deeper with its serrated edge. Instead of trying to distract himself from the pain, he descended deeper into it. He ground his teeth until his jaw hurt. He balled his fists until his nails cut his palms.

Good. Feel the pain. You deserve no less. May I never experience any beauty, any glory ever again without the remembrance of what I paid for it.

Swiftly as a hawk falling on a dove from the sky, a sense of impending danger skimmed over Parfyon's mind. In a flash, he saw, but his body froze in indecision.

Something cracked on the road downhill from Parfyon. Stone splintered, as though something were pushing up from the depths of the earth. Rocks fell in a scree from his army's left. In no more than three seconds, his entire vanguard was crushed under an avalanche of rock.

Parfyon's breath came in ragged bursts. *Idiot*, he thought. How could I allow myself to get so distracted?

He jumped down from his vantage point onto the road and pushed his men aside, rushing to get to the confusion at the front of his lines.

A warrior was lying on the ground, his head caved in. A bloody boulder lay not a foot away from him. The churning frustration in Parfyon's chest overflowed, and he lifted the rock over his head. He hurled it down the road with such force that it broke into a hundred smaller pieces on impact. It did nothing to relieve his frustration.

"Idiots!" he screamed.

Arms and legs poked out into open air here and there in the rock fall that had completely covered the road to Vasyllia. Silence hung in the air, thicker than the dust scattered by the falling rock. Behind the silence,

Parfyon sensed something wrong in the air around him. Not menacing, exactly, just not entirely natural. Was the rock fall...intentional?

Something squeaked, a sound completely strange in the mountains. It sounded like something...being stretched...*Oh, no!*

His body responded before his mind completely processed the information. He fell on the ground and covered his head. Just in time.

The arrows fell like a sudden hailstorm. That stretching sound—it was bows being pulled back, the tautness a squeaking no louder than a mouse. His body was clearly not yet accustomed to the extreme sensitivity of his newly enhanced senses.

His warriors surrounded him and made a wall of shields around him. He pushed them aside.

"Go, maggot-fodder! They're all around us."

The word rushed back along the lines to the rear, but before it arrived, the fighting had already begun. Parfyon saw it all with his expanded senses. He cursed. Around a hundred bear riders, a sword in each hand, appeared out of nowhere from the rocks above the road, cutting through his still confused rear lines. The Nebesti were running in every direction except the one they needed to. Many were trampled by their own.

Parfyon climbed up to a spur in the rock wall above him, allowing him a clear view of the pass, now teeming with steel-bearing men. The smears of blood were clear even from this distance. The bear riders were slaughtering his men.

Then he saw something, and it tickled that new depth in his awareness. Interesting... That spot right above the point of the pass where the most bear riders stood. It was very unstable ground. What if that spruce tree were to fall over just at that point...there! Extending the power of the giants outward, Parfyon splintered the spruce, and it collapsed.

The ground shook underfoot as the entire pass collapsed in on itself. All the bear riders were crushed in a moment, but the rocks didn't discriminate. They continued to fall. More and more of them gathered until the entire rear portion of his Nebesti army was also crushed. Parfyon ran to examine them, his warriors thick about him, their swords drawn, their shields angled up over his head.

Four of the bear riders had survived. They were archers with short swords and round shields, captured after their bears had been cut down. Parfyon jumped down from his perch just as an over-eager soldier was about to decapitate them.

"Stop!" Parfyon's voice echoed through the narrow pass. His warriors stood at attention, standing back to allow Parfyon a narrow path. The bear riders, though covered with gashes and bleeding profusely, stood taller than his own men. Their hands were tied behind their backs, but their expressions made it look like they stood at inspection before their own superiors. Again, Parfyon was impressed by these worthy adversaries.

"This is what comes of being merciful in a time of war," grumbled Bragadun, who had been recently promoted to head of the knyaz's household knights. "Forgive me, lord, but if you had not allowed that boy…"

"Silence," said Parfyon. "I require no one to state what my eyes tell me well enough. What's done is done." He caught the eye of the tallest of the bear riders. "Your name, warrior?"

"I am called Olgerd," he said, "of the children of the Priest-King."

Parfyon pulled out his hunting knife and buried it deep in the man's gut. Olgerd did not so much as cry out.

"As I thought," said Parfyon, unable to hide the admiration in his voice. "Look at this, Nebesti! And we thought we were the greatest warriors of the age. Watch, and learn. If we are to take Vasyllia, we will need some of that kind of mad valor."

He pulled out the knife, and Olgerd gasped slightly.

"Olgerd, I will make your death swift. You deserve a warrior's death. But I require information. What are the intentions of that brat who pretends to be Dar of Vasyllia?"

"What else can they be, but the calling he received at birth?" Olgerd's legs shook slightly, then he regained his posture with an effort. "He goes to claim the throne only he can sit upon."

"He'll have to get past us. And we have some very powerful friends."

"You know very little." Olgerd laughed, then coughed up blood. He tottered and fell on one knee. Parfyon caught him and steadied him on two knees. "Do the men of this land need roads built for travelers of other lands, merchants of other reaches?"

Parfyon slapped his forehead with his open palm. "Oh, Olgerd. I have been a fool indeed! Thank you for showing it to me."

Faster than an eye blinking, Parfyon unsheathed his greatsword. In only two strokes, he cut Olgerd's head off. The warrior fell torso-forward at Parfyon's feet.

"Clean deaths for the rest as well," said Parfyon to Bragadun as he turned around and walked back to the front line. His heart raced from excitement. He thought he understood Olgerd's implied words.

He sensed outward, down to the valley directly below them. *There*.

"What is it?" asked Bragadun.

"Bragadun, have you been to Vasyllia before the invasion? Do you know the land at all?"

"Well enough. The road below us passes through a valley, then narrows into a gorge between two peaks. It's narrow. Probably the most dangerous bit of road we'll encounter. If there's any Vasylli defense, it'll be there. Beyond it, there are nothing but plateaus and open roads all the way to the woods directly before Vasyllia."

"Well, that gorge? It's blocked."

"With Vasylli?"

"No, Bear riders."

"But... I don't understand. How did they get around us?"

"Clearly there are other paths through Vasyllia that you and I don't know about."

"So," Bragadun said with relish, "They want to decide this thing once and for all."

"They *are* Vasylli," said Zmei that night, as Parfyon perched on a rocky defile that overlooked the masses of encamped enemies below them in the valley. Underneath his feet, the Vasyllia River meandered, tendrils of fog writhing on its surface like sea-snakes.

"What are you saying?" countered Parfyon. "That they have a right to harass us? To stand in our way?"

"The young man, Antomír, has powerful friends. And all he's doing is coming to take his own. And as for the bear riders... They are much more than you think. They believe themselves to be the true Vasylli. They have not been in this part of the world for many centuries. Your people have long forgotten about them. The children of the Priest-King..."

Parfyon couldn't believe the wistfulness in Zmei's voice.

"You know them?"

"I knew the one they call the Priest-King, yes. Askoldír. He was a good man. History remembers him as Lassar's idiot brother. But he was not that. Oh no. He was much like you, Parfyon. In some ways, even more ruthless."

"I knew you giants were old, but..." Parfyon scoffed. "Why do I sense that you're about to tell me something I don't want to hear?"

Zmei, no more than a hulking shadow faintly glimmering silver in the starlight, sighed.

"My brothers and I...We had not anticipated this. When the riders first attacked you, we thought it was only another band of roving mercenaries left over from the Internecine War. But this is the legitimate Dar of Vasyllia who marches to his city. And his aims do not hinder our aims."

"But they hinder mine, Zmei! What are you saying? That you would renege on our bargain? After all I've sacrificed for it?"

"No, you fool." Zmei's outline flickered red to match the rising anger in his voice. "We serpents do not go back on our word unless there is extreme need."

"That is very comforting," Parfyon growled.

"Listen to me, Parfyon. There may be some wisdom in bargaining with this young Dar. You and he both want the removal of the contagion inside Vasyllia."

"He is part of the contagion! He is Vasylli. I will purge this land of their filth. I gave my word to wash the ground of Vasyllia with their blood, to build feasting platforms on the mounds of their dead. But I suppose you have no interest in my aims, do you, Zmei? Speaking of which, do you think perhaps you might tell me your own aims in Vasyllia? I had thought your feud was with Vasyllia as well."

"Not with Vasyllia, no. With a certain man who calls himself the Healer. But that is a private vendetta, and the disease at the heart of Vasyllia is more important than our annoyance with a small man. In any case, he is not with these Vasylli under Antomír's command. I've made sure of that."

"Have you been lying to me, Zmei?"

Zmei finally looked at him, and his eyes glowed. His voice simmered with anger, and Parfyon was more afraid of that cold fury than all of the bombastic displays of power that the giants were capable of.

"I care nothing for the idiotic power squabbles of you humans. If you wish to wash the streets of Vasyllia with Vasylli blood, you would not be the first. What we want to destroy is far more important. There is a great beast at the heart of Vasyllia Mountain. He... he is at the source of Living Water itself. And he is drinking it dry."

Parfyon scowled. "The great Changer. The one they call the Raven. I had thought it all a child's tale." But with his new intuition, he felt the truth of Zmei's words.

"Don't underestimate what you don't understand, Parfyon. Only a great fool does that."

"That's as it may be. So you backed me, believing the Nebesti to be your most effective opportunity to overcome the barriers to Vasylli and take over the city, only so that you and your brothers can go into the bowels of the earth to kill some overgrown leech?" Parfyon laughed aloud. "And now, you wish me to ally myself with the returning Dar of Vasyllia, probably no more than a pretender to that glorious throne, only to ensure your unimpeded entry into Vasyllia?"

"Look down the road, Parfyon. The bear riders control the only remaining pass into Vasyllia. Any battle in such terrain will result in catastrophic losses. There is no way for an army of your size to travel around, to seek smaller mountain paths. Not if you wish to come to Vasyllia before Antomír."

Parfyon flared in anger but choked down his response. It was going to be a long enough night without an extended argument with the prince of giants.

"Will you at least think about it, Parfyon?"

Zmei, the demonic serpent-giant capable of sacrificing an innocent woman to the fire merely for a bit of power, sounded like a placating old man, eager to rest from his labors. Parfyon gritted his teeth.

"No, Zmei! Are you mad? I have come too far for anything but the complete victory."

Zmei faded into the darkness. Only his outline continued to shimmer with red fire. "You will regret this. As shall I."

CHAPTER 45
BATTLE

Antomír stood behind the rows of banner-bearers and watched as the surface of the Vasyllia River burned with white fire, ignited by the monks of Raven's Bane.

"Olgerd will not come back, will he?" Antomír said aloud, partly to distract himself from the coming battle.

Veles, standing at his right, grunted. When Antomír turned to him, he saw that his old bodyguard's beard was wet with tears.

"It is the sign," said Veles in a ragged voice. "The white fire. They have done what they were sent to do. The knyaz of Nebesta must have decided to accept our invitation to the feast of slaughter."

Antomír's heart skipped two beats, then reignited, beating like a mad blacksmith at his forge. It was time.

A charge of energy passed through the bear riders and the monks. They formed ranks behind Antomír without prompting, and by the time he had turned around to face them, they were in position—several thousand of the most efficient killers this world had ever known.

"Highness," said a raspy voice among the monks in the front lines, robed and hooded as always. "May I approach?"

Antomír beckoned him nearer. The monk bent the knee before him, then uncovered his head. He was not much older than Antomír himself, though his olive skin and dark hair were a study in contrast to Antomír's typical Vasylli hair and skin.

"Lord Antomír, my name is Ratmir. I am the youngest of the monks of

Raven's Bane, but they have chosen me to speak for them. They say I talk too much as it is, so I may as well be useful." His mischievous smile endeared Antomír to him immediately. "Highness, you know what we face. Not merely men and steel, but the old powers of the earth. The giants will come at us first in serpent form, I believe, no longer content to wait in the shadows."

"Yes, I can understand that desire," said Antomír. "What do you suggest?"

"I think, Highness, that you cannot fail to recognize certain patterns in events. These so-called coincidences contain special blessings of the Heights to those who pay attention. We, the elite warriors of Raven's Bane, are fifteen."

Antomír understood. "And the giants are also fifteen."

Ratmir inclined his head. "We would engage them in direct battle, by your blessing, Dar of Vasyllia."

"You will not survive," said Antomír, his voice breaking. He could not bear the thought of losing his best even before the heat of the battle.

"No, I dare say not. But then, we do not live for this world. Everything we do is a preparation for the passage." The words were brave, but the olive face turned a shade whiter, and there was a quiver in the voice. *Even the monk fears death*, thought Antomír. At least before the war-wind seizes him.

"Lord?" prompted Veles, his shoulders tense.

"Yes," said Antomír, "it is fitting."

Veles relaxed into a grim smile. As Ratmir rose, the monks all uncovered their heads and unsheathed their swords. They raised them, hilt-first, toward Antomír, asking for his blessing. Antomír raised both hands and bowed his head.

"Thank you, my Dar," said Ratmir, his own voice thick with emotion. Then his eyes softened as all sound seemed to cease in the moment just before he began to sing. The noise cut through Antomír—intense and searing.

That young warrior sings his own funeral dirge, thought Antomír.

The other monks picked up the chant—an ancient, plangent melody. The high voices lamented at the limit of their range, while the low basses intoned a single note, invoking an image of an endless plain of grass-swept earth in Antomír's mind. Then Ratmir let his voice loose above the other high voices—a chilling keening in that same ancient language of the children of the Priest-King. It was like the soaring of an albatross over endless waves—Ratmir was the bird, and the other singers were the depths of ocean below him that pulled at him, but could never pull him in. In that tension, the music was born, and it was like light and fire and flowing water all in one. Then, Ratmir's voice shifted into accented old Vasylli, and Antomír recognized the words.

"The child-king stood on battlefield bare
Arrayed against a myriad strong.
Alone he battled while the day waxed fair,
Until he heard death's final song."

Antomír's tears gathered as he remembered the bear riders who had died for him, but Ratmir had not finished.

"Yet he was not alone that day,
For unexpected aid was sent.
And others rushed to take death's way,
And fate's decree to shreds was rent."

Ratmir finished, and the entire army of warriors stood silent, allowing the echoes of the song to wash over them. When nothing remained but the soft lapping of the white flames on the river, Antomír stood on his knees and raised both hands.

"O Silent Heights!" he intoned. "Beloved Adonais! If ever Vasylli have done aught that is virtuous or pleasing in your sight, let it be remembered today. May I and my bear riders labor in dearth for a hundred years, but let your extraordinary grace descend on these, your servants, the warriors of Raven's Bane. They go to fight the demons of old, whose power is as great as the earth is wide. But they are your warriors, Adonais! Be their fighting hand. Direct their blows! Vanquish those who would take the grace of the earth and turn it to the darkest of magic."

He stood and unsheathed his sword. The sun rose behind him, and he saw it reflected in the eyes of those watching him, as they ignited with the war-wind.

"Go, and pave our way home, my brothers."

The alarm horns sounded. Parfyon jumped up, his sword already in his hand. He thrust his helmet on his head and ran outside his tent. It was still dark, except for the Vasyllia River below them. The river was on fire with white flames. Parfyon closed his eyes and extended his awareness outward, toward the line of fire. But he could not pass the line with his senses.

Zmei materialized in a blaze of red flame near him.

"Last chance, Parfyon. Will you consider saving all these men's lives? Will you parley with Antomír?"

Parfyon spit on the ground. "I will not."

Zmei laughed at Parfyon. "You may have tasted of our power, little man, but don't think that you will ever be able to do anything without us. You think there is no price to pay for everything you have received and will yet receive?"

"I have paid enough!" screamed Parfyon.

Zmei looked away and shook his head.

"My brothers and I will go ahead."

Parfyon nodded at the giant.

As though that were the cue, all of Zmei's brothers materialized in blazes of red fire, all in their serpent forms. They were so fast that they looked like a river of fire flowing down the mountain. Before Parfyon could even count to ten, they stood in a single line before the near bank of the river of white fire. From the midst of the fire came fifteen hooded figures. Compared to the giants, they looked like ants, but even from this distance, the glint of their swords caught the light of the white fire. Then, each one of the fifteen caught fire. White fire.

They raised their swords as one man and ran at the serpent-giants.

"Lord, what sort of contest have we entered?" Bragadun gaped at Parfyon's side.

"One that we will win, Bragadun."

"Can we win this, Veles?" Antomír asked as he watched the monks walk on the flame-ridden water as though it were a grassy knoll. "We have gambled a great deal on this battle. Neither side has the advantage here. Why did we not lay more traps for Parfyon? Attack them in smaller skirmishes along the mountain passes?"

Veles took Antomír by the shoulders and shook him, much more gently than he would have on Ghavan. His eyes were hard. Antomír knew that look. He had used to call it "the old hag lecture face."

But rather than say anything, Veles merely enfolded Antomír in an embrace, then fell on one knee before him and kissed his right hand.

"Whatever they all say, you are my Dar now. Do not let yourself be swayed by doubt. You are our sun, our beacon of grace. Lead us—"

"Veles!" Antomír interrupted. "Look at that!"

All around him, the bear riders huddled together in shock and amazement. A huge horseman, twenty times the size of the giants, passed over the high summits ahead of them. His bulk filled half the sky. His raiment was red-gold, his hair was light, and his eyes were stars. As he passed, he stopped in the exact center of the sky and turned. The sun, rising in his wake, stopped in confusion.

"The horseman of the dawn," whispered Veles, amazed. "He's looking at you, Antomír." In the light of the rider, Antomír clearly saw Veles's wings of fire extend up and outward, like a shadow of the great warrior who faced them.

The horseman bowed, and the army of bear riders uttered a collective gasp. Whispers ran back and forth like mice in a winter storeroom.

"Omen!" They said. "Good omen!"

Antomír strapped on his helmet and went to find his bear.

For a moment, Parfyon forgot everything—his pain, his anger at the giants, his insistent drive to acquire power—in the wonder. The horseman of the dawn was a legend, a story. And yet, he bowed in deference to their enemy. It was the ultimate bad omen for him. In all the old stories, if the horseman of dawn appeared before battle, he always chose the winner. The assembled lines of bowmen were frozen in the same wonder. Their bowed sagged, their arrows drooped. No one stood at the ready. Some of the sword-and-shielders had even dropped their shields.

Parfyon gritted his teeth and stared at the two lines—red and white, serpents and hooded warriors.

"Lord! Look!"

Air hissed through Parfyon's lungs as he watched the serpents flap their wings and rise above the ground. Instead of flying at the enemy, the flew up and up, into the sky above. Each one of them spun around themselves as they flew, until each was a small, red sun spinning ever higher into the clouds. *The bastards are abandoning us*, he thought. His blood boiled inside him.

"Archers! On my mark! Damn the serpent-giants. This is *our* day!"

Parfyon's arm burned with pain, as though his blood were warmed over a fire. He looked at his new arm, and it was livid. The hairs stood extended and began to smoke.

No!

"Bragadun..."

His left eyelid twitched, then shuddered. A poker of fire seemed to grow from the back of his head, trying to come out of his eye.

No! No! No!

"Stop!" Parfyon screamed, but it was too late. His arm was burning, and he felt the warm blood streaming down his face from his left eye. "No!!!"

"Oh, by all the...My Lord, your... your..." Bragadun's face was grey, his expression horrified.

The pain crested and began to recede. Through the blurring in his one good eye, Parfyon saw the burnt stump where his right arm had been. *Not again*, he thought, and even through the pain, he couldn't help but chuckle at the absurdity of it all. It was not enough for Parfyon of Nebesta to lose his right arm and his left eye. No, for him fate had chosen a special end. He was to lose them twice!

Parfyon laughed and laughed and laughed.

The white fire on the river faded and dissipated with a breath of wind. Antomír strained to see the field of death. Every monk still stood, though no longer wreathed in white flame. But there was no sign of the serpents.

"Highness," said Severuk. "Look up!"

Fifteen small suns receded into the eternal blue of the sky. The giants had abandoned their allies.

"Go," said Antomír. "Sound the attack. Now!"

At Severuk's command, previously built pontoons were quickly laid along the river. As soon as the pontoons were in place, the banners crossed the waters and arranged themselves in a line along the river.

The monks waited for them, their swords bared and their faces intent.

"Sound the advance," called Antomír, still amazed at the sight of so many men.

As the oxhorns blared, he turned to Veles and embraced him. Then he mounted his bear and charged.

The arrows fell thick and fast among them, taking down many. But that only seemed to make the monks run faster, and some of them had begun to laugh as they ran. The bear riders sang their death song, and their bears all bellowed, making the earth shudder. The arrows fell again. Gaps began to appear in the lines, but they only came on and on.

Then the Nebesti did something Antomír had never seen before. They formed a wall of shields, all across the front ranks.

The monks crashed into the wall like a wave against a cliff. The wall held. The first wave of bear riders charged in. The wall bent but held. Antomír's own line was almost there. He crouched down and braced for the impact.

The wall held, but as he crashed it, he could feel it splinter. He stood on his bear's back and launched himself over the shield wall. He heard the cheers behind him as he fell on a mass of men.

The momentary confusion saved his life, as he hacked down three men, giving himself some breathing space. But his mad leap had done its trick. The wall broke behind him, and monks and bear riders poured in. They slaughtered the sword-and-shielders who stood holding the wall and the archers behind it.

When Antomír stopped to breathe, he saw that they had mowed down the front lines of Nebesti completely. Ahead of them, up an incline toward the pass road, the main force of the Nebesti army stood. They did not yet charge. They did not seem to want to charge. Antomír realized his chance.

"Veles!" He turned around, hoping to see his guardian near him. He almost didn't recognize Veles, his eyes were so wild, his face so spattered with gore. "Veles, come back to me!"

Slowly, the berserker eyes calmed, and Antomír's old friend stood before him again.

"Veles, take three of our best riders and hoist the white banner. Go to the Nebesti. I want to parley."

Two hours later, Antomír, Veles, and an honor guard of ten monks stood on the Nebesti side before a man who had been Knyaz Parfyon. But he was something else now.

His hair was completely white, his back had twisted and bent, and his right arm was a burnt cinder. His eyes—those bright, angry eyes that had so impressed and awed Antomír—were lumps of white coal, bereft of fire. He had been emptied.

"Well, I'm listening," he cackled, barely able to wheeze that much before the coughing took over again.

"My Lord," said Antomír. "You are not well. Will you not reconsider?"

"What are the terms of surrender?" This was not Parfyon, but a young voyevoda at his side. Parfyon looked up at him with disgust but seemed too tired to do anything else.

"Leave Vasyllia. Return to your New Nebesta. Live with your wives and children. And have your own knyaz."

The voyevoda visibly twitched. The last part he had not expected, evidently.

"I, the future Dar of Vasyllia, will not seek dominion over the other cities. Not while my own domain sickens and dies. It is my fervent hope to restore the old order, but I will not insist upon it. You may go in peace, and there will be no retribution."

"You cannot…" Parfyon coughed blood into his palm, then looked at it with surprise, as though he did not understand what it was. "We will never again bow… Ours will be the Mother of Cities!"

"Peace, Lord." The young voyevoda put a tentative hand on Parfyon's shoulder. "You are not well. I will take it upon myself to decide, while you recuperate."

"Bragadun, do not…" But he could not finish. The coughing took him, and when it finished, he doubled over on the ground, apparently unconscious.

Bragadun nodded at the other Nebesti, and they lifted Parfyon and took him to the back lines gently, as though he were an old man, as indeed he looked to have become.

"You are an uncommon man," said Bragadun, assessing Antomír. "I do not say this with any ill intent. I have great respect for what you have done. But will you not heed a last bit of advice? Abandon your claim to Vasyllia. Let it rot, let it consume itself. Come to our city. I believe you would have a fair chance of claiming a Veche of Choosing for yourself. As you see, we have lost our knyaz."

Antomír was struck dumb. For a brief moment, he saw that Nebesti and Vasylli could perhaps coexist in a new world, free from any taint of the Raven. But while that disease in Vasyllia persisted, every relationship between man and man, city and city, prince and prince would sour. Nothing other than Internecine War was possible while the Raven still feasted in Vasyllia.

"I honor you, Bragadun. I know that Veches are fickle and dangerous affairs. But I wish you luck. I hope Nebesta will choose you for her next knyaz. Then perhaps we will have the good fortune of feasting at the same table. I hear the mead is unparalleled in Nebesta."

***

It took most of the rest of the day for Nebesta's army to leave the valley and begin crossing the Pass of Ardovían. During that time, the bear riders rested. Antomír, however, did not move from his position at the bank of the river. He would not move until the very last Nebesti had crested the high pass, visible above them like a jaw with two broken front teeth.

"The real battle is still ahead," said Veles as the last Nebesti banner passed out of sight. "After today, any devilry is possible from our brothers, the Vasylli. You need to rest. Who knows? The first battle may be tomorrow."

"I am tired," said Antomír. It was as if the speaking of those words gave his body permission to lessen its vigil. He almost crumpled into a heap right there, on the spot.

"Easy, my Lord," said Veles, chuckling. "Let me help you back. I know you'll have a lecture ready for me tomorrow, but I still had the men pitch your royal pavilion."

Antomír was ready to lecture him then and there, but his mind gave out. There was nothing there but pudding.

"Thank you," he managed, barely slurring the words out.

He was asleep even before Veles covered him with a blanket. When he was jolted awake, what seemed to be only a minute later, he was annoyed, but Gamayun had taken to wakening him so often that he was almost used to it by now.

But it was not Gamayun. It was Veles.

"Up, sire. Up! Battle calls again." His eyes danced with the war-wind.

Antomír barely managed to put on his armor. His sword was unwieldy in his hand, and his vision blurred. Even sound came in waves, like he was drunk or taken with some sickness of the brain. When he came out, the camp was in confusion. It was deep night, but torchlight was everywhere. Horsemen ran to and fro, whooping as they hacked and charged at the bear riders, who found themselves at the receiving end of a surprise attack. Veles stood near him, his mace ready.

"Who is it, Veles?"

"Vasylli, I think. Foolish. We should have expected…"

A scream ripped the air in pieces. Veles doubled over with pain. Antomír's chest felt cloven in two at the sound. He found it impossible to breathe. His sword-arm moved of its own accord. It raised his sword above his head.

No…No!

Antomír's sword arm, outside of his control, hacked at the doubled-over figure of Veles. He felt flesh and bone under the slash. Veles fell and screamed.

No…No…No!

Antomír's feet took him into the maelstrom of men, then away from them, toward an unnaturally thick and tall column of smoke. It was clearly not natural. Antomír fought with everything he had left, but his body didn't listen to him.

Ahead of him, he saw three men, hooded and in black. They smelled terrible—something cloying and sweet, like rot.

Antomír did not have time to process that information. He ran to them, not able to control his movements, and they grabbed his arms and legs and tied them with the swiftness of professional slavers. Something dark obscured his vision, and when he tried to cry out for help, he breathed in bits of something rough like rope, and it choked him.

"None of that," said a voice with a surprisingly refined accent. "No one will hear you. No one will help you. Not ever again. I hope you've enjoyed your triumph."

Iron hands raised him onto the back of a horse. He struggled, but his bonds only tightened with every movement. He breathed in against the panic, and let the air out slowly, forcing his heart to beat at a manageable pace. He suddenly felt unbearably sleepy.

Antomír smelled roses. His left hand was in cool water. He snapped awake.

Rose petals fell on his upturned face. Giant trees seemed to regard him with curiosity. A river gurgled to his left. Antomír sat up, bewildered. What had happened to the battle? Where was he?

"It's time, my Antomír," said Gamayun in his head.

He looked up to see a shriveled figure approaching him. It was pitiful, like a hobbled old man with a disease. But then it looked at Antomír, and its eyes were like two windows into the land of the dead. Antomír stiffened and tried to scramble to his feet, but Gamayun reasserted control over him, and he sat down again, pushed against the trunk of one of the cherries. He spat in the direction of the creature.

"A bit of fire, eh?" It wheezed. "Good. Young and strong by the looks of it. You'll make me a fitting vessel."

Antomír pushed with all his remaining strength, but his hand moved only an inch. It grazed something hard and sharp. Out of the corner of his eye, he saw his fingers touching a knife-long rock amid the pebbles lining the riverbank. As the sweat beaded his upper lip and brow, he arduously twisted his right hand until the sharp tip pointed upward.

He thought of Khaidu, that strangely attractive Gumira with her fiery eyes. He would never speak to her again. That thought, more than any of the recent troubles, left him empty with sadness. But there was nothing to be done about it. Perhaps they would meet again in some other Realm, some other life.

"Gamayun," he said, forcing the word out. "I want to be myself when he comes for me. It is too late to fight back. I will accept it."

For a moment, nothing happened. Then, he felt her hold on him loosen.

His muscles were his own. His body was his own. His tongue was his to command.

"Burn in eternal fires, Raven," he said and fell onto the exposed tip of the rock. He felt it go deep and true.

Gamayun screamed in his head.

CHAPTER 46
INTO VASYLLIA MOUNTAIN

It seemed as though many years passed without anything happening. Then, a barely-heard scratch. Then, another one. Without warning, the chains suspending Sabíana in mid-air began to lower. Finally, with a soft thud, she landed on hard ground. She saw a very dirty, emaciated man with rope-like muscle in his half-uncovered arms. The details of his face were hidden by the torchlight on the wall behind him. He tore open Sabíana's cage and pulled her unresponsive body onto his chest. As soon as he carried her past the light of the torches, she gasped.

"No! No, no, it can't be. No!"

"Yes," said the man, his voice cracking and hoarse, "I've come back for you, my love."

Just behind him, the darkness shifted. Aglaia the wolf materialized out of the shadows and padded toward Khaidu.

"Well, you didn't expect me to just leave you to your own devices, did you?" asked Aglaia, smiling wolfishly. "Admit it, you can't do without me."

Suddenly, the tower was bathed in lightning-white radiance. Something winged and jewel-toned flew in the space above their heads.

"Come," said the Sirin, "we may be already too late."

Voran sat down on the bare stone of the cave, exhausted nearly to death. He still held Sabíana in his arms. All that day, their small company, led by Lyna and the light she scattered around her in waves, traveled deeper and deeper into Vasyllia Mountain through undisturbed caverns and tunnels. But the waves of Lyna's light faded as they went, until she was barely more than a reflection. Finally, they reached a cave large enough to house an army, or so Voran suspected in Lyna's dim light. As soon as they stopped, Aglaia, Khaidu, and the one they called Kipchak fell asleep.

Voran, his arms twitching with the strain, placed Sabíana against the rock wall. She was sleeping like a child.

You are still so beautiful, my love. The thought came unbidden, even though his rational mind told him she was anything but beautiful—her hair a matted mass of tangles, her face a mask of pain, her skin stretched and dry. She looked exhausted half to death. But she was still beautiful, and he loved her.

She stirred and opened her eyes. There, her beauty still remained, though as the reflection of the sun in a puddle of muddy water. Her eyes were still as large and rheumy and cow-brown as they had been twenty years ago.

"You took a long time coming back, my love," she said, a smile tugging at the corner of her mouth.

He said nothing, though his eyes never left her face. The words he wanted to say were like a full-term unborn child in his heart, not quite ready to come out. He hesitated, afraid of the pain, even though he knew that joy would follow.

"I have been so foolish, my love. I should have turned the world inside out to come back to you."

"Voran," she said, her real self trying to peck its way out of the shell of her sick, dying self, "do you know? I feel like I last saw you yesterday. But I also feel like I haven't seen you in a hundred years. How can both be true?" And she laughed, a silvery sound that seemed to increase the light of Lyna the Sirin.

Voran picked Sabíana up again, gently, and embraced her. She offered neither resistance nor encouragement with her body, though he sensed her need for this intimacy. He kissed her on the lips, three times.

Her tears gathered.

"I don't know how this will end, my love," he said. "But I do not think that we go to the end of our story. Something awful is about to happen, but if we come through it, I think there is a place for us somewhere to be quietly and completely together."

"If you believe that," she said, as a tear dropped from each eye, "then you are a greater fool than I thought."

Voran laughed and embraced her. "There's the girl I missed," he whispered. She melted into his embrace, and he realized with joy that she had more capacity for movement than he expected.

They remained intertwined for an eternity. The silence around them was only broken by the wheezing breath of the sleeping Aglaia and the short snores of little Khaidu.

"The testing will be horrible, I fear," said Lyna, alighting on the ground next to them without preamble. "Voran, I will go with you, onward until the end, as will all those who love you. But you must know. There is something so twisted, so wrong down there, that I am already losing my sight of the Heights. You can see it, can you not?"

"Your light," Sabíana said. "It's diminished."

Lyna inclined her head. "If we go much further, I may become entrenched in this level, stuck, unable to return to my sisters in the Heights."

"Lyna, please don't even think—" Voran began.

"It is not your choice to make, my falcon," said Lyna with a sad smile. "I make it willingly. It is my hope to sway Adonais by my sacrifice. I will brave death itself if there were a chance to restore Vasyllia."

Voran's heart surged at the thought. "As would I."

※

Something smelled so foul that Khaidu was wretched out of her sleep.

"Where is that smell coming from?" she asked Aglaia, who sat on her rump, breathing fast with her tongue lolling out.

"I think it's the far-right tunnel," said Aglaia.

"Please don't let that one be our road," Khaidu muttered to herself. But she knew it would be that one, and her absolute certainty made her irritable.

"Why are we even here, anyway?" In spite of herself, she could feel the pout forming itself around her lips.

For a moment, Aglaia had a too-human expression of mawkish sentiment in her wolf-face. "It is so pleasant to hear you so speak so clearly, wolfling."

Khaidu sighed *very* audibly, bringing Aglaia back from her pleasant reverie.

"Why are we here, you ask? Didn't I tell you? We are going to the Garden in the Heart of the World."

"What?!" Khaidu exclaimed.

THE HEART OF THE WORLD

She couldn't help it. It exploded out of her. But the sound of her cry echoed along the walls and down into every conceivable crevasse of this endless mountain.

Voran turned at her with fire in his eyes. Sabíana had more white than brown in her eyes. Even Lyna, though her expression was rarely anything but somber, looked ready to rain fire down at her from the Heights.

"I'm..." she began to apologize, but suddenly all she wanted to do was sing and dance and prance about like a fawn on a spring morning. "Don't you understand anything? You idiots!"

That checked their anger a bit. Good.

"The Garden in the Heart of the World! Sabíana, surely you remember."

Sabíana turned white, then red, then white again, in such quick, comic succession that Khaidu nearly burst into laughter. "By all that is...Khaidu, are you sure?"

"Yes! You are, and always have been, the Queen Who Walks the Skies. I knew it-I knew it-I knew-it! And you are leading us all to him."

"Him? Who is she talking about?" asked Voran.

"It's an old legend the Gumiren tell," said Sabíana. "A great queen who will take the Gumiren to a mountain city, where they will find the way to—"

"The Unknown Father!" interrupted Khaidu. "He who will show the Gumiren...no, not just the Gumiren—all people! —the right way to live."

"You stupid child!" screamed Kipchak. "You don't believe in all that nonsense? Isn't it enough? All that the Dark Father did? You still seek something sublime in this world of murder?"

The cave fell silent.

"Lyna," said Voran, deciding to ignore Kipchak for the moment, "maybe you can explain to Khaidu that there is no place higher than Aer, that no one supersedes the Creator and Lord Adonais..."

"Peace, Voran," said Lyna, and her eyes were shining. "We Sirin have long waited for this child. For the one who will find the Unknown Father."

Voran was struck dumb, as indeed were Sabíana and Aglaia.

"Yes, my falcon," continued the Sirin. "Even we do not know all the mysteries of the Heights. But among the eldest of our sisters there has always been a rumor that Adonais has a father. And that coming to know this father will reveal mysteries and realities that no race has yet tasted of. The ultimate purpose of all creation—from the fiery Palymi all the way to smallest worm that crawls in the dirt. How else do you think the Raven managed to convince all those Gumiren to follow him across the lands to some country in the mountains they had never heard of? Wealth and power, certainly, but there was more. He knew that of all the races, the Gumiren kept the memory of the Unknown Father the most fervently. He used them, but in that manipulation, he was revealing his own need."

"What? Are you saying the Raven seeks this Unknown Father as well?" asked Aglaia.

"No creature can fail to seek him," said Khaidu, suddenly inspired. "Every creature yearns for the place of its birth. And the birth of life is in the Unknown Father. Even as the Dark Father seeks for immortality, he reaches, unwittingly, for the greater purpose. He grasps at what he does not understand. Not knowing him, he thinks to usurp his place. Isn't that right, Lyna?"

Voran's eyes widened as he seemed to understand. "Yes, I see it now. His endless need for a form is actually the thirst for true existence. The same thirst we all have, only our bodies provide enough diversion for us to forget about it. But the Raven has become so twisted by his hunger that he will never seek it in the right place."

"And he will devour the whole world before he finds it," said Sabíana, "all the worlds, in his vain quest for immortality. Even if he were to become immortal, he would never find what he seeks. In the end, were he to remain the last living thing in all the world, he would eat himself."

"Oh, by the endless grasses," said Khaidu. "Why are we sitting here? We need to get to the Garden!"

Kipchak laughed, but the sound of it was as hollow as the cave.

Lyna chose the passage with the terrible smell.

Soon, the source of the smell became clear. Every few hundred feet, a huge, mangled monster lay amid piles of stones. Each was more horrifying than the next, nothing like Khaidu had ever seen.

"Changers," said Aglaia, as if that explained everything.

"But why would the Raven's own creatures be lying here, dead?" asked Sabíana. Khaidu's heart leapt to see that she embraced Voran's neck with arms that actually moved.

"Look at them," said Voran. "Look at how...desiccated they are. What does it remind you of?" This he asked of Aglaia. She nodded.

"Something like the blood magic of the giants. The Raven was using his own creatures to open the ways to the Garden."

"I think you are right, Aglaia," said Lyna, who looked even darker and paler. "But there are ancient wards, protections. Otherwise any curious princess might stumble into it. To break such old magic, you need..."

"Yes, well, I think we get the picture," said Aglaia, as if she were anxious to avoid the subject for the sake of Khaidu's innocent ears. Khaidu smiled. It was good to be pampered by a mother again.

They saw more than a hundred such monsters in the tunnels. With every monster they passed, Lyna faded a touch more. Soon she would fade completely, and how would they see their path then? Would they be forced to grope forward on their knees with outstretched hands until they collapsed from hunger and exhaustion? What a horrifying death! It would be like being buried alive. Khaidu shuddered and gripped Aglaia's thick nape even harder.

"Lyna," said Voran, "you must go back. What possible good can there come of you fading like this? Go back and intercede for us at the court of the Heights of Aer before it is too late."

"I will not leave you," said the Sirin, in a voice as human as Sabíana's. "I saw...in shadow...what awaits you, my falcon. I fear I will be of no help to you, not in the sense of any powers. But I will give you my love. As will all of us, I am sure of it."

The last dead changer was a horrifying lion-man creature, reduced to little more than fur and bones. He lay before a cave opening into darkness even deeper than the already lightless gloom of the interior of Vasyllia Mountain. Khaidu's heart began to beat like a hammer on an anvil, and she found it hard to breathe.

As they passed the monster, Lyna's light flickered and died.

"It's there," said Voran. "Just a little further ahead. I'm sure of it. Forward..."

The darkness opened before them like a door into another world. One moment, they were in blackness, the next, light blinded them, flooding in from all sides. Khaidu fell off Aglaia onto soft moss. She buried her face in it. It smelled slightly sweet and pleasantly musty, and the smell suffused her with a soft calm. This was a good place, she felt it down to the marrow of her bones.

A tremor shook the earth, and thunder rumbled behind them. Khaidu looked back and realized her eyes had already adjusted. The door through which they had entered was now a pile of fallen rock. No door to be seen, only a wall of stone that reached to the sky. She could not see where it ended.

"There's no going back that way," she said.

"Well, there's no need to be so painfully obvious about it," complained Aglaia.

"Where's Kipchak?" asked Aglaia.

"Gone back to her masters, I imagine," said Aglaia. "To tell them of the entrance to the Garden. Much good it will do her."

Even though it didn't surprise Khaidu, she was still saddened that her own countrywoman could prove to be so fickle.

"Look," said Sabíana, her eyes intent on what lay ahead.

Khaidu turned. Before them, not one hundred yards away, was something that was definitely not a garden. It was a forest of the tallest trees she had ever seen. They were so monumental that the bottom branches only began at the same height where most trees ended. They had dark red bark, striated and supple. Even from here, the cool scent of their needles wafted gently on a breeze so soft it was like the breath of a mother on her child's face as it nursed. Khaidu had an unexpected desire to weep.

"Forward," said Voran. His face was white with fear, and his hands shook at his sides.

CHAPTER 47
THE GARDEN

Voran walked through the line of trees first. He stopped.

The sounds had changed. In the bowels of Vasyllia, whispers bounced and cavorted and danced. Here, even shouts tiptoed. His footfalls were inaudible. The ground was carpeted in pillows of red needles, cushioning every step pleasantly. The light filtered through the trees, but not in rays and sheets as in normal forests. Here, the light spread in waves, giving the impression that the entire forest was underwater. Voran was mystified by it, but then he looked up. The trees—which at ground level seemed immovable as marble columns—gently swayed, but only at their very tips, changing the quality of the light with every slight sway.

Underneath these behemoth red-barks, smaller furs, maples, and alders reached toward the sparse light. Between them, spider webs the size of tapestries hung, bejeweled with dew. The spiders reclining in their centers were spattered with color. Rivulets ran between the trees, and the water was scented.

Voran remembered to breathe.

They approached a single red-bark, slightly set off from the rest. When they were close enough to see the crown, Voran heard Khaidu gasping. She had her head craned so far back, it looked like she might hurt her neck.

"It's not...possible!"

The tufts of needles were unlike any other conifers Voran had seen. They looked like green clouds floating about a red tower. Looking at them for too long made him dizzy.

Everywhere, animals came out of hiding. Large red squirrels with tufted ears stopped in front of Voran, inquisitive, before rushing off again. Birdsong was ever-present, so that it seemed to him that he was breathing it in and out.

Ahead of them and slightly to the right, five boles grew up and slightly bowed from a single, huge root. It looked like a crown sitting on the head of Mother Earth, its tips reaching up beyond the gathering clouds. Another such crown lay twenty paces farther, then another, then another. Then Voran realized they were not arranged in a line, but in a circle.

"The center!" said Aglaia, a little too loudly.

Voran had not seen it until then, though how he could have missed it, he didn't know. Three cherry trees with pink petals crowned a tall cone of rock. The trees were on fire, yet they were not consumed. From the root of that cone, a foaming fountainhead bubbled into a river, gathering strength as it fell down a slight incline to their right. Two of the cherry trees shed their petals at an alarming rate. It looked like the trees wept blood into the water. There were so many petals that the water at the source looked not like water, but like fire. The third tree bore a single red-gold fruit that shimmered in the dappled light as it hung over the river.

"Welcome," said a voice behind them. They turned, and it was as though the grove of trees parted. Coming at them, impossibly large, was a warrior. He wore silver chainmail adorned with a red-gold chestplate. The sun shone from the center of that breastplate. His helm's peak erupted into grey-blue hair that reached down to his waist. His beard and hair were grey, but he walked with the strength of a man in his prime. His helm had no noseguard, and his eyes glowed like beacon towers. A red cape flowed from his shoulders, on which also hung a jeweled belt and scabbard. The sword on his hip was encrusted with jewels the size of small animals. They throbbed with their own life, as though blood flowed through their veins together with fire.

Voran fell on his knees. He knew the warrior-god. He had waited for him his entire life.

"You have come at last," said the warrior in a booming voice that was at the same time kind, gentle, caressing. "Voran, my warrior and my healer, welcome. Here, you may forget all your troubles and rest."

"My Adonais..." whispered Lyna, whose own resurgent light was invisible in the light of the helmed god.

"Impossible," whispered Sabíana.

"Why not, my love?" said Voran, unable to tear his eyes away from the regal figure. "It makes sense. Why wouldn't Adonais come to the Heart of the World at the final hour? Perhaps this is a kind of ante-room to the Heights."

"But it's ... underground!"

Voran chuckled, remembering his conversations with Tarin about the analogy of the ever-increasing onion, so many years ago.

The warrior was close enough that he now dominated the skyline. Even the trees could not reach his height.

"But before you rest, my children," he said, "There is one final ordeal. One final act of trust. We must put the world to right. We must make a worthy adversary for the Raven."

He pointed at the trees and the fountainhead.

Voran turned and saw an unknown young man sitting, seemingly asleep, leaning against the cone of rock. His face was strangely familiar. Like Mirnían, but subtly different. He recognized shades of Lebía, his sister, in that face. So, this was young Antomír. He had grown much in the last ten years. But what was he doing in the Garden?

"There is the future Dar of Vasyllia. My chosen one," said Adonais. "But he is wounded."

Voran now saw that blood streamed out of a wound in his chest, mingling with the petals and the fountainhead of Living Water.

"Voran, my Healer," said Adonais. The voice seemed to come from the earth itself, from the leaves, from the air. "Your final task. You must take the fruit from the tree, you must give it to Antomír. You must heal him."

"But Lord!" Sabíana said. "The lifeblood of the worlds! It will cease flowing."

"The time has come for Vasyllia to die," he said. "Too many have been its sins. Raven's Bane will be the new Garden, the new source for the lifeblood of the Realms. But first, we must heal the only heir of Cassían capable of killing the Raven. Hurry, before the Raven comes to this place and takes it for himself! He is near, very near."

A sense of intense urgency overtook Voran, and he stumbled forward, toward the tree and toward the figure of Antomír half-sitting, half-lying by the waters. He saw Lyna fluttering by his side. She had a strange expression on her face, as though she were not quite aware of her surroundings. As though she were trapped in sleep, but still moving. She didn't look at him.

"Voran!" called Khaidu. "Wait. Something is wrong."

"My son," said Aglaia, "I would listen to the little wolf-child, if I were you."

"Do not tarry, my healer!" said Adonais, more commanding this time. "The Raven is near. Very near!"

Voran walked closer to Antomír but had to stop. Memories inundated him. Mirnían's bloody body on the top of a mountain. Lebía's crying eyes as she spoke to him for the last time, ten years ago. Both were there, in this boy, who looked so young, and yet, even in sleep, his face was pained and tense.

Something wasn't right. Voran couldn't put his finger on it. There was a half-shimmering quality to Antomír sitting there by the tree. Almost as if he wasn't quite there. Voran stood at the bank of the lifeblood of the Realms and hesitated. He would have to walk through the water to reach Antomír. Could he simply…wade through these hallowed waters?

"Voran, please," said Khaidu, and there was something pained in her voice. He didn't want to turn around to look at her.

"Go, my healer!" boomed Adonais. "Walk through the water. It is my command."

Voran obeyed. The water burned him as he entered it. But unlike the river of fire near Tarin's hut, this felt immediately wrong, so profoundly in violation of all the laws of the Realms, that he was sure he would be consumed in a moment. But no. Adonais had commanded him. Even if it meant being burned to death, he would do it.

"My love!" Sabíana called, as though feeling his pain. He refused to turn around. He would see this to the end.

"Voran!" screamed Khaidu, and she was clearly in intense pain. He turned around, in spite of himself. She held her head in her hands, and her eyes were bloodshot. Aglaia twitched in anticipation near Khaidu, whining. She looked torn between protection for her new charge, and a desire to come charging to Voran to save him. "Voran, listen to me! That is not Adonais. That is the Raven!"

Khaidu gasped for breath. The jagged distortion of reality twisted her from the inside. This was far worse than any sympathy with beast or human. For a moment, she saw the thoughts of that monster that called itself Adonais.

She saw a prison. Withered hands being held up by rusty chains. A curious princess with a cup of water in her hands, offering. A tree on top of a mountain, frothing with flowers. Voran, a young version of Voran, hacking at a tree that bled from every stroke of his sword. Every strike of that blade sent jagged waves of hatred through her body. Not her hatred. Adonais's hatred. Then the scene shifted back into this garden, but at a different angle. She saw

Voran picking the fruit, squeezing it. Blood poured out and into the open maw of Antomír, who was not Antomír at all, but a hybrid creature with black wings and a beak instead of a nose. As he poured the lifeblood into the creature's mouth, Khaidu felt a sense of balance, a sense of justice restored. But it was wrong, not justice. That was a future that must never happen.

"Voran, that is the Raven!" The words came out of Khaidu out of some place beyond thought. She was prophesying, and everyone held still to hear her words: "You chopped down the tree that wept Living Water. You escaped the invasion. You bear the bond of the Sirin. You have the Word imprinted on your heart. You are a living symbol of the Raven's futility. Of course, he wants *you* to be the one responsible for the death of the Realms. You must not take the last fruit!"

"Blasphemy!" boomed Adonais, and lightning bolts flew out of his beacon-eyes, striking Aglaia under Khaidu. Khaidu fell over, and her muscles froze up in rictus pain. Aglaia lay next to her, unmoving. Khaidu writhed in pain, but her mind was still clear, and she still felt the thrumming thoughts of the monster. Voran looked at her, and she pitied him. He was being torn apart from the inside.

Then, the images came again, thrust on her like a barrage of blows to her body and mind.

A temple under the open sky. Worshipers on their knees. An altar with a deer offered on it. Laughter, cold and sarcastic, laced with a drunken hunger to dominate, to consume, to feast.

"There is no Adonais, can't you see?" whispered Khaidu through her pain. "He has always been the Raven. The Raven's worst delusion. His best trick. He has fooled you Vasylli. Adonais is not the creator. Adonais is the Raven."

Lightning struck her again and continued to dance over her smoking body. The fit took her, and she lost consciousness.

For a moment, Voran stood dumbstruck. What did she mean, Adonais is the Raven?

But his thoughts were cut short as Khaidu's pain burst into his awareness. The agony she experienced—it was now his own. He had to heal her. It was his calling. But Adonais! Did he dare defy Adonais? What was he even thinking? How dare he consider doing anything other than obey his creator? He knew it, had thought of it often before: Adonais is not a soft god, not the effeminate father figure that Vasyllia had come to cherish. No. He was a god of power and authority, and he had to be obeyed.

"Voran," said Sabíana, her eyes reflecting her agony. "Help her."

In that last appeal, Voran thought he would go mad. Torn between two paths, between his love and his aspiration, he stood in place as the water burned him down to what seemed like the essence of his thoughts. He had to do something.

He turned away from Antomír and walked toward Khaidu.

"No! I command you to turn back!" Adonais shouted, but now there was something strident in the tone. Voran didn't stop. He ran to Khaidu, expecting at any moment to be a recipient of the same lightning bolts. But nothing struck him.

He took Khaidu in his arms. Her body shook out of control, her eyes rolling into the back of her head, and she foamed at the mouth. The sight horrified him more than any of the other people he healed. He felt his own body begin to shake. Panic reached for his throat to throttle him.

How can I do this? How dare I heal someone that Adonais himself has decreed worthy of punishment?

But he did it.

His muscles froze up, and his mouth opened wide, stuck in a wordless cry. It was unbearable, the agony of that Gumira. His legs gave way. He fell, and his body could no longer move. His legs were dead twigs that had no life to them. His mouth curved downward. His tongue was felt-like, heavy, a burden. His hands shook, and pins and needles seemed to run up and down them, driving deep to the bone. He breathed in deeply, and as he exhaled, he wept.

Khaidu relaxed and breathed more easily in his arms. Then her eyes flittered open and fixed on him, snapping back into awareness. She grabbed him with strength he never expected from someone so broken.

"No," she whispered, "No! We're too late." She pointed back at the fountainhead and the trees.

Adonais waded through the water toward Antomír.

Lyna hissed, a sound Voran had never thought to hear from the perfect face of his beloved Sirin. Voran followed her glance and saw a hideous, black parody of a Sirin who flew over their heads and landed in front of Antomír, shielding his body.

"Raven!" she cried, facing down the warrior-god. "Your promise to me! Fulfill it!"

"You!" Lyna screamed as though she were being cut. "How could you!"

The hideous black Sirin, her eyes already full of tears, groaned with anguish so deep, Voran felt it boring into him, reaching down into his gut, then into his stomach, then down to his hips. He breathed in sharply. This pain was worse even than Khaidu's.

"Lyna, Lyna, you will know my pain yet!" the black Sirin said. "Do you feel the tiny, narrow window connecting you to your sisters closing with every moment? Yes? Does it hurt?"

"It burns like liquid fire!" screamed Lyna. Voran bit his hand, forcing himself to be contained. He could not interfere here, no matter how much Lyna and Gamayun's pain were goring wounds into his heart.

"That is only a foretaste of what I have endured and continue to endure. This creature, this Raven, is the only one who can release me from it."

"And I will, my dear one," said Adonais, standing in the midst of the river of life. Behind his young voice was a growl older than the stones of Vasyllia. "As soon as I have finished."

He reached down a monstrous hand toward Antomír.

"No!" Gamayun screamed. "Now. Do it now. Before you pluck the fruit. Return me to my place.

He smiled. "Poor Gamayun. What makes you think I can return you there? No one can but the Unknown Father." He was mocking her, and the realization that she had been fooled was painted on her face in strokes of white. Voran wanted to look away from her pain. It was almost too much to bear, even only looking at her.

Gamayun flew into Adonais's face like a black arrow, but he swatted her off like a fly. She fell near Antomír, her wings twisted underneath her. Lyna keened, and the earth itself seemed to shake with the sound. Voran had to force himself to take a breath. It hurt his chest, as though someone were pushing his ribs in from all sides.

"Voran," whispered Sabíana, her face white. "Look."

Antomír's body spasmed suddenly, then he breathed out. His eyes opened and didn't close again. He lay still.

Adonais's scream drowned out Lyna's song, and two of the great trees cracked in half and fell over.

Voran picked Sabíana up and leaned her against one of the red trees that still stood. "Sabíana, my love. Be strong for me. No matter what you see, do not despair."

She kissed him.

Voran walked up to Adonais, still standing in the midst of the river, though the panic tried its best to throttle him.

"Raven! You have failed. Antomír is dead. Leave this place. Do not defile it with your filth."

Adonais laughed, froth foaming at the edges of his mouth. He reached down toward Voran, and as he did, he billowed out into a black cloud with two monstrous raven wings. Only the beacon-eyes remained alit. Two claw-like arms whipped out of the darkness and grabbed Voran's head. The nails bit deep into Voran's skin.

"You asked for it," the Raven voice whispered.

Voran smiled. "Yes. It is fitting. A fitting punishment for all my failures."

Already the Raven's presence slithered in Voran's mind. *Come inside me; I will heal you,* he thought. It was his last thought.

CHAPTER 48
STRANGE ALLIANCES

The bear-riders beat off the Vasylli incursion in the course of a few chaotic minutes. Severuk gathered his division to assess the damage. Most of the dead were Vasylli, not bear-riders. Only a few wounded, among whom was Veles, of all people. It was not a serious wound, and he seemed more upset than hurt.

"Severuk, I am an overgrown tree stump!" he bellowed. "I should be flogged publicly. Idiot, idiot! How could I have been so stupid?"

"Calm down, brother," said Severuk, chuckling. "What have you done this time?"

"Antomír," said Veles, and the tears came, as they always did with his overgrown child of a brother. "Gamayun forced a soul-bond with him. I had suspected it, but surely, I thought, all the blessings showered on Antomír would have been enough to sever that bond! She must have been truly desperate."

"She...wait, where is Antomír?"

Veles sat on the bare ground and wept into his hands. In between sobs, his words came out ragged and labored. "He attacked me, Severuk. She had taken control of his body. I think she has taken him into the Garden."

"Oh, by all that is holy," said Severuk, unsheathing his sword again. "We must go now. Storm the walls."

Ox-horns sounded on all sides. Cries of "they're back! Vasylli attack!" flew back and forth among the men. Severuk made out little in the confusion until young Cassían ran up to him and fell on one knee.

"They're holding the pass into Vasyllia. It looks like a sizable army. Everything up to this point must have been diversion."

Veles swore.

"We've been outwitted at our own game," said Severuk. "Well, we never thought it would be easy. Cassían, Veles, come. For our Dar, our young Dar."

<hr />

The last pass leading to Vasyllia was bristling with spears. Veles tried to count them, but he gave up when he reached a thousand. The bear riders could perhaps handle them, but only in the open field. So it was either lose most of their men trying to get through the pass or wait the Vasylli out until they decided to engage in the open field.

What about Antomír, you fat failure?

No, there was no question. There was no choice. They had to take Vasyllia, whatever the cost. Severuk nodded at him silently, as though hearing his thoughts.

"Well, it was glorious for a day or two," said Cassían at Veles's left. "Now for the real fight."

Veles ground his teeth, then unsheathed his sword. He missed the familiar weight of his mace, which was no weapon for this kind of war. He much preferred it to the finesse of a sword.

All around him, the bears tensed for the charge. Some growled, others quivered in anticipation. Their riders mirrored their readiness. It would be a bloodbath, yes, but it would be glorious.

Out of the sky fell fifteen suns, directly in the narrow space between the bear-riders and their Vasylli welcoming committee. Zmei uncurled from within a ball of flame, the fire still licking the edges of his giant human form.

"Protectors of the Realm of earth," he said with an edge of ridicule in his voice. "I come bearing gifts and news. The Dar of Vasyllia comes to reclaim his own." He pointed back toward the pass of Ardovían.

Veles, completely dumbfounded, turned around.

An army of mounted and walking warriors filed through the pass, already coming down the mountain toward the plain where the bear-riders stood. Banners rose and fell in the midst of the mass of men. A banner bearing a silver tree with white blossoms, with three streams of blue water pouring from the roots—Veles gasped. It was the banner of Mirnían. Interspersed with the banners of Mirnían were ragged brown standards on long sticks with no discernable sigil.

Severuk came to Veles's side. "Is that what I think it is? Gumiren spirit-banners?"

Veles laughed. "I think we've found little Khaidu's lost horse-clan."

"Time to draw up the new map of the world," said Zmei, and they turned back to him. "Will you come with me to the gates of Vasyllia?"

Before Veles could answer, the giants burst into flame and charged at the waiting Vasylli.

CHAPTER 49
THE REVELATION OF ADONAIS

Adonais dissipated into a cloud of dust that flew about like a swarm of bees, then entered into Voran's mouth. He collapsed, his eyes glazed over. He had stopped breathing. Khaidu wanted to scream. Instead, she focused on Voran. Something was happening to him. Something strange.

"There," said the voice of the Raven, deep inside Voran as he stood up on two unsteady legs. "That's better."

Then, Khaidu's heart seemed to explode in pain inside her. It was not her pain. It was the pain of the Raven.

Voran's body twitched and fell back on the ground, writhing. "Nooooooooooo!" The Raven groaned, and the trees in the grove shook from the sound.

Khaidu shut her eyes tight, her hands on the side of her head, her jaw cramping from pain that felt like every drop of her blood had suddenly boiled.

But Khaidu was still herself. That kernel of a thought was an anchor in a storm. *I am Khaidu.*

Then she knew what she must do.

She closed her eyes and breathed slowly. She spoke, and the feeling of her tongue, free and loose, was like cool water on burned skin.

"Voran, hear my voice. I am with you."

The sudden surge of pain as Voran opened himself up to her almost drowned her. *I am Khaidu.* The voices, so many, so many! She saw...

...A boy. A pockmarked, damaged child. A child who could not speak for the horrors done to him. The first healing of Voran the Healer.

Someone else—a bear of a man, weeping. Holding a dying child in the palm of his hand. Voran the Healer had given them both new life.

An old man, dying after a hard life of toil. Voran returned him his joy. He laughed almost to the end, that old man whom everyone forgot.

Five hundred and thirty-seven warriors healed after years of war.

Khaidu opened her eyes and seemed to awake.

The body of Voran stood before her, tense, ready to pounce.

"Raven," she said. "A man is not merely himself. A man is a world. This man whom you have possessed? He is a world of healed men and women and children. And they love him. They love him. They will not stand to have your presence befoul his world. His beautiful world."

Voran's body opened its mouth, and a moan issued from it like a foul vapor. He shook, shuddered, then thrashed about.

"No! No! I will have this body! I will have this body! I will become the Deathless!"

A scream tore through the earth, and several more of the great trees cracked. The sky turned black with roiling clouds. The fountainhead exploded, and the river flooded. Khaidu covered her ears.

Then, silence.

"Khaidu, my dear," said Voran. His voice was horse, but his own. "Thank you."

She opened her eyes. Voran was radiating white light, so bright she could hardly look at him.

A little way beyond him lay a shriveled, feathery creature. The Raven lay unmoving as the rising waters of life lapped at him gently.

"Khaidu, do you wish to be healed?" Voran said. "Do you want to walk again?"

❧

Voran was amazed at Khaidu's eyes. So childlike, in spite of her wisdom and her experience. So full of hopes, doubts, questions.

"You can do that?" she asked.

Her simplicity warmed him, and he smiled.

"I couldn't heal the Raven, dear girl. I did try. But I have a last healing left in me, I think. Will *you* be healed?"

The wrinkles in her forehead cleared, and she looked away from him.

She bit the lower left corner of her bottom lip. Too hard, and she flinched. Then she looked at him and shook her head.

"No. You must heal Sabíana."

"Khaidu!" called Sabíana from the tree where she reclined. Her voice was full of that playfulness Voran had loved so much in her as a girl. "I refuse to be healed. If this so-called healer cannot love me in my broken state, he does not deserve to love me when I am whole."

Voran heard what she was hiding—the long pain, the fear, the desire to rest—and he promised himself that once this was all over, he would do nothing but serve her for the rest of their days together.

"Khaidu," said Voran, "I want to heal you. You deserve it, perhaps more than anyone else."

Khaidu scrunched up her face. She clearly disagreed with him and all the "Vasylli idiots," as she called them.

Voran descended for a moment with his mind into his heart, where he found an ocean of Living Water bubbling, ready to flow forth. Like the monks in the mountain, his ordeal against the Raven seemed to have called down Living Water. Inside his heart, he saw the image he held there of Sabíana. Young, passionate, and very, very contrary.

He smiled.

All the stores of Living Water inside him—all of it—flowed into Sabíana, whose mouth and eyes snapped open. As it siphoned off Voran, the exhaustion crept up and began to pull down at him. He held on, letting the last of it leave him. The light that had surrounded him danced around Sabíana like the aureole around the sun. It lifted her off the ground until all her twisted bits had taken their proper form and shape. The light went inside her open mouth, and she gasped with the sudden pleasure of it. Her face changed. It was radiant as the lines of constant pain were smoothed away. She didn't quite look the same as his image of her—she was over forty, after all—but she was even more beautiful than he remembered.

Lyna sang, softly at first, then stronger and stronger, until her gem-toned wings glowed with their natural light, and her usual radiance mingled with the light of Voran's healing that still surrounded Sabíana. Finally, on a note that cut through the air like a sword, she stopped. Only then did the trees begin to move again, the humans to breathe again.

Sabíana walked, tottering a little, as though remembering how to use her legs, toward Khaidu, who still lay on the ground, leaning on Aglaia. The wolf was still unconscious.

Sabíana embraced Khaidu with tears in her eyes.

"You stubborn little wolf-girl," she said, half-sobbing. "Why didn't you let him heal you? You have your whole life ahead of you."

Khaidu half-smiled. "I'll show you why."

Khaidu took Aglaia's muzzle in her hands and closed her eyes. She breathed out in concentration, then gasped.

Aglaia snapped awake, then sneezed. "Wolfling? Did you ... *how* did you?"

Voran understood. Khaidu was a healer herself. It would be her place, her calling, to heal all the rents between the lands, the wounds in the fabric of the Realms. *Who better than a Gumira?* he thought. He looked back at the trees in the Heart of the World. The last fruit throbbed with light, still growing on the last tree.

Then...

"No!" Voran ran toward the trees. The shriveled, pathetic form of the Raven was already halfway up the cone of rock.

"If I cannot be the Deathless," he growled, "then let the Realms die."

A white sword of flame came down from the sky and struck the Raven down from the rock. Three towering figures stood behind the rock with the three burning trees. A warrior in red, a warrior in black, and Athíel of the Palymi, whom Voran had encountered once, when his master Tarin had died.

Standing over the smoking form of the Raven was the Pilgrim, the legendary Harbinger himself. He was in his young form as a man in golden robes, his face shining with white light. He held a sword of white fire. With his other hand, he lifted the head of the Raven. It dissipated into a brown vapor.

Seeing the Pilgrim, Voran felt emptied of everything. His entire life, he had been striving toward Adonais, seeking to become a better servant of his creator, to grow closer to him. But it seemed that creator was a lie, a ruse invented by their greatest enemy. What was true, then? Who had created the Realms? Was there an Unknown Father as Khaidu suggested? All he had left was the love of Sabíana. But even that was small comfort in the emptiness of his heart.

And here, at the end of all things, when there was no more hope left, the Pilgrim dared to show his face. Voran burned with anger.

"What, now? After all this? Only now do you come?"

The Pilgrim bowed his head. "Did I not tell you, my falcon? The answer to everything your heart seeks is in the Heart of the World. I never promised that the answer would be an easy one."

Lyna alighted next to Voran and stared with challenge at the Pilgrim.

"I am angry too, Harbinger. The Sirin were also fooled by Adonais. When he made himself known to us, during the reign of Cassían, we believed that the son of the Unknown Father had finally made himself known. We thought he would lead us further up, toward a better knowledge of our higher natures. But ever since he appeared, slowly, slowly, the Vasylli lost their love for our kind, and our bonds were all broken. Why didn't you warn us, you who are supposed to be our father and protector?"

"We did. But the Sirin are slow to change. You did not want to believe us."

"I do not know anything anymore," said Lyna. Voran had never heard anger in her voice before. He wanted to comfort her.

"Voran," said Khaidu, approaching on the back of Aglaia and bowing before the three Powers who stood impassive and silent behind the trees. "You shouldn't despair. Not yet. We Gumiren have made images of the three flaming trees crowning a monolith in water. It is the only symbol we have for the Unknown Father. I think you have never been on a surer path than you are now."

"Small comfort, little wolf, when your entire world has been destroyed."

"Not destroyed, Voran," said the Pilgrim. "Not yet. You still have time to rebuild. This much we can give you. We can take you back to Vasyllia in time to stop the war. To heal the wounds."

Something buzzed inside Voran's head, as though his right ear stopped hearing for a moment. He shook his head, and the feeling subsided.

"How can we return to Vasyllia?" he asked. "The way is shut."

The Pilgrim smiled and turned to the three towering figures behind him.

"Open the doors," he said.

At the feet of each figure, a spinning oval resolved into something like a curtain of water. Three doors into other Realms.

"You all have lost much in this war," said the Pilgrim, and now he was an old man in grey robes. "Though it is not in the nature of the Powers to intervene directly in the affairs of men, we are allowed to give this one gift. The left door will take you to Raven's Bane. The central door opens into Vasyllia. The right will take you to the parting of the ways, from where you may choose your own path."

Voran's vision blurred, as though he were weeping, though not a single tear dropped from his eye. His ears rang. He shook his head in frustration, and the sensation faded.

"Aglaia and I will go to the parting of the ways," said Khaidu. "We are going to the land of the dead to seek Antomír. We will find a way to get him out."

Sabíana put her hand on Voran's shoulder as she spoke. "You can't travel to the land of the dead. Only the dead go there."

"It has been done before," said Aglaia. "Veles, Antomír's protector, and his family. They passed through the land of the dead on their journey to the Heights of Aer."

"Did they reach it?" asked Voran. "The Heights of Aer?"

"So he has said. He and his family brought their petition directly to the throne of the Most High."

Voran's eyes grew wider. "I will go with you, for I have a grievance with the Most High."

"As do I," said Lyna.

"I would not advise you to go that way," said the Pilgrim. "It is too dangerous. You will never come through it. What Veles and his family did was extraordinary. But the king of the underworld has taken measures to prevent any such thing from happening. I cannot allow you to endanger the cause of Vasyllia."

Someone laughed next to Voran. Voran turned, but there was no one there. Something strange glimmered in the grass half a stone's throw away. Something metallic, definitely not belonging to the Garden. He approached, his every sense ringing with a rising dread. It was Llun's flask.

"How is that possible?" asked Sabíana, standing now on his right. She leaned on him, and the slight touch thrilled him with its intimacy.

"The Consistory had it. They must have given it to the Raven somehow." But that didn't make sense. Aspidían had said that they no longer had contact with the Raven.

Voran reached for it, happy to have it returned to him, even in such an unaccountable place.

"Voran, no!" Sabíana pulled back at his arm.

It was too late. Something sucked at Voran's stomach in a sensation so familiar, he almost laughed at his own stupidity. As had happened countless times in the last twenty years, Voran's world spun around him, blurring into an impression of all the Realms together. Then, slowly resolving into solidity, a snowy, frozen landscape asserted itself around Voran.

After all this time, Voran had blundered into another of the Raven's traps.

He tried to make sense of his surroundings as he wrapped his arms around his body and hopped in place, trying to warm himself. As he looked down, the world spun again as he reeled. He was on the edge of a precipice in the middle of a range of mountains. The wind hurled ice at him like darts.

Next to him lay the flask. He picked it up.

"I do apologize," said the Raven's voice. Voran turned to see a young man, around twenty years old, wrapped in fine, brown furs. His features were pleasing and symmetrical, but his eyes were two bits of emptiness. "I had hoped it wouldn't come to this. But just in case—"

"You put a bit of yourself into the flask?" interrupted Voran.

The young Raven's eyes widened in surprise. Then he laughed, as though Voran had said the stupidest thing in the world.

"No, no! Of course not. What a stupid idea. You were not able to expel all of me from your body when I took it. A sliver of my will clung inside the darkest part of your own heart, my dear Voran. Your heart does have a few untended rooms, you know. I took the smallest one. You wouldn't ever have noticed me."

"The flask?"

"Just a simple bit of illusion. A bait for the trap."

Voran shook with fear and exhaustion. "I don't understand. Are you real? Or does my mind conjure you up?"

The Raven smiled and put a finger on his lips.

"What do you want from me?" asked Voran, his voice hoarse.

"I only want to give you your heart's desire. To brave the Heights of Aer and demand an answer from the Powers. Just say the word, and I'll take you. You would avoid the land of the dead entirely. Secret paths, dangerous ones, yes, but I know them well. I am a Power of Aer, after all. Or have you forgotten?"

"And if I refuse?"

The Raven extended his arms, demonstratively indicating the sheer cliffs, the driving snows, the absence of any road anywhere in sight.

"I have nothing more to lose," the Raven said. "You, on the other hand..."

To Voran's own surprise, he laughed aloud. It was all too absurd. But the possibility of reaching the Heights, of finding the answers to all his questions... Even if he would be leading some small part of the Raven directly to the heart of the Realms.

He would have to take that chance.

"Lead on, then," Voran said.

Suddenly, he was wrapped in furs, there was a walking stick in his hand, and a road extended forward, hugging the mountain.

"After you," said a voice on the air. Or was it inside his head?

CHAPTER 50
THE LAND OF THE DEAD

Parfyon Krivoshey, once the greatest man in Nebesta and Karila, lay on his deathbed in the same palatial pavilion where he had made love to the fair Alienne. He had not even made it back to New Nebesta. Most of the army left him behind, but Bragadun, Baryan, and his honor guard remained to see him off to the land of the dead.

It was strangely peaceful to die. Most of his life had been a mad struggle —first to rise through the ranks, then to win the most beautiful woman in the world, then to amass power to himself. Honestly, it was exhausting. And his end was fitting. He had committed the ultimate abomination, and he should die for it in dishonor.

"Where do you want your body buried?" asked Bragadun, his eyes actually full of tears.

"Not buried," Parfyon managed to croak, though speaking was more and more difficult. "Burned. No honors. Just as I lie. Burn my pavilion, with me and all my things within."

He expected Bragadun to protest, at least for form's sake. But his first and most loyal follower only inclined his head.

"It shall be so."

The end came that evening. He found it increasingly difficult to breathe. It was his chest. It refused to move like it was supposed to. If only he could...

And then, he was plunging down through the earth. His body was whole —all arms and legs and eyes accounted for—though it had a slightly translucent quality about it. He was not breathing. No need. But he was aware. Down, down, through the dirt and stone and water and fire, until he saw, underneath him, a vast, shadowy continent. Not a tree in sight. He alighted on dark grass that stretched as far as he saw in all directions. No sun lit this land of shades. The silvery radiance that surrounded him came from something that looked like stars, but they seemed to be embedded in crystal far above the surface of this new place. It was not without a chilling kind of beauty.

"Are you Parfyon Krivoshey?" rasped a voice at his left, "Formerly knyaz of the great city of Nebesta?"

Parfyon turned to face the speaker—a monstrously ugly creature with the body of a vulture and the face of a woman.

"I am," said Parfyon.

"How would you like to gain your heart's desire? To sit on the throne of Vasyllia the Great?"

Parfyon's breath quickened as the old desire awoke in him again.

"I would, yes. I would do anything, anything to gain it."

The creature leered at him. "Good. Gamayun can provide that."

"How?"

She turned around and looked up at the twilit sky of the netherworld. Shimmering through it, insubstantial as a mirage, was the outline of a hill. On it stood three cherry trees in bloom. They were aflame, but the blooms were not consumed by the fire. Parfyon's skin prickled and his blood rush through his tingling fingers as he realized what it was. The vision on the battlefield. The vision in Veche Square. There it was.

Gamayun spoke in a faraway voice as she rocked back and forth on her vulture-feet. "That is the way back to the Garden in the Heart of the World. There is a wall blocking our way, but it is weakening. Your escape, and mine. But first, help me to become queen of this land of the dead, and you will see what we can do."

ALSO BY NICHOLAS KOTAR

The Song of the Sirin
The Curse of the Raven
The Heart of the World
The Forge of the Covenant
How to Survive a Russian Fairy Tale

ABOUT THE AUTHOR

Nicholas Kotar is a writer of epic fantasy inspired by Russian fairy tales, a freelance translator from Russian to English, the resident conductor of the men's choir at a Russian monastery in the middle of nowhere, and a semi-professional vocalist. His one great regret in life is that he was not born in the nineteenth century in St. Petersburg, but he is doing everything he can to remedy that error.

Made in United States
Orlando, FL
29 November 2023